THE GRAND GAME
BOOK 8: THE LOST RECLAIMED

THE GRAND GAME

Book 8: The Lost Reclaimed

Tom Elliot

COPYRIGHT

THE GRAND GAME

There is no one path to victory, but many. Which will Michael pursue?

Michael's plans have shifted, or rather, he has upended them. His once simple plans for raising House Wolf have morphed into something different. Will he succeed at his new goals? Will the Forerunners? Or will Michael's allies be made to pay for his overreach?

Join Michael on his epic journey and find out!

PRAISE FOR THE GRAND GAME:

"Interesting portal litrpg. Well-paced and the start of a new series. Curious to see where it goes..." —**Tao Wong on goodreads.com.**

"... Great action, great storyline and I honestly binge read it, start to end..." —**Alex Kozlowski on goodreads.com.**

"Smart MC. Great Tension. Full of Action." —**CookieCrumble on RoyalRoad.com.**

"Everything I look for in a LitRPG." —**CosmereCradleChris on RoyalRoad.com.**

"Oh I liked this very much!" —**The Enlightened Beard on amazon.com.**

"One of the best in this category this year." —**kindle customer on amazon.com.**

Author's Note

Dear Readers,

Thank you for reading the Grand Game. This is a self-published book. Even though care has been given to the review and editing of this novel, some mistakes may have slipped through. If you spot any grammatical errors or typos, please get in touch with me via email.

This book also contains game-like elements. They are generally unintrusive and integrated into the story, but beware, they exist. Otherwise, I hope you enjoy Michael's story.

Happy reading!
Tom (**TomLitRPG.com**)
Support me on PATREON

CONTENTS

MICHAEL'S EVOLUTION

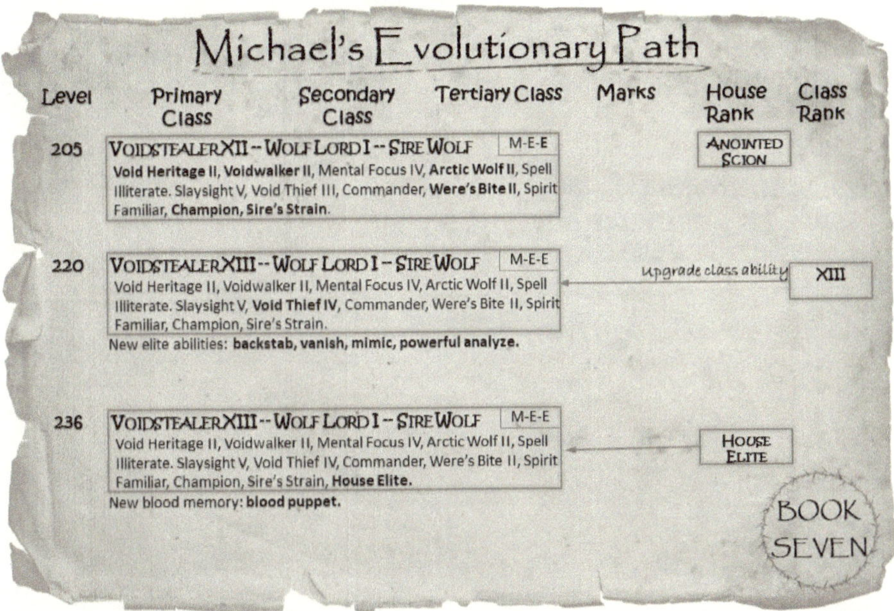

As always, Michael continues to grow during his adventures in the Forever Kingdom. The chart above only illustrates his latest achievements (as accomplished over the course of the last book). If you wish to view Michael's earlier evolutionary charts, please visit my site at the link below.

tomlitrpg.com/michael

THE SYSTEM OF THE GRAND GAME

The universe of the Grand Game continues to expand with every book in the series, and at this point, it no longer makes sense to include all the maps, charts, and diagrams in each new book.

If you wish to learn more about the world of the Forever Kingdom or understand the system of the Grand Game better, please visit my site at one of the links below.

tomlitrpg.com/game-lore
tomlitrpg.com/world-lore
tomlitrpg.com/glossary

Player Profile: Michael

Level: 236. Rank: 23. Species: Human. Lives Remaining: 4.
Ghost's Lives Remaining: 4.
True Marks: Powerful Initiate.
True Marks (hidden): Worthy Adversary, Wolf Protector, Wolf Progenitor.
False Marks (fabricated): Lesser Shadow, Lesser Light, Lesser Dark.
Followers: 2 / 200. Active Pacts: 5 / 20.

Faction Data: Forerunners

Office held: Faction Leader. Sectors claimed: 0 / 2.
Players pledged: Nyra, Ceruvax, Safyre, Terence, Teresa, Anriq.
Non-players pledged: Pack of the Reach (500), Bane Wolves warband (2,000), arctic wolves (200), dire wolves (130).

Active Buffs

** denotes boosts affected by items.*
Damage reduction (DR) (reduces damage incurred only):
Life: 20%. Death: 25%. Air: 55%. Earth: 55%. Fire: 55%. Water: 55%.
Shadow: 40%. Light: 40%. Dark: 40%. Nether: 100%. Physical: 62%*.

Resistances (RES) (negates damage and/or rebuffs spell effects):
Life: 10%. Death: 12.5%. Air: 27.5%. Earth: 27.5%. Fire: 47.5%*. Water: 27.5%. Shadow: 20%. Light: 20%. Dark: 20%. Nether: 70%*. Physical: 0%.

Ghost (DR / RES): Fire: 50% / 75%. Nether: 50% / 25%. Physical: 56%* / 25%.

Other Benefits derived from Items

Damage: +30% damage (ebonheart), +40% damage (faithful).
Abilities: perceive tier 6 spelled wards (sorcerer's coif), move soundlessly (wayfarer's boots), hands immune to hazardous substances (wayfarer's gloves), spellhold: none (mage's surprise), psi-feed (psi bracelet).
Traits: +20% aoe evasion (tiamaten vest).
Skills: +5 ranks in thieving (scoundrel's wristband).

Attributes

Available: 6 points.
Strength: 28 (20)*. Constitution: 36 (24)*. Dexterity: 137 (113)*.
Perception: 94 (90)*. Mind: 135 (123)*. Magic: 86 (65)*. Faith: 0.

Classes

Available (Michael): 0 points.
Available (Ghost): 8 points.

Primary-Secondary-Tertiary tri-blend: voidstalker (fabricated). voidstealer XIII (hidden).
Ascendant Class: wolf lord (rank I, hidden), sire wolf (rank I, hidden).
Familiar: stygian pyre wolf VI (unique, hidden).

<u>Traits</u>

void heritage II (wolf, hidden): +4 Dexterity, +4 Strength, +8 Mind, +8 Perception, +12 Magic.
voidwalker II (wolf, hidden): improved senses in all conditions, nethersight, immunity to blindness.
arctic wolf II (wolf, hidden): +10 Constitution, +4 Mind, +6 Strength.
were's bite II (wolf, hidden): 0 to 30% chance of granting another player the were-trait.
sire's strain (wolf, hidden): boosts your other wolf traits by +1 tier.

house elite (bloodline, hidden): bound to House Wolf, detect dormant wolf bloodline strains.
secret blood (bloodline, hidden): conceals the wolf blood of yourself, your followers, and your familiar.
blood puppet (bloodline, hidden): grants you the enslave ability.

beast tongue: can speak to beastkin.
Marked: can see spirit signatures.
inscrutable mind: +8 Mind.
mental focus IV: increases effectiveness of Mind skills by 40%.
budding explorer: all key points in newly discovered sectors logged.
spell illiterate: cannot cast mana-based spells.
potion resistance II: potency of potions reduced by 2 ranks.
spirit talker: can speak to spirits.
bold blood: +1 attribute per level.
higher evolution: can evolve Class beyond master ranked.
commander: can share bloodline traits or blood memories with your followers.
champion: increases the strength of blood memories.
spirit familiar: can bind a willing spirit as your familiar.
mage-host: +10 Mind, +10 Magic.
slip-through-shadows*: 20% chance to evade AoE damage.

spirit familiar (Ghost): mirrors player attributes and level, and shares ability slots with them.
psionic being (Ghost): retains telepathic skills and abilities from her former incarnation as a dire wolf.
free spirit (Ghost): can roam an unlimited distance from her host, but only within the same sector.
born again II (Ghost): grants your familiar 2 additional lives, will resurrect in spirit vessel.
pyreborn (Ghost): +50% fire magic resistance and +50% fire damage.

mirrored jewelry*: gains benefits of accessories rank 7 and below (rings, bracelets, and necklaces).

Skills

Available skill slots: 0.
light armor (current: 163. Constitution, basic).

dodging (current: 207. Dexterity, basic).
sneaking (current: 226. Dexterity, basic).
shortswords (current: 212. Dexterity, basic).
two weapon fighting (current: 186. Dexterity, advanced).
thieving (current: 150. Dexterity, basic).

chi (current: 185. Mind, advanced).
meditation (current: 214. Mind, basic).
telekinesis (current: 190. Mind, advanced).
telepathy (current: 222. Mind, advanced).

insight (current: 246. Perception, basic).
deception (current: 230. Perception, master).

channeling (current: 216. Magic, basic).
elemental absorption (current: 115. Magic, master).
null force (current: 82. Magic, master).
null life (current: 44. Magic, master).
null death (current: 53. Magic, master).
nether absorption (current: 204. Magic, master).

magma maw (Ghost) (current: 93. Magic, master).
stygian claws (Ghost) (current: 102. Strength, master).
ash armor (Ghost) (current: 103. Constitution, master).
telepathy (Ghost) (current: 94. Mind, advanced).
death magic (Ghost) (current: 76. Magic, advanced).

Abilities

Constitution ability slots used: 15 / 24.
greater load controller (15 Constitution, master, light armor).

Dexterity ability slots used: 101 / 113.
crippling blow (Dexterity, basic, shortswords).
minor piercing strike (5 Dexterity, advanced, shortswords).
deadly backstab (30 Dexterity, elite, sneaking).
improved trap disarm (5 Dexterity, advanced, thieving).
superior lockpicking (5 Dexterity, advanced, thieving).
superior set trap (10 Dexterity, expert, thieving).
superior whirlwind (15 Dexterity, master, two weapon fighting).
vanish (30 Dexterity, elite, sneaking).

<u>Mind ability slots used:</u> 111 / 123.
mass puppet (15 Mind, master, telepathy).
stunning slap (Mind, basic, chi).
improved windborne (15 Mind, master, telekinesis).
enhanced reflexes (15 Mind, master, chi).
superior astral shurikens (15 Mind, master, telepathy).
extreme shadow blink (15 Mind, master, telekinesis).
improved quick mend (15 Mind, master, chi).
improved fortified mind (15 Mind, master, meditation).
astral bite (Ghost) (5 Mind, advanced, telepathy).

<u>Perception ability slots used:</u> 86 / 90.
powerful analyze (30 Perception, elite, insight).
greater trap detect (15 Perception, master, thieving).
conceal small weapon (Perception, basic, deception).
mimic (30 Perception, elite, deception).
superior ventro (5 Perception, advanced, deception).
lesser imitate (5 Perception, advanced, deception).

<u>Magic ability slots used:</u> 1 / 65.
draining bite (Ghost) (Magic, basic, death magic).

<u>Other abilities:</u>
adept slaysight (hidden) (Class, elite, telepathy): paralyze, shatter, sleep, terrify, blind.
greater void thief (hidden) (Class, master, any void skill and telepathy): steal, siphon, negate, redirect on direct-damage, channeled, damage over time, aoe).
manifest (Ghost) (Class, advanced): explosive.
diresight (Ghost) (Class, advanced, telepathy).
direshield (Ghost) (Class, advanced, telepathy).
enslave (hidden) (blood memory, greater).

Known Key Points

Kingdom Sector 1 (Nexus) safe zone.
Kingdom Sector 12,560 (wolves' valley) nether portal and safe zone.
Kingdom Sector 18,240 nether portal 1 (guardian tower), and nether portal 2 (Draven's reach).
Kingdom Sector 75,172 nether portal 1 (Draven's Reach) and safe zone.

Dungeon Sector 101 (scorching dunes) exit portal and safe zone.
Dungeon Sectors 102, 103, and 104 (haunted catacombs) exit portals and safe zones.
Dungeon Sector 105, 106, 107, 108, and 109 (guardian tower) exit portals.
Dungeon Sector 14,913 (candidate's dungeon) exit portal and safe zone.
Dungeon Sector 73,102 (Draven's Reach) one-way entrance portal, safe zone, and exit portal.

sector 24,401 safe zone.

Equipped (28 / 30 Game items)

Weapons (2 equipped)
ebonheart (+30% damage).
faithful (+40% damage).

Armor & Clothes (12 equipped)
tiamaten scalemail vest (+32%, +4 Constitution, slip-through-shadows).
sorcerer's coif (perceive tier 6 wards).
ranger's kit (+24% damage reduction, 4 pieces).
bomber's belt (5 x acid bombs, 5 x smoke bombs, 5 x ice bombs, and 5 x fire bombs).
belt of the chameleon (10 x rank 4 nether protection crystals, 11 x rank 4 disease protection crystals, 7 scent concealment crystals, 5 x mental concealment crystals, 4 x rank 6 disease protection crystals, 2 x rank 5 poison protection crystals, 1 x rank 4 strength enhancement crystals, 0 x rank 4 dexterity enhancement crystals, and 2 x rank 4 magic enhancement crystals).
wayfarer's boots (legendary item, +8 Dexterity, move soundlessly).
wayfarer's gloves (legendary item, +8 Dexterity, hands immune to hazardous substances).
cloak of the Reach (legendary soulbound item, +10 Magic, +20% fire magic resistance, +20% nether magic resistance).
scoundrel's wristband (+5 ranks thieving, 300 / 300 trap-making crystals) (triggers: pressure plates, sound glasses, tripwires, motion pins, remote control, spell detector, psi detector. elements: lightning, poison clouds, fire, spring-coiled daggers, bear-trap clamps, small explosives, blots of darkness, ice, spiked-pit, hallucinogenic mist. guides: reflect, split, and funnel. keys: remote, timed.)

Rings & Accessories (12 equipped)
goliath's ring (+8 Strength).
acrobat's ring (+8 Dexterity).
sharpshooter's band (+4 Perception).
hale stone (+8 Constitution).
savant's ring (+4 Mind).
troll's talisman bracelet (+6% damage reduction).
mage's surprise (+10 Magic, spellhold: trigger-cast tier 5 spells).
psi bracelet (legendary item, +8 Mind, psi-feed).
simple potion bracelet (3 / 3 full heal potions).
aetherstone bracelet (1 / 5 stored locations, 3 stone charged).
jeweled pet (grants Ghost: mirrored jewelry trait).
farspeaker bracelet (Safyre set, 1 of 4).

Other (2 equipped)
large bag of holding (200 slots).

seeking eye of Sylvana (legendary item, +invisible, 4 hours use, track & scout).

<u>Ghost (1 equipped)</u>
shadow's friend (+4 ranks stealth).

<u>Backpack Contents (Key Items)</u>

<u>Money</u>: 1023 golds, 5 silvers, and 3 coppers.
1 x coil of rope.
cat claws.
5 x full healing potions, 2 x rank 4 cure poison, 1 x rank 6 cure disease potions.
simple map of Nexus.
commune rod.
10 x acid bombs, 10 x smoke bombs, 10 x ice bombs, and 10 x fire bombs.
small bag of hiding (tier 6 concealment ward).
stygian shortsword, +3.
stygian shortsword.
netherstone.
underworld promissory note (12,000 gold).
4 x upgrade gems.
piercing strike tier III, IV, & V.
trap disarm tier III.
lockpicking tier III.
ventro tier III & IV.
2 x greater portal scrolls.
packet of unrefined cynacilin powder.
ranger's kit vest (16% damage reduction).
veteran's trapper's wristband.
Blood Talisman.
small bag of hiding containing 100 x possessed finger bones.
farspeaker bracelet (Tyelin set, 1 of 15).

<u>Soulbound Items</u>
Tartan token.
Vivane token.
Kesh Emporium access card.
tavern bill of ownership.
BHG ID (junior member, 1 / 10 active jobs).
phoenix's feather shaft (soulbound, Sunfury's feather).
apprentice rogue's underworld token.
pioneer's compass (soulbound, attuned to safe zone).
unmarked chest key card (from Nicola).

<u>Miscellaneous Loot</u>

3 x legendary items.
73 x miscellaneous items reserved for use by Mammon's Sworn.

Alchemy Stone Contents

(14 / 500 ingredients stored).
4 x orbs of petrification, 10 x Shadow ectoplasm.

Bank Contents

Money: 1,655 gold, 0 silvers, and 0 coppers.
2 x full healing potions.
2 x full mana potions.

Tavern Money: 9,850 gold, 0 silvers, and 0 coppers.

Open Tasks

Heist in the Dark (steal chalice from the Power, Paya).
A Perverted Trial (stop the Triumvirate abuse of the Combat Trial).
Brokering Peace (establish peace in sector 12,560 within 4 months).
Brotherhood Obligations (report to the brotherhood after 4 months).
Restore the Nexus Guardian (replace Kolath with Adriel).
Revive the Guardians (awaken Draven's brethren).
Locate the Lost Prime (find the hidden Prime).
Resurrecting Death (make Adriel a scion again).
Seedy Side of Life (become a full member of the thieves guild).
Found a new House (persuade two non-Wolf Powers to join your House).

Open Pacts

Deliver cynacilin. Status: pact obligations fulfilled. Blythe owes Jasiah a favor equivalent to the worth of sector 75,172.
Inner Council Pacts with Safyre, Anriq, Teresa, and Terence.

If you wish to view Michael's earlier player profiles, please visit my site at the links below.

tomlitrpg.com/michael

CHAPTER 497: DIVERGING PATHS

"So, how do we run the stygians out of the sector?" Teresa asked.

For a moment, I didn't say anything. It had been only a few hours since House Forerunners—*or was that the Forerunners faction?* I still wasn't sure which we were yet—had made the momentous decision to reclaim sector 18,240.

To try reclaiming it, I amended.

Success was by no means guaranteed, especially with the sector playing home to a young void tree, four stygian overlords—all Powers in their own right—ten thousand stygians, and a rift that could end up doubling all those numbers or worse.

"We don't have a plan yet," I replied. "A strategy perhaps, but until we know what forces we can muster, I can't answer you."

"Alright, I get that," Teresa allowed. "But what are our next steps?"

"That's what we're here to decide," I murmured, surveying the seven figures arrayed around me.

Ghost, Adriel, Safyre, Anriq, Nyra, Terence, and Teresa each sat on their own pile of furs in what was quickly becoming the meeting hall of the Forerunners' inner council. Although, calling the igloo we sat in a hall was a stretch.

The pack elders and Snow had left. With the House's goals decided and the wolves unlikely to be involved in the Forerunners' immediate plans, they had turned their attention to internal matters—and readying the packs for war.

"You said earlier that we would have to leave the tundra," Teresa said. "What did you mean by that?"

Not answering her, I glanced at Safyre.

Correctly interpreting my look, the aetherist took over. "Our immediate goals are twofold: gathering allies and getting stronger. Adriel, Michael, and I will see to the first part, leaving you three—Nyra, Teresa, and Terence— free to focus on acquiring your second Classes."

Terence frowned. "What does that mean? Can't we just buy the Class stones we need?"

"You could do it that way if you wanted to," I allowed, "but don't forget what I said: the best Classes are always gained through dungeon dives."

"Michael is right," Adriel added. "In my day, acquiring a Class was as much a rite of passage for young scions as attaining their Marks were. If you want to follow in the footsteps of the ancients, if you want to become the most powerful versions of yourselves possible, searching a dungeon for a Class is the way to do it."

The lich's words had the desired effect, and the twins' expressions turned gratifyingly determined.

I smiled. "If you're lucky, it may not be just your second Class you acquire—but your third as well."

"So which dungeon are you sending us to?" Teresa asked eagerly.

"Not one anywhere close to Nexus," I replied. "For obvious reasons, those are too dangerous for you. But between them, Safyre and Adriel know of at least a dozen remote dungeons that may be suitable. Dungeons where three young players without any Force affiliations should go unnoticed."

"But why can't we get what we need here?" Nyra asked, a trace of unease in her voice. "Isn't the guardian tower a dungeon?"

"It is," Safyre agreed. "But the tower has only a single treasure chest, making it one of the worst dungeons for this sort of thing. Especially for a party of three."

"Oh," Nyra said, her shoulders slumping.

Unlike the twins, she appeared less enthused by the idea of entering an unknown dungeon, for which I didn't blame her. After growing up in Draven's Reach, she was understandably wary of dungeons. Still, it was important for both her own sake and the Forerunners that she did not shrink from the task.

Leaning forward, I held her gaze. "If you mean to follow Wolf's path, it's important you gain a psi Class. Atiras' Mind Trials await, and ideally, we want to send you through the Rings before we take on the void tree. But the Trials are dangerous. And we can't risk you entering ill-prepared. If you're not ready..."

Nyra's back stiffened. "I'll be ready," she said resolutely.

"What about me?" Anriq asked quietly.

Pursing my lips, I turned his way. Given the glaring omission of his own role in the coming days, Anriq had held his peace far longer than I expected. But matters were a bit more complicated when it came to the werewolf.

"You have three options," I said softly. "The first is to accompany the others in their dungeon delve. While your Class configuration is complete, both your skills and level could do with work."

"Which is the second reason we're sending the twins and Nyra to a remote dungeon," Safyre added. "As a were-player, you will attract attention wherever you go, that is inevitable. But in a remote sector, you will suffer less... scrutiny than you would in Nexus or any other major Force stronghold."

Anriq grimaced. "I'll pass on option one, thanks. What are my other choices?"

"You can stay here with the packs," I replied. "Given your level, the tundra will not make for an ideal training ground, but much like Ghost has, you can still use it to raise your skills."

Anriq nodded slowly. "That sounds more feasible."

"The third option," I went on, "is that you accompany me when I go to Nexus and lead me to the saltmarsh dungeon, Sickening Ooze."

Anriq's face shuttered so quickly that no one failed to notice the change that came over him. "How? I don't know where it is."

"Uh-oh, he's lying," Terence muttered.

Teresa nudged him. "Shh! Let Michael handle it."

Ignoring the pair, I kept my gaze fixed on Anriq. "Maybe you don't," I said.

The werewolf began to relax.

"But I'm positive you know the people who do."

Anriq's shoulders hunched over again. "I don't know who you're—"

"The marshmen," I said, cutting him off. This was too important a matter to let Anriq's evasions stand. "They are from the saltmarsh dungeon, I'm sure of it."

"The marshmen are nobodies," Anriq protested weakly.

"They're not," Adriel contradicted.

"They are so," Anriq insisted. "It's like I told Michael. They're just primitive non-players."

The lich shook her head. "The marshmen are *not* nobodies, and they are *not* primitives."

Anriq thrust out his chin. "Yeah? So, who do you think they are?"

"Scions of House Pestilence," Adriel replied evenly.

Anriq's face flushed. "Ridiculous!" he scoffed. "There is no evidence to suggest that!"

"It's far from ridiculous, young man, and there is plenty of evidence." Showing more patience than I credited her with, Adriel expounded further. "For starters, the 'marshmen' inhabit the same region as Sickening Ooze—a dungeon, mind you, that has always been Pestilence's stronghold.

"Then there is the fact that the Nexus plague quarter—and incidentally that was not the name it bore in my day—is overrun with diseases and maladies of one sort or another, and it should come as no surprise to you that pestilence was and *is* Pestilence's most potent weapon.

"But most damning of all is the fact that the Triumvirate co-opted *werewolves*—Pestilence's ancient enemy no less—to keep the 'marshmen' at bay. Given all these things, it beggars belief that the 'marshmen' and House Pestilence are unrelated. They are either descendants of the House or Pestilence scions themselves."

Anriq paled. "If you know so much, why don't you lead him—" he jerked his thumb in my direction—"to the dungeon yourself?"

The lich smiled. "I would, but in my day, the saltmarsh was but a thin strip along the coast bordering Nexus. From what Michael tells me, it has since swallowed up a good portion of the quarter, including it seems, the entrance to Sickening Ooze. I doubt I would recognize the district as it is now, much less be able to find the dungeon portal."

Anriq's gaze swapped to me, looking for all the world like a cornered animal. "I can't tell you anything," he gasped.

Solemnly, I studied his anxious face, wild eyes, and trembling fingers. Anriq was conflicted. I had expected that. What I had not anticipated was the strength of battle raging in him. "Did you swear a Pact to keep their secrets?"

"Something like that," he muttered, shying away from my gaze.

I frowned at the vagueness of his response but decided not to push him further. "What about relaying a message?"

He raised his head. "A message?"

"Yes. What if instead of leading me to the marshmen, you carry a message to them from me? Will the ties that bind you allow that much?"

Anriq thought for a moment. "What will the message say?"

"The truth, if only its barebones." I ticked off points on my fingers. "The bloodlines rise again. The Endless Dungeon is fading. The Guardian Draven has asked for our help. And finally, we seek allies. In exchange for the marshmen's help, we will provide them with a secure base away from the new Powers. It will say no more than that, though. If they wish to know more, they must agree to a meeting."

A relieved grin spread across the werewolf's face. "Such a message I can carry."

"Good," I said, feeling no small measure of relief myself. "Last thing: do you trust them?"

Anriq's brows furrowed. "How do you mean?"

I leaned forward. "Do you trust them to let you go no matter what?"

Anriq nodded firmly.

"Truly?" Safyre asked. "Will they let you walk away even if they want no part of us and wish to stay isolated?"

Again, the werewolf nodded.

"Even if they suspect it is Wolf, their ancient rival, who is making overtures?" Adriel asked.

This time, Anriq's reply was slower in coming. Nonetheless, his response remained unchanged. "I trust them."

I nodded, knowing I had no choice but to accept Anriq's judgment in the matter or else force him into making a choice he clearly did not wish to. "Very well, then it's settled. You will accompany me to Nexus."

"What about Adriel and Safyre?" Teresa asked. "What will they be doing?"

"I will go to Death's home and recover my body," Adriel replied before I could respond. "But not immediately. First, I must inspect the Rings and determine if the possessed can be rehomed in the manner we hope."

"I, too, must leave," Safyre added. "I will accompany Michael and Anriq to Nexus. But I will delay my departure to assist Adriel with her investigations." She glanced at the lich. "Assuming she finds that acceptable?"

"I do," Adriel murmured. "The help of an aetherist-elite will not go amiss."

"Should Safyre be returning to Nexus?" Terence asked, looking alarmed at the notion.

Safyre sighed. "Kesh is one of the potential allies we must reach out to. But it is not only Kesh herself that is important. Her agents—the other forsworn like me, who have taken shelter in the emporium—are just as crucial to our cause. Michael may already have established a relationship with Kesh, the old tyrant may even *like* him, but for a sensitive matter like this, it's best my former fellows deal with someone who they've known for decades." She paused. "That's why it will be me who approaches Kesh."

I stayed glumly silent, not liking the idea of Safyre returning to Nexus, but knowing she was right. If anyone could convince Kesh and her agents to join our cause it was Safyre.

"But you're forsworn yourself," Terence protested, stating the obvious. "How are you going to reach Kesh alive?"

Safyre shrugged. "I will resume my identity as—" her eyes flitted to me—"Cara and become just another anonymous emporium agent for a time again."

"But—" Teresa began.

"Enough," I said, cutting her off. "Safyre knows what she is doing, as does Adriel."

"What about Draven's Reach?" Nyra asked abruptly.

I glanced at her. "What about it?"

"Aren't we going to reach out to those inside?" she asked, looking troubled.

I hesitated, then shook my head. "I've thought about it," I admitted, "but I don't think it's a good idea. The only way to get into the dungeon is to assault the blocking force the void fathers have placed around the Reach Portal, which may have the unhappy consequence of causing them to increase their forces in sector 18,240 even more. Needless to say, that's something we don't want. It's best, in fact, if the stygians have no hint of what's coming. That gives us the best chance of success when we *do* eventually hit them."

Frowning, Nyra nodded in reluctant agreement.

I rose to my feet. "Right, now that everyone knows what's in store for us in the immediate future, Nyra, Terence, and Teresa, you three better get some rest. We will be leaving at first light tomorrow."

Nyra blinked. "We?"

I nodded. "Yes, I will be escorting the three of you to the dungeon."

"Why would you do that?" Teresa asked with a frown.

"Well, for starters, to ensure you don't run into any trouble along the way," I said, earning myself a trio of glares. I grinned. "But also to make sure you three are well-stocked with any gear you need—ability tomes and skillbooks especially."

"Oh," Terence said. "I guess that's alright then."

I smiled but didn't voice the third reason. If the trio ran into any trouble in the dungeon, it would be me who would be doing the rescuing.

CHAPTER 498: NETHERNESS

I rose early the next morning—a habit that had become deeply ingrained in me since my first year-long visit to the tundra. Untangling myself from the pile of furs I'd buried myself beneath, I let my awareness expand.

The rest of the 'human' den was still abed. Even most of the wolves in the surrounding igloos were asleep. *"Go back to bed, Prime,"* Ghost said groggily. *"It's too early."*

I grinned. The pyre wolf was in the adjacent igloo, sharing her warmth with the other wolves, yet her mind was too attuned to mine not to notice my rising.

"We have a busy day ahead of us," I said, slipping out of my room.

"Every day is a busy day," she complained.

I chuckled. *"True enough."* Bracing myself for the cold, I strode out of the human compound and onto the tundra.

It was snowing again.

"When is it not?" a voice demanded grumpily.

Turning my head to the right, I spotted two shapes emerging through the curtain of white. The larger was a void of darkness on which the falling snow found no purchase—Ghost—while the smaller was a near-indistinguishable smear of whiteness.

"Sulan," I greeted the elder. *"You didn't need to get up."*

She snorted. *"As if this one's restlessness left me any choice,"* she said, nudging Ghost in the shoulder.

Obligingly, my familiar danced sideways. It was not that Sulan could force the much stronger pyre wolf to move if she didn't want to, but Ghost was Sulan's pup in every sense of the word except the literal one, and I doubted she would ever seriously set herself at odds with the pack elder.

"You are leaving today?" Sulan asked.

"Only for a short time," I replied.

A spurt of sorrow, quickly suppressed, shot through the white wolf's mind. It was not for me, though.

"Ghost will be staying to continue her training," I added.

Sulan turned to glare at the other wolf. *"You didn't tell me that,"* she accused.

Ghost ducked her head. *"I was going to surprise you."*

"Hmpf." The elder's blue eyes found me again. *"Then why are we out here?"*

"Two things," I murmured. *"The first is seeing to Ghost's advancements."*

"I see. But you could've done that just as easily inside—where it's warmer," Sulan said pointedly.

That was true enough, but I wasn't about to let myself be drawn into an argument. *"Ready?"* I asked, turning to Ghost.

The pyre wolf bobbed her head. *"Yes, Prime."*

Without further ado, I turned my focus inward and called up her Class upgrade interface.

Assessing familiar's suitability for a Class upgrade...
Class points available: 8.
Familiar's rank: 6.
Upgrade requirements met.
Your familiar may advance her Class to rank 7 at this time by improving an existing Class benefit or by selecting a new one. Do you wish to proceed?

Responding in the affirmative, I half-heartedly scanned through the scrolling Game text that followed like I had on prior occasions, but without really expecting anything to catch my eye. It was the existing benefits that I was interested in.

Ghost and I had already agreed to upgrade her draining bite ability. Her death magic skill had reached tier two recently and was ready for advancement. Unfortunately, none of her other abilities were in a similar position. Otherwise, I would have had no hesitation in upgrading her class ability, manifest, again.

"It's like we discussed, Ghost," I began. *"Draining bite is—"*

I broke off.

Ghost tensed. *"What is it?"*

I scanned the hovering Game message again, making sure I'd not misread it.

I had not.

"One of the new benefits on offer is a skill," I murmured.

"Oh. A skill," Ghost said. *"I don't need another one of those, do I? Let's stick with upgrading draining bite."*

"Ordinarily, I'd agree," I replied, *"but this is no ordinary skill."* Focusing on the applicable Game text, I read it aloud for Sulan and her.

New benefit: <u>nether manipulation</u>. This skill allows Ghost to manipulate the nether.

The Game's description of the skill was damnably short, which perhaps explained why I'd almost failed to register its presence in the first place. But despite the Adjudicator's less-than-insightful explanation, I felt my interest piqued. This was the type of skill we'd been looking for.

Something different. Something rare.

Opening my eyes, I scanned the faces of the two wolves to see what they thought, but neither looked anywhere near as excited as I was.

"That's it?" Sulan asked eventually. *"That's all the Game has to say about the skill? It's for manipulating the nether? What's so good about that?"*

I chuckled. *"It doesn't sound like much, I agree. But I've only ever run across a handful of nether skills during my time in the Game—nether wizardry and nether absorption amongst them. There's no two ways about it; nether skills are definitely rare—and valuable."*

"It sounds like nether magic," Ghost put in cautiously.

"It might be that," I conceded. *"Or it might be a psi-based equivalent. There's no way to tell from the Game's description, but whichever it is, we can't afford to ignore it."*

"What about the ability you came out here to upgrade in the first place—draining bite?" Sulan asked.

I brushed aside the question. *"Ghost has plenty of Class points. We'll improve draining bite after this."* I turned back to the pyre wolf. *"So, what'll it be? Do you want to learn the new skill?"*

Ghost hesitated. *"Shouldn't we ask Adriel or Safyre what they think?"*

I shrugged. *"We could seek out their advice, but when it comes to the nether, their expertise is not any greater than our own."* I paused. *"There's one other consideration: jeweled pet and mage's surprise. Assuming nether manipulation is a mana-based skill like I hope, I will also be able to use whatever spells you acquire."*

Ghost bobbed her head, finally convinced. *"Alright, Prime, let's do it."*

I smiled. *"Excellent,"* I said and conveyed our choice to the Adjudicator.

Upgrade complete. Class points remaining: 7.
Ghost's Class has advanced to rank 7.
Ghost has gained the master skill: <u>nether manipulation</u>.

Due to the substantial amount of stygian matter woven into her being, Ghost is in some respects akin to the void's creatures. As such, she is one of the few Game participants able to learn nether skills.

Nether manipulation is a specialized school of nether wizardry that focuses solely on manipulating free-floating nether. This includes dispelling, moving, modifying, and eventually creating nether. The skill itself does not provide your familiar with any immunity from the nether's touch; however, abilities to this effect may be acquired.

Note, as a familiar, Ghost may only manipulate nether that she is in direct contact with. She is unable to affect the deadly mists from afar. Ghost has no more skill slots remaining.

"Well, well," I murmured. *"This sounds perfect—especially considering our plans for sector 18,240."* Just how perfect gave me momentary pause. Was Ghost's new benefit the Game's way of pushing its own agenda?

"You think so?" Sulan asked, distracting me from my musings. *"How is Ghost going to manipulate the nether if she has to immerse herself in it first?"*

"That bit is unfortunate," I admitted and, before the elder could grow more alarmed, added, *"but Ghost's ash armor already grants her a measure of nether resistance, and that will only grow as she advances the skill further."*

Sulan glanced meaningfully at the younger wolf. *"Then it's a good thing she is staying behind. I will have to intensify her training."*

"Aww, Prime, why did you have to tell her that?" Ghost asked on a whisper-thin mental channel.

"I heard that," Sulan snapped.

Ghost ducked her head apologetically.

Sulan rose to her feet, unimpressed. *"Come on then, pup. There's no time to waste. We will have to reorganize your training to focus on improving your ash armor."*

I winced. There was only one way to advance an armor skill, and that was by taking hits, and I had a feeling Ghost was in for a world of pain in the coming days.

"Prime?" my familiar asked, looking at me hopefully.

I shook my head, denying her implicit request. Even if I was willing to risk Sulan's wrath by rescuing my familiar, I wouldn't. The dire wolf elder was right, after all. Given Ghost's new skill, it made sense for her to focus exclusively on her armor training in the coming days.

"I'll finish up here without you," I said. Technically, I didn't need Ghost's permission when choosing her upgrades and besides, I could still contact her from a distance if necessary. *"I'll advance draining bite like we discussed and also get you a nether manipulation ability if one appears."*

And one was almost guaranteed to do so. The Game knew any magic skill was useless without an ability to train it, which would influence the new benefits it offered during Ghost's follow-up Class upgrades.

Sighing heavily, Ghost slunk dejectedly after Sulan.

Chuckling at the pyre wolf's antics, I sat down cross-legged in the naked snow and closed my eyes. I still had Ghost's progression to finish, and then I had my own to see to as well.

✳ ✳ ✳

Much to my relief, my supposition proved accurate, and on Ghost's very next upgrade, a nether manipulation ability appeared—or rather, two did.

3 new Class benefits are available, and 2 of 6 existing benefits are upgradeable.

New benefit: <u>mist-taken</u>. Your familiar can swallow a tiny portion of the surrounding nether, storing it for later use.

New benefit: <u>mist-thin</u>. This spell lets Ghost reduce the concentration of nether in the immediate vicinity.

New benefit: <u>pinning paw</u>. This ability allows Ghost to knock down her foe in a single hit.

Existing benefits that may be upgraded: <u>draining bite</u> and <u>born again II</u>. Existing benefits not available for upgrade: <u>manifest</u>, <u>astral bite</u>, <u>diresight</u>, and <u>direshield</u>.

"Two abilities," I muttered, rubbing hard at my jaw. It was not that I didn't relish the opportunity the choice provided, it was just that I was having a hard time deciding between them.

It had not escaped my notice that nether manipulation had one hard, limiting factor: it could only be used in a nether-infested sector. For all the skill's obvious benefits, it would be useless in an untainted sector. Mist-taken seemed to offer a solution in this regard. A partial one anyway.

Ghost being able to carry around even a tiny vial's worth of free-floating mists elsewhere could be invaluable, especially considering my own nether immunity. Much, however, would depend on the exact mechanics of the ability and if she could simply eject the swallowed mist. On the other hand, mist-thin would undoubtedly be more useful *while* Ghost and I were in the nether.

It would likely also be easier to train nether manipulation with mist-thin. And in the short term, raising the skill was what mattered most.

"Mist-thin it is," I murmured.

Ghost has gained the basic spell: <u>mist-thin.</u>

This is a channeled ability that allows Ghost to reduce the toxicity of the free-floating nether in a 10 yard radius by 1 tier. Mist-thin has no verbal or somatic components. Its activation time is slow, it consumes mana, and it can be upgraded.

Upgrade complete. Class points remaining: 6.

Ghost's Class has advanced to rank 8.

"*Ah,*" Ghost exclaimed from afar as the Adjudicator fed the new knowledge into her consciousness.

"*What do you think of the spell?*" I asked.

"*It doesn't feel very useful.*"

"It isn't," I conceded. "*Not yet anyway. But imagine what it will be like at tier five. I wouldn't be surprised if you could thin the nether into nothingness by then.*"

"*Now that would be useful,*" Ghost agreed.

I grinned. It certainly would.

CHAPTER 499: SETTING OUT

You have upgraded Ghost's draining bite ability to <u>improved draining bite</u>. The second tier of this ability allows your familiar to leech 20% of the damage she inflicts from a single bite attack, restoring her own health in the process. You and Ghost have 59 of 65 Magic ability slots remaining.

Upgrade complete. Class points remaining: 5.

Ghost's Class has advanced to rank 9.

After advancing Ghost's death magic ability, I turned my attention to my own progression. The first order of business was spending the six attribute points I had accrued over the last few days.

Your Dexterity has increased to rank 116. Other modifiers: +24 from items.

Your Mind has increased to rank 126. Other modifiers: +12 from items.

I split the points evenly between Mind and Dexterity, not-so-coincidentally increasing my available slots in each to fifteen—the exact number needed to advance a master-tiered ability to elite.

So... am I ready for more elite abilities?

To answer the question, I called up the relevant extracts from my player profile.

Status of Dexterity abilities (101 of 116 slots used)

Elite abilities (not eligible for upgrade): backstab, vanish.

Master abilities (not eligible for upgrade): whirlwind.

Expert abilities: set trap.

Advanced abilities: piercing strike, trap disarm, lockpicking.

Basic abilities: crippling strike (can't be upgraded).

Status of Mind abilities (111 of 126 slots used)

Master abilities (not eligible for upgrade): windborne, enhanced reflexes, shadow blink, quick mend.

Master abilities (eligible for upgrade): mass puppet, astral shurikens, fortified mind.

Basic abilities: stunning slap (can't be upgraded).

I sighed. Sadly, my sole master-tiered Dexterity ability—whirlwind—couldn't be advanced, since its governing skill—two weapon fighting—hadn't reached tier five yet. Nonetheless, I had another Dexterity ability in urgent need of attention: set trap.

The scoundrel wristband I'd looted from the Blade Haiken was able to deploy tier four traps, something I myself was incapable of doing just yet. If I wanted to utilize the item properly, improving set trap was necessary.

Taking an upgrade gem in hand, I did just that.

You have upgraded your set trap ability to <u>greater set trap</u>. This ability allows you to deploy tier 4 traps. Additionally, it increases the effectiveness

of your traps, enhancing their range, strength, and concealment. You and Ghost have 10 of 116 Dexterity ability slots remaining.

That takes care of Dexterity.

Turning my attention to Mind, I considered the three abilities ready for improvement: mass puppet, astral shurikens, and fortified mind. Which to advance?

Not mass puppet, I decided immediately.

Given my recent acquisition of blood puppet, I had an overabundance of mental domination abilities right now, which meant mass puppet could wait. And as much as I wanted to upgrade astral shurikens, tending to my mental defenses had to be my first priority. Especially, considering that I would soon be facing a telepathic stygian Power in the form of a void tree.

Crushing another upgrade gem in my hand, I saw to the ability's advancement.

You have upgraded your fortified mind ability to <u>impregnable mind</u>, transforming your consciousness into a veritable fortress. The fifth tier of this spell is a passive variant that requires no active intervention on your part and ensures your consciousness is always protected, even when you are asleep. It consumes no psi except when repelling hostile attacks.

You have 0 of 126 Mind ability slots remaining.

A slow grin spread across my face as I felt the new spell take effect. It required no casting and felt less like a spell and more like a... permanent buff.

Impregnable mind is active.

"Excellent," I murmured as I rose to my feet. I was as ready as I could be for the next few weeks. It would not be easy, I knew. Not only would I be entering Nexus, the beating heart of the Game, but I'd also be going up against five stygian Powers.

If I succeed, though...

If I succeeded, if I somehow managed to do everything needed—*without suffering any misadventures*, I thought wryly—then the future of the Forerunners would be secured. Come what may, the faction's people, *my people*, would be safe.

Swinging around, I turned my back on the tundra and headed into the den. It was time to rouse the others and get started.

✳　✳　✳

You have lost a Blood Talisman and a small bag of hiding containing 100 possessed finger bones.

A few hours later, my human companions, Ghost, and I were gathered at the portal to the nether-infested sector. The wolves had opted to stay at the den where it was warm, and I didn't blame them. I had made sure to leave the House's most prized possessions in their keeping as well.

"You three ready?" I asked.

Nyra, Terence, and Teresa nodded, the latter two bouncing on their feet.

Ignoring the twins' excitement, I performed one last check on the trio's gear. Nyra had the longbow quaker strapped across her back and the elite poisoning kit concealed somewhere about her person.

Terence was in his old armor. Malikor's legendary armor was too distinctive to wear around other players, and the young swordsman had wisely left it behind. He had, however, seen fit to bring along the mirror shield.

Teresa's garb was just as subdued as her brother's. She carried two rank six items on her person—icefang and healer's friend—but I could see no sign of either.

"Perfect," I pronounced. "You three look like just about any other party of young players I've come across."

"Not quite," Safyre murmured, her gaze resting on quaker and the mirror shield. "It'll be clear to anyone who thinks to look that you three have powerful backers, but that's not a bad thing."

Terence smirked. "Little do they know how powerful."

"Still, it's best you don't attract any undue attention," Adriel warned. "Most players are opportunistic by nature and absent benefactors—no matter how powerful—will not stop them from taking advantage of any weakness they sense."

"Adriel's advice is sound," I added. "Make sure you heed it."

The trio nodded again, more grimly this time.

"Good. Then there are just two last things to see to," I said and waved Nyra forward.

Looking puzzled, my apprentice approached slowly.

"I have one more gift for you," I said by way of explanation as I laid my hand on her shoulder. Closing my eyes, I willed my intent to the Game.

Commander ability triggered.

Do you wish to pass on the <u>blood puppet</u> memory to your follower, Nyra?

"Yes," I said aloud.

Analyzing player...

...

...

Analysis complete.

Nyra carries a major wolf bloodline strain that is as yet unawakened, and you may bequeath her with a less powerful variant of the blood memory. Do you still wish to proceed?

Willing my answer to the Game's query, I waited.

Nyra has been awarded the ability: <u>enslave (lesser)</u>. As a weaker variant of blood puppet, this blood memory will allow your follower to permanently enslave a single non-player subject whose level is equal to or lower than her own. This spell will only remain active while your follower and the dominated subject remain in the same sector.

Note, in the event that your follower binds herself to a bloodline other than Wolf, she will lose access to this blood memory.

I released my apprentice's shoulder, and she staggered back, her eyes wide with shock.

"Use it wisely," I replied in response to her look. "The blood spell should benefit you greatly in the dungeon, especially if you dominate the right creature."

"Thank you," she murmured.

"Now for the last thing," I said. Retreating a few steps, I nodded jerkily in Adriel and Safyre's direction. "Hit me."

Adriel's lips twitched. "You're going to have to step farther back than that."

"Give him some space," Safyre said, addressing the others.

The rest of my companions backed away hastily.

Adriel looked at me questioningly. "Ready?"

I braced myself. "Go for it."

The lich gestured to Safyre. "You first."

"I've been dying to see how this works," the aetherist murmured. Before I could reply, she flung up her wands, then brought them crashing down.

Safyre has cast furious storm.

In response, the clouds roiled into sudden turmoil, the air crackled with static, and flashes of light rent the darkening sky. Then a bolt sizzled downward, striking the ground mere inches away.

You have passed a magical resistance check! Safyre has failed to stun you.
A lightning bolt has injured you.

I flew backward, my limbs trembling and my thoughts befuddled as a result of the violent charge coursing through me. The bolt, though, was only the first of many.

A second, a third, and a fourth followed in its wake. Then dozens more.

A lightning bolt has injured you.
A lightning bolt has injured you.

...

Void thief triggered!
You have acquired the area-of-effect spell <u>furious storm (stolen)</u> and will retain memory of it for the next 16 hours.
Furious storm (stolen) is a tier 5 spell that rains down destruction in a circle 50 yards in diameter for 30 seconds. All entities in the target area will be randomly struck by lightning, and may be stunned, dazed, or killed outright.
Void negate activated! You are immune to furious storm for the next 16 hours.

Gingerly, I picked myself up, ignoring the lightning still falling all around me.

"Impressive," Safyre murmured, watching me dusting myself off.

"Wild!" Terence yelled, his eyes shining.

"Wow," Teresa exclaimed, for once at a loss for words.

"Psychotic," Anriq murmured under his breath. "That's what it is."

I threw them a lopsided grin. "It's all that and more, but believe me, it still hurts. I feel like I've been stomped on—repeatedly."

"A small price to pay for such a powerful ability," Adriel rejoined unsympathetically.

I chuckled. "Perhaps."

Adriel raised her arm. "My turn."

I held up my hand. "One second. Let me secure the spell."

You have successfully stored the <u>furious storm</u> spell in the ring, mage's surprise.

You have fully restored yourself with quick mend.

I straightened. "I'm ready."

I barely got the words out before streams of black smoke spewed out of Adriel's mouth to envelop me in their dark embrace.

A noxious vapors spell has injured you.

You have failed a magical resistance check! You are <u>rotting </u>(health decaying at 10% per second). Duration: 5 seconds.

"Wow," I muttered. I'd suffered under the effect of the selfsame spell the first time Adriel and I had met. Only then, it had just grazed me. This time, the damage was much worse, and in no time at all, my mana pool shrank as it fought to protect me.

Void thief triggered!

You have acquired the channeled spell <u>noxious vapors (stolen)</u> and will retain memory of it for the next 16 hours.

Noxious vapors (stolen) is a tier 6 spell that decays the flesh of all living entities to feel its touch. The health of every target subjected to the spell will decay at a rate of 10% per second for 5 seconds. Note, each subsequent touch from the vapors will increase the duration of the spell's debuff.

Void negate activated! You are immune to noxious vapors for the next 16 hours.

Stolen spell limit reached. You have lost knowledge of the tier 5 spell, furious storm.

"Well," I remarked as nonchalantly as I could while still reeling on my feet. "Now, I'm ready."

Adriel rolled her eyes, not impressed by my bravado. "Heal up and follow us through." Marching forward, she entered the portal.

CHAPTER 500: DUNGEON FOUND

You have entered sector 18,240 of the Forever Kingdom.
The nether toxicity at your current location is at tier 4.
Safyre has cast purifying dome. Duration: 30 minutes.
You have entered a purifying field. All environmental ill-effects have been nullified.

I stepped out of the portal, but not into the nether's familiar coils. Instead, I entered a space blessedly free of the void's mists and still bearing the electric tang of the spell used to clear it.

"That was fast," I remarked, studying the purified span of space a hundred yards in diameter around the portal.

Safyre threw me a quick smile over her shoulder. "I had the spell prepped and ready to go."

"Is the area clear?" Adriel asked, all business.

"Yes," I replied, having already checked the surroundings. "There are no stygians around for miles."

"I'll get started then," the lich replied. Not waiting for my reply, she closed her eyes and began casting.

I watched intently. Adriel was opening a portal—or rather, she was trying to.

She and Safyre had ranked the potential dungeons they'd come up with from most to least favorable, and first on the list was a location that had only been known to high-ranking members of House Death. Assuming the dungeon and the sector leading to it hadn't been rediscovered since, Nyra and the twins would have a long-abandoned dungeon all to themselves. An ideal scenario.

Alas, it was not to be.

The lich opened her eyes. "The portal refuses to open," she said tightly. Which meant the sector in question had been rediscovered, claimed, and was now shielded from unauthorized access.

I sighed. *I guess it was too much to hope for.* I swung to face Safyre. "Let's move on to option two."

Wordlessly, the aetherist began casting, but only a moment later, she, too, stopped. "No go. The sector is shielded."

I forbore comment. Option two had been nearly as perfect as number one. Unfortunately, the alternatives were, for one reason or the other, significantly less so. Still, everything on the list fulfilled the basic criteria we'd established and were all far outside the zones of control of the Game's most powerful factions.

"Run through the rest of the list until you find all those that work," I instructed grimly. Turning to the others, I added, "Best make yourselves comfortable. This may take a while."

✳ ✳ ✳

Ghost has taken the form of a level 236 stygian pyre wolf.

While I waited patiently for Adriel and Safyre to finish their investigations, the rest of my companions—Ghost, Nyra, Anriq, and the twins—made their way to the edge of the purifying dome to gaze upon the nether mist beyond. For two of them at least, this was their first opportunity to study the nether at leisure.

"Can I go past the dome?" Ghost asked.

I glanced at her. *"You plan on trying your new skill?"*

She bobbed her head.

"Go on," I said, smiling indulgently, *"but don't stray too far."*

Bounding forward, the pyre wolf slipped beyond the edges of Safyre's spell and into the mists.

Immediately, damage messages began scrolling across my vision. Ignoring them, I kept my gaze focused on my familiar as she wove mana.

Ghost has cast mist-thin, reducing the nether toxicity of the nether around her in a 10 yard radius to tier 3. Duration: infinite. The debuff will remain in effect as long as your familiar continues channeling the spell.

"It works!" the pyre wolf exclaimed.

I chuckled. *"Of course it does."* Narrowing my eyes, I studied the yellowish haze around Ghost as she raced along the outside of the purifying dome. The change was nearly imperceptible, but the mist around my familiar was *definitely* thinner.

Ghost's nether manipulation has increased to level 2.
Ghost's nether manipulation has increased to level 3.
...

"Keep at it," I murmured. *"You're doing well."*

"Where's Ghost gone to?" Adriel asked.

Swinging around, I found the lich and Safyre looking at me expectantly. Neither could see the pyre wolf in the mist, of course. "Training her nether manipulation," I replied.

I'd told the pair about Ghost's new skill on the way over. Surprisingly, neither had heard of it before nor of anything similar. Still, they'd both agreed with my assessment. Selecting it had been the right decision.

Safyre arched one eyebrow. "She's not wasting time, is she?"

"Time, I fear, is the one commodity we're always going to be short of," I replied.

Adriel laughed. "True enough."

My gaze darted from one to the other. "I take it you found an accessible dungeon?"

"We have," Adriel said.

I waited.

"Only number five and eight on the list are open for portal entry," Safyre said.

"Five and eight," I echoed, mentally running through what the pair had told me of the sectors in question.

Neither was ideal. Worse yet, number eight was controlled by a Light faction. A minor one to be sure, but one not averse to selling dungeon access to 'neutral' players—which was the only reason it was on the list in the first place.

"I guess it has to be five then," I said heavily.

Both women nodded solemnly.

I looked at Safyre. Number five was one of her contributions to the list. "Did you manage to glean anything of the sector's current conditions?"

She shook her head. "No, I let the spell unravel before the portal could fully form."

It was a justifiable precaution. One I couldn't fault. I sighed. "Let's go tell the others the good news, then."

✳   ✳   ✳

"We've found an accessible dungeon," I said, when the rest of the party rejoined us at the portal.

"Which one is it?" Teresa asked excitedly.

"Number five," I replied. "Korg."

Terence frowned. "Korg? But isn't that the sector with a one-way portal?"

"It is," I replied. The one-way dungeon portal was the primary reason sector 65,231—otherwise known as Korg—was as low down on the list as it was. The dungeon itself, Korg's Deep, was an ideal fit for the trio, but unfortunately, its exit portal was in a sector that neither Safyre nor Adriel had visited before.

That was the bad news. The good news was that both the entrance and exit nether portals from Korg's Deep were located in the safe zone of their respective sectors. The dungeoneering trio would therefore only be at risk while they were in the Deep itself.

"You've been to Korg, Saf," Teresa said. "What can you tell us about it?"

Safyre's lips turned down. "Nothing more than what I've already shared, I'm afraid. I visited Korg exactly once, and briefly at that. Then Korg Minor—the sector you'll be entering through—was owned by a small faction. I forget the name."

"You didn't enter the dungeon?" Terence asked.

Safyre shook her head. "I was in Korg for another reason. But I remember the dungeon's description well. The Deep is designed for a party of tier two players and is seeded with mostly non-magical creatures. It shouldn't be especially hard for you three to run through."

"But how will we get back when we're done?" Nyra asked worriedly.

It was the question on everyone's minds. "It should not be too complicated," Safyre remarked. "Korg Major—the sector with the dungeon exit portal—sits adjacent to Korg Minor, after all. If for whatever reason you can't teleport out directly from Korg Major, you should return to sector 65,231 and leave from there." She bit her lip. "Although, I'll admit that may be easier said than done."

I nodded. Much would depend on the current conditions in the respective sectors—of which we knew nothing. Nor would further speculation help. "We'll figure it out once we're in Korg," I pronounced.

Teresa bounced on her feet. "So, we're still going ahead?"

"We are." I paused. "Assuming you three are comfortable with the risks, of course."

"Yes!" the twins exclaimed in unison.

I glanced at Nyra who nodded firmly. "I am."

"Good. I guess we are a go, then." Removing the Cloak of the Reach, I handed it to Adriel who accepted it without comment. Kneeling, I ruffled the pyre wolf's coat. *"Take care, Ghost."*

"You, too, Prime."

"I won't be gone long," I assured her. *"Focus on your ash armor training with Sulan in the meantime, and perhaps Adriel will bring you back here sometimes so you can work on nether manipulation, too."*

"I'd like that," Ghost said.

I glanced at Adriel who nodded. *"I'll bring her,"* she agreed.

"Thanks," I said aloud as I rose to my feet. Turning to Anriq, I handed him the Sylvanain eye. "You remember what to search for?"

"I do," he replied.

"Don't go scouting in-person," I warned. "Use the eye." I grimaced apologetically. "It'll be tedious work, I know, but finding a—"

The werewolf waved aside my words. "Don't worry. I understand the importance of the task you've set me. I'll find what we need."

I clasped his hand, glad that I could depend on him. Turning around, I faced Safyre who returned my look.

"No need for goodbyes," she said with a smile. "We'll see each other soon enough."

Inclining my head in rueful agreement, I saw to my final preparations.

You have cast mimic, transforming your visage into that of Actus, a level 101 human brawler and concealing your Powerful Initiate Mark. Duration: 10 hours.

You have activated the simple mode enchantment of the belt of the chameleon. Your armor and weapons are now hidden.

Feeling out my new face—that of a player I'd run across in Nexus—I checked my clothing. Camouflaged by the chameleon belt, they were as non-descript as I expected. If anything, I wanted to attract even less attention than my younger companions. "Right, final check. Does everyone have their farspeaker bracelets equipped?"

Solemnly, the trio raised their arms, baring the gold bracelet on their wrists. I wore the last one. For this mission, we would be taking all four of Safyre's farspeaker artifacts, they being essential for the four of us to communicate easily with each other in Korg.

I glanced at Adriel and Safyre. "I'll head directly to the wolves' valley after seeing our dungeon team settled," I told them. "So, don't expect me to return for at least a few days yet."

"Give Saya my regards," Safyre replied.

"And bring her back if you can," Terence blurted.
Declining to reply, I nodded at Safyre. "Open it."

Safyre has cast supreme portal, creating a protected ley line to sector 65,231.

"Protected ley line?" I asked, my gaze flitting between the aetherist and the curtain of light that had materialized before her.
"It's exactly what it sounds like—a shielded portal," she explained. "No one will be able to pass through without my permission."
"Useful," I murmured.
"You four better go," Safyre instructed, waving me forward. "The longer the portal is open, the more attention it will attract."
I nodded in agreement. The time had come to put our plans in motion. Inhaling deeply, I ducked through the waiting gateway.

Transfer through portal commencing...
...

...
Passage completed!
Leaving sector 18,240 of the Forever Kingdom.

CHAPTER 501: KORG

You have entered sector 65,231 of the Forever Kingdom, an open sector forming part of the region known as Korg. This sector is under the control of the Silach.

The following restrictions apply to this sector: only silachens may purchase new buildings in the safe zone and only silachen civilians may trade in the safe zone. Note, a shield generator is in place around the sector, preventing portals from opening anywhere except in the designated teleportation areas.

You have entered a safe zone.

I stepped out from the portal and into a brightly lit world. The sun shone down from up high, the sky was deep cerulean, and the breeze had a salty tang to it. Wet white sand lay beneath my feet, and from behind, I heard waves rippling gently in and out. In front of me there were more sand dunes, palm trees, and what appeared to be a prosperous village.

Whatever else Korg Minor was, it was an idyllic-looking sector. *Island,* I corrected. *Korg Minor is an island.*

Turning around slowly, I confirmed what my senses were telling me. I was standing on a south-facing beach. According to Safyre, the safe zone encompassed the entire island, which made Korg Minor a player-only sector.

Unless, of course, the surrounding ocean is home to an aquatic species. Which, admittedly, was not far outside the realm of possibilities.

The gate behind me burped, and three more figures spilled out before it winked out of existence. My companions' tension was palpable. Bunching together behind me, they eyed the surroundings nervously.

"Is this the place?" Terence whispered.

"Of course, it is!" Teresa snapped back in a low voice. "Didn't you read the Adjudicator's message?"

"Should we draw our weapons?" Nyra asked, fixing her gaze on me.

I shook my head. "This is a safe zone. There is no need for that." I paused, then projected my words through the farspeaker bracelet. *"That is not to say the island will be threat-free. There is almost certainly danger here. But it won't be of the physical kind. Stay on guard, and don't utter anything revealing aloud. Who knows who may be listening."*

The trio nodded in grim understanding.

"Let's go," I said. "Whoever runs this place is probably in the village."

✳ ✳ ✳

The village was heavily populated.

However, the residents were not what I expected. Green-scaled and blue-gilled, they had webbing fanning out from behind their heads and a thick muscular tail in place of legs.

"Merefolk," Teresa muttered.

I tore my gaze away from the players sliding across the sand like upright snails to glance at the twins. The merefolk were everywhere, slipping in and out of the buildings but seemed disinterested in us.

"You've come across them before?"

"You could say that," Terence said. "We had a run-in with a mereman early on in our Game. He was a new entrant like us."

"He was also rude, curt, and standoffish," Teresa added bitingly.

"But a great fighter, nonetheless," Terence said.

Teresa nodded reluctantly.

"I see," I said noncommittally. The twins' remarks were hardly useful, nor did they explain the merefolk's presence on the island. Safyre had not mentioned them either, and I could only assume that was because they hadn't been here during her own visit. The amphibious nature of the sector's residents would've surely stuck in her memory otherwise.

What did it mean for our plans?

"Hail, two-legs."

Facing forward again, I saw that a large mereman wielding a harpoon had placed himself before us. He wore no armor, nor any clothing of any kind, but was draped in jewelry aplenty, each bearing the telltale spark of magic.

"Welcome to Korg," the mereman continued, seeing that he had our attention. "What brings you to our little corner of the world?"

"Greetings...?" I began, pointedly not using his name, though I knew it already.

"Wylton," he supplied easily, "silachen protector and resident of Korg."

I inclined my head. "Well met, Wylton. I'm Actus, and this is Nyra, Terence, and Teresa."

"What brings you to Korg?" Wylton asked again. "It is not often we get visitors of the two-legged variety."

"I confess I've never been to Korg before," I replied, "nor for that matter have I heard of the silachen."

Wylton laughed. "I'm not surprised. We are a new faction."

I let my surprise show. "Then Korg is a recent... acquisition?"

"Relatively," he allowed. "Silach claimed both islands a decade ago."

Hmm. So, they own Korg Major as well. "That explains it."

Wylton tilted his head to the side. "Explains what?"

"It's been many years since our friend, the one who directed us here, last visited the island," I said.

"Ah," Wylton remarked. "You were expecting a different sort of reception."

I smiled. "Actually, we had no idea what to expect. Our coming here was something of a gamble." I dipped my head again. "One which hasn't paid off it seems. Please accept my apology for the intrusion. We'll take our leave now." Not waiting for his response, I swung around. *"Let's go."*

"Wait!"

I drew to a halt. I'd been hoping we could make our escape without suffering further questioning. For all of the mereman's apparent affability, he was a rank nineteen player. And while not all the other players in the village were of comparable level, enough of them were to leave me in no doubt that the Silach were a powerful faction.

One, I did not want to trifle with.

Especially not with three under-leveled companions at my back, and *especially* not on their home turf. But I did not mistake the protector's words for anything but what they were: an order.

Sighing, I turned back around. "Yes?"

"You did not answer my question," Wylton said mildly.

I feigned ignorance. "Which one?"

The mereman chuckled, not fooled. "The only one that matters: what brings you to Korg?"

There was no point in denying the truth. "We came for the dungeon," I admitted. "Korg's Deep."

Wylton's gaze flitted from me to the others, studying our gear critically. "What Force are you affiliated with?"

"None yet," I replied, "as I'm sure you've already noticed."

Wylton's lips turned down. "Which Power then?"

"One who prefers to remain anonymous," I replied calmly.

The mereman frowned but didn't push the issue.

I stepped back. "Now that we've answered your questions, we'll take our leave."

"The dungeon is open to non-faction members," he declared abruptly.

My brows rose in surprise. "Really?"

He nodded. "There will be a cost, though."

"Naturally," I murmured. "How much?"

Wylton shrugged. "That's for the dungeon keeper to say. You will find him at the island's northern beach, in the tower housing the nether portal."

I hesitated. Wylton had displayed no sign of hostility, yet I remained wary of staying longer. The silachen appeared to be in absolute control of the sector, and the same likely applied to Korg Major. Then there was the strength of the protector's Marks.

The mereman was steeped in Shadow. As were many of the village's residents.

Wylton had not said so, but I was certain the Silach were a Shadow faction. Did I really want to leave my young companions at their mercy? But what other choice did I have? Right now, it was either this or a dungeon under the control of a Light faction.

"We should do it," Teresa said.

I glanced at her sideways. *"They're a Shadow faction."*

"So?" she demanded caustically. *"That doesn't make them any more—or less—dangerous than a Dark or Light one."*

Because of Loken, I viewed Shadow with more trepidation than I did Dark and Light, but Teresa was right. There was no objective difference between the three. Shadow factions could be as benign as Light or Dark ones—or just as brutal.

"That may be true," I admitted, *"but there's no denying they're a Force faction, and likely one with a Power nearby. Are you three sure you want to enter a dungeon controlled by them?"*

"We should at least investigate further," Nyra replied.

"I agree," Terence added.

I sighed. *"Very well."* Turning my attention outward again, I bestowed Wylton with another smile. "Thank you for the directions. We'll head that way now."

* * *

We made our way through the village without incident.

None of the players we passed—all merefolk—attempted to approach us, and while I spotted more than one shopkeeper, I kept my distance as well. As the only landbound players on the island, we were already too memorable, and the last thing I wanted was to create more of a stir.

Exiting the village, I spotted a blurred shape to the north. "Korg Major," I murmured.

"Where?" Teresa asked.

"There," I said, pointing out the large landmass on the horizon. "It looks huge."

Terence squinted at the island. "Well, at least we now know which direction to swim in if we have to."

"I don't think you want to do that," I said, picking out a deceptively small shape breaking through the surface in the far distance. "The ocean is not empty, and somehow, I don't think the wildlife is going to be friendly."

"Oh," Terence said, deflating.

"That must be the tower Wylton spoke of," Nyra said, drawing my attention.

Looking where she pointed, I spotted a squat wooden tower partially obscured by the surrounding palm trees. Changing course, I headed towards it.

* * *

The tower's ground floor was crowded with heavily armored and armed merefolk. *Dungeon teams,* I thought, *readying for their dive.* It was not only merefolk filling the room, though. Looking carefully, I spotted a handful of tratins, sirens, and even a few sea hags.

The sea hags gave me pause.

Our one prior meeting had not ended well, but even though our entrance had attracted the attention of everyone in the room, I sensed no animosity in any of the staring faces, hags included.

"Is there a line?" Terence asked worriedly. *"Because if we have to wait for all these people to go through first, it's going to be days before we enter the dungeon."*

"Don't be so impatient," Teresa retorted.

"You're calling me impatient?" Terence demanded incredulously.

I almost smiled at the pair's banter, but the approach of a slim merewoman distracted me. "You can head on down," she said peremptorily.

I blinked. "Down?"

She nodded. "Wylton told us you were coming. Dungeon Keeper Quartz is waiting."

"What about all of them?" Terence asked, looking pointedly into the crowded room.

The merewoman shrugged. "They're freeloaders. You're paying customers. You get preference."

Terence straightened proudly. "How about that."

Rolling her eyes, Teresa brushed past him and down the nearby stairs.

Nyra and Terence glanced at me.

"I guess we best follow her," I replied in response to their looks.

CHAPTER 502: REVISITING OLD HAUNTS

Except for a hulking and bearded mereman, the tower's basement was empty. But that was not to say I did not have cause for renewed surprise. In place of a single nether portal, I found *ten*—all shimmering and all active.

"Damn," Terence remarked, echoing my own sentiments.

"Welcome," Quartz, the dungeon keeper, said, smiling genially. "I take it from your expressions that this is your first visit to the Deeps?"

I nodded. "We were expecting, uhm, *one* dungeon."

"Oh, you're not wrong," he said. "Korg's Deeps is a single dungeon."

I frowned.

"One dungeon, ten levels," he explained. "What you see here are the one-way portals to each level."

I rubbed my chin. "I see."

"So, we can start at the last level?" Terence asked eagerly.

The mereman chuckled. "There is *no* last level, young man. Granted, there was such in the dungeon's original configuration. But we've changed all that. Each level now provides a separate and individual challenge.

I lifted an eyebrow. "Korg's Deeps is an owned dungeon?"

"It is indeed." Quartz rubbed his hands together. "And with ten levels to pick from, you four will be spoiled for choice."

"Three," I corrected him. "I will not be entering the dungeon."

The mereman didn't bat even an eye. "A party of three, very good. But before we get into the details, there is the matter of the entrance fee to settle."

"How much is it going to cost?" I asked.

"One thousand gold," he pronounced. "Each."

My companions' eyes bulged.

Quartz's smile vanished as he sensed their hesitancy. "The price is non-negotiable."

I sighed. "Of course, it is. But setting aside the matter of cost for the moment, where are the exits?"

The mereman turned my way. "There is a matching tower in the center of Korg Major. Your friends will emerge from the portal there."

I nodded. "And where can I get its coordinates?"

"I can open a portal to it right now if you like," he offered. "Assuming we conclude our transaction, that is."

"Hmm," I murmured noncommittally despite my pleasure at Quartz's offer. It simplified things greatly on my end and dealt with one of my major concerns, but we were bargaining I knew, and so I maintained a disinterested air. "What does that enormous entrance fee get my companions?"

The smile slid back onto the mereman's face. "Enormous? I wouldn't call it that. One thousand gold buys your friends two days in any level of their choice and guaranteed privacy. No one will be allowed to enter the level until their time is up or they slay its sector boss. And the best thing? They get to keep any loot they recover."

"Two days? One level? Those are ridiculous restrictions!" I scoffed. Turning around, I headed for the stairs. "Let's go."

As anticipated, I didn't get far.

"Wait!" Quartz barked. "Three days, then."

Ha! So much for 'non-negotiable.'

I turned around. "Five," I countered, "and as many levels as they want."

The merman glared. "That will be impossible to schedule. Four days. Two levels."

I pretended to think. "That would be acceptable if... you guarantee their privacy until they *exit*. No one must be allowed to enter a level until they leave it."

"Fine," Quartz muttered, "but any time they waste between killing a sector boss and exiting counts towards their four days."

I nodded. "That's agreeable." I turned back to my companions. "The decision is yours," I stated bluntly. "Do you wish to proceed?"

"Can we afford the fee?" Nyra asked.

"Yes," I replied simply.

"Do you think it's safe?" Terence asked cautiously.

I didn't laugh. *"No dungeon dive will ever be safe. But I think your question was directed more towards the Silach, yes?"*

He nodded almost imperceptibly.

"I wouldn't go so far as to say they're trustworthy. Motivated by self-interest? Maybe. Willing to cheat us out of every penny we have? Definitely. But out to get us specifically? I don't think so." I grimaced. *"If you ask me, the threats here are the everyday ones all players live with in the Game."* And as much as I wanted to protect them from such, it was not my place to do so.

"Let's do it," Teresa said firmly, and I glanced at the other two.

"I agree," Terence replied.

"Me, too," Nyra added.

Swinging back to the dungeon keeper, I found him grinning again. "Excellent decision!" he said and held out a bank keystone. "That will be three thousand gold, if you please."

Ignoring the keystone, I stretched out my own arm to reveal a purse and another item.

"What's this?" Quartz asked.

"Three thousand gold, just like you asked."

"There's only a thousand coins in your hand, friend," he stated flatly.

"*And* a legendary item worth much more than the two thousand outstanding," I added. "We can pay the fee."

The mereman chewed on his lip for a moment, then with a shrug, he moved to relieve me of the items.

I closed my fist. "Not so fast. Let's finish up our dealings first."

He scowled. "The negotiations are over."

I nodded. "So, they are. But you promised to open a portal to Korg Major, and there is also the small matter of the 'details' you mentioned earlier. Let's get all that out of the way before we conclude."

Quartz's scowl deepened. "Very well. Have it your way." Pointedly turning away from me, he scrutinized my three companions. "Which levels do you wish to enter?" Before they could answer, he added, "Given your levels, Class, and gear, I suggest attempting level one and four."

My brows rose in mute surprise, but I refrained from commenting. I'd done my bit, and it was time for the trio to take charge of matters.

"You said we'd have ten levels to choose from," Teresa pointed out when it became apparent I wouldn't speak. "What about the others?"

"Well..." the mereman temporized, "there *are* ten levels. But three are currently occupied, four are fully submerged, and the other has been designed for tier four players. That leaves only level one and four. Both of which will become available tomorrow morning."

"Tomorrow?" Terence demanded, his voice rising.

"Tomorrow," the dungeon keeper repeated, unruffled. "But if you prefer, you can wait another two days for level three and eight to become available. Both of those are also suitable for air-breathers of your ranks."

"Want to change your minds?" I asked the trio softly.

Teresa glared at me. *"No."* Swinging back to the mereman, she said, "Tell us everything you can about levels one and four."

✳ ✳ ✳

You have entered the safe zone of sector 65,232 of the Forever Kingdom.

An hour later, after our discussions with Quartz concluded, my companions and I entered Korg Major. Since the trio couldn't immediately start their dungeon dive, they'd managed to convince the dungeon keeper to waive payment of the fee until tomorrow morning—when they would *actually* enter the Deeps.

Quartz had then—with a not insignificant amount of grumbling—acceded to opening a gateway to Korg Major for all four of us.

Like its sister sector, Korg Major was protected by a shield generator and owned by the Silach. Neither of those things bothered me, though. As mercenary as the silachen appeared when it came to money, they didn't seem to care much about non-faction members wandering their domain, and as far as I could tell, the travel restrictions were minimal.

Korg Major itself was an eye-opener. It was many times larger and more cosmopolitan than Korg Minor. In my first few minutes alone in the sector, I saw dozens of 'two-legs' walking about unconcernedly.

"We don't stand out as much here," Nyra said, noticing the same thing.

"And there are plenty of shops around, too," I said, coming to stop in front of a tavern. "You three should make your purchases here before returning to Korg Minor."

"With what money?" Terence groused.

"Hold out your hands," I instructed.

The three did as I asked, and I dropped an item apiece in each's palm.

You have lost 3 x miscellaneous legendary items.

"Where did you get these from?" Teresa asked, looking down at the legendary artifact I'd given her in shock.

"Put them away before someone notices," I said gently. *"And as for where I got them, I looted them from the Devil Riders in the Eastern Marches."*

"What should we do with them?" Terence asked, taking another quick peek at his own item.

I smiled. "Sell them. I can't tell you their value because I don't know myself. Ask around—carefully. At a guess, I'd say each artifact is worth at least ten thousand gold."

Their eyes widened.

And no wonder, I'd just handed them a small fortune. But if the trio were going to succeed, they needed every advantage I could reasonably afford them.

I chuckled. "Use the proceeds from the sale for Quartz's entrance fee, a portal back to Korg Minor, and whatever gear you require. The rest you can store in a bank."

Nyra frowned. "It sounds like you're leaving."

"I am."

Concern replaced astonishment.

"Don't worry, you three have got this." I gestured to the tavern. "We'll meet back here in four days. By then, you should be done with your dungeon run." I glanced around. "And whatever you do, don't leave the safe zone with the artifacts still in your possession or while carrying anything of value. Hmm, better yet, don't leave the safe zone at all."

Unlike in Korg Minor, a whole city lay outside the Korg's Major safe zone—one I was sure the trio were tempted to explore.

"We won't venture into the city," Nyra promised.

I nodded. "See that you don't." Clasping their hands in turn, I bid them farewell and strode steadfastly away.

✳   ✳   ✳

After disappearing from the somewhat-forlorn trio's sight, I spent a few minutes walking around Korg Major's safe zone, trying to get a feel of the place, but if I was being honest, I was mostly wondering if I'd done the right thing.

Nyra, Terence, and Teresa would be alright, I had to believe that. Korg was as good a place as any for the trio to learn to deal with other players on their own. It was something none of the three had any real experience with, but they weren't alone. They had each other.

And for now, they had to suffice.

Setting aside further thoughts of my companions, I considered my next move. No walls separated Korg Major's safe zone from the city beyond, and for a split-second, I felt the urge to do what I had expressly forbidden my companions to do: go exploring.

But I reined in the temptation.

I had too much to do, and I couldn't afford to become embroiled in another misadventure. It was time to move on to the next leg of my journey: wolves' valley.

Ducking into an empty alley, I dropped into a crouch and wrapped myself in shadow. Then, I focused on the bracelet around my right wrist.

You have etched an aetherstone with the aether coordinates of the safe zone of sector 12,560.

Aetherstone bracelet activated. Connection to the ley line network formed.

Transfer commencing…

…

…

Passage completed!

❋   ❋   ❋

You have entered the safe zone of sector 12,560. This area is part of the Forever Kingdom's wild borderlands. It is currently neutral territory, unclaimed by any faction or Force. No additional restrictions apply to this region.

Aetherstone bracelet deactivated. Remaining stored locations: 1. Charged and unetched gems: 2. Uncharged gems: 2.

I emerged in the southern end of the safe zone, within the shadows of Mariga's log cabin, which even after all this time remained abandoned. Staying put, I considered the sector welcome message.

The wolves' valley was still unclaimed.

That pleased me. Despite the shift in my focus from sector 12,560 to the nether-infested one, I still wanted to see matters in the valley settled if I could. Although, for the foreseeable future it was pretty much a secondary concern.

Rising smoothly to my feet, I took a long look around.

And spotted smoke. *Lots* of smoke.

It surrounded the village on all sides. Raising my head, I sniffed the air and got the whiff of a familiar acrid tang. The smoke was close enough to smell, if barely.

War had broken out in the valley again.

The last time I'd been in the sector, Tartar, Muriel, Loken—and a host of smaller factions—had armies encamped in the valley, but outside of a few skirmishes, things had been relatively calm.

Has all that changed?

The smoke seemed to imply that it had.

I bit my lip. A lot could have gone wrong in the two months since I'd been away, and it seemed that at least some things had. Thankfully, though, I'd evacuated the dire wolf pack.

There was still Saya and Shael to worry about, of course.

But both players were stationed in the sector's safe zone, and there was no reason to fear that the chaos raging in the valley would touch them. Nonetheless, I needed to check on the pair.

Turning my attention inward, I checked the status of my disguise. My 'Actus' face was firmly in place and would remain so for a good while yet. There was no reason to delay.

Leaving the safety of the cabin's shadows, I headed for Wyvern's Roost.

✳ ✳ ✳

In stark contrast to two months ago, the village's streets were empty, as were the surrounding 'barracks.' It was another ominous sign of how hotly the war had to be raging that even the factions' reserves from the safe zone had been pulled in.

According to my mindsight, many of the shops were deserted as well. Even some of the merchants had left. *Just like rats abandoning a ship before it sinks.*

Merchants would only leave if they believed the sector was in imminent danger of falling, I knew. My dread rising, I hurried my steps.

Turning a corner, I spotted the tavern ahead, a brick and mortar building six stories tall. It was unchanged from the last time I'd seen it. Sharp relief sang through me at the sight of the Wyvern's Roost. Why, I couldn't explain. Maybe it was because the tavern and Saya were inexplicably linked in my mind.

If the tavern still stood, it meant the gnome was safe.

Not caring anymore who was watching, I dashed down the street. Bursting through the tavern doors, I drew to a stop.

The Wyvern's Roost was empty.

Or nearly so.

A lone figure sat with his head resting on a dusty table in the center of the common room. Shael.

At my entrance, the red bard raised his head and blinked owlishly. "Go away," he slurred. "We're closed."

My eyes drifted from the bard to the many empty bottles scattered around the table. Shael was drunk. My lips tightened. "Where's Saya?"

Shael threw back his head and brayed, the sound disturbingly discordant. "Saya? Saya's gone."

"Gone where?" I asked, my eyes narrowing.

Shael's laughter cut off abruptly. "Where? Why nowhere, of course. She's *gone,* gone."

My face blanked.

"That's right, fellow," the bard hissed. "Saya's dead."

CHAPTER 503: OLD NIGHTMARES REKINDLED

For an unaccountable time, I stared unseeing at Shael.

Saya dead? *Impossible.*

"That can't be right," I said inanely.

The bard cackled bitterly. "Ah, I wish it were so, friend, but it's true." He made a shooing gesture with his hands. "So run along and find somewhere else to stay tonight. Because the rooms in this here tavern of death are all full up tonight."

Rising to his feet and uncaring of the chair that fell flat behind him, Shael staggered up to the bar and rifled through the contents. Searching for another bottle, I suspected.

"Tell me how it happened, Shael," I ordered woodenly.

Maybe it was my use of his name or something in my voice, because the next moment, the bard jerked upright, bottles forgotten. "Do I know you?" he asked, squinting at me.

"It's Michael," I said softly.

The bard's reaction was not what I expected.

"Again?" he scoffed. "You're trying this again? What the hell is wrong with you!"

My brows furrowed. "I don't—"

Moving with surprising quickness, Shael picked up an empty bottle off the bar counter and flung it at me.

I ducked the projectile easily enough, but that didn't stop a message from the Adjudicator unfurling in my mind.

Violation of safe zone protocols detected. The player Shael has taken hostile action against you. Do you wish him punished?

Ignoring the Game alert, I glared at the bard. "Damnit, Shael, stop!"

"Go away, witch!" he roared. "Haven't you done enough already? Just leave me alone!"

"I don't bloody know what you're talking about!" I roared back. "Now, are you going to shut up and explain, or do I need to beat some sense into you first?"

Shael picked up another bottle.

"Don't," I warned. "It really is me—Michael."

The bard hesitated. "You don't look like him."

"Nor do I sound like me," I agreed. "But I'm a deception player. Hells, you are one, too. And you know as well as I do, faces are malleable."

Shael lowered the bottle. "Prove it. Prove you're Michael."

"How?"

The bard thought for a moment. "Where did we first meet?"

"That's easy. At the feet of the Adjudicator in Nexus."

Shael relaxed fractionally. "What's the first thing you paid me to do?"

"That's trickier," I allowed. "Do you mean the message I asked you to carry to the Shadow Quarter? Or the information I purchased from you about Nexus' dungeons."

The half-elf dropped the bottle. "It is you," he breathed.

I nodded grimly. "It is. Now, sit down and tell me where the hell Saya is."

✳   ✳   ✳

"I told you," Shael said softly when we'd seated ourselves at one of the tables. "Saya's dead."

I shook my head. "I can't believe that."

"Believe it," he said bitterly. "I saw it with my own eyes."

I stared at him searchingly. There was no denying Shael was a mess. There were bags under his eyes, his hair was disheveled, his clothes were torn, and he stank worse than a sewer. Worse yet, the minstrel's most prized possession—his flute—was nowhere to be seen.

All signs pointing to someone lost to the bottle.

Or in the throes of grief.

I closed my eyes. *No, it can't be.*

"Tell me," I demanded.

Shael shrugged despondently, his hands opening and closing as if searching for the comfort of a bottle. "There's not much to tell. You showed up here, convinced Saya and I to leave the safe zone with you, then killed her." He shuddered. "Over and over."

"*I* showed up?"

Shael nodded. "Someone wearing your face anyhow." He fell silent for so long I didn't think he would continue. "It was the envoy," the bard said finally.

"Whose envoy?" I asked sharply, but I knew already. Deceit and trickery had been employed in the attack, and only one Power in the valley was known for that.

"Loken's," Shael said in damning confirmation.

I rocked back in my chair, keeping a tight rein on the rage, anger, and grief boiling inside me. If I let it go...

No, I can't do that.

Exhaling slowly, I reviewed what I knew of Loken's envoy, which was little enough. Other than knowing she was *likely* a woman and a deception player, I knew naught else. The one time we'd met—after she'd laid a compulsion on the dire wolves—the envoy had managed to hide nearly everything about herself, including her Marks, face, and level.

I needed to know more. Much more.

"Explain," I rasped.

The bard raised his eyes—bloodshot and swimming with guilt—to meet mine. "Haven't I done so already?" he demanded. "Loken's envoy tricked us. And I, like a gullible fool, fell for it. What else can you possibly want to know?"

I leaned forward. "I want to know the details. For instance, how do you know it was Loken's envoy who lured you and Saya out of the safe zone?"

"Because that's what she named herself!"

But what's to say she was telling the truth? I wanted to ask but didn't. Letting the issue lie, I moved on. "You said Loken's envoy killed Saya—" I swallowed around the sudden lump in my throat—"'over and over.' That was the exact phrase you used. How did she manage that?"

After her first death, Saya would've been reborn in the safe zone, and I knew the gnome was smart enough not to fall for the same trick twice.

"She did it by taking us elsewhere," Shael said, his shoulders sagging. "The moment we crossed the safe zone's boundary, the envoy revealed herself and teleported us to another sector—one controlled by Shadow."

That would do it.

Still, I refused to believe. "You said 'we'? Does that mean you were captured as well?"

"Yes."

"Then why are you here?" I asked softly. "Did you escape?"

Shael laughed. "Escape? Hardly. I'm only here because the envoy needed someone to bear witness and carry her message."

I stiffened. "What message?"

Reaching into his pocket, Shael pulled out a thin slip of paper and laid it on the table between us. Looking down, I read what it said.

The tavern keeper is not dead, but she will be soon.
If you want her back, meet me where you and she first met.

The note was unsigned. But I knew who it was from. Loken's envoy. Or the trickster himself.

"It's all lies," Shael said stonily.

I raised my eyes to meet his. "What makes you say that?"

"I told you. I saw Saya die. Five times over."

Hope rekindled. "*Five* times? You're sure about that?"

"Of course, I'm sure," Shael retorted, looking outraged. "Do you think I would ever forget something like that?"

"There is no way Saya had five lives remaining," I murmured, ignoring his own question.

Shael's brows drew down. "What do you—" He broke off, his eyes widening. "Are you saying it was all an illusion? More deception at play?"

"It must have been," I muttered. It had to be, because if it wasn't, I wasn't sure what I would do.

"But why?" Shael demanded, the momentary glimmer of hope in his eyes fading. "It makes no sense. Why convince me Saya is dead, then send a note saying she is alive?"

"When do any of the trickster's actions ever seem to make sense?" I asked morosely. "Loken could be simply toying with us or trying to force my hand."

And get me to act irrationally.

Which admittedly I was on the verge of doing. And that was the damnable thing about Loken's ploy. Even knowing what he was about, I was finding it hard to pull back from the precipice, from dashing after the envoy to rescue—or revenge—Saya, and damn the consequences.

Shael stared at me tight-lipped for a moment. "Then you think this is Loken's doing?"

"Perhaps," I allowed. "Or it could be his envoy acting alone."

Weirdly enough, I found myself hoping it was Loken who was orchestrating affairs. The trickster would not kill Saya, I was fairly sure of that, and it was not because I didn't think he was capable of cold-blooded murder. Loken was certainly capable of such. No, it was because, in my experience, the shadow Power was always one to leave the door open.

Killing Saya was too... final.

There would be no hope of reconciliation between me and Loken after that. And the Power knew me well enough to know that would be the case.

Feigning Saya's death on the other hand... leaving me tied in knots and wondering if she was alive or dead... *That* was Loken through and through.

However, when it came to the trickster's envoy, I did not know enough to guess at her motivations. The woman was certainly ruthless, cruel even. Was she capable of killing Saya out of spite? *Definitely.* Had she done that? I didn't know. And at this stage, I could only hope she hadn't.

I inhaled deeply to calm myself again. "What I don't know," I went on, "is why Loken or his envoy would do something like this."

While matters between me and the trickster were tense, we had an understanding of sorts. More importantly, he *needed* me. Unless I was completely misreading the situation, Loken would not upset the status quo until *after* I stole Paya's damn chalice for him—or he learned the truth of my bloodline, and there was nothing to say he had.

I had also made a deal with Loken's envoy to broker peace in the valley, and she, likewise, had no reason to capture or kill Saya either.

Then again...

I had no concrete evidence that it *was* Loken or his envoy behind matters—my gaze shifted to Shael—nothing beyond what the bard himself had seen and heard, and I, of all people, knew only too well how truth and reality could be twisted.

I studied the bard anew. As befuddled by grief and besotted by drink as Shael was, he was far from a reliable witness. *And that assumes he is truly what he appears.*

"Did the envoy say anything?" I asked.

"She said plenty," he replied morosely. "And asked plenty, too."

Then he was interrogated, too. My eyes narrowed. A confused person was easier to question. Had the envoy only pretended to kill Saya to weaken Shael's resolve? It seemed plausible, but I was reaching, I knew—searching for reasons to believe the gnome alive despite everything.

"When did this all happen?" I asked.

"A month ago."

A month. A month ago, I was still stuck in Draven's Reach. But according to the deal Loken's envoy and I had struck, she'd given me four months to resolve matters in the valley. Why had she reneged on our bargain so quickly?

"What changed a month ago?" I wondered aloud.

"The war resumed," Shael said flatly.

I looked at him.

"No one knows who struck the first blow, but one day, the Light and Dark armies were camped in the center of the valley at relative peace with each other, except for the occasional skirmish, and the next day, they were trying to obliterate one another." Shael sighed. "It was soon after that that Loken's envoy turned up at the tavern. She came twice, in fact."

I stared at him. "She came in person?" That was out of character for the mysterious envoy.

He nodded. "The envoy came cloaked, of course, so no one got a peek at her face, but she came asking after you."

"Then what happened?" I asked intently.

"Saya spoke to her—on both occasions—and informed her that we had no idea as to your whereabouts. The envoy didn't believe her and got angry." He barked a laugh. "That's an understatement. She was so furious I thought she'd attack Saya there and then. Instead, she started spouting nonsense about wolves and went on about how since they were gone, it was Saya she would hold responsible."

"I see," I said hollowly. And I did.

Loken's envoy must have feared I'd betrayed her somehow, and with the pack absent, there was no one for her to take out her anger on. No one except Saya.

"I admit the envoy's words confused me," Shael said. He stared hard at me, the dull look in his gaze disappearing. "But I can tell they come as no surprise to you. What's going on, Michael?"

I sighed. "I will tell you everything, but first I need to know two things."

Shael's eyes narrowed. "Go on."

"Do you want to be part of this?" I asked bluntly. "You can walk away now, and we need never see each other again. Honestly, it will be better for you if you do. You won't walk away empty-handed either. I will recompense you handsomely for your time and… suffering."

The bard's face twisted in disgust. "Recompense me? By the Powers, no! Whatever is going on, I want in. I may not have known Saya as long as you did, but she was my *friend*. I cannot—*will not*— walk away!"

My own expression did not shift. "Even if it means tangling with Loken?"

"Even then," he retorted, glaring at me.

I inclined my head. "I had to ask."

Shael's anger did not abate. "What's the second thing?" he demanded.

"How many lives do you have remaining?"

Consternation flickered across the bard's face. "What?"

"Answer me," I said, not bothering to explain further.

"Three," he replied, "but what does—"

I didn't let him finish. Recalling the waiting Game alert, I replied in the affirmative to the Adjudicator.

Your response has been noted. The player Shael will be punished for violating the safe zone protocols.

A split-second later, the bard sitting across from me exploded, splattering me and everything else nearby.

Shael has died.

CHAPTER 504: A TESTING TIME

Eight hours later, I was at the rebirth well. Waiting.

I didn't search the village. I didn't explore the valley beyond. I didn't do anything except sit and stew. Over what I had to do next. What I needed to do next.

And Wolf forgive me, what I couldn't do next.

Around and around my thoughts circled, going over all the permutations, possibilities, false trails, ploys, and potential treacheries in store for me. Sadly, too much was uncertain, too much was unknown. And as much as I wanted to rush things, I knew I couldn't.

I would have to move carefully, with each step measured and thought out, else Loken and his envoy would get the better of me. And that would not only be to my detriment but that of all the Forerunners.

First, though, there was the matter of Shael to deal with.

Which was why I was sitting where I was. Waiting.

Exactly on the eight-hour mark, the rebirth well came to life. It was the first confirmation I needed. The second was seeing the minstrel's face as he surged out of the water. Shael looked exactly how I remembered him. But the bard's eyes remained glazed over, his mind still foggy after his gruesome death.

Reaching out with my will, I inspected him.

The target is Shael, a level 121 half-elf red minstrel. He bears a Mark of Moderate Shadow.

It was the final confirmation I needed. Shael was who he said he was. Saying nothing, I waited patiently for him to recover.

A minute later, the bard's face cleared. "You killed me!"

"Technically, the Adjudicator did," I murmured.

"But you could've stopped him!" he accused as he exited the well in a pair of white newbie shorts and shirt.

"I could have," I agreed.

"So, why didn't you?" he demanded.

"No spell survives death," I replied softly.

Shael blinked furiously as he processed that. "You didn't think I was me?" he asked at last.

I shook my head. "Not quite. I *worried* that you weren't. If the envoy could impersonate me, she could do the same with you, and who was to say that you weren't part of whatever elaborate plot she cooked up?"

"That's.... dastardly."

I shrugged. "It's the Game. Especially the way Loken and his people play it. And if you are truly going to utilize your own deception skills, it's the way you're going to have to learn to play it, too."

"But did you have to kill me?"

"I did," I said unapologetically. "I needed to see your face free of any misleading spells and witness how long you took to resurrect."

Shael crossed his arms over his chest. "And what if I hadn't thrown that bottle at you earlier?"

"Then I would have taken you outside the safe zone and killed you all the same," I said implacably.

"Hells," Shael muttered.

"It was necessary."

The bard shrugged. "I'll forgive you for killing me this time, but don't you dare do it again."

"I'll try not to," I replied solemnly.

"So, now that I've passed your test, will you tell me what's going on?"

"You haven't."

Shael frowned. "What?"

"You haven't passed my tests, not all of them anyway, just the first one."

The bard's eyes widened.

A small smile stole onto my face. "Don't worry, the second one won't require any dying."

He scowled. "Then what will it require?"

"A visit to Nexus," I said, rising to my feet and putting the package I held in his hands.

"What's this?" Shael asked, looking down.

"Clothes," I replied. "I doubt most of the stuff on your corpse is salvageable." I looked at him questioningly. "Unless you have something else to wear?"

He shook his head, looking lost.

"Then these will have to do until we reach Nexus."

"Nexus," Shael repeated, still baffled. "Why would we go there? Loken's envoy is here."

"The second test is there."

"Which is what exactly?"

"You'll see," I said, not elaborating further. "Come on, let's head back to the tavern and get what remains of your stuff."

"But what about Saya?" he asked, hurrying to catch up after he shrugged on the blue mage's robes I'd given him. "The note said—"

"Soon," I finished for him. "I know. But by your own admission, you received the note a month ago. It is already too late for 'soon.' At this stage, waiting a few more days won't matter." My lips thinned into a grim line. "In fact, if we don't want to fall prey to the trap the envoy no doubt has waiting, we damned well better do this carefully."

Shael had no response to that.

Marching through the still-open doors of the tavern, I seated myself at a table free of gore. "There's something else you need to do before we leave for Nexus."

"Oh, what's that?" Shael asked, seating himself across from me.

I leaned forward. "Finish your tale. Start from when you last saw me and leave nothing out. I want to know everything that has happened in the sector since."

*　*　*

Shael's tale was not a short one. He kept talking well into the night.

It turned out that Loken's envoy had kept her word, at least initially. The marauders that had been troubling Wyvern's Roost up to that point vanished, leaving the tavern to prosper in their absence.

Then, a month ago, something happened. What, Shael didn't know, but whatever it was, it was enough to cause the simmering tensions between the Light, Shadow, and Dark armies in the valley to boil over into a full-scale war.

So intense had the fighting been that the safe zone had been claimed thrice already. No one, though, had managed to hold onto it.

This was when the merchants had begun leaving. Most feared what would happen once the sector became finally owned, and rightfully so. There would be no place for non-aligned merchants then, and rather than stay and risk suffering further losses, most had moved on to other ventures.

The factions' barracks had also emptied during this time. Despite the security and convenience offered by the safe zone, it was too risky for the factions to house their soldiers in the area where the fighting was the hottest.

This had led to the current status quo: a deserted safe zone and a valley ripped asunder by war.

"Tell me again," I said. "How did the envoy manage to lure Saya out?"

"I told you: she was wearing your face. She went on—or rather you did—about some rare wyvern you'd found and killed, and how you trusted only Saya to harvest the ingredients."

I frowned. It was a plausible lie, if not one that accounted for my prolonged disappearance. "Did neither of you think to ask where I'd been?"

"Of course we did," Shael scoffed, "but Saya was not surprised when you held off explaining." He looked down his nose at me. "It seems keeping secrets is something you do often."

I winced. The jibe was all too accurate.

"That's all of it," Shael said, stifling a yawn. "Now, you know everything that I do."

I nodded slowly. I had a lot to think about and even more to do. "Use one of the rooms upstairs and get some rest," I instructed.

"We're not going to Nexus?" he asked in surprise.

"We are," I said, rising to my feet myself. "But not tonight. We could both do with some sleep. We'll leave at first light tomorrow."

✳　✳　✳

I met Shael in the common room the next morning.

I had slept fitfully and had contemplated ducking back to the tundra to report to the others several times over the course of the night. But, in the end, I decided the wiser course was to wait.

If I was careful, I would be in no danger in the Nexus safe zone, and it was imperative I didn't do anything to jeopardize the secret of the nether-infested sector nor that of the Forerunners' existence. Which returning prematurely to the tundra might just do.

"Sleep well?" I asked Shael.

"Better than I have in weeks," the bard admitted, which I could tell just by looking at him. Some of the shadows beneath his eyes had disappeared, and his face was no longer as guilt-ridden.

"That's good to hear," I said, removing an item from my backpack. "Shall we go?"

"What's that?" he asked, eyeing the parchment in my hand.

"A portal scroll," I replied.

"Huh. I was wondering how you planned on getting us to Nexus." He tugged at the robe I'd given him. "This almost made me think you'd become a mage."

I smiled. "Not quite."

"What about your face?" he asked.

I touched my cheek. "What about it?"

"You're going to go to Nexus looking like that?" He gestured at my false visage. "Who are you supposed to be anyway?"

"Actus," I replied. "Someone of no consequences. And yes, I do intend on wearing this face while in Nexus."

He tilted his head to the side. "You won't get past the Triumvirate knights at the gates of the safe zone looking like that," he predicted. "There is some strong magic woven into Nexus' walls. They'll strip you of your enchantments in seconds and alert every guard around."

I nodded. "I'm aware, but I don't intend on leaving the safe zone." *This time.* "Nor will it take us long to conclude our business in Nexus before we depart the sector."

He sighed. "You're still not going to tell me what this second test of yours is?"

"I'm not," I said. Cracking open the portal scroll, I drew on my magic and released its enchantment.

Item consumed.
You have opened a greater portal to sector 1.

The scroll vanished from my hands, and a moment later, a luminous white doorway appeared before me. "Let's go," I said and ducked through without hesitation.

Transfer through portal commencing...
...
...
Leaving sector 12,560. Entering Nexus!

✳   ✳   ✳

You have entered the safe zone of sector 1.
A shield generator is in place around the city, preventing portals from opening anywhere except in the designated teleportation zones.

My re-entry into Nexus was almost a replica of my first foray into the giant city. Emerging in a world of noise on the raised stone dais that served the city as its primary teleportation point, I wasted no time in shoving my way past other travelers and getting off the platform. This time, given the alacrity of my movements, none of the watching Triumvirate knights paid me any heed.

Shael, appearing behind me, quickly followed suit, and we were soon lost in the surging crowd at the platform's base.

"Where to?" the bard yelled in my ear, having to shout to make himself heard.

Not responding, I cut a path toward our destination.

The bard fell back, muttering under his breath about secretive fools when he realized I wasn't going to answer him. We traveled that way for the next few minutes. While we did, I scanned the passing buildings.

Nexus looked no different than it did during my first visit, unchanged and perhaps unchanging.

Uncaring mansions lined the streets, and rich players hurried to and fro. I was glad for it. In Nexus' multitudes, Shael and I were just two more insignificant specks, anonymous players and unworthy of attention. Finally, the south gate to the plague quarter came into view, and I slowed my steps.

"I thought you said we're not leaving the safe zone?" Shael asked, finally breaking his silence.

"We're not," I replied as I veered left and towards the water-logged building sitting there.

Shael stopped short. "We're going to a *bank?*"

"Yes. The Albion Bank specifically." I would have preferred using another bank, but the Bank owned by the Power Viviane was the only one whose layout I was familiar with, and now was not the time to slip up by crossing paths with unexpected wards or spells.

"Come on," I said, waving Shael forward. "Let's get this over with." Not waiting for his response, I strode across the thin stone bridge leading to the Bank's entrance.

You have entered a dampening field. Your mana, psi, and stamina abilities have been inhibited.

The Game alert did not give me pause.

I had not forgotten the dampening field from my previous visit. I also knew it wouldn't strip away my existing spells. And with my true face concealed by mimic, there was little danger of anyone inside recognizing me.

Strolling confidently into the bank's interior, I came to a stop in the middle of the marble foyer, and while I waited for Shael to catch up, I took a slow, long look around. Everything was exactly as I remembered.

"What are we doing here?" the bard hissed as he drew to a stop beside me.

"*We* are not doing anything," I replied in a low voice. "You, on the other hand..." I pointed out the rune-inscribed rectangular frames at the far end of the rooms. "You see those?"

Shael looked where I gestured. "The watchers. What about them?"

"Walk through one," I instructed.

He waited for me to go on, and when I didn't, he threw me an incredulous look. "That's it? That's your test?"

I nodded. "I'll explain in a bit. Now, go."

Looking perplexed, but complying nonetheless, Shael strode through the nearest watcher under my watchful gaze.

No alarms triggered. No hidden doors opened.

Nothing at all happened except for one of the tellers behind the counter glancing curiously in Shael's direction. The tension in my shoulders eased further.

Looping back to me, Shael drew to a stop before me. "Now what?"

I spun on my heel. "Now, we leave."

CHAPTER 505: A OR B

Shael didn't say anything until we exited the building. He didn't stay silent for long, though. "What was all that about?" he demanded once we were on the street again.

"That was me making sure Loken or his envoy didn't lay any spells on you."

"Why would they do..." he began before running aground. "Right, stupid question. But what made you suspect something like that?"

I smiled thinly. "Because that's what the trickster did to *me*. After our first meeting, Loken set a tracking spell on me—one that the Albion Bank's Watchers immediately picked up on. After that experience, it seemed prudent to check you after your own encounter."

"Huh... I guess." He paused. "So, does that mean I've passed your test?"

"You have."

"Good," Shael pronounced. He waited for a beat. "Well, go on then. Tell me what all this is about."

"I can't just yet," I murmured. "There's another one you have to undergo first."

"*Another* one?" Shael glared at me. "Just how many damn tests do you plan on subjecting me to?" he hissed.

"Just one more," I replied mildly.

The bard put his hands on his hips. "So, let's get to it."

"We'll do that in a bit," I replied. Taking my bearings, I crossed the street. "To get to the next test we'll have to leave Nexus, and before we do that, I have a short stop to make."

"And what stop is—" He broke off. "Wait, don't tell me. Let me guess: I'll *see*."

I smiled. "Now, you're getting the hang of things."

✻ ✻ ✻

We didn't have far to go. Just one street over in fact.

"The Emporium," Shael murmured as he caught sight of our destination. "You're going *shopping?*"

I laughed, somewhat darkly. "Believe it or not, this is no idle side trip. We wouldn't be here if the need wasn't dire."

Shael sighed, but he didn't say anything further as I drew to a halt before the gates of the walled compound. Two familiar giants stood guard over it.

"Lake. Ent," I greeted before either could get a word out.

Ent squinted at me. "Do we know you?"

"No," I said lightly, "but I know you." Pulling out the Emporium access card, I flipped it Lake's way. "And before you think to get rid of me, have a look at that."

After a moment of silent inspection, the giant berserker grunted. "It's the real thing."

Not questioning his companion, Ent swung back the gate, and I stepped through. "Come on, Shael," I called over my shoulder.

"Not so fast," Lake said, stepping in front of the half-elf before he could follow me in. "Where's his card?"

I sighed. "He doesn't have one," I said honestly. "He's my guest."

Ent shook his head. "No guests allowed," he said adamantly.

I glared at the giant.

"It's alright," Shael said. "I'll wait here."

I glanced at him. "You sure?"

He nodded.

"Don't wander off," I warned. "I won't be long." I turned my gaze on the giants. "And you two, you better keep an eye on him."

"Yessir," Lake drawled. "Whatever you wish." Waving me on, he shut the gate behind me.

✳   ✳   ✳

Like every other time I'd been in the emporium, I was met by a red-robed and hooded woman, one of Safyre's former colleagues. Ideally it should have been the aetherist standing here, going to meet Kesh, not me.

But matters in the wolves' valley had forced me to change plans.

And it was not just the matter of Saya's capture-murder that accounted for the unwanted change. Originally, I'd intended to obtain Safyre's red robes from the emporium agent in the wolves' valley. But, unsurprisingly, given the breakout of hostilities, the agent was long gone, necessitating this visit.

"How can I help you today?" the agent asked.

"You can direct me to Kesh," I replied politely.

The woman shook her head. "I'm sorry, but Kesh is unavailable."

It was the same response I'd received the first time I'd come here. Then, I'd used Viviane's token to get past Kesh's gatekeepers. This time, though, I hoped not to draw more attention than strictly necessary.

I smiled. "I believe I've heard that line before," I murmured, and before she could respond, I added, "Tell Kesh that Cara's friend is here." No one else in the emporium but Kesh knew the name I'd bestowed on Safyre when she still worked for the old merchant. Even Kesh had only heard me use the name once.

Hopefully, it stuck in her mind.

For a moment, the agent said nothing.

"Go on," I urged gently. "I'll wait."

Coming to a decision, the hooded woman bowed low and silently departed.

✳ ✳ ✳

A few minutes later, I was standing in Kesh's office.

The old merchant was ensconced behind her desk as always. At my entrance, she looked up. Kesh hadn't changed in the intervening time. Her face was just as seamed, her hands as wrinkled, and her eyes as sharp as ever.

"Michael?" she demanded bluntly, not fooled for a moment by the face I wore.

Not answering, I looked pointedly at the closed door at my back, then at the surrounding walls.

She snorted. "This room is better shielded than any bank. No one will overhear anything you say here."

"Ah, that's good," I said, relaxing. Letting the spell woven about my face dissipate, I sat in the chair opposite the old woman.

Kesh studied me in silence for a moment. "Do I even want to know what trouble you've gotten into this time?" she asked at last.

I shrugged. "Probably not."

"Hmpf. Where's Cara? Is she...?"

"Safyre is safe," I replied, deliberately using her real name.

Kesh sat back, some of her own tension easing. "So, it is not about her that you're here?"

"It is," I allowed. "But not wholly."

"Then it's about the valley," Kesh guessed.

My gaze sharpened. "You know what's happened?"

Kesh shook her head. "I know war has broken out, and I know Saya's disappeared." She threw me an apologetic look. "I am trying to find out what happened, but I haven't managed to uncover a single clue." She sighed, looking disheartened. "I'm sorry, Michael, I know how much she means to you, but I don't know where Saya is."

I inclined my head. "I don't hold you accountable. What's happened is not your fault."

"I'm not done yet," Kesh said grimly. "I won't give up on Saya; my people are still looking. But I don't want you to get your hopes up. After this long..."

I shook my head. "I appreciate the effort, but it's not necessary. I know what's happened."

Kesh's eyes narrowed. "You do? Tell me."

I hesitated.

"Tell me," she demanded. "Whatever it is, I want to know."

"This may be one of the things you're better off not knowing," I suggested delicately.

"No," Kesh refuted, glaring at me. "Saya and I may not have met, but we've corresponded for months, and I consider the young lady one of my own. She is as much mine to protect as any of the emporium's agents. Do you understand?"

I exhaled heavily. "I do."

"Then go on," she said peremptorily. "Tell me."

I slid the note Shael had given me across the table. "That was sent a month ago," I said softly.

Picking up the slip of paper, Kesh read the short message inscribed within. "Who is this from?"

"Loken's envoy."

Kesh inhaled sharply. "Loken. What interest does he have in Saya?"

I shifted uncomfortably. "You remember the marauders?"

"Yes, Kalin's people who blockaded the tavern," she said impatiently. "What about them?"

"I may have struck a bargain with Loken's envoy to get them to stop."

Bowing her head, Kesh pinched the bridge of her nose. "Foolish boy," she muttered. "It is never wise to trifle with the Powers, especially not one of Loken's caliber."

"Be that as it may, I had no choice in the matter," I said stiffly. "And for reasons I can't go into right now, the attention of the Powers is not something I'm ever likely to escape."

Kesh sighed but didn't pursue the subject further. "What deal did you strike with Loken's envoy, and when did you break it?"

"I *didn't* break my bargain with the envoy." I grimaced. "But circumstances in the valley changed while I was... away."

"The war happened, you mean," Kesh guessed.

"Yes. I'm not sure who or what started it, but Loken's envoy may have taken it as a sign I was reneging on our bargain."

Kesh pursed her lips. "Then this is all a misunderstanding?"

I breathed out heavily. "I'm not sure. Either way, I can't let things stand as they are."

"Of course not," Kesh said primly. "And Saya? Do you know if she is still..."

"Alive?" I completed for her.

Kesh nodded.

I barked a laugh. "I don't know," I confessed. "She may be. Or she may not be. With the trickster, one can never be sure."

The merchant did not refute my statement. "Do you have a plan?"

"Two actually."

Kesh leaned across the table. "Go on. Tell me."

"Are you sure you want to involve yourself in this?"

"Yes," she said simply.

I did not demur again. "Plan A is to sneak into the envoy's base and rescue Saya." A low, guttural growl escaped my throat. "And after I've seen her safe, I will burn Loken's envoy's house down around her and purge the valley of Shadow's minions."

"A noble aspiration," Kesh said acerbically, "if somewhat unrealistic."

I didn't argue. Kesh was right. Going to war with Loken—even if it was not him directly that I attacked—was madness. But it was the kind of madness I would not shrink from if it meant seeing Saya safe.

"Let's set aside Plan A for now," Kesh continued. "What's Plan B?"

For a long moment, I didn't say anything. Plan B was something I was still mulling over. It was risky and daring but admittedly had more chance of success than going scorched earth on Shadow.

"Michael?" Kesh prompted.

I sighed. "Plan B is reaching out to Loken."

Kesh searched my face. "You think that will work?" she asked skeptically.

"It might... I suspect his envoy is acting without his blessing."

"So why the hesitation?"

I grimaced. "Well, for one, there is no way of telling if my suspicions are correct. Asking Loken won't help us any. The trickster will certainly have no issue disavowing his envoy's action if it suits him."

"But if it gets Saya back, who cares?"

"There's that," I allowed. "But there is also the fact that meeting Loken is dangerous."

Kesh did not laugh as many likely would've in her place. Coming face to face with a Power like Loken was never safe. "Dangerous in what way specifically?"

"If he manages to analyze me, it will be disastrous," I said obliquely. "Not only for me but for everyone else I know—Saya and Safyre included."

"We can arrange for the meeting to happen in a shielded room. One with a dampening field," Kesh suggested.

I nodded. "That was my idea, too. But even so, the risk will not be completely eliminated."

Kesh stared at me. "You're that worried?"

I laughed. "No need to be polite about it. I'm not worried, I'm *afraid*." But it was not for myself that I feared. It was those who depended on me that concerned me. Endangering their lives was not as easy as risking my own.

Kesh drummed her fingers on the desk. "Plan B is still your best option," she said, gently nudging me in the right direction.

I sighed. "I know that. It's a large part of why I've come here."

"Shall I arrange the meeting then?"

I nodded. "Do that. Use the Wanderer's Delight."

"The hotel is a good choice," Kesh agreed. She paused. "Should I share any details in the invitation to Loken?"

I shook my head. "No. No need to forewarn him. I want to see Loken's face when I tell him the news." While trying to figure out if the trickster was lying or not was likely an exercise in futility, I might still be able to gain some insight into his thinking.

Kesh nodded. "I'll see it done."

"Thank you," I said. "Now for the next matter."

"Safyre," Kesh stated.

"Yes," I agreed. "It's time we discuss Safyre."

"Tell me," Kesh said.

Gathering my thoughts, I wondered how to phrase my request, then realized it was best to just come out and say it. "Safyre needs her robes back."

Kesh's eyes widened. "She wants to rejoin the emporium?"

I shook my head. "No. She wants to borrow a set."

The old merchant frowned. "That's not the way it works."

"I know and, more importantly, Safyre does, too. She doesn't need the robes permanently. Only long enough for a quick visit to Nexus."

The red robes of the emporium's agents weren't just ordinary pieces of cloth as I'd learned when I'd first met Safyre. They were high-tiered artifacts crafted by the Triumvirate. While Safyre wore the robes, her forsworn Mark would be concealed, letting her safely enter Nexus.

"Why would Safyre need to come here?" Kesh asked sternly.

"To speak to you in person." I paused, wondering how much to share. "And to speak with the other forsworn."

Kesh stiffened.

"Yes," I said quietly. "Safyre told me all about them. I know there are more like her within the emporium's ranks."

"She shouldn't have told you that," Kesh said tightly.

I shrugged. "Perhaps. But she did. And you have my word I will not share the secret with anyone."

The old merchant stared at me in silence for a moment. "Why does she want to speak with the others?" she asked eventually.

"To make them an offer," I replied.

"What offer?"

"A life free of persecution."

Kesh laughed hollowly. "Such does not exist," she scoffed. "Not for the likes of them. The Game and its players are everywhere. No sector is truly safe for a forsworn."

I inclined my head. "That may be true. But how about a faction that needs the forsworn as much as they need it? How about a Power who is willing to take them on as followers and who promises to protect them?"

"Bah! More foolishness. No Power will ever consider binding themselves to someone who has already forsworn their oaths. If they've done so once already, what's to stop them doing the same again?" She shook her head sadly. "That's how the Powers think, anyway. Few will even acknowledge that the fault may lie with the commander and not the commanded, that they themselves may have been the unjust ones, that what was asked was too onerous, and that the forsworn had little choice *except* to disobey."

I stared at Kesh thoughtfully for a moment. There was an ever-so-slight tremor to her voice that bespoke a deep-seated passion. The topic of the forsworn was clearly an emotionally charged one for her.

"Do you know what I am?" I asked softly.

"Trouble," she muttered. "Trouble I should have chased from my door the day our paths first crossed."

Unfazed, I tried again. "I was watching you carefully earlier, you know. When I told you that I didn't want Loken analyzing me, you didn't so much as bat an eyelid."

The merchant raised her chin. "What does that have to do with anything?"

"How old are you, Kesh?"

She blinked at the apparent non-sequitur. "Again, what does that have to do with anything?"

"Old enough to remember the ancients?" I asked quietly.

Kesh's face blanked. "We've drifted far enough afield," she warned. "You don't want to go down this path. Let's return to the matter at hand."

I shook my head. Kesh's response only confirmed what my intuition was telling me. "I think you suspect what I am," I went on. "I think you have for a long time."

"Enough," Kesh barked.

I was taking a dangerous risk, I knew. But the way matters were going, my bloodline would not stay secret much longer, and if I was going to be revealed, it was better for it to happen in pursuit of allies rather than when someone like Loken inevitably figured out the truth.

"I am a Power, Kesh," I whispered. "One willing to bind even forsworn to his cause. But I'm not just any Power, I'm one who will do everything I can to shield my Pack. If the forsworn join me, I promise you I will go to the same lengths to protect them that I do for Saya."

Kesh froze. "Wolf," she breathed.

"Yes," I said simply.

A riot of emotions flickered across the old woman's face, too many and too fast to decipher. "Why are you telling me this?"

"Because I think you care. Someone who has done what you have to protect so many forsworn women cannot *but* care."

Kesh laughed—bitterly I thought. "You think I care? That's a slim thread on which to hang your life on. If you only knew of the hundreds I failed to help. Or the deals I had to make to survive."

"That does not negate what you've done for those you've saved," I countered. "Each of us can only do so much." I thought of Adriel. "And we've all done things we'd rather not have."

Kesh's gaze hardened. "The Triumvirate will pay a fortune for the information you've just handed me. What's stopping me from turning you in?"

"Nothing."

Kesh waited for me to go on, but when I didn't, she rasped, "That's all you have to say? You're not going to even try and convince me not to?

I shrugged. "If I fall, others will take my place. Safyre amongst them."

Her gaze narrowed. "Then she knows about...?"

"My bloodline? Yes, she does. She knows that I intend on becoming Wolf Prime. She knows that I plan on raising the ancient Houses again. She knows

I will not stand idly by and let the new Powers destroy what's left of the Kingdom."

Kesh flinched at my bald statements, and despite her earlier professed confidence in the wards about the room, her gaze flitted left and right as if trying to spot any would-be eavesdroppers.

"I can't tell if you're mad or simply stupid," she muttered.

"Neither," I said gravely. "Some things need to be said no matter the risk so there is no ambiguity." I leaned forward. "And I have a plan. *We* have a plan—Safyre and the others who have joined my cause, I mean. It may seem far-fetched at the moment, but I assure you it's perfectly achievable."

"Oh, really? Let me guess you're going to take over Nexus. No, wait, you're going to defeat the combined might of the Forces." She shook her head. "It's all been tried before. Many times. No one has come close to succeeding."

"It's nothing so grand as all of that," I replied mildly. "What we intend on doing is claiming a sector and holding it."

She snorted. "Once the new Powers learn the truth of what you are, and they will, they will come banging on your doors. How do you plan on holding your sector then?"

I smiled. "Simple. With an Aether Cloaking Device."

Kesh's mouth snapped close.

Still smiling, I watched her working through the implications of my startling statement. I'd gotten the idea from the Awakened Dead, of all people. A cloaking device was the exact same artifact Ishita had used to hide the wolves' valley's coordinates from the rest of the Game—and that included Powers like Loken. For a newly discovered sector, it was the perfect solution.

"The sector you have in mind... It can't be the wolves' valley," she said at last, a hint of a question in her tone. "Its coordinates are known far and wide already."

"It is not sector 12,560," I agreed.

She blinked owlishly at me. "Then you have found another *hidden* sector?"

I nodded.

"One that is also closed off?"

Again, I nodded.

"Have you claimed it yet?" she asked sharply.

I shook my head. "Regretfully not. There is a minor problem." *Or perhaps a not-so-minor one.*

"What problem?" Kesh demanded when I didn't go on.

My lips twitched. "Does this mean you're in? You will help us?"

Kesh scowled. "Well, I certainly don't intend on letting Safyre suffer for whatever idiocy you've planned."

I laughed. It was not the most glowing of endorsements, but I was not fooled by the old woman's irascible response. Kesh had just committed herself. And if we were going to succeed, her help would be invaluable.

✳   ✳   ✳

"Don't tell me any of the details," Kesh said a little later. "I don't want to know."

"It's safer if you don't," I agreed. For both her and us.

She met my gaze, her own steely. "But I will need to know the broad strokes if I am to help."

I inclined my head. "Of course."

"Then let's start with the basics. Earlier, you claimed to be a Power. Is that true?"

"Technically, I'm not one yet," I conceded. "I'm a Powerful Initiate."

She nodded. "Good enough, I suppose. You've already formed a faction then?"

"I have."

"What about your blood?" she asked suddenly. "Have you awakened it?"

If Kesh had thought to catch me off-guard, she failed. "I have," I said evenly.

"What is your House rank?"

I raised one eyebrow, only mildly surprised by the question and the breadth of understanding it implied. If Kesh was as old as I suspected, then her knowledge of the ancients had likely been obtained firsthand.

"House Elite," I replied.

Something akin to respect flashed across Kesh's gaze. "Then you have managed to accomplish more than the others who have come before you," she murmured. "Perhaps your fate will be different from theirs."

It was an intriguing aside, but staying focused on the matter at hand, I didn't pursue it.

Kesh planted her elbows on the table. "Back to this sector you've found. Tell me, why haven't you claimed it yet?"

I sighed. "It's been overrun by the void."

Her eyes narrowed. "Is that the reason you were so desperate to purchase the nether absorption skillbook all those months ago?"

I nodded.

"You've been planning this for a long time then?"

"I have."

"And no one but you and your faction know the whereabouts of the sector?"

"Correct."

"Then why risk telling me about it now?"

I sighed. "Because, unfortunately, given the strength of the void's forces in the sector, we cannot fight them off alone. We need allies."

She steepled her fingers. "I see. And that's why you need the Aether Cloaking Device."

"Yes. The device is the only way we can keep the sector's coordinates hidden from any allies we teleport in."

"Procuring the device will not be easy," Kesh warned. "Nor cheap. Shield generators are sector-tiered artifacts."

"I'm aware. But I can afford it."

Kesh's brows rose in surprise, but she refrained from commenting further.

"The device is only part of what I need." I laid a parchment down on the table between us. "I need these things, too, or as many of them as you can get."

Personal Equipment
wayfarer legendary armor pieces,
rank 4 Perception & Mind rings,
tiamaten legendary armor pieces,
rank 6 spellhold artifact.

General items
farspeaker bracelets (set of 20),
10 x upgrade gems,
10 x greater portal scrolls,
100 x blank faction tokens,
20 x rank 5 nether crystals,
40 x miscellaneous tomes,
1 x steel door, 20 x beds, 20 x storage chests, 2 x cooking stoves, 100 x stores of preserved...

Once again, my shopping list was not as comprehensive as it could be, and I'd only included 'must-haves.' Assuming Nicola upheld his end of the deal we'd struck, I wouldn't need to be as circumspect in my purchase in future.

But until then...

"Tiamaten," Kesh muttered to herself as, head bent, she worked her way through the list. "Why am I not surprised?" But despite the comment, she didn't look up until she got to the general terms. "Faction tokens?" she asked, her brows rising. "And by that, do you mean what I think you do?"

"If you're thinking of stamped coins manufactured from unbound soulbound material, then yes."

Kesh pursed her lips. "I take it, you already know how expensive and rare such items are?"

I nodded. "I do. I must have them, nonetheless."

Soulbound items could not be created. They could only be found. And there was really only one dependable source of the artifacts: the Game. Typically, the Adjudicator only gifted players with soulbound items after they performed an extraordinary feat in a dungeon.

Which accounted for their rareness.

Soulbound items *could* be repurposed, though. Adriel had done just that when she'd created the Cloak of the Reach from the Magister's Cloak and Sunfury's feather. But by far the most common means of reutilizing soulbound items was in the creation of tokens.

Tokens like the ones I'd received from Viviane and Tartar.

While not exactly commonplace, the tokens were a simple, if effective, means of negating the deception skill. Unlike spirit signatures, they could not be forged, and all the major guilds and factions used them to verify their members.

"You have someone trustworthy who can work the tokens?" Kesh asked.

"Yes," I replied simply.

While soulbound tokens could not be counterfeited, their designs *could* be duplicated, but only by their original maker. It was their one weakness—and the primary reason why the identity of a faction's token makers was one of its most closely guarded secrets.

"And you're certain you can pay for all this?" Kesh asked doubtfully.

"Yes."

"You're sure? The money remaining in the tavern's accounts will not be nearly enough to cover everything."

"How much is there?" I asked curiously.

"Twenty thousand and three hundred."

"Impressive," I murmured. Saya had clearly gotten the tavern back on track before the untimely war. "But to answer your questions, yes, I'm fairly certain I will be able to pay for the items."

Assuming Nicola comes through.

Kesh slipped the scribbled note into one of her pockets. "Then, I'll begin the process of acquiring them." She shook her head. "But some of these items, I warn you..."

"I understand, they'll be hard to come by."

She nodded. "Exactly." She studied me for a moment. "Just so you know, I've found a player willing to sell his wayfarer item. His asking price is well above the market rate, though."

"Which piece does he have?" I asked eagerly. "And how much does he want for it?"

"The pants—for forty thousand gold."

I winced. That was a lot of money, but even at the exorbitant asking price, I was not about to pass up the opportunity to add to my own set. "Get it."

"Very well. I'll make the trade," Kesh said, looking unsurprised. "In the meantime, can I offer you some advice?"

"Please. Go ahead."

"You mentioned coming to Nexus to find allies."

I opened my mouth, but she held up her hand, forestalling me.

"Don't tell me. I don't want to know who you will be approaching. But if I can make a suggestion: speak to the brotherhood."

The stygian brotherhood was already on my list of potential allies, but wanting to hear Kesh's own reasoning, I made no mention of that. "Why?"

"Every nether-infested sector is of interest to them, and like it or not, they are amongst those best equipped to fight the void's creatures. If nothing else, they will have the gear others you recruit require."

"That's a good point," I allowed. "I will consider visiting them."

"Good. Now back to the matter of Safyre's robe." Reaching beneath the table, she extracted a slim package. "Here you go."

CHAPTER 507: BLIND DROP

I stared at the garment sitting on the table but made no move to take it, admittedly more than a little surprised by how easily Kesh was offering up one of the emporium's famed red robes.

"That's it? You're just giving it to me? With no strings attached?"

"I trust Safyre to use it wisely," Kesh said simply. "She understands the danger, not just to me but also to her fellows in the emporium if she misuses them." She paused. "Besides, the robes come with their own 'strings,' so to speak."

I frowned. "What does that mean?"

She gestured at the package on the table. "Go on, take it. I've unshielded the robes' properties so you can see for yourself."

Still frowning, I stretched out my hand.

You have acquired a set of <u>emporium robes</u>. This item is a rank 12 artifact created by the Power Herat and has been designed to shield its user from attacks and conceal their identity. It has no minimum requirements to equip.

Warning: a location beacon has been concealed in this artifact. It will automatically activate if the user suffers any damage or on request by the item's creator.

I pursed my lips. "Urgh. It has a locator beacon."

"Yes, that strictly limits the item's use." Kesh paused. "It should not bear mentioning, but I'll say it anyway: *don't* take the robes to your hidden base."

"I won't," I murmured, still unhappily studying the robes in my hands. "Safyre didn't mention the beacon."

"She doesn't know about it."

I looked up in surprise.

"None of my agents do," Kesh continued. She smiled thinly. "In fact, I'm fairly certain that the Triumvirate never intended I find out either."

I blinked. "Then how...?"

She laughed. "Like you said, I've lived a long life. Not all of it has been spent frivolously. I've managed to acquire a few tricks of my own along the way."

"I see." Turning back to the robes, I wondered how to factor this latest wrinkle into my plans. I couldn't take the thing back to the nether-infested sector. I would have to store it elsewhere. Somewhere that wouldn't surprise the Triumvirate—if they ever thought to look—and somewhere Safyre could easily reach.

"Tell Safyre not to return to Nexus," Kesh said.

My brows furrowed. "You *don't* want her to come here?" I raised the robes. "Then why give me this?"

"Safyre will need it to visit the emporium vaults. Don't ask me where that is, the location is secret, but Safyre knows. I will arrange for the other forsworn to rotate through the vaults in the coming days so she can speak to them there. Safyre can also collect your purchases while she's there." She glanced at me sidelong. "Assuming you've managed to arrange payment before then, of course."

I nodded in understanding. Kesh might be willing to help us, but she still had a business to run. "You'll have your money," I promised. I paused, struck by another thought. "In fact, I can fetch it right now if you allow me to wear the robes."

Kesh frowned.

"Just this one time," I added hastily. "And only to get past the safe zone's wards." If the robes could hide Safyre's forsworn Mark, they would just as easily conceal my Power Mark from the detection spells the Triumvirate had placed around the safe zone walls and gatehouses.

The old merchant sighed. "Alright, I'll make an exception." She threw me a stern look. "But just this once."

I bowed my head. "Thank you."

"You'll be taking your companion with you?"

She meant Shael. "Yes..." As tempting as the idea of leaving him behind was, that wouldn't do. For all his faults, the bard was a savvy operator and knew his way around the Game and its players, more so than most of my other companions. If he was going to be a full-fledged member of the Forerunners, I had to use every opportunity to learn his strengths—and weaknesses.

Kesh nodded. "I'll reach out to Loken in the interim. It should not take long to get an answer."

I rose to my feet. "Then I best be on my way."

✳   ✳   ✳

You have equipped a set of the <u>emporium robes</u>, concealing your identity.

Before exiting Kesh's office, I put on the red garment, transforming myself into just another faceless emporium agent, and as I left the compound, none of Kesh's employees gave me a second glance, not even the two at the gate.

"Come with me, Shael," I whispered to the bard slouched against the compound's outer wall as I strode past.

"Thanks for the offer, friend," he began. "But I'm—"

Breaking off, he threw me a sharp look, no doubt finally recognizing my voice, before his gaze flicked to the two giants watching us. "Whatever you wish, friend," he said, starting again. Keeping pace beside me, he waited until we were out of earshot before speaking again. "Michael?"

"The one and the same," I whispered back.

"How did you get those robes?" he hissed. "Please don't tell me you stole them."

"Of course, I didn't steal them. And the how is unimportant."

"Alright, what about the why?"

"I've got to leave the safe zone, and I prefer my identity not to be revealed," I replied.

Which was true enough.

I was fairly certain that the spells embedded in the safe zone exits—like those in the banks—were powerful enough to see through my mimic spell *and* detect my Power Mark. And while I was not a criminal in Nexus—yet— I wanted to avoid the attention my Mark's revelation would bring.

"Worried about Loken, are you?" Shael asked, throwing me a shrewd look.

"You could say that," I murmured.

The half-elf sighed. "Are we still on your—what did you call it?—'short stop'?"

"No," I admitted. "This is another detour, but it's the last one, I promise. We just need to fetch something."

Shael didn't say anything, but I could sense his unhappiness. Still, I only needed him to be patient for a little longer, and then he'd learn the truth about everything.

✳ ✳ ✳

You have left a safe zone.

We passed through the south gate with only a cursory nod from the Triumvirate knights on guard for my red robes.

"Where to?" Shael asked.

I glanced around, searching the streets of the plague quarter for a likely alley. I was uncomfortably aware that my every movement was potentially being tracked—not that I thought the Triumvirate would bother with such without real cause—and had to be doubly careful of my movements.

"There first," I replied, pointing out a narrow and heavily shadowed street that my mindsight reported as empty. "Wait at the entrance."

Not commenting, Shael watched as I ducked into the alley's depths and drew the shadows around me.

You have unequipped a set of the <u>emporium's robes</u>.
You have cast mimic, renewing your Actus visage. Remaining duration: 10 hours.

Stuffing Kesh's robes into an empty bag, I buried them in the trash and rubble littering the alley. Leaving the garment behind was a risk, but it was not as large a one as taking it to Nicola's drop point. And besides, I didn't intend on being gone long.

My disguise in place, I strode out of the alley, and with Shael close on my heels, I headed deeper into Nexus' poorest quarter.

✳ ✳ ✳

Heading due south, Shael and I cut a wide arc through the plague quarter. As we did, my gaze idly drifted to the Triumvirate citadel dominating the skyline, and I wondered which emporium agent had replaced Safyre in the knights' castle. Was it another forsworn?

"What are we doing here?" Shael muttered. "A rift could open at any moment."

I glanced at him sideways. The bard's gaze rove restlessly, darting from the pockmarked cobblestone streets to the dilapidated buildings, and from the wary residents to the heavily armored groups of passing players.

"You haven't spent much time in the plague quarter, have you?" I guessed.

"No."

My brows rose at the curtness of his response. "Have you been here at all before?"

Tight-lipped, he said nothing.

His silence was answer enough. Taking pity on him, I attempted to set him at ease. "Rifts aren't that common here. Yes, they appear, but not every day, and not in multiple locations at once. Although," I added in fond reminiscence, "after my first day here, I had a somewhat different picture of the plague quarter."

Despite himself, Shael looked intrigued. "What happened?"

I laughed. "I ran into a rift. Quite literally."

Shael's eyes widened.

"But in hindsight, it was probably for the better." My thoughts drifted as, not for the first time, I wondered what things would be like if I had not run into Simone's party that day. Would I have still entered the guardian tower? Would I have still discovered the nether-infested sector, survived my next brush with the stygians, and met Draven, Adriel, and the others?

Possibly not.

"I *have* been to the plague quarter before," Shael volunteered finally, "but never this deep."

I nodded, unsurprised. "Then, you'll need this," I said, handing him a small crystal.

You have lost a crystal of rank 4 disease protection.

Withdrawing another crystal from my belt, I crushed it in a closed fist.

You have activated a single-use enchantment, casting a ward of disease protection around yourself. For the next 4 hours, you will be shielded from tier 4 and lower infections.

Silently copying me, Shael did the same.

"Good, now we're ready," I said.

"For what?" he wondered.

"For the saltmarsh," I replied.

✳ ✳ ✳

Nicola's drop point was not in the saltmarsh proper.

Rather, it was in one of the many abandoned houses along its edge. "We're here," I said softly as we rounded a corner, and the building in question came into sight.

"Here?" Shael asked, looking around in confusion. "Here, where? All I see are—"

Yanking the half-elf back, I cut him off.

"Wha—"

"Shh," I hissed. Drawing the shadows around me, I edged up to the closest building.

On my prior visits to the plague quarter, I'd always found its southeastern section—the region overrun by the saltmarsh—to be vacant. Few players ever ventured here. It was why Nicola and I had chosen the faded yellow house on the rim of the saltmarsh as our drop point.

Unfortunately, the region was no longer empty.

Mindsight reported twenty players ahead, and not just ahead, but *in* the very same yellow house where I hoped my money was. It could not be a coincidence, of course.

Has Nicola betrayed me?

Sadly, that seemed like a distinct possibility. But I couldn't let the thought distract me. I had more important things to worry about at the moment. Moving slowly, I peered around the corner.

Multiple hostile entities have failed to detect you.

My second look at the north side of the yellow house was no more revealing than my first short glimpse. None of the players that my mindsight reported as being inside were visible from this distance. Drawing back from the corner, I closed my eyes and refocused on the mindglows I could sense.

The players were lying motionless all along the edge of the building, and at a guess, I'd say the nearest six were peering out of the second floor's dirt-stained north-facing windows.

Lookouts, I concluded.

It was a good bet, too, that the other fourteen were watching the western and eastern approaches, and perhaps even the southern one from the saltmarsh.

More and more, this was looking like an ambush. But whether of Nicola's making or someone else's, I couldn't say for certain yet.

Did they see me?

I couldn't tell that either.

The yellow house was about two hundred yards away, placing the players at the very limit of my mindsight range. Shael and I hadn't been in direct line of sight for long, a couple of seconds at worst. And importantly, none of the players had altered position since I'd spotted them.

"Michael," Shael whispered. "Talk to me. What's going on?"

I glanced his way. The bard had dropped into a crouch—unconsciously, I thought—but he hadn't faded into the shadows like I had. "There are at least twenty players lying in wait inside the house at the end of the street,"

I replied, not willing to conclude yet that I'd accounted for all the ambushers.

Shael's eyes narrowed. "Lying in wait for whom? Us?"

"Not us. *Me.*"

"How do you figure that?" he asked.

"Because they're sitting right on top of where I need to go."

The bard licked his lips. "I guess we better withdraw then and get a party together. I know more than a few players who are quite capable in a fight, and I daresay many of them are still in Nexus."

"Retreat?" I smiled bleakly. "I've no intention of doing that."

The bard stared at me. "You can't be serious? You can't really expect the two of us to take on twenty players by ourselves!"

"I said *at least twenty*. There may be more," I murmured. "And it's better if I did this alone."

"Saya was right, you are crazy," Shael muttered under his breath. In a louder voice, he added, "I'm not letting you do this on your own."

I shook my head. "I'm serious. It's better if you stick this one out. I'm no stranger to this sort of fight."

"I can help," he insisted stubbornly.

I ran my gaze over the bard. He wasn't in newbie clothes anymore, but he lacked both armor and weapons. "How?"

Shael shifted. "Well..."

"Can you sneak?"

He shook his head. "I can't, but I have Shadow magic."

That sounded promising at least. "What rank is your skill at?"

"Tier three," he replied.

I grunted. "Not bad. What else?"

"I have deception, thieving, and even some fire and life magic—all at tier two. It's music, though, that's my strongest asset." His fingers twitched as if searching for something. "But I'm ashamed to say that I've lost my flute. Without it..."

I pursed my lips. "And you *still* want to help?"

He nodded firmly. "Yes."

I sighed. "Tell me about your abilities."

The bard straightened. "Then, you'll let me help?" he asked hopefully.

"We'll see," I replied noncommittally. "But go on, describe your abilities and leave nothing out. I need a detailed breakdown."

"That's fair," Shael acknowledged. He breathed in deeply. "Alright. For starters, there's guile, which you already know about. It's a deception ability which..."

* * *

It turned out that Shael's Class—red minstrel—was an unusual one. It was a thief-caster hybrid but with one important distinction. Nearly all of Shael's magic—both offensive and defensive—had to be cast through his flute.

Meaning that without his instrument, Shael was effectively powerless.

Minstrels, it seemed, were prevented from adopting *any* psi skills and nearly all physical skills. The bard couldn't even use a wand, nor acquire a simple weapon skill, like daggers, or a basic defensive one, like light armor. All of which, in Shael's own words from long ago, made the half-elf 'not particularly combat-efficient.'

On a positive note, most of Shael's abilities were of the rare and exotic variety. And he did have dodge. *And* he could use my old trapper's armband.

"Alright," I said, when Shael was done. "I think we can make a half-decent support caster out of you—" I paused—"*after* you've regained your instrument."

Shael nodded vigorously. "I agree, which is why our best recourse is to retreat and find a merchant. We wouldn't even need to visit the emporium. Any old merchant from the knights' citadel will do."

I shook my head. "If we leave the area, we'll give our would-be ambushers a chance to reposition."

"You don't even know if they saw us," Shael pointed out.

"I don't," I conceded. "But I also don't want to risk that they might have. And besides, like I said, I can do this without you."

Shael sighed. "Alright. Alright. I'll just sit here and watch then."

I eyed him speculatively. "Well, there is *one* role you could fulfill, if you really wanted to. It will make things easier."

The half-elf perked up. "What's that?"

I grinned. "Bait."

*　*　*

You have lost a veteran's trapper's wristband.

You have cast mimic, transforming your visage into that of Henry, a level 132 human scout.

You have cast enhanced reflexes, load controller, vanish, and trigger-cast quick mend.

A short while later, we were ready.

I had used the intervening time to cast my buffs and change my face. While doing so wasn't strictly necessary, I didn't want anyone attempting to trace Actus's movements—however hard that would be.

Shael, meanwhile, had repositioned and trapped a derelict warehouse. If everything went according to plan, the building would serve as our killing ground.

Nestled in the shadow of a broken-down shop west of the yellow house, I watched the minstrel stroll closer. I'd already scouted the surroundings and was certain that it was only the yellow house that our ambushers occupied. Their true numbers, though, remained a mystery.

Whistling a meaningless, if cheerful, ditty, Shael passed me by. Blades at the ready, I waited to see what the enemy would do.

We were still some hundred yards distant from the yellow house—I wasn't about to let my unarmed companion get any closer—but even so, striding down the middle of the street, Shael was in plain sight.

Unmissable, really.

But the ambushers did not react.

I cursed softly. Either the players in the yellow house bore Shael and I no ill-will—unlikely—or they really *had* spotted us earlier and smelled a trap.

Staying where I was, I watched Shael loop back to the abandoned warehouse. We'd planned for this eventuality, even if neither of us had truly believed it necessary.

The bard disappeared from view, and I rose to my feet. Shael would wait out the rest of the encounter in the trapped building. If things took a turn for the worse, I would retreat to him. But if they didn't, my own mission would be simple.

Search and destroy.

Padding forward, I crept towards the yellow house. It was time for a closer look.

✱　✱　✱

Fifty yards from my target, I paused. None of the twenty players I'd detected earlier had moved. Nor were they talking. Or if they were, their words were too soft to carry to even my wolf-sharpened senses.

Raising my left hand, I rubbed at the side of my head.

You have activated a sorcerer's coif.

You have detected a hostile spell! The target is a tier 4 ward: <u>proximity warning</u>. This working will notify the caster in the event that a physical object crosses the spelled boundary.

Hmm. The ward's presence was another sign that the players inside the yellow building were up to no good. They almost certainly had to be here for me or the loot. Or both.

How do I do this?

One option was tripping the alarm. Another was trying to circumvent the ward altogether. Doing so wouldn't be hard either. The spell only stretched nine yards in height. With windborne, I could easily evade the ward *and* reach the second floor of the yellow house.

That, though, would put me in the enemy's midst without a full understanding of their numbers or capabilities. The twenty players I could see were all between rank fifteen and nineteen—high leveled enough to pose a real threat, especially if there were more of them than I anticipated.

I'll trip the spell, I decided. Shael had failed to draw the players out, but perhaps breaking the ward would do the trick.

Picking up a loose stone, I flung it directly into the ward.

You have triggered a proximity warning!

Tense and crouched, I waited.

But no response was forthcoming, not even after a full minute. Frowning, I released the hilt of my blades. The Adjudicator's message made clear that the alarm had sounded, even if there had been no audible indication of such.

Those inside had to know I was close, yet they were choosing to remain where they were. Why? Either to draw me in or because they were too smart to fall for my ploy.

Well, there's more than one way to skin a cat.

Marshaling my will, I sent strands of psi reaching into the mind of one of the twenty players.

You have charmed Hugo, a level 170 human priest.

Despite his level, Hugo's mental defenses were not up to the task of repelling my casting, and he quickly fell under my spell. I could've attempted to charm more of the players in the yellow house, of course, but one minion or ten, it made no difference for what I had in mind.

Sending my consciousness into the priest, I spent a precious few seconds trying to gain a better sense of his position. Mindsight told me where Hugo was and who was nearby, but it did not tell me what lay around him. Nor, sadly, did the charm spell let me see through my minion's eyes. *"Stand,"* I ordered.

A shadow crossed a window.

Hugo was pressed up against one of the second-floor windows, and before his bespelling had likely been staring directly in my direction, I judged. Listening intently, I waited.

A second passed.

Five more, then ten.

Finally, someone spoke.

"Hugo, you fool! What's wrong with you? Sit down and answer Sintar on the farspeaker link."

My eyes narrowed. Farspeaker bracelets would explain the players' silence, but the artifacts were not cheap and meant the enemy was well-equipped.

"Hugo!" the unknown speaker barked again. "I said get down! The marks will see you!"

Hugo, of course, did not do as ordered.

"God damnit, Hugo!" someone else hissed.

For a moment, I contemplated letting the priest do as his fellows wished, but only for a moment. Instead, I shouted, *"Jump!"*

Obedient to my will, Hugo flung himself against the glass pane he had so recently been looking out of and threw himself out of the second floor.

You have taken hostile action against your minion and have lost control of him!

The hapless priest landed in a tangle of limbs. The fall was far from fatal, though, and a second later, he rose to his feet, dazed and angry. A face peered out of the broken window, and Hugo's head jerked upward—perhaps in response to a telepathic query.

I gave him no chance to inform his companions about what had happened, though.

You have cast slaysight.
You have successfully terrified Hugo.

Dread suffused the priest's face as my spell took hold, and ignoring the cries of his fellows, he bolted heedlessly south, in the direction of the saltmarsh.

Smiling, I rose into a half-crouch and followed after.

✻   ✻   ✻

Hugo is no longer terrified.

I caught up with the hapless priest not long after he became mired in the swamp. I didn't go to his rescue immediately, though. Letting Hugo flail helplessly, I watched our rear.

But no pursuit followed.

Which was not altogether surprising given the enemy's seeming determination to stay entrenched in the yellow house. Shrugging, I strode toward Hugo. It was time to get some answers.

Too caught up in his struggles to free himself, the priest didn't notice my approach. Not that he would've, anyway. My stealth was too good. Catching hold of Hugo by the scruff of the neck, I tugged hard, pulling him off balance.

The priest fell flat on his back. "Wha—?"

Hugo's outraged scream was cut short as my blood came alive.

You have cast enslave.

In a manner reminiscent of a casting performed by my void armor, spell weaves rippled into being. Yet this time the spell was not being recreated from stolen knowledge but rather long-dormant memories.

Memories residing within *me*.

Memories whose echoes reverberated across my spirit, blurring the lines between me and my distant forbearers.

Memories that tasted of Wolf.

It was my first blood casting, and through it, I felt a spirit-deep connection to the Primes that came before—to Atiras, to Zumen, and to...

Ole?

Or was that Ordor?

But the name of the distant Prime in question escaped me as my connection to the past snapped, and my blood spell took shape.

You have successfully dominated Hugo, a level 170 human priest. Duration: permanent until death.

Hugo is now tied to you by bonds of blood that are unbreakable as long as he lives. As your creature, Hugo is compelled to obey your every command, no matter how unreasonable or onerous. While under your spell, Hugo's ties with all other entities have been disabled, and you will not be able to command them through him. On death—yours or Hugo's— the blood ties between you and him will be severed, restoring his autonomy and wiping his mind of all memories of his time under your spell.

Enslave is not a telepathic spell, however. No weave of psi has been laid upon Hugo to bespell his thoughts. Instead, you have imposed your will on

him through ties of blood. As such, Hugo retains full control of his mental faculties, and for all purposes, including dungeoneering, he will be accounted a full-fledged player.

Note, too, that if an enslaved player enters a safe zone, they will be automatically freed.

As the spell completed, a wave of dizziness passed over me, and I almost fell atop the prone priest. Catching myself, I staggered back and let my gaze drift downward to my new... minion.

But calling him that was wrong.

He was more than that but less, too. The priest still lay flat on his back in the mud. Beyond that, though, I could tell nearly nothing of his condition. Unlike when I employed charm, no mental connection had formed between me and Hugo.

He *was* under my influence, I knew that much. The Game's report made that much clear. Still, to be certain, I analyzed him again.

The target is Hugo, a level 170 human priest. His health is at 73%, and he is currently suffering under the <u>dominated</u> debuff.

I rubbed my chin, admittedly surprised by the manner in which the blood spell had manifested. I could sense no connection—of any sort—between the priest and me. On the one hand that would make relaying commands to him problematic, but on the other, it meant my influence over Hugo would be more difficult for others to sense.

After all, it would take a successful tier five analyze to reveal the priest's dominated state. And even amongst elites, such an ability would be rare.

Of course, it did also make me wonder how blood puppet would work on a non-sentient creature. How would I, or Nyra for that matter, be able to command them?

Hugo's eyes opened, cutting short my ruminations. "What happened?" he asked, staring straight at me.

"You've been enslaved," I replied as I helped him up.

The priest's eyes narrowed. "By you? Is that why I can't attack you?"

I lifted one eyebrow. "You've tried?"

He nodded.

"Well, don't bother trying again," I ordered calmly. "The spell will stop you from doing me any harm." After a second's thought, I added, "You will not tell anyone what has befallen you nor warn your companions either."

Hugo's brows furrowed.

"You can hear them?" I guessed.

He nodded reluctantly. "They're shouting at me over the farspeaker link, demanding to know what's happened."

"Don't answer," I instructed.

He shook his head. "I can't now that you've ordered me not to." He frowned again. "What spell did you use on me? I've never heard of any that works like this."

"That's unimportant," I said, waving aside his question.

Hugo's frown deepened. "Who are you? And why have you done this to me?"

"Also unimportant." Swinging back around, I headed out of the saltmarsh. "Come with me."

"Where are we going?" Hugo asked, scrambling to obey.

"Somewhere we can continue this conversation in more privacy."

Five minutes later, Hugo and I entered the building where Shael waited.

"Who's this?" the bard demanded, shooting to his feet.

"My minion," I replied laconically.

"Your minion—?" Shael's mouth snapped closed, and a moment later, a Game message dropped open in my mind.

Your blood-bound slave has been analyzed.

Now that's interesting.

While I could perceive no connection between Hugo and myself, the Adjudicator clearly deemed that we were linked and was sending me Hugo-related Game alerts.

"He's no ordinary minion," Shael commented, his eyes narrowing. "He's a player, too."

"An astute observation," I said with a straight face.

The bard glared at me.

"What else did your analyze tell you?" I asked, forestalling his retort.

"Nothing. Just his Class and level. Why?"

"Oh, no reason," I said, concealing my delight. My earlier conjecture had proved correct, and even Shael—a player with both deception and insight—couldn't 'see' Hugo's dominated debuff.

The bard's scowl deepened at my evasion. "Are you going to tell me who he is?" he demanded. "Or why have you—"

"I'm Hugo," the priest growled through clenched teeth, "and you can stop talking about me as if I'm not here."

Shael's eyes widened. "He can talk?"

"Of course I can talk!" Hugo snapped. "What sort of idiot are you?"

I chuckled. "Hugo is no ordinary minion, Shael. My hold on his mind is light, and he retains full control of his faculties."

The half-elf pursed his lips. I could see my words alarmed him, but perhaps constrained by the priest's presence, he did not give further voice to his concerns. "I see," was all he said in the end. "And why is Hugo here?"

"That's what I want to know, too," the priest put in grumpily.

Shael eyed him sideways but didn't comment on his interjection.

"Hugo is from the yellow house." I smiled. "And he is here to tell us all about the ambush his friends have prepared."

✳   ✳   ✳

The enslaved priest frowned. "They're not my friends."

"Companions, then," I said, acknowledging his point. "But I have surmised accurately, haven't I? It *was* an ambush?"

Hugo nodded curtly. "Yes."

I leaned forward. "For me specifically, correct?"

This time, the priest's response was more ambivalent. "That I can't say. You don't look like him."

I tilted my head to the side. "Like who?"

"Like the one we were told to watch out for," Hugo replied.

My fingers tightened into fists. The ambushers had my description, and they'd know where to find me. All of that pointed to one person only: Nicola. Things were not looking good for the under-dweller. "Told by whom?" I asked softly.

"Dinara."

I stiffened, surprise warring with relief—Nicola had not betrayed me. Maybe. *"Who?"*

"Den chief Dinara," Hugo expounded.

Folding my arms, I rocked back on my heels while I thought through the priest's answer. I didn't doubt his words. Hugo might have retained all his mental faculties, but just like he couldn't attack me, he couldn't lie to me either. The blood spell would not allow it.

"Who is Dinara?" Shael wondered aloud.

"The underworld's representative in Nexus," I murmured.

"The thieves guild?" Shael asked. "How did you get mixed up with them?"

That the red bard knew about the underworld did not surprise me. "It's a long story," I replied absently, "and one for another time." Lowering my head, I began pacing the floor.

"Dinara," I muttered. I'd never met the man and only knew of him through Nicola. So, why had he sent his people to ambush me? There could be multiple answers to that question, but there was only one obvious one.

Money.

Given the amounts involved, anyone would be tempted, much less a self-proclaimed thief. No, that Dinara was trying to rob me didn't surprise me. What did, though, was how he knew about the drop point in the first place. There was no reason for Nicola to tell him about it.

Unless, of course, the under-dweller was in on the scheme, too.

But that made no sense either. If Nicola wanted to steal my money, all he had to do was keep it. There was no need for an elaborate charade like this.

Perhaps this is the under-dweller's famed honor at play. Perhaps, Nicola feels honor-bound to keep his word. If only the letter of it and not the spirit.

My lips turned down unhappily. It made sense—in a twisted sort of way. Still, if that was really what was going on here, it meant I'd read the under-dweller merchant all wrong.

Drawing to a halt, I rounded on Hugo again. I had to be certain. "How did Dinara find out about the drop point?"

The priest looked at me in confusion. "What drop point?"

My own brows furrowed. "The one in the yellow house."

He shook his head. "I don't know anything about a drop point."

I bit my lip. "So why were you in that house?"

"To capture the merchant's accomplice."

My gaze sharpened. "What merchant?"

Hugo shrugged. "I don't know. Some under-dweller."

"The under-dwellers are mixed up in this, too?" Shael muttered. "Why am I not surprised?"

Ignoring him, I stayed focused on Hugo. Whatever was going on, matters didn't appear as straightforward as I first assumed. "Start at the beginning and leave nothing out: what led you and the others to the yellow house?"

Hugo shrugged. "There is not much to tell. Five days ago, an under-dweller merchant came into the Crooked Man, a tavern not too far from here. He was looking for the den chief. Anyhow, the two spent some time talking—about what, I don't know—but after the merchant left, Dinara rushed to our gang's table. I was there so I overheard everything. Dinara's instructions were quite clear. We were to track the under-dweller and capture anyone he met with."

"Capture, not kill?" I asked.

Hugo nodded.

"And then what happened?"

Hugo shrugged. "Nothing. Nicola came here, went into the house we're holed up in, spent a few minutes inside, then returned to the safe zone and left Nexus. With nothing else to go on, Sintar—that's our gang boss—decided to sit on the house in the hopes that someone would turn up." He met my gaze. "We were just about to give up when you showed up."

"I see," I murmured. On the face of it, it seemed Nicola had not betrayed me. "So, you don't know about the money?"

Hugo's confused look was answer enough.

"What money? Shael asked loudly.

I shifted in his direction. "The money I came here to collect."

Shael's eyes narrowed. "You thought the thieves were trying to rob you," he guessed.

I nodded. "But now it appears they know nothing about the money."

The bard frowned. "Then, what is it that they want?"

I turned back to Hugo, a thoughtful look on my face. "That is the question, isn't it?"

✳ ✳ ✳

I spent the next few minutes interrogating Hugo about everything he knew about his fellows and their abilities.

Sintar's gang was one of the larger and more experienced bands of thieves in Nexus, and Sintar himself was someone Dinara often turned to when it came to fulfilling many of his more sensitive commissions. But something else Hugo's information made clear was that despite the gang's undoubted expertise at thievery, they were somewhat lacking in combat abilities, and I was confident of being able to take them down.

"Tell me again, why do we have to do this?" Shael asked. "And why right now? We should come back after they've left. If you believe the priest, all we have to do is wait them out."

"I believe Hugo," I replied, "and unfortunately, we can't afford to wait." I held his gaze. "Or have you forgotten about Saya?"

"Of course I haven't forgotten about her," Shael retorted crossly. "But what if—"

"Besides which," I said, speaking over him, "it's equally important I find out what Dinara is up to."

"How will ambushing Sintar's men help do that?" Shael demanded. "Hugo has already told you everything they know."

"Sintar may know more," Hugo interjected.

"He might," I allowed, "but I am not depending on him. I have a plan."

"Of course, you do," Shael muttered. "And let me guess. It begins with killing everyone?"

I grinned unrepentantly. "Actually, it does."

Seeing my look, Shael groaned. "Alright, let's get this over with."

✳ ✳ ✳

Five minutes later, I was inside the yellow house.

Sintar's men had not reset the wards around the building, and thanks to Hugo, I knew why that was the case. The player who'd laid the spell had done so using a scroll and had not thought to bring more. As specialist thieves, the gang had no true mages.

That lack would make things easier.

However, it was about the only good news Hugo delivered. The bad news was that there were thirty gang members, not twenty. The other ten had mind shields. Hugo was convinced, too, that at the first sign they were outmatched, the gang would flee. They were thieves after all, not fighters, and a stand-up fight was something they were very much averse to. Complicating things further was the farspeaker link. All thirty thieves were connected to it.

Unfortunately, if my plan was to work, I couldn't allow any of the gang's members to escape. Which was why I was going to do things as quietly and stealthily as possible. And why, I'd decided not to involve Hugo and Shael directly.

You have cast vanish. You are <u>invisible</u>. Duration: 5 minutes.

My final buff in place, I focused my senses on the room directly atop me. Hugo had given me the layout of the second floor, and I knew that four players waited inside, two of whom were mind shielded. For obvious reasons, they were the biggest threat in the room, and I would have to deal with them first.

Drawing ebonheart, I shadow blinked.

You have teleported into Cari's shadow. You are hidden.

I emerged from the aether in a heavily shadowed room. Before me was the broad back of the player whose mindglow I'd used to teleport. She was exposed. Vulnerable. Easy prey.

Nevertheless, I did not lunge forward. Staying stock still, I swept the room with my gaze.

The two shielded players were less than three yards away, sitting on the floor with their backs to a wall and with their eyes closed. They were not asleep, though.

The pair were speaking, but not in an ordinary way.

You have passed a Perception check!
Mental sendings detected. Narq and Agtor are communicating telepathically.

No sooner did the Game message unfurl in my mind than a faint buzzing began in my ears. It was no true sound though, but rather a telepathic spillover from the pair's conversation, and interesting enough, it wasn't just random noise I was hearing. Concentrating on the not-noise, I sensed an almost-familiar pattern buried beneath. Intrigued, I focused harder.

You have passed a Mind check!
You have successfully eavesdropped on Narq and Agtor's conversation.

A moment later, the buzzing resolved itself into words—the very words spoken by Narq and Agtor mind-to-mind. Shamelessly, I listened in.

You have passed a mental resistance check! Your mental intrusion has gone undetected.

"... Hugo?"
"Bah! Hugo was an idiot. Good riddance, I say."
"Still, you have to admit it's concerning. What the hell happened to him?"
"Like I said, who cares. I just want to get back to my..."
Frowning thoughtfully, I dropped out of the pair's mental link. Narq and Agtor were not speaking over the gang's farspeaker link. I knew this for certain because I was wearing Hugo's own bracelet—and right now, all was quiet on that link. Which was all to the good and meant the pair's abrupt cessation of chatter would go unnoticed.

Blade in hand, I crept closer to Narq.

It was time to clear the room.

CHAPTER 510: THE INVISIBLE MAN

There was no easy way to deal with Narq and Agtor.

Killing the pair would be simple enough but slaying them *before* they could cry out in warning—whether verbally or through the farspeaker link—was going to be a little trickier. I would have to rely heavily on both my stealth and speed.

The other two players in the room were not an issue though. Reaching out with my mind, I sent psi delving into their minds.

You have cast slaysight.
You have paralyzed 2 of 2 targets for 60 seconds.

I smiled in satisfaction. *That'll keep them out of the fight.*

Crouched on my haunches in front of Narq, I refocused on the thief. Despite my proximity—I was close enough to reach out and strangle him— Narq was blissfully unaware of my presence. As was Agtor who was immediately beside him. Moving with deliberate care, I drew faithful.

Two targets. Two blows.

I would have to strike cleanly and fast, killing instantly with each attack.

Fortunately for me, Narq and Agtor were close enough to each other to make that possible. Sliding soundlessly along the floor, I shifted position until I was between the pair, then took a moment to plan my attack, picturing the arc of my blades and the exact spot I needed to land each hit.

And when I was certain, I moved.

Uncoiling as fast as a striking viper, I rocked forward half a step and struck—first with ebonheart, then with faithful.

A split-second, that was all the time my targets had to react and save themselves. But neither player sensed death rushing down on them, and my swords crashed home without resistance.

You have killed Narq with a fatal blow.
You have killed Agtor with a fatal blow.

Blood spurted as I ripped open the thieves' throats, coloring my hands and blades red. I paid the mess little heed, though. Frozen in position, I listened intently.

All remained quiet on the farspeaker link.

Perfect, I thought. As messy as the killings had been, they'd gone unnoticed and that was all that mattered. Wrenching free my swords, I rose to my feet and swiveled around. My work was not yet done.

Dripping blades in hand, I advanced on the paralyzed thieves.

*　*　*

You have killed Cari and Inaya.

There were six rooms on the second floor of the yellow house, and one long corridor joining them all. There were traps aplenty too, but thanks to Hugo, I knew where they were and how to bypass them, and slaying the gang members in chambers two to four went as smoothly as killing those in the first one.

However, as I was about to teleport into room five, a new wrinkle presented itself.

"Everyone, report in," a voice—Sintar's, I guessed—barked through the farspeaker bracelet.

"Still here, boss," someone else replied lazily.

"Where else would we be?" another quipped.

"Cut that shit out," Sintar snarled. *"Or have you clowns already forgotten about Hugo and the player who killed him? I doubt he just upped and left. The bastard must still be nearby."*

"Sorry," someone said contritely.

"You think Hugo's dead, boss?" another asked worriedly.

"I said report in, not pester me with pointless questions," Sintar retorted sharply. *"Narq, Chez, how are things on your end? Any sign of the mark yet?"*

I grimaced.

My presence was about to be uncovered, and I still had fifteen gang members to deal with. Room five held four thieves, and room six—the large central chamber which I was leaving for last—housed Sintar himself and the gang's reserve, a full squad of ten.

"Damnit, Chez. Stop ignoring me!" Sintar growled. *"What's going on there?"*

Chez had been one of the players in room two and, being dead, couldn't answer, of course.

Time to move, I decided. Weaving psi, I shadow blinked.

You have teleported into Lyle's shadow.

I emerged from the aether behind a rail-thin thief who appeared more interested in inspecting his nails than watching the street below. Knowing things were about to get loud soon, I didn't hesitate. Lunging forward, I drove ebonheart straight through his heart.

You have killed Lyle with a fatal blow.
Three hostile entities have failed to detect you! You are hidden.

"Chez, I'm warning you... if you're toying with me, I'll have your head! Now, report in, you whoreson!"

Retracting ebonheart, I spun around to find the room's other three occupants staring in horror at their lifeless companion. Grim-faced, I advanced on the closest.

"Chez—"

"The intruder is here, boss!" a thief named Khamalin shouted.

A pregnant pause. *"What did you say, Kham?"*

"He's here!" Khamalin shrieked again. *"The bastard has just killed Lyle and—"*

Khamalin's warning was cut short as I sliced open his throat.

"Kham?"

"Kham's dead!" Orly, one of the two remaining thieves yelled at the top of his lungs. *"The mark killed him! Help!"*

Turning away from the corpse, I faced the surviving pair. Standing back-to-back, they were scanning the room fearfully. They couldn't see me, of course, which, no doubt, accounted for a large part of their terror.

On the farspeaker link, Sintar was still speaking, alternating between issuing orders and demanding answers. Ignoring him, I rushed forward to deal with the room's remaining threats.

A task that was altogether too easy.

Orly was weaving his sword around in a misguided attempt to keep me at bay. Unfortunately for him, the arcs he moved his blade through were too large and too wild. Ducking beneath the swinging blade, I ripped open Orly's gut with ebonheart.

You have critically injured Orly.

Shouting incoherently, the large man clamped his hands to his sides to keep his innards from spilling out. It was no use, of course. Death was inevitable. Flowing past, I struck at the last thief, plunging faithful through the nape of his neck before he could react to my assault on Orly.

You have killed Menzo with a fatal blow.

And that quickly it was over.

The room was clear—or nearly so. Leaving Orly to his noisy struggles, I exited the room.

✳ ✳ ✳

"They're all dead, boss, they must be," I heard someone whisper as I crept toward the last room.

"We should flee!" another hissed.

"No!" Sintar declared. "There's eleven of us. Even if that bastard somehow managed to kill all the others, there's no way—"

The gang leader broke off as I stepped through the door and strangely enough, his eyes darted to my exact location.

I paused, too, surprised that the gang leader had sensed me—and that he had I was sure of, the man was staring straight at me! But I had not been dispelled and both vanish and my stealth were still active. Nor had there been a ward on the door. None that I could detect anyway.

"What is it boss? What are you staring at?"

Following Sintar's gaze, the other thieves in the room turned to face the doorway.

Yet, they still failed to see me.

Ten hostile entities have failed to detect you! You are hidden.

Ten, not eleven, I mused. The Game message was revealing in what it had not said and could only mean that the eleventh player—Sintar—*had* detected me.

"Run," Sintar whispered, his face as pale as a sheet.

"What's that, boss?"

"Run!" the gang leader repeated more loudly. "The bastard is invisible."

"What's that?"

"Invisible. How can he—"

Sintar's face devolved into a scowl. "Fools! Heed me or not, but on your heads be it!" Tucking tail himself, the gang leader raced toward the closest window.

"Not so fast, Sintar," I said lazily over the farspeaker link.

The gang leader missed a step and almost stumbled, but he managed to keep his balance, and if anything, he ran even faster. Sighing, I drew psi.

You have teleported 9 yards.

I stepped out of the aether on Sintar's left flank, with my right hand fully outstretched and ebonheart cutting a wide backward arc.

Blade met neck.

And tore through.

You have killed Sintar with a fatal blow.

"Goddamn!" a thief shrieked as the gang leader's head went flying.

"Did you see...?"

"What did that?"

"It's the intruder! Sintar said he was invisible."

"Run! Flee! Warn the chief."

I chuckled softly. *"No one is going anywhere,"* I said with deliberate menace. *"This is where you die."*

Unleashing the spells I held ready, I got to work.

✳   ✳   ✳

You have paralyzed 8 of 10 targets for 60 seconds.
You have cast windborne.
You have killed 10 hostile players.
You and Ghost have reached level 237!

Despite the thieves' best efforts to flee, it did not take me long to chase down and finish them. After I was done, I leaned out the closest window and gave Shael and Hugo the all-clear. I had tasked the pair with watching the building from afar in case any of the thieves made it out.

An unnecessary precaution, it turned out.

Returning my attention to the blood-spattered room, I picked out Sintar's body. As eagerly as I wanted to check out Nicola's stash, I was admittedly just as curious about the gang leader. Somehow—either through an ability or item—he'd managed to see through my invisibility, and I wanted to know how.

Bending over the headless corpse, I rifled through Sintar's gear until I found what I was looking for.

You have acquired the rank 5 ring: <u>true-seer</u>. This item allows the wearer to pierce illusion and concealment spells of tier 5 and below. It requires a minimum Perception of 20 to use.

I sighed as I read the ring's properties. *Of course.*

Truesight was the obvious counter to invisibility, and I'd known that sooner or later I'd run into a foe equipped with the ability, or in this case, one with an item that granted a lesser variant of it.

Removing Hugo's farspeaker bracelet—I didn't need it anymore—I equipped Sintar's ring in its place. Hopefully, the artifact would serve me better than it had the gang leader.

You have equipped the ring, <u>true-seer</u>, gaining the <u>true-seeing</u> ability. Equipped items: 27 / 30.

Next, I turned my attention to the rest of the gang leader's gear. But sadly, except for a pair of rank five daggers, the thief had little else of note. And unfortunately, as nice as the daggers were, they were of no use to me.

Still, I can sell them, I thought, pocketing the items. *Or maybe Nyra will find them handy.*

You have acquired a cache of miscellaneous items.

You have acquired the rank 5 dagger: <u>snake bite</u>. This item increases the physical damage you deal by 50% and bears the enchantment, <u>weaken</u>, which slows your opponent on every successful hit. This item requires a minimum Dexterity of 20 to wield.

You have acquired the rank 5 dagger: <u>ghoul-maker</u>. This item increases the physical damage you deal by 50% and causes any wound you inflict to become infected and the surrounding flesh to rot. This item requires a minimum Dexterity of 20 to wield.

Rising to my feet, I moved to the next corpse. Nicola's stash could wait a little longer. For now, it was better to get the more laborious—and messy— chore of looting out of the way first.

CHAPTER 511: ASKING DIFFICULT QUESTIONS

You have acquired a cache of 28 miscellaneous items.
You have acquired all 30 farspeaker bracelets that form part of the matching set named: Sintar's link.

Looting the corpses was as unappealing and tedious as I expected. Some of the equipment the thieves carried was intriguing, but ultimately nothing I looted was superior to my own gear. In fact, the most interesting items I found were the farspeaker bracelets.

My encounter with Sintar's gang had made apparent something I'd not given much thought to before this: the vulnerabilities within the farspeaker bracelets. That the bracelets were not keyed for use by specific players meant that any enemy who got their hands on one could use it to eavesdrop on the entire network—just like I had.

Understandably, this realization made me less enthused than I otherwise would've been about my find.

I can't use the bracelets, I decided despondently, *not unless Safyre and Adriel can come up with an enchantment to protect them from being misused.*

I wasn't sure how it could be done, but in my mind, I was imagining something like the Sworn-locked items I'd found in the Eastern Marches. Something like a set of faction-locked bracelets. "Now those would be ideal," I murmured. "Or even better, maybe we could—"

"Yikes!" someone exclaimed.

Turning around, I spotted Shael and Hugo entering the room.

"You weren't kidding," the bard said, his face devoid of color.

I frowned. "Huh?"

"I thought it an idle boast. A prideful jest." Shael shook his head. "Never did I imagine..."

"How is it that you're capable of all this?" Hugo whispered.

Bemused, I let my gaze drift from the shocked pair to where they looked. Was it the lurid streaks of red painting the room that had caught their interest? Or the floor full of corpses?

Probably both.

"Ah that," I said. "That's just combat. Walk any battlefield and you'll see the same."

Shael shook his head, whether in disbelief or disagreement, I couldn't tell. Hugo was more forthright in his response. "What level are you?" he demanded bluntly.

I raised one eyebrow.

"Come now," the priest chided. "After all this, you can't truly expect me to believe you are 'Henry,' a level one hundred and thirty-two scout. No mere scout could have slain this many so easily, and certainly not one at rank thirteen! Tell me your level."

"I'm sure you can work that out for yourself," I replied evenly.

He tilted his head to the side. "You're an elite?"

"Maybe," I said, rising to my feet.

Hugo nodded. "I thought so. It's the only explanation for whatever charm spell you used on me. Only an elite would have an ability that powerful."

Shael eyes widened. "You're an elite? Truly?"

I shrugged. "Like I said, maybe." Not wanting to discuss the matter further, I changed the topic. "What do you know of this?" I asked Hugo, showing him true-seer.

The priest's brows furrowed. "That's Sintar's ring." His eyes darted to the headless corpse. "That him?"

"Yes," I replied shortly. "So, you know about the ring. Why didn't you tell me about it?"

It was the priest's turn to shrug. "You only asked me about their abilities," he said, gesturing at the dead players, "not their equipment."

My eyes narrowed. What Hugo said was true enough. I had not thought to question him directly about the gang's gear—an oversight on my part. It was a timely reminder that as cooperative as the priest appeared at times, he was *not* a trusted companion. It was only the blood-binding that forced his compliance. He would obey me, but only to the letter of my instructions. And no further.

"Why would Sintar need such an item?" I asked, deciding not to pursue the matter further.

Hugo smirked. "Sintar was a thief. We all were, and in our line of work true-seeing is a necessity. You wouldn't believe how many marks think it wise to use illusions to conceal their valuables."

I nodded slowly. That also made sense.

"And besides, there's also our *fellow* thieves to consider," Hugo went on. "If the gang ever came into possession of a valuable enough prize, no denizen of the underworld would hesitate before robbing us. Under the right circumstances, we are all of us marks. Sintar trusted no one completely, not even Chief Dinara."

I grimaced. I'd had a somewhat rosier picture of the underworld and had—naively, it turned out—imagined most of them to be like Nicola.

There's truly no honor amongst thieves, it seems.

"How would a true-seeing ring be of any use to Sintar against the den chief?" Shael asked in a puzzled tone.

Hugo ignored the question.

"Answer him," I ordered sharply.

"Dinara is a master of stealth," the priest replied easily and as if nothing untoward had happened. "Some say he can turn completely invisible too, though I've not witnessed him do so myself."

I stiffened. "Turn invisible... you're sure about that?"

"Like I said, I'm not," Hugo replied. "But Sintar believed the rumors."

Frowning, I bowed my head. I had not questioned Hugo about Dinara earlier, deeming it more prudent to focus on the immediate threat that the gang represented—another oversight—and now it seemed my plans were in danger of unraveling. I'd intended on using Hugo to lure Dinara here, then to enslave him like I had the priest.

Now, though... that appeared too risky.

"What is it, Mi—" Shael broke off and quickly corrected. "Henry, I mean. What's wrong?"

"Dinara is an elite," I pronounced. Raising my head, I looked straight at Hugo. "Isn't he?"

"He is," the priest confirmed.

"What level?" I asked softly.

"Two hundred and forty-seven," Hugo answered. "According to the rumor mill, he's been at that level for decades."

"Damn," I murmured as the priest confirmed my fears.

Shael's eyes fixed on me waiting for me to explain the source of my unhappiness, but when I stayed silent, he turned to Hugo again. "That sounds decidedly odd. Why would he stop leveling like that?"

This time the priest didn't wait for me to force him to answer. "Who knows? The den chief doesn't venture out much these days. Most believe he's retired."

"Again, that makes no sense," the bard said. "Why retire when you're so close to tier six?"

I was keeping quiet, but I knew why, of course. At level two hundred and fifty, Dinara would earn the Powerful Initiate Mark whether he wanted to or not—assuming he had an evolved Class, of course—and I was guessing the den chief very much *didn't* want that. After all, why would he risk his comfortable existence for a life on the run, and with Powers for hunters, no less?

"No idea," Hugo replied, unaware of my musings. "Again, everything I told you is just gossip. No one but Dinara knows why he does what he does."

"Which Power has Dinara sworn himself to?" I asked, rejoining the conversation.

"No Power," Hugo said confidently. "Dinara is beholden to no one."

My brows drew down. "What makes you so sure?"

Hugo shrugged. "It's not strictly speaking a requirement, but most of those who join the underworld are what you call... independent-minded. There's no way someone like Dinara would have risen as far as he has in the underworld if he had any allegiances outside of it."

Shael nodded. "I've heard much the same thing."

I glanced at him questioningly.

"Not about the den chief, per se," he explained. "But about the underworld's denizens in general. They have a reputation for being aloof. Many of them scorn the Powers, even going so far as refusing to join their factions." He paused. "It's partly why the thieves guild is more poorly treated than say... the bounty hunters guild."

"I see," I murmured. That Dinara was not a Sworn was at least one thing to be thankful for. However I dealt with him, I need not fear repercussions from an angry Power.

Shael looked at me expectantly. "So, what does all this mean for us?"

I sighed. "At the very least it means I have to rethink our plans." I couldn't blood-bind Dinara anymore. Even if I did manage to lure the den chief away from his base, enslave wouldn't work on him. He was too high leveled.

"If Dinara is an elite *and* hunting you..." The bard trailed off, leaving unsaid the rest, but I knew what he was thinking: we should leave Nexus post-haste.

"Soon," I promised, responding to his unspoken suggestion. There were a few odds and ends to tie up first, though—like Hugo. The priest had outlived his usefulness, and it was time to deal with him.

✳   ✳   ✳

You have killed Hugo.
You have acquired a cache of miscellaneous items.

"Why did you do that?" Shael asked quietly.

The bard had sat still, watching in a kind of stunned silence as I dispassionately slew then looted the priest.

I shrugged. "I was going to kill him eventually, and sooner was better. This way there's still a good chance the rest of the gang won't realize how long he's been under my spell. And the less they figure out about *that* the better."

Shael studied me with a serious expression. "You still haven't told me what spell you used on him. Nor how you managed to become an elite in such a short span of time."

I met his gaze. "I'll tell you everything, but first—"

"—I have to pass your tests," he finished for me, his expression twisting. "But how am I going to do that if you keep delaying our departure from Nexus?"

I didn't say anything for a moment. Shael had a point. I hadn't intended on being in Nexus this long, and the way things were going, it was conceivable my departure would be delayed even further.

And I could already sense that the bard's patience was waning. *I can't keep holding him at arm's length,* I realized. At this point, it was either cut Shael loose or trust him.

"We'll do it here," I said at last.

The half-elf frowned. "What?"

"We'll conduct your final test right here and now."

"But I thought you said we had to leave Nexus for that!"

"Things have changed," I replied, not explaining further.

"How?" Shael demanded.

"Hugo happened for one," I said bluntly. "His example taught me that I can force my minions to be truthful."

Shael's brows furrowed. "How did you not know that before?"

I opened my mouth to respond, but before I could answer, the bard threw up his hands. "Never mind, don't tell me. I don't want to know." He glared at me as the rest of what I said caught up with him. "So, you think I've been lying to you all this time?"

"I don't," I replied honestly. "But given the circumstances, I have to be certain that you haven't been."

"And to achieve this... certainty you seek, you want to interrogate me, is that it?"

"Yes," I replied candidly. "I'm sorry Shael, but I can't let you in on any of my secrets until I know how far I can trust you."

For a drawn-out moment, Shael stared at me, his expression opaque. "How will you do it?" he asked finally.

"I will bewitch you the same way I did Hugo."

"What if I refuse to be bespelled?" Shael demanded.

"Then we part ways," I replied evenly. "Here and now."

The half-elf exhaled unhappily. "Fine. I'll let you conduct your bloody test. Go on, get it over with."

I held up my hand. "Hold on. There's a catch. Something you should be aware of before we start."

The bard looked at me sharply. "You're going to hurt me, aren't you? Stick me with needles or something."

I shook my head. "Nothing like that. I'm going to *question* you, nothing more." I paused. "But you'll remember none of it."

Consternation flickered across Shael's face.

"The spell I'll be using will wipe your mind when it's done. You won't remember anything of the time you spend bewitched."

My explanation did nothing to assure the bard and if anything, his expression grew more baffled.

"I promise it won't hurt," I added.

Shael still looked unconvinced, but he waved me on anyway. "I understand... I think. Do what you must."

"Thank you," I whispered. Stepping forward, I placed my hand on his shoulder. "Just relax. This will all be over before you know it..."

You have successfully dominated Shael, a level 121 half-elf red minstrel. Duration: permanent until death.

Warning: you have cast enslave twice in one day and cannot recast it again today. The blood memory requires a full sleep cycle to recharge.

Releasing my grip on Shael's shoulders, I staggered back and nearly fell. The dizziness from casting enslave was much worse this time around, and if the Game message was anything to go by, it was the blood memory itself that was responsible for my momentary wave of weakness.

This is not a spell I want to cast in the midst of battle, I thought.

"Did it work?" Shael asked.

Rubbing at my temples as I regained my equilibrium, I focused on the bard once more. "You tell me. Try attacking me."

A second ticked by.

The bard bit his lips. "I can't. My limbs won't obey."

I smiled. "Then I guess the spell's working. How does it feel?"

"Not like I imagined it would," Shael conceded. "I don't feel any different." He paused. "Except when I think of hurting you."

I laughed. "Well, don't think that!"

The bard smiled, but his amusement was short-lived. He was too anxious for that. "So now what?"

"I ask you a few questions, none of which you will remember after we're done," I replied calmly.

"That's it?"

"That's it," I assured him. "Are you ready to begin?"

He nodded nervously.

"Good. First question: did you kill Saya?"

Shael rocked back on his heels, his expression equal parts shock and outrage. "No!"

"Did you play any part in her capture or death?" I asked, ignoring his reaction.

"No," the bard growled from between gritted teeth.

"Do you know who took Saya?"

A momentary pause. "I *thought* it was Loken's envoy, but after everything we've discussed, I can't be certain anymore."

"Fair enough. Have you met Loken?"

"No."

"Do you work for him?"

"No."

"*Are* you Loken?"

"Don't be ridiculous!"

My expression did not shift or otherwise change. "Answer the question."

The bard stared at me disbelievingly. "That was a serious question? Truly?"

I nodded curtly.

"You can rest easy then. I'm *not* Loken!"

"Good to know," I said, not easing up. "Are you working for any other Power or envoy?"

"No."

"Have you ever worked for one before?"

Shael shifted. "Well, that depends."

My eyes narrowed. "On what?"

"On how you define 'work'," he replied.

"Explain."

The bard sighed. "I've performed in the safe zone mansions on multiple occasions. I didn't always know who my clients were, but I'm sure that at least some were Powers or envoys."

I pursed my lips. "By perform, you mean musically?"

He nodded.

"What about outside of your musical performances? Did you do any other sort of work for a Power?"

"Hmm." Shael rubbed his chin. "I did bring that message back to you from the Shadow Keep that one time. I suppose that could be considered—"

I waved dismissively. "Forget that. That was at my behest. Anything else?"

Shael shook his head. "No."

I nodded, relaxing fractionally. Things were going well, and thus far, Shael was everything he said he was. However, now it was time to venture into murkier territory.

"Will you risk your life to save Saya's?" I asked after a moment's thought.

"Without hesitation," the half-elf said.

"What about a lifetime spent on the run? Being hunted forevermore by Loken and his kind. Would you risk that?"

"I would," Shael replied just as firmly.

I inhaled. That established how far Shael was willing to go for Saya, but what about rebelling against the established order? Would he risk that?

"What do you know of the ancients?" I asked.

The bard's face creased in confusion. "Uh... I'm not sure what you mean."

"Have you heard of the Primes?"

Shael cocked his head to the side. "That's not a title I'm familiar with."

"What about the Houses, the bloodlines, scions, or the guardians? Heard of any of them?"

He shook his head. "No. I have absolutely no idea what you're talking about."

I exhaled. *So far so good.* "What if I told you that the new Powers didn't always stand ascendant in the Kingdom, that before them, the ancients—led by their Primes—were the ones who ruled? What if I told you that I and those allied with me are determined to break the hold Loken and his kind have on the world?"

To my surprise, the bard laughed. "Well, for starters, I'd say you got your hands on the good stuff." He chuckled again. "But if by some huge stretch, you're not hallucinating, joking, or otherwise, pulling my leg. *If* you're asking what I think you are, then yes." His expression turned grave. "I'd join your cause if it means saving Saya."

I eyed him speculatively. "And that would be the only reason?"

Shael hesitated as he gave the matter more serious thought. Patiently, I waited.

"I'm not one for grand causes," he said eventually. "Living in Nexus for as many years as I have, I've seen lots that is... wrong with the ways things are. But I've never felt it my place to fix things." His gaze rose to mine. "I suspect however that's not the answer you were looking for. I'm sorry."

I shook my head. "Don't be. Your perspective is no different from most other players in the Game. Indeed, I felt much the same way when I first started."

"What changed you?" Shael asked quietly.

I shrugged. "Circumstances. Power." I smiled. "Or perhaps I'm just more contrary than you are. It sticks in my craw to submit to the likes of Loken and his fellows."

Shael grinned. "*That* I can understand."

I glanced at him. "Would you follow me?"

Shael opened his mouth to reply, but I held up my hand forestalling him.

"Would you follow me even *after* we rescue Saya and knowing I plan on overthrowing the new Powers?"

This time the half-elf did not hesitate. "Yes."

The last of my tension eased. "Then I guess we'll not be parting ways, after all."

✳   ✳   ✳

My interrogation did not end there, of course.

I plied Shael with many more questions, but they all revolved around the same topics, and in the end the bard proved to be exactly what I always thought he was: a dependable, sincere sort trying to make his own way through the Game.

"I think we're done here," I said, rising to my feet.

Shael studied me, a thoughtful look on his face. "That was easier than I expected."

I chuckled. "Really? Were you expecting me to break out the torture-kit or something?"

He smiled. "When you put it like that it does sound foolish, but I'll admit I was anticipating *some* degree of pain. This was... effortless." His amusement faded. "What happens now?"

"I release you, and we go back to doing what we were before."

"And I won't remember anything from this conversation?"

"You won't," I confirmed.

"But you'll tell me everything?" he asked worriedly. "About your allies—" his voice dropped to a whisper—"the Primes, the ancients, and all that?"

"I will," I assured him. "But not here. Once we get to a secure location, I'll share all the details with you."

I'd taken a minor risk in mentioning the ancients and the Primes during my questioning. If anyone had been listening in, they would have everything they needed to brand me both a rebel and criminal. But they would have no more than that. I'd shared no specifics with Shael and wouldn't do so until we returned to the tundra.

"The important thing," I went on, "is that I now know I can trust you." I squeezed the bard's shoulder. "You ready to proceed?"

Shael squeezed his eyes shut. "Do it."

Doing as he bade, I reached within myself and severed the blood ties keeping the half-elf bound to my will.

✳   ✳   ✳

You have freed Shael from enslavement. He is no longer dominated.

The bard's eyes flickered, then opened.

"Well, what are you waiting for?" he asked, throwing me a puzzled look. "Go on, charm me or do whatever it is you intend."

I grinned. "It's already done."

Shael frowned. "What?"

"It's over," I replied. "You were bespelled for about an hour. The interrogation is done."

"Really?"

"Really," I confirmed.

Still looking dubious, Shael glanced downward and began patting himself down.

"You passed, by the way. Congratulations."

"Thanks," Shael muttered, not looking up.

"What are you doing?" I asked curiously.

"Looking for dagger holes," he replied, only half-jokingly.

I laughed. "Well, when you're done with that, join me. I've a chest to find."

Shael looked up. "A chest?"

"Remember the money I told you about? Nicola has stashed it somewhere in this building. All I have to do is locate it."

"Nicola," Shael repeated. "He's the under-dweller merchant Hugo mentioned?"

"Correct." Pulling out the key card Nicola had given me, I held it up in the air.

"What's that?" Shael asked, slipping closer to inspect the item.

"A soulbound key card," I explained. "It's supposed to warn me when I'm close to the chest. Nicola would have hidden it well." I glanced at the corpses on the floor. "To prevent any would-be thieves from stealing its contents."

"Nice," the bard remarked, looking impressed. "Your merchant friend seems quite the professional."

I nodded. "I got the feeling this is not his first blind drop. More like his hundredth." Waving the card before me, I began circling the room.

Shael shot me a quick look as he kept step beside me. "You're being surprisingly free with your explanations all of a sudden."

I glanced at him. "You prefer I stay closed mouth?"

He rolled his eyes. "Please no!"

My lips twitched, but only a moment later, I grew serious again. "I told you, you passed the last test," I said softly. "I will not withhold anything from you now."

Shael nodded slowly. "I see that."

Finishing my circuit of the room, I drew to a halt. "Well, wherever the chest is, it's not here." The key card had remained steadfastly inert in my hands the entire time.

"The next room, maybe?" Shael suggested.

"Maybe," I agreed. Striding out the door, I made my way down the corridor. "Come on, let's go find this thing."

✳   ✳   ✳

Thirty minutes later, the card in my hand finally buzzed.

"It's here," I declared.

"Where?" Shael asked, scanning the surroundings.

We were in the half-collapsed basement of the yellow house—and the very last place I'd thought to check. Under pressure of the adjacent saltmarsh, the south-facing wall had caved in, letting in its semi-liquid sludge. Gingerly picking my way through the room, I kept my focus on the key card in my hand and did my best to ignore the ankle-high muck I was wading through.

The card's buzzing reached a crescendo.

I drew to a halt. "It's in there," I said, pointing.

Shael's gaze darted from me to the sludge heap I stood in front of. "You're joking. Why would your merchant friend bury the chest in *there*?"

I didn't blame the bard for his reaction. The heap in question looked truly revolting, and even I had a hard time stomaching the smell wafting off the delightful pile of excrement, rotting corpses and other filth that had washed in with the marsh. "I suppose because it's the last place anyone would want to look," I murmured.

Shael shook his head in disgust. "I take back what I said earlier. That under-dweller of yours is entirely too professional for my liking."

I chuckled. "He could have been less... thorough," I allowed. Opening my backpack, I retrieved my shovel.

Shael's eyes fell on the implement in my hands. "Well, you seem to have matters under control here. I should go up and keep watch."

I smiled. "You do that. I'll join you soon." Bending down, I got to digging.

✳   ✳   ✳

It took me far longer than I would've liked to find Nicola's chest, but eventually, after an hour of back-breaking work, I pulled a heavy metal box out of the muck. Prudently deciding not to open the chest in the filthy basement, I dragged the box upstairs.

"You found it?" Shael asked from where he lay stretched out on the floor.

"No thanks to you," I muttered, feeling far less charitable towards the bard now than I had earlier.

"But you only had one shovel," Shael protested innocently.

Not deigning to dignify his statement with a response, I set the chest down and began cleaning myself.

"What's inside?" Shael asked, chuckling unrepentantly at my lack of reaction.

"A whole lot of money," I muttered. "Or so I hope, anyway."

Shael scratched his head. "All of this seems like an extraordinary amount of effort to go through simply for collecting a payment. Was there a reason you and the merchant chose not to use a bank instead?"

I nodded as I finished wiping off the worst of the basement's muck. "Banks can't be fully trusted, and given the amounts of money involved, the transaction would undoubtedly have been flagged by someone for a deeper look."

The bard cocked his head to the side. "How much are we talking about here?"

"A million," I said casually as I kneeled before the sealed chest.

Shael's mouth dropped open in shock.

"A *m-million?*" he gasped when he finally got it working again. "What in hells did you do to earn that much?"

"You wouldn't believe me if I told you," I said with a smile. Placing the key card against the chest, I flipped it open, eager to see what lay inside.

CHAPTER 513: STASH

You have unlocked an unmarked chest with a key card.

The chest didn't hold one million. Studying the paltry contents, I could immediately tell it was less than that—a *lot* less.

"Two bags," I muttered. *Why in hells are there only two?*

"What's in the pouches?" Shael asked, peering over my shoulder.

"Stygian powder," I murmured, staring despondently at the mostly empty chest.

"Nether dust?" Shael asked curiously. Leaning forward, he inspected the pouches with analyze.

"There's two kilograms of the stuff in here!" he exclaimed a moment later. "That's more dust than I've ever seen in one place before! Each pouch must be worth thousands!" He paused. "No, that can't be right. Tens of thousands!"

"Almost correct. All told, the two bags are worth two hundred thousand gold."

Shael blinked, taken aback by the astronomical amount. "Then why the long face?"

"It's less than I was expecting," I replied glumly.

His eyes widened incredulously. "Really?"

I nodded.

"Alrrright... but it's still two hundred thousand gold! That's a fortune by anyone's reckoning, Michael. You're rich!"

"Not rich enough," I muttered.

Shael's delight waned as he sensed the depths of my frustration. "There's a note," he pointed out helpfully. "Two of them actually. Perhaps one of them has an explanation?"

Peering into the steel box again, I saw that he was right. A thin slip of paper had been tucked beneath each bag. Reaching into the chest, I retrieved bags and parchment both.

You have acquired 2kg of stygian powder.
You have acquired an underworld promissory note for 200,000 gold.
You have acquired a penned missive.

Ignoring the stygian powder and promissory note for now, I opened the letter and began to read.

Jasiah (or whoever you really are),

I have bad news. No doubt, you've already counted the pouches in the chest and noticed their lack. I apologize for failing to live up to my end of the bargain, but unfortunately, I've run into a few problems.

The biggest one being Mammon.

Yes, the Power himself contacted me, and let me tell you, he was not happy (an understatement if there ever was one)!

His people informed him that I refused to sell them back their gear on day zero. As you can imagine, Mammon had some choice words for me and a few not-so-subtle threats. He didn't threaten my person, but he did strongly suggest my days as a merchant were numbered. But don't worry on my behalf, I don't fear Mammon.

At the end of the day, he is only a minor Power, and his threats are just so much hot air. However, Mammon does have an iron grip over his people. And unfortunately, the Devil Riders are enough of a force in the Eastern Marches that they've managed to block the sale of your items. Worse yet, they're also refusing to buy back their own Sworn locked items.

It's a petty sort of revenge, seeing as they're hurting only themselves by not reacquiring their gear, but in the short term their strategy is proving…. effective.

To cut a long story short, I've only managed to sell a third of your loot so far (the least valuable items), the proceeds of which are in this chest. Do not despair, though. The Riders will come around eventually. I'm hoping their current stalling is just a bargaining tactic to drive the prices down when they do concede to the inevitable and buy back their Sworn-locked items.

Beware, though, the final sum may be less than you expect.

I didn't want you to think I betrayed you, hence the partial payment. Make sure to keep this drop point secure, and once I have the second half of your payment, I'll put it in the selfsame chest. But if you feel the need to change the drop point, contact me through Dinara.

Regards, Nicola.

P.S I almost forgot. Tyelin handed over his promissory note without fuss. I admit that surprised me. Anyway, you will find it in the chest too. I know that doesn't make up for the shortfall, but perhaps it will help tide you over until I can sell the rest of your stuff.

My brows furrowed unhappily, I read the note again.

But my impression the second time around was no different from the first: Nicola's words appeared heartfelt. I could sense no trace of deception in them, and the problems he described were entirely too believable. In hindsight, I realized I should have foreseen something like this happening.

"What is it?" Shael prompted.

"Further delays," I replied obliquely. "Nicola needs more time to gather the rest of my money."

"I see," Shael remarked and left it at that, for which I was grateful.

"So, what does that mean for us?" he asked, shifting focus to the present.

I pursed my lips as I pondered the question.

On one hand, I was now two hundred thousand richer—four hundred, if you counted Tyelin's note, but I was not sure I could depend on cashing it in anymore.

On the other hand, I was still short of the sum I required to procure the Aether Cloaking Device. By Safyre's estimate, the artifact would set us back half a million.

The shield generator was a must-have item, though.

So, how to get it?

Tyelin's money would make up a good deal of the shortfall, but collecting on it meant visiting Dinara. And for whatever reason the den chief was trying to capture or kill me—I wasn't sure which yet. I also hadn't failed to notice that Nicola's note had not alluded to why that would be the case. Either the merchant was pretending innocence, or he was truly ignorant of whatever machinations the den chief was involved in.

"Michael?" Shael prompted.

I rose to my feet. "We have another stop to make in the plague quarter."

"Where to this time?" Shael asked, appearing resigned to the fact of more delays.

"The Crooked Man," I replied. "It's time to pay Den Chief Dinara a visit."

✱　✱　✱

Before heading to the tavern, we stopped by the Triumvirate citadel to purchase Shael some gear. We were on a time schedule—ideally, I wanted to deal with the den chief before Sintar and his gang revived and warned him—but it was not a severe one, and we could afford a short detour to re-equip the minstrel.

"You've been here before?" I asked Shael as we drew closer to the knights' main stronghold in the plague quarter.

"A few times," he admitted, having to shout to make himself heard. The square around the citadel was always crowded and hundreds of players were dashing to and fro. "Are we going to enter the keep itself?"

I shook my head. "It's better we avoid unnecessary scrutiny," I replied, recalling the all-too-perceptive constable and the knights standing guard over the entrance to the inner citadel.

"Agreed," Shael said. "We should find something suitable amongst the merchants in the bailey."

Nodding wordlessly, I fell silent as we joined the long line of players waiting to enter the citadel.

✱　✱　✱

You have sold 30 x miscellaneous caches of items for 3,100 gold.

You have lost: 2,000 gold, 5 silvers, and 3 coppers. Total money carried: 3,223 gold.

Our visit to the citadel courtyard passed without incident.

I sold all the gear I'd looted from Sintar's gang—except for the tier five daggers, of course—and while the merchants' rates were less desirable than I wanted, I still managed to make a profit after outfitting Shael.

Killing players was certainly profitable.

"We're done?" I asked, glancing sideways at the bard.

Shael tore his eyes away from his new flute. He hadn't been able to keep his fingers away from the thing since he'd purchased it. The instrument had cost a thousand gold on its own, fully half the money I'd given the half-elf but judging by the bard's smile and firm step since, I judged the flute well worth the price.

"We are," he said emphatically. "And thank you again. I doubt I'll ever be able to repay you."

I waved aside his protest. "You will," I replied. "If not in gold then in deeds." I paused. "Don't forget where we're going and what we're about to do."

Shael straightened. "Of course. This time around you'll find me a more useful companion, I promise."

I smiled. "I'm counting on it."

✳ ✳ ✳

The Crooked Man was on the west side of the plague quarter. I'd visited the area before—both the entrance to the scorching dunes and haunted catacombs were in the same vicinity—yet that did not mean the tavern was easy to find.

Unusually, for the type of establishment it purported to be, there were no signposts leading the way nor bright lights. Nor any rowdy music to follow.

The Crooked Man was clearly an establishment that chose not to announce itself to the world, but then again, given the nature of some of its patrons, that was only to be expected. In fact, according to Hugo, there were two sides to the Crooked Man. The public-facing tavern—a true den of iniquity that catered to every vice known to both players and non-players— and the private club beneath—the beating heart of the underworld's Nexus branch.

There were two entrances, too.

The tavern's front doors, usable by anyone, and the thieves-only backdoor. But finding the second, even with Hugo's explicit instructions to guide me, proved troublesome.

And in the end, it was only the pair of thugs idling outside the rusted steel door at the end of a darkened alley—where neither they nor it had any purpose in being—that gave away the second entrance. Invisible, and crouched in the shadows as an added precaution, I studied the pair thoughtfully from the mouth of said alley.

The target is Ince, a level 160 half-orc brawler.
The target is Hagfyr, a level 171 dwarven scoundrel.

Both dwarf and orc had wrapped themselves in shadow, but their stealth was insufficient to hide them from my keen sight. Nor did the alley's darkness do anything to conceal the door itself.

This must be it, I thought. *The back entrance to the Nexus underworld.*

I could see nothing of the Crooked Man's interior from the outside but that was of little consequence. Courtesy of Hugo, I had a detailed description of its internal layout. Unfortunately, I also couldn't pick out the mindglows of any of the tavern's undoubtedly many patrons either. Both the building's lower and upper floors were obviously shielded. And given that this was a *thieves'* hideout, I knew to expect traps aplenty.

I sighed. Breaking in through the backdoor was going to be too risky.

That left only one other option. Retreating from the alley, I crept back to where I'd left Shael waiting.

＊　＊　＊

"I've found it," I said without preamble as I emerged from the shadows in front of the bard.

Shael did not startle, obviously getting used to my abrupt comings and goings. "Where?" he asked, straightening from his slouched posture.

"Five blocks away and tucked away deep inside an alley," I replied.

The bard frowned. "Can we use it?"

I shook my head. "*We* can't. Like I suspected, breaking in is not an option. We're going to have to go with Plan B. You'll enter through the front, and I'll bluff my way through the back."

Shael grimaced. "Then you're still determined to go ahead with your madcap plan?"

"I need that money," I said stiffly. "*And* I need to know why Dinara is so eager to find me."

Shael raised his hands palms up. "I'm not arguing. I'll do my part. It's you that I'm worried about. You're going to be alone down there, and if you get into trouble, there's not much I can do from upstairs."

I sighed. "Don't worry, I'll be fine. Just keep watch for my signal. When you hear it, don't hesitate or improvise. Do your bit and get out."

Shael nodded. "Then we're a go?"

"We are," I said, drawing psi. "Let's do this."

You have cast mimic, transforming your visage into that of Jasiah, a level 152 human duelist. Duration: 10 hours.

You have cast enhanced reflexes, load controller, and trigger-cast quick mend.

I returned to the alley wearing Jasiah's face. All my buffs—except vanish—were cast, and I strode down the center of the narrow street, making no attempt to conceal either myself or my gear.

The two thugs noticed me immediately, but they didn't break cover until I closed to within five yards of the tavern's entrance. Then the first crept through the shadows toward me.

Pretending to be oblivious, I let him come. Right up until he circled around me and tried to put a knife to my throat. Sidestepping the maneuver, I let the thug stagger past.

You have evaded Ince's attack!

The half-orc stumbled forward, arms flailing. Reaching out, I grabbed him by the hair and yanked his head back. "This is the correct way to do it," I whispered in his ear, pressing faithful against his bare neck.

The second thug rushed out of the shadows. "Let him go!" he hissed.

My gaze shifted to the dwarf, and sensing an opportunity, the orc under my blade tensed fractionally.

"Don't," I warned, nicking his skin and drawing blood.

Ince stilled.

"Better," I praised before turning my attention to his companion, Hagfyr, again. "Now, you were saying?"

The dwarf scowled. "Let him go, you bastard. I'm warning you. You don't know who you're messing with here."

I chuckled. "Please! Do you think I just happened on this alley by accident? Of course, I know what you two are. Underworld thugs." I cocked my head to the side. "Right?"

Hagfyr's scowl deepened and out of the corner of my eye, I spotted his hands curling into fists.

"If you're thinking of triggering any traps," I said, guessing what he was about, "don't. Matters will only get messy then, and I assure you it will serve no purpose."

I knew no such thing of course, but the dwarf didn't need to know that. That there were traps, I didn't doubt. Unfortunately, they were beyond my ability to detect—I'd tried and failed already.

Hagfyr's eyes narrowed, and for a moment, I feared he was going to call my bluff, but before he could do anything foolish, the half-orc spoke up. "Who are you?" he croaked.

"A fellow thief, of course," I replied lightly, not taking my gaze off the dwarf.

"Is that so?" Hagfyr scoffed. "I don't recognize you."

"I'm from out of town," I said evenly. "A friend directed me here."

"Yeah? And who might that be?" the dwarf demanded.

"An under-dweller by the name of Nicola."

Hagfyr was no actor, and I recognized the exact moment he connected the dots. At the mention of Nicola's name, the dwarf's eyes widened fractionally before darting across my face. Then, his expression smoothened so quickly it was almost comical.

"Why didn't you say so in the first place?" he asked with barely concealed eagerness.

Somehow, I kept from laughing. "Your friend here didn't give me a chance," I said with a pretended frown at the orc. "He attacked without warning."

"I wasn't trying to kill you!" Ince growled.

"Oh? What were you trying to do then?"

"Hold you for questioning!"

"Like I am doing now?" I asked, deadpan.

"Exactly!" he exclaimed, seemingly oblivious as to the irony of the situation.

Withdrawing, faithful, I shoved him forward. "Well, then," I said expansively, "I guess we are all friends here." I eyed the two. "Aren't we?"

"Of course," Hagfyr said, looking like he wanted to rub his hands in glee.

Ince glared at me. "We still need to see your chit before we can let you in," he said, feeling gingerly at his throat.

I smiled at the half-orc. He was either a better actor than the dwarf or ignorant of what was going on.

"Come, Ince, there's no need for that," Hagfyr said with oily smoothness. "He's a friend of Nicola's. Of course, he can—"

"Here you go," I said, tossing Ince my underworld token.

The half-orc snatched the chit out of the air and examined it closely. "You're an *apprentice*?" he asked in a tone that was equal parts outrage and disbelief.

I shrugged. "What can I say, I'm a late bloomer."

Hagfyr chortled. "Huh-oh. You let a little bitty apprentice get the better of you, Ince? You're not going to live this one down!"

Ince's glare swapped to his companion.

Stepping forward, I reached out and plucked the token from the half-orc's hand. "Everything is in order then?"

"Yessir, mister apprentice!" Hagfyr replied before Ince could say anything. Reaching behind him, he unlocked the steel door. "Come on in. I'll escort you."

✳   ✳   ✳

The tavern's main door opened into a narrow corridor that sloped gently downward. Affecting a relaxed air, I trailed after the dwarf.

The thieves' main hideout lay beneath the tavern, which accounted for the passage's sloping. There was more to its design than that, though. The corridor served the thieves as both a backdoor *and* an escape route. And while there were no guards, that did not mean the passage lacked defenses.

It was trapped, of course.

Given the passage's length and narrow confines, it would be a death trap for any assaulting force. However, based on Hugo's information, I knew the front entrance was even *more* heavily guarded—and not just by traps. There were multiple thief squads roving above, all tasked with watching the patrons and the entrances to the below-ground level.

It was why I had chosen to 'sneak' in through the backdoor. This way, there was a decent chance I'd come face to face with Dinara *without* having to wade through each and every one of his minions.

And all it took was offering myself up as bait.

You have crossed through a tier 6 concealment barrier. All entities within the barrier are hidden from outside detection.

You have entered an adept dampening field. Your tier 1 to 4 mana, psi, and stamina abilities have been inhibited.

Your spells, load controller, quick mend, and enhanced reflexes have been dispelled.

Impregnable mind and mimic have resisted dispelling.

My musings came to an abrupt end as the Game messages dropped into my mind. Hugo had warned me about the field and barrier, and I'd known to expect them. However, I hadn't been entirely sure how accurate his information was, and it was a relief to find out he was spot on.

My wariness about the dampening field was another reason I'd chosen to make my entry through the backdoor. If it had stripped me of my false visage, I knew I would have an easier time of concealing my face from Hagfyr and Ince than a tavern full of people while I made my escape.

Thankfully, that was no longer necessary.

Admittedly, though, the strength—or lack thereof—of the dampening field surprised me. On a positive note, it meant I'd have access to my tier five abilities: backstab, vanish, mimic, and slaysight amongst them. On the other hand, it *also* meant Dinara and any other elites in the basement would enjoy the same advantages.

Which could be both good or bad.

It all depended on what abilities the other elites had.

"Caught you by surprise, did it?" Hagfyr asked with a knowing smile. "Don't worry, though, the barrier and field are there for everyone's sake."

Ha! That was unlikely to be true. Given the field's design, it had probably been configured solely for Dinara's protection. With the other thieves' abilities inhibited, the den chief wouldn't have to worry about being stabbed in the back.

I didn't pursue the subject further, of course. "Where are we going?" I asked instead.

"To visit the chief," Hagfyr answered airily. "He'll want to see you."

"Oh, why's that?" I asked, concealing my delight.

"Dinara—that's his name—always insists on meeting any newcomers to the city," Hagfyr replied easily. "You know, to make sure you're properly welcomed and all that stuff."

I bet.

"I see," I murmured. "Well, I look forward to meeting him myself."

✳   ✳   ✳

A little later, we entered the underworld complex proper, and despite thinking I knew what to expect, I drew to an involuntary stop. Hugo's words had not done the place justice. He'd labeled it a private club. But the underworld den was more than that.

Much more.

The passage had spilled out into a wide-open seating area. Couches, divans, and even throne-like armchairs were strewn across the chamber. The carpet underfoot was plush, translucent silk curtains pretended to partition off the room, trays heaped with extravagant dishes graced every table, drinks were in abundant supply, and everywhere I looked there were muscular and near-naked servitors—non-players all—serving the guests.

"Impressive, isn't it?" Hagfyr asked proudly.

"That's one word for it," I muttered under my breath.

"What's that?"

"Nothing," I replied, studying the 'guests' again. They were all players. High-ranking thieves was my guess, but none of them was the one I sought. "Where's Dinara?"

Hagfyr snorted. "Not here amongst the riffraff, of course. He has a private suite farther back for his own enjoyment and that of his... special guests."

"Of course," I murmured. Extending my arm, I waved the dwarf on. "Lead on."

Turning around, the dwarf proceeded to do just that, but he didn't get far before a hulking brute barred our progress. "Hagfyr," the thug greeted the dwarf before turning my way. "Who's this?"

"A friend of Nicola's," the dwarf replied, beaming from ear to ear.

The brute blinked slowly. "Nicola?"

Hagfyr nodded with ill-concealed smugness. "That's right. This one here is an acquaintance of the under-dweller. I'm taking him to see the chief."

The brute raked me over with a lazy gaze.

You have passed a mental resistance check!
Hed has failed to pierce your disguise.

Snorting softly, Hed stepped out of the way, clearly perceiving me as no threat. "Go on ahead."

✳   ✳   ✳

We crossed the chamber without incident.

Along the way, I spotted more lurking thugs but none of them attempted an approach. No doubt, they'd spotted Hed's earlier interception and noted his decision to let us pass unhindered.

It was clear that despite the obvious opulence of the lounge, the thieves had not forgone their security measures altogether. A fact I was reminded of again when I spotted the two elites lounging outside the shut door that was our destination.

The target is Darkdawn, a level 225 elven fencer.
The target is Horus, a level 230 human blademaster.

"What are you doing here, Hagfyr?" Darkdawn drawled, not bothering to get up from the couch he was sprawled across.

"Yeah," Horus chipped in, sipping deeply from his mug. "Aren't you on door watch?"

Hagfyr rocked back on his heels, his excitement barely contained. "I have a present for the boss."

"Oh?" the elf enquired.

The dwarf stuck his thumb in my direction. "This is the one."

Horus barely glanced my way while Darkdawn didn't even bother with that much. But despite the pair's seeming insouciance, I did not miss the keenness of their gazes, nor the many buffs layered over their persons. The elites were alert and ready to act on a moment's notice.

"The one?" the human repeated, stifling a yawn. "Is that supposed to mean something? 'One' what?"

"Yeah, Hagfyr, tell us what's got you so all hot and bothered," Darkdawn added. "And don't deny that's the case. You're practically oozing—" He paused, then widened his eyes theatrically. "Wait, don't tell me. Has Hagfyr finally found a partner? Is he *the* one? Have you come to ask the boss' permission?" The elf got no further. Clutching his sides, he broke down into laughter.

"Congratulations, Hagfyr," Horus said solemnly. "But I hate to break it to you, the boss doesn't go in for that sort of—"

The dwarf's face grew heated. "Shuddup, you fools!"

Darkdawn's mirth vanished as quickly as it appeared. "Easy, Hagfyr," he said softly. "Don't forget your place."

The dwarf gulped audibly.

"Now report," Horus rasped, his own face scrubbed clean of expression. "*Properly*. As you should've done in the first place."

Visibly stiffening, Hagfyr inhaled sharply. "This here fool is the mark the boss is looking for. The under-dweller's associate. Walked right up to the door, he did."

Two sharp gazes fell on me.

You have passed a mental resistance check!
Horus and Darkdawn have failed to pierce your disguise.

Ignoring the elites' scrutiny, I stared at the dwarf, affecting shock and confusion. "What's going on here?" I demanded. "Your boss is looking for me? You didn't mention that! What does he want?"

Ignoring my outburst, Horus addressed the dwarf, "How do you know he is the mark?"

"Uhh... he said so."

Darkdawn rolled his eyes. "He just upped and turned himself in, did he?"

Hagfyr's flush deepened. "No. He claimed to be the under-dweller's friend, and I saw no reason to doubt him. He fits the description, after all."

The elf pursed his lips, but he didn't mock the dwarf further. "Hagfyr is right about that," he murmured in an aside to Horus that I was sure I wasn't supposed to hear. "He does look like the one the chief is after."

Horus nodded minutely. "Go tell the boss. I'll keep an eye on him so long."

Not saying anything further, the elf slipped through the closed door behind them.

"Is someone going to tell me what's—" I began.

"Shut up," Horus ordered. "And don't move."

Glaring at the elite with what I hoped seemed like helpless outrage, I let my right hand slip closer to my hip.

"Don't," Horus warned. "You'll be dead before your blade leaves its sheath."

I doubted that, but my gambit was working and there was scarce need for further playacting. Folding my arms in front of me, I set myself to wait patiently.

But only a moment later, the door behind Horus opened again and Darkdawn stepped out. "The boss will see you now," he said, staring straight at me.

Concealing a smile, I stepped forward. It looked like I was finally going to get my wish: a private meeting with Dinara. And all without killing anyone or a single slipup.

I must be getting better at this.

CHAPTER 515: A POLITE CONVERSATION

The den chief's office was huge but surprisingly lacking in the opulence of the rest of the level. Bookshelves lined the walls, a sturdy leather rug lay underfoot, and magelights floated near the ceiling. It was the large oak desk on the opposite side of the room that dominated the space, though. Sitting behind it and facing the door was a gray-haired man.

Dinara.

The moment my eyes alighted on him, a Game message opened in my mind and screamed for attention.

The target is Dinara, a level 247 trapsmith.
Warning: this player has been branded a criminal by the sector's ruling faction, the Triumvirate. Aiding him in any manner may result in charges being brought against you.

I continued my advance into the room, with only the tiniest of hitches betraying my surprise at the Game alert. My stutter, slight as it was, did not go unnoticed, though.

The den chief's eyes tightened fractionally. "How did you analyze me so quickly?"

Ignoring the question, I strode deeper into the room and seated myself across from the slim figure. Dinara sat with his arms casually resting on the table. Moving carefully, I mimicked his pose.

The den chief didn't say anything, but the slight upward tick of his lips conveyed his appreciation of the gesture. I didn't want the encounter devolving into violence—not until I got the answers I sought—and it seemed Dinara was inclined the same way, too.

Sitting back, I considered the man. It was early days yet, but my first impressions tallied with Hugo's—Dinara was dangerously perceptive. I would have to be careful.

"Answer me," Dinara ordered mildly.

"I'm sure you can work that out for yourself," I replied evenly.

"You used a tier five analyze," Dinara said with no hint of a question in his tone.

I inclined my head in acknowledgment, seeing no point in denying it. The den chief had already worked out that much for himself, and the closer I skirted to the truth, the less likely he was to uncover my other secrets.

"You're an elite," he stated flatly.

I shrugged. That, too, stood to reason. Knowing what was coming next, I waited.

Sure enough, an electric tingle rippled over me a moment later.

You have passed a mental resistance check! Dinara has failed to pierce your disguise.

"Boss?" a startled Darkdawn asked from the door. "Want me to stay?"

The den chief's eyes flickered to the elf. "No. Close the door on your way out. But stay vigilant."

"Got it." Slipping out of the room, Darkdawn paused in the doorway. "We'll be listening," he warned me before shutting the door behind him.

Ignoring the byplay, Dinara's gaze slid back to me. "Who are you?"

"Jasiah," I replied innocently.

The den chief snorted. "We both know that's not true. Your analyze data is patently false. What spell are you using to conceal your identity? Mimic?"

I chuckled. "Come, Dinara, you know I'm not going to reveal that."

"Then tell me why you are here," he demanded.

I cocked my head to the side. "Didn't your bodyguard tell you?"

The den chief's eyes hardened. "Don't take me for a fool. Darkdawn's report counts for naught. As does Hagfyr's. Everything you told them was likely lies. But whoever you are, you didn't come all this way for nothing. So, I repeat: why are you here?"

Not answering immediately, I took a second longer look at the den chief. Dinara was exactly as Hugo had described. A slight unassuming man, who if he were not a player, I would've judged to be around fifty. As it was, I imagined the den chief had been around for at least a few centuries and was almost certainly better versed in the Game than me.

Dinara carried no visible weapons, and his clothes, while immaculate, looked ordinary. He wore almost no jewelry to speak of either and despite his obvious ire, his posture remained relaxed and assured—a king in the heart of his demesne.

Rightly or wrongly, Dinara did not fear me.

"They were not lies," I replied finally. "I *am* Nicola's acquaintance." I paused. "And I heard you were looking for me."

The den chief seemed to take my answer at face value. "How did you learn about that?"

"Sintar's gang," I replied laconically.

Consternation flickered across Dinara's face. "Sintar would not have—" Breaking off, he studied me keenly again. "He's dead, isn't he?"

"Yes."

"The rest of the gang?"

"Dead too."

Dinara leaned back in his chair, his hands sliding to the edge of the desk but still visible. "And did you think I would be as easy to slay? Is that why you're here? To kill me?"

"Not at all."

He frowned. "I admit you confound me. You eliminated Sintar and the men I sent after you, then you come here alone into the heart of my base. Why? What's stopping *me* from finishing the job they started?"

I quirked one eyebrow.

"Ah, I see. You don't think I can." Dinara shook his head. "Well, believe what you wish, but I assure you, in the Crooked Man, only one man rules. Me. Your fate is in my hands now."

I said nothing, not caring if Dinara believed *he* was the one in control.

Dinara smiled. "I see my words fall on deaf ears. But even given your misplaced confidence, you must surely perceive the precariousness of your situation? Why risk coming here in the first place?"

"Because I want answers."

Dinara studied me inquisitively. "And what makes you think you're entitled to any?"

I tossed him my underworld token. "This for one."

The den chief caught the chit easily. Opening his palm, he inspected it carefully. "Who gave this to you?"

"Nicola."

Dinara blinked slowly. "Of course," he murmured. "The timing is unfortunate, though." He slid the token back to me. "If I'd known you were a member of the underworld before this, it might have changed things. Now, it's too late. I've already accepted the commission." His eyes glittered. "And I always fulfill my commissions."

Now we were getting to the heart of the matter. "A commission to secure my death," I mused, deliberately placing the darkest possible interpretation on the nature of his interest. "And here I thought the underworld did not deal in death."

"The commission is for your capture, not death," the den chief replied stiffly.

"Hmm. So, you say." I leaned across the table. "Who is paying you?"

Dinara took a long time answering. "I suppose that—" he glanced at the chit still on the table between us—"earns you the right to an answer on that much at least."

Patiently, I waited.

"The commission is from Tyelin."

I exhaled softly. Things were starting to fall in place. The puzzle was far from complete though. "What does he want with me?"

Dinara shrugged. "I don't know, nor did I bother asking. Blythe's envoy is willing to pay handsomely for you. And in the end, that is all that matters."

"What did he offer you?"

"Enough with the questions," Dinara said, his expression turning impatient. "I've already been more obliging than necessary. I will tell you no more."

"Was it, by any chance, a sum of two hundred thousand gold?" I asked, ignoring his dictate.

The older man's eyes narrowed. "Who told you? It couldn't have been Sintar. He didn't know."

Sliding a thin slip of parchment across the table, I sat back. "I know because of this."

The den chief let the promissory note lie where I left it, yet he did not fail to register what it was—nor the number 'two hundred thousand' etched boldly upon it. "Where did you get that?" he asked, his eyes darkening.

"From Tyelin," I replied offhandedly. "As payment for services rendered. Nicola was acting as my intermediary on the matter, which I gather is why Tyelin had you following him." I paused. "I'm guessing your commission was also for all the items on my person?"

"Yes," Dinara said in a clipped tone, making the same connections I had.

Blythe's envoy had acted more shrewdly than I expected. Exploiting my reliance on Nicola, he'd used him to get to me. And the beauty of it was that Tyelin's commission wouldn't leave him any further out of pocket than he already was. If Dinara managed to fulfill it, then instead of me collecting on the two hundred thousand gold, Dinara would. And, as an added bonus, the envoy would also get his looted legendary items back.

Was that the sum total of Tyelin's calculation, though?

Or was there more to the matter that I was not seeing? There were other considerations, too. *Like, for instance, how did Tyelin know I'd be—*

"So, the little snot played me," Dinara mused.

I glanced up at the den chief. "It seems so," I agreed.

He sighed. "It does not change things, though."

"Oh?"

Instead of responding, Dinara reached out to the underworld token and touched it lightly.

Your underworld token has been updated.

You have been designated a journeyman rogue by den chief Dinara, marking you as a full member of the underworld.

My gaze flickered downward in time to spot the numeral "1" stamped on the top side of the chit change to a "2."

"What was that for?" I asked, my brows rising.

"Consider it compensation for what I must do next," Dinara murmured.

I held his gaze. "You still intend on fulfilling Tyelin's commission then."

He nodded. "I do."

"Why?"

The den chief sighed again. "Because if there is one thing that's sacrosanct in the underworld, it's a commission. If word got around that I reneged on a deal, I'd be done for."

I rubbed my chin. "Have you considered the risks?"

Dinara's lips quivered in amusement. "From where I'm sitting there *aren't* any."

"You're a criminal," I said bluntly. "When I kill you, you'll end up in Nexus' safe zone and never make it out again—at least not as a free man. The knights will spawn kill you until your final death."

"*If* you kill me," he pointed out.

"Is that a chance you're willing to take?"

"It's a chance I *must* take."

It was my turn to sigh. "I see." Sweeping the token off the table, I returned it to my backpack. "What about the whole induction thing?" I asked suddenly. "Isn't there supposed to be one before I can become a full thieves guild member?"

Dinara barked a laugh. "Brazen, aren't you?"

I smiled. "I've been called worse."

"I don't doubt it." Reaching into his pocket, the den chief extracted a pamphlet and handed it to me. "Read that, and you'll be inducted."

"Sounds easy enough," I murmured, storing the item away.

He grinned. "It is. You're bypassing all the difficult tests that come before. No small concession on my part, I may add."

"A gesture I will not forget, I promise," I said with the same air of affability he had.

"Good," Dinara pronounced, his hands still resting near the desk's edge. "Then shall we get down to business?"

I held up my hand for patience. "One last thing." I gestured to the promissory note. "Can I get my money please?"

Dinara gaped at me, momentarily flummoxed by my audacity. "I think not."

"Why not?" I challenged.

"That's my money," he retorted, his veneer of politeness disappearing.

"No, it's not," I countered instantly. "It's Tyelin's."

He stared at me.

"Think about it. What do you have to lose? If you capture me after this—as you seem certain you can—you've lost nothing but a bit of time exchanging that note for gold. And if you fail and I get away? It's Tyelin who bears the cost, not you. He will still have to pay you if you complete your commission."

"*When* I complete the job," Dinara retorted automatically, "not if."

But despite the den chief's protest, a gleam had appeared in his eyes, and I could tell he was giving serious consideration to my proposal—as I suspected he might. He hadn't sounded too happy about being played by Blythe's envoy earlier.

"Assuming I do as you ask," Dinara said, looking up at me again, "I take it you don't intend on giving yourself up thereafter?"

I chuckled. "If that's your way of asking if I'm going to surrender, then the answer's no. You won't take me alive. If at all."

Dinara smiled—a little too toothily, I thought. "I'll fulfill your request. As a den chief, I'm obligated to do so after all. What currency do you prefer?"

"Bags of stygian powder will do nicely," I replied.

Dinara's brows rose. "Interesting choice."

Removing a second promissory note, I placed it beside the first. "And while you're at it, exchange that for me, will you?"

Laughter bubbled in Dinara's eyes, but this time he chose not to comment. Leaning across the desk, he swiped both notes, and a moment later, two hefty pouches appeared in their place. "Your payment in full, exact to the gram."

You have lost Tyelin and Nicola's promissory notes.
You have acquired 2.12 kg of stygian powder.

Although I was curious about how he'd managed to measure out the exact quantity needed in such a short span of time, I refrained from inquiring. I'd gotten everything I'd come for, and there was no point in pushing things further.

"Thank you," I murmured, dumping the two pouches in my bag of holding.

Dinara inclined his head. "Now, is that all?" he asked sardonically. "Or is there something else I can do for you today?"

"You could let me go," I quipped.

The den chief grinned. "Why would I do that? You are in the center of my..."

Dinara kept speaking, but I stopped paying attention. My focus had swapped to something else—his hands.

They were moving again.

The motion was slow and smooth and ordinarily, it would not have impinged on my awareness, but throughout the conversation, I'd made certain not to lose sight of them.

Dinara was a trapsmith.

Not a pure combat Class by the sounds of it. Yet, he continued to evince no nervousness at being *alone* in a room with me—an unknown player who was quite possibly higher-ranked than him. I didn't believe his calm confidence was feigned either.

All this told me one thing.

Dinara's office was trapped to the nines. And the moment the den chief triggered his ambush, I was a dead man.

Which was why I had to act first.

Palming the remote trigger concealed in my left hand all this time, I pressed down on it before Dinara's hands could slip off the desk.

You have activated a trap.
You have activated a trap.
You have activated a trap.

The building shook as explosions rocked the perimeter of the building.

Dinara froze. "What was that?"

I grinned. "A signal."

Realization dawned in the den chief's eyes. "You didn't come here alone."

I shook my head, playing for time. Any second now... *C'mon, Shael!*

A tier 6 concealment barrier has been disabled.
An adept dampening field has been disabled.
Your tier 1 to 4 mana, psi, and stamina abilities are no longer inhibited.

"No, I did not," I agreed and, releasing the psi I held ready, blinked away.

CHAPTER 516: DENIED

You have teleported 97 yards. You are hidden.

I teleported out of the Crooked Man using the furthest mindglow visible in my consciousness. I'd been tempted, for just a moment, to stay within the confines of the tavern and exact revenge on Dinara's men.

That would've been petty though—not to mention dangerous.

But more importantly, it wouldn't have served my goals.

The den chief wasn't an enemy, nor were the rest of the thieves. Yes, for the near future I had to avoid Dinara because of his commission and yes, I would have to stay vigilant in any further dealings I had with the thieves— they were truly the mercenary sort. But I'd already gotten what I'd sought.

Money and answers.

Once my present troubles were resolved... well, then, I could see about returning to the underworld. Its denizens and I had more than a few things in common. For now, though, some distance would be good.

Slipping out of the shadows, I made my way to the agreed upon meeting point, and to my relief, I spotted Shael heading the same way from afar. *Good, he's made it out in one piece.* And by the looks of it, no one was tailing him.

"Any problems?" I asked as I caught up to the half-elf.

"None," Shael pronounced with satisfaction. "I was out before anyone even realized anything was wrong."

I nodded. Hugo's inside knowledge of the Crooked Man had made all the difference. His gang had long since figured out the location of the focus crystals controlling the tavern's wards.

Knowing all too well the nature of his fellow players, the den chief had chosen not to place the artifacts in a locked and guarded room but had hidden them away where no one would ever think to look—in a secret compartment in one of the guest rooms. Unfortunately for him, Sintar had found it.

"What about getting in?" I asked.

"A breeze," Shael replied. "I walked in through the front door, hired the room, and bypassed the alarms. Hugo's information was spot on."

"Excellent," I murmured.

Shael glanced at me sideways. "Where to now?"

I smiled. "Not onto another detour if that's what you're thinking. It's time we left Nexus. We'll stop by Kesh on the way out to drop off the money, but then it's straight to the teleportation platform."

Shael grinned. "Excellent," he echoed.

✳ ✳ ✳

You have equipped a set of the <u>emporium robes</u>, concealing your identity.

Shael and I recovered Safyre's robes and made our way to Kesh's compound without incident. When we got there, the half-giants waved me in without comment. "He stays with us," Lake said, pointing at Shael.

Nodding agreeably, the half-elf made himself comfortable while I continued onward. The inside of the emporium was quieter than usual, and I passed no one on my way to Kesh's office.

"Come in," the old merchant said as I raised my hand to knock on the door.

Doing as she bade, I shut the door behind me before lowering the hood concealing my face. "I have your money," I said, beaming at Kesh. "Most of it anyway."

She did not return my smile. "Sit," she ordered perfunctorily.

"What's wrong?" I asked, my good mood evaporating.

"Sit," Kesh repeated, and this time I didn't fail to mark the weariness in her tone. "You'll want to be seated for this."

My trepidation rising, I slipped into the chair facing her. "Tell me."

"I've received a response from Loken."

"And?" I asked, stilling.

"He's denied your request."

I blinked. "What?"

"The trickster does not want to meet."

Kesh's words made as little sense the second time around as it did the first. I knew what she meant, of course. What stymied me was the nature of Loken's reply.

After asking Kesh to reach out, I had considered and planned for every possible response from the Shadow Power—or so I'd thought. Everything from a demand to change the meeting spot, questions about why I wanted the meet, demands for assurances, and questions about where I'd been. I'd even anticipated and planned for Kesh being unable to reach Loken.

What I'd not expected was a flat refusal.

"He doesn't want to meet—at all?" I asked, still trying to wrap my head around Loken's rejection.

Kesh nodded.

I bit my lip. "You're sure it was Loken who replied? Not one of his lackeys trying to—"

"I'm sure," she cut in. "The trickster's answers came back almost immediately, and I've spent the better part of the day working my contacts to verify the source. There's no doubt. Loken is in Nexus. My letter was hand delivered to him. The response is his."

I nodded slowly. "How exactly did he phrase his refusal?"

"*No.*"

I stared at her. "That's it? One word? No explanation?"

"That's it," she replied, her own expression tight. "What do you think it means?"

"I'm not... sure," I replied, leaning back.

Why was Loken refusing to meet?

Had not telling him about Saya been a mistake? The last time the Shadow Power and I had spoken—many weeks ago—he'd seemed almost desperate for me to steal Paya's chalice, and I'd assumed he'd jump at the chance to check on what progress I'd made in the interim. I'd either misread the situation or...

Loken was toying with me.

It would not be the first time either. *What game is he—*

"Michael?"

My eyes darted back to Kesh.

"What are you going to do?"

"The only thing I can," I replied slowly. "Resolve matters in sector 12,560 myself."

She stared at me searchingly. "Can you?"

"I must," I said grimly. "I don't know what game Loken is playing, but I don't have time to indulge his love for theatrics. I've wasted enough time as it is. I will rescue Saya and deal with the envoy myself."

Kesh did not question my choice further. "Tell me what you need."

Removing the pouches of stygian powder I'd obtained from Nicola and Dinara, I set them down on her desk. "This is all the money I've been able to acquire. I know it's a bit short, but if you can—"

"Don't worry," Kesh said, running an expert eye over the bags. "I'll make it work. You'll have your shield generator."

I bowed my head in gratitude. "Thank you."

"It's the least I can do." Kesh frowned. "But with regards to the legendary artifacts and other gear you wanted, I'm afraid I can't complete their delivery until you come up with the money."

I sighed. "I understand. And trust me, I'm working on it."

"I can, however, give you this much," Kesh added. Waving her hand, she materialized a small cache of stone coins. Turning my gaze downward, I inspected the objects that had appeared on the desk.

This is a set of unmarked soulbound faction tokens. Except for being indestructible, each token possesses no further properties.

The tavern has lost 20,000 gold. Money remaining in the Wyvern Roost's bank account: 300 gold.

There were far fewer tokens on the desk than I'd requested, but even so, they were more than welcome, and I swept them into my backpack without complaint.

You have acquired 20 x unmarked soulbound faction tokens. Do you wish to soul-bind the items?

Ignoring the Adjudicator's question, I turned back to Kesh. "They cost one thousand gold each?"

She nodded. "That's the discount price too."

I winced. "Thanks."

Kesh inclined her head. "Is there anything else you need?"

Pausing for thought, I mentally reshuffled my priorities. For the next few days, weeks, or however long it took, I would be tied up in the wolves' valley.

That meant many of the tasks I planned on completing in the short term would have to be put on the back burner or allocated to my allies. Reclaiming the nether-infested sector was too important to just ignore.

"Yes," I replied at last.

"Go on," Kesh encouraged.

Running through my mental list, I identified the tasks I could safely ask Kesh to handle. "Do you know of a crafter capable of working with soulbound items?"

If the old merchant was surprised by the question, she didn't show it. "Of course, I know many such crafters. What sort are you specifically looking for?"

"A bladesmith," I replied, laying down Sunfury's feather shaft on her desk. "One capable of creating a shortsword from this."

"Ah," Kesh exclaimed, her eyes gleaming as she picked up the shaft. "A phoenix's feather. Fascinating. I know someone capable of forging this into a weapon. He will be quite excited at the opportunity, I assure you." She paused. "I can't give you a time or cost estimate, though."

"It doesn't matter how long it takes or how much it costs. Just see it done, please."

"I will," she promised. "Do you have any requirements for the blade?"

I shrugged. "Tell your crafter to do the best he can. As long as it's a shortsword."

"Noted. What else can I do for you?"

"Contact the stygian brotherhood," I replied.

Once again, Kesh evinced no surprise. "I'd thought you might ask that. I assume you want me to negotiate on your behalf for their help in closing the rift in that sector of yours?"

Exhaling heavily, I nodded.

Ideally, I didn't want to depend on the stygian brotherhood, at all. If I had my way, the army we forged for our assault on the stygians would be made up of werewolves, rehomed possessed, and scions from House Pestilence. But there were still too many unknowns with all three groups.

I didn't know yet if I could convince the werewolves to our cause, let alone Pestilence, nor if Adriel could rehome the possessed. And unfortunately, I didn't have the luxury of doing everything in a stepwise fashion anymore.

"I'll reach out to Huntmistress Kartara," Kesh said. "How much can I tell her?"

"Tell the huntmistress the rift is guarded by four overlords, a young void tree, and a nest numbering in the thousands. If she feels her people are up to the challenge of facing such a force, I will welcome their aid. Needless to say, don't share my name with her."

"Of course not."

"Assuming the brotherhood is willing, ask them to begin gathering," I went on. "They must be ready to move on my call and should not expect more than a day's notice."

"Got it. Where should they assemble?"

"Any sector, just not Nexus. We'll provide the portals to take them to the rift."

Kesh nodded. "And what are you offering the brotherhood in exchange for their aid?"

"All the stygian remains from the nest, including the bodies of the overlords," I replied, knowing I had little choice in the matter. "But not the void tree itself."

Kesh rubbed her chin thoughtfully. "Kartara may deem your offering insufficient."

I grimaced. "Negotiate with her as you see fit. I'll trust to your discretion."

"Very well. Huntmistress Kartara will likely want an upper limit on the time her people spend waiting for your call."

I nodded. "That's fair." I couldn't expect the brotherhood to wait forever. "Tell her, we'll make contact within a month." I paused. "If I can't do so personally... Safyre will act on my behalf."

Kesh frowned. "You're rushing things," she noted.

"I am," I admitted, "but I don't have much choice in the matter. If the rift is not closed soon, the sector will be lost."

"I see," Kesh murmured. "Then I won't tell you to slow down. Securing that sector is vital."

"Agreed."

Kesh sighed. "You've given me more than enough to do, but I'll ask again, what else do you need?"

I didn't answer immediately. "There is one more thing."

Kesh waited expectantly.

"I need information on a sector."

Kesh frowned. "Information is not something I usually deal in as you already know. But I'll do what I can. Which sector?"

"Sector 90,830," I said, rattling off the number of the sector that in times gone by had been Death's home.

To my surprise, recognition sparked in Kesh's eyes. "Don't you think you have enough to deal with already?" she asked reproachfully. "Why tangle with the Awakened Dead further?"

"I don't want to— Wait! What?" Understanding dawned. "Are you saying," I asked slowly, "that sector 90,830 is owned by the Awakened Dead?"

Kesh looked at me strangely. "You didn't know?"

I shook my head.

"Oh. Then no doubt, you'll be interested to learn that Erebus' main stronghold is in sector 90,830."

Bowing my head, I stifled a groan. House Death's former home and Erebus' base were one and the same?

That could not be a coincidence.

You have acquired 6 x greater portal scrolls.
You have lost 3,000 gold coins.

Before leaving the emporium, I restocked my supply of portal scrolls, almost draining my remaining funds to the dregs. Money was tight again, unfortunately, but the added mobility the scrolls gave me made their hefty price tags worth it.

"Bad news?" Shael asked as I rushed out of the compound.

"What?" Looking up, I saw him scrutinizing my face. "Oh. Yes, sort of."

"We're still leaving, though, right?"

Nodding, I turned my steps in the direction of the teleportation platform. "We are."

"Good," he pronounced, then fell silent as we made our way to our destination. Reaching the stone platform, I wasted no time in cracking open a portal scroll and releasing its enchantment.

Item consumed.

A moment later, a luminous white doorway appeared, and I ducked through without hesitation.

Transfer through portal commencing...
...
...
Leaving Nexus.

✻   ✻   ✻

You have entered the safe zone of sector 12,560.

I stepped out of the crowded portal platform and into the deserted common room of the Wyvern's Roost. Shael, following close on my heels, staggered out a moment later.

"The tavern?" the bard asked, his face crinkling in confusion. "Why are we back here?"

Swiveling about, I made my way to the still-open entrance. "You'll see," I replied, pulling on the door.

It refused to budge.

Putting my back into it, I tugged harder. Still nothing. "What's wrong with this thing?" I growled.

"Saya had it reinforced," Shael said from behind. "The door may look like wood, but that's just paneling. It's solid steel on the inside. It took two men to close it every night."

"Huh," I grunted. "Come and help me then."

Doing as I bade, the bard lent his efforts to mine, and with much groaning and shoving we finally got the damn thing closed. "Where are the keys?" I asked, studying the imposing lock on the door.

"Beneath the bar counter."

"Go get them. It's time we locked this place up."

Shael moved to comply. "Not that I mind, but are you going to tell me why you're bothering to do that?"

"In a minute," I replied, moving to the closest window. As I sealed its shutters, I noticed in passing that they too had been reinforced. "I've got the windows on this floor. Shut the rear door, and then do the ones on the next level."

"Why?" a puzzled Shael asked.

"I want the tavern shut from top to bottom," I said, ignoring the question. "And let's hurry. We have six floors to work through."

Sighing, the bard got to work.

✳ ✳ ✳

An hour later, we were done.

After double-checking Shael's work, I sat down in the common room, finally satisfied that there was no opening into the tavern that could be exploited to gain unauthorized access.

"So, now are you going to tell me what all that was about?" Shael asked, sitting down opposite me.

"I don't want any strangers entering the Wyvern's Roost," I replied.

Shael rolled his eyes. "I figured out that much, but it's a tavern, remember? Serving strangers is the Roost's entire purpose!"

"Not anymore, it isn't," I replied tightly.

He frowned. "What does that mean?"

Removing the tavern's bill of ownership, I laid it down on the table. "It means the Roost is no longer open for business. From today, it will serve as the private barracks of my army."

"So, we're an army now?" Shael quipped. "Just the two of us? That's a bit rich, don't you think?"

My expression did not alter, and after a pregnant pause, the bard's humor faded. "You're serious," he breathed. "You have an *actual* army? Really?"

"Only a small one," I said, deadpan.

"What! Where? And more importantly, how?"

Ducking my head before he could see me smile, I studied the parchment I'd unrolled on the table.

One of the key benefits to owning property in a safe zone was that it could be used as a form of secure storage. The same Game laws that prevented a thief from pickpocketing a player in a safe zone also stopped said thief from robbing a house in one. It was why merchants were so enamored of safe zones.

Of course, property in a safe zone was only as secure as the safe zone itself. If a rival faction claimed sector 12,560, I would lose everything I left in the Wyvern's Roost, including the building itself.

But it was not for the purpose of storing stuff that I intended on using Wyvern's Roost.

Another upside of having property in a safe zone was that it gave me the ability to control my surroundings—in this case, that meant deciding who was allowed to enter or stay in the Roost. Sadly, the Game did not prevent magical eavesdropping or detection spells, but for that there were wards.

Still, even as it was, the Roost was the safest place for my allies to come and go from the nether-infested sector. This held doubly true for the forsworn. Even though the Game wouldn't protect them personally, it would stop any intruders from getting into *my* building and harming any forsworn sheltering inside.

And while a waypoint to the nether-infested sector wasn't strictly necessary, the Roost would make traveling to sector 18,240 easier for those who couldn't create their own portals—like Anriq for instance. The werewolf could hitch a ride from any mage to the wolves' valley, and thereafter have a forerunner mage—one stationed in the Roost, ideally— open a portal back 'home.'

Of course, all the pieces weren't in place for what I planned yet, but it was always better to lay the groundwork early. Returning my attention to the scroll unrolled on the table, I inspected it carefully.

The target is a bill of ownership for 'The Wyvern's Roost' in the safe zone of sector 12,560.

All safe zone building bills of ownership are Game-created items that grant you full control over the building and cannot be stolen or lost, even upon death. Note, if the building is unoccupied or unused for an extended period, ownership will revert to the Game.

This item must be freely gifted or traded to pass on to another. On final death, it will drop and be freely lootable.

Now for the next step, I thought. Closing my eyes and holding the Game artifact in one hand, I willed my intent to the Adjudicator.

By rights of your bill of ownership, you have repurposed the Wyvern's Roost from tavern to private hostel.

Notice added: 'The Wyvern's Roost has been indefinitely closed to the public. Only authorized guests may enter.' Note, this notice will be issued as a Game alert to all unauthorized players who approach the building.

Do you wish to alter the list of allowed occupants? The list is private and only visible to the building owner.

Replying in the affirmative to the Adjudicator's query, I relayed a string of names to the Game.

The Wyvern Roost's list of allowed occupants has been successfully updated.

Allowed occupants: 9. Michael, Saya, Safyre, Anriq, Nyra, Ceruvax, Terence, Teresa, and Shael.

Assigned managers: Saya, Safyre.

Smiling, I opened my eyes. It was done.

The Roost was as physically secure as I could make it. The magical defenses I could do nothing about. Safyre would have to sort that out once she got here. Thinking of the aetherist reminded me of the emporium robes stuffed in my backpack. Removing them, I placed them behind the bar counter.

"You're leaving that here?" Shael asked, watching me.

I nodded.

"Why?"

"There's a tracking device inside the robes. The Triumvirate can find it wherever it goes. And where we're going, no one can know about."

Shael's eyes widened. "The Triumvirate!" he whispered. "You're swimming in deep waters, Michael."

I shrugged. "Not by choice."

The bard's face grew puzzled. "But... won't the Nexus trio find it strange to discover the robes here?"

I smiled. "Have you forgotten already? Kesh posted one of her agents in this very tavern not so long ago."

"Of course!" Shael exclaimed, smacking his forehead. "That's clever of you. Diabolical even. I understand now why we came here." He paused. "*Not that I can claim to know what you want with the robes in the first place.*"

"You'll find out soon enough," I said brightly. "We'll leave for our final destination at first light tomorrow."

"Tomorrow?" Shael asked, looking crestfallen. "I thought..."

"You'll thank me for it come morning," I promised. "Where we're going is colder than cold. Tonight, at least you'll get to sleep in a warm bed."

✳   ✳   ✳

My rest was broken the next morning by a set of surprising Game messages.

You and Ghost have reached level 239!
You have slept 7 hours. Your blood memories have been recharged.

For a moment, I stared stupidly at the alerts, wondering who I'd managed to kill in my sleep. Then reason penetrated.

It was Ghost's doing, of course.

Stifling a yawn, I sat up. *Two whole levels? What has she killed to earn us that?*

I rolled off the bed, excited and worried in equal measure. Ghost was fine, I knew that much. The Game would have reported had she died. Still, the niggling concern remained that a new threat has arisen to plague us.

Slipping out of the room I'd claimed as mine on the sixth floor, I strode into the hallway. The door opposite mine—Shael's—was still shut.

"Time to go!" I yelled, thumping hard on its wooden surface. "I'll meet you downstairs. And hurry!"

Heading into the common room, I sat down and schooled myself to patience. Whatever was going on in the tundra was already over. *Another ten or twenty minutes will make no difference.*

Accepting the truth of that statement, I eased back into my chair and considered the emptiness about me while I waited for Shael.

Without Saya's bright presence, the tavern—*former tavern,* I corrected—was a forlorn looking place. The tables were dusty, empty bottles littered the floor, and thanks to the newly shuttered doors and windows, the place was beginning to smell. Even the flowers the gnome had planted everywhere had wilted.

I will have to get the twins to clean the place before she gets back.

And Saya would be back. I was certain of it. No other outcome was acceptable. Closing my eyes, I considered what I might have to do to rescue the gnome.

Slay the envoy for one, I thought morosely.

It was not the idea of killing the treacherous player that bothered me, though. It was how Loken would react. Thus far, I'd managed to walk a fine line with the trickster—avoiding his enmity while at the same time *not* doing his bidding.

That was all about to change, I suspected.

I couldn't imagine that even a Power as fickle as Loken would let the killing of his envoy go unavenged. And even if I somehow managed to keep my role in upcoming events secret, Loken would guess the truth.

The trickster would hunt me, I was sure. And not just him, all the Powers in that Shadow Coalition of his would do likewise.

So be it.

Exhaling softly, I made my peace with the consequences. Soon, I would be in direct conflict with Shadow. I could see no other way around that fact. The only viable option had been to approach Loken directly, and that avenue was closed now.

My only consolation was that Loken and his allies would not know the true nature of their foe.

Perhaps that will make their hunt less relentless.

I snorted. *As if.*

Banishing my worries of the future, I turned my mind to the present and more specifically to my player profile. Thanks to whatever Ghost had done, I had a small cache of attributes to spend, and I didn't have to think hard about how to invest them.

Your Dexterity has increased to rank 122. Other modifiers: +24 from items. Available ability slots: 16.

I smiled. I now had enough ability slots to upgrade whirlwind when I finally did manage to raise my two weapon fighting skill above level two hundred. "Well done, Ghost," I murmured.

"Who's Ghost?" Shael asked, hurrying down the stairs.

I glanced over my shoulder at him. "You'll meet her soon enough. Ready to go?"

He nodded firmly.

I rose to my feet. "Then let's be about it."

Chapter 518: A Serpent Rears its Ugly Head

I tossed Shael a nether protection crystal. "You don't have to use it but keep it somewhere safe."

The half-elf stared incredulously at the object in his hand. "You're taking me into the nether?"

"Not quite," I replied. "The void *is* present in the sector we're going to, but we won't be staying long."

"I don't understand any of this—" Shael shook his head—"but alright."

Withdrawing a scroll from my backpack, I began casting. On the off chance an unknown player was hiding nearby, I deemed it safer to open the portal inside the tavern rather than outside. Admittedly, the possibility that someone would try to dash through the portal was remote, but it was still not one I wanted to risk.

Item consumed.
You have opened a greater portal to sector 18,240.

"Let's go," I said, beckoning Shael as I strode forward.

"Wait!"

Checking my stride, I glanced at him.

"Shouldn't we buff or something? What if we run into stygians?"

"Don't worry, it's safe," I assured him. "And like I said, we won't be in the sector long. Now, come on. The portal won't stay open forever." Advancing once more, I slipped into the luminous doorway.

Transfer through portal commencing...
...
...
Leaving sector 12,560.

* * *

You have entered sector 18,240 of the Forever Kingdom.
Warning: this region is under assault by the nether and is in impending danger of being pulled into the Nethersphere!
The nether toxicity at your current location is at tier 4. Your health, psi, stamina, and mana are degenerating at a rate of 0% per minute (damage reduced by 100% due to void armor).

I emerged out of the portal, at ease and relaxed.

Like I'd told Shael, there was nothing to fear. The last few times I'd been this way there had been no stygians for miles around, and everything I'd seen and learned from Anriq's scouting excursions—and my own—led me to believe the status quo would stay unchanged *until* the void claimed the sector.

It took only an eyeblink for me to realize my folly.

The space around me was *not* empty. It teemed with mindglows—some friendly, most not.

We had walked straight into a battle.

Damnit, I cursed. Ignoring the swords sheathed on my hip, I dug out my stygian blades from my bag of holding and glanced over my shoulder. Shael had yet to emerge.

And isn't he going to be happy when he does?

I grimaced at the thought. Still, it was too late to rectify my error, and not wanting to compound my mistakes further, I spread my awareness and took stock of the battlefield while I wove psi.

The sector had not fallen into the Nethersphere, that much was clear. But the status quo *had* changed. The two nearby gatherings of stygians made that much obvious.

The first pack—the smaller of the two—was less than ten yards away and on the opposite side of the nether portal to the tundra. The group wasn't close enough to stop us from escaping into the guardian tower but some of its members were already drawing closer and would soon be a threat.

Still, it was to the second stygian pack that I turned my attention.

They were about two hundred yards beyond the first group and congregated around four familiar shapes—Safyre, Anriq, Adriel, and Ghost.

Why in hells are they so far from the portal? I wondered.

Equally pertinent was the question of what the four were doing fighting a pitched battle here in the first place. The idea had been for them to lay low and *not* risk the void learning about our invasion plans!

It mattered little that the four seemed to be faring well enough. Despite the dozens of stygians surrounding them, my allies were untouched. Answers would have to wait, though, until the stygians were dealt with.

Almost unnoticed, a shape reared up silently on my left.

Stygian serpent.

Whipping around, I lashed out with the sword in my right hand. My motion triggered the nether creature's own attack, and it snapped at me with bared fangs.

Too slowly.

My own blow landed first, the smoky blade cleaving through the stygian's less-than-solid form as easily as through butter, decapitating it.

You have killed a level 110 stygian serpent with a fatal blow.

The snake's head flew free, flying in the direction of my portal and for a moment I feared it would go all the way through—and what would Shael make of *that?*—but happily, it fell short.

Less happily, the bard chose just then to transition through the portal. And, of course, he immediately noticed the head.

"I thought you said—" Shael began, staring down in horror at the head resting against his boots.

"I was wrong," I replied tightly. "Get ready to move! The others need us."

"Others? What others? Who else would possibly—"

I slashed my hand downward even as I eyed the pair of hydras approaching from behind the portal. "Save the talk for later! Buff up and put your back to mine!"

"Got it," Shael growled.

I was being a little harsh on the bard, I knew. Unlike me, Shael couldn't see through the mists to the beleaguered party two hundred yards away, nor for that matter could he perceive many of the stygians near the portal. And truly, it was not Shael I was annoyed with, but myself.

The situation was less than ideal—for Shael in particular. One ill-timed attack and he would suffer final death. And I would have no one to blame but myself.

Next time don't be so cocky, Michael.

"Prime!" Ghost exclaimed suddenly. *"You're back!"* A fractional pause. *"I can't see you. Where are you?"*

"At the nether gate to the tundra," I replied calmly. *"But don't come to me. I'll come to you. And warn the others."*

The party could no more see me than Shael could them. Safyre had a purifying dome up, of course, but its outer edge still fell about a hundred yards short of our current position, and once again, I wondered why they'd ventured so far from the gate to the tundra.

The question was of secondary import, though. My spell was ready, and just in time too. The hydras were almost in striking range.

You have cast windborne.

"Hang on!" I yelled to Shael.

"Wha—?"

His question went unfinished. Wrapping my arms about the bard, I yanked him onto the windslide and towards my embattled allies.

*   *   *

You have trigger-cast quick mend.

Twenty yards later, Shael and I dropped back to the ground. I'd only had enough time while on the windslide to cast one of my buffs, and I'd gone for the most defensive one.

"Run!" I shouted, shoving the bard in the back.

"W-which way?" he mumbled, staggering forward drunkenly.

"Dead ahead," I replied. I'd purposely set the ramp of air to deposit us in an area clear of danger, but the stygians near the nether portal were already turning our way once more, and we couldn't afford to tarry. "Don't stop when you hit the purifying field. Keep going! I'll guard your back."

No doubt, Shael found my instructions confusing, but he didn't stop to question me again and simply did as I bade. I raced after, blades out and scanning the mists.

The safer option *might* have been to send Shael into the tundra, of course, but not knowing if some calamity awaited on the other side, I'd chosen not to risk doing that. As dangerous as the nether sector was, I was confident I could protect the half-elf until we reached the others.

A bubble of dark energy sailed in from somewhere up ahead.

It was a ranged magical attack and an atypical one for the stygians.

But I'd already noticed a few unrecognized forms amongst the more familiar hydras and serpents, and it was a safe bet that the attack had originated from one of them. I'd not had the chance to analyze the 'new' nether creatures yet, and ordinarily, I would have simply blinked out of the unknown missile's path. But the evil-looking ball was homing in on Shael, and the odds of him surviving a strange magical assault were not good.

Angling left, I placed myself in the missile's path.

A voidball has hit you. Nether damage repelled!
Void armor charge remaining: 83%.

The spell's dark energy washed over me, but thanks to my void armor, I endured none of its effects. That did not prevent me from feeling unclean, though.

Shael stumbled to a stop, his eyes widening in horror—I was still close enough for him to perceive me through the mists. "Michael! Are you alright? What was that thing?"

"Keep going!" I replied. "I'm fine."

Another voidball launched.

This time, I picked out the source. Focusing on the creature, I scrutinized it intently. In most ways, the caster was identical to a stygian serpent. Only bigger. *Much* bigger.

A giant stygian serpent?

That didn't sound too bad. The serpents were easy enough to kill, after all. But I wasn't about to underestimate the threat level again, not so soon after being caught out by my false assumptions. Reaching out with my will, I analyzed the new nether creature.

The target is a level 238 stygian naga.
Stygian serpents are perhaps the most common and prevalent of all the nether's creatures. Lithe and agile, they are feared for their speed and cunning. Yet even so, a single snake is usually of no danger to an experienced player.
The same cannot be said of the nagas.
Of all the creatures in the stygian serpent's evolutionary chain, none is more feared than the naga. Larger than a hydra and faster than a serpent, nagas also wield the void's magic with an ease that even nether wizards envy, making them deadly at both ranged and close quarter fighting.

"Damnit," I muttered. "It's an elite."

Worse yet, there were four nagas accompanying the stygian packs. Two were behind us—with the first pack—while the other two flanked the besieged party ahead. I suspected that at some point there had also been a *fifth* naga, one that Ghost had killed. It would account for the two levels she'd so recently acquired.

The picture was becoming clearer.

Given the disposition of the stygians and the surprising appearance of elites amongst their number, there could be no doubt about what was going on.

This was an ambush.

And that meant that not only was the void aware of our presence in the sector, but they had just seized the initiative, too.

Caught unawares, Safyre, Adriel, and the others had likely been forced away from the tundra portal before they could regroup. That they had done so and were managing to hold the stygians at bay was encouraging. But I could not forget the lone stygian overlord that only a few days ago I'd spotted lurking near the river. At a guess, it was already moving this way.

With reinforcements in tow, no doubt.

The only thing in our favor was how slow the overlords were. The damnable thing would take hours to get here — *if* it hadn't repositioned itself beforehand.

But there was no way to divine that, not in the thick of battle. *Gah. There's no choice. We have to retreat.*

And before the overlord gets here.

Dashing right, I moved to intercept the incoming voidball. In the process, another realization came to me. It was more than Shael's life that was at stake. All our lives were.

And quite possibly, my plans for the sector too.

Chapter 519: A Ball of Void

Before the stygian naga's attack hit, I managed another buff. And once again, it was *not* vanish.

You have cast enhanced reflexes, increasing your Dexterity by +16 for 20 minutes.

I *wanted* the stygians to see me; I *wanted* them to focus their attacks on me rather than my allies. The battle would be easier that way.

There was no time for further calculation, though. The naga's attack was almost upon me. Blades out and arms spread, I braced myself for its touch.

A voidball has hit you. Nether damage repelled!
Void armor charge remaining: 66%.
Void thief triggered!
You have acquired the direct-targeted spell <u>voidball (stolen)</u> and will retain memory of it for the next 16 hours.
Voidball (stolen) is a tier 5 spell that inflicts direct necrotic damage to the targeted area on impact. The nether's version of the ubiquitous fireball spell, voidball, is especially deadly to living creatures.

I exhaled sharply, hoping somehow that doing so would rid my mouth of the spell's foul aftertaste—alas, it did not—then turned my back on the naga. As much as I wanted to take the fight to the creature, my first priority was escorting Shael to the others.

Jogging alongside the bard, I refocused on the group ahead. We'd covered more than half the distance to the party, but while I could easily see Safyre's purifying field and the glimmering black dome that protected the four—Adriel's doing, presumably—my allies were less visible. Stygian hydras and serpents were pressed tight against the lich's shield and hacking at it with tooth and claw.

Getting Shael through that mess is not going to be easy.

But there was no need to go through the stygians. *Over* would do just as well.

I glanced upward. There was still no sign of the overlord or any flying snakes. As yet, this was strictly a ground battle. *Good. Windborne should do the trick again.* It would get us to Adriel's shield with limited risk.

But how were we going to get inside once we arrived?

I couldn't ask Adriel to drop the black dome. *That will be a recipe for—*

"Prime," Ghost interrupted, "*Adriel says she and Safyre will clear a path for you. Just say the word.*"

I smiled. Clearly, my allies had also been working on the problem and had figured out what needed to be done.

Glancing left and right, I took stock of the stygians before responding. Shael was moving at a good pace, and I judged none of the hydras and serpents from the first pack would catch us before we reached the others. Even better, the nagas ahead had yet to launch any further attacks.

Interestingly enough, the two nagas behind us had *not* joined the rest of the first pack in their chase and appeared more interested in the tundra's portal than us. Whatever they were up to, I was sure it wasn't anything good, but dealing with the pair would have to wait.

"*Tell Adriel to go ahead,*" I replied. "*Light them up. We'll be there soon.*"

✳   ✳   ✳

Over the next few seconds, death stalked the stygians.

Safyre has cast furious storm.

The mists roiled uneasily as storm clouds boiled overhead, unleashing bolt after bolt in a breathtaking spectacle of sound and light.

A level 145 stygian serpent has been stunned.
A level 131 stygian serpent has died.
A level 167 stygian hydra has been stunned.
...

...

The nether creatures unfortunate enough to be caught out by Safyre's magic were flung aloft, wreathed in coils of glittering energy. Most were stunned senseless. An unlucky few—struck multiple times or critically hit—simply died.

Then, a heartbeat later, Adriel joined the fray.

Adriel has cast Death's righteous fury.

In stark contrast to the lightshow Safyre was putting on, the lich's own contribution lacked any fanfare. Cold gray fire leaped silently from her hand, through the black dome, and into the massed stygians pressed up against it.

Whatever the fire touched died.

Instantly.

A level 140 stygian serpent has died.
A level 183 stygian hydra has died.
A level 187 stygian hydra has died.
...

...

"Wow," I murmured, recognizing Adriel's casting for what it was: a blood memory. I'd seen her use it only once before—against the archlich's wards, and that time it had been equally devastating.

"Err..." Shael stuttered to a halt as we passed through the outer edge of Safyre's purifying field and finally saw where we were going. "Should we be running *to* that?" he asked, panting for breath.

"Don't stop," I ordered. "The fireworks show is our allies' doing. They're opening a path for us."

The bard looked like he wanted to protest further but wisely refrained and resumed running. I kept my own gaze fixed on the slaughter ahead. Walking a slow circle around the perimeter of her shield, the lich was purging it of stygians. Any moment now, I expected the creatures would break and flee—temporarily, of course.

Sadly, though, the two nagas flanking the party were unaffected by Safyre and Adriel's spells. The elites' own shields stopped the aetherist's stunning bolts and, positioned as far back as they were from the black dome, the pair were also out of reach of the lich's killing flames.

The nagas in fact seemed completely indifferent to the fellows' fate. Ignoring the destruction Adriel and Safyre were wreaking they released another pair of voidballs my way.

"I can see you!" Ghost sang out.

"I see you too," I assured her, keeping a wary watch on the incoming missiles. *"Is Adriel planning on lowering her shield?"*

"Yes, but only long enough for you to enter."

I frowned. I would be of limited help inside the lich's shield. Just like Anriq and Ghost, I would be forced to stand around doing largely nothing while the mages ran amok with their spells.

"I'm not coming inside," I stated, arriving at a decision.

"What! Why?"

My reply was of necessity delayed. The voidballs were almost upon us. Accelerating ahead, I opened the distance between Shael and me so that when the missiles hit, he would be unaffected.

Then, I braced myself and waited.

2 voidballs have hit you!
A voidball has failed to harm you. You are immune to this spell.
A voidball has failed to harm you. You are immune to this spell.
Void armor charge remaining: 32%.

Void siphon activated!
You have siphoned a portion of your foes' mana. Mana remaining: 36%.

I grimaced at seeing how little mana I had remaining after suffering the double hits. Void siphon had barely done anything to restore my reserves either, and I knew I couldn't risk intercepting further voidballs.

But perhaps I won't need to.

Reaching out to the Adjudicator, I queried the Game on the status of the spells my void armor had recently absorbed.

Currently stored spells: 2 iterations of the voidball (stolen) spell.
Remaining storage time: 8 seconds.

Excellent. Delaying no further, I unleashed the two captured spell imprints in quick succession.

Void redirect activated!
You have successfully reconstituted the stolen spell, voidball, and redirected it at a level 238 stygian naga.

You have successfully reconstituted the stolen spell, voidball, and redirected it at a level 236 stygian naga.

I had no idea if the nagas were immune to their own spells, of course, but at the very least the voidballs I'd sent sailing back at the pair would keep them distracted long enough for Shael to reach safety.

"Hells, if that is not the damnedest thing I've ever seen," the half-elf muttered as he caught up to me.

I waved aside his words. "I won't be able to do that again," I warned as I resumed running. "We'll have to reach the others before we're attacked again." I paused for effect. "Or else."

The bard didn't say anything, but digging deeper into his reserves, he found an extra burst of speed.

Smiling grimly, I resumed my conversation with Ghost while I kept pace with Shael. *"Tell Adriel I suspect an overlord is on the way with reinforcements. We have to clear the field of the stygians before they arrive."*

"An overlord!" Ghost exclaimed. *"You'll need my help, then. I'm coming out."*

"I could use the help," I admitted, and after a second's thought, I added, *"Bring Anriq too."* My eyes darted left and right. Both voidballs were halfway to their targets. And while the nagas were not fleeing, their gazes were glued to the onrushing missiles.

Good, I thought, returning my attention to the scene in front. We were only forty yards away from the others now. Yanking open my bag of holding, I rifled through its contents.

Beside me, I heard Shael gulp audibly as he finally made sense of what lay ahead. "Is that— Is that a... lich?"

"Yes," I replied shortly, still searching the bag.

"And she is an... ally?"

"Oh yes."

Thirty yards. I began drawing psi.

"What about the werewolf?" Shael gasped. "And is that a stygian? Don't tell me they're allies too!"

"Ghost is not a—"

I broke off as a string of Game alerts demanded attention. The voidballs had just struck their targets.

You have critically hit a level 236 stygian naga.
You have critically hit a level 238 stygian naga.
No damage inflicted. Your targets' shields have blocked the attacks.

I smiled tightly. I still had no idea whether the voidballs would hurt the nagas, but I knew now at least it would damage their shields.

Severely damage, I amended, eyeing the much dimmer glow surrounding the pair. *That'll make killing them later easier.*

"Ghost is not a stygian," I said turning back to Shael, "she's my familiar." My searching hand finally found the items I was looking for in the bag of holding. Extracting them, I closed the bag and re-secured it on my belt again.

"Your familiar!" Shael exclaimed, his confusion making itself known even through his heaving breaths. "Since when do rogues have—"

"Here, hold this," I said, shoving two of the four objects I'd removed into Shael's open hands.

You have lost 2 farspeaker bracelets from the named set: Sintar's link.

"What's this?" Shael asked, looking down.

"Farspeaker bracelets," I replied. "Give one to Cara—" that was the name he knew her by, at least—"and put the other one on yourself." Heeding my own instructions, I did the same.

You have equipped a farspeaker bracelet from the Sintar link set.

"Cara? As in the emporium agent, Cara?" Shael asked, his gaze darting from me to the dome ahead. We were only twenty yards away now, and just like I'd anticipated, the serpents and hydras had begun to scatter.

"Yes, she goes by Safyre now," I replied across the farspeaker link.

"I would say I'm shocked, but I think we're beyond that now," Shael said numbly. Before I could respond he went on, *"Why do we need the bracelets, anyhow? And why do I have to give—"*

He broke off as he figured out the answer for himself. *"You're not entering the shield?"*

"I'm not," I confirmed and released the spell I held waiting.

You have cast windborne.

Grabbing hold of Shael again, I pulled him onto the windslide. *"Here we come, Ghost."*

The windslide took us all the way to the edge of Adriel's black dome which flickered off just as we arrived.

Great timing, I thought, scanning the surroundings. The survivors of the second stygian pack, while still sizable in number, remained scattered. They were of no threat yet. The pursuing serpents and hydras from the first pack, on the other hand, were closing in rapidly.

And the nagas...

I didn't think I was imagining the hungry gleam in their eyes as they eyed the downed shield. We'd have to hurry.

Spinning back, I nudged Shael forward. "Go," I urged. *"I'll see you again soon."*

The bard advanced tentatively just as Anriq and Ghost rushed by the other way. The werewolf tossed me a thick garment in passing. Catching it, I pulled it over my shoulders in one smooth motion.

You have equipped the <u>Cloak of the Reach</u>, gaining +20% fire resistance, +20% nether resistance, and +10 Magic.

"These are for you," I told Anriq and tossed him two items in turn.

You have lost 1 nether protection crystal and 1 farspeaker bracelet from the named set: Sintar's link.

"Thanks," Anriq growled, simultaneously equipping the bracelet and cracking the crystal.

"Much better," he added a moment later over the farspeaker link. *"What's the plan?"*

"We'll get to that in a bit," I replied. *"Watch my back."* Swiveling about, I began waving my arms to get our spellcasters' attention, only to find the pair staring at me intently already. "Raise the shield!" I shouted.

Adriel nodded curtly and Safyre threw me a lopsided smile. She knew as well as I that greetings and explanations would have to wait. Besides which, I was sure the pair would get the gist from Shael soon enough.

A split second later, the black dome snapped back in place, and my shoulders sagged in relief. *"Now we can get to work,"* I told Anriq.

He nodded curtly. *"Our targets?"*

"The nagas." Turning about, I dashed away from the shield and straight toward the first pack.

The werewolf's expression did not shift, but he couldn't conceal the note of worry in his tone as he and Ghost jogged after me. *"They're elites and hard to kill."*

I jerked my chin toward the naga on the left. Its shield looked the most damaged. *"That's why you and Ghost will double up on that one. Adriel and Safyre will handle the elite on the right."* In an aside to my familiar, I added, *"Protect Anriq. Make sure he doesn't die."*

Not only was Ghost higher leveled than the werewolf, but unusually, she and Adriel were *less* at risk in this sector than me and the other players. The lich and familiar had somewhere to resurrect.

The rest of us didn't.

"Will do," the pyre wolf replied.

"What are you going to do?" Anriq asked, his eyes beginning to glow. He was shapeshifting, I knew.

"Take out the two elites near the guardian gate," I replied.

"Is tackling them on your own wise?" Safyre asked, abruptly joining the conversation as she put on the bracelet Shael had given her.

"Not especially," I acknowledged, *"But we don't have the luxury of time. An overlord is likely on the way even now."*

Safyre sighed. *"Understood."*

I drew stamina in readiness. *"Can you and Adriel handle the naga on the right?"*

"Of course," she replied confidently. *"We'll see to what's left of the hydras and serpents too. Don't bother with the group heading for you. We'll take care of it."*

Not questioning her, I began casting.

Anriq has shifted into wolf form.

Glancing over my shoulder, I met the gazes of the two huge wolves bounding in my wake. *"Go,"* I ordered, and they peeled off to the left.

Turning back to the approaching stygians, I saw they were almost upon me. Unfortunately for them, I was about to cheat them of their quarry.

You have cast vanish. You are <u>invisible</u>. Duration: 5 minutes.

The hydras and serpents ground to a halt as I disappeared from sight. Chuckling quietly to myself, I drew psi again and shadow blinked past and onward to my own prey.

✻ ✻ ✻

You have teleported into a level 241 stygian naga's shadow. You are hidden.

I slipped unnoticed behind the giant stygian elite.

From here, the sounds of the battle almost two hundred yards away were muted. Not that my targets seemed to care much about it.

Both nagas remained transfixed by the guardian portal.

The impulse to strike immediately was strong, but I held myself back for a moment. *What are they doing?* I wondered. From the pair's near-constant hissing, they were obviously casting.

But what spell? And to what end?

My gaze drifted to the portal beyond. A string-like lattice of dark energy was wrapped tightly about it, evidence enough that the first elements of the stygian elites' casting were already in place.

I frowned. I'd not noticed anything wrong with the portal when I'd initially arrived, but then again, I hadn't taken the time to study it in detail.

"Safyre, do you know what the nagas are doing to the portal?"

"No," she replied, *"but the first thing the stygians did when we clashed was to push us away from the gate. Those two have been there for close to an hour."*

My frown deepened. Even with analyze, I couldn't tell the purpose of the elites' weave, but in just the few seconds that I'd been watching, two more strands had joined the magical construct surrounding the portal.

The nagas were reinforcing their work.

I had to stop them, of course. But how to go about it quickly? Taking a few steps back, I studied the pair anew.

As expected, both elites were shielded. But that was only part of the challenge I faced. Even at ease, and with the bottom halves of their bodies loosely coiled and their broad triangular heads raised high, the two nagas still loomed over me. At a guess, they measured all of thirty yards from head to tail.

And unlike their smaller brethren, the elites were depressingly *solid.* Their bodies had real bulk and their scales were hardened. I suspected hacking through with my stygian blades was not going to be easy.

"Ghost, you killed one of the nagas before, didn't you?"

It took the pyre wolf a moment to shift focus from the battle she was embroiled in to answer. *"I did, Prime, but it wasn't easy. Adriel kept the creature paralyzed while I chewed through its neck."* A pregnant pause. *"It took a while."*

I grimaced. I'd feared as much. *"Thanks,"* I murmured. *"One last thing before I let you go."*

"Yes, Prime?"

"You see the spell stored in mage's surprise?"

"What about it?"

"Use it if it helps take down your target faster," I ordered. *"Don't try to do things the hard way."*

Before the pyre wolf could answer, I sensed her focus jerk away. Simultaneously, her emotions spiked in intensity. I knew what that meant. The pace of Ghost's skirmish had picked up, and she had no more attention to spare. But that was alright. I knew she'd heard me.

I refocused on the nagas. It was time to begin my own battle too.

✳   ✳   ✳

I had multiple options for dealing with my targets.

Close-up bladework.

A mental assault.

And even magic.

My swords would make quick work of the nagas' shields, but going on what Ghost had said, I knew they would have a much harder time penetrating the creatures' scaled-hides.

A mental assault from afar was the safest option but also the slowest. Before I could paralyze or charm the nagas, I would have to shatter their mental defenses first and that would take time.

Lastly, while the idea of flinging voidballs at the nagas was tempting, my mana reserves were already down to a third, and I wasn't fond of the idea of walking around without my void armor.

There was another option, of course: blood puppet. But it was not one I gave serious consideration to. Enslave's casting time was too long to use on an unrestrained subject, especially in the thick of battle.

In the end, I settled on an option that was a mix of my first two choices: bladework to destroy the nagas' shields and astral shurikens to bypass their physical armor and kill them from afar thereafter.

With my tactics decided, I advanced on the closest elite.

You have cast whirlwind and piercing strike.
You have backstabbed your target for 10x more damage.
You have backstabbed your target for 5x more damage.

By any measure, my opening salvo was devastating—even if blades didn't actually manage to touch the stygian.

A level 241 naga's shield has blocked your attacks.
Two hostile entities have failed to detect you!

Ignoring the Game messages, I kept battering at the naga's shield. I attacked with my two feet planted firmly on land. It mattered little *where* I struck, the damage to my foe's shield was the same.

You have backstabbed your target for 5x more damage.
You have backstabbed your target for 5x more damage.

...

...

With every slash and thrust, the health of the naga's shield plummeted, and finally the creature took note. Breaking off from its sibilant casting, the naga stabbed downwards with its triangular head.

The elite couldn't see me, but I wasn't going to hang around on the off chance it would miss. Mid-strike, I drew psi and shadow blinked.

You have teleported into a level 240 stygian naga's shadow. You are hidden.

Stepping out of the aether behind the *other* naga, I resumed my attacks.

You have backstabbed your target for 5x more damage.
You have backstabbed your target for 5x more damage.

...

...

My second foe reacted quicker than the first, and after suffering no more than a handful of hits, it sent its head skimming low along the ground in search of me.

In response, I threw myself flat.

You have evaded a level 240 stygian naga's attack.

The moment the danger passed, I popped back up and unleashed another flurry of blows. One way or the other, I was determined to destroy the nagas' shields before I retreated.

The naga's searching head returned, its forked tongue tasting the air. Walking a slow path in the opposite direction, I kept striking at the now-perceptibly dimmer bubble encasing it.

A level 241 stygian naga has cast cloying nether.

Not breaking off my assault, I glanced over my shoulder at the first naga. After I had blinked away, the creature hadn't resumed its original casting. Instead, the elite had begun a new spell—one that had the surrounding mists swirling in agitation.

My brows furrowed. *What's it trying to do?*

It didn't take me long to find out.

In the next instant, every speck of free-floating nether in a fifty-yard radius burst into motion.

Towards me.

I flinched, anticipating the worst. But the tiny particles didn't harm me as I feared. No, they merely clung on—*all* of them—and in an eyeblink, the many millions of nether specks transitioned from not-quite innocuous free-floating bits to solid particles that weighed down on my limbs.

You have failed a magical resistance check!
You are <u>nether-cloyed</u> (-50% speed and revealed). Duration: 1 minute.
Two hostile entities have detected you! You are no longer hidden.

Goddamn, I cursed. *Of all the luck!*

With the Cloak of the Reach equipped, my overall nether resistance was seventy percent. That meant the naga's spell had only a one in three chance of succeeding.

Yet, it still had.

And no matter my annoyance at that fact, I had to deal with the consequences. *I have to cut this short,* I decided. *Time to retreat.* Moving slower than I was used to, I began backing away from my foe while drawing psi in readiness.

The elite wasn't keen on letting me go, though.

With its maw opened wide in anticipation, the naga brought its head racing around to chomp down on my unmissable yellow-form.

But even at half-speed, I was no slouch. Sidestepping the attack, I didn't let the opportunity the creature had given me for another 'free' attack to go abegging. Lashing out with both swords, I struck its passing body multiple times in quick succession—once, twice, thrice.

A level 240 naga's shield has blocked your attacks.

Sadly, the triple blows did not shatter what remained of the elite's shield as I'd hoped, but knowing I couldn't hang around any longer, I released the weaves I held ready.

You have cast windborne.

I would've preferred to teleport out, but one of the unhappy effects of the first pack's earlier pursuit was that there were no longer any handy targets within shadow blink range—except for the two nagas themselves, of course. Still, the windslide would serve well enough.

Directing the ramp of air away from the two nagas, I hopped on.

But no sooner had I gotten onto the windslide than a looming shadow drew my attention.

Crouched low on the air ramp, I glanced up. While I'd fought its companion, naga number one, uncoiling fully, had reared up to its full height. Now, it fell sharply, attempting to use its body as a weapon.

It's too late, I thought, judging the trajectory of its descent. My position had already shifted drastically, and I was no longer where the naga was aimed at. Nevertheless, I kept my eyes glued upward while the windslide carried me to safety and away from the falling shape.

But I'd forgotten one crucial fact.

The naga was not just a free-falling body.

Using its still ground-bound rear to course-correct, the stygian elite adjusted its descent at the last minute.

And fell squarely atop me.

A level 241 naga has critically injured you!

Chapter 521: Flattened

The naga fell on me like a ton of bricks, its weight crushing.

A level 241 naga has critically injured you!
Your health is now at 42%.

Trapped by the naga above and the solid cushion of air beneath, my bones broke. My body compressed. My eyes bulged. The air from my lungs was squeezed out. And the pressure... the pressure ratcheted upward with every passing fraction of a second the naga's body settled more deeply atop me.

In a heartbeat, my head would explode.

Quick mend triggered! Your health has been restored to 55%.
A level 241 naga has critically injured you!
Warning! Your health is dangerously low at 17%.

Quick mend bought me another split second. Long enough to realize there was nowhere to go, nowhere to dodge, and nowhere to hide. So, I did the only thing that came to me in the moment.

I dissolved the windslide.

Windborne has been dispelled.

My body fell. And the naga's body fell with me.

The gap I'd left between the bottom of the ramp and the ground was not large, three yards maybe. But those three yards were a lifeline, and transformed what would otherwise have been an insta-kill into a viable window of escape.

Drawing psi, I shadow blinked.

✻ ✻ ✻

You have teleported into a level 240 stygian naga's shadow.

I emerged out of the aether, flat on my back, ribs broken, mind befuddled, and in indescribable pain. But importantly, I was alive.

I was in no fit state to fight. And worse yet, I was visible. The nagas would be back—and soon. Dropping my swords uncaringly, I fumbled at my belt, searching by feel alone for the items I wanted.

Spying a slip of motion on the periphery of my vision, I ignored it. More motion appeared on the other side. I ignored it, too.

The nagas were back already.

Knowing I was out of time, I yanked free the first bottle that came to hand and flung it as far away as possible.

You have ignited a firebomb!

Wrong one, I thought woozily as a bonfire mushroomed up less than ten yards away. The sudden surge of flames did have the happy effect of surprising the nagas, though, and they both instinctively flinched back.

I'd earned myself a temporary respite. Using it, I randomly drew four more bottles and threw them away, too.

You have ignited a firebomb.
You have ignited an ice bomb, creating a frozen surface.
You have ignited an ice bomb, creating a frozen surface.
You have ignited a smoke bomb, creating a smoke cloud.

Better, I wheezed at the appearance of the thick plumes of smoke, and as soon as the first tendril touched me, I cloaked myself.

Two hostile entities have failed to detect you! You are hidden.

Even battered and half-senseless as I was, I didn't fail to mark the angry hisses of the nagas as I vanished from their sight once more. But I knew the smoke cloud wouldn't fool them for long. It was not nearly large enough for that.

I needed another plan.

"Prime, use spellhold!"

"But—"

"Do it!" she commanded. *"We're on our way. Look out for me, I'm almost in range."*

To my surprise, I realized she was right. Ghost and Anriq's mindglows were only one hundred and twenty yards away and closing rapidly. *When did that happen?* I wondered.

Had they killed their naga already?

But whether they had or not mattered less than the fact that the pair were almost in position to be of help. Doing as the pyre wolf bade, I reached into the ring on my right hand and drew forth the spell stored within.

Mage's surprise activated. Spellhold casting released.
You have trigger-cast furious storm.

The response was instantaneous. The sky darkened, and angry bolts of white shot down.

A lightning bolt has hit a level 241 stygian naga. Your target's shield has blocked the attack.
A lightning bolt has hit a level 240 stygian naga. Your target's shield has been destroyed!
A lightning bolt has hit you. Air damage repelled!

The triple strikes were only the beginning, and already the next wave was incoming, but I didn't hang around to watch. Weaving psi, I fell into the aether again.

✻　✻　✻

You have teleported 99 yards. You are no longer hidden.

Shadow blink dumped me unceremoniously back into the 'real' at my familiar's feet. I didn't stay there for long, though. Swooping down, Anriq scooped me up.

"*Got him,*" the werewolf reported over the farspeaker bracelet. Slinging me over his shoulder—he was in half-form—Anriq reversed course, heading for Adriel's shield, I suspected.

"*No,*" I whispered.

"*What?*" he demanded.

"*Don't head back,*" I replied, weaving more psi. "*I only need a minute to recover. Just keep me out of trouble that long.*"

"*You want to return to the fight?*" he growled. "*That's—*"

"*—necessary,*" I interjected.

"*Michael's right,*" Safyre chipped in before Anriq could say anything. "*Do as he says.*" Her attention swapped to me. "*Can you heal yourself?*"

"*Working on it as we speak,*" I replied from between gritted teeth. Bouncing along on the werewolf's shoulder was not helping my injuries but I didn't ask Anriq to stop. A moving target was harder to hit than a stationary one.

"*Have it your way,*" the werewolf said. Changing course abruptly, he cut a wide arc around the elites, presumably to stay out of their immediate range.

"*What's going on with the nagas?*" I asked, fielding the question to Ghost.

"*Both their shields are down now,*" she reported in satisfaction. "*They're trying to dodge the bolts.*" She barked a laugh. "*But they're not having much success.*"

I managed a weak smile. At least my efforts had not been in vain. "*What about the other two nagas?*" I asked over the farspeaker link. "*The ones near the purifying barrier.*"

"*They're both still alive,*" Safyre reported. "*But Adriel and I are keeping them occupied. The serpents and hydras are done for, though.*"

"*Excellent,*" I murmured. The final weave of the spell I was spinning fell into place, and I released it posthaste.

You have restored yourself with quick mend. Your health is at 47%. You are no longer bleeding or dazed.

I exhaled in relief as the greater part of the agony riddling my limbs fled. I was far from whole, but no longer was I crippled. "*You can put me down now,*" I told Anriq.

Skidding to a halt, he set me down gently.

I clasped his hand. "*Thanks for the rescue. I don't know if I would've managed to escape on my own. You two saved me.*" I inhaled deeply, drawing more psi. "*But your part here is done. Return to your fight.*"

The werewolf eyed my empty hands in concern. "*How are you going to manage without swords?*"

I smiled bleakly. "*Don't need them now.*" Spinning around, I turned to face my foes.

"*Alright people, I'm back in the fight. Let's finish this.*"

$$* \quad * \quad *$$

Furious storm had run its course.

And while the two elites hadn't exactly been left reeling, they had certainly been hurt.

A level 240 stygian naga is lightly injured.
A level 241 stygian naga is barely injured.

In the storm's aftermath, the nagas had coiled tightly together, forming a single mound of hardened glistening scales. It was a daunting defensive posture and one that presented a foe with no easy angle of attack—at least physically.

Magically, I suspected, the pair were even now replenishing their spent defenses, and no doubt their shields would be back up soon.

But I wasn't going to allow that.

Gathering psi, I pulled my arms back. Interestingly enough, despite losing their shields, both nagas' consciousnesses remained opaque to me. Evidence enough that their minds were protected.

Attempting to shatter the stygians' mental defenses was one option. But there was no reason to bother with that. Notwithstanding its near fatal outcome, my original plan was still workable.

You have cast astral shurikens.

Two three-pointed stars appeared in my empty hands, each a deep shade of translucent purple and thrumming with energy. Whipping my arms forward, I sent them racing towards their targets.

The flattened discs whizzed through the mists, arcing to the nagas a hundred yards away. Neither creature saw the psi projectiles coming and a heartbeat later, they struck.

Your astral shuriken has hit a level 241 stygian naga.
Your astral shuriken has hit a level 240 stygian naga.

My aim proved true—not that it required any great effort on my part to hit the motionless creatures—and both shurikens slipped soundlessly *through* the nagas' outer shells to attack the nerves beneath.

Your astral shurikens have inflicted psi damage!
Nerves at the point of contact have been weakened. Inflict further psi damage to deaden them entirely.

The nagas shuddered. They'd felt the touch of the ethereal blades, but their only response was to coil more tightly together.

It availed them little.

Because, of course, the shurikens were not done yet. Reemerging from the nagas' bodies, the psi projectiles bounced to the adjacent target.

Your astral shurikens have inflicted psi damage!
Your astral shurikens have inflicted psi damage!
…

Five consecutive times, the blades bounced. Five consecutive times during which they eked away a little of the elites' health. It mattered not that the damage was minuscule.

My next pair of shurikens were already airborne.

Taking off running, I circled around the nagas. I was not about to close in on the pair and risk another physical confrontation. Such was no longer necessary. But sooner or later, I expected the two elites to switch from defense to offense, and when that happened, I had to be ready.

✳ ✳ ✳

It was only after bearing the brunt of three full volleys that the nagas chose to react. Uncoiling with vicious speed, they lobbed two voidballs my way.

But if the pair had thought to catch me off guard, they'd miscalculated.

The voidballs were slow—in comparison to my shurikens, anyway—and I observed their approach with a distinct lack of concern as I kept up my own assault.

Your astral shurikens have inflicted psi damage!
Your astral shurikens have inflicted psi damage!

...

Three seconds later, the voidballs closed to within striking range. Breaking off my assault, I set down a windslide and darted away.

You have cast windborne.
You have evaded a voidball.
You have evaded a voidball.

Ignoring the nagas' angry hisses at their attacks' failure, I dropped down from the air ramp and resumed my steady jog.

A level 238 stygian naga has died.

I smiled. I didn't need to look behind me to know that Adriel and Safyre had just killed one of the elites. *Only three to—*

You are no longer nether-cloyed.

My grin broadened. Now, the outcome of my own fight was assured. Weaving stamina, I prepared to vanish once more.

A level 236 stygian naga has died.
A level 240 stygian naga has died.
A level 241 stygian naga has died.
You and Ghost have reached level 243!
For achieving rank 24, you have been awarded 1 additional attribute point and 1 Class point.

Your sneaking has reached rank 23 and your two weapon fighting rank 19.
Ghost's magma maw has reached rank 10, her stygian claws rank 12, her ash armor rank 12, her telepathy rank 10, her death magic rank 8, and her nether manipulation rank 5.

The battle drew to a close without fanfare. The two nagas died without managing to land any further blows, and with Safyre and Adriel's help, Anriq and Ghost made quick work of their own foe.

While I waited for the others to finish mopping up, I scanned the skies. They were clear. The stygian overlord had not made an appearance as yet. *That gives us some time, at least,* I thought in relief.

Turning my attention inward, I reviewed the post-battle messages. Ghost and I had advanced four levels, which was about what I'd expected given the pyre wolf's earlier gains for killing a naga. What I found more startling, though, was the progress of Ghost's skill. Most I knew had occurred during her training with Sulan. Still, the degree to which she had improved was impressive.

"*Did you think I was just lazing around while you were gone?*" the pyre wolf joked as she drew up alongside me.

"*Of course not,*" I murmured. "*But maybe I'm a bit jealous. You seemed to have got a lot more done in the two days than I have.*" In fact, other than securing Kesh's help, I had to wonder what I'd really achieved since leaving the tundra. Worse yet, I'd made little to no headway rescuing Saya.

Ghost's ears pricked up as she picked up on my surface thoughts. "*Something's happened, hasn't it? Something bad.*"

"*Yes,*" I admitted. "*But the tale must wait for the others. It's not one I want to repeat.*"

Ghost didn't push the issue, for which I was grateful. "*Whatever the case, I'm glad you're back, Prime.*"

"*As am I,*" I replied, running my hand through her coat. "*I missed you.*" My gaze drifted to the others. "*And everyone else too.*" Things were much simpler here. There was no question of who the enemy was, our goals were clear, and even the path to achieving them was relatively straightforward.

Back in the heart of the Game, everything had been... murkier.

I sighed. I knew there was no escaping the greater Game, though. One way or the other, I'd have to deal with Loken and his envoy, and rescue Saya. And it was not like we didn't have problems aplenty in this sector either.

My gaze fell upon Shael and Anriq once more. Under Safyre's direction, the pair were hauling the nagas' corpses to the lich who was…

I frowned. "What is Adriel doing?" I wondered aloud.

"Skinning them," Ghost supplied helpfully.

I glanced at my familiar. "And why would she be doing that?"

"For use in the golems' bodies, of course," she replied brightly.

It took me a moment to process that, and when I did my eyes widened. "Adriel has figured it out," I breathed. "She knows how to rehome the possessed."

The pyre wolf bobbed her head. *"Yes."*

The news cheered me. It was at least one bright spot in what had otherwise been a mostly disappointing few days. *"Saf,"* I said through the farspeaker link, *"I have an alchemy stone. It might make collecting the ingredients Adriel wants easier."*

"Won't work," the aetherist replied. *"Adriel needs the nagas' scales more than she needs their reagents, and the alchemy stone won't collect skin. In fact, using the stone on the nagas will likely destroy the scales."*

I deflated. *"Oh."*

Across the distance, I saw Safyre turn in my direction, a smile playing on her lips. *"Although… you could make yourself useful and loot the other stygians."*

I ducked my head sheepishly as I rose to my feet. *"Right. Ghost and I are on it."*

❋ ❋ ❋

"I don't see why you needed me for this," Ghost grumbled as she kept pace beside me.

"Why, did you have somewhere else to be?" I asked innocently as I ducked down and retrieved the alchemy stone from the last corpse.

You have retrieved an alchemy stone. New ingredients acquired: 100 x lumps of necrotic plasma and 70 x vial of nether residue.

"I could be training my nether manipulation!"

"Aren't you doing that already?"

"That's not the point," Ghost protested.

I smiled. *"No, you're right. It isn't. Say rather, I wanted your company."*

It was the answer Ghost had been looking for all along, and I sensed her brighten immediately. *"You're shameless,"* I said, chuckling.

"There's nothing wrong with expressing your enjoyment of another's company," the pyre wolf retorted.

It felt like a more pointed remark than the situation warranted and suspecting what she was alluding to, I changed the topic. *"How did Anriq do?"*

Ghost rolled her eyes at my evasiveness before replying. *"He fought well. He'd make an excellent wolf."*

I nodded, pleased by her assessment. I already knew from analyze that both Shael and Anriq had advanced significantly during the battle, with the bard netting eight levels and the werewolf six. Safyre, too, had progressed, if not as much as the two lower level players.

"We're all done here," Anriq said suddenly, drawing my attention. Glancing to my left, I saw my four companions standing next to a tall pile of stygian scales.

Stepping through the aether, I appeared beside Safyre. "What's all this for?" I asked without preamble.

Adriel threw me a wry look. "Too lazy to walk?"

"More like I'm in a rush," I replied, glancing upward again. "We might have company soon."

The lich nodded. "Safyre said so."

"You checked the gate?" the aetherist asked, sensing my unease.

I shook my head. "I was waiting for you and Adriel to finish up before risking an approach. Whatever spell the two nagas cast is still active. Unfortunately, the weaves didn't dissipate with their deaths."

"Damn," Anriq said softly.

Safyre frowned. "That does not bode well. Not on top of everything else."

"This was not a random encounter then?" I asked, wanting to confirm my suspicions.

Adriel snorted. "No. This was an ambush. Carefully conceived. And well executed."

I sighed, not happy about being proved right. "What happened? I would have thought you four would know better than to try and take on four elites. Why didn't you retreat?"

"It was only one to begin with," Anriq muttered sourly.

My gaze flickered in the werewolf's direction. "Meaning?"

"Meaning I was careless," Anriq replied, meeting my gaze unflinchingly. "I was escorting Ghost while she trained her nether manipulation skill when we spotted the naga. It was alone, so instead of retreating immediately back to the tundra like I should've, I decided to investigate further. That's when the rest of the stygians showed themselves." He hung his head. "I'm sorry, Michael, I let them lure me and Ghost away from the portal."

"It's not all his fault," Ghost said, speaking up on Anriq's behalf. *"I also failed to smell the stygians hiding in the mists."*

"The boy is not to blame," Adriel said, unconsciously echoing Ghost's sentiment. "I didn't sense the stygians until too late either."

"Me neither," Safyre agreed.

Adriel ran a lazy hand through the yellow smog. "It's this damn mist. It makes hiding all too easy for the stygians. The nagas used that to their advantage with their cloaking spell."

I winced. It was one more thing to worry about. "But how did you two wind up here?" I asked, looking expectantly at the two spellcasters. By Anriq's reckoning, only he and Ghost had been in the sector when the stygians had sprung their ambush.

"We were checking out the caves," Safyre replied, "when Adriel heard Ghost's telepathic cry."

The lich nodded. "That was a bit of good fortune we can all be thankful for. Our arrival was the only thing that fouled the nagas' ambush."

Still focused on Safyre's words, I barely heard her. "Checking out the—" Breaking off, I whipped around to face Anriq. "You found something?"

The werewolf smiled tentatively, his glum look disappearing. "I did. Two somethings, actually."

"*Two?*" I asked in disbelief.

"Yes, two separate cave systems," he confirmed. "The first is small and beneath the riverbed itself. The second is also near the river but extends deeper into the earth. We've only just begun exploring its depths."

"And you're sure their entrances can be sealed?" I asked breathlessly.

"Already done," Safyre murmured.

I glanced at her, not daring to voice my next question lest she dash my hopes.

Her lips quirked upward. No doubt, she sensed my excitement.

"We dispelled the free-standing nether from inside and caved in all the entrances," Safyre confirmed. "They're covered in so many layers of rock now, it will take weeks to dig through."

Saying nothing, I waited.

"And you were, right, Michael," she finished, "the nether did not return."

I rocked back on my heels, elated. I had suspected, but hadn't been certain, that solid rock would be proof against the ingress of the invasive mists. It was the river that had given me the idea. The river into which I'd fallen into during my first foray in the sector, and the river that had been blessedly *free* of nether.

It was why I'd left the Sylvanain eye with Anriq, and it was why I had tasked him with finding a deep and, ideally, closed cave system.

Because, of course, we needed a base in sector 18,240.

Not just to hide the shield generator but also to serve as our shelter until we expelled the void from the sector. Using the tundra itself was impractical. Especially once more players joined the Forerunners.

"What about air?" I asked. "Are the caves—"

"They're breathable," Adriel confirmed. "Where the air is coming from, we can't say for certain, but the nether's taint is not seeping in with it."

"Excellent," I pronounced. "Well done, Anriq. Well done, everyone."

That drew smiles all around, temporarily alleviating my companions' somber demeanors, but predictably, it did not last.

"You know what the ambush means, right?" Safyre asked, throwing me an intent look.

I nodded slowly. Unfortunately, I did.

"Well, I don't," Shael said, speaking up for the first time.

The others looked at him.

The bard's face creased into an unhappy frown. "I have no idea what any of this means or even where the hell we are. Or for that matter, what any of this has to do with Saya!"

Safyre's brows rose. "Saya?" she asked, looking at me questioningly.

I grimaced. Obviously, Shael had not shared his tale with the others yet. "I'll tell you in a bit," I told her before turning back to the bard. "And you'll get an explanation too, I promise. Just be patient a little longer. For now, it's imperative we check on the portal."

"Agreed," Adriel said. Not waiting to see if anyone followed, she marched in the direction of the gate.

I glanced from the pile of discarded stygian scales to the retreating lich. "What about all this?" I called after her.

"What about it?" Adriel asked, glancing back. "It'll keep. I highly doubt the stygians are going to try carrying it off."

Muttering under my breath, I hurried to catch up to her.

Chapter 523: Allegiances

The target is a nether portal leading to sector 107 of the Endless Dungeon. Warning: an unidentified stygian infestation has taken root in the ley line connected to this gateway. Infection type: unknown. The portal may still be used, however the consequences of doing so cannot be predicted.

Remaining time until the infestation is purged: 4 hours.

I stared despondently at the Game alert hovering in my mind for a moment before turning my attention to the nether portal itself. The blackness besmirching it had not abated.

"'...unidentified stygian infestation,'" I quoted. "That sounds less than promising. Anyone know what it means?"

There was no response.

"Safyre?" I prompted, focusing on the aetherist beside me.

She shook her head. "I have no idea."

I glanced at Adriel, but even after repeating the Adjudicator's words verbatim to her, she, too, looked just as perplexed.

"I've never heard of something like this before either," the lich murmured.

I grimaced. "That's just great."

"Do we flee?" Shael asked, eyeing the opaque surroundings suspiciously, his discomfort obvious.

"We will if we need to, but we're not there yet." I turned to our spellcasters again. "What if you—"

"Dispelling doesn't work," Adriel said.

"Neither does restoration, rejuvenation, nor any of the other spells I've tried," Safyre added.

"How about we cut the black strings?" Anriq suggested, flexing his hands. "That might do the trick."

"Don't," Adriel and Safyre snapped simultaneously.

The werewolf held up his hands. "I wasn't going to," he protested.

My gaze darted from the chastened werewolf to the two women. "What are you afraid of?"

Safyre's brows crinkled. "As resistant as the... infestation is to spellcraft, I doubt hacking at it with a sword is going to have any effect."

"And," Adriel added, her lips pursed, "simply touching the strands may transfer the infection."

I rubbed my chin. "Hmm, in that case, maybe Anriq *should* try."

Both spellcasters glares swapped to me.

"He's a werewolf," I reminded them. "I doubt any infection, no matter how severe, will be able to take hold in his body for long."

Adriel frowned. "Perhaps," she muttered. "But is that a chance you want to take? Don't forget there is no safe zone for him to resurrect in."

I thought about that for a moment, then shook my head. "No. You're right. It's an unnecessary risk."

"But—" Anriq began.

"No," I repeated more firmly, and he subsided. "That leaves us with only two other options," I went on. "Retreat or wait it out."

No one said anything for a moment.

"Four hours is not all that long," Safyre said at last.

She was right, it wasn't. But four hours was likely long enough for the overlord to get here, and by this point, I was all but certain that that had been the nagas' intent all along—to trap us in the sector until reinforcements arrived. Staying would be playing into their hands. There was something else that concerned me too. "What about the wolves?"

Safyre took my meaning at once. "The elders aren't expecting us back before nightfall," she assured me. "They have no cause to worry yet, and Duggar knows better than to allow the Pack to enter the gate."

I sighed. That was one less worry at least. "Alright then," I said, coming to a decision. "We wait. But not here."

"That would be an especially bad idea," Safyre agreed. "Let's relocate to the cave." She glanced sideways at Shael. "We have a lot to discuss in any event, and there, at least, we'll be safe."

I hoped that was true. "Let's go."

"Not so fast," Adriel interjected. "We've got to retrieve the naga remains first. If we're going to use the cave system as a base, we might as well start transferring the scales now."

Careful not to sigh, I turned about and headed back to the discarded pile, beckoning Shael and Anriq. Somehow, I got the feeling that we would be the ones doing the lion's share of the work.

✳ ✳ ✳

Safyre has cast supreme portal, creating a protected ley line to a secondary location in sector 18,240.

Transfer through portal commencing...

...

...

Passage completed!

The nether toxicity at your current location has decreased to 0. No environmental ill-effects experienced.

I stepped out of a world filled with yellow smog and into the cool, welcoming darkness of an underground cave. "Ah," I exhaled, set immediately at ease.

The others trickled in after me, both Adriel and Safyre bearing magelights. "Feel at home?" Safyre teased, spotting my expression.

"Actually, I do." Releasing my end of the impromptu sled we had assembled, I turned about in a full circle and examined our surroundings. We were in a large cavern. It was about a hundred yards from end to end and stretched nearly as high. And even with my mindsight extended to its fullest, I could sense no mindglows but our own.

"Is all of it this empty?" I asked as Safyre's portal closed behind us.

There was nothing living in the cave, not even moss or lichen. And except for my five companions and the two sleds overflowing with naga scales, everything else was cold, barren stone.

Anriq nodded. "Near as we can tell. We're about a thousand feet below ground." He pointed to a darkened passage to the right. "That used to go to the surface." He spun around. "And those openings all lead to tunnels that delve deeper into the earth, but like I said earlier, we've explored only a tiny fraction so far."

"Why did we come here?" Shael asked rhetorically. Rubbing his arms, he tried in vain to stop shivering. The cave was appreciably colder than the surface. "This place doesn't look like any sort of improvement over what's above."

Anriq scowled. "Really?" he asked sarcastically. "You'd rather hang out in the nether?"

"The Roost would've been better," the bard mumbled under his breath, perhaps unaware that both Anriq and my own hearing was sharp enough to catch his offhand comment.

"He complains a lot, doesn't he?" Ghost remarked.

"Not usually," I replied, defending the half-elf. *"He's had to put up with a lot from me, and I guess he's feeling out of sorts."* Out aloud, I said, "The tavern might be more comfortable, but not everyone can enter it."

Shael's gaze darted to Adriel as he took my meaning. "Oh." He hugged himself tighter. "So, what do we do now?"

"Sit for starters," I said, dropping into a cross-legged stance. It was finally time for a frank discussion, and this was as safe a place as any for it. I patted the bare rock to my left. "You sit too."

The half-elf sat gingerly, eyeing the pyre wolf on my other side with a fair bit of trepidation. "That's Ghost, I take it," he said, as the others took their places.

"It is." I smiled. "And be careful of what you say next, because not only can she understand everything you say, but she can also speak, too."

The bard's eyes widened. "I... see."

Gesturing at the others, I began making introductions. "Safyre, you know already."

The aetherist nodded politely in response, but Shael refused to meet her gaze.

I frowned. "What's wrong?"

"She's a forsworn," he muttered stiffly.

"She is," I said evenly. "And?"

The bard stared at me, taken aback by my lack of surprise. "Don't you know what that means?" he hissed. "We can be killed just for knowing her!"

I laughed. I couldn't help it.

"What's so funny?" Shael demanded.

My mirth died. "I'm sorry. I forgot you don't remember our previous conversation."

His eyes narrowed. "You told me she was a forsworn while I was enslaved?"

That got the others' attention.

"You used blood puppet on him?" Safyre cried. "Why would you do that!"

I waited a beat before responding, realizing that matters could quickly devolve if I said the wrong thing. "I used it to administer a truth test."

Safyre blinked. "A truth test?" she repeated, seemingly at loss for words.

Adriel chuckled as she caught on. "Oh my. That was clever."

"I don't get it," Anriq said, his brows drawing down.

"An enslaved subject is spell-bound to obedience," Adriel explained, still smiling. "All Michael had to do was command Shael here to tell the truth and he would have had no choice but to."

Anriq's frown deepened. "Not even the Wolf Torc is powerful enough to enforce that level of obedience." His gaze met mine. "That's a scary spell."

"It certainly is," I said. "Which is why I obtained Shael's consent before employing it." I glanced at the bard. "Right, Shael?"

"I was a willing subject," he agreed, further allaying any fears the others might have.

Not wanting to dwell further on the subject of blood puppet—Anriq still looked perturbed—I moved the conversation on quickly. "And as to your question," I said, addressing the bard again, "yes, I did tell you Safyre is a forsworn. I also told you what I am, which in the eyes of the new Powers is infinitely worse than what Safyre is."

The bard's eyes rounded at that.

"Don't worry, we'll get to that in a moment," I said. "The point being, you're going to learn a whole lot of secrets today. Many of which will not only get your throat slit but ours, too, and that of everyone you know and care about as well. If I were you, I'd withhold judgment until you've the full picture." I held his gaze. "Sound reasonable?"

Shael nodded slowly. "It does."

"Excellent," I said, rubbing my hands together. "Then let's begin. For starters, let me tell you about a group known as the ancients..."

✴　✴　✴

"That's a lot to take in," Shael said when the others and I finally finished our tales.

"It is," I agreed. "Now the time has come to make your choice."

"My choice?"

"Whether to join the Forerunners or not. Whether to tie your fate with ours. And whether to become Pact-bound and allow me to direct your movements."

Shael shook his head. "You're a Power..." he marveled. "I still find that bit hard to believe. You can truly form Pacts?"

"I can," I replied simply.

Shael's gaze drifted to the rest of the party. "Everyone here is part of the Forerunners?"

"Technically, yes."

"Technically?"

"Adriel hasn't formally joined yet," I replied.

"A matter we should rectify today," she interjected.

I raised an eyebrow in surprise. The lich hadn't been overly keen on the Forerunners and my idea of 'one House.' Her attitude had been more one of 'wait and see,' and I'd been willing to let her be until she was ready to join.

Which appeared to be now.

"You're sure?" I asked.

She nodded. "The time for half-measures is over." She paused, seeming to mull over her next words. "And I tried returning to Death's home sector but failed. I fear it will be a while yet before I can recover my body and become a Death scion anew."

"What happened?" I asked quietly.

She shrugged. "The portal refused to open."

"The sector is shielded," I surmised.

"Yes," Adriel said bleakly. "Someone has claimed Death's bastion."

I pursed my lips, wondering how she'd react to the news I bore. "I know who."

The lich leaned forward intently. She didn't ask, but I could see the demand in her eyes.

"The Awakened Dead," I said softly.

"Ah," Adriel exhaled, but despite the calmness of her response, there was a sudden fierceness to her gaze that boded nothing good for Erebus, Ishita, and their ilk. "That makes sense, funnily enough."

"Does it change your decision?" I asked.

It took the lich a moment to refocus on me. "About joining the Forerunners, you mean?"

I nodded.

"No, I'm still committed."

"Good. We'll talk more about the Awakened Dead and Death's sector soon, I promise. But for now..." I turned back to Shael. "How about you? Are you ready to make your choice?"

He bit his lip, hesitating. "I assume you gave me this choice before?"

"I did."

"And what decision did I arrive at?"

I smiled. "I'm sure you can figure out that one for yourself."

Shael sighed. "I suppose I can." He fell silent for a moment, then nodded decisively. "I'm in."

I grinned. "Perfect."

Chapter 524: Scaly Matters

I took Adriel's pledge first, but I didn't just induct her into the faction, I assigned her to office too.

You have accepted Adriel, a non-player, into the Forerunners faction and have furthermore appointed her to the role of <u>custodian</u>. Only a custodian may create items bearing a faction's name.
Note, the custodian designation is a hidden one that cannot be revealed by any Game abilities.

Custodians could fulfill various roles in a faction but primarily, they acted as its caretakers. Only a custodian could bestow a faction's mark on an item. Adriel, as a crafter in her own right, was perfectly suited to the role. Then, too, given the lich's near-unique nature and vast experience, she was also the least likely person in the faction to fall prey to torture or extortion.
All of which made her the safest choice for the Forerunner's custodian.
Once I was done with Adriel, I accepted Shael's oath, and despite his earlier standoffishness, the bard was welcomed with open arms into the faction.

You have accepted Shael, a player, into the Forerunners faction.
You have sealed a Pact with Shael. In exchange for a place on the inner council of your House and being privy to its secrets, the red minstrel has agreed to let you direct his movements from here on, limiting the sectors he may visit. This Pact may be terminated at any time but only at your discretion.
You have 6 / 20 active Pacts.

"I guess this makes me as much a rebel as the rest of you lot," Shael joked once we all finished congratulating him.
The half-elf's words drew smiles from the others, but my own face stayed somber. Now that the immediate threat of the stygians had been dealt with and Shael properly inducted, my worries had returned to plague me.
Seeing my expression, Shael's smile faded. "It's time to talk about Saya," he guessed.
I nodded solemnly.
"What's this about Saya?" Safyre asked, concern flitting across her face. "This is the second time you two have mentioned her. Is she alright?"
I took a deep breath, then stated bluntly, "No. No, she is not."
"She has been taken hostage," Shael added.
Safyre inhaled sharply.
"Who would dare do such a thing?" Anriq growled.
"Loken's envoy would," the bard replied softly.
The werewolf's eyes widened. "Loken...?"
I sighed. "Unfortunately, yes," I said, knowing exactly what fears the news had conjured in his mind—and everyone else's, for that matter.

Adriel recovered first. "Why would the trickster's envoy do that?" she asked, her face expressionless.

I met her gaze. The lich had never met Saya, but I'd spoken often enough of the gnome in the past that she knew Saya's capture was not something I could—or would—let lie. "I don't know. To lure me out, I suspect."

"You better tell us everything," she said, her tone studiedly neutral.

I glanced at Shael. "Go on, tell them. This is more your tale than mine."

The bard lowered his head in acknowledgment. "Where to begin?" he wondered, biting his lip.

"At the beginning, I suppose," he added, before anyone could think to answer. Taking a moment, he gathered his thoughts. "It was not long after Michael left the valley that matters started changing. First, the Tartans went to..."

Sitting back, I closed my eyes and let the bard's words wash over me. His tale was not one I relished hearing again.

✳ ✳ ✳

"Damn," Anriq growled when Shael was done. "So, we don't even know if the tavernkeeper is alive?" he asked, cutting to the heart of the matter.

I winced at his bluntness. "We don't," I admitted, "but I'm convinced the envoy hasn't killed her."

"You don't know that," Adriel said, almost gently. "You *can't* know that."

"You're right," I conceded again. "I can't know that for certain, but I *believe* she is alive.

Anriq blinked. "You believe? You're joking, right? That can't be all you have to go on!"

I pinched the bridge of my nose, and before responding, I had to remind myself that the werewolf hadn't met Saya either. "Saya is worth more alive than dead. The envoy will know that. She won't do anything foolish."

Anriq opened his mouth to retort, but Safyre waved him to silence. "Your concerns are valid, Anriq," she said. "But Michael's stance is equally valid. We don't know *if* Saya is alive, but we have to *assume* she is. Doing otherwise means abandoning her to her fate."

No one was able to find fault with that.

"Thank you, Saf," I murmured. "You've put it perfectly. The question facing us now is what do we do next?"

For a drawn-out moment, no one said anything.

"You plan on rescuing her," Adriel said eventually. It was not a question.

I inclined my head. "I do. I've already tried approaching Loken in the hopes of getting him to intervene, but—"

"What?" Shael demanded, looking as astonished as the rest of my companions. "When was this?"

I held up my hands. "Calm down, everyone. I did not contact Loken personally. I used an intermediary."

"Who?" Anriq asked with a heavy frown.

My gaze darted to Safyre. "Kesh."

"Ah," she exclaimed softly. "That was a good choice. What happened?"

"Loken refused to meet," I replied. "Why, I'm not sure. But it's Loken and who can—"

"Know what game the trickster plays at," Adriel finished for me.

"Exactly," I said, surveying their faces. "Given all that, I don't see how I—*we*—have any choice but to take direct action and rescue Saya ourselves."

"Assuming she is still alive," Anriq pointed out.

"Assuming that, yes."

Safyre and Adriel exchanged glances. "What about this sector?"

My lips turned down. "That is a complication," I conceded. "The good news is that I've managed to procure the shield generator."

My companions sat up straighter at the news. "You have?" Safyre exclaimed. "How?"

"Through Kesh."

Safyre's brows crinkled. "B-but wasn't she—? Didn't she—"

"I told her who I am," I replied, suspecting what was running through her mind. "Kesh is now aware of our plans to bring about the return of the Primes." I held her gaze. "And what's more, we have her *full* support."

Safyre covered her mouth in astonishment.

I smiled, pleased by her reaction. "Not only will Kesh get the Aether Cloak for us at a discount, but she has also agreed to you using your emporium robes again." I paused. "Unfortunately, the Triumvirate embedded a tracking device inside the garment which forced me to leave it in the Roost for safekeeping."

I waved my hand, dismissing the matter from further consideration. "But getting back to Kesh, she will also see to it that your fellow forsworn are rotated through the emporium vaults. She has made arrangements for you to meet them there."

"Oh my," Safyre said, her eyes shining. "You convinced Kesh to do all that? How!"

I chuckled. "It wasn't as hard as we imagined. I got the distinct impression that our cause is one Kesh sympathizes with. The difficulty—if you can call it that—was convincing her our rebellion has a chance of success."

Safyre's eyes narrowed thoughtfully.

"That reminds me." Retrieving a string of items from my bag of holding, I dropped the first batch into Adriel's hands and the second in Safyre's. "I got these too."

You have lost 20 unmarked soulbound faction tokens.
You have lost 28 farspeaker bracelets from the named set: Sintar's link.

"You know what to do with the tokens, Adriel," I went on. "Those are all I managed to get for now. But I'll get more soon, promise." I turned to Safyre. "Those bracelets complete the farspeaker set we've been using. They need to be modified to prevent an intruder from using them to eavesdrop on us, though."

"My, my," Adriel said, examining the tokens. "You *have* been busy."

I shrugged. "I got some things done." I exhaled. "Unfortunately, not everything went our way."

Anriq leaned forward. "What's the bad news?"

"We're broke again for the foreseeable future," I replied, and went on to explain the situation with Nicola and the den chief.

Safyre sighed. "That's unfortunate, but I'm sure we can make do."

I nodded. "We'll have to. In any case, given recent events, we'll have to alter our plans."

Adriel arched one eyebrow. "By recent events, I take it you mean the nagas' ambush?"

"Correct," I replied grimly. "We can't ignore the implications."

"That the void now knows we're here?" Anriq asked.

I nodded again. "We've lost the luxury of time. Stockpiling resources, making contact with House Pestilence, and visiting the Nexus werewolves will have to wait until after we've reclaimed this sector." I paused. "And *before* we can get to that, we have to rescue Saya."

Safyre and Adriel traded glances again.

But before I could question them about it, Shael interrupted. "You expect the six of us to defeat a void tree, four overlords, and an entire nest?" he asked aghast. "All by ourselves?"

I turned the bard's way. "I don't, actually. Kesh is reaching out to the stygian brotherhood. I'm hoping we can secure their aid."

"The brotherhood," Anriq murmured. "They could give us a decisive advantage."

I nodded. "And don't forget that in three more days, Nyra and the twins will be done with their dungeon dive." I glanced at Adriel. "Then there are also the possessed to consider."

"The Rings of Astral Walking will work as we hoped," she confirmed, correctly interpreting my look. "The possessed can be rehomed in construct bodies."

I nearly sagged in relief. "That's good. How long will it take?"

Adriel shrugged. "Now that I have sufficient material to work with? Eight, maybe, ten days."

"You will create their golems from the naga scales then?" I guessed.

Nodding, the lich pulled one the scales from the sled and examined it anew. "Interesting stuff, this."

"How so?" Safyre asked, looking intrigued.

"As far as I can tell, it's a composite formed from pure nether that's been compressed, solidified, and combined with void crystals, surprisingly enough."

I tilted my head to the side. "Void crystals. What are those?"

Adriel didn't answer directly. "You once told me you visited a stygian nest inside the Nethersphere."

I nodded. "That's right. I entered through a rift in Nexus."

"Do you recall seeing any obsidian crystals there? They can sometimes be mistaken for black rock."

"I remember those. They were all over the nest." The necrotic spikes the overlord had used had been made from the same substance as well. I glanced at the scale in her hand. "Those were void crystals?"

"That's what we called them in my day," Adriel said. "Most scholars considered them largely useless. The crystals are harder than steel but inflexible. They can't be worked because they shatter under pressure, and they have no special properties that anyone can divine." Holding the scale by its ends, the lich pressed down firmly. "This is different."

"It bent," Anriq noted observantly.

Adriel nodded. "It did. Pure void crystals won't do that." She studied the scale quizzically. "I don't know what strange evolutionary path the nagas took to end up with void crystals infused with nether for scales, but I'm glad that they did—because these scales are near-perfect."

I rubbed my chin. "I take it that means you've not encountered the nagas before?"

"I haven't," the lich confirmed and glanced questioningly at Safyre who also shook her head. "I haven't either."

"Hmm, so either the nagas are a 'new' development—something I highly doubt—or..." I ran aground. *Or what?* "Anyone care to speculate?"

"Or they're incredibly rare?" Shael suggested.

"Maybe," I allowed, not convinced.

"Rare or not, I would've heard of a creature with scales like this," Adriel objected.

"And don't forget what they did to the nether portal," Safyre added. "I've not heard even a whisper of a rumor of something like that being done by the stygians before." She shook her head. "Whatever spell the nagas used was too noteworthy *not* to set tongues wagging."

"Safyre is right," Shael said, conceding the point. "Players gossip, they can't help it. Word of the nagas would have gotten out before this."

"Which means no player has encountered them before," Anriq concluded.

"Or if they have, they didn't live to tell the tale," Shael added.

I nodded slowly. "All that makes sense. Unfortunately, it's still only speculation." Reaching into the sled myself, I slipped a handful of scales into my bag of holding.

You have acquired 5 x naga scales. You are unable to discern their properties.

Adriel looked at me quizzically. "What are you going to do with those?"

"I was thinking we should consult an expert," I replied.

"Like the stygian brotherhood perhaps?" Safyre guessed.

I nodded. "It will be interesting to hear what they have to say about the nagas and having a few samples on hand to show them can't hurt. Assuming Kesh's negotiations with their huntmistress are successful, I'll ask them about the nagas."

"Good idea," Safyre agreed.

Considering the topic closed, I turned back to Adriel. "Let's return to the matter at hand: the possessed. What do the scales mean for them?"

"It means their golem forms will be unique," the lich answered. She glanced at the pyre wolf beside me. "Almost as unique as Ghost's. In fact, I wish I had this stuff when I crafted her body. I could've given her a far more *solid* presence."

"*That's alright, Adriel,*" Ghost said. "*I'm quite content with how I am.*"

Adriel smiled. "*I know you are, little one, but we'll talk more later.*"

"Are there enough scales for all one hundred possessed?" I asked, ignoring the pair's aside.

"Oh definitely," Adriel replied. "But you will have to retrieve the rest, of course."

The scales we'd brought in the two sleds only accounted for a small fraction of what had been skinned from the nagas, and there was still a small mountain waiting above ground. It would take many more trips of back-breaking work to retrieve the remaining scales.

Shael sighed audibly as he came to the same realization.

"Of course," I murmured. "We'll get right on it."

CHAPTER 525: A DIFFERENCE OF OPINION

The task of hauling the scales fell not unexpectedly to Shael, Anriq, and myself. That was not to say, Adriel and Safyre did nothing. Working in tandem, the pair kept a portal open between the cave and the surface, and even Ghost was put to work, hauling a sled.

Working thus, we made steady progress, and by the end of the first hour, nearly all of the scales had been successfully relocated. Just past the two-hour mark, though, something changed.

Pausing in my work stacking one the sleds, I stared across the horizon.

"What is it?" Safyre asked, noticing my sudden stop.

"Company," I replied, studying the distant dot in the sky.

"The overlord?" she asked.

"I think so." Even with my enhanced sight, the far-off shape was too indistinct to identify. "What else could it be?" I asked rhetorically.

Safyre glanced at the pile of remaining scales. "Do we have time to haul the rest?"

Not answering immediately, I took my time judging the enemy's approach, but even after a full minute of watching there was barely a perceptible change in its size. "Yes," I said at last.

"Then let's get to it," she said. "The sooner we're done, the sooner we're gone."

✳ ✳ ✳

Twenty minutes later, the last of the scales disappeared through the portal. Stopping beside Adriel who was on portal duty, I turned around to study the skies one last time.

There was no longer any doubt about our enemy's identity. It was an overlord. Nor was the stygian Power alone. Perched all around its crater-like body were dozens of flying serpents.

"Do you think they can see us?" Adriel asked.

I shrugged. "No idea."

None of my companions could see the incoming stygians, of course. The mists were impenetrable to their sight, and while I doubted the void creatures labored under the same handicap, the distance between us was still appreciable.

"The overlord hasn't sped up, though, or altered its trajectory in any way," I added.

"Good enough, I suppose," the lich replied, waving me toward the portal. "Go on, then. Let's not tempt fate further."

Doing as she bade, I stepped through the luminous doorway. Adriel followed quickly after and a moment later, the portal winked out.

The others were already gathered in the center of the cave. Joining them, Adriel and I sat down to complete the circle. "Now that that is all out of the way," I began without preamble, "let's talk about how we go about rescuing Saya."

Adriel and Safyre exchanged glances.

"Will you two stop that," I snapped in exasperation.

Startled, the pair turned my way. "Stop what?" Safyre asked innocently.

I waved my hand, demonstrating. "You know, staring at one another as if..." I sighed. "Forget it. Whatever it is you have to say, just spit it out."

This time the two managed not to look at each other before answering.

"Alright, if that's what you want," Safyre said, fielding the question. She paused to gather her thoughts. "We know this is a sensitive topic, so we've been trying to find a delicate way to approach it," she added by way of apology.

I frowned. "What is?"

"Saya," Adriel said bluntly.

I turned to stare at her. "I'm not sure what you mean."

Instead of answering, the lich looked to Safyre, who once again became the pair's spokesperson. "You said earlier you want to rescue her. Is that still true?"

"Of course."

"And you want to do it before we claim sector 18,240?"

"The timing works," I replied, thinking that was what they were concerned about. "Adriel needs ten days to create the golems. That gives me enough time to return to the valley, find Saya, *and* finalize things with the brotherhood."

"The timing works," Safyre agreed. "That's not the problem."

"Then what is?" I demanded.

Before she could answer, Adriel spoke. "What is your plan?"

My gaze darted to her. "My plan?"

"For rescuing the gnome," she clarified. "I know you. You have something in mind, already."

I chewed on the inside of my cheek for a moment, wondering if this was the right time to explain. Safyre and Adriel would not like my plan, I knew, but considering the pair's expressions, perhaps they'd already guessed what I intended.

My gaze darted to Shael and Anriq. The pair were sitting back—both figuratively and literally removed from the conversation. I would get no support from either. I glanced to my right. Ghost knew what I intended, and she, at least, I could count on.

"Always, Prime," the pyre wolf replied sleepily. *"You can always count on me."*

Silently conveying my thanks to her, I turned back to the two women and braced myself for what was sure to be a difficult conversation. "My plan is to return to the valley—alone."

Neither Adriel nor Safyre evinced any surprise at the pronouncement.

"I know the terrain well," I went on, making my case. "I especially know the wyvern caves to the west where I believe the envoy and Shadow's troops are based. A frontal assault won't work, but one man? Alone and in the dark? That man, I think, has a good chance of slipping in unnoticed, finding Saya, and returning with her unharmed."

For a drawn-out moment no one said anything.

Folding my arms, I waited. I didn't need Safyre and Adriel's permission to do what needed to be done, of course. But I'd made a pledge to them not so long ago. No more secrets and no more going at things alone. So, while I didn't *need* their permission, I *wanted* their buy-in.

Because I believed strongly in my plan.

It made sense. I had a better chance of infiltrating the envoy's base on my own than an army had of overwhelming it. Safyre and Adriel might argue, they might rail, but eventually they would see that I was right.

"You realize it's a trap, don't you?" Safyre asked at last.

I nodded. "I do. But I'll be going into it with my eyes open. I'm prepared for whatever surprises come my way."

Adriel laughed hollowly. "You're not. Have you forgotten this is the trickster you're dealing with?"

I shook my head. "I haven't. And Loken is *not* involved. This is all his envoy's doing."

"You don't know that!" the lich snapped. "He denied your request to meet. Why would he do that if he had no hand in matters?"

"There could be many reasons for his refusal," I replied stubbornly. "It does not mean—"

"He's toying with you, boy!" Adriel interjected.

"You don't know that!" I retorted, throwing her own words back at her.

Adriel scowled at me. Not backing down, I glared right back at her, and once again it fell to Safyre to mediate. "We don't disagree with your plan, Michael," she said softly.

Tearing my gaze away from Adriel, I turned to her. "What?" I asked, puzzled. "If you don't disagree, why the—"

"We don't disagree," Safyre said, speaking over me. "Your plan is better than anything we've been able to come up with, and as much as we may dislike the idea, this is a task you're best off doing alone." She paused. "But there are risks."

I nodded in heartfelt agreement. "There are. And I'm open to discussing ways to mitigate them."

"Risks," Safyre went on as if I hadn't spoken, "that are too great to ignore and that make your plan unviable in the short term."

I blinked, trying to make sense of her words.

My confusion did not go unnoticed. "We believe you should wait," Adriel stated bluntly.

My incomprehension grew. "Wait?"

Safyre nodded sympathetically. "Yes, wait. Until we've claimed sector 18,240 for the Forerunners."

I knew from the look in Safyre's eyes that she knew what she was asking. Still, I couldn't help protesting. "B-but, but that would mean—"

"—leaving Saya in the envoy's hands for another two weeks," Adriel finished for me. "We know."

I rounded on her. "She might not survive that long!"

"It's been a month already," Safyre interjected gently. "If you're right, if this is all some plan by the envoy to lure you into a trap, then another two weeks won't make a difference. She will keep Saya alive that long."

"And if I'm wrong?" I whispered.

Safyre's expression firmed. "Then Saya is dead already," she stated flatly. "And nothing you do will change that fact."

I bowed my head, having no counter argument ready.

"You don't need to heed us, of course," Adriel said abruptly. "But we tell you this not just for our sake, but yours. The wiser course is to wait."

I raised my head, my face expressionless. "I need to think." So saying, I turned around and walked away.

✳　✳　✳

Randomly choosing one of the descending tunnels, I descended its black depths. Alone, I walked aimlessly. Not even Ghost accompanied me, staying behind with the others at my request. While I walked, my thoughts churned.

Logically I could find no fault with what the others had said.

But it was not logic that motivated me. It was... instinct. A desire to protect the Pack. I could not—would not—abandon Saya. But Safyre and Adriel were not asking me to do that. They were asking me to wait.

An altogether reasonable request.

And one difficult to deny. What was wrong with waiting? Nothing. Nothing *except* that every day I delayed, the chances of Saya dying increased. How much... who could say?

Weighing up the lives and risks involved was easier. Unfortunately, though, the results were not in my favor. Venturing into the valley would, at best, save *only* Saya. At the same time, the risk of discovery was high. If I failed in my mission, was captured, or otherwise revealed, the life of everyone I considered Pack would be put at risk.

Claiming sector 18,240, on the other hand, had the potential to permanently secure the future of every Forerunner, had minimal risk of discovery, and only put one life in jeopardy—Saya's.

I exhaled heavily. It was a grim equation.

And for the sake of the Forerunners and the Pack, there was only one path forward.

Waiting.

"Hells," I muttered. "Safyre and Adriel are right."

Delaying my rescue attempt by two weeks, though, was unnecessary. We had to claim the sector faster. Narrowing my eyes, I considered how we could go about that.

There was a way.

It would not be easy, but all the pieces were already in place. It was only a question of nudging them along.

Nine days, I decided.

We'll do it in nine days. Then I'll rescue Saya.

As my resolve grew and my path firmed in my mind, a pair of Game messages unfurled before me.

The Adjudicator has allocated you a new task: <u>A Place to Call Home</u>!
As Wolf, a Prime-in-waiting, or a leader, protecting one's followers is usually synonymous with securing one's domain. It has been your bad fortune to find these goals in conflict. The wise leader knows his limits and does not reach beyond. You, however, have not only chosen to pursue both of the conflicting objectives before you, but you have also further constrained yourself with an ambitious time limit.
Is this hubris or wisdom? Only time will tell.
Objective: Claim sector 18,240 on behalf of the Forerunners within 9 days.

The Adjudicator has allocated you a new task: <u>Rescue the lost Pup</u>!
The fate of one of the first souls you claimed as Pack is in doubt. Saya is either dead or in the hands of your enemies. Objective 1: Ascertain if Saya is alive. Objective 2: Rescue Saya if she lives or punish those who have taken her if she is not.
Note, this task is linked to <u>A Place to Call Home</u> and cannot be fulfilled until that task is successfully concluded. Furthermore, if the task, <u>A Place to Call Home</u>, fails, this task will automatically fail as well.

My lips twisted. The Game was raising the stakes. But the stakes were already high enough to make failure inconceivable. Who cared if the Adjudicator sought to up the ante further? One way or the other, I would succeed.
At both my goals.

Chapter 526: Preparing for War

Day 1 of Michael's Deadline

"I've come to a decision," I said as I walked back into the cavern.

Safyre and Adriel's expressions were resigned. They weren't expecting good news, I realized.

"You two were right," I stated bluntly. "Rescuing Saya must wait."

Adriel's brows rose, Safyre's mouth dropped open in shock, and out of the corner of my eye, I saw Shael shift uncomfortably. Only Anriq didn't react. Glancing at the bard, I threw him an apologetic look.

"I won't pretend not to be disappointed," he whispered, "but I understand."

Grateful for his support, I turned back to Adriel and Safyre. "I have one condition, though."

The lich's face shuttered. "And that is?"

"We do it on my timetable."

"Your timetable?" Safyre asked, puzzled.

"Nine days. That's how long I will allow us."

Adriel grimaced. "Nine days will be tight, but at a push, I can have the golems ready in that time."

I shook my head. "You misunderstand. In nine days' time, I expect the Forerunners to *own* this sector. That means, the stygians must be vanquished by day eight at the latest. Which, in turn, implies the possessed must be rehomed before then."

Palpable silence.

"Impossible," Adriel rasped.

"No. Merely difficult."

The lich made to speak again, but Safyre laid a restraining hand on her. "Nine days," the aetherist said carefully. "That's an oddly specific number. Is there a reason for it."

I nodded. "By my calculation, it's the minimum time to get everything done."

Adriel frowned. "You have a plan in mind then?"

"I do," I replied and began to outline it step by step...

✷ ✷ ✷

Safyre inhaled sharply when I was done. "That's a bold plan," she murmured.

"But doable," I pointed out.

Not answering, the aetherist glanced at Adriel who nodded slowly. "It *is* workable, there's no denying that, but only if we can get all the pieces in place. And—" she sighed—"although I shudder at the speed with which you want to move, I can understand your desire for haste."

I leaned forward, more relieved than I cared to admit by her support. "Then you'll be able to complete the golems in seven days? That was the only part I wasn't certain about."

Adriel's lips thinned unhappily. "I can. The possessed's bodies won't be pretty, but they'll be functional. And I'll need help operating the Rings."

I nodded. "The Pack elders can assist with that." I glanced around at the others. "Then, are we agreed?"

One by one, they nodded.

"Excellent," I said, rising to my feet. "Then see to your preparations. In one hour, we begin our campaign against the stygians."

"Where are you going?" Shael asked, as I made my way to the far end of the cavern.

"To see to my progression. You should address yours as well," I replied without looking back.

"Come, Ghost, we have a few things to discuss."

✳ ✳ ✳

After finding a comfortable spot to sit, I decided to complete the pyre wolf's advancement first. The choices we faced when it came to my familiar were easier ones. *"Shall we begin?"*

"Yes, Prime," Ghost replied, and without further ado, I called up her Class upgrade interface.

Assessing familiar's suitability for a Class upgrade...
Class points available: 6.
Familiar's rank: 9.
Upgrade requirements met.
Your familiar may advance her Class to rank 10 at this time by improving an existing Class benefit or by selecting a new one. Do you wish to proceed?

Willing my response to the Game, I waited for the list of available benefits to appear. I only skimmed through the new ones—none was especially appealing and besides now was the time for consolidation, not further development—and focused on the existing ones.

6 of 7 existing Class benefits are upgradeable.
Existing benefits that may be upgraded: <u>born again II</u>, <u>manifest</u>, <u>astral bite</u>, <u>diresight</u>, <u>direshield</u>, and <u>mist-thin</u>.
Existing benefits not available for upgrade: <u>draining bite II</u>.
Choose Ghost's rank 10 Class benefit now.

"What shall we start with?" I asked with a small smile, knowing full well what her answer would be.

"Manifest!"

"As you wish," I murmured, and relayed her answer to the Adjudicator.

You have upgraded Ghost's manifest ability to <u>adept manifest</u>. The third tier of this ability allows your familiar to leave her spirit vessel and take shape as an <u>adept stygian pyre wolf</u>. When in this form, Ghost gains the trait: <u>voidborn</u>.

Ghost is a being of both fire and the void.

The second tier of this ability granted your familiar access to the fire woven into her being. This tier does the same for the stygian half of herself, granting her +50% nether resistance, +50% damage with all necrotic-based attacks, and the special manifest variant: <u>necrotic wake</u>.

When Ghost emerges in the physical plane using necrotic wake, she will leave a trail of mist residue behind her. The residue column will have a maximum length of 10 yards, will persist for 1 minute, and will cause the health, psi, stamina, and mana of all entities who feel its touch to degenerate by 0.5% per second. As residue only, and not true nether, the mist will not be fatal to non-players.

Adept manifest, additionally, increases the distance from her spirit vessel that your familiar may materialize to 20 yards. Note: there is no restriction on unmanifesting. Ghost may disassociate no matter how far she is from Cloak of the Reach.

Adept manifest consumes psi or mana, and it can be upgraded with Class points. When using necrotic wake, its activation time is average. This is a Class ability and does not occupy any ability slots.

Upgrade complete. Class points remaining: 5.

Ghost's Class has advanced to rank 10.

Ghost's physical form has changed to that of an adept stygian pyre wolf.

"Ah," I exclaimed, both pleased and disappointed by the changes wrought by the new manifest variant. On the one hand, the pyre wolf's nether resistance had become even higher than my own—her nether damage reduction was lower though—and that would stand her in good stead over the next few days. On the other hand, while necrotic wake would likely perform excellently against players, it would be of no use against the void's creatures.

"How do you feel?" I asked.

"Better," she said, examining her new paws and coat. *"And both tougher and meaner."*

I smiled. *"You're definitely all those things."*

Last time, it had been Ghost's teeth and coat that had changed. This time it was her claws that grew. Her coat had also been altered, but only subtly, its red gleam darkening a touch.

"Ready to go again?" I asked when she was done examining herself.

Her eyes twinkled. *"Yes!"*

Closing my eyes, I called upon the Adjudicator again.

✳　✳　✳

You have upgraded Ghost's mist-thin ability to <u>improved mist-thin</u>. The second tier of this ability allows your familiar to reduce the toxicity of any free-floating nether in a 20 yard radius by 2 tiers. You and Ghost have 55 of 65 Magic ability slots remaining.

You have upgraded Ghost's direshield ability to <u>fortified direshield</u>. This variant is a significant improvement over its lower tiered counterparts and grants your familiar access to her offensive psi abilities without compromising her mental defense. When fortified direshield is active, only one half of Ghost's psi pool is used to shield her mind. The other half remains available to her for psicasting. This is a Class ability and does not occupy any ability slots.

Upgrade complete. Class points remaining: 3.

Ghost's Class has advanced to rank 12.

After due deliberation, Ghost and I had decided not to upgrade diresight and astral bite, and instead to focus on her defensive abilities: mist-thin and direshield.

Direshield, in particular, was necessary considering that in the not-too-distant future we'd be tackling a psionic Power, namely the young void tree. A tier three mental defense would likely still not shield Ghost from the Power, but at the very least it would provide her with a greater degree of protection.

Her remaining points we saved for future use.

"Now, let's do me," I murmured, turning my attention to my own player progression. Thanks to the nagas, I had gained one Class point and nine attribute points. And when it came to the matter of my Class there was little to ponder.

Void thief *had* to be advanced.

Signaling my intent to do so to the Game, I waited patiently for the Adjudicator's response.

Commencing Class upgrade...

...

...

Upgrade halted!

Urgh. Was something wrong? Did I not fulfill the requirements somehow?

But before my worry could set in, another message unfurled in my mind.

There are 3 elite tier variants available for the void thief ability. Your Class upgrade cannot proceed until you select one.

Option 1: <u>mirror armor</u>. This variant causes your void armor to reflect a percentage of any damage absorbed back onto the caster.

Option 2: <u>void aura</u>. This variant expands the range of your void armor, allowing it to protect any allies in close proximity.

Option 3: <u>void thief extraordinaire</u>. This variant allows your void armor to effect multiple thefts simultaneously.

Choose your tier 5 void thief variant now.

"Well," I thought, rocking back. *"This is a surprise."*

For the first time, the Game was giving me a choice when it came to how I upgraded my Class ability—and it was a difficult one too.

All three variants on offer were good.

Naturally, I was drawn to the extraordinaire variant the most. Void thief's biggest handicap had always been that it only worked against a single spell. By allowing me to steal—and negate—multiple spells simultaneously, extraordinaire addressed that weakness in the best possible way.

Void aura was nice as well, seeing that it afforded my allies the same level of protection as me, and if I was the stand-and-fight type, I'd have no hesitation in choosing it. However, I moved around the battlefield too extensively for the variant to be an option. Then, too, there was also the possibility that the aura itself would compromise my vanish ability by warning my foes when I was close to my allies.

Mirror armor confused me initially. On first glance, what the variant did appeared to be no different from the tier four void thief effect, redirect. But after reading the Game's wording a second time, I realized my mistake.

Mirror armor did not just reflect or redirect damage from a successfully stolen spell, it reflected *any* damage absorbed. That meant from the moment a foe attacked me with magic, they would feel the effects of their own spell! "Yikes," I muttered, running a hand through my hair.

I wanted *both* mirror armor and void thief extraordinaire.

But I couldn't have both.

So, which do I choose?

Being able to reflect damage meant I could conceivably kill my foes by merely letting them attack me. But I'd still have to survive their hits first. And that meant investing heavily in Magic to strengthen my void armor.

I didn't want to do that, of course.

Mind and Dexterity was where the bulk of my attribute points had to go, otherwise my other abilities—backstab, shadow blink, and so on—would fall behind.

Void thief extraordinaire, on the other hand, was not as dependent on the size of my mana pool. Once I stole the spells I wanted, I could avoid further hits, letting me conserve my void armor with not too much effort. And of course, multiple thefts meant multiple new methods of attacking.

Hells, if I stole enough spells, I could conceivably out-cast some mages!

Another Game message flashed for my attention, a not-so-subtle reminder that the Adjudicator was waiting on my decision.

Choose your tier 5 void thief variant now.

"Variant three it is," I whispered, willing my choice to the Game.

Upgrade complete. Class points remaining: 0.

Congratulations, Michael, your voidstealer Class has advanced to rank 14!

You have upgraded your void thief ability to <u>void thief extraordinaire</u>. The elite tier of this ability makes it easier for you to filch knowledge from

your foes by reducing the damage your void armor needs to sustain for a theft from 20% to 10%.

The range of hostile spells that can be stolen has also expanded to include trigger-cast spells and wards. Additionally, the memory capacity of your void armor has improved, allowing you to remember any stolen knowledge for 48 hours instead of 16. Void thief extraordinaire also increases the number of spells you can steal and retain knowledge of to 3.

"Three spells," I marveled. "And retained for two whole days, too!"

I had been anticipating an incremental increase to both aspects of the ability, but I'd forgotten that the step up from tier four to five was a big one—as was the accompanying jump in spell power.

Still grinning, I turned my attention to my other abilities.

Unfortunately, I had less to smile about when it came to them. None were ready for upgrade to tier five yet. My two-weapon fighting had still not reached rank twenty so whirlwind couldn't be improved, and while I had a few mental abilities that *could* be advanced, I lacked the necessary Mind ability slots for that.

A state of affairs I should correct.

Reaching out to the Adjudicator, I communicated my intent.

Your Mind has increased to rank 135. Other modifiers: +12 from items. Available ability slots: 9.

I still didn't have enough Mind ability slots for another elite ability, but in only three more levels I would, and for now, that had to suffice.

My progression completed, I moved on to my next chore: reading the den chief's pamphlet.

Chapter 527: A Failure to Conform

The thieves' pamphlet was a quick read.

It contained a rundown of the underworld's structures, its officers, and the guild's code of conduct, which unsurprisingly, was not very stringent, and by the end, I could not claim to have learned much of value.

Importantly, though, my perusal triggered a response from the game.

You have completed the task: <u>The Seedy Side of Life</u>!

You have finished your induction into the thieves' guild and have been designated a journeyman rogue by Den Chief Dinara. By completing this task, you have aligned yourself with the underworld, an organization notorious for being fiercely independent and for its disregard of the rule of law.

As such, your new House has gained an affinity for renegades, outcasts, and criminals. Accepting these sorts of individuals as followers will deepen your Wolf Mark in the future.

Note, the converse applies as well. Turning those in good standing with the established order into followers will weaken your Wolf Mark.

I couldn't help but chuckle after reading the task completion message.

Renegades, outcasts, and criminals, huh?

These were terms that could be readily applied to the Forerunners. Over half of our player-members could be labeled as such, the only exceptions being Terence, Teresa, and Shael—although Shael's designation was questionable. The descriptors fit many of the non-players in the faction too. Algar and the other Bane Wolves were exiles from New Haven, while Regus and the wolfmen—former possessed and scions all—were at best renegades, and at worst, criminals.

Hells, both my current followers—Nyra and Ceruvax—were convicted criminals. I shook my head ruefully.

We truly are a bunch of rebels, aren't we?

And somehow, I doubted I was going to have much trouble finding new followers who fit the bill. Still smiling, I returned the pamphlet to my backpack and rose to my feet. My chores were done, and now it was time to return to the others.

We had a Power to kill.

✳ ✳ ✳

I found my companions sitting and eating around a campfire fueled by hot stones and small logs.

"Where'd you get the wood from?" I asked curiously.

"Brought it with us," Anriq replied laconically.

"We *were* expecting to be here the whole day," Safyre added. "Want some?" she asked, holding out a ration.

Accepting the morsel, I sat down beside her. From across the fire, Adriel tossed me something else.

You have acquired a Forerunner faction token. This item is soulbound, and cannot be stolen, traded, or lost, even upon death. Hidden properties: this item's faction ID is 0001.

Note, only faction members are able to discern its token's hidden properties.

I looked at the lich in surprise. "That was fast."

She shrugged. "The work was simple enough to perform." She gestured to the others. "Everyone already has theirs." A pause. "Well, everyone except Safyre."

I nodded in response. As a forsworn, the aetherist couldn't use any soulbound items. Lowering my gaze, I studied the granite coin in my hand. A wolf's head had been etched onto its surface in sharp glittering black lines that looked remarkably like—

I turned back to Adriel with a frown. "A stygian wolf? *That's* the symbol you chose?"

She smiled. "It seemed appropriate given—" her gaze darted meaningfully from Ghost to our surroundings—"everything."

I sighed. First the bane wolves, now the Forerunners. It seemed there was no escaping my association with Wolf.

Ghost chuckled in my mind. *"But you knew that already, didn't you?"*

Deciding to let the matter be, I changed the topic. "Everyone ready?" I asked, scanning their faces.

"As ready as we can be considering we don't know how you intend on bringing down the overlord," Safyre responded dryly.

"I have a strategy in mind," I replied. "But before I get into it, let's review what we know about the creatures." I glanced to my left. "Shael, let's start with you."

His response was not slow in coming. "Sorry. Never heard of them before today."

"I've nothing to contribute either," Anriq added. "Everything I learned about the stygians, I learned from Safyre."

I turned to my right. "Saf?"

The aetherist sighed. "What I know is little enough. The overlords are slow, easy to outrun, and are usually employed against defensive structures. Their main attack is the blob of nether spell." Her eyes darted to mine. "But you already know more about it than I do."

I grimaced. "Unfortunately, that's true. My knowledge was hard come by too." In fact, I'd almost died as a result of the spell.

"The blob spell," I explained to the others, "is a composite one with two stages: noxious fumes and necrotic spikes. Both can be deadly." Expanding further, I went on to describe both stages in as much detail as I could.

"That spell sounds... nasty," Shael said when I was done.

"And impossible to avoid," Anriq added, before shifting his regard to Safyre again. "You said 'main attack.' What else should we watch out for from the overlord?"

"I'm sure they have other spells," Safyre answered. "But the nether blob is the only one I've heard of." She threw me a questioning look.

"It was the only spell it used against me," I confirmed. Realizing that I'd reached the limit of what I knew, I turned to the only member of the party who'd yet to contribute anything. "Anything to add, Adriel?"

The lich chuckled dryly. "My information may be a little out of date. But like Safyre, I've only ever heard of the overlords using one spell: blobs of nether." She shrugged. "Given the creatures' nature and purpose, though, that's not surprising. They don't *need* any other forms of attack."

I frowned. "Why's that?"

"In my day, the overlords only appeared in a sector during the final stages of the void's takeover," she replied. "Their purpose was always twofold. Firstly, to flatten any remaining player structures still standing, and secondly, to drastically increase the nether toxicity in the region. Usually, by the time an overlord arrived, it was already too late to repel the stygians. But on the rare occasion a House *did* manage to push them back, the overlords invariably escaped death."

Anriq scratched his chin. "How's that possible? As slow as the creatures are, I would have thought they'd be easy to run down."

The lich barked a laugh. "You'd think that, wouldn't you? But nothing could be further from the truth. An overlord threatened will simply float upward, placing itself beyond the reach of most players. From up high, its blob spells remain devastating. Attacks launched from the ground on the other hand... well, I'm sure it won't come as a surprise to learn that most fall short of their target."

My frown deepened. "No one's killed an overlord then?"

"I didn't say that," Adriel said primly. "A few Houses have. But it required concerted effort to do so."

I leaned forward. "How did they do it?"

She laughed harshly. "With great difficulty. The overlords have no eyes or limbs to disable. And the tentacles beneath them? They serve no purpose other than anchoring the creature to the ground."

"But the thing is so big," Anriq protested. Surely it must be vulnerable somewhere!"

"It isn't," Adriel said flatly. "An overlord's entire body is covered by a hardened outer shell—like a turtle's, only thicker, *much* thicker. Nor do the creatures feed, so they have no need of mouths either."

"Physical attacks are out then," I murmured.

Adriel shot me a shrewd look. "You're thinking of using psi against it, aren't you?"

I nodded.

"Well, that might not work as well as you think," she replied. "An overlord lacks a nervous system."

My brows furrowed.

"Why would it need one?" Adriel asked rhetorically. "It has no limbs, and every inch of it is covered in nearly impenetrable hide armor."

"What about its mind?" Safyre asked quietly.

"That I'm less certain about," Adriel admitted.

"So how *did* those Houses you mentioned do it?" Shael asked.

"By splitting the overlord open," the lich replied grimly. "It took time as you can imagine. Cracking an overlord's shell requires repeated blows to the same spot—which is not easy when the damn thing is flying a few hundred feet above you."

I sat back. "Alright, I'll admit taking down the overlord might be a tad harder than I expected."

Laughter followed, if of the uneasy type.

"I still think it can be done, though." I pursed my lips as I ran through the options. "What if we…"

✳ ✳ ✳

Ghost has unmanifested.

A little later, our small party—minus Ghost—was back on the surface. We had a plan of attack, if not one that everyone entirely bought. Still, I'd been convincing enough that they all thought it was worth a shot.

In preparation, I'd cast my buffs, replenished my mana, and loaded my void armor with two powerful spells.

You have cast enhanced reflexes, load controller, and trigger-cast quick mend.

You have acquired the tier 5 spell, <u>furious storm (stolen)</u>, and the tier 6 spell, <u>noxious vapors (stolen)</u>, and will retain memory of them for the next 2 days.

You have successfully stored the <u>furious storm</u> spell in the ring, mage's surprise.

More importantly, though, our two elites had painstakingly buffed every member of the party. Their effect was tangible and left me buzzing with anticipation.

Adriel has cast undead's champion (+100% damage inflicted) and warrior's boon on you (+20 to all physical attributes).

Safyre has cast aether grace (+50% chance physical evasion) and aether protection on you (+50% reduced nether damage).

The party was sheltering inside a veil of concealment cast by Adriel—no purifying dome was in place as yet—and thus far, the stygians, some five hundred yards away, were unaware of our presence.

"Everyone ready?" I whispered, surveying the others.

Shael, Adriel, and Safyre nodded. Anriq, though, stepped forward, a small object in the palm of his hand. "Before we start, you should have this back."

Glancing down, I saw it was the Seeking Eye of Sylvana.

"I don't need it anymore," he explained. His look turned sheepish. "I know you think we can do this, but I'm less certain we'll all come out the other end alive."

Solemnly, I took the proffered item. "Follow the plan and everyone will be alright," I said, projecting as much confidence as I could as I addressed the group at large.

"We will," Safyre replied on everyone's behalf.

"Then let's not waste further time." Drawing stamina, I cloaked myself.

You have cast vanish. You are <u>invisible</u>. Duration: 5 minutes.

"Here I go," I said for the others' benefit before turning about and cutting across the barren plain.

My destination?

The nether portal and the hovering overlord.

✳ ✳ ✳

The stygian Power had taken up position over the portal itself. Hanging high above, it discharged a blob groundward every so often, ratcheting up the nether toxicity in the vicinity to tier twenty-four.

The void tree, overlord, or whatever was in charge of the stygians, had clearly changed tactics. No longer did the void seem interested in ambushing us. Now, it appeared content to simply besiege the portal.

We couldn't afford to let the status quo stand, though.

Not because the stygians had us trapped in the sector—they didn't—but because retrieving the Rings and the Pack were crucial to the rest of my plan. And of course, by killing the overlord, we would not only weaken the stygians, but we would strengthen our own side too.

The nether toxicity at your current location has increased to tier 24! Damage negated by void armor.

I drew to a halt the moment I entered the enormous plume of dense yellow surrounding the gate. Two things concerned me. The second stage of the nether blob spell being one and the overlord the other.

The last time I'd encountered the Power, my stealth had been insufficient to conceal me from its gaze—or whatever means it used to perceive its surroundings. This time, though, my sneaking was elite-ranked—and I had vanish, too. Would they suffice?

Only one way to find out.

Moving haltingly, I advanced farther into the near-solid sludge of the nether.

Multiple hostile entities have failed to detect you.

Tense, alert, and with one wary eye on the incoming messages and the other on the floating overlord, I crept closer to the nether portal.

Despite my wariness, though, the Game alerts remained reassuringly consistent.

Multiple hostile entities have failed to detect you.
Multiple hostile entities have failed to detect you.

...

...

So far so good, I thought. I was already thirty paces into the plume and about as deep as I thought I needed to go. The overlord hung about six hundred feet in the air, beyond the range of even my shadow blink.

On this excursion, though, it was not my target.

You have found an anomaly!
You have failed a Perception check. Anomaly unidentified.

Mid-step, I froze.

Despite the Perception failure, I knew what had to be waiting ahead. Given where I was, it could be only one thing.

A necrotic spike.

Clenching my teeth, I lowered my foot directly onto where I suspected it lay.

A necrotic spike has been activated! Damage negated by void armor.

Logically, I'd known the ebon shard would not be able to injure me, but rationality counted for little when it came to remembered-pain, and I had been unable to contain my trepidation.

See, I told myself, *it doesn't hurt. Your defenses are better this time around.*

Forcing myself to relax, I resumed my advance.

I managed only a single step, though, before motion drew my attention. I glanced up. The overlord had started spinning on its axis.

I frowned. Had it sensed the spike's activation?

Probably.

Multiple hostile entities have failed to detect you.

But despite being able to sense something amiss, the stygian Power was still unable to pierce my stealth. Comforted by that fact, I took another step.

"Are you sure it's wise to keep going?" Ghost asked quietly from her shelter inside the Cloak.

It was not just the overlord that worried her, I knew. It was the mist too. A nether toxicity of tier twenty-four was no joke, and staving off its effects was draining my void armor fast.

"Maybe not wise," I replied. *"But necessary."* Ghost had a point though. I had to speed things up. Quickening my pace, I triggered another spike.

The overlord spun faster.

Ignoring the creature's reaction, I found and deliberately stepped onto a third ebon shard.

Void thief triggered! You have acquired the spell, <u>necrotic spike (stolen)</u>, from an unknown entity and will retain memory of it for the next 2 days.

Necrotic spike (stolen) is a tier 6 spell that, when triggered by a hostile, will drain 5% of the target's health. The damage inflicted is magical in nature and will bypass all physical defenses and armor. The spikes will remain manifested for 5 minutes before dissipating.

I smiled in pleasure. I'd completed another of my goals. The first one—verifying the ability of my stealth to hold up against the overlord's scrutiny—was also a success.

I spared the creature another glance.

The overlord's tentacles were wriggling vigorously. Clearly, it was agitated. My grin widened. No doubt its inability to pinpoint me was driving the Power more than a little crazy.

"Objective one and two completed," I reported over the farspeaker link. *"It's time to move onto objective three."*

"We're ready," Safyre replied.

I drew psi. *"Alright, here—"*

I broke off as the last thing I expected happened.

"Michael?" Safyre asked worriedly. *"What's wrong?"*

"It's the portal," I replied absently, my gaze fixed on the luminous doorway in the distance. *"It's opening."*

There was little doubt in my mind what was happening. The wolves were coming.

Why the Pack would do something so foolish, I had no idea, but it was the only thing that made sense. And unfortunately, there was no time to stop them. The gateway was already spilling out its first passenger.

A familiar shape stepped out. It was not a wolf, though.

"*Damn,*" I muttered.

"*Who is it?*" Anriq demanded. "*It's Duggar, isn't it? You've got to stop him. Doesn't he know—*"

"*It's a naga,*" I interjected.

Startled silence.

I sympathized with his reaction. I'd been struck speechless for a bit myself.

The void could *not* use nether portals.

This was an intractable truth of the Game. The Adjudicator himself protected the gateways.

So, what was a stygian doing stepping through one?

"*Did you say a naga?*" Safyre asked after a protracted silence.

"Yes," I replied, my gaze fixed on the giant serpent as it began to scan the mists—in search of me, I suspected.

The gate flickered again.

My expression tightened. "*Make that two nagas. Another is coming through.*"

Stygians emerging through the gateway was almost as bad as the idea of the Pack doing so. It could destroy all my carefully laid plans. What if an entire nest's worth of nether creatures came through? What then?

My face hardened. *You'll deal with it. Just like always.*

Eyes peeled on the gateway, I watched and waited.

But as the seconds ticked by and no more stygians emerged, my tension eased a little. "*It looks like it's just the two for now,*" I reported back. "*Do you know how they are doing this, Saf?*"

"*Hang on,*" she replied, sounding harried. "*Adriel and I are discussing the situation.*"

But I couldn't afford to delay any further.

It couldn't be happenstance that it was nagas that had emerged from the gate. Suspecting what the two elites were about, I began my retreat, backstepping through the plume while my gaze remained firmly fixed on the pair.

A level 235 stygian naga has cast cloying nether.

You have passed a magical resistance check! Your void armor has repelled your foe's attack.

I grimaced. The Game message confirmed my suspicions. The elites were trying to reveal me. I'd evaded their first attempt, but I suspected many more were on the way.

It was only a matter of time before I was discovered.

"I'm moving on to phase three," I informed the others.

"But we don't know what's going on with the portal," Safyre protested. *"It might be better to—"*

"We don't know, but we can both guess," I said, cutting her off as I exited the plume.

The nether toxicity at your current location has decreased to 4.

"It has to be the 'unidentified stygian infestation' that's responsible," I went on. *"By my estimate, it'll take the Game another hour to clear out the infection. And who knows how many more stygians will have come through by then? If we're going to do this, it's better if we move now."*

"Alright," Safyre conceded reluctantly. *"Go ahead. Do what you have to. We'll be ready."*

"Here goes nothing," I replied. Inhaling deeply, I let the shadows around me dissipate and dispelled vanish.

Multiple hostile entities have detected you. You are no longer hidden.

The reaction was immediate.

The entire flock of flying serpents launched themselves from the overlord and set off in pursuit. The two nagas spun to face me as well—but neither they nor the overlord stirred from the portal.

That's alright, I thought, setting off in a sprint. *We'll take care of them later.*

✳ ✳ ✳

I didn't flee directly toward the party.

Instead, I raced south, away from the river and any potential reinforcements coming from the stygian nest in the far north. And I wasn't exactly fleeing either.

Two magic missiles sailed in from behind.

Cutting left, I dodged the first, then threw myself forward and out of the way of the second.

You have evaded a voidball.
You have evaded a voidball.

Rolling back to my feet, I glanced over my shoulder. The hundred-odd flying serpents that had set off in pursuit were closing fast, but more importantly, the distance between me and the overlord had opened up appreciably.

It was time to get started.

Releasing the weave of psi I held ready, I flung it upward.

You have cast mass puppet.

The strands of my will crashed into the flock of serpents, and delving into the minds of the twenty targets I'd chosen at random, swiftly overrode their defenses.

You have charmed 19 of 20 targets for 30 seconds.

I smiled toothily at the spell's near-perfect success.

Behind me, I sensed my new minions falter, their wingbeats slowing. *"Attack!"* I shouted, my mental command echoing loudly in their minds.

As one, the eighteen flying serpents so-ordered dove at their former companions. Serpent attacked serpent, raking each other with tooth and claw. Not all the stygians became embroiled in the impromptu airborne battle, though. Fully a third continued their attacking dives, barreling straight toward me.

But I paid them no heed.

Drawing stamina, I cloaked myself anew.

You have cast vanish. You are <u>invisible</u>. Duration: 5 minutes.
You are hidden.

In a flurry of angry hisses and furiously flapping wings, the freefalling serpents pulled out of their dives while they tried in vain to relocate me. Behind them, chaos reigned.

And all but unnoticed in the confusion, a lone form flapped west.

The nineteenth serpent.

The one I had given an altogether different order.

I watched it go, a small smile on my face. Then, I stole away myself and headed back to the party.

✳   ✳   ✳

Your minion has died.
Your minion has died.
...
...

Hopelessly outmatched, the bespelled serpents died one by one, until only the lucky nineteenth remained.

Then it, too, slipped the leash.

You have lost control over a level 151 flying serpent.

The stygian's escape didn't bother me, though. Its fate was already sealed. Behind me, the other flying serpents had given up their chase and had returned to the overlord. And from what I could tell, the nagas had also called off their search.

Excellent, I thought.

All in all, things had gone even better than I had any right to hope for, especially given the nagas' unexpected arrival.

Approaching the spot where I knew the party was encamped, I slowed my steps. The cloak Adriel had woven around the group was near-perfect, and it was only when I was almost on top of the spell's outer edge that I perceived it.

You have passed a Perception check!
You have pierced a veil of darkness. An illusion has been lifted.

Paying the Game message no heed, I continued my advance.

You have entered a tier 6 concealment field. All entities within this field are hidden from outside detection.

Slipping into Adriel's veil, I sensed five mindglows—not four.
Adriel. Safyre. Anriq. Shael.
And the flying serpent I'd sent the party's way.
"Any problems?" I asked lightly.
Adriel glanced over her shoulder and away from the stygian she and Safyre were keeping contained with powerful spells. "Nothing worth mentioning," she replied. "What about you?"
"None if you discount the nagas' appearance." Looking behind me at the creatures in question, I saw that they remained at the portal. Nor had any further stygians emerged from the gateway to join them.
That's puzzling, I thought, my brows furrowing in consternation.
"What's wrong?" Shael asked.
"The void hasn't sent anything else through the portal," I replied.
He pursed his lips. "Maybe they can't?" he suggested.
I shrugged. "Hells, if I know."
Dismissing the matter, I strode forward and joined the circle the others had formed around the immobilized serpent. Its eyes were glazed over, and its wings hung listlessly. "You've stunned it?" I guessed.
Safyre nodded. "Stunned. Frozen. Petrified. You name it, we did it. You will have plenty of time."
I nodded in silent appreciation.
"You think your ruse worked?" Anriq asked.
"I don't know," I admitted. "But none of the other stygians reacted when it fled, so maybe."
Objective three had been to capture one of the flying snakes alive, of course.
But not just that.
I'd deemed it equally important that we do it *unnoticed.* The ploy we'd devised might have been overly complicated, but neither Safyre nor Adriel had been able to hazard a guess as to the overlord's level of intelligence.
If the creature was like the harbinger, then it might be as smart as a player. That being the case, the overlord would likely have noticed something amiss if I simply charmed a flying snake and sent it to a remote location.
And given the overlord's behavior to date, I was certain that at the very least it had a rudimentary level of cunning.
Which was why I'd decided to err on the side of caution.

"Well, go on," Adriel said, waving me forward. "Enslave it already."

Rolling my eyes at her impatience, I stepped past the others and toward my prize.

✳   ✳   ✳

You have cast enslave.

You have successfully dominated a level 151 flying serpent. Duration: permanent until death.

Blood-binding the stygian was child's play.

"It's done," I gasped, staggering away from the creature. "You can dispel your spells now. It's not going anywhere."

"You sure about that?" Safyre asked, her gaze darting between me and the stygian.

I nodded wearily, and a moment later, a litany of Game messages scrolled through my vision.

Your blood-bound slave is no longer stunned.
Your blood-bound slave is no longer petrified.
Your ...

...

The flying serpent stiffened the second the last of the debuffs fell away. Furling its wings, it arched its neck and reared up ominously.

"Stop!" I barked.

The creature froze.

"Impressive," Adriel murmured.

"Down," I commanded, staying focused on the stygian.

Its eyes swimming with some unidentifiable emotion—hate, most likely—the flying serpent prostrated itself on the ground.

"This might just work, after all," Safyre whispered in an aside to Adriel.

"It's a crazy plan nonetheless," Adriel replied grumpily.

Ignoring the pair, I advanced on the flying serpent and laid my hand on its snout. Remaining stock still, the stygian didn't so much as flinch.

"*Up,*" I ordered, projecting the command mentally.

No reaction.

"*UP,*" I demanded, louder and more insistently.

Still no response.

"Damn," I muttered. "It won't respond to telepathic commands."

"Inconvenient," Adriel said, "but not an insurmountable problem."

I nodded in agreement.

"We're going ahead, then?" Anriq asked.

Turning about, I surveyed the group. "We are," I confirmed. My gaze darted to the luminous doorway in the distance. "But only after the Game clears out the infestation on the portal. I don't want the stygians to spring any more surprises upon us. In the meantime, let's return to the cave."

The werewolf's eyes slid to the flying serpent. "What about that?"

"It comes with us, of course." I smiled. "Consider it part of the team from here on."

Chapter 529: Taking the High Road

The next hour passed quickly.

Making good use of the time, I experimented with the flying serpent, getting a feel for where the limits of its understanding lay.

Anything beyond the most basic of commands was beyond the creature's ability to comprehend. Still, it understood enough that I was certain I could get it to do what was needed.

The others watched me with a mixture of amusement and apprehension. But despite Adriel's earlier remarks, I sensed their confidence growing as the hour passed. They were starting to believe—as I did—that we could do this.

That we could truly slay the overlord.

And beyond that, vanquish the void tree itself.

"It's time," I said, rising to my feet and popping a crystal.

You have activated a scent concealment crystal.

The others nodded solemnly.

Bounding forward, I leapt onto the serpent's back. While my perch was not exactly comfortable, the creature had grown used to my weight and did not protest.

"I'll wait for you to begin your assault before starting my own approach," I said to Adriel and Safyre.

In the midst of a casting, the lich nodded absently.

"Good luck," Safyre added.

"To you as well," I replied, drawing stamina in readiness.

Adriel has created a ley line to a secondary location in sector 18,240. You have cast vanish.

"Forward," I whispered, tightening my grip as the serpent snaked forward.

The others, watching silently, waved me on as the flying serpent—alone and unaccompanied by all appearances—returned to the mist-filled world above.

Transfer through portal commencing...

...

...

✳ ✳ ✳

Passage completed!

The moment we passed through the luminous doorway, the flying serpent snapped open its wings, the reaction likely an instinctive one to finding itself midair and three hundred feet above ground.

"Wow," I murmured, luxuriating in the sensation of flying, even if it was in a nether-filled sky.

"It worked?" Safyre asked.

"It did." I laughed. "I'm flying!"

"Hmpf," Ghost groused from inside the Cloak. "I don't see what the big deal is. This looks dangerous."

I chuckled. "You're just jealous you can't experience this for yourself," I retorted as the stygian glided through the air, borne upward by unseen air currents.

"Adriel wants to know if there are any stygians about?" Shael asked in a tone devoid of humor. This, I gathered, was the bard's first major battle, and dread and anticipation filled his mindvoice in equal measure.

Before responding, I scanned the skies a second time, verifying what I'd already ascertained. We were alone. By design, Adriel's portal had deposited us five miles south of the nether portal, far enough away that neither the overlord nor its escorts could spot the lone serpent winging through the air.

"There's nothing nearby," I confirmed.

"Good," Safyre replied. "Then we'll begin."

Saying nothing, I angled my mount northward, using a combination of words and gestures to convey my instructions. The entire time, I kept my gaze fixed on the ground, watching and waiting.

A few seconds later, an expectant glimmer appeared—about three miles south of the overlord and just outside of what I judged to be the limit of the Power's awareness.

"I see you," I murmured as the party emerged through the portal.

They didn't respond, but I saw their defenses go up—starting with Adriel's black dome, followed by Safyre's purifying field. My gaze flickered back north. "No movement from the stygians yet," I reported.

"When should I begin?" Shael asked anxiously.

"As soon as Adriel and Safyre give you the word," I replied.

"Go," Safyre ordered. "We're ready."

The bard did not respond verbally, but a second later, a strange sound filled the air.

The notes of a song.

And one undoubtedly foreign to the stygians.

Shael has begun playing <u>Shaten's Call to War</u>. You have been <u>inspired</u> (+15% to all attributes). Duration: infinite. The buff will remain in effect as long as the song can be heard.

Note, this song cannot be resisted. All entities who hear it will be affected. Allies will be inspired, and enemies will be <u>demoralized</u> (-15% to all attributes).

The buff conferred by Shael's song was nice, but that was not its true purpose. The music itself was. My gaze drifted back to the nether portal.

A dozen flying serpents had already taken flight, leaving their perch on the overlord. The rest of the flock were not far behind either. I smiled.

The stygians had taken the bait.

"You have incoming," I reported. *"A hundred flying serpents, maybe."*

"We'll handle it," Safyre said. *"Just make sure you stick to their outskirts. We don't want to strike you by accident."*

"You won't," I replied confidently and urged my mount onward.

We had a battle to join.

✳   ✳   ✳

The flying serpents swooped down on the party from up high.

They uttered no sounds. Not even an errant hiss escaped the flock. And with their wings furled as they dropped, the serpents made for silent and deadly missiles. Only the telltale whoosh of air gave warning of their approach, but that, too, went unheard, washed over by the notes of Shael's song.

It would've been the perfect ambush—ordinarily.

Instead, courtesy of me watching from afar, the party got regular updates on the flock's movements. And so, in the end, it was the flying serpents who were ambushed.

Waiting until nearly the last minute, Safyre and Adriel unleashed their spells when the leading edge of the flock closed to within thirty feet.

Adriel has cast noxious vapors.
Safyre has cast furious storm.
Adriel has cast death's finger.
Safyre has cast devilish winds.

Predictably, the flying serpents failed to avoid the storm of spells, and death and destruction rained down amongst them.

A level 153 flying serpent has died.
A level 140 flying serpent has died.

...

Shael, meanwhile, kept up his music. Only Anriq stood by idly. With no ranged attacks of his own, he was forced to stand aside and watch the rest of the party deal with the threat.

I, too, did not participate.

Making sure not to descend too far, I gently eased my mount into the upper reaches of the flock, a part, yet apart, of the whole. *"I'm almost in position,"* I reported to Anriq, who for lack of anything better to do was acting as the party's communications officer.

The werewolf's face turned skyward. *"I've lost track. Which one are you?"*

"You see the circling trio? I'm the one drifting toward them."

"Ah. Got you now." He paused. *"Is it time?"*

"No. I want to get closer first." My next test was a fairly simple one. If the other flying serpents sensed aught amiss, then the plan was a bust and we'd have to return to the drawing board.

Urging my mount on, I swept closer to the other stygians.

Multiple hostile entities have failed to detect you.
Multiple hostile entities have failed to detect you.

...

My satisfaction grew. None of the serpents were reacting to my invisible presence. Nor did any of them seem to realize the stygian I rode was blood-bound.

"The plan's working," I reported.

"Outstanding," Anriq growled.

I ran a practiced gaze over the flock. Only half their number remained. In just a few short seconds, Adriel and Safyre had wreaked untold destruction on the serpents. The battle had been—and remained—completely one-sided. Despite striking Adriel's shield multiple times, the stygians looked no closer to breaking through the lich's defenses.

Shaking my head in silent appreciation of our spellcasters' efforts, I refocused on Anriq. *"It's time. Break off."*

"I'll inform the others," he replied. *"Do we retreat all the way?"*

"Yes. Go back to the cave. I've got it from here."

The werewolf didn't reply, but I saw his head drop as he turned to the others. A moment later, a portal opened inside the black dome, and moving unhurriedly, the party withdrew from the field of battle.

A few seconds after that, the portal, black dome, and purifying field vanished, leaving me alone on the surface with forty-odd unhappy stygians.

✳   ✳   ✳

The serpents did not depart the area immediately.

Hissing angrily, they sniffed at the ground, upturned loose rocks and even dug up the soil in search of the party. Their dead companions, they ignored completely.

Content to wait, I kept my own mount circling aimlessly. None of the other serpents seemed the least bothered by its presence.

Eventually, though, the stygians broke off their fruitless search, their heads jerking up near-simultaneously as if in response to an unheard command.

"Interesting," I mused.

"What is?" Safyre asked from the cave.

"The flying serpents just received a telepathic order," I replied as all the stygians still on the ground pushed themselves into the air. *"I suspect the overlord has recalled them."*

"What about your mount?" Anriq asked. *"Did it react in any way to the order?"*

"Nope. My control appears absolute." Leaning low, I whispered a command into the stygian's ear. "Follow."

Turning about, the stygian obediently winged after its former companions, just another flying serpent in the flock.

We were on our way.

*   *   *

In an amazingly short span of time, the flock reached their destination.

Which, just like I'd suspected, was the overlord.

I held myself still, barely breathing, as we approached the colossal Power. It hung motionless in the air, almost a planet unto itself.

From this angle, the overlord's sheer size could not be ignored. The thing was truly immense. Hells, on foot, it would probably take me hours to circle its rim.

No wonder few overlords ever fall in battle, I thought. This close to the thing, I could believe it. And for a moment—just a moment—the idea of us felling such a creature seemed absurd.

But no more absurd than bringing down the harbinger. Or Sunfury. Or the archlich.

We'll do it because we must.

Tearing my gaze away from the looming overlord, I studied the two coiled nagas beneath. It was hard to fathom what the pair were thinking, but judging from their body posture, they sensed nothing amiss.

My eyes rose again to the surrounding mists. Interestingly enough, the thickened plume from below did not reach this high, and the nether toxicity in the vicinity remained at tier four.

At least there is that much to be grateful for, I thought as we entered the overlord's orbit.

Multiple hostile entities have failed to detect you.

The flying serpents began landing. Back flapping, they braked midair and, one by one, touched down lightly onto the overlord's pockmarked surface.

Then it was my mount's turn.

Bracing myself, I readied psi. Despite all the preparations and guesswork, there was no telling what would happen next. Would the overlord be able to sense me when I was mere inches away? What about when I dropped off the serpent and walked on its surface?

It sounded ludicrous that it wouldn't.

But Adriel had said the creature lacked a nervous system. The overlord's shell was for all intents and purposes... nonliving. Dead hide, nothing more. It should make no difference if I walked atop it.

But *should* didn't always translate into *would*.

Time to find out if all of this was for naught, I thought, urging my mount forward.

CHAPTER 530: MAKING A HOLE

A Game message flashed for attention as my mount alighted on the stygian Power.

A hostile entity has failed to detect you.

I bit back a sigh of relief. My blood-bound serpent's landing had gone unremarked. Following the example of its fellows, my minion curled itself into a ball, furled its wings, and was shortly indistinguishable from the rest of the flock—the only difference being its invisible passenger, of course.

Time to dismount.

Every movement slow and deliberate, I unwrapped myself from my minion. I had three choices for getting where I needed to—windborne, shadow blink, or walking.

I chose option three.

There was no indication that the overlord would sense my psicasting, but this close to mission completion, I was not about to risk it. My hands clenched tightly about the serpent, I lowered myself gently down the creature's side until my feet made direct contact with the overlord.

There, I paused, poised for... anything.

A hostile entity has failed to detect you.

I exhaled slowly. *So far so good.* Releasing my hold on the serpent, I transferred all my weight to my legs.

I was down—fully and completely.

A hostile entity has failed to detect you.

Right, things were going well. A little *too* well for my nerves, perhaps. Rotating my head slowly from left to right, I searched for an appropriate spot. Somewhere that was safe to work.

I almost snorted at the thought.

As if there was anything about my current situation that could be labeled safe. *Alright, not a safe spot, then.*

Somewhere—anywhere—I can set my traps undisturbed will do. I really didn't want to have to worry about being stepped on by one of the flock. *Speaking of...* My gaze flitted to the nearest flying serpent.

Incredibly, it was already asleep. My eyes darted to the next creature. It, too, was dead to the world.

I smiled. *That'll make things easier,* I thought and got moving.

✱ ✱ ✱

Creeping through the sleeping stygians proved only slightly nerve-wracking. The creatures slumbered deeply, and with the scent crystal and vanish enhancing my already-potent stealth ability, the chances of detection were truly minuscule.

Nonetheless, I worked in silence, communicating with neither Ghost nor the rest of the party back in the cave. For the selfsame reason I forbore using psi, I didn't want to risk any mindspeech. At the forefront of my mind was a singular thought: the overlord was a Power.

It would not do to underestimate it.

Multiple hostile entities have failed to detect you!
Multiple hostile entities have failed to detect you!

...

In any case, I emerged unscathed from the sleeping flock. A safe distance away, I unbent slowly and surveyed the hellish 'landscape.'

The pockmarks riddling the overlord's reddish hide were not of uniform size nor depth. Nor were they the creature's only blemishes. From my new perspective, I noticed something else too: a spidery network of cracks and seams that connected the crater-like holes together.

Hmm... those could be useful.

Moving faster now, I padded toward the biggest seam. My fear of discovery had waned somewhat. If the overlord hadn't detected me by this point, it likely wouldn't—unless I did something foolish, of course.

The seam in question looked for all the world like a fault line along a solid block of rock. Reaching it, I lowered my head and peered in. The seam was only about three inches thick but drove downward at least two feet into the overlord's hide. It was long, too, and from end to end measured at least ten yards.

This'll do, I thought.

Stretching out flat on my stomach, I activated the blue rune on the band on my wrist and got to work.

✳ ✳ ✳

You have removed a trap-making crystal from your scoundrel's wristband. Remaining trap-making crystals: 299 of 300.

Deftly slipping my hand into the seam, I embedded a crystal as deep as I could.

You have concealed a <u>funnel</u> guide.

I'd not used the funnel trap guides before, and truthfully, I'd never expected to, since their effect was the *opposite* of what I usually aimed for—which was dealing damage to a large number of foes.

This time around, though, I needed to concentrate the raw damage of my traps on a single point, and hopefully in the process, I'd blow a hole in the overlord's shell that reached all the way to its vulnerable innards.

For such a task, the funnel guides were perfect.

Drawing more trap crystals from my wristband, I emplaced them near the funnel.

You have concealed 1 <u>remote control</u> trigger.
You have concealed 2 <u>poison cloud</u> elements.
You have concealed 1 <u>fire</u> element.

Two clouds of poison for fuel, a fire to ignite them, a trigger to initiate the reaction, and a funnel to direct the resulting explosive energy *downward* and deeper into the crack.

Looks good, I thought, completing the spell-linkage between the five crystals.

A tier 4 trap has been successfully configured!

Imagining the cataclysmic impact of the trap, I couldn't help but smile. It was hard to judge what the impact on the overlord would be, though. Would the explosion widen the seam? *Probably.* But would it be enough to split open the Power's shell? I had no idea.

Still, I didn't plan on placing just the one trap.

I intended on setting *thirty.*

Removing more trap crystals, I resumed work.

✻   ✻   ✻

29 tier 4 traps have been successfully configured!
Remaining trap-making crystals: 150 of 300.

A little later, I was done.

Fully half of my trap-making crystals had been spent mining the seam. Moving stealthily, I crept away until I was a safe distance from the crack—not that I could pretend my estimate was anything but a guess.

What mattered, though, was that I was finally ready to begin the battle-proper.

"It's done," I whispered over the farspeaker link.

The overlord did not stir beneath me as I half-feared it would as I broke communication silence.

"We move?" Safyre asked crisply.

"Yes," I replied just as curtly. Now was not the time for explanations or unnecessary questions. Safyre knew that as well as I did.

"Moving," she reported.

Crouching down small, I set myself to wait. It wouldn't be long now.

✻   ✻   ✻

The first inkling I got of the party's arrival was from the overlord itself. It vibrated, nearly imperceptibly so, and if I had not been on the thing, the motion would've gone unnoticed.

My second warning came from the serpent flock. In one motion, all remaining forty-three creatures took flight—the only exception being my blood-bound slave. For a moment, I contemplated sending it after its fellows to avoid notice, but then I decided against it. Soon, it wouldn't matter, and if things went horribly wrong, I might need the creature to escape.

The overlord trembled again. This time more violently.

"We've begun our assault," Safyre reported, as right on cue, the notes of Shael's song cut through the air.

Shael has begun playing <u>the Epic of Ganesh</u>. You have been <u>windswept</u> (speed increased by +25%).

From where I sat, I could not see the party, but I knew that they would have teleported in closer than last time—just outside the overlord's plume of thickened nether in fact. The Power itself would be invisible to them through the mist, but even unseen, as big as the creature was, it would be hard to miss.

Their attacks were only a decoy though, and purely a means to distract the overlord and draw the attention of its escorts.

"The nagas?" I prompted.

"Engaged," Anriq replied. *"You can begin."*

Not responding, I rose to my feet and flexed my hands. My buffs were all cast, and I'd no more preparations to make.

"Should I manifest?" Ghost asked.

"Not yet," I murmured. *"We don't know how the overlord is going to react, and until we do, I want to hold you in reserve."*

The pyre wolf sighed but made no protest.

Removing the remote trigger from my pocket, I inhaled deeply—*here goes,* I thought—and pressed down hard.

A trap has triggered!

Light, so bright it hurt, flashed before my eyes. I squeezed my eyelids shut. It helped—but only a little. A heartbeat later a roar of noise washed over, forcing me to slap my hands over my ears.

It was only the beginning, though, and I couldn't afford to stop now. Ignoring my discomfort, I pressed down on the remote again.

A trap has triggered!

More bright light followed. And more noise.

Somewhat dazed and deafened, I huddled small and rocked back and forth. "Keep going," I muttered. "Got to keep damn going!" Squeezing the remote in my hand, I pumped it over.

And over.

And over.

A trap has triggered!
A trap has triggered!
...
...

A staccato of explosions rocked the smog-filled world as the remaining twenty-eight traps detonated in quick succession. Most of the lightshow passed by without me noticing, the repeated assault on my senses leaving me half-catatonic.

But my stupor faded as quickly as it set in, and when I opened my eyes again it was to the sight of flames and thick black smoke mushrooming out of the seam, while beneath me, the overlord shook with ever-increasing violence. My elation remained tempered, though.

Because, while there was no question that the overlord had felt the explosions, something was missing, something crucial.

Damage messages from the Game.

I had received none.

My brows furrowed in consternation. What did it mean? Had the traps failed? Despite the explosion of light and sounds, had I not succeeded?

"Yikes!" Anriq exclaimed over the farspeaker link. *"Was that you? We felt it even down here!"*

"It was," I rasped, my mental voice unaccountably hoarse.

"Are you alright?" Safyre asked worriedly.

"Well, I'm still in one piece if that's what you mean," I replied, in what was admittedly a feeble attempt at humor.

"Of course you are!" Shael declared, the tune he was playing on his flute not faltering one iota despite his split focus. *"You're our fearless leader. Nothing can stop you!"* A pregnant pause. *"But on a more serious note, Michael, did it work?"*

Despite the situation, a half-smile slipped onto my face. The bard sounded more relaxed than he'd been only a little while ago. His confidence in both the party and his own abilities were growing, I suspected.

"We're about to find out," I replied. Regaining my feet, I padded toward the crack. It was still belching smoke and fire, which gave me pause for a moment. *How am I going to see through all that muck?*

I didn't have long to ponder the question though, because just then the 'ground' beneath me stirred. This time, it was not from any random shaking.

This time, the overlord was moving—rising to be precise.

And rotating.

"Hells," I cursed, breaking into a flat-out sprint. *"The overlord is fleeing."*

"That's a good sign, isn't it?" Shael asked.

"Not if we don't kill it," I muttered. *"Or if I fall off."*

"Fall off?" Anriq asked in alarm.

"The damn thing is rotating. But don't worry, I was joking. I'll be fine." I hoped. The overlord wasn't turning all that fast, and it would be a few minutes before I was forced upside down. And while that might complicate things, there were plenty of handholds on its shell. The chances of me falling were minimal.

I snorted. *Yeah, keep telling yourself that.*

Ignoring the morose thought, I skidded to a halt as I reached the edge of the seam. If the bombs had failed to do anything else, they had at least widened the seam appreciably. Not pausing to deliberate or consider further, I shoved my head into the crack.

In hindsight, that was not the smartest thing I'd ever done.

Another puff of smoke billowed out and straight into my face and half-open mouth.

I swore. "By all that is—"

I broke off, overcome by a coughing fit. Yanking my head back, I scooted backward and waited for my chest's heaving to stop before reconsidering the seam.

While the smoke emanating from within had lessened somewhat—it was only rushing out in fits and starts now—something was still clearly burning somewhere.

And what in hells could that be?

Uncovering that mystery was less important than determining when the smoke was going to clear, though.

Unfortunately, it looked to be in no danger of dissipating anytime soon. And if I couldn't clear the air, I had no way of assessing the results of my handiwork. For all I knew the traps had failed abysmally—which would leave me in a pretty pickle.

Damn, damn, and damn.

My thoughts racing, I assessed my options. How did I clear the smoke? Would an ice bomb work? *Perhaps.*

But if I threw a bomb blindly into the seam, the chances of it landing on the source of the flames were minimal. *Ten bombs then.* I grimaced. That could work but—

My thoughts ground to a halt as something else occurred to me.

Did I really need to clear the smoke?

No. No, I don't.

"Ghost, you're up," I said, coming to a decision. The only real way to ascertain what was going on was to enter the seam, and I was loath to do that myself, not because of the risk, but because doing so would leave me blind to whatever was happening on the overlord's surface.

And truthfully, this was a task the pyre wolf was better suited to. *"Use explosive manifest."*

"You're sure?" she asked, sounding startled.

"Yes." At this point, a little more smoke and fire couldn't hurt—hells, it might even help. *"Time is of the essence."* I paused. *"Manifest in the seam itself."*

"On it," she replied.

I backed away hurriedly, and a heartbeat later, another blast rocked the overlord.

Ghost has cast explosive manifest.

Raising an arm, I shielded my eyes as more flames gushed out of the seam. *"Talk to me, Ghost."*

"I've fallen," she replied. *"How far, I'm not sure, but I think I've reached the bottom of the seam."* A pause. *"It's big enough down here for me and another dire wolf to walk side by side."*

I whistled softly. *"The seam has grown that big?"*

I sensed Ghost's silent assent.

"So, what's the problem?" I asked, suspecting there was one.

"The traps have not broken all the way through the overlord's shell," she reported, not pretending otherwise. *"We've got more hide to puncture through."*

I swallowed. *"More?"*

"More," she confirmed despondently.

A metallic screech cut the air.

I didn't react, knowing that it was Ghost who was responsible for the sound. She was clawing at the overlord's shell.

"The hide underfoot feels softer than the bits lining the sides of the seam," the pyre wolf said. *"It smells newer too. As if freshly-made."*

Freshly-made? How could she tell? The question was of no consequence, though.

"I think... I think I can claw through," Ghost added a moment later.

It was good news, better than I had expected. Still, my brows furrowed as I wondered how long Ghost would need. *"Then do that. As quickly as you can. In the meantime, tell me about the fire. Can you see what's burning?"*

More metallic screeches followed, a veritable song of them.

"There's no fire," Ghost said between her frantic pawing. *"Nor any flames to speak of. The smoke is coming from the hide itself. Parts of it are still smoldering."*

My frown deepened as I tried to figure out what to make of that little tidbit. I was more concerned, though, about what we did if—

A level 308 stygian overlord has cast the composite spell, <u>shield of nether</u>.

The first spell-stage has been activated, spreading <u>noxious fumes</u> over the targeted area.

I whipped my head around, scanning the surroundings.

The nether was thickening in an unhappily familiar way all about me. And at a guess, the same thing was happening over the rest of the Power's surface.

Warning: your surroundings have been contaminated with a concentrated dose of nether. The nether toxicity has increased to tier 24!

"Hells," I swore.

"What's wrong?" Anriq asked, overhearing me on the farspeaker link.

"The overlord has figured out it has a stowaway," I replied. *"It's trying to get rid of us."*

"Will you be alright?" he asked worriedly.

"We'll manage. How are things proceeding on the ground?"

"As well as can be expected," Anriq answered. *"The first naga is almost dead. And the second is not far behind."* A pause. *"What about the overlord's shell?"*

"We're working the problem," I replied, not wanting to bother him—nor the others, who were also likely listening—with the details. *"Stick to the plan,"* I reminded Anriq. *"As soon as all the overlord's escorts are dead, retreat. Don't worry about Ghost and me. We'll make our own way out."*

"But—"

"Gotta go," I said, closing the link and glancing to my left.

The blood-bound stygian serpent was still where I left it. "Come here!" I yelled. It had not escaped my notice that the spell the overlord had cast was a composite one, and if it was anything like the Power's other composite spell—blob of nether—then I could expect its second stage to include necrotic spikes.

Or something worse.

Which was the main reason I wanted my best means of escape within easy reach.

"Prime," Ghost called out, drawing my attention, *"scratching at the hide is not helping. What do you want me to do?"*

I inhaled deeply, trying not to let the latest dose of bad news unsettle me. But it was hard. The overlord's defenses were a lot tougher to penetrate than I'd anticipated.

Was it time to retreat?

No, not yet. There was still time for one last gamble. I exhaled, letting the plan taking shape in my mind germinate.

"Ghost, you said the shell looks weaker down there, right?"

"Right. But like I said, clawing at it is having no effect."

"Forget about that," I said, dismissing her words. *"What I want you to do is to unmanifest—"*

"But—" Ghost began in protest.

"—and then immediately re-manifest," I continued, speaking over her. *"Keep at it until you break through. Understood?"*

"Ah," she exclaimed, her form already unraveling as she heeded my instructions. *"I understand now."*

"Good, then after that, I want you to—

The noxious fumes have reached maximum dispersion. The first spell-stage is complete. Second stage spell(s) released.

I broke off as the Game interrupted me for a second time. Swinging about, I focused on the flying serpent making its way closer. *If I'm right...*

Right on cue, an ebon sliver shot out of the overlord's shell to pierce the stygian.

A <u>necrotic spike</u> has been activated.
Your blood-bound creature has been injured. Remaining health: 95%.

I grimaced. As resistant as the flying serpent was to the free-floating nether, it was not immune to pure necrotic damage. I had suspected as much, however it did further complicate matters.

"Fly over," I roared.

The stygian obeyed instantly and, flapping its wings, went airborne.

Ghost has cast explosive manifest.
Your familiar has injured a level 308 stygian overlord!

A damage message! I exulted. Whipping about to face the seam again, I whispered breathlessly, *"Ghost?"*

Her response was a moment in coming. *"It worked, Prime! The final layer of the overlord's hide has given way. I'm through!"*

My eyes shone. *"Excellent! You know what to do."*

"Yes, I'm venturing beneath now."

Your familiar has injured a level 308 stygian overlord!
Your familiar has injured a level 308 stygian overlord!

...

...

I grinned, my excitement knowing no bounds as Ghost forced her way inside the stygian Power and attacked its vulnerable insides with tooth and claw. And if the Game messages were anything to go by, already she was inflicting huge swathes of damage.

The overlord heaved, its spinning growing more frantic.

I laughed. "That's not going to save you anymore," I taunted. "You're done for!" Unsheathing my blades, I drew psi and prepared to join my familiar. With the two of us working in tandem, things would go even faster.

A level 308 stygian overlord has cast <u>tentacle guard</u>.

My brows crinkled. *Tentacle guard?* What sort of spell was that?

Breaking off from my casting, I lowered my blades. *"Ghost, is everything fine down there?"*

"It's not pleasant, if that's what you're asking," the pyre wolf replied easily. *"It smells truly awful! But really, there is no danger."* She paused. *"Why? Is something wrong?"*

I was about to reply when a slip of motion around the corner of my right eye drew my attention.

I spun about. A gray, elongated shape had appeared in the distance. It was drawing nearer, if not fast, then steadily, its upper end wriggling in the air while its thickened base propelled it across the overlord's surface.

My eyes narrowed. *A tentacle.*

Nor was the tentacle alone.

Hundreds more accompanied it, all making their way from the overlord's underside. Reaching out with my will, I inspected the closest one.

The target is a level 105 stygian overlord's tentacle. It is currently benefiting from the buff: <u>awakened</u>.

An overlord's tentacle is not a separate organism. It cannot survive prolonged separation from its host, and when asleep, it serves no purpose other than to anchor the overlord.

But nor is a tentacle a mere appendage of its host. In dire circumstances, an overlord can rouse its tentacles, detaching them and imbuing them with a limited form of self-will. The tentacles so awakened will instinctively and vigorously guard their host.

My mouth twisted sourly. We had well and truly underestimated the overlord's defenses. Or I had.

"Prime?" Ghost prompted when I failed to answer.

"We have incoming," I replied, hefting my swords. *"I'll deal with it. You take care of the overlord."*

Glancing to my left, I took a moment to assess the condition of the flying stygian that had landed beside me. The blood-bound creature was only lightly injured, but I didn't think it was going to be much use in the upcoming fight.

My gaze flickered back to the seam. I was fairly certain the tentacles were not here for me. According to the Game, I was still invisible and undetected, after all. And besides as threats went, I was the lesser one by the Power's reckoning.

No, the tentacles had to be here for Ghost.

That was why they were converging on the hole we'd made in the overlord's shell. I had to keep them from getting in, of course. But a standup fight was not my forte.

Far from it, in fact.

Which left me wondering how much use *I* was going to be in the upcoming battle.

An idea sparked.

Unless...

My gaze darted from my minion to the seam, comparing their relative length and widths. The repeated explosions had widened the seam and the serpent should just about fit.

The blood-bound creature, I realized, was better suited to acting as a physical barrier than serving as another defender. I didn't have much time to enact my plan, though. The tentacles would be here soon.

Galvanized into motion, I began shoving against the creature.

Amazingly, I completed my task in time.

The flying serpent complied with my wishes, albeit not without a few angry hisses of protest. And no wonder, since its delicate wings suffered untold damage in the process.

Still, by the time the first group of tentacles reached melee range, the seam was blocked—leaving me free to engage them. And I did just that as they bypassed me altogether and converged on the helpless flying serpent.

Lunging forward, I plunged the sword in my right hand through the thickened base of a tentacle. In the same motion, I pivoted about and cleaved through another with my second blade.

You have destroyed an overlord's tentacle.
You have destroyed an overlord's tentacle.

Dashing right, I slashed upward, then downward and two other tentacles died. Activating whirlwind, I unleashed another flurry of blows.

More tentacles died.

Killing the things were easy, but this was just the beginning, and the main horde was yet to arrive. Once they did... my mouth thinned into a grim line. Matters would grow more complicated then.

Still, I had a few tricks up my sleeve. I did not kid myself, though. Eventually, I *would* get swamped.

"You better hurry, Ghost," I said. *"Things are about to get hairy."*

✻　✻　✻

You have cast noxious vapors.
You have cast furious storm.
Your blood-bound creature has died.
You have ignited 5 acid bombs and 5 firebombs.
You have destroyed 372 tentacles of an overlord.

A few minutes later, the battle for the overlord was still raging.

Down below, at my insistence, the party had retreated to a safe distance. By this point, the overlord was already over one thousand feet high, and there was nothing those on the ground could do to affect the outcome.

Time and again, the tentacles had threatened to overrun me—but only threatened. Thanks to vanish, shadow blink, and windborne, not only was I still alive, but I was also still managing to hold the tide at bay.

Sadly, though, my minion had died.

Notwithstanding my expansive use of bombs and stolen spells, I'd not managed to prevent the tentacles from killing it. Yet, even dead, the creature fulfilled a vital role, and the seam remained blocked. This, despite the tentacles' frantic efforts to haul out its corpse.

But most crucially of all, Ghost was almost done with her own task.

**Your familiar has injured a level 308 stygian overlord!
It is near death.**

The stygian Power teetered on the very edge. I just had to keep my own efforts going and buy Ghost a little more time. *It can't be long now,* I thought as a tentacle wrapped itself around my torso. The things couldn't see me, but that didn't stop them from flailing about in an effort to trap me.

Plunging my sword downward, I buried it deep in the meaty appendage, then blinked away before a second tentacle could repeat the first's feat.

I emerged out of the aether behind yet another tentacle pack massing around the dead stygian. This group had somehow managed to wrap themselves around the serpent's neck and were attempting to drag it out of the seam.

Damn, if these things are not smart.

Wading in, I cleaved a tentacle in half, hacked through another, then tossed a bomb and fled.

**You have cast windborne.
A firebomb has ignited! 6 tentacles of an overlord have been destroyed and 5 injured.**

Somersaulting off the windslide, I plunged straight into another mass of tentacles. This pack was much larger than the previous one and already had their snaking ends buried *inside* the serpent's corpse—doing what, I had no idea, but I couldn't let them continue.

Rushing into their midst, I activated whirlwind and laid about with abandon. My blades a blur, I struck and struck, heedless of what I hit, how hard, or where.

**A level 104 overlord's tentacle has been injured.
A level 113 overlord's tentacle has been destroyed.
A level 107 overlord's tentacle has been destroyed.
A level 105 overlord's tentacle has been critically injured.
...
...**

Realizing their nemesis was within reach, the tentacles flung themselves at me.

I slew them as they came, cutting through the thin bodies as easily as a farmer reaping stalks of wheat. But the tentacles' numbers were limitless—or so they seemed in the moment.

And no matter how many I hacked down, or how fast, the press of thin, wriggling bodies reaching for me grew greater every second, and with no other choice, I fled.

Not without leaving my foes a parting present, though.

**You have ignited an acid bomb!
You have teleported 8 yards.**

I emerged from the aether feet set and blades at the ready. *Where shall I strike next?* I wondered.

There were no more attacks to fend off, though. All but unnoticed, the battle had drawn to a close.

Your familiar has killed a level 308 stygian overlord!
569 tentacles of an overlord have been destroyed.

The overlord was as silent in death as it had been in life. No sound escaped it, and except for the Adjudicator's message, nothing marked its passing.

I lowered my blades, stunned. As incredible as it seemed, we'd slain the overlord, and without suffering any losses.

"*Excellent work, Ghost,*" I murmured, my chest heaving as I surveyed the suddenly empty battlefield.

"*Thank you, Prime,*" she replied smugly. But only a second later her tone turned plaintive. "*Can I please unmanifest? It smells ghastly in here!*"

I smiled. "*Go ahead. I'll let the others—*"

A resounding thunderclap interrupted me.

I froze, fearing the worst.

A second crack cut through the air. Then a third.

Realizing the source of the sound, my gaze whipped downward. It was the overlord's shell.

It was finally cracking.

More Game messages vied for my attention. Ignoring them, I focused on my latest dilemma. How to touch down safely. Step one was obvious enough: flee the imploding titan. Breaking out in a flat-out run, I gathered psi.

"*Saf, I've news...*"

✳   ✳   ✳

Ghost has unmanifested.
You have cast windborne.
You have cast windborne.

...

Returning to solid ground turned out to be simple enough, the most complicated part was getting the timing right. Breaking my fall with a series of windslides, I turned what would likely have been a fatal freefall into a controlled crash.

You have been injured! Health remaining: 67%.

"Oof!" I exclaimed as I rolled to a stop in an untidy heap inside Safyre's purifying field.

Leaning down, Anriq helped me up. "You did it!"

I grinned as the others added their praises. "It was as much Ghost's doing as mine. I gestured to the pyre wolf manifesting beside me. "Don't forget to congratulate her."

Safyre smiled. "We will."

"Where is it?" Adriel asked, peering blindly into the mist beyond me.

"Somewhere back there," I replied, knowing she referred to the overlord. "Quite a ways back in fact," I added, having made sure to make my own landing as far away as possible from the overlord. "In about a million and one pieces."

"Oh," the lich said, deflating slightly. "Its shell cracked then?"

"Before it even hit the ground," I told her. "When the overlord died its hide lost all remaining integrity."

"That's too bad. It could've been useful," she replied wistfully.

"We can still gather the pieces," I said, ignoring the unhappy looks Shael and Anriq were throwing me.

Adriel shrugged. "We can, but the pieces will be far less useful." The ghost of a smile touched her lips. "And somehow I doubt Shael and Anriq are too enthused by the idea." She shook herself. "But enough of the overlord. What did the kill earn you?"

I tilted my head to the side. "I haven't checked yet, actually."

"You haven't—" Shael sputtered. "What's wrong with you? Go on, find out!"

Smiling, I turned my focus inward and called up the waiting Game messages.

You and Ghost have reached level 250!

Congratulations, Michael! You are now a tier 6 player. For achieving rank 25, you have been awarded 1 additional attribute point.

Your light armor and thieving have reached rank 17, your chi rank 19, and your insight rank 25.

Ghost's magma maw has reached rank 11, her stygian claws and ash armor rank 13, and her death magic rank 9.

Congratulations, Michael! You've slain your second tier 7 creature, deepening your Power Mark. Slay further Powers to evolve your Mark further.

"Wow!" I exclaimed. "Ghost and I advanced seven levels. That's unbelievable!"

Shael looked affronted. "Unbelievable? C'mon, you soloed a Power! I'm amazed you didn't gain *more* levels."

I shook my head. "This is not the first Power I've killed and when we slew the harbinger—"

I broke off, realizing what was different about this time. Ghost and I had dealt *all* the damage to the overlord—as opposed to before where the bulk of the damage had been inflicted by Adriel and Farren—and the Game didn't consider the pyre wolf a separate entity when it came to leveling.

"Is there another message?" Adriel asked intently, interrupting my musing.

Turning my attention inward again, I saw to my surprise that she was right.

Congratulations, Michael! You have accomplished the feat: <u>Solo your First Power!</u> Requirements: slay a tier 7 creature on your own. As only the

8th tier 5 solo player to defeat a Power without external aid, you have been offered a choice in the matter of your reward.
Option 1: A Fate's Key.
Option 2: +1 ascendant point.
Option 3: +5 Class points.
Make your choice now.

I inhaled sharply, stunned by the sheer scale of the Adjudicator's offerings.

"What is it?" Anriq asked eagerly. "What did you get?"

Breathlessly, I recited the Game alert for everyone's benefit, leaving them equally shocked in turn.

"How did you know?" I asked, turning to Adriel.

"I didn't," she replied. "I suspected you would earn a feat, though. The bard was right. You and Ghost took down a Power on your own. That seemed like an accomplishment worthy of recognition by the Adjudicator." Her look turned pensive. "But an ascendant point... I would never have guessed the Game would offer you that."

I nodded, sharing her awe. I knew what ascendant points were, of course. Adriel and Ceruvax had lectured me too hard on the subject of higher evolutions for its significance to pass unnoticed.

Starting at legendary rank—ascendant rank two—players received ascendant points that let them upgrade existing ascendant benefits or receive new ones. In this way, they worked very much like Class points.

Only, ascendant points were much rarer.

Over the course of an entire Game and assuming they reached the pinnacle of advancement—that being Primehood—a Power could expect to acquire, at most, *four* ascendant points.

But that was during the ordinary course of events.

And these were not ordinary circumstances.

As a result of what Ghost and I had done, the Adjudicator was offering me a free ascendant point. Or rather the option of one. But there was little doubt as to my choice. As wonderful as five Class points and the Fate's Key sounded, both paled in comparison to an ascendant point.

"You will take the ascendant point, of course," Adriel said.

"Of course," I agreed.

"*Should* he do that?" Safyre asked quietly. I'd already shared everything I'd learned about higher evolutions and ascendant Classes with Safyre, and she was now as knowledgeable on the subject as I was. "Will he be able to use it at his current ascendant rank?"

I pursed my lips, knowing what she was getting at.

If I had to wait until I reached legendary rank to use the ascendant point, then the five Class points or even the Fate's Key would be of more immediate benefit.

"I'm not sure," Adriel admitted. "We've reached the limit of my understanding on the subject. Only another Power will be able to answer that question with any certainty, and I'd wager that not even most of them can do so." She paused. "I do know that ascendant benefits are *usually* capped by rank. That means a rank three Power should not be able to acquire rank four ascendant traits and abilities, but…" She shrugged. "Sire's strain, the ascendant trait Michael gained from his sire wolf Class, has already broken that restriction."

I nodded slowly. Sire's strain had advanced all my wolf-type traits by one tier. That included were's bite, which was *also* an ascendant trait. "Maybe the Game will allow me to use the ascendant point to advance sire's strain?" I suggested hopefully.

Adriel snorted. "I'd be surprised if it does."

I sighed. She was right. If the Adjudicator allowed me 'free' upgrades of the sire's trait, I could become wildly overpowered before even becoming a Power. "So, what *will* I be able to do with the ascendant point?"

The lich frowned. "Best guess? The Game will let you acquire another rank one ascendant benefit."

I rubbed my chin, pondering. "Hmm. That might not be so bad." None of the rank one ascendant benefits the Adjudicator had offered me when I'd first chosen my champion and commander Classes had been what I would label a poor choice.

Adriel smiled. "I'd say. There's only one way to find out, though."

"Agreed," I said, willing my choice to the Game.

Chapter 533: The Old One

Your choice has been made.
You have gained 1 ascendant point.

"It's done," I announced.

Adriel blinked. "What, already? Isn't that a bit hasty?"

"Nine days, remember?" I shot back, a trifle grimly. "We're on the clock. That being the case, none of us can afford to hesitate. We must use every advantage at our disposal to get done what needs doing."

The lich sighed. "You're right, I suppose." She paused, then asked with more animation, "Can you use the ascendant point?"

"Let's find out." Closing my eyes, I conveyed my intent to the Adjudicator.

Assessing player's suitability...
...
...
Assessment completed.
Warning: you have not evolved your champion and commander Classes beyond rank 1, therefore your existing ascendant benefits are not eligible for advancement. You may, however, learn a new rank 1 ascendant benefit.
Do you still wish to proceed?

"Ah," I exhaled.

"What?" Adriel and Safyre demanded at the same time.

I smiled. "Adriel was right. I can't upgrade any of my existing benefits, but the Adjudicator *is* allowing me to choose a new one."

Anriq's brows furrowed. "Is that a good thing?"

I shrugged. "It depends on what's on offer." I paused to relay my answer to the Adjudicator. "Let's see what they are."

Commencing ascendant Class upgrade...
...
...
Viable ascendant benefits determined.

As a result of your new ascendant point, you may choose 1 of the following 5 ascendant benefits:
New commander benefit: <u>wolf's howl</u>. Your howl is a mighty weapon that can wreak havoc across an open battlefield, momentarily confusing, terrifying, and sometimes even charming those who hear it.
New commander benefit: <u>bloodlust</u>. This trait grants you a permanent aura that fortifies the attack and defensive strength of your followers and Sworn whenever they are near you.
New champion benefit: <u>lycan renewal</u>. This trait enhances your shapeshifting blood memories by fully restoring your energy pools whenever you shift form.

New champion benefit: <u>blood caster</u>. This trait reduces the cooldown of your active blood memories, allowing them to be used more often.

New champion benefit: <u>elder form</u>. This trait allows you to transform once a day into an elder wolf, the most powerful of all wolven subspecies.

Existing benefits not available for upgrade: <u>commander</u> trait (not upgradeable), <u>champion</u> trait (not upgradeable), <u>were's bite</u> (requires ascendant rank 2), and <u>sire's strain</u> (requires ascendant rank 2).

Choose your desired ascendant Class benefit now.

I rocked back on my heels. "Now, isn't that interesting?" I murmured, as much to myself as to my companions.

"What's that?" Shael asked.

Still perusing the choices on offer and just as importantly what wasn't—namely sire's strain and were's bite—I didn't immediately answer.

"C'mon," the bard demanded, "don't keep us in suspense!"

Turning my focus outward, I found everyone staring at me with ill-concealed impatience. I smiled. "All the 'new' benefits are familiar. They are the ones I *didn't* choose during my previous higher evolutions."

"That's bad, right?" Anriq asked, scratching his head. "I mean if you didn't choose them before—"

"On the contrary, it's great news," Adriel interjected. Her eyes darted to mine. "Elder form is one of the options on offer?"

I grinned. "Yes."

"Choose it," she shot back immediately.

"Yes, Prime," Ghost encouraged. *"Do that!"*

"Elder form?" Anriq mumbled, looking confused.

"What's that?" Shael asked.

"You're about to find out," I replied.

The elder wolf form was, of course, the best option on offer—especially considering what we planned on doing in the next nine days. There was no way I was *not* choosing it.

Safyre held up her hand. "Perhaps we should reconvene in the cave first?" She glanced meaningfully at the impenetrable mists surrounding us. "It'll be safer and who knows what's lurking out there. Let's not give away any secrets we don't have to."

She had a point. "Good idea, but..." My gaze slid in the direction of the guardian tower portal. "Let's return to the tundra rather. That way we can also get going with the Packs' migration."

Safyre cast me a somber look. "Are you sure you want to relocate the wolves so soon?"

"I don't think we have much choice," I replied. "We can't take the chance that the nagas will disable the portal again. And next time, we might not be in a position to interrupt their spell. Completed, who knows how long it would have lasted? Besides, we need the Rings and all the stores we've stockpiled on the tundra to begin the next phase of the plan."

She inclined her head. "All good points. Very well, the tundra it is."

"What about the stygians' corpses?" Shael asked. "Shouldn't we loot them first?"

I sighed. Despite my determination to speed things along, there were a hundred little things—all important—that needed doing beforehand. And truthfully, as enthused as I was about the waiting elder form, I was more eager to move on and take the fight to the stygians. Doing so would have to wait a little while longer, though.

"You're right, we should," I agreed heavily. "Let's split up. Adriel and Safyre, take Shael to the tundra and start preparing the Packs for the move. Anriq, Ghost, and I will see to the looting, then join you."

✳   ✳   ✳

You have retrieved an alchemy stone.
New ingredients acquired: 150 x lumps of necrotic plasma and 50 x vial of nether residue.

In the end, the Packs' evacuation got underway without me.

Looting the stygians took longer than expected, especially since Adriel insisted that we retrieve one of the naga corpses fully intact. Why she would want that, she wouldn't explain, and realizing our protests were getting us nowhere, Anriq and I capitulated and did as she desired.

Sadly, nothing remained of the overlord itself except for tiny shards of shell that would take days to collect, so I decided not to even bother trying.

Even so, by the time Anriq and I were done collecting the stygians' reagents, Adriel and the Pack elders—with the Astral Rings in tow—were back in the cave, and when I checked in on them, they were already hard at work golem crafting. Glad that they didn't need me to hurry things along, Anriq and I let them be and made our way to the guardian tower.

✳   ✳   ✳

You have entered sector 107 of the Endless Dungeon.

Ignoring the sideways falling snow, I drew to a halt as I entered the tundra's windswept plains.

It took Anriq a few steps to notice. "What's wrong?" he asked, glancing back in surprise. "I thought you were in a hurry."

"I am," I replied, gazing in the direction of the wolves' den. It was too far away to see, of course, but I was fairly certain that Safyre—ably assisted by Shael, no doubt—had matters well in hand.

"You go on," I told Anriq, urging him toward the distant den.

The werewolf turned about fully. "Aren't you and Ghost coming?"

I shook my head. "It's time I begin the hunt."

"The hunt... you mean against the stygians?"

I nodded.

Anriq's face fell. "You won't wait for the rest of us?"

"I can't," I replied. "Ferrying the wolves, not to mention all the supplies we've left in the den, is going to take Safyre and Shael the rest of the day." I smiled. "It *might* go a bit quicker if you helped them, though."

He nodded, seemingly resigned to being relegated to the role of a pack mule. "What do I tell the others?"

"Adriel and Safyre won't be surprised to hear of my plans, I suspect. But tell them, I'll return by nightfall."

"I'll do that." He hesitated, then blurted, "You're going to use the elder form, aren't you?"

I smiled. Anriq had since learned what the form entailed, and needless to say, his interest had been piqued. "Yes."

"I want to see it before you go."

I chuckled. "Alright. Let me get it first." Calling up the message, left hanging open all this time, I willed my choice to the Game.

"Done. Now, I can—"

I broke off as an avalanche of text poured through my mind.

You have gained the wolf trait: <u>elder form</u>. This trait grants you +10 to all attributes, the alternate form, <u>elder wolf</u>, and the <u>shapeshift</u> ability. Note, elder form is a trait unique to the sire wolf Class and cannot be bequeathed to any of your followers who themselves are not sire wolves.

Shapeshift (epic) is a self-use ability that can be used once per day to physically alter your body and shift into one of your learned forms. The transformation is permanent, and while psi is required to effect the change, there is no accompanying spell duration, nor is any energy expended to maintain your new form. Currently known forms: 2, human, elder wolf.

Note, shapeshift is an ascendant Class ability. It does not occupy any ability slots, and its activation time is very slow.

The elder wolf is an ancient and primal wolf, considered to be the precursor of all other wolfkin. They're hardier than werewolves, more mentally adept than dire wolves, and as magically gifted as hellhounds. Rare, and nearly hunted to extinction, they are universally feared by their foes.

While you are in wolf form you cannot equip any additional gear or use any consumables. However, all your equipped gear's benefits are retained irrespective of your form. Transforming into an elder wolf also grants you the following: <u>primal creature I</u>, <u>hide armor</u>, <u>tooth and claw</u>, <u>regeneration I</u>, <u>lacerating bite</u>, and <u>everburning (unavailable)</u>. These benefits are only applicable while you're in wolf form. Note, everburning is unusable due to its incompatibility with your spell illiterate trait.

Furthermore, while shapeshifted, you will lose access to your human-form-only abilities, these being: greater load controller, crippling blow, piercing strike, trap disarm, lockpicking, set trap, stunning slap, astral shurikens, conceal small weapon, and mimic.

Hide armor: While shapeshifted, your light armor skill is transformed into the primal equivalent, hide armor. Any skill progression you achieve in either wolf or human form is retained and applicable to both skill variants.

Tooth and claw: While shapeshifted, your shortswords skill is transformed into the primal equivalent, tooth and claw. Tooth and Claw is a beast-only skill that, depending on the nature of the creature involved, can be governed by Dexterity alone, Strength alone, or both Dexterity and Strength. Any skill progression you achieve in either wolf or human form is retained and applicable to both skill variants.

Primal creature I: This epic trait modifies your primal skills and size. In elder form, you will measure 12 feet from nose to tail and stand 6 feet tall. At this tier, your tooth and claws skill is governed by the higher of the two attributes: Strength and Dexterity. Additionally, you gain the ability to alter your tooth and claw attacks at will and inflict fire damage instead of physical damage. Furthermore this tier also makes your hide armor more resistant, granting you +25% resistance to all types of attacks.

Regeneration I: This epic trait grants you a health regeneration rate of 1% per second.

Lacerating bite is an epic bite-based attack that causes bleeding damage. The bleeding damage will be sustained for a duration equal to the rank of your tooth and claw skill. Lacerating bite is an ascendant Class ability and does not occupy any ability slots. Its activation time is near-instantaneous, it consumes stamina, and it cannot be upgraded.

Everburning is an epic mana-based spell and unusable by you.

My mouth dropped open in shock as I struggled to process the implications—some alarming, others astounding—of the elder form trait.

Staggeringly, the least noteworthy aspect of the new trait was the *seventy* attributes I'd gained. Sadly, though, they'd been split equally amongst my attributes. And while shapeshift did about what I expected, when it came to the elder form...

...there was a lot to digest.

And the Adjudicator was not done yet. Barely had I dismissed the first series of messages than the Game dumped another lot upon me.

Secret blood trait has triggered! To conceal your bloodline, your new trait will be hidden.

Sire's strain trait has triggered! Elder form has advanced to tier 2!

The second tier of elder form grants you +20 to all attributes, the alternate form, greater elder wolf, and the legendary variant of the shapeshift ability.

Shapeshift (legendary) is a self-use ability that increases the maximum number of shifts possible to 2 per day. Known forms: 2, human, greater elder wolf.

Transforming into a greater elder wolf grants you the following benefits: primal creature II, hide armor, tooth and claw, regeneration II, lacerating bite, everburning (unavailable), stunning paw, and fearsome aura.

Primal creature II: The legendary variant of this trait increases your physical size to 18 feet from nose to tail and 9 feet from head to claw. Additionally, your tooth and claw attacks are now modified by both Strength and Dexterity and can also inflict poison damage. Furthermore, your hide armor's resistance to hostile attacks has increased to 30%.

Regeneration II: The legendary variant of this trait increases your health regeneration rate to 2% per second.

Stunning paw is a legendary paw-based attack that stuns a foe for a duration equal to the tier of your tooth and claw skill. Stunning paw is an ascendant Class ability and does not occupy any ability slots. Its activation time is near-instantaneous, it consumes stamina and it cannot be upgraded.

Fearsome aura is a legendary channeled spell that causes foes that approach within a distance equal to the rank of your telepathy skill to freeze in fear. Fearsome aura is an ascendant Class ability and does not occupy any ability slots. Its activation time is average, it consumes psi, and it cannot be upgraded. Note, fearsome aura is a wolf-only-form ability.

I don't know how long I stood there—gaping at nothing for all intents and purposes. The elder form was powerful, and definitely worthy of its 'legendary' tag.

"Michael?" Anriq called out loudly.

"Sorry," I muttered, wrenching my gaze away from the Game text to focus on him. "I got distracted."

The werewolf's mouth quirked. "I figured. That was the third time I tried to get your attention."

I shrugged. "What can I say, there is a lot more to the elder wolf form than I expected."

"It's powerful then?" he asked eagerly.

"You could say that," I replied, then proceeded to share with him the Adjudicator's description.

"Wow!" Anriq exclaimed, looking as stunned as I'd been. "Thirty percent resistance? Across *all* types, that's... that's..."

"Insane," I finished for him. And it was.

Because, crucially, the primal creature trait granted my wolf form damage resistance, *not* damage reduction. The two were not to be confused.

A thirty percent damage reduction would decrease the damage I sustained from a hit by about a third, whereas a thirty percent damage resistance meant one out of three attacks launched against me would fail—completely. And the best part was that it applied equally to hostile spells as it did to direct damage!

"Will the trait stack with your void armor?" Anriq asked.

I nodded. "Undoubtedly."

"Wow. Resistance. Regeneration. And three legendary attacks." He shook his head. "You'll be unstoppable!"

"Not quite." I grinned. "But close. And not to quibble, but lacerating bite is only an epic ability." I chuckled at hearing myself say that.

Only an epic ability? Riiight!

Anriq was equally disdainful of my qualification. "Who cares. It's damn powerful."

I smiled. "I won't disagree."

"You forgot the best part, Prime," Ghost said, chipping in for the first time.

I glanced at her. *"Oh, what's that?"*

"You'll be huge!" she replied, letting her tongue hang out in a wolfish grin.

I laughed. *"Now that, I'm less sure about."* I'd grown used to fighting colossal enemies many times my size, but if the elder form tier-increases were anything to go by, by the time I reached tier five, I'd be as big as a dragon in wolf form.

And wouldn't that be something.

Anriq gestured impatiently. "Well, go on, do it! Let's see you in wolf form."

I closed my eyes. "Alright. Here goes."

Chapter 534: Changing for the Better

You have cast shapeshift.

The moment I released the psi weaves, I began to change.
Skin rippled.
Blood churned.
Bones softened.
And little by little, my body dissolved, its solid, distinctive bulk transforming into a misshapen and malleable lump.
It was frightening to say the least, and I could only imagine what the process looked like from Ghost and Anriq's perspective. But to me, it felt as if I would pop at the slightest provocation.
Next, I began to swell.
Like a bag of air inflating, my skin expanded. Bones stretched. And organs grew. *Urgh, this can't look pretty from the outside.*
"It isn't," Ghost replied primly—and somewhat snidely, I thought. But before I could retort, she added more reassuringly, *"It'll be over soon, I think. You're already larger than me."*
She was right, I realized. While all my senses had shut down and my awareness of the outside world had vanished, I could still feel myself. I was bigger. *Definitely* bigger.
Then the process began to reverse.
Skin smoothened. Bones solidified. And my blood's roiling quietened.
And then—finally—I began to change.
Fur replaced hair. Claws grew out of fingernails. Arms stretched. Legs shortened. Bones creaked as joints shifted. My torso lengthened. And lastly, my jaw popped.
Opening it, I felt around the inside of my mouth with my tongue. The sensation was wholly different from what I'd expected.
I have a snout, sharp teeth, and—
I broke off. My transformation was complete, I realized.
"It is," Ghost affirmed, and a heartbeat later, the Adjudicator's own confirmation arrived.

You have taken the form of a level 250 elder wolf.
2 new traits gained.
2 skills have been transformed into their primal equivalent.
3 new abilities gained, and 10 existing abilities disabled.

Congratulations, Michael, your nether resistance has reached 100% as a result of your active buffs (+20% from Cloak of the Reach and +30% from elder form). You are now immune to all hostile nether spells and effects.

My vision cleared, and the world came into focus again.

But my perspective had shifted.

Anriq and Ghost were both shorter than me now. In fact, I practically loomed over the pair.

My senses hadn't changed, though. They were no sharper than before—even if the story they told was a different one. *Frozen paws and cold nose. That's what I felt most keenly.*

Then there was the feedback from the rest of my body. I was more aware of myself than I'd ever been before. The heaving of my belly, the swish of my tail, the flick of my ears—I felt it all, but strangely enough, none of the hundred different sensations impinging on my awareness struck me as weird.

Time to take that all-important first step.

Not quite certain of the mechanics involved, I willed myself into motion, fully expecting to stumble.

But my new body displayed no hesitation, and I slunk forward gracefully, head dipped, tail extended, and paws padding lightly across the snow.

"Damn," Anriq whistled, craning his neck back to stare up at me. "That's one impressive wolf form."

I chuckled—or tried to, anyway. Instead, what emerged from my mouth was a nasty-sounding growl.

Raising his hands, Anriq backed away. "Nice doggy."

I snarled again—deliberately this time. *"That's not funny,"* I snapped over the farspeaker link.

He tried but failed to hide his smile. *"Sorry, I couldn't resist. Consider it an old werewolf joke. You won't believe how many times I've heard that one myself."*

"Hmpf." Turning my head this way and that, I walked about in a slow circle, inspecting myself from as many angles as I could.

My fur was ice white, much like Snow's. *Is white an elder wolf's natural color?* I wondered. Or had the Adjudicator made me this way to signify my relationship with the arctic wolves? The question was only a bit of idle speculation though, and I quickly dismissed it.

The rest of me was equally impressive. Muscles rippled with every stride I took. My claws were black and deadly looking. My teeth, I already knew, were sharp and long. And my eyes... what color were they?

"Black," Ghost supplied helpfully.

Nodding to her in thanks, I drew to a stop before Anriq again. *"Final thoughts?"*

"I wouldn't fight you, that's for sure," he said with a smile.

I glanced at Ghost, keen to hear what she thought as well.

"You look like how I always imagined," she replied. *"Just like a true Prime should."*

I sat on my haunches, basking in their feedback. Still, my feelings of pleasure did not last, and after only a handful of seconds, I began glancing at the waiting portal behind me again. My new body was functional, more than that really, and there was no more reason to delay further.

"It's time you got going," Anriq guessed.

"Yes," I replied simply.

"Which way will you head?"

I thought about the question for a moment. The ambush attempted by the overlord and nagas had changed things. Where before it had been imperative to keep our presence a secret, secrecy was no longer a factor.

The void knew we were in sector 18,240.

That being the case, there was no reason to avoid the stygians, and in fact, there was every reason to seize the initiative and thin their numbers while we still could.

I had a choice when it came to my targets, too.

The nest in the north. Or the stygians encamped in the south, near the Draven Reach's portal.

"South," I said finally. *"South is better for now."*

Anriq grunted approvingly. *"Fewer stygians there. I agree."*

That wasn't exactly my reasoning, but I didn't disagree.

"Well, I won't urge you to be careful," Anriq said. *"That goes without saying."*

I rose to my feet.

"Good hunting," Anriq said in farewell.

Ducking my head in acknowledgment, I spun about. *"Let's go, Ghost. We have some stygians to kill."*

✳ ✳ ✳

You have entered sector 18,240 of the Forever Kingdom.

I trotted through the portal fully at ease in my shifted form. The secret, I realized, was not to think too much about the mechanics of my motions. If I simply focused on what I needed my body to do, it would take care of the rest.

Ten yards beyond the gateway, I drew to a stop.

"What is it?" Ghost asked from where she paced on my left.

Not answering immediately, I turned about in a slow circle and studied the horizon in all directions. But despite how hard I looked I could spot no sign of the enemy.

"The stygians haven't returned," I murmured finally.

"You expected them to?"

I mimicked a shrug—something hard to do in a wolf's body. *"It won't do for us to underestimate the void again. We have to assume the void tree—or whichever of the nether's creatures is in charge here—is aware of the overlord's demise. That being the case, we should expect a reaction. What that'll be though, I can't tell."*

The pyre wolf cocked her head to the side. *"Which is why we need to scout the force to the south?"*

I growled softly. *"Oh, I have more than scouting in mind, but essentially, yes."* Turning in said direction, I broke out into a steady jog.

We had a long journey ahead of us.

*   *   *

While Ghost and I raced through the mist, I passed the time completing my player progression.

Thanks to my new elder form trait, I had a sudden abundance of ability slots, but I knew they wouldn't last, and I couldn't afford to be careless about how I spent my new attribute points.

So, what will it be? I wondered. *Mind or Dexterity?*

Piercing strike was the only one of my Dexterity abilities ready for upgrade to tier five. Sadly, whirlwind was still not where it needed to be.

On the other hand, I had two Mind abilities—mass puppet and astral shurikens—that could be advanced to the elite tier, and it wouldn't be much longer before the other *four*—windborne, enhanced reflexes, shadow blink, and quick mend—were also ready for upgrade. And even with the boost provided by elder form, I was far short of the ability slots I needed to advance all six abilities.

It has to be Mind, I thought. *I have to invest further in it.*

Momentarily turning my attention inward, I willed my intention to the Adjudicator.

Your Mind has increased to rank 170. Other modifiers: +12 from items. Available ability slots: 44.

Better, I thought in satisfaction after reviewing the Game message. Soon, I could expect to add more elite abilities to my repertoire.

Sadly, though, 'soon' was the best I could aim for. Ideally, I would have liked to advance astral shurikens immediately, but unfortunately, my shifted form made that impossible.

As a wolf, I had no access to any of my gear—including my consumables.

It was a definite limitation of my new form, and it was one I would have to carefully manage going forward.

"*Why must you always dwell on the negatives?*" Ghost protested. "*Especially seeing as there are so many advantages to your new form!*"

I chuckled mentally. "*You're right about that. And speaking of, let's see how my resistances have changed.*"

Reaching out to the Adjudicator again, I pulled up the applicable Game data on my damage reduction and resistances.

<u>Damage Reduction (DR)</u>

DR reduces damage incurred only.
Life: 20%. Death: 25%.
Air: 55%. Earth: 55%. Fire: 55%. Water: 55%.
Shadow: 40%. Light: 40%. Dark: 40%.
Nether: 100%.
Physical: 62% (from armor and items).

<u>Resistance (RES)</u>

RES negates damage and rebuffs hostile spells and abilities.
<u>**Physical Resistances**</u> (all): **30%.**

<u>Mental Resistances</u> (all): **30%**.

<u>Magical Resistances</u>:
Life: 40%. Death: 42.5%.
Air: 57.5%. Earth: 57.5%. Fire: 77.5%. Water: 57.5%.
Shadow: 50%. Light: 50%. Dark: 50%.
Nether: 100%. Aether: 30%

<u>Special</u>: **20% chance to evade area-of-effect spells** (derived from Tiamaten armor. This buff stacks with other resistances where applicable).

Reading my Game data, I felt like grinning. Not only was I now immune to nether magic, but the chances of any other type of spell or ability affecting me had drastically decreased. This included physical abilities like charge and knockdown.

"*Well?*" Ghost demanded.

I laughed. "*You were right. It's much better to consider the positives.*' Still laughing, I increased my pace—more eager than ever to face the stygians.

Somehow, though, I didn't think they were going to enjoy facing me as much.

Chapter 535: On the Offensive

The journey south was longer than my first one—then I'd been carried by the river. Still, it was not significantly so. As an elder wolf, I could maintain an impressive ground-eating pace, and the miles flew by with barely any notice.

Around noon—or just after—Ghost and I reached our destination. Cresting another rise of barren soil, I spotted a luminous glow on the horizon.

The portal to Draven's Reach.

And above it, another overlord.

I bit back a mental sigh. I'd known about the Power, of course. But I'd been hoping that Anriq and Safyre had been wrong about the creature besieging the gateway, or that it would have withdrawn in the interim.

No matter. We'll deal with it.

The overlord's absence would've made things easier, but the schedule I'd formulated already accounted for killing the creature. Besides, there were other obvious benefits to dealing with the void's Powers in a piecemeal fashion.

"What do we face?" Ghost asked quietly.

"One overlord." Letting my gaze drift downward, I turned my attention to the hydras and serpents massed around the gateway. *"And three hundred— no, make that four hundred—lesser stygians."*

"No nagas?"

"No nagas," I confirmed.

"That's good news at least," Ghost commented.

I bobbed my head. *"I'm going to take a closer look."*

"You want me to unmanifest?" the pyre wolf asked.

Glancing back at her, I hesitated. Ghost lacked the stealth necessary to sneak closer to the overlord, so she would have to stay behind or dissociate. But there was another consideration, too. *"How are you managing with the mist?"*

"Oh, it hardly bothers me anymore," she replied. *"Since becoming an adept stygian, I resist more of the mist's effects than I feel. My health has barely dropped since we started traveling south."*

I nodded slowly. *"Then unmanifesting is not necessary. You can wait here if you prefer."*

"I'd like that," she replied, flopping down on the ground.

Drawing psi, I padded forward. *"Alright, stay alert. I'll report back soon."*

* * *

You have cast enhanced reflexes, vanish, and trigger-cast quick mend. Multiple hostile entities have failed to detect you.

I slunk toward the portal, a silent and unseen menace.

Ahead, the hydras and snakes were piled atop one another, asleep and oblivious of the approaching danger. Above, the overlord and his escort of serpents were equally still. Meanwhile, the river rushed on noisily behind the stygians, masking all lesser sounds.

I didn't hesitate in my advance. Given the situation, I was confident I was impervious to detection. Only the overlord's thickened plume gave me pause, and I drew to a halt as I entered its depths.

The nether toxicity has increased to tier 24.

I had little fear for myself. It was Ghost I was concerned for. How would she fare once the battle started?

Not well.

"What's wrong?" the pyre wolf asked, sensing the direction of my thoughts.

"We'll have to draw the stygians out of the plume," I told her. *"You won't last long fighting in here."*

"That should be easy enough," she stated confidently. *"If I let them see me, they'll give chase."*

"Some would," I allowed. The only questions were how many would remain to guard the gate and would Ghost be able to handle those who chased after her.

"Should I do it?"

"One moment," I replied and took a minute to conduct a longer survey of the massed stygians.

But my initial evaluation had been correct. There were no nagas amongst them. We could proceed.

"Do it," I instructed. *"And make sure you lead the stygians toward the river."*

"Why that way?" Ghost asked curiously as she began her approach.

"If you get into trouble, or if the overlord itself gets involved, you can use the river to escape. The stygians don't appear to like water. Only unmanifest as a last resort."

"Got it," the pyre wolf acknowledged. *"What about you?"*

My upper lips lifted in a silent snarl. *"I'll hang around here and deal with the stragglers."*

✳ ✳ ✳

It was nearly a full minute before the first stygian stirred. From atop the stygian mound, a sleepy serpent uncoiled and glanced in Ghost's direction.

Then hissed.

Its response was a catalyst, and in short order, the entire pile of stygians unraveled.

Multiple hostile entities have failed to detect you.

I stayed where I was, my gaze fixed skyward. While the ground-bound serpents and hydras were certainly a danger, it was the overlord that was the true threat.

But the Power did not stir. Nor did its escorts of flying snakes launch off. *Hmm. Why's that?*

Meanwhile, the uncoiling serpents and hydras had split into two packs. The smaller group, slithering about in a frenzy of motion, set off after Ghost.

But the second group, remaining behind, were spreading out rapidly in all directions—as if to protect the ground-bound approaches to the overlord. Soon, they would overrun my position. And once that happened, I would be detected.

Even crouched low and with my belly hugging the ground, I made for a big obstacle, and whether by chance or not, one of the awakening stygians would brush up against me.

Nonetheless, I didn't move.

Letting my gaze drift beyond the approaching tide, I picked out the stygians that were pursuing Ghost. *"You have one hundred on your tail, mostly serpents, but there's a few hydras too."*

"Ha, so few? I'll handle them easily."

"Don't discount them," I replied sternly. *"No matter their levels, a hundred stygians is a lot. Take the threat seriously."*

"Sorry, Prime," she replied, more soberly. *"I will."*

I glanced upward again. *"The overlord still hasn't moved, but that doesn't mean it won't once you engage. Be careful and use the river to escape if you must."*

"Got it, Prime."

"Good luck, then," I said, rising to my feet. The serpentine wave was about to break over me. Crouching back on my haunches, I readied myself.

It was time I, too, went to work.

✳ ✳ ✳

You have set your teeth and claws alight. Duration: infinite. Your attacks will now deal fire damage.

I waited until the last moment before attacking. Then all it took was a single bound forward and a snap of my jaws to bring an end to the first of my foes.

You have killed a stygian serpent with a fatal blow.

I didn't pause to celebrate. Whirling about, I sprinted flat out, my paws flying across the ground. Another stygian was almost within striking distance. Leaping through the air, I landed atop the hydra's broad back.

A level 179 stygian hydra has been knocked down.

The large stygian crumpled beneath me, driven into the ground by my greater weight, and before it could do more than squawk in surprise, I got to work.

You have cast whirlwind, lacerating bite, and stunning paw.
You have backstabbed a stygian hydra for 5x more damage.
You have critically injured your target.
A stygian hydra is <u>stunned</u> (duration: 5 seconds) and <u>bleeding</u> (duration: 21 seconds).
You have backstabbed a stygian hydra for 5x more damage.
You have backstabbed a stygian hydra for 5x more damage.
...

...
A level 179 stygian hydra has died.
Multiple hostile entities have failed to detect you.

It took only a handful of seconds to slay my prey, and not unexpectedly, its death did not go unnoticed. What took me aback though, was the stygians' reaction.

They did *not* converge on the site of their fellow's death, seeking to overwhelm its slayer with numbers alone. Instead, in the short span of time it had taken me to effect the kill, the space around me had emptied, leaving no stygian within easy reach.

My nose wrinkling in confusion, I lifted my burning muzzle to take in the wider surroundings.

Only to be surprised anew.

Everywhere I looked, the stygians were... *fleeing?*

That couldn't be right, though. The nether's creatures didn't retreat. They fought to the death. I bent back my head further to see what the overlord made of its minions' cowardice.

It, too, was in motion—upward.

Withdrawing, as well.

"Damn," I muttered.

"What's wrong, Prime?" Ghost asked.

I glanced in her direction. The stygians chasing after the pyre wolf were receding too, if at a slower rate than those about me. *"The enemy is fleeing,"* I replied. *"Even the overlord is withdrawing from the fight. I'm not sure why, though."*

"That's easy enough to figure out," Ghost said, even as she turned about to snap at the closest stygian. *"It must be because of you."*

"What?" I asked, startled.

"The stygians are learning to fear you," she replied, as if it was the most obvious thing in the world.

"Nonsense," I scoffed. *"The stygians don't learn. They—"*

I broke off as I realized how foolish my words sounded. Of course, the stygians learned!

And nowhere was that more apparent than in this sector. The void had changed tactics multiple times already—not always for the better, perhaps—but unquestionably, it had managed to surprise us.

Not once. But repeatedly.

My gaze found the retreating overlord again. Its trajectory had altered infinitesimally. Now, not only was the Power rising, it was also floating northward. The ground-bound stygians had changed course too. Where before they'd been fleeing in random directions—to get away from me as fast as they could—now they streamed after the overlord, gathering beneath it as if seeking shelter.

"What do I do now?" Ghost asked as the last stygian in range of her paws died. *"There's nothing left for me to kill. The other stygians have fled. I know in which direction they went though. Do I pursue?"*

Still surveying the battlefield, I said nothing.

"Prime?" Ghost prompted. *"If I don't close the distance soon, I'm going to lose them in the mist. Let me go after—"*

"No, don't," I ordered, sitting back on my haunches. *"Stay where you are. I need a moment to think."*

It was clear the battle was over. Or at least, the opening sequence was.

I'd barely gotten into my stride. My plan had been to suck in the enemy, and once I was immersed hip-deep in stygians, to activate fearsome aura and freeze them in place.

It would have been a bloodbath. On the ground at least.

I'd had no intention of killing the overlord itself during this outing. My goal had been purely to thin the size of its escort, ground-bound or otherwise, and train as many skills as I could in the process.

Instead, the stygians had chosen to surrender the field, leaving the Draven portal unguarded.

Why?

Closing my eyes, I pondered the question. I didn't think the answer was as simple as Ghost made out—there was no way something as powerful as the overlord feared the likes of me—however, there was a kernel of truth to her words.

The stygians *had* learned. How though?

I reviewed the recent sequence of events, truncated as they were, in my mind. First, Ghost had revealed herself and a contingent of stygians had set off in pursuit. Nothing unexpected there.

Then I had attacked—while invisible—and the enemy had fled. *Immediately*, too. That was the most surprising part. There had been barely any time for panic to set in, much less for it to become so widespread as to simultaneously affect hundreds of stygians.

Which could only mean that it was not fear that had driven the nether creatures but a telepathic order from the overlord. And the only reason for the stygian Power to give such an order so quickly was if it *knew*.

Knew what had happened clear across the sector at the Guardian Tower portal.

Knew that an invisible foe had killed a fellow overlord.

And that implied... *communication*. Sector-wide instantaneous communication, no less.

I exhaled noisily. The failure of the overlord to send its flying serpents after Ghost finally made sense. *This* overlord clearly knew how the other one had died. Not only that, it had probably also figured out one of the key weaknesses we had exploited.

Namely, its fellow Power's airborne escorts.

This overlord, wary of its flying serpents being enslaved, had chosen to keep the creatures close. Hells, I wouldn't be surprised if any unknown flying serpent approaching the Power was killed out of hand.

All of which spelt trouble for us.

I'd been fully expecting to reuse the same tactics we'd successfully employed against the first overlord on the other *three* overlords in the sector.

I snorted. *So much for that idea.* We'd have to come up with another way of dealing with the remaining overlords.

I shook my head. It was a problem for another day. Today, we still had stygians to kill.

I rose back to my feet. *"I've thought it through, Ghost. Let's run those stygians down."*

"Happy to!" the pyre wolf replied cheerfully. She paused. *"What if they scatter again?"*

"Then they'll learn another lesson," I growled. *"There's no outrunning a wolf. Not today. Not ever."*

CHAPTER 536: VALUABLE LESSONS

The next hour flew by. If not for my nethersight, it was possible the stygians could've outrun us, but with it, catching the creatures was child's play.

Nor was what followed any harder.

Four hundred stygians were a lot to face head-on. But four hundred stygians fleeing and steadfastly refusing to engage? Well, that was as simple as picking stragglers from a herd.

Lurking around the edges of the stygian formation, I charmed, paralyzed, or slept small groups of the creatures, isolating them from the rest. Then, Ghost and I laid into the bespelled stygians with tooth and claw.

The overlord didn't try to stop us.

Keeping up its relentless retreat, north, northeast, the stygian Power didn't so much as throw an errant nether blob our way. Nor did it release any of the flying serpents perched on its surface.

I could still have charmed them from afar, of course, but not wanting to reveal any more of my capabilities to the void tree—which I had to assume was 'watching' the battle from afar—I didn't try.

For the same reason, I stayed invisible and reconsidered my decision to use fearsome aura. I would have to put all my abilities in play eventually, no doubt, but for now, the less the stygians knew about my wolf form the better.

Two hours into the skirmish—battle was too grand a word for it—the overlord crossed the river, leaving the remaining ground-bound stygians stranded on the same side of the river as my familiar and me.

"Where is it going?" Ghost wondered.

"Back to the void tree and the stygian nest, I suspect," I replied.

Ghost turned my way. *"Why?"*

I gave a lupine shrug. *"Probably because it realizes it's too vulnerable out here alone."*

The pyre wolf's head swung back to the river. *"We're just going to let it go?"* she asked, sounding disappointed.

"Today we are. But it won't reach its destination today. Or even tomorrow for that matter. The overlord moves too slowly for that."

"What happens tomorrow?" Ghost asked, sensing something in my voice.

"Tomorrow, it dies," I replied flatly.

The pyre wolf bobbed her head, taking me at my word. *"And them?"* she asked, gesturing toward the hydras and serpents still milling about the water's edge.

"Them, we kill today," I growled.

✳ ✳ ✳

The remaining stygians chose to scatter.

I wasn't sure if that was because of some final command by the overlord or whether it was a result of the stygian Power finally losing its hold over the creatures. Still, Ghost and I weren't about to let our prey get away so easily.

Tracking the stygians, we hunted them down one by one. It was a task that was tedious and time-consuming but without any real danger, and deciding to make the most of the opportunity, Ghost and I trained as many skills as we could. I even went so far as to use ventro again and limit the use of my more powerful abilities.

A few hours before midnight, we ran down the last stygian. But despite the lateness of the hour and the day's surprising turn of events, I was pleased by what we'd accomplished. Both Ghost's and my own skills had advanced appreciably.

You and Ghost have reached level 252!

Your tooth and claw (shortswords), channeling, and meditation have reached rank 22, your two weapon fighting and telekinesis rank 20, and your nether absorption rank 21.

Ghost's magma maw and telepathy have reached rank 12, her ash armor rank 14, her death magic rank 10, and her nether manipulation rank 6.

"Well, Ghost," I said, turning to my familiar, *"that took longer than we expected, but I can't say we have any cause for—"*

I broke off as another string of Game messages scrolled through my mind.

Your nether absorption has increased to level 213, increasing your chance of resisting harmful nether effects by 52.5% and decreasing the damage you suffer from the void by 105%.

Congratulations, Michael! Your nether damage reduction has surpassed 100%, transforming it from a reduction buff and into a regeneration one. In future, any nether damage you sustain will restore a portion of the applicable energy pools.

Your current <u>nether regeneration</u> rate is: 5%.

The nether toxicity at your current location is at tier 4.

Based on this, your health, psi, stamina, and mana are regenerating at a rate of 1.25% per minute.

My nostrils flared in surprise, and if I had been in human form, I would've laughed out loud, too. It was not so long ago that I'd been singing the praises of resistance and recounting—if only to myself—why it was better than damage reduction.

The latest series of Game messages gave me cause to reevaluate.

Was it better to enjoy total immunity—inclusive of spells—or to be healed every time I was attacked?

Damn, if I know, I thought.

Picking between resistance and reduction would be horribly difficult, and I was just glad that, having both, I didn't need to.

Ghost yawned mightily. *"Are we done here?"* She prodded the corpse at her feet with her nose. *"Or are you planning on looting these?"*

I shook my head firmly. The four hundred-odd stygian bodies were spread out over an area of a few square miles, and I was not about to tramp back and forth between them, collecting reagents—and certainly not in human form.

"No, it's time we rejoin the others," I said, drawing psi. *"Let me shift back. Then, we can leave."*

✳ ✳ ✳

You have taken the form of a level 252 human.
Warning: you have cast shapeshift twice in one day and cannot recast it again today. The ascendant ability requires a full sleep cycle to recharge.
Ghost has unmanifested.

Portal scroll consumed.
You have opened a greater portal within sector 18,240.

I stepped directly from the mist-filled plains and into the cool darkness of the cave that was to be our new home.

Only it was not so dark—nor cool for that matter.

You have entered a tier 5 concealment field.
You have triggered the ward: fly-trap!

Before I could react, strands of steely silk wrapped around my torso. Yanking me off my feet, they pinned me against the closest wall.

You are <u>stuck</u> (duration: 25 seconds).

I sighed. *This again?*

"I see you're not wasting time, Adriel," I said loudly, the words reverberating from the stone walls. "You've fortified the place already?"

The lich's rich laugh floated from somewhere out of sight. "Oh, that's not my doing."

I frowned. Fly-trap didn't sound like a spell that would belong in an aetherist's spellbook. "Saf?"

Her chuckle echoed Adriel's amusement. "The ward is not mine either."

My consternation grew. "Then who—"

You have passed a Perception check! You have detected a neutral entity.
Lucius is no longer hidden!

The shadows unraveled and a shape appeared above me. Craning my neck back, I tensed, drawing psi, and was about ready to shadow blink when I realized what—or who—I was staring at.

A possessed.

Or rather a former possessed in a new golem body.

It had taken inexcusably long for my brain to catch up with what my eyes were seeing. But in my defense, everything about the golem screamed of danger, and my instincts had taken over.

Then, too, the golem in question—Lucius—was upside down.

My eyes flitted from Adriel's silently descending creation to the silk threads holding it—him—up. Each of the six steel-like bands was as thick as a rope and affixed to the roof of the cavern itself.

How did he get all the way up there? I wondered. Lowering my head, I tracked Lucius as he descended from the stone ceiling.

The golem was humanoid in shape and slightly larger than me. In texture and color, his skin—*is that the right word?* Somehow, it didn't feel correct— was identical to the nagas' scales. But I could perceive no joints. The golem's outer layer was one seamless whole—unblemished and bearing an ebon sheen.

But for all that, Lucius looked... unfinished.

For one, the golem was completely hairless, and for another, while all his limbs appeared meticulously crafted and as about as supple and flexible as any player's, they lacked the finer details that often characterized people.

Lucius' eyes were orbless, his head bald, his face unwrinkled, and his limbs unlined. More telling yet, the golem was androgynous, and his torso bore no genitalia of any sort.

Adriel spoke truly, I thought.

She'd given Lucius a functional body, if not a human-appearing one. Certainly, there was no mistaking the golem for anything other than what it was—a construct.

The former possessed drew to a stop at eye level with me and our gazes met. "Lucius, I presume?"

The golem nodded. "Well met, Wolf." Lucius' tone was warm and smooth, and surprisingly lacking in any mechanical overtones.

I tugged on the silk cords binding me. "Mind letting me down?" I jerked my head toward him. "And while you're at it, how about turning yourself right side up? Conversing this way is far from comfortable."

Lucius shrugged. "As you wish."

While the golem set about unraveling his spell, I looked past him and took in the cavern at large. A lot had changed in the hours I'd been away.

The left side of the cavern had been reconfigured as a storeroom. Heaps of furs, bone sleds piled with food, ebon mounds of naga scales, and even huge blocks of ice sat there, all carefully sorted and arrayed in neat lines.

The right side of the cavern had been claimed by the Packs, and everywhere I looked, I spotted dire and arctic wolves lounging at rest and pups gamboling in play. To my great relief, all the wolves were present and accounted for.

Safyre, Shael, and Anriq have done well, I thought. Not only had they evacuated both Packs, they'd even managed to relocate the bulk of our supplies, and all in less than a day.

Speaking off the trio...

My gaze drifted to the far end of the cavern where Adriel, the pack elders, and Safyre were gathered around the Astral Rings. They appeared deeply involved in another rehoming ritual, which explained their truncated greetings and resulting silence.

Shael and Anriq meanwhile were busy in the center of the cavern doing...

I squinted. From the looks of it, the pair were building something made from bone, metal, and bits of wood. *Hmm, now what are—*

A fly-trap has dissipated. You are no longer stuck.

I broke off as my silken cage vanished. Controlling my fall, I dropped lightly onto the cave floor. A second later, the golem flipped himself over and thumped down beside me.

I winced as the ground shuddered at the impact.

"I do not like this body," Lucius said flatly, noticing my expression. "It's too heavy."

I shrugged. "It was the best we could do under the circumstances."

"You promised us flesh bodies," Lucius said, not letting the matter go.

I folded my arms. "I did. But I also promised that you would serve out the rest of your lives as soldiers of New Haven. That's not happening either." I held the golem's eerily-dead gaze. "A lot has happened since my speech in the archlich's court, and none of us have any choice but to adapt to the situation we find ourselves in."

The golem's expression did not shift, not even a little, and I got the sense that it could not. *No facial muscles?* I wondered.

Lucius tilted his head to the side. "Adapt or die, is that it?"

"Pretty much," I said evenly. "You can either pledge yourself to our cause or choose to end your life here and now—a life, mind you, that you artificially extended at the expense of countless innocents."

For a drawn-out moment, Lucius said nothing, leaving me to wonder what he was thinking. The choice I'd bluntly offered him was a harsh one, deliberately so. I could have sweetened the deal, I suppose. But that would have been an injustice.

The former possessed were criminals. I could not forget that, nor would I allow them to. Yes, I was offering them a chance at redemption, but until they had proven themselves, I would trust them no further than necessary, nor would I pander to their wants and desires.

"You speak plainly," Lucius said at last. "I like that." Before I could say anything, he went down on bended knee. "To whom or what do I pledge?"

My eyes darted to the back of the cave. "Did Adriel not explain?"

Lucius chuckled. "The lich does not explain. She commands, she instructs, and sometimes she may even stoop to asking. But explain? Never. I was *told* simply to guard the cave and await your return."

I stroked my chin. "I see. Then, in that case, we'll need to have a longer conversation. But that can wait for later. For now, you will make your pledge to the Forerunners faction."

"A faction," Lucius murmured. "How fascinating." Without needing further instruction, he bowed his head and made his pledge, which I accepted.

You have accepted Lucius, a non-player, into the Forerunners faction. Lucius is free to break his pledge of loyalty at any time and without

consequences. As are you. However, until such time as the Forerunners disavow the golem—or vice versa—he will be considered the faction's sworn servant, and his actions will reflect on it.

His oath made, Lucius rose smoothly to his feet. "Now that that is out of the way, will you tell me what I am?" he asked plaintively. Extending his arms, the golem stared down at them. "This substance... I do not recognize it."

My brows rose. "Adriel did not tell—" I broke off. "Forgive me, it's obvious from your question that she didn't. Let me analyze you."

Reaching out with my will, I inspected Lucius.

The target is Lucius, a level 210 nagian mage hunter.

Nagians, so-named for the nagas which birthed them, are a new type of flesh-construct. Created from bestial remains, pure void crystals, and condensed nether, they are equally at home in the Nethersphere as they are in the Kingdom.

Nagians are heavily resistant to physical damage and also suffer no damage from free-floating nether. Moreso, while surrounded by mist, nagians require neither food nor drink, and take sustenance directly from the nether itself. Note, a nagian's immunity to free-floating nether does not extend to other forms of necrotic attacks and spells.

I read the Adjudicator's response aloud for Lucius' benefit and could feel his shock. I was a little bemused myself. Adriel had created something unique—again. Was there no end to her creativity?

"How did Adriel make me immune to the void's touch?" Lucius demanded. "And why would she bother?"

"That's part of the wider discussion we need to have," I replied carefully. "Come on, let's rejoin the others, and I'll explain."

The golem came willingly enough.

I studied him surreptitiously as we walked. Lucius' expression was impossible to decipher but from his muttering, I could tell he was still preoccupied by what I'd told him. "I didn't think to ask before," I began, "but what House do you hail from?"

For some reason, the question set the golem chuckling despite his distraction. "Can't you tell?" he asked, gesturing behind us.

It took me a moment to figure out that he was pointing to the silk strands, then it clicked. "You're a... Spider?"

Flattening his lips, Lucius stretched them in what I suspected was meant to be a smile. It was a particularly poor imitation, but diplomatically, I refrained from saying so.

"That's right," he confirmed. "House Spider and Death are ancient allies." His tone turned morose. "Or we were. It's why Adriel rehomed me first. She trusts me more than the others."

"And is she right to?" I asked casually.

Lucius laughed. "Another blunt question. But I'm curious, do you truly expect me to say anything other than yes?"

It was my turn to smile. "Don't mistake me for a naïve fool, Lucius. I have ways of compelling the truth from you, and before the night is out, I will almost certainly do so. Consider this your only opportunity to speak freely before then."

The golem tilted his head. "'Speaking freely'—is that what they call interrogations these days?"

"You're still dodging the question," I pointed out mildly.

Lucius bowed his head and fell silent for so long I didn't think he was going to answer. "I'm not sure," he said finally.

It was an honest-sounding answer, and that was all I could ask for. Further questions would have to wait, however. We'd reached the center of the cavern. Anriq and Shael were still tinkering with whatever they were building and had not looked up yet. Instead our welcome was left to the two wolves approaching from the right.

"Welcome back, Michael," the larger one greeted warmly.

"Thank you, Oursk." Going down on one knee, I held out my hand to the arctic wolf accompanying him.

Snow snuffled my palm and sent a mental image that was his own greeting.

"How are the Packs doing?" I asked both wolves.

"We're settling," Oursk replied. *"Many of the pups are confused, but excited at the change nonetheless."* Raising his snout, the dire wolf looked meaningfully upward. *"Then there are those who want to know when we can leave."*

I winced. *"I'm sorry, Oursk, but the Packs aren't going anywhere. The caves will be your home for the foreseeable future."*

Both wolves lowered their gazes, clearly unhappy about the news. *"Duggar said so,"* Oursk began, *"but I thought you would…"* He shook his head. *"Never fear, scion, we will adapt. As always."*

"I'm sorry I had to uproot you from your home again."

My words prompted a flurry of images from the arctic wolf alpha that washed over me too quickly to decipher.

"Home is where the Pack is," Oursk translated. *"The rest is just a place to live."*

I chuckled. *"Very wise."*

I sensed the wolves' answering grins. *"Where is Ghost?"* Duggar asked, changing the topic.

"Sleeping," I replied. *"She's had a long day."*

"Pups these days have no stamina," he joked.

"Don't let her hear you say that," I murmured and glanced sideways at the golem lurking beside me. I wondered what he made of the wolves.

Lucius' body language screamed of wary watchfulness, but he exhibited no impatience or surprise. But then again, all the possessed—as former scions themselves—would have an intimate understanding of the relationship between a scion and their animal brethren.

"What do you make of him, Oursk," I asked softly.

"His mind is opaque," the big dire wolf replied so quickly I knew he'd been expecting the question. *"His awareness is too well shielded for even an errant thought to slip through."*

"Hmm. What do the elders think?"

"They have not been able to get a read on him either. Duggar instructed me to watch him until you returned."

"I see," I said, rising to my feet. I wished I'd spent more time getting to know the possessed before this, but truthfully there had been no time for that. I would have to rely on Adriel's counsel. I suspected, though, that further insight would have to wait until morning.

The lich and the others didn't look like they were quitting any time soon. Shael and Anriq, though, had, and they were finally approaching.

"We'll talk more later, Oursk," I said, turning to face the pair.

"See that you do," the dire wolf replied, accepting the dismissal. *"The pups are anxious to reacquaint themselves with you and Ghost."* On that note, the two wolves slunk off leaving me alone with Shael, Anriq, and Lucius.

"How did it go?" Anriq asked obliquely after a brief glance in Lucius' direction.

"There were complications," I replied in the same vein. "And on this end?"

"The evacuation is complete," Shael replied. "All the wolves have come through safely."

"Evacuation from where?" Lucius asked. He surveyed the cave. "And for that matter, where are we? Not in Draven's Reach, I don't think."

Shael glanced curiously at the nagian but didn't respond to his questions. "As you can see," the bard continued, addressing me again, "Adriel has begun rehoming the possessed."

I nodded. "How many so far?"

"Three," Lucius answered before the others could.

"Three?" I asked, startled "Where—"

"Hail, scion!" The words rang out hollowly from the left.

Turning in that direction, I spotted two nagians emerging from behind one of the 'storeroom's' fur piles. Like Lucius, their minds were shielded, which explained why I'd not noticed them before this.

Wanting to know who I was facing, I reached out with my will and analyzed the approaching pair.

The target is Bacheus, a level 208 nagian sorcerer.
The target is Zekiel, a level 206 nagian psi knight.

"Meet Bach and Zek," Lucius said grandly as the two drew closer. "My fellow captains."

I glanced at him sharply. "Captains?"

He nodded. "Adriel has chosen the three of us to serve as the leaders of the former possessed. Although, I suppose we should be calling ourselves nagians from now on."

My eyes narrowed. "Is that why all three of you are elites?"

Lucius attempted another gruesome smile. "Partly. But it's also because the lich trusts us."

I grunted noncommittally.

"Safyre asked us to watch them—discreetly," Anriq said over the farspeaker bracelet.

"Why?" I asked. Folding my arms behind my back and pretending to watch the approaching nagians, I betrayed no sign of our mental conversation. *"Does Safyre not trust them?"*

"No, that's not it," Shael replied. *"Adriel is confident of their loyalty—and that's good enough for Safyre—but given the precariousness of our situation, she felt it only prudent we watch them."*

"An understandable precaution," I murmured, then closed the link as the two nagians finally reached us.

"Well met, Bach, Zek," I said, nodding to each in turn.

Physically, the three nagians were nearly indistinguishable from each other, but as I looked closer, I noticed almost imperceptible differences in their facial structures and bodies that set them apart. Still, in the ordinary course of events it would be impossible to tell the nagians apart.

Thankfully, I have analyze, I thought.

Dropping into a cross-legged stance, I gestured for the others to seat themselves. "I guess it's time for some explanations."

"That would be appreciated, Wolf," Zekiel replied, his words a dry rumble.

"Yes, please," Bacheus added. "I hate being kept in the dark."

I nodded, understanding the sentiment. "For starters, as Lucius has already guessed, we are not in Draven's Reach."

Bacheus leaned forward eagerly. "Then where are we? Somewhere sunny I hope?"

I held up my hand. "We'll get to that in a bit." I glanced at Lucius. "If you don't mind, please share with your fellow captains what you've learned of your new body."

Inclining his head, the former Spider did just that.

"Void crystals!" Bacheus exclaimed when Lucius was done. He stared down at his arms in what I expected was fascinated wonder. "Is that what this is? I thought I recognized it, but working the crystals is supposed to be impossible! How did Adriel do it?"

Zekiel was studying his hands too. "I think... I like it."

Lucius snorted. "Of course, you would. You Bears were always overly enamored of size." His eyes found mine. "Are you going to answer Bacheus?"

Retrieving a naga scale from my backpack, I tossed it to Lucius. "Your bodies are made from this."

The nagian studied the item curiously for a moment before handing it to Bacheus.

"What is it?" the sorcerer asked.

"A naga scale," I replied.

"A naga," Zekiel repeated slowly. "What is that?"

"A stygian," Shael answered.

"Of course, it's a stygian," Bacheus said impatiently. "But what type? I've never heard of the creature before."

I shrugged. "Neither have we, nor Adriel for that matter. As far as we can tell we're the first to encounter its like."

Lucius glanced at the roof of the cave. "I take it we're in the Nethersphere then?"

I shook my head. "Not exactly."

The three nagians stared at me intently, waiting for me to go on.

"We're in a sector infested by nether. One we hope to claim for our faction," I said.

Lucius made the connection immediately. "That's what you meant by changing circumstances, isn't it? You need our help to defeat the stygians. *That's* why Adriel is rehoming us in these bodies."

I nodded. "Correct."

"But you're the scion of a dead House," Zekiel protested. "How can you belong to a faction?" The nagian's hands tightened into fists. "Unless... unless you've thrown in your lot with the new Powers?" He locked gazes with me. "Is that what you've done, Wolf?"

Anriq snorted derisively. "Michael would never do such a thing!"

But neither Zekiel nor I broke off from our impromptu staring contest to glance his way. "No, I have not," I said, enunciating each word carefully.

Zekiel didn't look convinced, but Bacheus took me at my word. "Then how?"

"Isn't that obvious?" Lucius asked quietly. "Our scion has become a Power himself."

The other two nagians froze, making their shock clear.

"A good guess," I said, turning Lucius' way. "But not quite correct this time. I'm only a Powerful Initiate."

Bacheus laughed. "Only an Initiate he says."

Zekiel bowed his head. "Then there is hope," he said hoarsely.

"Hope?" Shael asked, perplexed. "Hope for what?"

"Hope for restoring the Houses," Zekiel replied, his gaze staying fixed on me. "Is that what you intend, Wolf? To bring back the Primes."

"Call me Michael," I said. "And yes, that is my intent." I spread my arms to include Safyre, Adriel, and the others in the gesture. "That's why we are all here."

"Then you will have my help," Zekiel replied, his voice thick with emotion. "And gladly."

"And mine too," Bacheus added more softly, but no less fervently.

Pursing my lips, I studied each of the nagians in turn. Bacheus and Zekiel both seemed sincere, and even the more reserved Lucius was nodding along with the others. My instincts were telling me I could trust them, but I couldn't take any chances. "You know I will have to test the truth of your words."

Lucius inclined his head. "We would expect nothing less."

I rose to my feet. "Then I will leave it to Shael and Anriq to share our tale. Tomorrow, I will put your words to the test and take your oaths."

Anriq's brows furrowed. "Where are you going?"

"Bed," I replied, stifling a yawn. "It's time I got some rest."

I didn't go to bed immediately. Before I could fall asleep, I needed to attend to my player advancement. To start with, I pulled up my skill and ability statuses for review.

Available Strength slots: 40. **Upgradeable abilities:** none.
Available Constitution slots: 29. **Upgradeable abilities:** none.
Available Dexterity slots: 36. **Upgradeable abilities:** whirlwind, piercing strike, trap disarm, lockpicking.
Available Mind slots: 44. **Upgradeable abilities:** mass puppet, windborne, astral shurikens, shadow blink, astral bite (Ghost).
Available Perception slots: 24. **Upgradeable abilities:** analyze, conceal weapon, ventro, imitate.
Available Magic slots: 75. **Upgradeable abilities:** draining bite (Ghost).
Available Faith slots: 20. **Upgradeable abilities:** none.

Upgrade items in backpack: 2 x upgrade gems.
Ability tomes in backpack: piercing strike tier III, IV, & V, trap disarm tier III, lockpicking tier III, ventro tier III & IV.

The first thing that became immediately apparent to me was that I didn't have nearly enough upgrade gems nor ability tomes. Thanks to the elder form trait, I had a sudden surplus of ability slots that I was not equipped to use... yet.

The second thing that struck me was the forty Strength ability slots that were languishing unused. On their own, they were enough to acquire an elite ability. I had no strength abilities, of course—largely because I lacked any strength skills.

But that was no longer strictly true.

At least not when I was in wolf form.

If I understood the Game's description of the primal variant of the tooth and claw skill, it was governed by *both* Dexterity and Strength. And that meant I could acquire Strength abilities for my wolf form.

Definitely something to keep in mind during my next shopping trip.

The Magic slots were for Ghost to use, and the Faith slots, I could do nothing about unfortunately. Still, the additional Faith attribute points meant a nice increase to the size of my mana pool, and if there ever came a time again to bequeath attributes to my followers, I knew it would be from Faith that I drew.

I returned my attention to the text floating in front of me. It was time to refocus on what I *could* advance. *Mind abilities first,* I decided. I had two upgrade gems, and there was no question in mind that I had to employ them on my scion abilities, and unfortunately or fortunately, only two of them were ready for upgrade—astral shurikens and shadow blink.

So be it.

Picking up the first gem, I willed my choice to the Adjudicator.

Ability gem activated.
Creating ability tome...
You have acquired a tier 5 astral blades ability tome.

The ability gem vanished, leaving a small leatherbound book in its stead. Picking up the book, I absorbed its knowledge.

You have upgraded your astral shurikens ability to <u>sentient shurikens</u>. The fifth tier of this spell grants your astral shurikens limited intelligence and semi-permanence. They now function as an extension of your will, and for as long as they exist, they can be controlled by your mind.

You may summon a maximum of 4 shurikens at any one time. Each blade will remain manifested for a maximum duration of 5 minutes, during which time, they can be ordered at will. Note, your shurikens are not indestructible, and can be destroyed by your foes.

"Now, that was unexpected," I murmured. I'd been anticipating more bouncing shurikens, not mind-controlled ones—not that I was unhappy about the change. Being able to order my astral blades the way I did my minions, made them more versatile.

"Right, on to the next," I thought and activated the last gem.

Creating ability tome...

...
Tome creation halted. There are 2 elite variants available for the shadow blink ability.

Variant 1: <u>shadow jump</u>. This variant increases the range of shadow blink to sight range. You can blink to any creature you can see.

Variant 2: <u>blink</u>. This variant halves the spellcasting time and removes the restriction forcing you to teleport to a location occupied by another creature. You can blink to any visible location within 100 yards.

Choose your tier 5 shadow blink ability tome now.

An involuntary sigh escaped me and not because I disliked the options on offer. On the contrary, I wanted both. And that was not possible.

So, which to choose? I wondered.

Bowing my head, I pondered the choices before me. Was the ability to teleport anywhere—albeit only within a hundred yard radius—more valuable than being able to blink an unlimited distance to any creature within sight range? One option offered greater versatility, the other near limitless range.

Blink in combat would be amazing. With it, I could constantly change position, altering the angle of my attack. I could also use blink as an escape tool, to jump onto a nearby ledge, into a shadowy corner, or simply farther away from my foe.

But I could already do those things with windborne and vanish.

Yes, using windborne would be slower and more cumbersome, especially in combat. But truly, I was primarily a melee fighter. Changing position in a fight mattered less than if I were a ranged combatant.

And finally, while I disliked basing my player progression decisions on short-term goals, I could not ignore the fact that shadow jump would allow me to reach the overlord unhindered.

And the void tree too.

As long as I could see the Powers, I could teleport to them. Being able to do that simplified everything and let me bypass more obstacles than I cared to imagine. And as valuable as shadow jump would be against the overlord, I could see it being equally valuable against future foes too.

Shadow jump is the one.

Decision made, I communicated my desire to the Adjudicator.

You have acquired a tier 5 shadow jump ability tome.

You have upgraded your shadow blink ability to <u>shadow jump</u>. The fifth tier of this spell allows you to teleport to any living entity within sight range. Note, this applies only to creatures in your direct line of sight or within mindsight range, and not to entities observed via other magical means like scrying.

You have 14 of 170 Mind ability slots remaining.

"Excellent," I smiled, unbothered by the Game's qualification. It was a minor one and would hardly affect how I used shadow jump.

My mind abilities seen to, I turned next to Perception, but the only Perception tomes I had in my backpack were for ventro, and I was uncertain yet about the wisdom of upgrading ventro—especially, seeing as analyze was already ready for advancement to tier six.

I'll wait until I visit a merchant, I decided.

Next, I turned to Dexterity. Thanks to some careful preplanning, I had ability tomes for all the abilities ready for advancement—piercing strike, trap disarm, and lockpicking.

But do I really need to upgrade any of them right now?

In the nether-infested sector, I could hardly expect to encounter any enemy traps or locked doors. Only piercing strike bore immediate consideration. The ability could be advanced to the elite tier, consuming twenty-five more ability slots in the process.

Yet I found myself hesitating.

Piercing strike was a human-form-only ability, and there was no doubt in my mind that when it came to pure combat, my wolf form was superior. That made a piercing strike something of a liability, and as yet, my investment in piercing strike was minimal—the ability was at tier two and occupied only five Dexterity slots.

All of which begged the question: was it time to stop investing in piercing strike?

It is.

It was better to change tack now rather than later. Instead of advancing piercing strike, I would acquire another Dexterity ability. One that was usable in *both* human and wolf forms.

I turned back to the trap disarm and lockpicking ability tomes. Since I was not going to spend my Dexterity slots on piercing strike, I saw no reason not to acquire them now, and as utility abilities, it mattered less that they were only usable in human form.

You have upgraded your trap disarm ability to <u>greater trap disarm</u>. The third tier of this ability allows you to deactivate tier 3 traps.

You have upgraded your lockpick ability to <u>greater lockpicking</u>. The third tier of this ability allows you to open tier 3 locks.

You have 26 of 142 Dexterity ability slots remaining.

That was my abilities taken care of. *Now for Ghost's.*

The pyre wolf had only two upgradeable abilities—astral bite and draining bite—of which only one needed advancing—the death magic one. I didn't need to consult Ghost on the matter either since this was something we'd discussed previously.

Closing my eyes, I willed my intent to the Game.

You have upgraded Ghost's draining bite ability to <u>superior draining bite</u>. The third tier of this ability allows your familiar to leech 30% of the damage she inflicts from a single bite attack, restoring her own health in the process. You and Ghost have 70 of 85 Magic ability slots remaining.

Upgrade complete. Class points remaining: 2.

Ghost's Class has advanced to rank 13.

Perfect, I thought. *Now to spend my attribute points.* Turning my attention inward again, I relayed my choice to the Adjudicator.

Your Mind has increased to rank 174. Other modifiers: +12 from items. Available ability slots: 18.

Phew, that's everything, I thought. Closing my eyes, I lay my head down on my pillow and finally let sleep claim me.

CHAPTER 539: THE NEXT DAY

DAY 2 OF MICHAEL'S DEADLINE

Ghost has manifested.

Ghost awoke early the next morning, well-rested and eager to get going, and I reluctantly dragged myself out of bed at her insistence. I was still yawning, though, as we reached the center of the cave.

To my surprise, the area had been transformed, and where yesterday there had been only a single firepit, today there were three raised fire-beds.

"What are those?" Ghost asked, curiously eyeing the contraptions made out of bone, metal, and stone. About hip height, they were filled with brightly burning coals, atop which a line of cauldrons bubbled merrily.

"They're... for cooking, I think," I replied.

"Look who is awake," Shael said, looking up from one of the bubbling pots. "Have a seat, Anriq will bring you some food in a jiffy."

I glanced from the scowling werewolf—he looked none too happy to have been conscripted as a waiter—to the large bone table on the left. Adriel and Safyre were seated there, eating their own breakfast. They were not alone either. Behind the pair, seeming to chat idly amongst themselves, were the nagians.

And not just the three I'd met last night, but another seven too.

That makes ten possessed already rehomed, I thought with a pleased smile. *Adriel looks set to finish on time.* Nodding in acknowledgment to Shael, I made my way to the table.

"Are those the ones you told me about?" Ghost asked from beside me.

The nagians, I noticed, were looking our way now, and as many eyes were upon the pyre wolf as me. *"Yes. They're the former possessed."*

"Can we trust them?" she asked, making no effort to conceal the suspicion in her voice.

"That's what you're going to have to determine." I couldn't do so myself, not even with blood puppet. Questioning two golems a day—the maximum I could enslave in a day—would simply take too long. *"We'll deal with them after breakfast,"* I said, reaching the table and sitting down.

Safyre looked up from her bowl. "Morning," she said tiredly.

Returning her greeting, I glanced at Adriel. She, too, had dark circles under her eyes. I winced, knowing my tight timetable was to blame. "Long night?"

"Yes," Adriel replied simply.

I glanced at the silently watching nagians. "You've made good progress, I see."

The lich nodded.

"Any problems?" I asked.

Adriel shrugged. "None that bear mentioning. You will have your hundred golems, and with time to spare." She looked over her shoulder. "They are well-suited to fighting in the nether."

Lucius bowed. "You do excellent work, as always, Adriel."

A smile peeked through the lich's weary expression. "And you, my friend, have not changed. Still a flatterer, I see."

The golem laughed.

"Lucius is right," I said, ignoring the banter. "You've outdone yourself once again, Adriel."

She inclined her head, accepting the praise.

I glanced around. "Where are the Pack elders?"

"Still resting," Safyre answered. "We wore them out yesterday, I'm afraid."

"Oh." I bit my lip, wondering if the elders would be able to continue today, and if not, what it would mean for our schedule.

"Don't worry," Safyre said, sensing my concern. "Sulan and Duggar have come up with a workaround. Oursk and some of the other wolves will assist with operating the Rings today. We'll make the deadline."

"Ah. That's good."

Adriel stirred her bowl listlessly. "How did your own tasks go yesterday?"

"The stygian's siege of the Draven portal has been lifted," I reported. "The overlord's escorts have been defeated and the Power itself is fleeing north."

"Fleeing?" Adriel asked, looking up in surprise.

I nodded. "Correct. It refused to engage me at all."

Safyre's eyes narrowed. "What do you make of that?"

"There's only one possible explanation," I replied grimly, then went on to relay my thoughts on the matter. "Not only must we assume the stygians are in constant communication with one another," I concluded, "but we must also expect them to adapt quickly to any future tactics we employ."

"Damn," Adriel muttered as Anriq set a bowl down in front of me.

"Damn indeed," I agreed.

"What about your new form?" Safyre asked. A teasing note entered her voice as she glanced at the werewolf standing behind me. "Anriq couldn't stop gushing over it."

"I wasn't gushing," he replied stiffly.

Adriel raised one eyebrow. "Then what would you call it?"

"I..." Flushing red, the youth ran aground.

Chuckling, I came to his rescue. "Oh, it performed admirably." I took a sip of Shael's broth. It was surprisingly excellent. "In fact," I went on, dabbing my lip, "I expect my wolf form will prove instrumental in today's battle."

The gazes of both women slid my way. "What battle?" Adriel asked warily.

"The one against the overlord, of course," I replied. "We can still intercept it before it reaches the stygian nest in the north." If that's where it was going. I had only conjecture to go on, but I didn't think I was mistaken about the stygian Power's destination.

Safyre and Adriel exchanged glances. "Shouldn't we leave well enough alone?" the aetherist asked. "I mean if it's retreating..."

"No," I replied firmly. "The overlord has to die." I held her gaze. "And you know why."

Biting her lip, Safyre looked away.

"Are you sure about this?" Adriel asked. "You said yourself the stygians are adapting. What if—"

"The tactics we employ will be different this time," I interjected.

The lich didn't look reassured. "But what if something goes wrong?" She gestured to the Astral Rings at the far end of the cave. "I won't be able to break off the rehoming ritual and come to your aid." She frowned. "If you're dead set on going ahead, maybe it's better if I accompany Safyre and you."

I shook my head. "That won't be necessary." I glanced behind her. "And besides, we won't be alone."

Adriel took my meaning at once. "You will take the nagians with you?"

I sensed Lucius, Bacheus, Zekiel, and the others stiffen with interest, but it was to Adriel whom I directed my response. "Yes."

"So soon?" she asked.

Although she didn't elaborate further, I knew what she'd left unsaid: did I trust the former possessed enough to take them into battle?

"They will have to prove themselves first, of course," I said, addressing the nagians directly this time.

"How?" Zekiel asked, stepping forward eagerly.

I pointed to Ghost. "Pass her truth test."

Bacheus' gaze fixed on the pyre wolf. "Your familiar is a truthsayer?"

"You could say that," I replied. "Answer all my questions forthrightly and without deceit while Ghost probes your thoughts, and I promise that not only will you have my trust, but you will also be treated as full and valued members of the Forerunners." Scanning the nagians' faces, I tried to gauge their reaction, but their expressions remained as opaque as ever. "Do we have a deal?"

Lucius nodded. "Yes."

I rose to my feet. "Good, then let's be about it. We still have a battle to fight today."

*　*　*

You have accepted Lucius, a non-player, into the Forerunners faction.
You have accepted Bacheus, a non-player, into the Forerunners faction.
You have accepted Zekiel, a non-player, into the Forerunners faction.
...
...

All ten nagians passed Ghost's test, which was hardly surprising given that Adriel had started with those she deemed most trustworthy. After I took their oaths, we went over my plan for the overlord.

"So what does everyone think?" I asked when I was done.

"It's a bit unorthodox," Bacheus admitted.

"But a sound plan nonetheless," Zekiel added.

Lucius nodded. "We can make it work."

I glanced at Safyre, Shael, and Anriq. The bard and werewolf would also be joining us on today's venture—more for the experience than anything else. Only Adriel—who was already hard at work rehoming more possessed—was staying behind with the wolves.

Safyre cast me a wry look. "Don't look at us. We're well-used to these crazy schemes of yours by now."

I threw her an answering grin. "Good, then since we're all agreed, let me get going."

"One second," the aetherist said, holding out her hand. "Before you leave, put this on."

Curiously, I took the pair of items she held out for me. The first was familiar, the second less so.

You have acquired a <u>Forerunner bracelet</u> from the council farspeaker set.

You have acquired a <u>Forerunner collar</u> from the council farspeaker set.

Both the collar and bracelet may only be worn by members of the Forerunner faction. Likewise, only faction members may discern their properties.

"You did it!" I exclaimed. "You faction-locked them! How?"

Safyre smiled. "I had some help," she said, glancing at Bacheus. "He is quite the enchanter."

The nagian bowed. "You honor me, milady."

I shook my head, bemused. "But why change this one into a collar? I don't need a separate device for my wolf form. My equipped items still—"

Safyre laughed. "It's not for you!"

"Not for me?" Finally, realizing what she meant, I glanced at the pyre wolf at my side. "It's for Ghost?"

"Correct," she replied. "While technically Ghost is not a player, as your familiar she can use Game items, which means she is as capable of joining the farspeaker link as you are."

I rubbed my chin. "That makes... sense, actually."

"Of course it does," Safyre said with a grin. Kneeling before Ghost, she held out her hand for the collar. "May I?"

Handing it back to her, I watched as Safyre gently clasped the device around the pyre wolf's neck while I put on my own bracelet.

Ghost has unequipped <u>shadow's friend</u> and has equipped a <u>Forerunner collar</u>, joining the council farspeaker link.

You have unequipped a Sintar bracelet and have equipped a <u>Forerunner bracelet</u>, joining the council farspeaker link.

Almost on the exact instant, the bracelet closed around my arm, a mindvoice, shockingly loud, reverberated across the farspeaker link.

"THANK YOU, SAFYRE!"

Across from me, I noticed Shael and Anriq wince. They, too, it seemed, had the modified bracelets. Safyre, though, betrayed no adverse reaction to the pyre wolf's exuberant words.

"You're welcome, Ghost," she said softly. *"It's nice to finally hear you."*

"And you too!" the pyre wolf replied, her tail wagging furiously. *"Can you believe this, Prime? I can finally talk to everyone!"*

"Almost everyone," I corrected gently. Being non-players, neither the nagians nor Adriel could use the farspeaker link, but the lich already had her own means of communicating with Ghost, and I suspected some of the nagians were equally capable of telepathic communication.

Which reminds me.

"Did any of you overhear that?" I asked aloud, and even though I'd directed the question to the nagians at large, it was Zekiel on whom my gaze rested. As a psi knight, he'd no doubt invested heavily in psi skills.

The nagian did not miss my look. "I presume you mean the mental conversation you and the others just conducted over your farspeaker link?"

I nodded mutely.

"I did not," Zekiel replied.

Shael frowned. "Then how did you know they were speaking?"

Glancing at him, the golem shrugged. "I guessed. The farspeaker bracelets and the Wolf's earlier words made it obvious what was going on." He turned back to me. "You are worried about how secure your farspeaker link is?"

"I am," I admitted.

"Don't be," Bacheus said firmly. "All farspeaker bracelets are sophisticated magical devices. Penetrating their protections requires a telepathy skill of at least tier seven."

My brows furrowed. "Tier seven? That's a—"

"—Power-level skill," Zekiel finished for me. "Which is why the risk of being overheard is minimal. Even amongst the new Powers, I imagine, there can't be many capable of eavesdropping on a farspeaker link."

Ghost who up to this point had only been following the conversation with half an ear sat up attentively. *"But didn't you overhear those two thieves' mental sending, Prime?"* she asked, confused. *"How did you manage that?"*

It was the exact same question I was pondering.

"Are you sure—" I began, then closed my mouth as realization set in. My baseline telepathy was only at tier five, but I also had an almost-forgotten trait that boosted its power by forty percent.

The mental focus trait. That's how I did it.

Running some quick calculations in my mind, I realized my effective telepathy had likely already been in the low three hundreds at the time.

Damn. No wonder, I managed to eavesdrop on Sintar's farspeaker link.

Safyre lay a hand on my arm, dragging me away from my musings. "Michael? Is everything alright?"

I smiled to show her it was. "Sorry, just got a bit distracted there." I handed her the old, unenchanted farspeaker bracelet. "I suppose you'll want this?"

She nodded. "Yes. Bacheus and I will modify it tonight and add it to the new council network."

"Well then," I said, turning about to address everyone, "now that we've got all that out of the way, shall we begin?"

There were no objections.

I glanced back at Safyre. "Then if it pleases you, milady," I said in a teasing tone that mimicked Bacheus' earlier words, "open the portal, and I'll be on my way."

CHAPTER 540: IT TAKES TWO HANDS

You have taken the form of a level 252 elder wolf.
Passage completed!

I emerged from Safyre's portal crouched on all fours and with my senses trained for danger.

But the area was empty.

"Looks like we're alone," I murmured to Ghost.

"I'll tell the others," she replied eagerly.

Smiling to myself, I let her. The rest of the battle party was still in the cave. They would only join Ghost and myself later—assuming we located the overlord, of course.

"We've reached the portal to Draven's Reach," Ghost reported formally over the farspeaker link. *"There is no sign of any stygians."*

"Thank you, Ghost," Safyre replied solemnly. *"Message received. Let us know if anything changes."*

Ghost preened under the aetherist's praise. *"I'll do that, Safyre,"* she said gravely.

My mouth dropping open in a wolfish smile, I orientated myself northward. That was the direction the overlord had last been heading in. *"C'mon,"* I told her over our private link, *"let's go find our prey."*

*   *   *

Traveling in wolf form was infinitely easier than walking on two legs, and the miles flew by as Ghost and I set off in pursuit of the stygian Power. The journey was by and large easy, the only complication being crossing the river.

As near as I could tell, the river was sector 18,240's only major waterway and neatly split the region down the middle. It extended all the way from the stygian nest in the north to the Draven gate in the south. Still, Ghost and I managed the river crossing without undue difficulty, after which we raced northward once more.

Ghost kept her nose trained to the ground in the hopes of picking up a scent, while I kept my own gaze fixed skyward. The hours passed with little talking and, for the most part, we encountered nothing living—either stygian or otherwise.

Just past noon, as my concern mounted that I'd underestimated the overlord's speed and would need to use the Sylvana Eye to run it down after all, I spotted a dark smudge in the distance. Reaching out with my will, I inspected the distant form.

The target is a level 309 stygian overlord.

I padded to a halt.

"What is it?" Ghost asked, staring blankly into the mists.

"We've found it," I replied. *"Tell the others."*

"Is it alone?" Safyre asked, after Ghost relayed her report.

"The overlord's escorts are still with it," I answered. *"But I can't quite make out their number from here. I'm going to go closer for a better look."*

"Be careful," she added unnecessarily.

"I will," I replied. Drawing psi, I cast my buffs while I waited for Ghost to disassociate.

Ghost has unmanifested.
You have cast enhanced reflexes, vanish, and trigger-cast quick mend.

Moments later, invisible and alone, I dashed forward again.

✳   ✳   ✳

The overlord was not taking any chances.

It floated more than three thousand feet above the surface, well beyond the previous range of my shadow blink. Standing almost beneath the Power, I peered upward, counting the smaller forms latched onto its shell.

"I can make out one hundred flying serpents," I reported over the farspeaker link. *"It doesn't appear as if the nest has sent any reinforcements."*

"That sounds promising," Safyre replied, the relief in her mindvoice evident.

"There are large swaths of the overlord's body that I can't see from down here," I warned. *"My count may be off."*

Safyre sighed. *"Understood."*

I sympathized with her frustration, but sadly there was nothing I could do to alleviate it—not until I walked upon the overlord myself. *"Is everyone ready?"*

"They are."

"Initiating phase two then." Not waiting for Safyre's response, I turned tail and headed for the crevice I'd spotted on the way over. Diving within, I wrapped myself in shadows and began to shift.

You have cast shapeshift.

Ideally, I would've wanted to make my way onto the overlord while still in wolf form, but for many reasons, that was not a good idea. Once I reached the overlord, I would need access to both my traps and consumables.

And that meant shifting.

Unfortunately, unlike a werewolf's shift, my own transformation was neither quick nor easy. Mid-shift, I was blind to the world and achingly vulnerable—neither were conditions I could afford while standing upon an enemy Power.

No, the best place to undergo a change was on the ground and in the embrace of my shadows.

You have taken the form of a level 252 human. Further shifting is not possible until your next sleep cycle.

Gingerly picking myself up from the sprawl I'd ended up in, I renewed my buffs and climbed out of the crevice. Glancing up, I relocated the stygian overlord. Its position had barely changed.

"Michael?" Safyre called. *"Are you in place?"*

"Not yet," I replied. *"There is one more precaution I need to take."* Reaching into my pocket, I withdrew a small, rune-inscribed object—the Seeking Eye of Sylvana.

I'd not used the legendary artifact myself, but Anriq who had had plenty of practice with the device had shared what he'd learned about its operation. Closing my fist around the Eye, I brought it to life.

You have activated a Seeking Eye.
To enable all tracking features, provide the spirit signature or mental imprint of the target.

Focusing on the overlord in the distance, I inspected it while simultaneously willing my intent to the gray orb in my hand.

Target identified.
Analyzing a level 309 stygian overlord...
...

...
Failed to acquire a mental imprint. The target's consciousness is shielded. Tracking this target's mindglow is not possible.
Spirit signature acquired. Ready to spirit track.

I stowed the artifact in my pocket again. Now, even if the overlord somehow managed to escape, we'd be able to run it down wherever it fled to in the sector. It would've been better if I could've also used the Eye to watch over us during the battle, but unfortunately, the orb did not possess nethersight.

I'll just have to remember to stay on the lookout for trouble myself. Unsheathing my blades, I wove psi. It was time to move.

"Blinking in," I reported back and stepped into the aether.

✴ ✴ ✴

You have teleported onto the surface of a level 309 stygian overlord. You are hidden.

I emerged on a familiar pockmarked landscape, crouched, and prepared for anything. But my arrival point was well chosen, and none of the overlord's escorts were close enough to be of immediate threat—even if they could see me.

Exhaling slowly, I rose to my feet. *"I'm in position,"* I said over the farspeaker link, *"and so far, all appears—"*

An unknown entity has detected you! You are no longer hidden.
You have failed to detect an unknown entity.

I broke off, less than pleased by the Game alert, but before I had time to fully process it, more messages followed.

A level 309 stygian overlord has detected you.
A level 162 flying serpent has detected you.
A level 140 flying serpent has…
…
…

Swallowing bile, I banished the near-endless litany of alerts that followed. It didn't take any great powers of deduction to figure out what had happened either.

There was a stygian spore about.

Not only had the damnable creature's truesight penetrated my stealth—invisibility notwithstanding—its aura was *also* allowing the nearby stygians to do the same. Thankfully, though, I hadn't forgotten about my earlier run-ins with the things.

And while I hadn't thought it likely spores would be accompanying the overlord, I hadn't discounted the possibility that they might either. Then, too, this time around I was carrying a piece of equipment that I hadn't had the last time.

It might make all the difference. Pivoting on my heel, and ignoring the rousing serpents, I scanned the vicinity.

The area ahead was clear.

As was my left flank.

So, too, was the region to my rear.

And on my right…

You have failed to detect an unknown entity.

I sighed, disheartened by the repeated failure. It seemed that not even Sintar's tier five true-seeing ring was good enough to pierce a spore's invisibility. Now, I had no choice but to abandon the slow, careful approach and to speed things up.

"Saf, we're going to Plan C," I ordered in a clipped tone as I re-sheathed my swords.

"Acknowledged," she replied crisply. *"We're waiting to come through."*

I turned my attention inward. *"Ghost, I need you."*

"Already manifesting," she replied.

Leaving her to it, I withdrew a portal scroll from my pocket. It was time to call in reinforcements. Cracking open the scroll, I drew on my magic and began feeding mana into it.

Item activated.

Around the corner of my eye, I spotted motion. Wings were snapping out to my right, to my left, and in front of me. Everywhere really. The overlord's escorts were going airborne.

I couldn't afford to worry about the creatures just yet though. Ghost would have to keep them at bay until I opened the portal.

Ghost has cast explosive manifest.

The pyre wolf coalesced in a blaze of glory twenty yards away, causing flames to belch out and engulf the three serpents rushing at me from behind.

Ghost has taken the form of a level 252 stygian pyre wolf.
3 of 3 hostile entities have been critically injured.
A level 309 stygian overlord has cast <u>tentacle guard</u>.

I grunted, not bothered by the threat posed by the flying serpents so much as I was by the last message. The stygian Power was already reacting to our incursion.

"The overlord has awakened its tentacles," I informed Safyre even as I funneled more mana into the spelled parchment in my hands. *"You know what comes next."*

"We'll be ready," she promised.

Ahead of me, two flying serpents appeared, skimming low above the overlord's surface. They were going to reach me before I was done. *"Damn,"* I muttered. *"Ghost, can you—"*

"I'll deal with them," she interrupted.

"Thank you," I replied fervently while I tried to force mana into the scroll at an even greater rate. But it was no use. The item would charge only so fast, and the spellcasting would take as long as it needed.

A level 309 stygian overlord has cast the composite spell, <u>shield of nether</u>.

I sighed. I'd known the spell was coming, of course, and while it bothered me little, my allies would need to take greater care. *Let's hope they really are ready,* I thought grimly.

My gaze flickered back to Ghost.

Despite their best efforts, the incoming serpents had failed to evade her. The first stygian lay dead beneath her paws, while the second—stunned and dazed—was still trying to pick itself up from where it had been forced aground.

The pyre wolf had dealt admirably with the initial threats. But wherever I looked more threats were appearing—far too many for Ghost to deal with.

A greater portal scroll has been fully charged.

"Finally!" I exclaimed, almost shuddering in relief. For a moment, I'd feared I had miscalculated, and Ghost and I would be forced to retreat before I was done, but despite the spores' surprise appearance, my plan was coming together nicely.

And though the overlord didn't know it yet, its fate was already written.

Releasing the scroll's enchantment, I directed its spell weaves to the cave where the others awaited.

You have opened a greater portal inside sector 18,240.

This portal is large enough for 4 entities to pass through and will remain open for a maximum of 30 seconds.

No sooner was the portal up, than someone stepped through—Safyre. Barely pausing to acknowledge me, she cast.

Safyre has cast purifying dome.
You have entered a purifying field. All environmental ill-effects have been nullified.

The three nagian captains followed on Safyre's heels, each with their own carefully prepared spells at the ready.
And they, too, wasted no time, releasing them.

Lucius has cast <u>warding web</u>.
Warding web is a spell that entangles all hostiles coming in contact with it within a cocoon of silk.

Sticky white strands exploded outward from the nagian to enclose our small party in a dome of silk strands that appeared deceptively delicate.

Zekiel has cast <u>levitating disc</u>.

Air solidified beneath my feet. But unlike my own windborne, the psi knight's spell was a persistent one that formed a circular cushion of air large enough to levitate the entire party three feet above the overlord.

Bacheus has cast <u>supreme portal</u>.

A second luminous doorway appeared. It had fallen to the nagian sorcerer to bring in the rest of our waiting allies—Shael and Anriq included. Sadly, my own portal was not up to the task of transporting so many.
Spinning away, I drew my blades. My own part in securing the party's entry was done. Safyre and the others would see to it that the rest of the defenses were erected, leaving me free to help Ghost.
My familiar was all alone outside Lucius' web and could do with some help.
"Coming to you, Ghost," I said and shadow blinked into battle.

Chapter 541: Passing on the Torch

Shael has begun playing <u>Shaten's Call to War</u>.

Under the inspiring notes of the bard's song, Ghost and I roved across the overlord's pockmarked surface, killing serpents and tentacles alike with abandon.

In doing so, we ensured Anriq and Zekiel—who were guarding the party's perimeter from inside Lucius' web—were not swamped. Safyre and the other nine nagians, meanwhile, had turned their attention downwards—to the overlord's shell.

Working together, the ten forerunners punched a hole through the Power's thick hide faster than I'd anticipated, and in short order, I had damage messages scrolling through my mind.

"Excellent work, Saf," I said as I bobbed beneath a slashing tentacle and punctured a hole through a nearby serpent.

"Thanks," she replied tiredly. *"It won't be long now."*

"Just make sure you get in the last hit," I warned.

"I will," she answered, *"although I am still not convinced of the wisdom of that."*

The whole point of this entire exercise was making Safyre a Powerful Initiate.

Admittedly, I'd been tempted to kill the overlord myself, and perhaps even to attempt another solo run. It would've quite possibly earned me another feat and would have almost certainly caused my Power Mark to evolve.

But as important as it was for me to get stronger, it was equally important for the Forerunners to add another Power to our ranks. If nothing else, it would secure our budding House's future. Then, too, with two Powers to lead the faction, so much more became possible.

And when it came right down to it, there was no one I trusted more than Safyre with custodianship of the Forerunners.

"It's necessary," I replied gently, understanding the source of her self-doubts. As a Forcesworn, Safyre could not acquire any blood memories. Worse still, as a forsworn, she had been stripped of her Force abilities and couldn't use soulbound items.

All of which were undoubtedly debilitating restrictions.

Yet Adriel believed some—if not all—of Safyre's constraints would fall away if she transitioned into a Power. It was only guesswork on the lich's part, but Adriel didn't consider Safyre's status as a forsworn compatible with the Powerful Initiate Mark.

After all, Safyre had only become a forsworn after betraying the Power she followed. And Safyre's status as a former Sworn would no longer be relevant once she became a Power. Still, there was no certainty the Adjudicator would see it that way, which was why Adriel predicted one of two things would happen.

Either Safyre gained a Power Mark and lost her forsworn status.

Or the Game would prevent her from becoming a Powerful Initiate.

There was only one way to know for certain which way the chips would fall, though—and that was for Safyre to evolve.

"But the risk—" Safyre began.

"What risk?" I interrupted as I charmed one pack of serpents and paralyzed another. *"There's none."*

"You're oversimplifying matters," she accused. *"If I slay the overlord and fail to acquire the Mark, then the kill will be wasted. And not just any kill, a* Power *kill, Michael. Can we afford that?"*

"Don't worry," I replied airily—more to assuage her doubts than because I believed the loss negligible—*"there are plenty more stygian Powers to go around."*

Safyre sighed, and not in concession of the point. This was an old argument, one we had hashed out a few times already, and we always came back to the same point—the potential rewards were worth the risk.

A level 309 stygian overlord is near death.

Even mid-fight, I paused on receipt of the Game message. *"Saf...."*

"I've got it too. The others have backed off." She sighed again. *"Alright, here goes."*

Safyre has cast aether bolt.
Safyre has cast aether bolt.
...

...

Safyre has killed a level 309 stygian overlord!

✳   ✳   ✳

You have teleported into Anriq's shadow.

The overlord fell, but the rest of us did not.

Held aloft by Zekiel's levitating disc, we watched the few remaining flying serpents flee north—and back to the stygian nest, presumably.

"That's the most one-sided battle I've ever been in," Lucius said as he and the other nagians walked up to join me.

Bacheus shook his head. "And against a Power too."

Only half-listening, I nodded absently. I'd not even taken the time to check my own battle messages from the Game. Instead, I kept my gaze trained on Safyre, keenly searching for some clue as to the outcome of our gambit.

"Did it work?" Anriq asked, realizing what the source of my preoccupation was.

"I'm not sure," I replied, biting my lip. Safyre's eyes were still closed, and her attention was turned inward.

"I'm sure it did," Shael said, in what was an obvious attempt to be reassuring.

Leaving the others behind, I strode closer to the aetherist.

"We'll make sure the area remains secure," Zekiel called after me.

"Do that," I replied, not bothering to mention that Ghost had already assigned herself the selfsame task. "Saf?" I murmured as I drew to a stop before her.

"Check your alerts," she whispered back, not opening her eyes.

Right on cue, a new message buzzed for attention.

The player, Safyre, wishes to temporarily share her Game messages with you. Do you accept?

Despite my surprise at the unexpected request, I wasted no time in replying in the affirmative.

Your fellow Forerunner, Safyre, has slain her first tier 7 creature and accomplished the feat: <u>A Mighty Player</u>! Requirements: be unsworn to any Power, possess an evolved Class, and reach player level 250. Or be unsworn to any Power, possess an evolved Class, and slay a foe above level 300. Her spirit signature has been etched with a new Mark!

Safyre has acquired the Mark: <u>Powerful Initiate</u> and has begun to tread the ways of Power herself. The path to greatness is paved by death, and no player can rise to prominence in the Game without pitting herself against its strongest contenders. She has done so and emerged victorious.

Safyre is no longer forsworn! For achieving a Power Mark, her former misdeeds have been forgiven, and she has regained 1 greater and 2 lesser Force abilities. Note, however, that any further transgressions will result in more severe punishment.

I drew in a sharp breath. "It worked. It actually worked!" I could hardly believe it, Safyre was a Power now!

"You sound surprised," Safyre said, a radiant smile on her face.

"Say elated rather," I quipped. We had little time to savor the moment further, though.

More Game alerts were vying for Safyre's attention.

As a result of Safyre's new Power Mark, she has gained the trait: <u>Higher Evolution</u>. This is a trait granted to all would-be Powers and allows her to evolve beyond the limits imposed on ordinary players.

Safyre is ready to experience her first higher evolution. As the bearer of both a Supreme Light Mark and a Powerful Initiate one, she may acquire an epic Class.

Higher evolution commencing...

...

...

Analysis of Safyre's player Marks completed. Viable ascendant paths determined. Three new paths lie before her.

The first path is that of a <u>Maverick Light</u> and will grant her the ascendant trait, <u>champion</u>. As a champion, the power of all her Force abilities will be doubled. She will also gain 30 attribute points and may choose 1 additional benefit unique to her chosen Class.

The second path is that of a <u>Light Crusader</u> and will grant her the ascendant trait, <u>commander</u>. As a commander, she can share weaker variants of her Force abilities with those who follow her. She will also gain 20 attribute points and may choose 1 additional benefit unique to her chosen Class.

The third path is that of a <u>Bastion of Light</u> and will grant her the ascendant trait, <u>governor</u>. As a governor, she gains access to a unique branch of Force abilities that focuses on sector-wide buffs and spells. She will also gain 20 attribute points and may choose 1 additional benefit unique to her chosen Class.

"Which should I choose?" Safyre asked softly, her gaze still turned inward.

"The choice is yours as always," I replied cautiously and though I was tempted to add a 'but,' I left it at that.

This decision was for Safyre alone to make.

Safyre's lips bent upward in another smile. "Now why did I know you were going to say that?" Before I could respond, she went on, "but I know what to choose. There is only one option that serves the faction best."

A moment later, another series of Game messages unfurled before me.

Safyre's higher evolution has been completed. She is now a bastion of light.

Safyre has gained the base trait: <u>governor</u>. As a governor, she gains access to a powerful branch of Light spells that only Lightsworn governors may acquire, the first of which may be chosen now.

Safyre has gained the epic Class, <u>Bastion of Light</u>.
Those who fight for the Light are legion. This has always been Light's strength. Where Darksworn often fight alone or in small groups, Light's soldiers invariably rally together when threatened. As a Bastion of Light, Safyre gains access to an array of abilities that allow her to summon her allies—wherever they may be in the Kingdom or Nethersphere—to aid in the defense of the faction's territories.

Safyre has accomplished the feat: <u>Ascending to New Heights!</u> Requirement: acquire her first ascendant Class. She has been awarded 2 additional lives!

Safyre has accomplished the feat: <u>Eager for Power!</u> Requirement: adopt an ascendant Class before reaching level 250. Not many in the Game dare to assume a Mark of Power early. As a reward for Safyre's brave choice, she has been awarded the trait: <u>Driven Force</u>. This trait grants her 1 additional attribute point every two player levels.

Safyre is now a rank 1 Bastion of Light and may choose 1 new ascendant trait and 1 new governor ability.
New trait: <u>aware bastion</u>. This trait places a permanent sector-wide ward over one of your faction's owned sectors. You will be immediately alerted to any portal openings in the sector.

New trait: <u>bastion of healing</u>. This trait bestows one of your owned sectors with a permanent sector-wide buff that increases the health regeneration of all faction members in the sector by +0.25% per second.

New trait: <u>blighted bastion</u>. This trait curses one of your owned sectors with a permanent sector-wide debuff that drains the stamina of all hostiles in the sector by 0.1% per second.

New governor ability: <u>call to arms</u>. This ability allows you to recall a maximum of 10 allies from anywhere in the Forever Kingdom to defend your sector.

New governor ability: <u>archon summoning</u>. This ability lets your envoy manifest 6 lesser aspects of yourself to defend your territories.

New governor ability: <u>eternal light</u>. This ability enables you to summon 30 light wisp lords to defend your sector.

"Wow," I gasped.

I'd been somewhat dismissive of the governor path during my own higher evolutions, but seeing the choices the Adjudicator had provided Safyre with, I realized a governor was every bit as powerful as a commander or champion, and gave new meaning to the term 'home advantage.'

And this time around, I had no compunction about advising Safyre. "You definitely want call to arms," I said.

She nodded. "I agree."

I rubbed my chin. "As to the traits... I can see benefits to all of them."

She sighed. "Yes, but the sticking point is that we have to *claim* a sector first."

I couldn't disagree. "Given that we intend on installing a shield generator here, I'd say it's a toss-up between bastion of healing or blighted bastion." I paused. "Personally, if I had a choice between buffing our allies or debuffing the enemy, I'd go with the buff—who knows what protections our foes will have to negate the debuff."

Safyre pursed her lips. "That's true. In that case, I'll go with bastion of healing and call to arms."

Saying nothing, I waited, and as expected another Game message appeared.

Safyre's ascendant Class upgrade has been completed.

The aetherist opened her eyes. They brimmed with unshed tears. "That's it," she said.

I returned her smile. There was only one thing for me to do. Turning my focus inward for a moment, I willed my intent to the Adjudicator.

As the original founder and leader of the <u>Forerunners</u> faction, you have designated Safyre as its co-leader. She has now the same breadth of faction powers as you, is able to appoint officers on her own, and is also able to recruit others into the faction.

My smile widened. "Now we are truly on our way to becoming a House to be reckoned with."

It was only much later, when we were safely back on the ground, that I thought to check my own Game messages.

You and Ghost have reached level 254!
Your light armor has reached rank 18, and your telepathy rank 23.
Ghost's stygian claws have reached rank 14 and her nether manipulation rank 7.

Congratulations, Michael, your faction has gained its second ascendant player! The number of sectors your faction may own has increased to 3.
Your task: <u>Found a new House</u>! has been updated. Safyre, a Lightsworn Power has joined your burgeoning House. Revised objective: Convince 1 other Power not of Wolf blood to join your House. Note: completion of this task may have unpredictable consequences.

Ghost and I had only gained two levels from the battle, less than everyone else involved. *"Ah well,"* I remarked to my familiar. *"That's to be expected. In the end, the others did most of the damage."*

She bobbed her head. *"I'm happy for Safyre."*

I nodded. *"Me too."* I glanced across at the aetherist. Safyre, understandably, was still coming to terms with her new status, and right now her whole focus was turned inward, exploring her new Class, traits, and abilities. Reaching out with my will, I analyzed her anew.

The target is Safyre, a level 217 human aetherist and Bastion of Light. She bears a Mark of Supreme Light, a Mark of a Powerful Initiate, and is Lightsworn.

A Bastion of Light, I mused. Safyre had become more deeply entrenched in Light than I'd expected, and while it did not unsettle me, the same could not be said for the nagians.

The former possessed had withdrawn into their own circle a few yards away, and every now and again, one of them would shoot nervous glances at Safyre. I did not begrudge them their anxiety. The world they came from was different. In *their* minds, the new Powers were persecutors and destroyers.

And while not much had changed in the present day, the fault did not lie with the new Powers' Force affiliations. No, it was the enmity that existed between the two groups—new Powers and old—that was the cause of the ancient strife.

New Powers and Primes *could* work together, I was sure of it. And if anyone was able to demonstrate that fact to our allies and enemies alike it would be Safyre and I.

They will learn, I thought.

In the meantime, it had become even more imperative that we claimed sector 18,240. With Safyre as its governor, and an Aether Cloaking device for protection, the sector would assure the future of the Forerunners. *We're so close.*

But we were not there yet.

And there were still some fairly hefty obstacles in the way. Sighing anew, I left off my musings and turned my thoughts back to more immediate concerns—like investing my new attribute points.

Your Mind has increased to rank 178. Other modifiers: +12 from items. Available ability slots: 22.

"So what now?" Ghost asked when I opened my eyes again.

I glanced from the scattered remains of the stygians to the rest of the party. *"First, we loot the corpses."*

"And then?" Ghost prompted.

"And then..." I paused, exhaling heavily. Once we took the next step, there was going to be no turning back. But we couldn't back down now. *"And then,"* I repeated, *"we decide who goes where."*

✳   ✳   ✳

Your alchemy stone is full.

I grimaced at the Adjudicator's message. It had come too early for my liking. I was only little more than halfway done looting the stygians. Sadly, the rest of the reagents would have to languish where they lay.

It's just as well I am returning to Nexus soon, I thought as I bent down.

You have retrieved an alchemy stone. New ingredients acquired: 116 x vial of nether residue. Total stored ingredients: 500 / 500.

Straightening again, I idly scanned my surroundings. Bits and pieces of the overlord's shell lay everywhere—but only of its shell, the rest of the creature had seeped into the ground already.

I had spent some time idly picking through the Power's remains, but I'd found nothing of value. It was like Adriel had said, the overlord corpses were useless.

Which was unfortunate. I'd been hoping to find more netherstones. Adriel had disabused me of that notion, too, but that hadn't stopped me from wishing she was wrong.

It turned out that harbingers were the only void creatures that could freely travel from sector to sector *without* using a rift. And that was why they were the only stygians to yield netherstones.

I sighed. Still, I had the one stone already. It would have to do.

"Michael, are you done?" Safyre asked across the farspeaker link. *"Everyone's waiting."*

"Coming," I replied. Turning around, I fixed my gaze on the party and shadow blinked.

You have teleported into Safyre's shadow.

No one appeared surprised at my appearance in their midst. They were well-used to my sudden comings and goings by now.

"Good, you're here," Shael said. "Let's head back to base."

I shook my head. "We're not returning to the cave."

The bard blinked. "Not even for a short nap? But I'm tired."

"You'll manage," I replied, ruthlessly squashing his objections. I turned to Safyre. "Open the portal."

Already knowing our next destination, she gave a clipped nod.

Safyre has opened a greater portal inside sector 18,240.

❋ ❋ ❋

Safyre's portal didn't take us far.

In fact, we covered only a few dozen miles with it, but it beat walking. Striding forward, I placed myself squarely in front of the other portal we'd arrived at—the dungeon entrance of Draven's Reach.

Turning around, I addressed the others. "This is it, people; this is where we commit fully. No matter the precautions we take, once our allies emerge from Draven's Reach, the possibility exists that someone will notice their sudden appearance in the Eastern Marches. It may take weeks, or even months, for anyone to connect the dots thereafter, but eventually, the new Powers will realize the dungeon is still active. And you can bet everything you own that the Reach will pique the interest of every high-level player who hears about it. They will not rest until they find a way inside."

I inhaled deeply. "But like I said, discovery is only a possibility, and whether or not it materializes is out of our hands. Still, we should be prepared for the worst—and the worst is that the secret of the Forerunners' existence will get out."

I paused to survey the faces arrayed around me and to reinforce the gravity of the situation. "Before this happens, before the forerunners are discovered, or Draven's Reach is, we have to isolate sector 18,240 from the rest of the Game. No one that is not a Forerunner must ever be allowed to enter. Failure is *not* an option."

"We understand the stakes, Michael," Safyre said softly.

I nodded. "Then, let's begin." Shifting my stance slightly, I faced the nagians.

Zekiel stepped forward.

Wordlessly, I placed two letters in his waiting palm. The first missive was penned in my own hand and was addressed to Ceruvax. The second was from Adriel and was for Farren.

Both letters bade the Pack of the Reach and the Bane Wolves to abandon the Reach.

"I will not fail you in this, Wolf," Zekiel vowed.

I scrutinized the nagian anew, wondering if I was making the right choice. Zekiel would have to travel the breadth of Draven's Reach to get from the hidden portal to the archlich's court where Ceruvax and the others were encamped.

And he would have to do it alone.

But the psi knight was better suited to this task than almost anyone else. Thanks to his telekinetic skills, he could traverse the dungeon the same way I had and bypass nearly all the elite creatures within.

The other option—and the original plan—had been to send a party so large it would be practically invincible. And while such a party would have little to fear from the Reach's denizens, it would still have to fight the dungeon's elites every step of the way—which would inevitably result in delays.

And delays were the last thing we could afford.

Still, sending Zekiel alone was a risk. Much depended on him safely carrying the messages to their recipients. Then, too, I was also depending on Ceruvax and Farren's foresight. Hopefully, they had already made the necessary preparations and were ready to leave Draven's Reach at a moment's notice.

Because if they hadn't and weren't, it could put all our other plans in jeopardy.

I clasped the psi knight's hands. "Remember speed is of the essence. But so is arriving safely." I smiled to show him I was aware of the inherent conflict between those two imperatives. "Get there fast but get there safely."

The nagian bowed. "I will."

I stepped aside. "Then let me not keep you."

Zekiel flowed forward and without further ceremony vanished into the portal.

Doing my best not to let my worry show, I turned back to Safyre. "Right, that's done. Let's move on."

✳ ✳ ✳

Safyre has opened a greater portal inside sector 18,240.

Once more, we used Safyre's portal to hop across this sector. And once more, we emerged beside another nether portal.

This one led to the Guardian Tower.

Unbidden, Shael and Anriq stepped forward. Their own task was simpler than Zekiel's but no less important. And although the Tower was significantly less dangerous than the Reach, the biggest challenge the pair faced was not the dungeon's denizens—but time.

My gaze came to rest upon the bard. "Are you sure you can do this?"

He nodded stoutly. "I promise I will not be a drag on the werewolf." He eyed his companion sideways. "I may even help speed him along like I said I would." He sighed heavily. "But if I've overestimated my... uhm, resilience, Anriq will leave me behind. We've discussed it already. Neither of us will jeopardize the mission."

I inclined my head in reluctant agreement. The biggest challenge the pair faced would be in getting from the hidden portal in the far north of the tundra to the gateway hundreds of miles to the south. It had taken me many weeks to make the same journey, but then I'd been alone and without guidance of any sort.

Anriq had already made the journey once—in the reverse direction—and he was confident he could do it again, and significantly quicker too. Shael had volunteered to go with the werewolf, claiming he could be of help.

I'd agreed, not so much because I believed the bard's claim, but because once Anriq left the tundra, he would require assistance to get through the next two levels. Neither the wyverns of sector 108 nor the savant grandmaster of sector 109 could be defeated by the werewolf's strength alone.

But I wasn't sending the pair on their own either. They would have help.

Letting my gaze drift beyond the waiting two, I scanned the faces of the nagians. One of them would have to accompany Shael and Anriq. I had not prescribed who it should be, though. That decision was too onerous, and truthfully, it was not mine to make on anyone's behalf.

Bacheus stepped forward. "We've reached consensus amongst ourselves," he stated without preamble, "and for many reasons, we believe I am the one best suited for this task."

I didn't ask him why. The nagians had been briefed on the challenges the trio would face getting to the Guardian Tower's final chamber, and in the short time I'd known him, Bacheus struck me as a more than capable sorcerer.

He would be an asset to the others.

I shook hands with each of them. "Remember, if I am not there in five days, proceed without me."

The trio nodded.

"Then I'll see you three on the other side," I said in farewell.

✳ ✳ ✳

After the trio disappeared through the portal, Safyre turned to me. "I guess we should part ways here as well."

I nodded, not missing the wistful note of regret in her tone. I felt much the same way, but sadly, the time had come for Safyre to reunite with her former forsworn, and it was a journey she best made alone.

"Be careful," I warned.

She smiled. "That's my line." Stepping forward, she drew me into a heartfelt hug.

I allowed myself a moment to savor the feel of her in my arms before pulling back. "You will escort Lucius and others back to the cave first?"

"I will." She smiled. "And I'm sure Adriel will want to hear how the battle went." Her gaze drifted north. "You still intend on revisiting the stygian nest?"

"I must," I replied, knowing she was not in favor of the idea. "Before we launch our assault on the void tree, we have to learn everything we can about the remaining forces it has under its command. And you know I am the best scout we have."

"I do know that." She sighed. "But that doesn't mean I have to like the fact that you insist on endangering yourself time and again."

"I don't do it deliberately!" I objected.

Safyre looked at me reproachfully.

"Not often, anyway," I added weakly, not meeting her gaze.

She paid my protests as much heed as they deserved—which was to say, none at all—and closing her eyes, wove mana.

Safyre has opened a greater portal inside sector 18,240.

"Let's go," the aetherist said, ushering the nagians through. Silently obeying, they stepped through the glowing gateway. Following behind, Safyre paused on the portal's threshold.

"Good luck, Wolf," she called over her shoulder. "And don't do anything foolish."

"I'll try not to." My lips curled upward. "But I can't make any promises."

Safyre laughed. "You're hopeless," she said before stepping forward and vanishing from sight.

The smile still plastered on my face, I stood staring at nothing long after she was gone.

CHAPTER 543: SCOUTING THE ENEMY

Alone once more, but for Ghost resting in her Cloak, I removed an item from my backpack. It was a twelve-hour journey to the stygian nest in the north, and I was not about to waste that much time simply walking.

There were better ways to reach my destination—as Safyre had just demonstrated.

Feeding mana into the portal scroll in my hand, I created a ley line to a spot about an hour away from the nest. The chances were minimal that any stygians were nearby. Even so, my mission was not entirely a stealth one, and it would not unduly trouble me if I was discovered.

The portal snapped open, and I wasted no time in dashing through.

Transfer through portal commencing...

...

...

Passage completed!

I rolled to a stop at the other end. My mindsight was active but no entities—hostile or otherwise—impinged on my awareness. Staying crouched, I turned about in a slow circle.

My natural sight confirmed my mindsight's findings. The area was empty.

Unbending, I rose to my feet. The river—the same river I encountered time and again in the sector—was to my left. It was close enough, in fact, for its waters to lap at my feet. Striding forward, I began my march north. A series of rolling hills lay ahead and, beyond them, was the nest itself.

Won't be long now, I thought.

✳   ✳   ✳

Only dead trees and large boulders inhabited the hills.

There was no path to navigate by and the best route was rarely straight ahead. If not for my nethersight, traversing the area would've been a nightmare. As it was, I managed the journey without mishap and was soon cresting the tallest hill. Dropping down to all fours, I crept forward and peeked down.

Below me, the stygian nest spread out in all its glory.

Little had changed since my last visit. The two overlords accompanying—*protecting?*—the void tree remained ground-bound and puffing out plumes of nether. The void tree itself was as tall and imposing as ever. And the rift... the rift's black depths still fouled the landscape.

Then, too, there were the lesser stygians.

Their numbers had grown to twelve thousand. And they were not all exactly 'lesser' stygians either. Some familiar serpentine shapes were wrapped around the base of the tree.

Nagas. One hundred of them.

I sighed, the forlorn hope I'd been clinging to that our work in the sector had made things easier dying. If anything, the void tree's defenses had improved.

"But we are stronger," Ghost said.

That was true. I'd advanced significantly, and the others were improving too. And then again, we were only on day two of my timetable—which left us six more days to thin the stygians' numbers.

But how best to do that?

Dragging my gaze away from the center of the nest, I took in the rest of the surroundings.

The void's minions had established themselves in a horseshoe-shaped valley bordered by the river on three sides. It was an interesting choice, especially given the stygians' seeming-apathy for water.

Could I use that to my advantage?

Maybe, I thought, biting my lip.

The fourth approach was from the east, and through the very hills I'd just traversed. And while the march itself would prove difficult for a non-player army, any half-decent group of players could teleport directly onto its heights. And once gathered on the hilltops, an attacker would have the advantage of elevation over the stygians in the valley below.

My initial assessment was wrong, I realized. The terrain did *not* make the nest unassailable. Quite the opposite. Given the stygians' peculiarities when it came to water, the terrain actually favored us.

Which begged the question: why had the stygians chosen the location they had?

The nether itself was not mindless, even though many of its minions were. All the stygian Powers I'd run into—void tree, harbinger, and overlords—seemed possessed of a malevolent cunning. They would not have willingly chosen such a patently unfavorable position for the nest.

Unless they were forced to.

Thinking back on the void sapling I'd encountered in Draven's Reach, I realized its position had *also* left much to be desired. So, what had driven the nether's choice there? Proximity to the guardian and... the safe zone.

Hmm. Could that be the answer?

Was the sector's safe zone—former safe zone, rather—located in the valley below?

It wouldn't surprise me if it was. And while that fact did nothing to help my cause, the realization did provide me with a small measure of comfort. The nether had chosen to locate its nest in the valley for no other reason than it had to. Which meant there was nothing to fear from the terrain. In fact, it behooved us to exploit it as much as we could.

We can attack from the hills or from across the river.

With either approach, the terrain would help safeguard our forces. Venturing into the valley itself would be a death sentence for most of my allies, though. And it was not just because of the twelve thousand-odd stygians there.

The entire region was saturated in concentrated nether, and the plumes the overlords were emitting ensured it stayed that way. I scanned the valley from end to end again, searching for a break in the thick fogbank.

But there was none.

The thick plumes of mist stretched from the shores of the river to the very foot of the hills I was perched upon. I sighed, realizing my allies' sights would be even more impaired than usual in the coming battle. So much so, I doubted our forces would be able to target the tree from across the river — or from atop the hills, for that matter. All anyone but me would see was a wall of yellow smog.

That's problem number two then.

And as if two nearly insurmountable problems were not enough, there was the rift to consider, too.

Like on my previous visit, the void of oblivion was still active. A near-continuous stream of stygians were passing through it in both directions. But sadly, I could not see what lay beyond. The rift's inky darkness was opaque to my sight, and for all I knew, there were another twelve thousand stygians waiting on the other side.

Sighing again, I tagged the rift as obstacle number three.

Nest. Smog. Rift.

Three problems I had to find solutions to over the next few days.

I had the bare bones of a plan, of course. I wouldn't have come this far without one. But there were still a lot of details to flesh out. And seeing what awaited us made depressingly clear how hard that was going to be.

Would my plan work?

I hoped so. Otherwise, we were…

I shook my head. There was no need to go down that route yet. *One step at a time, Michael.*

Slipping down the slope, I advanced on the nest. It was time to test the strength of the stygians' defenses.

✻　✻　✻

Multiple hostile entities have failed to detect you.

I reached the bottom of the hill without incident. Standing tall, I surveyed the area. The outer edge of the fogbank was less than two yards away, and nothing else living was close by. I was clear to proceed.

Steeling myself for the mist's unclean touch, I resumed my advance.

The nether toxicity has increased to tier 30, boosting your health, psi, stamina, and mana regeneration rates to 7.75% per minute.

"Damn," I whispered to Ghost. *"It's even worse than I thought."*

"The fog can't hurt you though," she said comfortingly.

It couldn't. But it wasn't me that I was worried about. Dropping into a half- crouch, I pushed forward. The closest visible stygian was more than three hundred yards away. But it wasn't the ones that I could see that worried me. It was the ones I couldn't.

And only three yards later I found the first.

An unknown entity has detected you! You are no longer hidden.
You have failed to detect an unknown entity.

My lips tightened unhappily. Just as I had suspected, the void tree had seeded the rim of the nest with its spores. It was what I would have done. *But what about beyond the perimeter?* I wondered. Were there spores there too?

It bore investigating, but not immediately. There was something else I had to deal with first—namely, the stirring stygians.

Drawing psi, I reversed course. More than a thousand lesser stygians had turned my way, intent on pursuit. But they did not concern me overly much. If the nether creatures dared to follow, I would lead them on a merry chase across the foothills where neither the tree, the nagas, nor the overlords would likely venture.

Step one, though, was slowing my pursuers down.

Directing my will at the nearest clump of stygians, I unleashed the spell I'd prepared.

You have cast mass puppet.

Rushing across the intervening space, my psi delved into the minds of my chosen targets and assaulted their defenses.

You have failed to charm 20 of 20 targets.
Your targets are shielded from mental manipulation by the protective aura of a level 340 young void tree.

I grimaced at the spell's abysmal failure.

A protective aura. I'd not expected that.

Unsheathing my blades, I kept up my steady retreat. How far did the stygian Power's touch extend? *At least to the end of the thickened fog bank, I bet.*

Attempted mental intrusion detected!

My gaze darted to the void tree in the distance. I'd no doubt *it* was the source of the attempted mental intrusion. Shoring up my defenses, I braced myself for what was sure to follow. *"Ghost, if I—"*

"Don't worry, Prime," she interjected bleakly. *"I know what to do."*

On the heels of her words, another Game message arrived.

A young void tree has failed to enthrall you!
Impregnable mind has fended off your foe's assault.

My breath exploded out of me in a rush of palpable relief.

Testing the strength of my mental fortifications against the void tree was always going to be necessary, and I'd done what I could to prepare— upgrading impregnable mind and investing in Mind—but there had been no way to actually know if my defenses would hold up.

Not, without exposing myself to the stygian Power.

It failed!" Ghost exclaimed from the safety of her spirit vessel. "

"You don't have to sound so surprised about it," I replied drily, but only a moment later, I turned serious again. *"Anyway, now we know for sure my psi defenses are sufficient. That's one less thing for us to worry about during the assault."* It meant, amongst other things, that I could approach the void tree without fear of being bespelled.

Test one was over, and while the results were mixed, I was nevertheless pleased by the outcome. Now, though, it was time to leave.

Scanning the nest again, I checked to see if there were any more surprises heading my way. But except for the thousand odd serpents and hydras closing in, none of the other nether creatures had bestirred themselves.

Turning about, I jogged towards the foothills. *"Ghost, once I'm out of the spores' sight, I want you to—"*

An etheric lash has struck you.

An etheric lash has failed to damage you. The attack has been blocked by your impregnable mind, consuming 3% of your psi in the process.

The telepathic blow struck my mind with the force of a hammer, leaving me reeling for a moment. But only for a moment. It was the unexpectedness of the attack more than anything else that surprised me.

Well, that, and the appreciable dent it made in my remaining store of psi Regaining my footing, I kept running.

An etheric lash has failed to injure you. 3% psi consumed.

Damnation, I muttered as the second blow landed. I kept my balance this time, though, and breaking out into a flat-out sprint, I dashed for the safety of the hills.

An etheric lash has failed to injure you. 3% psi consumed.
An etheric lash has failed to injure you. 3% psi consumed.

...

Ignoring the now near-constant rain of attacks on my mind, I stormed up the hill. How long could the void tree keep up its assault? And how could it still see me? Was the unseen spore trailing me?

An etheric lash has failed to injure you. 3% psi consumed.

It must be, I thought. Cresting the first hill, I scrambled over and descended the steep slope on the other side as agilely as any mountain goat. While I did, I conjured up strategies for dealing with the pursuing spore—or was that spores? Who knew how many of the damn things were on my trail?

"Ghost, get ready to explode," I ordered tersely.

"I'm ready," she replied serenely. *"Where do you want me to manifest?"*

"See that ravine ahead? I'm going to dash through. If the spores are following, they should—"

You are hidden.

Startled, I fell on my rear and slid to a halt.

"Prime?" Ghost queried worriedly.

"I'm fine," I assured her. *"Vanish just reactivated."* Glancing over my shoulder, I peered up the slope. *"Looks like the spores gave up."*

"What about the rest of the stygians?" she asked.

The pursuing serpents and hydras had not crossed into mindsight range yet, but I was not about to ascend the hill anew to look for them. *"We'll wait here to see if they appear."*

"What if they do?"

I shrugged. *"Then we kill them."*

"And if they don't come?"

I sighed. The answer to that was more complicated. What would I do if the void tree did the smart thing and recalled the lesser stygians?

I didn't know yet, but I knew it would make my job of thinning the enemy's numbers tenfold harder.

✳ ✳ ✳

Ghost has taken the form of a level 254 stygian pyre wolf.

While I waited to find out if the stygians would appear over the hill, I sank down into a cross-legged stance and, under Ghost's watchful eye, began the laborious process of restoring my spent psi.

A little later, I opened my eyes, fully restored.

Meditation completed. Your psi is now at 100%.

I blew out a troubled breath. The fact that my meditations had gone undisturbed could only mean one thing: the stygians had called off their pursuit and retreated to the nest.

Glancing at Ghost, I could see the same disappointment reflected in her own eyes. *"Did they appear at all?"* I asked quietly.

She shook her head. *"No. Not even for a little peek over the crest,"* she replied forlornly. *"Should we head back to the cave?"*

I rose to my feet. *"No. We still have more tests to run."*

Ghost's ears pricked forward. *"We're going into the valley again?"*

"We're not—but I might." I glanced at the nearby hilltop. *"I won't be going this way, though. It's time to try a different approach."*

"Oh? You mean from across the river?"

"Yeah," I agreed glumly. *"It looks like I'm going for a swim."*

✳ ✳ ✳

Ghost has unmanifested.

Cutting west across the hills, I crossed the river. All things considered it was not an arduous swim. Reaching the river's west bank, I dragged myself ashore and took stock.

There were no stygians in view, not a single one, and the nest to the north was still out of sight. Wringing out the worst of the water from my clothes, I headed north.

"How does approaching from this direction help us?" Ghost asked.

"It may not," I admitted. *"It all depends on how the stygians react to an attack from across the river."*

"An attack?"

"Not a real one. More of a probe to see how they respond. The big question is: will the lesser stygians cross over? Will the spores? And what about the tree and the overlord? What will they do?"

"Why wouldn't the spores cross?" Ghost asked, sounding puzzled. *"They could simply fly across. As could the winged serpents."*

"They might at that," I agreed. "But will the void tree's protective aura extend past the nest and to this side of the river? If it doesn't, I suspect the Power will hold the flying serpents back."

"What about the spores then?"

"The spores are a different matter," I conceded. "Don't forget, though, that the river borders the nest on three sides—north, west, and south. That's a lot of ground for the spores to surveil. If the void tree is going to have any hope of revealing me, it'll have to dispatch a small army of spores. Which it likely won't do, for fear of leaving the nest—and itself—unprotected."

Ghost ruminated over this for a moment. "So, we'll be safe on this side of the river?"

"I won't go that far. But an approach from across the river should be less dangerous than one from the hills."

"Will I have to swim across too?" she asked doubtfully.

I smiled. Ghost wasn't overly fond of getting wet either. "Not this time. And before we begin our probes, there's something else we have to do first."

"Oh? What's that?"

"Establish a base camp."

✳   ✳   ✳

About half a mile from the river's edge, I found a gully that met our needs. It was large enough to fit me, Ghost, *and* a sizable number of our allies.

It wasn't perfect but it would do.

Dropping into the gully, I turned around to face the distant nest. None of its denizens were visible and only the upper rim of the rift could be seen. "You can manifest here," I told Ghost. "Even if the stygians could see this far, we're hidden from view down here."

"On it, Prime."

While the pyre wolf went about her casting, I turned my attention to the farspeaker bracelet on my wrist. "Saf? You're still there?"

"I am," she replied. "I have a few more things to take care of before I can leave for the emporium's vault." A pause. "Why? Is something wrong?"

"Nothing like that," I assured her, then proceeded to give her a rundown of the events of the last hour.

Safyre sighed and even across the farspeaker link I could feel her concern. "You still think we can claim the sector? The odds you describe... they sound insurmountable."

"I'll admit I have my doubts too," I replied honestly. "But I'm not ready to give up. We can do this."

"I know you believe that, but if a time comes when you don't, don't be afraid to sound the retreat. We still have other options."

"I won't," I promise. She was right, we did have other options—just not any as great as sector 18,240.

"I'll hold you to that," she warned. Before I could think of a response, she went on, her tone businesslike once more. *"So, what do you need at the moment?"*

"The nagians," I replied. I would've preferred to request Safyre herself come, but the aetherist's own mission was too important to disturb. *"I'm going to open a portal to the cave. Send Lucius and three of his fellows through. Make sure they're all strong mages. It will be up to them to open portals for the rest of the group when the time comes."*

"I'll do that. What about the new ones?"

I wrinkled my nose. *"New ones?"*

"Adriel has already rehomed another eight possessed."

I grunted in surprise. *"Ask the wolves to watch over them. Ghost and I will truth-test them tonight."*

"Alright."

Removing a portal scroll from my backpack, I began casting.

✳ ✳ ✳

Ghost has manifested.
You have opened a greater portal to sector 18,240.

A few minutes later, there were six of us in the gully as Lucius and three other nagians I knew less well strode through my portal.

"Ward the area," the mage hunter ordered his fellows.

The three golems spread out, muttering the words of their spells under their breath. Curious to see what they were about, Ghost followed on their heels.

"Wolf," Lucius greeted as he drew to a halt before me.

I smiled, then replied in kind. "Spider."

I sensed more than saw the golem's grimace. "No longer," he corrected.

My lips turned down. "Sorry, that was thoughtless of me." I doubted any of the possessed wanted to be reminded of what they'd lost.

"What can you tell me?" Lucius asked, changing the subject. "Safyre didn't have time to brief us."

"First, look there," I said, gesturing over the nagian's shoulder, "and tell me what you can see."

"I don't see anything but mists," Lucius said, glancing in the direction I pointed. "Why? What lies there?"

I sagged in disappointment. It would've been advantageous if the nagians shared my nethersight. "A rift," I said.

Lucius swung back to face me. *"The* rift?"

"Yes, we're about half a mile from the edge of the stygians' base. The nest measures about a mile on each side. That puts us just over a mile away from the void tree and the rift."

There was no perceptible change in Lucius' stance, but his sudden tension was unmistakable.

"Relax," I said before he could speak. "We're out of the stygians' direct line of sight. And besides, the river is in between us."

"Ah," Lucius intoned. "You expect the water to shield us from the creatures?"

I shrugged. "I've yet to see a stygian enter any body of water. Have you?"

The nagian shrugged in turn. "I have not. But my knowledge of the void is limited." He paused. "I suppose that I will have to rectify that lack now."

I nodded. "And that is partly why you are here. I intend to probe the nest's defenses from this side. But if things go wrong, it'll be up to you and the others to extract us to safety."

"That'll be difficult to do without us being able to communicate directly," he pointed out.

Frustratingly, as non-players, the nagians couldn't use the farspeaker bracelets.

I grimaced. "Agreed. That's why Ghost will stay behind. She will act as my voice." The nagians wouldn't be able to speak to her, but the pyre wolf was more than capable of communicating her desires through physical gestures. "We'll set up a few prearranged signals."

"That could work," Lucius allowed, "but it might be better if we brought Elise across."

I blinked. "Who?"

"Elise is from the group Adriel rehomed today," he explained. "She has the beast tongue trait."

I rubbed my chin thoughtfully. I knew Adriel was prioritizing mages in her rehoming, which was why Zekiel was the only psionic amongst the nagians. So far, he was the only one of their kind able to communicate telepathically with me and the wolves. It brought up an interesting point, though. "What about the rest of you?"

"You mean how did we talk to our beastkin when we were scions?"

I nodded.

"Most scions favored the kinship trait—not only did it allow us to speak to our animal brethren, it provided a host of other benefits too. Unfortunately, the trait is linked to a scion's Marks and will only allow communication between a scion and a beast that shares the same Mark."

"I see. In that case, go ahead and bring across the one you mentioned. But before you do, let me share what I've learned about the stygians so far..."

Ten minutes later, I was back in the river.

Ghost and the others remained in the gully—the pyre wolf practicing her nether manipulation and the six nagians laboriously scrying the surroundings. While the nagian mages' magical sight was no more acute than their physical ones, scrying allowed them to remotely—and safely—map the terrain.

"I'm drawing close to the shore," I informed Ghost.

"Have the stygians spotted you?" she asked.

"Not yet." And I didn't expect them to, not until I was back on solid ground, anyway.

In keeping with the nether's aversion to water, a clear stretch of ground at least twenty yards in width separated the edge of the nest and the fogbank from the shoreline. And while I could not see the spores, I expected that they, too, were maintaining their distance from the river.

My feet brushed against the muddy ground beneath the water, and I halted my slow careful swim to take stock.

None of the stygians in the nest had stirred. Nor had any Game messages dropped into my mind. I remained invisible and unseen. *Perfect.* I was now certain that if it became necessary, I could cross the river without being spotted.

That's another test completed.

Reversing course, I backed away until I was treading water again and scanned the shoreline anew.

Thanks to the ubiquitous mist, the reeds and other foliage that had once graced the river's banks were long gone—leaving my sight unimpeded. From where I floated, I could easily see the rift, overlords, void tree, and nagas. The lesser stygians—smaller in size—were hidden by the riverbanks. But that was alright. It was not them I was interested in right now.

"I'm about to begin my attack," I reported to Ghost.

"I've informed the nagians," the pyre wolf replied after a noticeable delay. *"They're ready."*

Drawing on my mana, I cast—or rather, I let my void armor do so.

You have cast furious storm.

Between one breath and the next, the sky darkened, and bolts of lightning flashed down, striking the void tree and the nagas wrapped around its trunk. I didn't wait to behold the results. Delving into the ring on my right hand, I drew forth the spell stored within.

Mage's surprise activated. Spellhold casting released.
You have trigger-cast furious storm.

A second black cloud materialized, adding its fury to the first. I was still not done, though. Drawing more mana, I let the spell weaves of a third instance of Safyre's spell take shape under the direction of my mana. While it did, I took the time to observe the results of my opening salvo.

The stygians had been caught completely off guard. None of the nagas had their defenses up, and bolt after bolt mercilessly pounded into them.

A lightning bolt has critically hit and stunned a level 241 stygian naga.
A lightning bolt has critically hit and stunned a level 245 stygian naga.
A lightning bolt has...
...

Unfortunately, the void tree weathered the assault much better.

A level 340 young void tree has partially resisted your attack. Minor damage sustained.

The storm's lackluster performance against the void tree did not deter me though. Killing it—or the nagas for that matter—was not the point of the exercise. Gauging the stygians' reaction was. More damage messages poured through my mind, but I ignored them in favor of observing the nest.

Serpents rustled and hydras hissed. The entire nest was rousing.

The question, though, was which way would they go?

A second later, I had my answer as I spotted a pack of stygian mindglows heading east—toward the foothills. I smiled. It was the final confirmation I needed. The stygians had no idea where I was.

Finally, some good news, I thought.

My third spell reached completion, and without hesitation, I unleashed it over the void tree.

You have cast furious storm.
A lightning bolt has critically hit and stunned a level 244 stygian naga.
A lightning bolt has critically hit and stunned a level 240 stygian naga.
...

Once more, I drew mana. I had no intention of stopping, not until the stygians found me—or I ran out of mana.

The nagas had begun dispersing, and fully half of them were already out of the area impacted by the triple storms. A few of the quicker-thinking ones even had their shields up. Nonetheless, there were more than enough vulnerable—or stunned—targets for my lightning bolts to strike.

Better yet, when I analyzed some of the nagas who had the misfortune to have been struck multiple times, I realized there was a good chance of me scoring some kills after all.

A level 241 stygian naga is stunned and badly injured.
A level 244 stygian naga is severely injured.

Giving myself over fully to my spellweaving, I concentrated on chain-casting Safyre's stolen spell.

You have cast furious storm.
You have cast furious storm.
...

Ideally, I would've preferred using the noxious vapors spell against the nagas. It was the more powerful spell. Unfortunately, Adriel's spell lacked the range I required, and worse yet, it was a directionally cast spell. Which meant that if the stygians followed the black smoke back to its source, they'd find me readily enough.

You have cast furious storm.
You have cast furious storm.
Warning. Your reserves of mana have dropped below 25%. Void armor charge remaining: 24%.

Panting for breath—spellcasting was more arduous than I'd thought—I stopped my wanton expenditure of mana and turned my gaze upon the distant tree. My efforts had not been in vain, I saw.

4 stygian nagas have died.
You and Ghost have reached level 258!

"Prime, what's going on? Did you kill something?"
I smiled wearily. *"I did. Four nagas to be precise."*
"Four!" she exclaimed in jubilation.
"Inform Lucius and the others that all is going well," I instructed, not wanting the nagians to get worried.
A pause.
"Elise wants to know what is going on. She says it sounds as if the whole nest is on the move."
"Not quite," I murmured, smiling. *"But the stygians do appear at a loss about what to do."*
The nagas were widely dispersed now, and nearly all of them had their shields up. Sadly, I would not be scoring any more quick kills. What's more, the nagas' had gone on the offensive and were unleashing voidball after voidball.
At the empty hills to the east.
If the need to remain hidden wasn't so dire, I would've laughed. Even the void tree had joined in on the assault and was showering the selfsame hills with stygian thorns.
I did not kid myself, though. Sooner or later, the stygians would figure out the truth of the matter, and then they would begin searching the riverbanks in earnest. And with my mana reserves as low as they were, I didn't want to be still hanging around when that happened. It was time to leave.
Kicking off, I swam for the river's western shore.

✴   ✴   ✴

The trip back to the gully was uneventful. Inside, I found the five nagians waiting patiently for my arrival.
"Elise, I presume?" I said, greeting the newcomer first.

The golem bowed low. "It's a pleasure to finally make your acquaintance, Wolf," Elise said.

Inclining my head in response, I reached out to inspect her.

The target is Elise, a level 170 nagian were-druid.

"You're a werewolf?" I asked, startled.

Elise chuckled. "Not quite. I'm of Fox's line."

My brows furrowed. "That would make you... a werefox?"

"Exactly right." Elise hesitated, then added, "In times gone by, Fox and Wolf were closely aligned. It gladdens me to see Wolf rising again." She shook her head sadly. "If only you could bring about Fox's return too."

I cocked my head to the side. "My efforts are not only bent towards Wolf. I, and those allied with me, seek to resurrect all the ancient bloodlines. One day, who knows, a Fox Prime may walk the Kingdom again."

Elise exhaled. "I eagerly await that day."

Nodding in acknowledgment, I was about to turn away to address Lucius when something else occurred to me. "I'm curious... can you still shift?"

Elise pressed her hands together. "I couldn't before," she said softly. "According to Adriel that was because my spirit and possessed body were not completely melded."

I waited for her to go on but when she didn't, I prompted, "What about now?"

"It's been so long... I've been afraid to try," she confessed.

"Then perhaps the time to do so has come?" I held her gaze. "Not knowing is worse, I think."

For a drawn-out moment, Elise said nothing. Finally, she gave a clipped nod. "As you wish, Wolf," she said, sounding at one time both reluctant and eager.

Stepping back, I waited. The other nagians and Ghost said nothing, content to remain silent observers.

A moment later, Elise rippled. Her limbs contorted and her face dissolved.

"By the ancients," Lucius breathed. "She's doing it."

"I can't believe it!" another nagian exclaimed. "It's actually working!"

Ignoring their commentary, I kept my gaze fixed on Elise. Her shift was occurring quicker than my own, and from the looks of it, less painfully. Surprisingly, though, no fur appeared. Nor did Elise's skin change texture or color.

Finally, the were-druid's shift ended, and a fox stood before us. But it was like no fox I'd ever seen before.

I glanced sideways at Lucius. "Is this what her fox form was like before?"

"No," he replied succinctly.

I turned back to fox-Elise, studying her intently. Ghost was doing the same, circling the smaller creature. *"What do you think?"* I asked my familiar.

"She still smells like a nagian," Ghost replied, wrinkling her nose.

And looks much like one too, I thought. While Elise's shape had changed to resemble one of her House's four-footed brethren, her skin had not. In fact, she was very much the nagian version of a fox.

"*How do I look?*" Elise asked, her mindvoice ringing excitedly in my head.

My brows rose. "*How are you speaking to me mind to mind?*" I was sure she hadn't been able to do so before.

The fox tilted her head to the side. "*You have the beast tongue trait yourself, don't you?*"

I nodded.

"*Well, technically, I'm a beastkin—in this form, anyway.*"

"Ah."

Elise danced on her feet. "*So... how do I look?*" she asked for the second time.

"*Like a nagian fox,*" Ghost replied laconically, drawing closer to sniff at the were-druid.

Elise's head whipped around in my direction. Her eyes were no longer orbless, I noted in passing. "*Is that true, Wolf?*"

"*It is. It seems that even in fox form, you will retain your nagian traits.*" I paused. "*Congratulations.*"

"*Thank you!*" Spinning about faster than even I could manage, Elise put herself nose-to-nose with Ghost—she had to stretch her neck to do it, though. "*Come, Ghost, let's run!*"

The pyre wolf glanced at me for permission, and I smiled indulgently. "*Go on, but stay in the gully.*"

Without further delay, the pair dashed off, and I turned back to Lucius. "Will you and the others watch the perimeter? I need to regain my spent mana."

The nagian tilted his head curiously. "Don't you want to do that back in the cave? It will be safer there."

"Oh, we're not leaving yet," I murmured. "There's still much to be done before we can call it a day."

Your Mind has increased to rank 186. Other modifiers: +12 from items. Available ability slots: 22.
Your sneaking has reached rank 24.
You have replenished 100% of your mana.

Elise and Ghost returned from their run just as I finished replenishing my mana. Opening my eyes, I beheld the pair stretched out on the ground and panting heavily.

"Good run?" I asked Ghost.

"It was," she replied contentedly. *"The fox is fast."* She smiled smugly. *"I still beat her, though."*

Chuckling, I turned away to find Lucius' gaze resting on me. "Are you ready to tell us what you plan on doing next?" he asked.

I nodded, my amusement fading. "I must swim across the river again."

If Lucius was surprised by my response, he didn't show it. "Why? Are you going to kill more nagas?"

"If they are so foolish as to give me that opportunity, then yes." I sighed. "But no, that's not the main reason. I have to cross the river so that I'm discovered."

Lucis stared at me as he tried to process that. "You *want* the stygians to find you?" he asked finally.

"Yes."

"Why?" he demanded flatly.

I blew out a troubled breath. "Because when the time comes for us to launch our assault, we must know how much of a barrier the river will pose to the stygians."

Lucius rubbed his chin while he considered this. "I can see the value of determining that. But are you willing to give up the element of surprise in exchange? Won't it be better to catch the nest unawares during the main battle rather than warn them beforehand of a potential hole in their defenses?"

I shrugged. "I've underestimated the stygians too many times to want to do so again. We're assuming they have cause to fear water, but how much of that is grounded in truth, and how much is mere... distaste? I don't know, and I will not risk not-knowing before committing our forces to what may very well be a trap."

I shrugged again. "And besides, I think it's already too late to count on surprise carrying the day. My first probe today may have fooled them. But I doubt they will stay fooled. You'll see. I give it four or five more invisible-attacks before the void tree realizes their foe is not hiding in the foothills."

The nagian bowed his head, conceding the point. "You're probably right. But so what? What can the tree do? Send its spores to surveil the river? That's a perimeter more than four miles long and impossible to cover entirely."

"I won't argue differently. But don't forget, on the day of the main assault, there will be no disguising where our forces are deployed. The void tree will *know* that the storm of magic raining down on it is coming from across the river. What will it do then?"

Lucius rubbed his chin thoughtfully but said nothing.

I'd not meant the question rhetorically, though, and I waited for his response.

"I don't know," the golem finally admitted.

I leaned forward. "And that's the point—we don't know. But we *have* to know. The risk to our people is too great otherwise."

The lives of too many were at stake for me to take the forthcoming battle lightly. Hundreds, if not thousands, of forerunners would be involved on the day of the main assault, and there was no way I, Safyre, or even Adriel would be able to protect everyone if the stygians caught us unprepared.

I had to ensure that didn't happen.

"There is no such thing as a bloodless battle, Wolf," Lucius said quietly. "Tell me you are not trying to fight one?"

I sighed. "I know that. And I'm not. But I will bend the odds in our favor as much as I can. To do that I need information."

"And to get it you will needlessly endanger yourself?"

I smiled. "I would argue your use of the word 'needlessly,' but essentially, yes."

Rising to his feet, Lucius bowed low from the hip. "Then we will do it your way, Wolf Lord." He paused. "But if I may make a suggestion?"

I waved him on. "Go ahead, please."

"The next time you cross the river, perhaps it's best you do so with a better arsenal of spells."

✳   ✳   ✳

You have successfully stored the <u>furious storm</u> spell in the ring, mage's surprise.

You have acquired the direct-targeted spell, <u>disrupting ray</u>, from Lucius and will retain memory of it for the next 2 days. Disrupting ray (stolen) is a tier 5 spell designed to destroy an enemy spellcaster's shield. This spell will not harm the target themselves but will deal 5x more damage than you ordinarily would against any magical wards or shields they have erected.

You have acquired the direct-targeted spell, <u>mana strike</u>, from Lucius and will retain memory of it for the next 2 days. Mana strike (stolen) is a tier 5 spell that attacks an enemy's mana pool, consuming and setting a portion of it ablaze, thereby injuring the target itself. The damage inflicted by mana strike is directly proportional to the size of the target's mana pool.

You have acquired the direct-targeted spell, <u>fireball</u>, from Elise and will retain memory of it for the next 2 days. Fireball (stolen) is a tier 4 spell that inflicts fire damage to the targeted area on impact.

Thirty minutes later, I was back in the river, and this time around, I was armed with three wholly different spells.

"Lucius is asking for an update," Ghost said, her mindvoice ringing loudly in my mind.

I rolled my eyes. The nagian mage hunter was fast turning into a mother-hen. Still, I did not refuse his request. *"I'm approaching the river's east shore, but I've yet to encounter any sign of the spores."*

"What about the rest of the stygians?" Ghost asked after a noticeable delay as she first fielded my response to Elise, then relayed Lucius' next question.

"They've settled down," I reported. *"The nagas haven't returned to the tree, though. They're roving the nest in ones and twos now—and their shields are still up."*

"What are you going to do?" Ghost asked, speaking for herself this time and not the nagians.

It was the same question I was asking myself.

I had two options: stay in the river and bombard the nagas with my stolen spells or climb up the riverbank and see how far I could get before being spotted by a spore.

Both choices had merit, and in the end, I expected the net result would be the same: the stygians would find me. But the second approach was one I had already enacted, and I could well predict the tree's response. It would send hordes of lesser stygians my way and flood the area with spores.

And besides, I was eager to try my new spells.

"I'm going to launch another assault," I told Ghost. Fixing my gaze on one of the nagas, I drew on my mana.

You have cast disrupting ray.

Motes of energy danced in the air in front of me as the spell took shape, and a moment later, a liquid bar of luminous purple shot out from my still-invisible hands to the distant naga.

Striking the black dome surrounding the elite, the viscous beam latched on as a leech would, then spread itself all around the shield, smothering it in a layer of purple for a brief instant.

You have hit a level 227 stygian naga's shield for 5x more damage.

The shimmering dome of blackness surrounding the elite dimmed noticeably—a fact that neither the naga in question nor the rest of the nest failed to notice. And given the spectacular light show accompanying my spell, none of the stygians had any trouble tracking the source of the attack.

Multiple hostile entities have failed to detect you.

Of course, the stygians still couldn't see me. But that didn't stop all ninety-six remaining nagas from targeting my location.

A level 234 stygian naga has cast voidball.
A level 246 stygian naga has cast voidball.
...

Ignoring the wave of spells sailing toward me, I cast anew.

You have hit a level 227 stygian naga's shield for 5x more damage.

There was no way I would survive contact with the horrifying wave of spells descending my way. My nether immunity depended on my void armor, and my void armor would be drained with every spell it repelled.

When it eventually failed—as it inevitably would—I would lose my immunity.

But I still had time before I needed to retreat. For all their destructive might, the voidballs were slow-moving. Focusing on my target, I kept casting.

You have hit a level 227 stygian naga's shield for 5x more damage.
You have hit a level 227 stygian naga's shield for 5x more damage.
Your target's shield has been destroyed!

I did it! Grinning in triumph, I glanced upward. The closest voidball was three-quarters of the way to me. Not delaying further, I faced downstream and set down a windslide.

You have cast windborne.

Propelled by the ramp of air, I rushed through the river three times faster than normal. It was certainly a novel experience. Exhilarating too.

And when I finally slowed down twenty yards away, I was sure I was clear of the expected impact zone.

Still, I kept swimming as fast as I could. It was not only the naga's assault that I had to worry about—

You have evaded a voidball.
You have evaded a voidball.
...
...

—and eventually the message I'd been waiting for arrived.

Multiple hostile entities have detected you. You are no longer hidden.

I stopped swimming. At least two spores had found me.
Now, to find out if I can get rid of them. Drawing mana, I unleashed another spell.

You have cast fireball.

Growing out of nothing, a ball of flames leaped from my hands to the riverbank, where it detonated.

Unfortunately, I'd guessed incorrectly as to the spores' position and the flames fizzled out sadly. Undaunted, I drew more mana.

An etheric lash has failed to injure you. 3% psi consumed.

Ignoring the void tree's telepathic assault, I kept casting.

You have cast fireball.

My second attempt did no better than the first and also raged away at nothing but empty mist and air. *One more try,* I thought stubbornly.

An etheric lash has failed to injure you. 3% psi consumed.
An etheric lash has failed to injure you. 3% psi consumed.
You have cast fireball.
2 stygian spores have died. You are hidden once more.

As abruptly as they began, the psionic attacks ceased.

The two spores that had been tracking me were dead. Still, I knew I didn't have much time. More spores were likely already on their way, not to mention that the area would soon be saturated with voidballs and stygian thorns as well.

Swimming away and attempting to put as much distance as I could between me and the marked area, I drew mana and cast again.

You have cast mana strike.

In contrast to disrupting ray, mana strike was a 'quiet' spell. Leaping soundlessly from me to the target—and without any telltale trails to track— the casting detonated in my foe's mana well.

A level 227 stygian naga has failed a magical resistance check! It is mana burned (mana and health consumed). Duration: 5 seconds.

In the distance, flames leaped out of the elite. Shrieking in sudden pain, the naga turned about in a frenzy, searching for the source of the conflagration.

But *it* was the source.

And there was no putting out the flames—not until the spell had run its course.

Continuing my swim downstream, I drew more mana.

A level 227 stygian naga is no longer mana burned. Total mana consumed: 5%. Total damage dealt: 15%.

Unfortunately for the hapless naga, my next spell was already ready, and I didn't hesitate to strike at it again.

A level 227 stygian naga is mana burned. Duration: 5 seconds.

Chuckling quietly to myself, I kept swimming. Sooner or later the elite would be dead.

CHAPTER 547: A TEST OF WILLS

My prediction proved accurate and only a little while later, my foe expired in a wash of flames.

A level 227 stygian naga has died.

Not entirely unexpectedly, I did not advance in level. The level disparity between me and the nagas was growing—and my chosen target had been especially weak. Going forward, I knew my gains would slow even further.

Still, it was not all bad news. The stygians had not found me yet.

Partly, I expected, this was because I was in near-constant motion, my location always changing. Then, too, the deaths of the two spores earlier might have spurred the void tree to caution. But this was not to say it was taking the slaying of the naga lightly.

The lesser stygians had been driven into motion, and now they patrolled the river in large groups of forty to fifty. The two overlords, interestingly enough, had not taken to the skies as I'd half expected.

But the flying snakes had.

"Ghost, inform Lucius he may have incoming soon. The winged serpents are airborne."

A pause. *"He asks if you want us to portal out."*

I thought about that for a moment. I knew Lucius was a capable sneak. I wasn't sure about the rest of the nagians though. *"Are they able to hide?"*

"Lucius says that except for Elise the others lack stealth. But he has a concealing web spell that can cover everyone in the gully. He cautions, though, that it's only a tier three spell and may not hold up under the scrutiny of the flying snakes."

I spent a few seconds considering the best way forward. Should I risk the stygians discovering my allies encamped in the gully? Or do everything to keep our forward base a secret?

But the gully was only one of many such locations on the west side of the river, and if it became necessary, we could always relocate the base. The gully was also over half a mile from the river, and given the risk my hidden presence posed to the nest, the void tree might not let the flying serpents range that far.

"Tell Lucius to stay put and raise his concealing web," I instructed finally. *"If the serpents discover you and the others, we'll deal with it."*

"Got it, Prime."

✳   ✳   ✳

In the end, it turned out the void tree had no intention of sending its minions past the river's western edge. The hydras and serpents maintained their patrols, always coming close to, but never quite touching, the water.

The flying serpents followed a similar approach. In groups of ten to fifteen, they skimmed low over the water from the top to the bottom of the horseshoe-shaped stretch of river. Then they winged aloft and repeated the entire maneuver.

The nagas, too, were put to work casting cloying nether, and while I had no way to tell which exact areas they were targeting, I was certain they were also systematically working their way across the river's length and breadth as they tried to reveal me.

The void tree's strategy had little chance of working, of course.

There was just too much river to cover. It was interesting nonetheless that it had chosen not to risk the overlords and further spores. That had to make them valuable and rare commodities. Equally noteworthy was the fact that none of the stygians were straying into the water.

"*What now?*" Ghost asked from the gully.

"*It's time for another probing attack,*" I replied while bobbing gently in the river.

"*You're going to kill another naga?*"

"*Yes. I am going to slay as many of them as I can before my mana runs dry again.*" This, admittedly, was the biggest limiting factor when it came to my stolen spells. By most non-caster's standards my mana pool was large, but it was still a far cry short of what dedicated casters like Adriel and Safyre had at their fingertips.

The simple truth was that I could not maintain the same intensity of attacks with magic as I could with psi. Nor could I afford to spend long stretches of time channeling between attacks.

Time itself was a rare commodity.

And as much as I would like to spend the rest of the afternoon and evening thinning the stygians' numbers, I couldn't. I had to wrap things up—and soon.

"*What about the overlords?*" Ghost asked curiously.

"*What about them?*" I asked absently as I ran my gaze over the nagas in search of a target. They had stopped roving the nest and were now drawn up in a line parallel to the river, chain-casting nether cloy.

"*Why don't you use mana strike against them?*"

I smiled. "*It won't do much good, I'm afraid. Lucius tried that on the overlord Safyre slew, but the damage the spell inflicted was minimal. According to Lucius, the Power has a surprisingly small mana pool.*"

"*Oh.*"

"*It was a good idea nonetheless,*" I assured her as I picked out a target. "*I'm about to begin.*"

"*Go ahead, Prime. The others and I are ready.*"

Drawing mana, I did just that.

✳   ✳   ✳

A level 240 stygian naga has died.
A level 235 stygian naga has died.

You and Ghost have reached level 259!
Ghost's nether manipulation has reached rank 8.
Your dodging and nether absorption have reached rank 22.
Your nether regeneration rate has increased to 10%.

In the end, I didn't actually drain my mana pool dry. Before that happened, the nagas withdrew—and not just to the void tree. No, they retreated all the way into the rift.

It was damnably frustrating.

Especially since I knew the nagas were not a spent force. Far from it. In all likelihood, they were hovering on the other side of the rift, waiting to return when required. Still, I had no choice but to be satisfied with my efforts and pull back.

Sopping wet again, I dragged myself out of the river and onto its western shore. There was no longer any reason to launch my attacks from the water. I'd originally intended on using the river to conceal myself from the spores in the event they swarmed around me. Diving beneath the surface—all the way to the riverbed if needed be—there was little chance I would remain in any spore's line of sight.

Unless, of course, they followed me into the water.

Which it had since become clear they wouldn't. The void tree appeared unwilling to let the spores fly over the river, and there was no way it was going to allow them to submerse themselves in water—where they would be vulnerable. There was no mist beneath the river's surface, after all, and without the nether to disguise their presence, the spores would be revealed.

All of this meant that the western river shore was 'safe' territory—while I remained invisible at least. What the stygians would do when I revealed myself was yet to be determined.

"Ghost, I have two final tests to conduct, then we can call it quits for the day."

"More tests?" she asked, sounding desperately bored by the idea.

I nodded unrepentantly, even though she couldn't see the gesture. *"They shouldn't take long."* I paused. *"But they might create more of a stir than my previous attacks. Warn Lucius and the others to be ready."*

Alarm shot through our bond. *"What are you going to do?"*

"For starters: attack the void tree." Not waiting for her response, I wove psi and cast.

You have manifested 4 sentient shurikens.

The ethereal blades coalesced in front of me. Spinning rapidly around their centers, the psi constructs bobbed gently in the air as they awaited their orders. *"Attack,"* I breathed, directing them at the void tree.

Rising smoothly into the mists, the astral projectiles whizzed toward their target. Crouching down, I watched intently.

The four shurikens crossed the river and sped over the patrolling stygians unnoticed. Zipping past the now mostly empty nest and motionless overlords, they swooped down on the void tree.

The stygian Power, though, did not fail to notice the approaching threat, and before the shurikens could complete their attacking run, a brace of black thorns shot out from the tree.

Your shurikens have been destroyed!

I grimaced. The attack's failure made clear that the void tree was sensitive to psionic threats. I would not be able to blindside it or kill it from afar with psi. And I already knew that the tree was heavily resistant to most elemental magics. But what about Lucius' mana strike?
Would the spell work against the void tree?
Only one way to find out.
Drawing mana, I began spell weaving anew.

You have cast mana strike.
You have failed to mana burn a level 340 young void tree. The target lacks mana and is consequently immune to this spell.

"Bloody hell," I muttered.
The number of viable options available to me when it came to assaulting the void tree were narrowing sharply. So far, the only potential strategy appeared using Force attacks—like the one I'd used against the sapling in Draven's Reach. Still, perhaps, someone else—Ceruvax, Farren, or even the brotherhood—would be able to come up with a better solution.
Rising to my feet, I changed position—just in case. I was still invisible, but there was no point taking chances. *"Final test,"* I informed Ghost, and drawing psi, I cast again.

✳ ✳ ✳

You have manifested 4 sentient shurikens.

This time around, I didn't send the astral projectiles raging against the tree. Instead, I targeted one of the lesser stygians patrolling the river.

Your shuriken has injured a level 167 stygian hydra.
Your shuriken has injured a level 167 stygian hydra.
...
You have inflicted irreparable nerve damage on a hydra.
1 of 6 of your target's heads has been permanently damaged.

My face expressionless, I watched the shurikens work.
The hydra didn't suffer the attacks lightly. But its snapping jaws—and that of the other stygians in the patrol who sought to assist—were too slow to land more than the occasional blow on the ethereal constructs. Yet even a glancing blow was enough to destroy a shuriken.
Of course, when that happened, I simply summoned another.
And bit by bit, the hydra began to die.
Towards the end, I could tell the nether creature wanted to flee, but the void tree's hold on it was too strong, and instead it died ignominiously where it stood.
"That was easy," Ghost remarked when I informed her of the kill.

It was, but slaying the hydra wasn't the test, only the precursor to it. Breathing in deeply, I stepped right up to the water's edge, then revealed myself.

You are no longer hidden.

Immediately, the gazes of hundreds, if not thousands, of stygians fixated on me. But I didn't flee. Folding my arms, I watched and waited.
Would they cross over?

An etheric lash has failed to injure you. 3% psi consumed.

My lips twisted. I'd been expecting the attack. Even so, I didn't move. Instead, I stilled my mind and began to meditate. In response, my subconsciousness stirred, and energy surged out of it and into the impregnable walls around my mind.

You have replenished 6% of your psi. Your psi is now at 100%.

A smile stretched across my face. The tree's telepathic blows would wash harmlessly off my defenses—so long as I had an opportunity to meditate between them.
More attacks followed.
I meditated through them all, my breathing slow and even.
All the while, I kept my steely gaze on the lesser stygians across the river and the flying serpents above. But despite me standing out in the open, and to all appearances defenseless, neither group ventured to attack.
My smile widened. So far, my test was going about as well as could be expected.
Around the corner of my eye, I spied a shower of glistening ebony slivers heading my way. *Stygian thorns.* The void tree was doubling down on its assault.
And still, I didn't move.
Instead, I braced myself and waited.

A stygian thorn has failed to injure you. The attack has been blocked by your impregnable mind, consuming 0.1% psi in the process.
A stygian thorn has failed to injure you.
...

...
Your psi is now at 70%.

I rocked back, staggered by the combined psychic strength of the thirty thorns. But crucially, I had weathered the assault, and already my subconsciousness was working to restore my mental defenses.

You have replenished 6% of your psi.
You have replenished 6% of your psi.
...

Another etheric lash hit me. Then another.
But the attacks did nothing to dim my satisfaction.

While I might not have the void tree beat in a test of wills, any advantage the stygian Power had over me was slim at best. And considering all the other abilities in my arsenal, if it came down to a battle between the two of us, I fancied my chances.

But of course, the void tree and I were not going to be the only contenders in the upcoming battle. My gaze drifted back to the lesser stygians.

Now that I had stymied their 'Chosen's' assault, what would they do?

Chapter 548: Schooled in War

Your psi is now at 100%. Your meditation has reached rank 23.

Five minutes on, I was still at the river. The entire time, the void tree's assault did not abate. It struck me with lash after lash, and repeated salvos of thorns. The thorn attacks were further spread apart, though, which allowed me to restore my lost psi between salvos.

The other stygians, meanwhile, did nothing.

None of the hydras braved the water. No flying serpents swooped down. No spores crept up on me. And no overlords nether-bombed the region.

It defied expectations.

I'd anticipated the Game pinging me with failed detection messages as the odd spore snuck closer or a flight of serpents dove down. What I had *not* expected was nothing.

Tiring of the lesser stygians' inaction, I launched a series of my own attacks between bouts of meditation.

You have cast mass puppet.
You have cast slaysight.
You have cast sentient shurikens.

Much to my disgust, all my telepathic abilities failed bar one—sentient shurikens.

It was proof, if I needed it, that the void tree's protective aura encompassed the river. It was possible, though, that it did not extend beyond—which would be as good an explanation as any for why the stygians were not attempting to cross over onto the west riverbank.

And while my shurikens claimed more than one stygian scalp, the damage they inflicted was not enough. Far from it. There were just too many of the nether creatures and killing them one by one was not going to make any difference in the long run.

Eventually, I swapped over to mana spells.

You have cast fireball.
You have cast fireball.

...

This, at least, drew a response from the stygians. But again, it was not the one I expected. Instead of advancing, the nether creatures retreated and... dispersed.

I sighed, finally accepting the truth. My tactics were proving ineffective. *"This is not working,"* I told Ghost.

"Why not?"

"The void appears willing to accept the losses I'm inflicting. And to be honest, there's little reason for it not to, especially not with the rift close by to provide reinforcements."

A pause. *"Elise and Lucius are asking if you want us to join in on the attack."*

I hesitated, then shook my head. *"No. Let's not reveal more of our hand just yet."*

I had been circumspect in the use of my own abilities too. I'd not used blood puppet for instance. I was fairly certain the blood memory would work despite the tree's protective aura—it being a blood-blinding and not a mental domination spell, after all—but like I'd told Ghost, I didn't want to tip our hand too much.

"So, what's next?" the pyre wolf prompted after the prolonged silence.

Drawing the shadows about me, I vanished from sight, causing the void tree's attacks to cut off abruptly. *"We go home."*

✳ ✳ ✳

The cave was much quieter on our return. With Shael, Anriq, and Safyre gone, Adriel busy with the rehoming rituals, and many of the Pack elders exhausted from the same, it fell to Lucius to take charge of the camp.

After supper and a mostly monosyllabic conversation with Adriel, Ghost and I truth-tested the new nagians—all fifteen of them.

You have accepted 15 non-players into the Forerunners faction.

"How many does that make now?" I asked Lucius after I was done accepting the nagians' oaths.

"Twenty-five," he said softly.

I grunted. "Adriel has done better today." The lich, bone-tired, had gone to her bed. Ghost, too, was asleep, and at the moment it was just the nagian captain and me sitting around the campfire.

"She has," Lucius agreed. "No doubt, you'll have your hundred bodies in time for the big finale."

I eyed him from across the fire. Was that a note of bitterness I detected in his tone? "Is there something you want to say to me, Lucius?"

He met my gaze squarely. "Trust us."

I blinked. "By 'us' I take it you mean the former possessed?"

He nodded.

"What makes you think I don't?"

"Today does. You held us back, sidelining us when we could have helped."

"That's not what I was doing," I objected.

"No?"

"No," I said firmly, then grimaced. "At least not deliberately. I'll admit to having a certain tendency to want to do things on my own."

Unexpectedly, Lucius laughed. "You're definitely too much of a lone wolf."

My lips turned down. "That's not what I said."

"But it's true, nevertheless," he countered.

I opened my mouth to retort, then closed it with a sigh. "You're right." I sipped from my cup, then scrutinized the nagian again. "So, what is it that you think I did wrong today?"

"I didn't say you did."

"But you thought it," I accused.

Lucius chuckled. "Fair enough." He met my gaze again. "You really want to know?"

"I do."

Lucius raised his index finger. "You left everyone in the dark about your plans right up until the end. If something went awry, we would not have been in a position to help until too late." Another finger went up. "You focused only on your own strengths, ignoring what we could do." A third finger. "And lastly, your approach to the problem has been too... direct."

My eyebrows rose. "No one has ever accused me of taking the direct approach before," I remarked.

The nagian shrugged indifferently.

"I'll allow you the first two points," I said when he didn't seem inclined to go on, "but what do you mean by the third?"

"The river," he said succinctly.

I frowned. "What about it? I've already factored it into our plans. Given the stygians' hesitancy to cross the water, we can array our forces on the western shore and attack—"

I broke off, noticing Lucius was shaking his head. "You disagree?"

Instead of replying, the nagian pulled a piece of char from the fire and began drawing on the ground.

Patiently, I waited for him to finish.

"You said the terrain looks like this?" he asked when he was done.

I glanced down at the crude map Lucius had drawn. It showed the nest in the middle, the hills to the east, and the river enclosing the valley on the other three sides.

"That looks about right," I agreed.

Picking up the charcoal stick again, Lucius made another mark. "Then all we need to do is this."

My frown deepened. Lucius had drawn a line that ran from north to south along the hills. "I'm not sure I understand. You want to divert the river and trap the stygians in a circle of water? How will that help us defeat them?"

The nagian shook his head. "That's not what I'm saying, no." He drew a big 'X' across the nest. "We should flood the valley."

My eyes widened. "Flood the valley? You can do that?"

The nagian laughed. "I can't, but there are more than a few water magic specialists amongst our number. They *should* be able to do it." He paused. "We'll have to wait for them to be rehomed, though."

"Flood the valley," I repeated—and by implication the nest—"that's ingenious." Pursing my lips, I thought through Lucius' suggestion.

"We still don't know what effect the water will have on the stygians," I pointed out after a moment. "For all we know, they just don't like to get their feet wet."

Lucius inclined his head. "There is that. It is something we will have to figure out beforehand."

I nodded absently. "And flooding the valley won't help with the overlords. They will simply go airborne."

"Hmm." Lucius stroked his chin. "Not if we cause a flash flood and freeze the water soon after."

"Freeze—" I broke off again. "Of course. Can it be done, though? Can we flood the valley and freeze a body of water that large?"

Lucius shrugged. "The only way we'll know for certain is if we *ask* the water mages."

I didn't fail to mark the subtle emphasis he placed on the word 'ask.' My gaze flitted back to him, my expression somber. "You were right to... chastise me. I should have consulted more widely before running my tests."

"I will not belabor the point except to add one last thing." Lucius leaned forward, his gaze intent. "We possessed are more than simple armsmen. Between us we have hundreds of years of experience in combat and war. Use it. Use *us*."

It was another valid point. I'd been thinking of the nagians as a force multiplier only and had not considered deeply enough what their many years of experience meant. "You have further suggestions?" I asked gravely.

Lucius did not hesitate. "I do. Let us handle the problem of how to deal with the nest. Grant me and the others permission to scout its environs more fully, and after a few days I'll be able to give you a more definitive answer about our ability to flood the valley and how to go about it."

I pursed my lips, pondering his words. It was a bold request. I, myself, only planned on spending a single day more scouting the nest. There was just too much else to do. But the nagians lacked nethersight. "How will you deal with the mists? None of you can see past your noses in the nether."

Lucius chuckled. "There are spells for such things. Granted, none of them are anywhere near as perfect as your own ability, but we'll figure it out."

Frowning, I began to reply.

"Trust us," he repeated.

I closed my mouth with a snap. "Alright. I will. You have my permission."

"Thank you," Lucius breathed.

"You realize, though, that flooding the river will only take care of one— maybe two—of our four problems."

Lucius sat back. "Four problems?"

This time it was me who began ticking off points on a hand. "Nest. Fog. Tree. Rift. We'll have to deal with all four. Flooding the river will possibly neutralize the lesser stygians, and it may even help with the overlords—and by extension the fog—but that still leaves us with the rift and tree to contend with."

"Ah, those I will leave to you," Lucius allowed grandly. He threw me another of his atrocious-looking smiles—someone should really tell him to stop doing that. "You can't expect us to do *all* the work, after all."

"Thanks," I muttered sourly.

Rising to my feet, I stifled a yawn. "Well then, I guess I better go to bed. Tomorrow, I will have to see about investigating one of those problems."

If Lucius had eyebrows, I was certain that in that moment they would've drawn down. "I was joking," he protested. "I didn't mean—"

I laughed. "I know. But I was planning on revisiting the nest tomorrow even before our little talk." Turning about, I walked away. "Night, Lucius."

"Which problem?" he called out suddenly.

Glancing over my shoulder, I looked at him questioningly.

"Which problem do you plan on investigating tomorrow?" he asked.

"Why, the rift, of course."

CHAPTER 549: THE BLACK VOID

Safyre was still not back when I woke up the next morning, and Adriel had already resumed work on the golems. So, deeming it past time, Ghost and I visited the wolves for breakfast.

"How is everyone doing?" I asked between spoonfuls of broth.

Duggar, Aira, Snow and I were sitting together watching the Packs' pups chase Ghost around. The other senior wolves—Oursk and Sulan included—were with Adriel, working the Astral Rings.

Duggar shrugged. *"We've adapted. While not ideal, the cave is safe."*

"The boredom is the worst," Aira added. *"Many of the younger wolves don't know what to do with themselves, and I'm half-afraid they're going to start stalking the golems—or even the lich."*

I sputtered, imagining the consequences of that. *"Have them explore the cave system,"* I suggested. *"According to Anriq, there is an entire network of tunnels beneath us. Who knows? They might even find something useful."*

Duggar and Snow exchanged glances, then the dire wolf alpha bobbed his head. *"That may work."*

"There is something else we must discuss," I said, my expression growing serious.

The three wolves turned my way.

Removing my cloak, I folded it neatly and set it down before Duggar. *"Take care of Ghost while I am away."*

You have lost the Cloak of the Reach.

Aira's gaze flitted from the black garment to me, a puzzled look in her eyes. *"That is something you need not ask. Ghost is Pack. She will always have a home with us."*

I nodded. *"That is good, because I'm not sure when—if—I will be back."*

I sensed Duggar's frown. *"What is it you're going to do, Scion?"*

I blew out a troubled breath. *"Enter the rift."*

All three wolves' emotions spiked with concern.

I jerked my chin in the direction of the Cloak. *"The risk is too severe for Ghost to accompany me, which is why I ask that you keep her here and hold her spirit vessel safe."*

"If it's so dangerous, why go yourself?" Aira asked worriedly.

I sighed. *"Because we must know what lies on the other side of the rift. We can't launch the final assault against the void tree otherwise."* I pressed my hands together. *"Is it a harbinger that's waiting? Or two? Or something else?"*

"You fear an ambush," Duggar stated.

"I do. There is no reason for the void to gather the greater part of its strength on this side of the rift, after all. They only need enough numbers to make sure they are not immediately overrun. No, as powerful as the nest's forces are, I fear what's waiting to come through from the other side may be worse."

"But... will knowing what that is help us?" Aira asked.

I laughed darkly. *"It might not. Information is power, though, and if necessary, I will call off the assault, and we will abandon this sector."*

"But you have a plan, don't you?" Duggar guessed shrewdly. *"A strategy for dealing with what lies on the other side of the rift."*

My lips twisted. *"I do. It's a crazy one. But it might work—if I survive the journey."* And if I could convince the Brotherhood to help.

"Which brings us back to my first question," Aira said. *"Why go yourself? Why not send someone else?"*

Duggar and Snow bobbed their heads in agreement. *"An alpha must know when to delegate,"* the dire wolf said, speaking on behalf of both of them. *"For the good of the Pack."*

I shook my head. *"Believe me, I don't want to go either. I know how much of the plan rests on my shoulders, and I would not jeopardize everyone needlessly. But there is no one else who can do this. No one else can enter the rift and survive long enough to return. It has to be me."*

Silence. But hearing the conviction in my voice, none of the wolves tried to dissuade me further.

Finally, Aira turned to consider Ghost and the pups romping around her. *"Have you told her?"*

"I have. Ghost is not happy." That was an understatement. *"But she will follow her orders."*

Aira sighed, seeming to understand the subtext. *"I will speak to her. And Sulan too."*

"Thank you," I said gratefully.

"When do you leave?" Duggar asked.

I rose to my feet. *"Now."*

✳ ✳ ✳

Passage completed!

Elise opened a portal for me to the gully, saving me the use of one of my own scrolls.

The nagians would be visiting the gully themselves, but only much later in the day. According to Lucius, they had some preparations to complete beforehand. What those could be, I had no idea, but conscious of my resolution to 'trust' the nagians, I didn't ask.

Alone, for what felt like the first time in forever, I sank down to the floor of the gully and contemplated the task ahead: scouting the rift.

Reaching the black void would not be an issue.

For all that three stygian Powers lay in close proximity to it, they would prove no obstacle. I could simply shadow jump to an overlord—or one of the many nearby lesser stygians—and dive straight into the rift.

The problem, though, was I wouldn't be able to do so undetected.

The area around the void tree was likely saturated with spores. I *would* be found out. I could count on that much. But this fact did not unduly trouble me. I only needed to survive long enough to dive through the rift. What lay on the other side, though, I could neither predict nor prepare for.

All of which meant it was best to conduct my scouting as a 'wolf.' In wolf form I was not only faster, I was also stronger and harder to kill. On this mission, speed would be my ally, not stealth.

So be it. Closing my eyes, I saw to my preparations.

✳   ✳   ✳

Your Mind has increased to rank 188.

You have lost a smoke bomb.

You have taken the form of a level 259 elder wolf, gaining primal resistance (+30% against all damage types) and health regeneration (2% per second).

You have cast enhanced reflexes, vanish, and trigger-cast quick mend.

A little later, with my attribute points invested and my buffs cast, I was ready to begin.

Reaching down, I gently grasped the dropped bottle in my jaws. While in wolf form, I couldn't access any of the items in my bag of holding—or on my human person for that matter—but a smoke bomb was an easy item to use.

All I needed to do was break the bottle holding the alchemical concoction and its smoke would be released. Simple really. So simple even a wolf could do it.

Assuming, he didn't need his mouth for anything else, of course.

Mindful of the smoke bomb trapped between my jaws, I climbed nimbly out of the gully and trotted towards the river. One of the downsides of leaving behind Ghost and the Cloak of the Reach was that my nether resistance was no longer at one hundred percent—even though it was close—and while the probability of me being disabled by a void spell was extremely low, it was not zero.

I would have to be wary of the void's spellcasters, creatures like the nagas, a hundred of whom I was all but certain waited on the other side of the rift.

Reaching the river's western shore, I took a moment to survey the nest. The opposite riverbank was still being patrolled by the lesser stygians, but there were fewer of them today than there had been yesterday. The rest had returned to the nest and looked to be slumbering. Everything else about the stygians' disposition remained the same.

Padding forward, I entered the cold water.

Crossing the river was not necessary, but before braving the rift, I wanted to see how far into the nest I could sneak when entering from this side. The information might prove useful at a later stage.

I made it to the far bank without incident. Now was when matters became a bit trickier. Staying low and with my belly almost hugging the ground, I slunk forward.

Three yards into my advance, I drew to a halt. A stygian patrol was approaching from the left. Deciding to let them pass, I waited.

Multiple hostile entities have failed to detect you.
Multiple hostile entities have failed to detect you.
...

...

The lesser stygians passed within a scant few feet of my outstretched paws yet failed to detect me. *No spores with them, then,* I concluded. Advancing once more, I crossed over the invisible line walked by the patrols.

The outer edge of the nest was less than twenty yards away and there I was sure I would encounter spores. Moving glacially slow, I crept on.

Fifteen yards.

Ten.

Five.

An unknown entity has detected you! You are no longer hidden.
You have failed to detect an unknown entity.

I didn't hesitate. Releasing the psi I held in readiness, I shadow jumped.

You have teleported 397 yards.

I emerged out of the aether in the shadow of a stygian serpent about to enter the rift. Unfortunately, my stealth had not reactivated. Which could only mean...

Multiple unknown entities have detected you!

More spores, I thought morosely. But I had come prepared. Closing my jaws, I crushed the bottle between my teeth.

You have ignited a smoke bomb, creating a smoke cloud.

Thick plumes of gray mushroomed out, wreathing my body in smoke before the serpent I'd teleported behind—or anything else for that matter— could think to attack.

You are hidden.

That simply, I blocked the spores' truesight. The smoke was not an illusion. It was real, and the spores could no more see past it than they could through a wall of solid rock.

Of course, the smoke cloud was small and would soon dissipate, but I didn't intend on hanging around. Leaping forward, I cleared the distance to the black void ahead in a single bound.

You have entered a rift.

* * *

The smoke bomb had not been necessary, of course. I'd employed it only to confuse the stygians as to my whereabouts and on the off chance there were no spores on the rift's other side.

Alas, I was not so lucky.

Multiple unknown entities have detected you!
You are no longer hidden.
You have set your teeth and claws alight. Duration: infinite. Your attacks will now deal fire damage.

There were a whole host of other Game messages blaring for my attention, but I ignored them. I had more important matters to deal with.

Like the sea of mindglows crowding all around me.

A level 234 stygian naga has cast voidball.
A level 190 stygian weaver has cast blight thorn.
A level 241 stygian naga has cast cloying nether.
...
...

A plethora of spells descended on me from nearly every direction, but there was no time to make sense of anything other than the fact that I was surrounded and, void armor or no, about to die.

Picking a direction at random, I fled.

A shape reared up in front of me. Not bothering to aim, I bashed it aside with one massive paw.

Another form swooped down. Darting left, I evaded its reaching talons.

A spell hit from the right. Another from the rear. And a third from the left. Repelled by my void armor, they failed to affect me, and I kept running.

A massive shape rushed in from ahead, too big to avoid. But the psi spell I wove was ready. Not bothering to meet the onrushing creature, I blinked away.

My target? A blurred, half-seen shape in the distance.

You have teleported 957 yards.

Chapter 550: Failed Experiments

I emerged from the aether in the shadow of a hydra, but I barely registered the creature's presence. Open ground lay ahead of me, and without hesitation, I hurtled toward it. Behind me, the hydra did not react. In fact, it appeared completely oblivious to my presence.

You are hidden.

The Game message explained it all, and if I could've, I would have exhaled in relief. My shadow jump had put me out of range of the spores.

But I didn't stop running. Before I investigated what lay behind me, I needed to make sure I was truly safe. I did slow my flight, though, and took more time to study the surroundings more closely.

The ground underfoot was soft and gritty, and with every stride, my paws sank deeply. Turning my head left and right, I spied more dry sand, entire dunes of them. Only in the far distance was the landscape different. There, tall peaks reached for the sky. But they, too, appeared barren.

Whatever this place was before, it's a desert now.

There was nothing living in sight. Even the stygians to my rear had fallen out of mindsight range. Worse yet, there was little in the way of cover.

Coming to a halt, I glanced over my shoulder. In the far distance, partially obscured by the dunes, I could just about make out the rift. Most of the stygians were out of my line of sight, though. Only those winging aloft were visible, and while they appeared to be in something of a frenzy, none were flying my way.

It looks like I've gotten away.

Turning around fully so I faced the creatures, I flopped down on the ground, and finally spared the time to peruse the many Game messages waiting for my attention.

You have entered sector 30,199 of the Nethersphere. This area is outside the boundaries of the Endless Dungeon and has been claimed for the Nethersphere by a mature void tree. Warning: the ley line connecting this sector to the Kingdom is under the control of a young void tree in sector 18,240 and may close at any time.

You have entered the nether. The nether toxicity at your current location is at <u>tier 10</u>. Your health, psi, stamina, and mana are regenerating at a rate of 5.5% per minute.

You are the first player ever to have visited this sector!

Congratulations, Michael! You have accomplished the feat, <u>Realm Explorer</u>. Requirement: enter 2 previously unexplored sectors. Your budding explorer trait has advanced to: <u>intrepid explorer</u>.

This rare trait is normally reserved for rank 5 rangers and in addition to the benefits provided by the rank 4 variant, it further grants you

knowledge of the safe zone location in any sector you visit, automatically adding it to your Log.

Analyzing key points in sector 30,199...
...
...

Nether portal found. Current status: disabled. This portal has been closed to safeguard the dungeon sector on the other side from the void. Its location has been added to your Log.
Safe zone not found. Current status: destroyed. Its location cannot be logged.

In the wake of the Game messages, a faint pulsing impinged on my awareness. It came from the north—the far north. *It was my explorer trait at work,* I thought. The pulsing was coming from the disabled nether portal.

The portal's existence was a curiosity, certainly, but not especially noteworthy. As far as I knew there was no way to reactivate a disabled nether portal. Of more interest was the fact that I was the first player to visit sector 30,199.

How long has this sector been in the grip of the void? I wondered.

Centuries? Millenia? Given that no other player had visited the region, there was no way to tell. I sighed. That didn't make my task of figuring out the strength of the void's forces in the sector any easier. My gaze drifted back to the rift. I'd been right to suspect an ambush.

Even in the mad rush to escape, I'd gotten the impression of great numbers. There had to be at least a few thousand stygians assembled near the rift.

And that could not be happenstance.

Rising to all fours, I crept forward. Cataloguing the stygians at the rift was my first priority, and the sooner I got that done, the sooner I could leave.

✳   ✳   ✳

After a short internal debate, I decided to retain my wolf form for the upcoming scouting mission. It wasn't strictly necessary, but it was still too early to tell if I would need to flee again.

Slinking through the dunes, I made my way southward. But I'd barely begun retracing my steps when I was forced to a halt.

Topping a rise, I spotted stygians ahead.

Multiple hostile entities have failed to detect you. You are hidden.

Damn, I cursed, freezing in place. A pack of hydras and serpents almost a thousand strong were heading straight for me. How they'd found me was no mystery either.

The damnable creatures were following my tracks.

I hadn't thought the lesser stygians were intelligent enough to do that, but I had not reckoned on a smarter stygian accompanying them. My gaze drifting to the back of the pack, I reached out with my will and inspected the colossal shape lumbering after its smaller brethren.

The target is a level 320 stygian harbinger.

My eyes narrowed. The monster ahead was a harbinger? It looked nothing like the one I had encountered in Draven's Reach, though. For one, this harbinger was *bigger*. For another, it lacked wings. But in one disturbing respect, the two creatures were similar.

They were both a grotesque blend of multiple beasts.

Chimeras.

That was what the harbingers truly were. Well, that and death magic users. I refocused on the monster ahead. She had the head of a bull, the body of a woolly mammoth, and the tail of a scorpion.

A formidable foe, I thought. But not one outside my ability to kill — even if she did have a thousand lesser stygians escorting her.

Still, it was not to hunt that I'd ventured into this sector. And I especially didn't want to become embroiled in a fight so close to the rift and the rest of the stygian horde.

No, it was best to retreat.

Slipping back down the dune I'd just scaled, I escaped the harbinger's sight and drew psi. It was time to obscure my trail.

✻ ✻ ✻

I spent the next hour travelling across the dunes by windslide. I barely set a paw down on the sands again, and when I did it was only to transition from one air ramp to another.

My strategy worked.

While the harbinger's party was able to unerringly follow my original trail, none of the stygians could track me further. And soon I was lost in the dunes. As far as the void was concerned, anyway.

Cutting a wide arc around the mammoth-harbinger — still vainly searching for me — I made my way back to the rift.

What I found was not a... nest. Not precisely.

It was more properly a war-party. For one, no void crystals littered the ground. Nor was there a void tree or any seeds to be seen — and thank the ancients for that — but in numbers alone, the stygians encamped around the rift rivaled those on the other side. I spotted everything from nagas, hydras, and serpents to crawlers and weavers. There was also a sprinkling of more unfamiliar stygians — horse-like nightmares, devil-hounds, death crows, torpid scorpions, and the like.

None of them were Powers, though.

And in the end, while I judged the lurking stygian army to be sizable and certainly a force to be reckoned with, it was no worse than what awaited us in sector 18,240.

Still, I mused, *the question remains, where did all these stygians come from?*

My eyes dropped to the pristine sand of the adjacent dunes. I was on the east side of the rift, and by this point, I had already circumvented the encamped stygians twice over and knew with certainty that it was only to the south that the sands of the almost-perfect dunes had been thoroughly displaced.

As if by the passage of some great army.

South, I decided. *If there is a stygian nest anywhere in this sector, it's to the south that it lies.*

Turning about, I headed that way.

✳　✳　✳

It took me five hours to track down sector 30,199's nest.

I begrudged every wasted second. Still as much as I hated the time lost, mapping out the void's forces in the region was important—essential even.

My plan, of course, was to assault the rift from both sides.

It was the only way I could think of to stop sector 18,240's void tree from being reinforced mid-battle. To pull it off, however, I needed to send a small army into this sector—where there were dangers aplenty.

Discounting the region's heightened nether toxicity—which could be managed, albeit not easily—there was also the risk of whatever force I sent into sector 30,199 being ambushed in turn by a *third* stygian horde.

Which was why I had resolved to find the region's stygian nest.

Knowing its location would tell me how much time we would have during the battle. And so, as much as I hated the idea of losing nearly half a day tracking down the nest, I drew comfort from the fact that it would take any nest-reinforcements at least as long to make the same journey back to the rift.

And there were a *lot* of potential reinforcements to be had—as evidenced by the sight before me.

Going down on my lupine belly, I inched along a dune to inspect the nest ahead. There were serpents and hydras aplenty, of course. At a guess, they numbered in the tens of thousands. But equally populous were a type of stygian I'd not seen before.

Although, I was not sure if they could really be classified as a single 'type.' The nether creatures in question shared only one distinguishing characteristic—they were all amalgamations of other creatures.

Be it hounds mixed with serpents.

Scorpions with crows.

Spiders with bulls.

The variations were as endless as they were perplexing. Yet, despite the fear threatening to swamp my mind—not even in my darkest nightmares had I imagined we'd be facing thousands of harbingers!—my churning thoughts outpaced my terror, and I noticed an oddity.

There was something off about the chimeras.

The hound-serpent was missing two legs. The scorpion-crow was short a wing. The spider-bull looked too heavy to move. *They're not just chimeras,*

I thought. *They're* failed *chimeras.* Reaching out with my will, I inspected the three creatures in question.

The target is a level 105 crippled stygian snake-dog.
The target is a level 145 flightless stygian scorpion-bird.
The target is a level 87 immobilized spider-bull.

I panted in relief. Most of the chimeras in the nest were no threat and looked to be the result of mad experiments gone wrong.

But most was not all.

And a few chimeras in particular were larger, sleeker, and more powerful than their less hale fellows. Three in particular drew my attention.

The target is a level 301 stygian harbinger.
The target is a level 303 stygian harbinger.
The target is a level 341 stygian harbinger.

That made four harbingers in the sector I had to worry about. Then, there was the tree, of course. Tearing away my gaze from the ominous chimeras, I let my eyes rest upon the colossal tree in the center of the nest.

The hellish thing was big.

Its trunk alone was three times the height of the young void tree in sector 18,240, and its leafless branches extended so far out it was a wonder that the tree was still standing. But then again, who knew how far its roots' unclean touch extended? Hells, for all I knew, even the dune beneath me was infested.

Repressing a shudder at the disturbing, if improbable, possibility—my lookout point was too far out for that—I reached out with my will and inspected what was very likely the preeminent stygian Power in the sector.

The target is a level 421 mature void tree.
Your analyze attempt has been detected!

I was only mildly surprised that my target sensed my analyze.

Given its size and stature, I had expected the stygian to be powerful. However, that was not to say my inspection results did not disturb me.

The tree was *only* a mature one.

It was this fact that bothered me more than anything else and left me wondering how much *more* powerful a void father was going to be.

Void fathers, if recollection served, were the nether's rulers—the malign intelligence behind the void—and from what Adriel had intimated, they were as far above the void trees as the trees themselves were above lesser stygians.

The void fathers were obviously a challenge I was not ready to face. Hells, at this point, I wasn't even certain if killing the void tree in sector 18,240 was something I could accomplish. That wouldn't stop me from trying, though. Banishing my doubts, I turned back to the nest.

The stygians within were aflutter, hissing and cawing. The three harbingers had snapped alert and, patrolling around the tree, were scanning the surrounding dunes suspiciously.

I was unconcerned, though.

I was over a mile away from the nest and too far away for even the tree— or its spores—to reach me, much less for any of them to uncover my stealth. Letting my gaze rove idly over the stygians, I contemplated my next move.

It was time to leave.

Of that I had no doubt. I had accomplished what I'd come here to do and had a firm grasp of the enemy's numbers and disposition. Now, the only thing to decide was where to launch the second prong of our assault.

It will have to be at the rift, I decided after musing over the options. The distance between the rift and the nest in front of me made any other choice impractical.

Still, I hesitated.

The choice was a big one and had implications beyond the battle itself and hinged largely on the workings of the netherstone—because, of course, we'd be using my netherstone to launch the second prong of our assault. Indeed, it was only the black stone that made such an attack possible.

Netherstones were like aetherstones, but while they served the same purpose as those brighter stones, their operation was fundamentally different. A location imprint on an aetherstone was fleeting and usable only once. Thereafter, the stone forgot the etched coordinates and could be reimprinted with a new location.

Not so with a netherstone.

Once etched a netherstone could not be reimprinted. The coordinates I scribed onto the black stone would stay there for eternity to be reused as many times as I desired, and it would always, always, take me back to the same location.

This was the main reason for my reluctance.

The terrain surrounding the rift was flat and barren, and while from the perspective of the upcoming battle, it made sense for our forces to make entry as close to the rift as feasible, beyond the battle itself there was nothing to recommend the sandy dunes as a teleportation point.

Because, of course, once we banished the stygians from sector 18,240, it was to this sector that we would turn our attention. Sector 30,199 would make for a rich hunting ground. Unfortunately for my future intentions—and admittedly, they were somewhat grandiose—once the forerunners claimed sector 18,240, the rift would close, making the netherstone the only means of entering this sector.

And ordinary portals did not operate in the Nethersphere.

This was as true of dungeons as it was of anywhere else in the nether. The only way to travel to and from a sector fallen to the void was by means of a netherstone.

Of which I had only the one.

Still, I was getting ahead of myself. There was no point dreaming up plans for sector 30,199 until *after* we claimed sector 18,240. If we failed to win the battle, my future ambitions for the new sector were a moot point anyway.

And in the end, that was what decided me. Our upcoming assault on the rift was all important. And if we wasted the netherstone in the process, so be it.

My course set, I slunk away from the nest.

✳ ✳ ✳

Your channeling and nether absorption have reached rank 23.
Your chi has reached rank 20.

It was early evening when I reached my destination—a shallow dip less than half a mile from the rift and out of the immediate line of sight of the stygians arrayed around it.

This'll do, I thought.

Flopping flat onto my lupine belly, I took a second to rescan the surroundings. What I was about to attempt next was dangerous—but necessary. The nether creatures around the rift had quietened down again. The lesser stygians were asleep, the nagas were curled up tightly, and most importantly, the mammoth-harbinger had abandoned her patrols and was sitting at ease in front of the rift.

It was about as safe as it was going to get.

Closing my eyes, I began to shift.

To portal out of the sector, I had to be in human form. Only then, could I use the netherstone and other items stored in my backpack. There was simply no way around the restriction—unless I wanted to brave the rift again, and even I was not so foolish to attempt such. My first venture through had caught the void by surprise, but I doubted they would be as complacent the second time around.

No, the best way out of the sector was using the netherstone, and for that I had to shift, regardless of the risks of doing so.

Despite my concerns, though, I completed my transformation undisturbed and undetected.

You have taken the form of a level 259 human.
Warning: you have cast shapeshift twice in one day and cannot recast it again today.

Excellent, I murmured as I unwrapped my limbs from the contorted position I found them in. Feeling uncharacteristically vulnerable—I'd grown used to being a big bad wolf—I set about my remaining tasks swiftly.

Reaching into my bag of holding, I withdrew the netherstone and placed it on the ground. The black stone was already brimming with mana and ready to be etched. I'd made sure to charge it before setting out this morning. Touching a single finger to the item, I willed my intention to the Adjudicator.

You have permanently etched a netherstone with the coordinates of an arbitrary location within sector 30,199. This location will henceforth be designated: Rift-X.

An involuntary sigh escaped me. It had worked, and with less fuss than I'd anticipated.

Right, time to get out of here.

Returning the netherstone to my pocket, I pulled out a portal scroll and began feeding mana into it. What ordinarily stopped portals from working in the nether was the lack of anchor points. The way Ceruvax and Adriel had explained it, nether sectors were shrouded, their coordinates hidden in a similar if more complete fashion than a Kingdom sector protected by a shield generator.

I had an anchor, though—namely, the netherstone in my pocket.

As long as I was at the location designated Rift-X, the stone would anchor any ley line I created—effectively allowing me to open a portal to the world beyond.

Portal scroll consumed.
You have opened a greater portal to sector 18,240.

Despite wanting to, I didn't immediately dive through the waiting gateway.

A second passed, then another. But there was no reaction from the stygians encamped by the rift. My shoulders sagged in relief. They'd not sensed the portal. *Now* I could go.

Striding forward, I entered the luminous doorway. It was time to rejoin my companions.

Transfer commencing...
...
...
Passage completed!

                              *   *   *

You have entered sector 18,240.

An Aether Cloaking Device is in place around this sector. Only designated entities may open portals in this sector and only at allowed locations. Note, all coordinates in this sector will be masked from anyone entering the region after the shield generator was emplaced.

Once more, I found a surprise waiting for me in the cave. This time, though, it was a decidedly pleasant one.

Safyre was back.

And she'd brought the Aether Cloaking Device with her. Grinning in pleasure, I marched forward. "Saf," I called out, "when did you—"

"Halt!"

Checking my stride, I glanced down at the sharpened tip of the poleaxe pressing against my chest.

"Identify yourself!" the same voice snapped again.

More than a little bemused, I raised my head to stare at the player before me. In my preoccupation, I'd not noticed him earlier. But now that I had, his analyze data flooded my awareness.

The target is Keros, a level 205 human windknight and a member of the Forerunners faction. He is a Lightsworn and forsworn and bears a Mark of Greater Light and a Mark of Safyre. Note, only a faction's leaders can identify its members through the analyze ability.

My brows rose. Keros was both a forerunner and a follower already.

Saf's been busy, I see.

"I said identify yourself," Keros growled, prodding me again with his weapon.

Before I could respond, Safyre herself intervened. "Stand down, Ker. This is Michael. The one I told you about."

The scarred warrior glanced over his shoulder at the approaching aetherist, but he still didn't lower his blade, I noted.

"You're sure?" he demanded harshly.

The aetherist rolled her eyes, undaunted by his tone. "Of course, I am," she said, striding closer.

Keros' gaze swapped back to me, and I did not miss the baleful look in his eyes. For whatever reason, it seemed like I'd already earned the man's dislike. "Sorry," he bit off, sounding not the least bit.

I pushed down on the poleaxe still pressing into my chest with one finger. "You mind lowering this now?"

Grudgingly, Keros did as I bade.

"Thank you," I murmured, and took a moment to study the newcomer.

He was obviously one of the forsworn Safyre had gone to meet, and from his new Mark, a loyal adherent of hers too. Everything else about the man defied my expectations, though.

His gaze was fierce, his hands rough and workmanlike, and his face was split by a long diagonal scar. About my own height, Keros' shoulders were broader than mine—much broader—and his legs and arms were thick and stout. In fact, everything about the windknight screamed 'hardened warrior.'

How in hells did he pass for a merchant all these years?

But despite my curiosity, I didn't voice the question aloud. Somehow, I got the feeling it would only make the warrior dislike me even more.

Safyre drew to a stop between us. "So, you're finally back." She looked me up and down, an amused glint in her eyes. "And in one piece too."

I smiled. "I told you I wouldn't do anything foolish."

She snorted. "Now, that's a lie and you know it." A pause. "Ghost told me *everything.*"

I sighed. "I imagine I have some explaining to do, then."

"That you do," she said emphatically.

Turning my head from left to right, I searched the cave, but I already knew my familiar wasn't nearby. "Where is she by the way?"

"Ghost, you mean?" Safyre asked.

I nodded.

"At the forward base with Lucius and the others. They're still scouting the nest."

"Ah." Projecting my thoughts into the farspeaker bracelet on my wrist, I reached out to my familiar across the distance. *"Ghost, I'm back."*

Stark silence was my only response.

I winced. I knew Ghost had heard me, but she was deliberately choosing not to reply. *I guess she's still mad.*

"No answer?" Safyre asked, correctly interpreting my look.

I shook my head glumly. "She's still angry, I expect."

Keros chuckled. "Boy, it seems like you have the knack. You're even more talented at angering those of the female persuasion than me!"

I glared at him.

Unfortunately, that only increased the warrior's amusement. "Since I've gotten here," he went on, "I've heard no less than three of them rail at your stupidity. That takes real talent, you know."

My brows drew down. *Three?*

I knew Ghost was mad at me, but who were the other two? Glancing at Safyre, I saw that her cheeks had reddened.

"Guilty as charged," she said apologetically. "I'll admit to expressing a certain measure of frustration when I learned where you went."

Keros laughed uproariously. "A measure she says!"

Ignoring the warrior's inexplicable happiness, I kept my gaze fixed on Safyre. She made two. Who was the third?

"Adriel wasn't happy either," she informed me. "After all, you left without telling her what you intended."

My shoulders slumped. Right, now I really was in for it. Striding forward, I marched deeper into the cave. "Let's get this over with," I muttered.

CHAPTER 552: WHAT THE STONES CAN DO

Adriel's scolding began every bit as fiercely as I expected, but I weathered it stoically, and in the end, her tirade was short-lived—the lich was too exhausted to stay worked up for long.

"It had to be done," I said quietly when she finally ran down.

Adriel, Safyre, and I were sitting alone around the cave's main campfire. The lich had not made any effort to hide her ire, and not wanting to risk her wrath, the nagians and even the wolves had withdrawn to the cavern's outskirts.

"Oh, I know that," Adriel growled, "but not in the manner you attempted. I could've helped."

I shrugged. "You were busy. Both of you were," I replied, including Safyre in my response. "Neither of your tasks could have been put on hold for this."

"That does not excuse your stupidity!" Adriel snapped, her ire seeming to find a second wind. "And what were you thinking by leaving Ghost behind?"

"I was thinking of protecting her," I growled, my own irritation growing. "If the worst befell, and I died, she at least would not have to suffer the same fate."

"Nonsense," Adriel retorted. "If you died, Ghost would be just as dead!"

I stiffened. "No, she wouldn't. I left the Cloak behind to stop exactly that from happening!"

Adriel threw up her hands. "You fool! Have you forgotten soulbound items are destroyed upon final death?"

I deflated. I *had* forgotten. "Oh," I exhaled, bowing my head as I realized what she was getting at.

"Ghost cannot survive without the Cloak," Adriel went on, unrelentingly, her every word as sharp and unyielding as stone. "When you died, her spirit vessel would've vanished, and she would be just as dead as you were! By going alone, all you were doing was subjecting her to—"

"Enough," Safyre ordered. She threw me a sympathetic look I was not sure I deserved. "I think he gets the idea."

Adriel shook her head despairingly. "I'm sorry, Michael. I don't mean to beat you with this, but the risks you took..." She shuddered. "They were unnecessary."

Safyre nodded in agreement. "We can't afford to lose you, Michael," she said softly. "Not now, not ever."

I sighed mournfully. "I'll admit leaving Ghost behind was a mistake." I raised my head. "But what I did—entering the rift—is no different from other things I've done. It's the way I've always played the Game, you both know that. And if we're being brutally honest, it's the way I have to keep playing if we're going to survive in the long run." Someone had to take the unconscionable risks, and for more reasons than I could recite, it was best that that person be me.

Adriel's jaw tightened and she looked ready to argue further, but Safyre waved her down. "It's done," she said quietly. "And he's back. Let's move on."

Nodding reluctantly, the lich addressed me again. "Tell us what you've discovered."

"Gladly," I replied, eager to move the conversation on. Leaning forward, I proceeded to lay out in exacting detail what I'd found.

✳   ✳   ✳

"Four harbingers," Safyre murmured when I was done.

"But there's likely only one that we'll have to contend with," I pointed out. "The other three are too far away to affect the outcome of the battle." Or so I deemed, but my knowledge of the harbingers was incomplete, and I needed Adriel's expertise on the matter. "Am I right about that?" I asked, looking at her sideways and with more than a little trepidation.

But the lich's earlier ire had vanished, and in the wake of my tale, she was calm and composed again. Her brows furrowed. "You're worried about their netherstones?"

I nodded.

Each harbinger carried a black stone inside them—like the one Ceruvax had harvested from the harbinger we'd killed in the Reach—and it gave the stygian Powers the ability to jump from sector to sector without the aid of a rift.

But would they be able to do so in this instance? That was the crucial question. "Will the shield generator stop the harbingers from opening a gateway between the two nests?" I asked aloud.

The lich took her time replying. "It should... theoretically."

I grimaced. Adriel's answer lacked the unyielding certainty I was seeking. "You care to expand on that?"

The lich pressed her finger to her lips as she gathered her thoughts. "Now that the shield generator is in place—and well done to you, Saf, on getting it set up so quickly—this sector should be completely cut-off from sector 30,199."

"Except for the rift," I pointed out.

"Except for the rift," Adriel agreed. "But the rift only allows physical passage between the two sectors at predefined points. What I was getting at, though, is that the shield generator should prevent the harbingers from 'seeing' this sector's coordinates and portaling into it."

I rubbed my chin. "Why only 'should'?"

Adriel sighed. "It depends on whether the three creatures in question have already visited this sector. In that case, they will already 'know' its coordinates and be able to assault the shield from afar."

My brows rose. "Assault how?"

"With magic," Safyre replied succinctly. "I know for certain that there are aether spells that would allow such an assault." She bit her lip. "And I can only assume that similar nether magic spells exist too."

"Right," I muttered. "So... assuming the harbingers are able to attack the shield, how long will we have before it falls?"

Adriel and Safyre exchanged glances.

"There is no straightforward answer to that," the lich said, answering for the duo. "Unlike a mage's personal shield, the sector-wide shield generated by the Aether Cloaking Device is a channeled spell, and mana must near-constantly be poured into it."

I nodded, recalling witnessing Xrex and Ishita's other Sworn doing the same for the shield they'd placed around the wolves' valley. "Go on."

"Because of the mana flowing into it," Adriel continued, "the shield around this sector is constantly being repaired. So, not only will the three harbingers have to damage the shield, they will have to do so at a rate greater than its repair rate."

"I see," I mused. "Then we can control the outcome by feeding the artifact with more mana?"

"Exactly," Safyre replied. "At worst, we should have a few minutes' warning before the shield collapses."

Adriel nodded. "And in the best-case scenario, the harbingers will not be able to bring enough force to bear to overcome the mages we have operating the shield generator."

I looked curiously at Safyre. "Who *is* manning the shield generator at the moment?"

"The forsworn from the emporium," she replied. "Ten of the eleven I brought back are mages."

I blinked. "You brought back *eleven* forsworn?"

Adriel chuckled. "Not only that, she has already convinced all eleven to become her followers. Our dear Safyre can be quite persuasive when she wants to be."

Safyre blushed. "I hope you don't mind," she said, keeping her gaze fixed on me. "They're all Forcesworn, and seeing as they don't know you, I thought they would be more comfortable with me leading them."

"I don't mind," I said firmly. "Not at all." I paused. "But do you trust them?"

"Unequivocally," she replied just as firmly. "I've known all of them for years, and although some of us may have started out in rival factions, that's all well in the past now. Becoming forsworn changed who we are, and now we are bound more tightly to each other than we ever were to our former Powers."

My gaze drifted to Keros. The scarred warrior was still where I'd first encountered him, standing stiffly at attention and staring at nothing. I had a better inkling of the source of his dislike now. I'd intruded on the close bond the forsworn shared, and worse yet, I had taken Safyre away from them.

It's a good thing I didn't have to bind him as my follower.

I jerked my chin toward the player in question. "I presume he is the non-mage?"

Safyre nodded. "Correct. Keros has little magic, and what few spells he does have, are all geared towards enhancing his melee combat abilities."

"He's guarding the teleportation point, I presume?"

A smile flickered across Safyre's face. "He is. Keros is very... martial in his disposition and he insisted we not leave the teleportation point unprotected."

I grunted. *So, he's paranoid too.* That, though, was a mark in the windknight's favor. "How did he ever manage to pass for a merchant?"

Safyre laughed. "He didn't. Keros never left the vaults. In fact, he served as guard commander there."

"Ah, that makes sense." I paused. "What about the other forsworn? Are they all his rank?"

Safyre shook her head. "Not all. Five are elites, while the other five range between rank fifteen and nineteen."

"A force to be reckoned with," I noted, impressed. Especially with Safyre to lead them.

The aetherist simply nodded. "Do you wish to meet the others?"

I waved aside her offer. "Not tonight. Tomorrow, perhaps." I turned back to Adriel. "Getting back to the harbingers... we'll have to come up with a plan for dealing with them in case they manage to break through the shield and into the sector."

"That we will," she agreed.

"What about the other sector—30,199?" Safyre asked.

Adriel glanced at her. "What about it?"

"Can the harbingers portal directly from the mature tree's nest to the rift, bridging the gap between the two points instantly? Do we need a contingency for sector 30,199 too?"

I frowned. The possibility Safyre was raising had not occurred to me. If the harbingers could do as she was suggesting, the consequence for any force we sent to the far side of the rift would be... ruinous.

Adriel's response, though, quickly set my mind at ease.

"No, they cannot," the lich said emphatically. "Two netherstones are needed to open a portal from one nether destination to another. Not only that, but to do as you suggest, the caster must simultaneously be at both the target and start locations—a physical impossibility."

"And thank the ancients for that," I muttered. "So, we can safely assume the force attacking the far side of the rift is unlikely to face more than one stygian Power."

Adriel inclined her head. "We can."

"Which brings us to the next question," I said. "The composition of the warband we send to sector 30,199."

Safyre leaned forward. "I have news on that front."

I glanced at her in surprise. "You do?"

She nodded. "Kesh reports the brotherhood is amenable to your proposal."

I stared at her. "You went to Nexus?" I asked slowly. "I thought it was the emporium vaults you were visiting?"

"I *did* go to the vaults," Safyre replied, "and no, I didn't visit Nexus."

I shook my head. "Then I don't understand. How did you speak to Kesh?" The old merchant was confined to the Nexus safe zone and couldn't leave even if she wanted to.

Safyre smiled. "I used an aether spell to talk to her."

My eyes rounded in alarm. I knew some of what aether magic could do, of course. Most mages—like Adriel—merely dabbled in it, investing only enough in the skill so that they could open a portal. Safyre, though, was a specialist aether mage. Her entire Class was built around the skill, and she had given me a rundown of its capabilities many times already.

Although primarily a non-combat skill, aether magic was essential to any large organization in the Game. It facilitated not only the transfer of goods and people across sectors, but communication too.

The problem, and the source of my alarm, was that aether spells that reached between sectors were loud and noisy—Safyre's words, not mine— and the ley lines they formed could be tracked. This applied equally to those used for transport *and* communication. Now, ordinarily, no one would bother attempting to trace the source of some random ley line.

But of all the sectors in the Game, Nexus was the most watched.

The Triumvirate was fanatical about tracking all incoming and outgoing traffic in Nexus. It was why Safyre had not risked contacting Kesh directly before, and why we still shunned remote contact with the merchant. And it was why I'd not teleported directly to the city either. A portal opening in Nexus from a previously undiscovered sector would be sure to raise eyebrows.

Seeing my expression, Safyre's smile faded. "The risk was minimal," she explained. "Communication between the vaults and the emporium offices in Nexus is commonplace. One more message would have gone unremarked, and just to be certain, Kesh and I kept our conversation short and vague."

I nodded in recognition of the precautions she'd taken. "Alright, so what's this about the brotherhood? Have they agreed to our terms?"

Safyre shook her head. "No. Their huntmistress hasn't gone that far yet. She won't commit until she's met you."

I sighed. Of course, it wouldn't be that easy. "I'll head off to Nexus tomorrow then." I'd planned on doing so already, but it would've been nice if I could have avoided the trip.

But Safyre was shaking her head. "Not necessary. The huntmistress is waiting for you in sector 45,104—that's the brotherhood's home sector. I have the coordinates and can teleport you there directly."

"Ah. Thanks, that'll make things easier." I paused. "I still have to go to Nexus, though."

She looked at me questioningly

I grimaced. "To shop."

Surprisingly, Safyre smiled again. "Also not necessary."

My brows rose.

"You remember I said I brought eleven forsworn from the emporium?"

I nodded.

"Well, I brought one who is not forsworn—a civilian."

My eyes widened. "A civilian? Why would you—" I broke off as realization hit.

Safyre smiled. "That's right. He's a merchant, and he, too, has pledged himself to the faction."

I rocked back. "Oh my. That's great," I murmured, already mentally rearranging my plans for the next few days. At the very least, Safyre had saved me a day of travelling back and forth to Nexus. And while at some point, I would still have to visit city, that day was not today. "How does your merchant's wares compare to Kesh's?"

Safyre's eyes twinkled. "That's where it gets even better. Sedgwick—that's his name, by the way—is still in Kesh's employ and has full access to the emporium's vaults. You'll no longer need to visit Nexus to shop. You can do it all from here."

I had to meet Sedgwick immediately, of course.

After promising Adriel I'd greet the new nagians tomorrow—she'd rehomed another fifteen during the course of the day—I bid good night to the weary lich and followed Safyre away from the campfire.

"Where are we going?" I asked. Safyre was leading me toward the left side of the cave, but I'd already analyzed every player in the cavern and knew there was no one named Sedgwick about.

"Into the tunnel network below," she replied.

I nodded, on reflection, unsurprised. "Is that where you've hidden the Aether Cloaking Device?"

"It is. The wolves have done a good job of mapping the tunnels and we selected one of the more remote sections to conceal the artifact."

My brows rose. "Sedgwick is at the shield generator?"

Safyre shook her head. "No. No one outside of the eight forsworn operating the device—and myself—knows its exact location." She sighed. "Perhaps I'm being overly paranoid, but I didn't think it wise to share the generator's location further than strictly necessary."

"Oh, I don't think you're being paranoid," I murmured. "You did the right thing."

The artifact itself was the Aether Cloak's biggest vulnerability, and the easiest way to destroy a sector's shield was from within—just like I had done in the wolves' valley. And as much as I wished to believe no forerunner would ever betray us, I could not discount the possibility that at some point, someone would—no matter how many truth tests Ghost and I subjected them to.

Safyre shot me an uncertain look. "You think so? I don't want to make the others feel like I distrust them. It's not good for—"

I cut her off. "The fewer that know the device's location, the better. In fact, you don't need to tell me where it is either."

Consternation flickered across Safyre's face.

I raised my hand, forestalling her objections. "It's not like I'll be much help powering the device, and if anyone is disgruntled about the secrecy, our shared ignorance might make them feel a bit better."

She nodded hesitantly.

"Although..." I rubbed my chin. "At some point, we're probably going to have to put in additional measures to secure the thing. Keeping its location hidden will not work forever."

Safyre smiled. "I'm ahead of you there. I've given the matter some thought and have a few ideas on how to better protect the artifact."

"Good," I pronounced in satisfaction. "Then, I'll leave it in your hands." I paused. "So, if Sedgwick is not at the Aether device, where is he?"

"Inspecting another large cavern we've found. He thinks it may serve as our vaults."

My eyebrows shot up. "*Our* vaults?"

Safyre grinned. "You'll understand when you meet him, but our dear merchant has big plans already."

✳   ✳   ✳

We found the merchant in question a little later.

Sedgwick was a dwarf, older and frailer than most others I'd met, and unusually, his graying beard was neatly trimmed and almost non-existent. Alone in a cave flooded with magelights, Sedgwick was puttering about the empty void of space, drawing lines on the floor and taking measurements, all while whispering quietly to himself.

"What's he doing?" I asked Safyre softly.

She shrugged. "Knowing Sedgwick? Probably planning the layout of his warehouse."

I frowned. Why did we need a warehouse?

But before I could get my question out, Safyre raised her chin and called out. "Sedge! Come here. Michael would like to meet you."

Startled, the dwarf froze for a second, then caught sight of the aetherist's white-clad form. "Oh. It's you, Saf. I thought for a second it was those damnable wolves again."

My eyes narrowed. I hadn't sensed any of the Pack nearby, but then I hadn't thought to look either. Almost as if realizing they were about to be discovered, two sets of yellow orbs appeared from the tunnel mouth at the far end of the cavern.

"Stormdark? Shadetooth?" I yelled, recognizing Oursk and Aira's offspring. "What are you two doing here?"

"The elders asked us to watch the skinny one," the darker of the two wolves replied.

My gaze flickered to the 'skinny' one. Alerted by my shout, the dwarf had spotted the skulking wolves, and in response, his face turned as pale as a sheet. Something had given Sedgwick cause to be afraid, and I was fairly certain I knew what. My lips tightened.

"Is that what you were doing?" I asked, swapping to mindspeech. *"Watching him?"*

The pair had the grace to look embarrassed. *"We were bored,"* Shadetooth replied sheepishly.

I folded my arms. *"So? You decided to stalk a harmless dwarf?"*

Neither wolf had the temerity to question my categorization. *"Don't tell Sulan, please,"* Stormdark near-whined.

I didn't say anything for a moment, letting their worry and alarm build. *"Go, then,"* I instructed, finally relenting, *"but don't let me hear of this again."*

Both wolves touched their noses to the ground. *"Thank you, Scion,"* they replied in chorus before tucking tail and fleeing.

Shaking my head in rueful amusement at the pair's antics, I turned back to find a more composed Sedgwick standing before me. Under Safyre's ministrations, he'd calmed quickly.

"Wolf lord," the dwarf greeted. Looking me up and down, he smacked his lips. "You are everything Saf described. A truly tasty-looking—"

Safyre elbowed him in the ribs.

"Ow!" Sedgwick exclaimed, rubbing vigorously at his side. "That hurt," he complained.

Glancing sideways at the aetherist, I found her blushing.

"Sedgwick is an old friend," she said hastily. "I've known him since before I joined the emporium."

"Ah," I said, nodding sagely, even though her words did nothing to explain the strangeness of the dwarf's greeting.

Sedgwick laughed. "That means we talk." Leaning closer, he whispered conspiratorially. "We talk *a lot*."

"Uh-huh," I replied, no less enlightened.

Safyre pushed the dwarf away. "Enough of that now, Sedge. Michael is here to talk business."

The amusement vanished from the old merchant's face so quickly I would have thought I'd imagined it—if not for the twinkle that remained in his gaze. "Business? Why didn't you say so." He rubbed his hands together. "So, what can I sell you today, Wolf Lord?"

"Call me Michael," I said.

"Michael it is," he replied grandly. "See, Saf," he added, turning her way, "we're friends already."

She rolled her eyes. "If you believe that, you haven't been listening very well to me. Michael is not so easily won over."

The dwarf studied me shrewdly. "Is that right? Then, I'll guess I'll just have to work harder," he murmured. "So, what shall it be, Wolf? A mighty sword? An unbreakable suit of armor?" His gaze darted over my equipment. "Alas, I have nothing so fine as a Tiamaten Vest. Wherever did you find that exquisite piece, by the by?"

Already grown used to Sedgwick's mannerism, I paid his question no heed. Normally, I'd view his inquisitiveness with more suspicion, but it was clear Safyre trusted him wholeheartedly. "We'll get to matters of trade soon enough. Before that, though..." I turned to Safyre. "It just occurred to me to wonder if this is safe."

She studied me quizzically. "Safe? In what way?"

I waved my hands in the air, not quite sure how to explain my concern. "Uhm, won't the Triumvirate be able to track his... uh, transactions?"

"We won't complete our dealings here, of course!" Sedgwick exclaimed, sounding offended. "That'd be foolish."

"Foolish?" I repeated, looking to Safyre for an explanation.

"Sectors that wish to remain hidden generally cut-off all access to Nexus and other institutes outside of their control," Safyre said. "That's why you couldn't use a bank or the global auction in the wolves' valley when it was under Ishita's control."

"Because ley lines can be tracked," I said, nodding along. "Right, understood. But we're still going through Nexus, aren't we?" I jerked a thumb at the dwarf. "Because of him."

"We aren't actually," Safyre contradicted. "Even though Sedge is technically Kesh's representative, none of the trades he concludes will touch Nexus. The Triumvirate will have no idea what you're about."

I scratched my head. "How's that?"

"Your transactions with Sedge will be affected through the emporium vaults—which are *not* in Nexus," Safyre said. "And while the Triumvirate may watch over the city, they have no jurisdiction in the sector in which the vaults are located."

I nodded slowly. "That makes sense." I paused. "But Sedgwick said we won't be trading here?"

"Sedge will be using the Roost," Safyre replied.

"Ah."

"Your idea of using the former tavern as a waypoint was a good one," Safyre said. "Not only will it serve as a good base for Sedge, it will also make it impossible for anyone to track our portals to and from here."

I arched one brow. "It will? How?"

"Tracing a ley line's source—or destination—requires access to the *other* endpoint." Safyre explained. "And since you own the Roost..."

"No one will be able to get to the tavern's endpoint without us knowing," I finished for her. "Brilliant. In that case, we should make sure everyone always uses the Roost whenever they enter or leave sector 18,240."

Safyre smiled. "That's the policy already. I have stationed two forsworn at the former tavern. It will be their responsibility to portal our people to and from sector 18,240."

I shook my head ruefully. Trust Safyre to have thought of everything already. I turned back to the patiently waiting Sedgwick. "Well, since that's all settled, how about we relocate to the Roost?"

✳   ✳   ✳

You have entered the safe zone of sector 12,560.

Ten minutes later, after greeting the two forsworn on duty, I seated myself opposite Sedgwick at one of the tavern's—former tavern's—tables.

Safyre had already left to arrange for the retrieval of the twins and Nyra. By now, the trio should've completed their dungeon dive and, assuming all had gone well, would be waiting at the rendezvous point.

The aetherist herself would not be going to Korg Major—her Powerful Initiate Mark made that too dangerous. Instead, she would be using one of Sedgwick's contacts to deliver them somewhere she could safely meet the trio. Still, I couldn't help but wonder if I shouldn't have seen the task done myself...

"Worried about Saf?" Sedgwick asked, catching sight of my expression

I nodded.

"Don't be. She can take care of herself."

I couldn't argue with that. Eyeing the dwarf carefully, I studied him anew.

The target is Sedgwick, a dwarven merchant. He is a player and bears a Mark of Lesser Light and Lesser Shadow.

Unlike Keros and the two forsworn I'd just met, Sedgwick did not bear Safyre's Mark. "You haven't sworn yourself to Safyre," I stated bluntly. "Why?"

If the dwarf was perturbed by the abrupt demand, he did not show it. "Safyre and I both agreed it was better if I did not. This way I can move about more freely in the Kingdom and with less scrutiny."

Which was true enough. "What's your story then?"

"My story?"

"You're not forsworn. How did you come to work for Kesh?"

He chuckled. "Kesh doesn't *only* employ forsworn. She's a merchant. As am I. It seemed appropriate."

"It can't be that simple," I objected. "I've no doubt there are hundreds of merchants clamoring to work for Kesh. Why did she pick you?"

Sedgwick's smile faded. "Because of Saf."

"Safyre asked Kesh to employ you?"

The dwarf shook his head. "No. I followed Safyre into her... exile and offered the emporium my services." He threw me a quicksilver smile. "They were smart enough not to refuse."

I tilted my head to the side. "That's right. Safyre said she knew you from before." I hesitated for a moment, wondering if I should probe further, then pushed ahead anyway. "Which Power did she serve?"

The dwarf's brows flew up. "Saf didn't tell you?"

"I didn't ask."

Sedgwick shrugged. "It's no secret. Safyre served Ganelle."

I frowned, not recognizing the name. "I don't know that Power."

"No reason you should. She's dead."

I blinked. "What?"

The dwarf contemplated me in silence for a moment before responding. "As Powers go, Ganelle was not a major one. She ruled over a single sector and was not affiliated with any other Light faction—which in the end proved her downfall."

I leaned forward. "What happened?"

"A more powerful rival—I forget his name—invaded her territory. With no one to call on for aid, Ganelle quickly fell."

I frowned. "That's it?"

Sedgwick shrugged. "That's it. I'm afraid there was nothing particularly remarkable about Ganelle, or her story. In fact, her fate is one many minor Powers share."

I sat back. "What about Safyre? How did she..."

"Become forsworn, you mean?"

I nodded.

Sedgwick grimaced. "That's where it gets ugly. Ganelle had a particularly vengeful streak and foreseeing her fate, she ordered her followers to scour her domain's capital before the enemy could get his hands on it." He paused. "Fortunately for me—and the dozens of other civilians trapped in the town at the time—Safyre refused Ganelle's command. Instead, she helped us flee the sector."

I sighed. "Thus sealing her fate and becoming forsworn."

The dwarf nodded.

"Thank you for telling me," I murmured.

"You had a right to know," Sedgwick said. "Safyre knows she made the right decision. "That, though, does not stop her from feeling shamed by her betrayal. It's likely why she has not spoken of it yet."

I didn't say anything, but I agreed with the dwarf's assessment. I'd felt Safyre's uneasiness with her past on more than one occasion, for which reason I'd chosen not to probe.

The dwarf slapped his hands against the table. "But enough of the past, that's all behind us now. Shall we get down to business?"

Nodding, I extended a piece of parchment across the table. "This is what I need…"

"I can get you all this," Sedgwick said once he was done perusing my list.

"You can?" I asked, a little surprised by his easy confidence.

The merchant nodded. "Provided you can pay, of course."

"Of course," I murmured. Money was tight at the moment—a state of affairs I didn't expect to change until Nicola fulfilled his debt. Nonetheless, I foresaw no problems paying Sedgwick.

My shopping list was hardly what you would call extravagant—at least not in comparison to the gear I'd requested from Kesh. Seeing the expectant look on the dwarf's face, I set down two items on the table.

You have lost a bag containing 73 x miscellaneous items reserved for use by Mammon's Sworn.

You have lost an alchemy stone containing: 4 x orbs of petrification, 10 x Shadow ectoplasm, 250 x lumps of necrotic plasma, and 236 x vials of nether residue.

Sedgwick's brows rose as he sifted through the bag's contents. "Sworn-locked gear..." he murmured.

"Is that going to be a problem?" I prompted.

Kesh, I knew, was quite fastidious in how she dealt with equipment looted from players, which is why I'd not sold the Riders' gear to her during my previous visit to the emporium. The only other option was to use something like the thieves' market.

And I'd planned on doing just that, but after the way things had panned out with Den Chief Dinara, I'd lost the opportunity to do so. And as cash-strapped as I was, I had no choice except to sell the gear for whatever pittance Sedgwick was able to get from more mainstream buyers.

The dwarf surprised me, though.

"Not at all," he replied smoothly. "I will be able to match these items to the... uhm, right buyers—anonymously, of course."

I eyed Sedgwick speculatively. "You have access to the thieves' market?"

"Ah, you know about that. Good, it will make things easier."

I pursed my lips. So, Sedgwick wasn't *only* an emporium merchant—Kesh wouldn't touch the thieves' market herself. "Does Kesh know about your..."

"Side hustle?" he finished for me, his eyes twinkling.

I nodded.

"She does, and while it does not please her, she tolerates it as long as I don't try recycling anything through the emporium." He held a hand to his heart. "And that I would never do. It would be a betrayal of all the good lady has done for me and Saf."

"Uh-huh," I said, not sure how much I trusted his protestations of innocence.

Leaning forward, Sedgwick whispered conspiratorially. "But tell me, how did you acquire the equipment?" He held up a hand, forestalling any objection I might raise. "I ask, not out of any sense of misplaced morality, I assure you, but so that I know what precautions to employ during the sale."

I was unamused. "I did not steal the gear, if that's what you're getting at." I paused. "But I did kill—murder some would say—the owners. So, extreme caution would be advisable."

"Ah, I see." Tapping the end of his nose with one finger, the dwarf pondered the equipment strewn negligently on the table. "In that case, I can offer you... one hundred thousand gold for the lot."

"Deal," I said, not hesitating in the least, even though I knew what Sedgwick offered was likely only a fraction of the gear's true value. I'd looted the items off Malikor, Leafbright, and Zultan, after all—all three Sworn and elite players in their own right.

Despite my instant acceptance, though, Sedgwick felt the need to explain further. "The items are worth more, of course—a lot more. But considering the precautions I must take, the risks inherent with transacting on the thieves' market, and the need to soothe your... uhm, victims' egos, that's the best I can offer."

I waved off his words. "I understand." Nicola, too, had complained about his overheads when dealing with the thieves' market. "What about the alchemy stone?"

Sedgwick picked up the object in question. "This is a more straightforward transaction. I'll give you fifteen thousand for all five hundred reagents." He looked at me questioningly.

"Acceptable." I nudged my list. "Let's double the quantities of all the consumables listed here, then." It seemed like I could afford it.

The merchant inclined his head. "As you wish." Closing his eyes, he began materializing the items on the table.

You have acquired 20 greater portal scrolls, 14 upgrade gems, and 58 bombs.

You have acquired the ability tomes: load controller V, whirlwind V, trap disarm IV & V, lockpicking IV & V, set trap V, mass puppet V, windborne V, enhanced reflexes V, trap detect V, ventro V, lesser imitate III, IV, & V, charge I, II, III, IV, & V, overpowering blow I, II, III, IV, & V, and stomp I, II, III, IV, & V.

Your trap crystals have been fully replenished.

"Thank you," I murmured, sweeping my purchases into a bag of holding.

"You're welcome," the dwarf replied. His eyes fell on the disappearing books. "That's a lot of tier one strength ability tomes. Excuse my curiosity, but why would a player of your level need so many new abilities?"

"I'm experimenting," I said, which was true enough.

"Ah," Sedgwick said and left it at that. "What about the rest of your money? Do you want me to deposit it in a bank?"

"How much remains?"

"Sixty-one thousand and three hundred gold exactly."

"Hmm..." I drummed my fingers on the table, thinking. "What's the price of a moderate healing potion these days?"

Sedgwick raised one eyebrow. "A moderate potion? Not a full one?"

I nodded, not explaining.

"Thirty gold."

"Thirty gold," I mused. "And what if I buy them in bulk?"

The dwarf cocked his head to the side. "What sort of quantities did you have in mind?"

"Sixty-one thousand, three hundred gold's worth—to be exact."

For a moment, Sedgwick looked nonplussed, then realization dawned in his eyes. "Ah, I see now. They're not for you." He closed his eyes, calculating. "If you're willing to buy in such numbers, I can reduce the price to twenty-five gold per bottle. That'll work out to approximately two thousand, four hundred potions."

My lips turned down. It was fewer potions than I would've liked, but the quantity was still a sizable one and should make a material difference in the forthcoming battle. "I'll take them."

"I can't promise immediate delivery," Sedgwick cautioned.

I shrugged. "As long as you can have everything here in five days."

"Five days I can do."

"Good. Then, see that the potions are delivered to Safyre. She will know what to do with them." Rising to my feet, I headed for the Roost's upper floors.

It was time to put my new ability tomes to use.

* * *

Sitting down cross-legged on my bed, I considered the items arrayed in front of me. I'd bought far more ability tomes than I could hope to use, but the books were relatively cheap, and I'd seen no reason not to buy them.

Where to begin? I wondered.

I picked up the whirlwind tome. I'd been chasing after whirlwind's tier five variant for a long time now, and beginning with it made sense.

Yet, I hesitated in opening the tome.

I had no doubt that the ability contained in the book would be an improvement over the tier four variant I currently used. But was there a better variant to be had?

Setting down the tome, I picked up an upgrade gem.

Upgrade gems, I'd come to realize, were not just expensive replacements for hard-to-find tomes. Sometimes—not often—they offered something else.

Like unanticipated variants.

It was a truism of the Game that there existed more abilities—and variants—than any one player could ever hope to discover in a single lifetime.

Which is what made upgrade gems handy.

I turned over the small crystal in my hand. Using an upgrade gem meant I didn't need to know all the possible variants of an ability beforehand, nor did I need to find the right tome to match the option I wanted.

The upgrade gem would find it for me.

Of course, there was no guarantee that any tier five variants of the whirlwind ability existed. Or if they did, that they were more suitable than the one in the ability tome I'd just bought.

Still, it was worth finding out.

Closing my fist around the upgrade gem, I willed my intent to the Adjudicator.

Ability gem activated.
Creating ability tome...

...
Tome creation halted.
There are 3 elite variants available for the whirlwind ability.

A small smile stole across my face. I'd guessed right! More text scrolled through my sight.

Variant 1: <u>whirlwind</u>. This variant increases the speed boost provided by the buff, allowing you to attack 6x faster than normal for 3 seconds.
Variant 2: <u>bladedancer</u>. This variant increases the buff's duration to 5 minutes, but only works while you are dual-wielding bladed weapons.
Variant 3: <u>wind daemon</u>. This variant modifies the buff so that it increases not only your attack speed but your movement speed as well, doubling both.

"Interesting," I murmured as I considered the three options on offer. Variant one was clearly the stock-standard one and doubled the boost the buff provided to attack speed.

Variant two didn't boost attack speed at all. Instead, it increased the buff time significantly. Unfortunately, it also restricted how I could use the ability.

The last option was the most intriguing. Assuming you discounted enhanced reflexes, I had no pure speed buffs—at all. Enhanced reflexes increased my Dexterity, and while that did provide a small boost to my overall speed, it did not increase it anywhere near by a factor of two.

Which wind daemon promised to do.

However, wind daemon also provided a smaller attack speed boost than either of the other two variants on offer. Nor had the Game made any mention of its duration. Would it remain at three seconds or would it last longer?

I didn't know. Nor did there appear to be any way to find out before I made my choice.

I sighed. Ultimately, though, the question boiled down to whether I was willing to sacrifice attack speed for movement speed. And the answer to that was...

Yes. Unequivocally, yes.

There were too many benefits to be had from moving faster. My decision made, I willed my intent to the Adjudicator.

You have upgraded your whirlwind ability to lesser <u>wind daemon</u>. Wind daemons are famously hard to hit and, just as famously, hard to block. They are preeminent fighters who rely on speed to carry through their

attacks and dodge incoming blows. The tier 5 variant of this ability doubles the speed of all your movements for 1 minute. Its activation time is fast, it consumes stamina, and it can be upgraded. You have 11 of 142 Dexterity ability slots remaining.

I smiled. The ability's description assuaged my doubts. I'd made the right choice. Lowering my head, I considered the rest of the objects on the bed.

So, what to continue with next?

Chapter 555: Choices

I spent the next few minutes improving the two tier three Dexterity abilities I'd marked for advancement.

You have upgraded your trap disarm ability to <u>superior trap disarm</u>. The fourth tier of this ability allows you to deactivate tier 4 traps.
You have upgraded your lockpick ability to <u>superior lockpicking</u>. The fourth tier of this ability allows you to open tier 4 locks.
You have 1 of 142 Dexterity ability slots remaining.

I didn't use a gem for either upgrade—and not because of how costly they were. I'd come a long way in the Game and the price of the upgrade gems were no longer a determining factor.

Still, the gems were rare and not easily come by. For which reason, I'd decided to restrict my use of them to abilities at tier five and above.

Lowering my gaze, I refocused on the ability tomes. I didn't have many low-tiered abilities anymore. In fact, only four upgradeable ones remained—piercing strike, conceal weapon, ventro, and imitate—and I'd already decided not to upgrade piercing strike and conceal weapon.

Which left only ventro and lesser imitate to consider.

I rubbed my chin thoughtfully. I was tempted to advance the imitate ability. But doing so would require a drastic shift in strategy—and reneging on previous decisions I'd made.

Given how little I could afford to invest in Perception, I had resolved to stop advancing lesser imitate and focus on mimic instead. And while my Perception slots were still limited, something else had happened to make me reconsider my approach.

Namely, I'd gained the shapeshift ability.

Mimic was useless to me in wolf form. But imitate wouldn't be.

With lesser imitate, I could, for instance, pretend to be a stygian hydra— my elder form was certainly large enough to pull off such a deception.

Hells, if I advanced lesser imitate all the way to tier six—transforming it into the doppelganger ability—I could conceivably *become* a hydra. Then, even the spores would not be able to detect me!

However, doing so would exact a hefty toll in Perception slots.

I bit my lip, pondering the cost. Was it worth it?

In the short run—definitely. The doppelganger variant of imitate would allow me to sneak up on the void tree, something I could not do presently and that could prove pivotal in the battle ahead.

Oh, my deception was not quite where it needed to be, but the skill was almost at rank twenty-four, and I foresaw no problems getting it to tier six in the next few days.

The bigger question, though, was whether imitate be useful beyond the forthcoming battle.

The answer to that was yes, too.

There was sector 30,199 to consider—and who knew how many other stygian sectors beyond that? All, no doubt, had spores aplenty.

My elder form itself was another consideration. As a doppelganger, not only would I be able to hide from the void's spores, I would also be able to conceal my spirit signatures *and* the elder form itself, which in turn, would allow me to walk freely amongst players in wolf form without fear of detection.

I sighed. In hindsight, I shouldn't have invested as heavily as I had in mimic. But to be fair, without mimic, I would never have survived my visit to Nexus—nor the Eastern Marches.

I picked up the tier three lesser imitate tome. *For now, I'll improve the ability to tier four,* I decided. There was no need to go further—yet.

Opening the tome, I began to read.

You have upgraded your lesser imitate ability to <u>improved imitate</u>. The tier 3 variant of this ability expands the spell's versatility, allowing you to disguise not only your voice, apparel, and appearance, but also your scent.

You have upgraded your lesser imitate ability to <u>superior imitate</u>. The tier 4 variant of this ability improves the spell's durability, allowing you to maintain the illusion around yourself for an entire day and even during combat.

You have 14 of 110 Perception ability slots remaining.

Closing my eyes, I contemplated the new knowledge sitting in my mind. Lesser imitate would work while I was in wolf form; I knew that for certain, and now I'd improved it to the point where I could use it in combat. The spell's potential effectiveness against my foes was still questionable, though.

The tier four variant wouldn't work against the spores—the spell remained illusion only—and players would still be able to see my spirit signatures—revealing my own player status. But even as limited as it was, imitate should still confound my foes for a few crucial seconds, and in the end, that could make all the difference.

With a mental shrug, I dismissed the matter from my mind. It was time to move on. Looking down, I considered the three Strength ability tomes I'd purchased: charge, overpowering blow, and stomp.

I had a fair idea what all three abilities did, and how they would synergize with my existing abilities, but I wasn't certain which one to focus on yet—so for now, I planned on learning the tier one variants of all three.

Opening the books in question, I absorbed their knowledge one after the other.

You have gained the basic ability: <u>charge</u>. This is a Strength ability that allows you to ram all targets in a 5 yard straight-line path, knocking each down for 1 second. Its activation time is very fast, it consumes stamina, and it can be upgraded. Note, this ability can only be used when you are in wolf form.

You have gained the basic ability: <u>overpowering blow</u>. This is a Strength ability that causes your next attack to deal 1.5x more damage than normal.

Its activation time is very fast, it consumes stamina, and it can be upgraded. Note, this ability can only be used when you are in wolf form.

You have gained the basic ability: <u>stomp</u>. This is a Strength ability that staggers all foes within 3 yards of you for 1 second. Staggered foes lose concentration and for the duration of the debuff can neither attack nor cast. Its activation time is very fast, it consumes stamina, and it can be upgraded. Note, this ability can only be used when you are in wolf form.

You have 37 of 40 Strength ability slots remaining.

I smiled in satisfaction. How effective the new abilities proved was yet to be seen, however their Game descriptions were promising.

There was one last matter to attend to: my mind abilities. Turning my attention inward, I called up the relevant Game information.

<u>Status of Mind abilities (156 of 188 slots used)</u>

Elite abilities (not eligible for upgrade): sentient shurikens, shadow jump, and impregnable mind.

Master abilities (eligible for upgrade): mass puppet, windborne, enhanced reflexes, and quick mend.

Basic abilities: stunning slap (can't be upgraded).

I sighed. The Adjudicator's response confirmed my fears. I only had enough Mind slots to advance two of my master abilities.

Mass puppet. Windborne. Enhanced reflexes. Or quick mend.

Which two did I advance?

Quick mend definitely. Its healing had proved lifesaving on more than one occasion. But what else?

Enhanced reflexes, I decided after contemplating the matter. Seeing that I didn't need better escape options just yet and the void tree's protective aura had effectively nullified my charm spell, upgrading windborne and mass puppet could wait.

Picking up an upgrade gem, I willed my intent to the Adjudicator.

Ability gem activated.

Creating ability tome...

...

You have acquired a tier V quick mend ability tome.

I sagged in disappointment. This time around, there were no variants on offer. Still, an elite version of the quick mend ability was nothing to scoff at, and opening the newly-acquired tome, I devoured its contents.

You have upgraded your quick mend ability to <u>greater quick mend</u>. The fifth tier of this spell increases the restorative effects provided by each trigger-cast to 50%. Additionally, the number of trigger-cast events generated has increased to 2.

"Wow," I murmured. The tier five variant of quick mend was even better than I'd anticipated. Not only would the spell trigger twice, it would restore half my health each time.

Definitely worth it, I concluded as I picked up the next ability gem.

Ability gem activated.
Creating ability tome...

...

Tome creation halted.
There are 2 elite variants available for the enhanced reflexes ability.

A wry chuckle escaped me. Using the upgrade gems for advancement was already yielding dividends! Stilling my impatience, I waited to see the options on offer.

Variant 1: <u>acrobat</u>. This variant increases your Dexterity by +30 ranks for 1 hour.
Variant 2: <u>engine of war</u>. This variant increases all your physical attributes: Strength, Constitution, and Dexterity, by +20 ranks for 30 minutes.

Ah, well, I thought, deflating slightly.
Both variants were nice, if not as good as I wanted them to be. But I didn't take overly long in making my decision. My Dexterity buff had served me well in the past, but the new engine of war variant offered better benefits, and I chose it without hesitation.

You have upgraded your enhanced reflexes ability to lesser <u>engine of war</u>. The tier 5 variant of this ability expands the reach of your chi to boost all 3 of your physical attributes by +20 for 30 minutes. Its activation time is slow, it consumes psi, and it can be upgraded.
You have 2 of 188 Mind ability slots remaining.

That'll do nicely, I thought with a pleased grin.
Scooping up the rest of the books and gems, I returned them to my bag of holding. I was done with my player progression, and now it was time to get some much-deserved sleep. Lying flat on the bed, I rested my head on the pillow.
Tomorrow would be another long, hard day, and hopefully by its end, our plans for dealing with the rift would be concluded.

Chapter 556: Reunions

You have slept 8 hours. Your stamina, mana, and psi reserves have been fully restored, and your blood memories have recharged.

You have lost knowledge of the stolen spells: mana strike, disrupting ray, and fireball.

Ghost's magma maw has reached rank 13, her ash armor rank 15, her death magic rank 11, and her nether manipulation rank 9.

You and Ghost have reached level 260!

I awoke, rested and refreshed, and to a surprising set of Game alerts. Ghost had obviously been fighting, and while I found the news initially alarming, I calmed quickly when I spotted no accompanying death message.

The pyre wolf was fine.

More than that, she was accompanied by the nagians. Elise and Lucius would not let any harm befall her. Sitting up and rubbing the sleep away from my eyes, I considered the rest of the Game alerts.

However, she'd done it, Ghost had earned us another level and, more importantly, a Class point each. Sadly, though, neither of my Class abilities were ready for upgrade. Advancing them would have to wait.

Swinging my legs off the bed, I rose to my feet. It was time to get the day started.

✱   ✱   ✱

The soft murmur of conversation greeted me as I made my way down to the former tavern's common room. I picked out Safyre's voice immediately, and then three more familiar voices. I sighed in relief. The dungeoneering trio had made it back safely from Korg.

With a smile on my face, I entered the common room.

Six faces turned my way—Safyre, Terence, Teresa, Nyra and the two forsworn on duty.

"Morning!" Terence called out exuberantly.

"Morning," I replied just as cheerfully. Nodding in greeting at the forsworn duo, I seated myself at the table with the other four.

"Where's Sedgwick?" I asked Safyre after we'd exchanged pleasantries.

"Sedgwick?" Nyra asked, a curious look on her face.

"Our new merchant," Safyre replied offhandedly. Receiving only blank stares from the trio, she smiled. "I'll explain later, but there have been more than a few changes since you three left."

"We can see that," Teresa said, her eyes drifting in the direction of the two silent forsworn at the far end of the room.

"But as to Sedge," Safyre went on, refocusing on me, "he's returned to sector 18,240 to poke around the tunnels."

I nodded in understanding before turning back to address the returning trio. "How was Korg?"

"Interesting," Nyra replied laconically.

"Quite," Terence echoed.

Teresa rolled her eyes. "These two... I don't know what's gotten into them, but they've been like this the past two days." She turned to face me. "We had a few hiccups," the young Lion admitted. "But nothing that we weren't able to deal with, and in the end, we achieved what we went in for."

"So... mission accomplished?" Safyre asked.

"Absolutely," Nyra confirmed with a sharp nod.

"Most definitely," Terence agreed.

Concealing a smile, I ran my gaze over the three, rechecking their analyze data.

The target is Nyra, a level 103 virulent witch.
The target is Terence, a level 117 arcane knight.
The target is Teresa, a level 119 priestess of the Blade.

The Game's feedback confirmed the trio's responses.

"A virulent witch. An arcane knight. And a priestess of the blade," I pronounced aloud for Safyre's benefit. "Congratulations. Those sound like excellent melded Classes."

Safyre whistled softly. "They're bi-blends?"

Teresa nodded smugly. "We each still have one more Class to get." She rubbed her hands together gleefully. "I, for one, cannot wait." While the other two didn't say anything, I could see the same hungry desire in their gazes.

They've grown, I thought. *And in more ways than one.*

Sitting back, I examined the three anew. Besides their second Classes, Nyra, Terence, and Teresa had each gained more than thirty levels from their time in the dungeon. That was not the entirety of the changes the trio had undergone, though.

Each carried themselves differently. More... confidently. Their gazes were steady and their movements sure. Gone was Nyra's tentativeness. Gone was the twins' self-doubt. Often masked by their brashness, it had always lurked beneath the surface.

There was none of that in evidence now.

And even though I'd only just reacquainted myself with the trio, I was sure their new self-assurance was not a passing fad. They'd changed—permanently—and for the better. Now, Nyra, Terrence, and Teresa were players.

In every sense of the word.

I smiled broadly and in genuine pleasure. "Tell us about your new Classes."

That drew a flurry of responses—even from the thus far mostly-monosyllabic Terence and Nyra.

I held up my hand, laughing. "Wow, slow down. Start at the beginning and leave nothing out. And while you're at it, give us a rundown of your journey through the dungeon too."

The three exchanged glances, then Teresa inclined her head solemnly in Nyra's direction. "You should start," she told my apprentice.

Nodding, the former assassin inhaled deeply. "I suppose I should begin with our shopping trip." Her eyes found mine. "After you left us in Korg Major, we..."

✳   ✳   ✳

It took two hours for the trio to finish reciting their tale, and though I felt the press of time, I didn't begrudge them their moment.

"Well," I said, when they at last fell silent, "that is quite the tale."

"You've done well," Safyre added warmly. "All three of you."

I nodded. "Agreed."

The three stiffened proudly.

Smiling, I turned to Safyre. "You've given them their faction tokens?"

"I have," she replied. "We are running low on them, by the way. There's just one left."

I grimaced. I would have to find the money to purchase more soon. "What about the farspeaker bracelets?"

"We could do with more of those too, but we still have some spares." Safyre gestured to the trio. "I've given them their bracelets as well."

"I don't need it," Nyra volunteered. "I have telepathy now!"

I grinned. "You do, true."

Nyra's second Class was that of a hedge witch, and in addition to granting her the herbalism and deception skills, the Class had also made her a psionic. She now had the same psi skills I had.

My smile faded. "That also means you can enter Atiras' Mind Trials. Do you think you're..."

"Ready?" she prompted when I ran aground.

I nodded.

"Yes."

For a moment, I said nothing, measuring her resolve, then I nodded decisively. "Very well. Inform Sulan you have my permission to enter the Rings."

Safyre glanced my way. "You are not returning to the cave with us?"

I shook my head. "It's better if I head straight to the brotherhood. Tell Adriel I'll take the new nagians' oaths when I return." I had delayed my meeting with the Brotherhood's huntmistress long enough as it was. "With every passing day, it becomes more urgent to find out where they stand." And if they would aid us as I hoped.

Safyre sighed but did not question my priorities. "What about Ghost?"

I grimaced. Hopefully, by now the pyre wolf's anger had subsided. Still, as evinced by this morning's Game messages, she appeared to be faring well

333

enough. "It's better she keeps doing what she is doing in the nether. The training will do her good."

Safyre didn't argue, but I could see she didn't agree with my decision. "Very well. I'll see these three back to base."

"What about us?" Terence asked abruptly. "What are our orders?"

I exchanged glances with Safyre.

"We could use them," she allowed, but didn't push the matter further.

"The Eastern Marches?" I asked obliquely.

She nodded.

I bowed my head, pondering the matter for a moment, then blew out an exasperated breath. Only hours ago, I'd been admiring the twins' newfound confidence, yet here I was hesitating to send them into danger.

Trust that they are capable. Trust that they can do what you ask.

Raising my head, I glanced from Terence to Teresa. "You recall what I told you of the Eastern Marches?"

Teresa nodded eagerly. "Every word," she promised. "You were trapped there for days."

"And you gave the sector to the Blades before you left," Terence added.

"Not quite, but close enough," I replied. "It's been about two weeks since Nyra, Adriel, and I escaped from sector 75,172." I paused. "You know what that means, right?"

Teresa nodded. "The Blades claim on the sector is still new."

"Which means they can't yet restrict who teleports into or out of the sector just yet," Terence added.

"Correct—on both accounts," I said. "But more crucially, it means our information on the sector is two weeks out of date. We don't know what's happened since we left. The Blades may not even be in control anymore. The Riders may have returned in force and kicked them out." I shrugged. "Or, who knows? A third party like the Reapers may have decided to take a hand in matters."

Teresa pursed her lips. "Alright, I get that. But why do you care? I thought we were done with the Eastern Marches?"

"That's right," Nyra put in. "In fact, the only relevance sector 75,172 has is—" Breaking off, she inhaled sharply in realization. "You're bringing them back!"

Terence frowned. "Bringing back who?"

I turned his way. "Tomorrow—or perhaps, even as early as today— Ceruvax, Farren, the Pack of the Reach, and the Bane Wolves will exit Draven's Reach and enter the Eastern Marches."

Teresa's eyes widened. "Oh my!"

"And as Michael has pointed out," Safyre began, "we don't know what they will find when they do. Odds are that nothing has changed at the portal tower. The town around it is probably still deserted. But it will be good to have confirmation."

Teresa nodded slowly. "You want us to scout the sector?"

"Not the sector," I corrected firmly, "just the environs of the town housing the exit portal. Once you've confirmed it's still vacant, you'll wait for Ceruvax and the others to arrive, then escort them back to sector 18,240." I paused. "Do you think you two are up to the task?"

The twins stiffened to attention. "Of course."

I rose to my feet. "Good. Then, you best be about it."

✳   ✳   ✳

You have lost snake bite and ghoul maker.

Before the others left, I gave Nyra the two rank five daggers I'd looted from Sintar. She had the daggers skill, and they would serve her better than they did me.

The trio's return was yet another worry shed from my mind. *Now,* I thought wryly, *I've only three other things to stew over.*

Shael and Anriq's expedition.

Zekiel's.

And the brotherhood.

Still, I had a fair idea what the outcome of the first two would be. The third though... that was the wild card. Notwithstanding Kesh's involvement and Safyre's assurances, I knew things with the brotherhood could go either way. Convincing them to help was crucial.

So, let's hurry up and do that.

Drawing psi, I saw to my final preparations.

You have cast mimic, transforming your visage into that of Havick, a level 187 human scout and concealing your Powerful Initiate Mark. Duration: 10 hours.

You have activated the simple mode enchantment of the belt of the chameleon. Your armor and weapons are now hidden.

Disguise in place, I spun on my heel and made for the forsworn at the end of the room.

Safyre had given the two the coordinates of the sector where I was meeting the brotherhood. "I'm ready," I told the pair.

Inclining their heads in silent acknowledgment—the two were some of the most reticent players I'd met—the first began chanting.

While I waited for the portal to open, my gaze drifted idly across the Roost's shuttered windows. I'd not so much as glanced outside the building to see what was going on in the sector. And while I was eager—desperate even—to gain more insight into Saya's fate, I knew now was neither the time nor the place to investigate further. Until sector 18,240 was reclaimed, I couldn't afford to be distracted.

Llewyn has opened a greater portal to sector 45,104.

"Thank you," I murmured, turning back to face the newly opened gateway. *This was it.* The biggest unresolved piece for my grand plan. Would the brotherhood cooperate?

Time to find out.

Inhaling deeply, I stepped through the portal.

Transfer commencing...

...

...

Passage completed!

CHAPTER 557: THE CORAL ISLANDS

You have entered the safe zone of sector 45,104 of the Forever Kingdom, an open sector forming part of the region known as the Coral Islands. It is currently neutral territory, unclaimed by any faction or Force.

Note, a shield generator is in place around the sector, preventing portals from opening anywhere except in the designated teleportation areas.

I stepped out of the gateway, blinking in surprise. The sector welcome message had me confounded.

Sector 45,104 was both unowned *and* protected by a shield generator? Just like our own sector 18,240? And the region's name, Coral Islands... it tugged at my memory. I'd heard of it before or of somewhere similar. But where?

Setting aside these troubling questions, I glanced around.

Not unexpectedly, I was on a teleportation platform—just like the one in Nexus. But this one was many times less busy. And no city lay beyond. Instead, I was in what appeared to be a bustling town.

A seaside town.

Lifting my head, I tasted the sea breeze. Wind tugged at my hair and spray brushed my face. *The platform must lie right up against the shoreline*, I thought. And sure enough, when I glanced around, I spotted waves of dark green, topped by frothing white, crash against the rocky beach.

"Are you quite done taking in the sights, friend?" a bored voice asked.

Turning around, I found a player attired in what looked like a uniform patiently waiting for my attention. "Customs official," he said, identifying himself before I could ask.

I'd been aware of the player, of course—Texalo was his name—but seeing that I was in a safe zone, I'd not considered him or any of the other nearby players a danger.

Texalo waved his arm in front of my face. "Well? Aren't you going to say anything?"

Finding myself wondering if I was in the right place, I stayed silent.

You have passed a mental resistance check!
Texalo has failed to pierce your disguise.

The custom official sighed. "If you didn't know, friend, this is where you tell me your name, Class, rank, Force affiliations, and faction."

"Where am I?" I asked instead.

Texalo rolled his eyes. "The brotherhood port town of Sango."

"Ah," I breathed. So, despite the unexpectedness of the surroundings, I was in the right place, after all. Taking a moment to compose my response, I gave the official the answer he sought. "Havick. Rank eighteen scout. Unaffiliated and factionless."

Texalo quickly scribbled down the information on the board he was carrying. "Good. Are you here to buy or sell?"

I blinked. "Neither."

He shook his head. "The form only has space for one or the other. Choose."

"I'm here to buy then, I suppose," I replied in bemusement.

"Got it. Which merchant do you represent?"

"None."

Sighing again, the official put down his board. "Look, friend, I'm not sure how you got here or who told you to come here, but Sango doesn't cater to independents. This town is for *bulk* trading only." He threw me a sympathetic look. "None of the brotherhood merchants here are going to sell you—"

"I'm here to see Huntmistress Kartara," I interjected.

Texalo's eyes widened fractionally before narrowing again. "The huntmistress does not see anybody without an appointment."

"I was invited," I replied tersely.

Picking up his board again, Texalo scanned it. "I don't see a Havick listed here."

I pinched the bridge of my nose. Of course, there wouldn't be. And truly, I had no idea what name Kesh had given the brotherhood during her negotiations. *Perhaps you should have asked, eh?*

I turned back to the official. "Hmm, maybe it's better if I speak to someone higher up the food chain?"

Texalo smiled. "Sorry, friend, I'm it. Now, seeing as you don't have an appointment, I'm afraid I'm going to have to ask you to leave. If you don't, I'll be forced to summon the—"

"Kesh," I said abruptly.

He blinked. "What?"

"I'm here as a representative of Kesh's Emporium. If you look, I'm sure you'll find an appointment listed in the emporium's name." I was sure of no such thing, but there was a good chance I'd guessed right. If not, I would have to take more drastic measures to gain the brotherhood's attention.

Texalo didn't inspect his board again. Instead, he stared at me in steely assessment. "Are you sure? Because if you're lying, I warn you the guards will not go lightly on you."

"I am," I replied, showing no trace of uncertainty.

Texalo nodded slowly. "On your head be it, then." Not waiting for my response, he shouted over his shoulder. "Gorn, take over. I'm going to escort this here fellow up to the castle. The huntmistress will want to see him."

✳   ✳   ✳

You have left a safe zone.

The castle was outside the bounds of the safe zone, and while security in the town was lax, the same could not be said for the fortified structure sitting atop a seaside cliff that served as the brotherhood's headquarters in this sector.

The castle bristled with towers and ramparts, dozens of guards patrolled the perimeter, and using the sorcerer's coif, I spied no less than a dozen tier six wards.

Which left me wondering if there were not even more powerful wards that I could not see.

Still, I did not let the castle's menacing appearance trouble me. This sector was unowned, and even if the brotherhood meant me harm, they would not be able to keep me trapped in the region.

Texalo drew to a stop before the castle's barred doors, and following on his heels, I did, too.

"Who's this?" one of the players on guard demanded. He, too, was in uniform—a simple garb shaded a deep purple. Proudly displayed on his chest was the silver medallion of the brotherhood.

"No idea," the custom official replied cheerfully. "Calls himself Havick."

I glanced sideways at the man. He'd said nothing the entire trip, and I'd thought nothing of it. Yet it seemed I'd done something to raise his suspicions.

The guard yawned. "So, why bring him here, Tex?"

Texalo shrugged. "He claims to be from the emporium."

The guard's gaze shifted to me. "One of Kesh's, eh?"

"Not quite," I replied. "I'm a customer of the emporium. Kesh, at my request, is acting as my intermediary with the brotherhood."

The guard turned to his partner. "What do you think?"

"He must be the one we were told about," he replied equably.

The first guard grunted. "Doesn't look like much." Not waiting for my response, he turned around and pushed open the door. "Follow me, and no dawdling!"

✳   ✳   ✳

You have entered the dampening field: <u>brotherly shield</u>. This is a tier 6 shield keyed to members of the stygian brotherhood.

You are <u>ability-locked</u>. While ability-locked, you are prevented from casting any psi, mana, or stamina abilities of tier 5 and below.

You are <u>scry-locked</u>. While scry-locked, you are prevented from using any remote observation abilities of tier 5 and below.

Duration: infinite. Both debuffs will remain in effect as long as you are within the confines of the dampening field.

The dampening field came as no surprise.

I'd detected it from outside. And while letting myself be disarmed so left a sour taste in the mouth, I accepted it as the cost of doing business. I, too, would be as wary of any strangers entering the heart of my demesne.

More troubling, though, were the eyes I felt upon me, following me every step of the way on my journey through the castle. I was being watched, and the gazes of the watchers did not feel kindly, at all. Ignoring the tingling touch of magic on my skin, the inquisitive mental probes against my mind, and the scrutiny of the guards lining the corridors, I strode nonchalantly behind my escort.

To my surprise, the guard led me not to a receiving room or an audience chamber as I expected, but back out into a courtyard flooded with bright sunlight.

I drew to a halt.

I was in a training yard.

On the hard-packed sands ahead, a tall woman was sparring against three others. She wielded two curved stygian swords and was armored in dull purple scale mail—also forged from a stygian composite, I thought. Her long black hair was tied back in a bun, and a trio of silver brotherhood medallions graced each of her gauntlets. Moving lithely between her foes, she dodged their blows while launching her own ripostes.

As I watched, the analyze information of the four combatants slipped into my awareness—analyze was not a psi, mana, or stamina ability and, therefore, was unaffected by the dampening field.

The target is Cait, a level 230 elven nether witch.
The target is Duskar, a level 218 orcish voidknight.
The target is Senzo, a level 219 human spymaster.
The target is Kartara, a level 276 human dread summoner. She bears a Mark of Greater Shadow, Greater Light, and Greater Dark.

My eyebrows rose. The huntmistress was over rank twenty-five and yet possessed no Powerful Initiate Mark. That could only mean she lacked an evolved Class.

Well, that or she was concealing the Mark, and not her level—which would make no sense, at all.

"He's analyzed us," the spymaster said, breaking off from the skirmish.

Four pairs of eyes turned my way.

"Has he?" Kartara murmured, sounding not at all put off by that. "Even you?"

Senzo hesitated, then gave a clipped nod. "I think so."

"And what can you tell about him?" the huntmistress asked.

The spymaster's eyes tightened fractionally as he inspected me.

Senzo has failed to pierce your disguise.
Your deception has reached rank 24.

The spymaster grunted. "Less than Fiona. According to the Game he is a level 187 scout named Havick."

Fiona? I wondered, keeping my expression studiously neutral in the face of the four's examination. *Who is that?*

"Interesting." Sheathing her blades, the huntmistress strode toward me. "Return to the barracks and await my orders," she called over her shoulders in what was a clear dismissal of the trio.

"Are you sure?" the orc growled. "We don't know—"

"I'm sure," Kartara interjected, not bothering to look back. "Go."

The three went, leaving me alone with the huntmistress and my escort.

Kartara's eyes flickered to the guard, and bowing low, he too, retreated from the training yard.

"So," the huntmistress began when we were finally alone, "you are the one Kesh spoke of."

There was no hint of a question in her tone. I inclined my head. "I am."

Tilting her head to the side, Kartara scrutinized me from head to toe. "You are not what I expected," she murmured.

Neither was she, but I kept that observation to myself.

Summoning a towel from somewhere—a bag of holding most likely—the huntmistress began wiping off the sweat beading down her face. "Walk with me, please," she said as she did so.

I did as she bade, and we strode through the courtyard. Maintaining my counsel, I waited for the huntmistress to begin, but she, too, remained silent while she gathered her thoughts.

Eventually, realizing Kartara was waiting for me to start, I asked curiously. "Why the training?"

The huntmistress blinked. "Excuse me?"

I gestured to the now empty sparring field. "Why train? The Game will not award you any skill gains from such bouts. So, why bother?"

A smile tugged at Kartara's lips. "Then it is a good thing I don't have any martial skills."

My brows crinkled, not understanding.

Seeing my mystified expression, Kartara chuckled. "What I mean to say is I have no Game-gifted skills with either a sword or medium armor."

I gaped at her. I'd just seen the huntmistress fight, and I could say with certainty she was no novice of the blade. I'd even go so far as to say that Kartara was nearly as good as any blademaster I'd encountered. "Then all that—" I waved my hand airily—"is self-taught?"

"Not entirely," Kartara murmured, her eyes twinkling. "I had some excellent tutors."

"Damn," I said, unexpectedly impressed. "How long did it take you to learn to fight like that?"

"Decades," she replied softly, her amusement fading.

The huntmistress looked not a day older than thirty, but I knew players in the Game aged slowly. That did not lessen her achievement, though. Spending years mastering a single skill... that took real discipline.

Intellectually, I'd always known learning a skill without the aid of the Game was possible, yet I'd always wondered about its practical benefits. "How well do your sword skills perform? In actual combat, I mean."

Kartara threw me a wry look. "You mean would I have been able to defeat those three in a 'real' fight?"

I nodded.

"Not likely," she replied. "At least, not with my blades alone. In a *real* fight, Duskar, Cait, and Senzo would use their abilities." She paused. "But then so would I, and then it wouldn't be a simple swordfight anymore."

"I see."

"That does not make my sword skills superfluous, though. In a pinch, I can use it to surprise my foes." She eyed me thoughtfully. "And as I'm sure you know, sometimes surprise alone can carry a battle."

"That it can," I murmured. Whatever else the huntmistress was, she was clearly a dangerous player, and not just because of her Game-granted abilities. My initial impression was that Kartara was not only a student of war, but also someone who honed her skills incessantly.

She's definitely someone I want on my side.

I slowed to a halt. "Shall we get down to business, then?"

Stopping beside me, the huntmistress studied me gravely for a second, then shook her head. "No."

I stared at her in surprise. "No?"

"No," she repeated firmly. "I will not deal with someone whose intentions I do not understand, and who by all appearances knows nothing of the brotherhood, what we are capable of, or what we do."

My lips drew into a thin line. "I assure you I know everything I need to about your brotherhood."

Kartara raised one delicate eyebrow. "You do? Tell me then."

The request caught me off guard, but I forged ahead anyway, "I know the brotherhood is not beholden to any faction or Power. I know you are the foremost experts on the void. I also know you have a near monopoly on stygian artifacts. And finally, I know you are not above capturing and binding nether creatures for your own use."

The huntmistress' eyes darkened. "'For our own use' and what use do you suppose that may be?"

"Profit," I said, seeing no reason not to be transparent about it.

This time there was no mistaking the anger clouding Kartara's expression. "Profit," she spat. "You know nothing of us at all!"

I opened my mouth in protest.

The huntmistress held up a hand. "Quiet!" Spinning on her heel, and not waiting to see if I followed, she headed for the nearest castle entrance. "If you wish to learn the truth about the brotherhood, come with me. Otherwise, you may leave the same way you came in."

Left with no other choice, I hurried after her.

✳ ✳ ✳

Kartara led me through what I thought to be the castle's east wing. The passages were small and dark with no doors leading off them. Nor did I sense any watchers, nor spy any guards. It left me to speculate as to the purpose of the wing.

I wasn't left wondering long, though.

Turning a corner, we entered a windowless hall, one large enough to house the hundreds of stygians inside.

All roaming freely.

On catching sight of me, the creatures hissed in anger. My hands dropped to my waist, ready to disengage the chameleon belt's enchantments and draw my blades.

"There's no need for that," Kartara said.

I glanced warily from the huntmistress to the stygians drawing closer to me. Already, some two dozen of the creatures were within striking range, hydras and serpents mostly, but also a few weavers too. "Why? Are they tame?"

"Tame?" Kartara's lips curved upward in another smile, her earlier anger seemingly forgotten. "Definitely not, but they *are* leashed."

Suddenly, all three hundred odd stygians in the hall froze—near simultaneously.

My tension did not ease. "How did you do that?" I demanded tersely. That the huntmistress had done something was obvious, but what? It couldn't have been a charm spell she had used, there were too many stygians for that.

Kartara tapped the back of her gauntlets. "I used these."

Glancing at the objects in question, I noticed that the silver medallions inset in them were glowing gently. "The medallions? I've used one of those before. I thought all they are good for is summoning stygians?"

The huntmistress tilted her head to the side. "You have? How curious. But it was not the medallions I was referring to, but the gauntlets themselves. They're soulbound—so don't get any ideas—and they allow me to control any brotherhood-collared stygian."

I finally relaxed. Whatever was on Kartara's mind, it didn't appear to include murder. "Collared? What do you mean by that?"

She jerked her head in the direction of the closest stygian. "Have a look for yourself."

I studied the serpent in question but failed to see what the huntmistress was referring to.

Kartara rolled her eyes. "Go closer. It won't bite—promise."

Not amused by her tone, I stepped up the stygian serpent, nonetheless.

"Look between the head and the torso," Kartara instructed. "*Beneath* the surface."

I leaned forward. The void's creatures—the lesser ones especially—were not truly solid, which was how I'd missed the thin strip of black metal in the first place. Like the huntmistress had said, it was buried inside the serpent's shadowy form.

Reaching out with my will, I inspected the device.

The target is a tier 4 <u>obedience collar</u> crafted by Orwel, an enchanter from the stygian brotherhood. The artifact is embedded with a netherstone fragment and allows members of the brotherhood to impose their will on the collar's subject. This item may only be employed on a nether creature below level 150.

I straightened. "Are all the stygians in the hall similarly leashed?"
"Yes."

"How did you manage to collar so many?"

Kartara shrugged. "We outsource most of the work, offering bounties and the like to any player who cares to try."

At the mention of bounties, I recalled the bounty I myself had taken up— but never fulfilled—during my first trip to Nexus. It was a small, but important, confirmation of the huntmistress' words.

"I still don't get it," I said, shaking my head. "You've used a netherstone fragment in the collar's making, which means the device itself must cost a pretty penny. Not to mention the cost involved in capturing and subduing a stygian." The bounty in question had been for one hundred and fifty gold, I recalled. "Why go through all that trouble? Are you building an army here?"

"An army? Not at all. These stygians are only a tiny fraction of the creatures the brotherhood has captured over the years."

I frowned. "A fraction? Where are the rest?"

"Back in the void."

My eyes widened. "Back in the—?" I broke off, my gaze darting between the collar, the gauntlet, and the medallion as I finally made the connection.

I inhaled sharply. "You recall them at need from the void using the medallion. The netherstone fragment in the collar allows a summoning portal to lock on the creature. And the gauntlet ensures their obedience once they answer the call."

The huntmistress smiled in genuine pleasure. "Exactly right. Congratulations. You've worked it out much faster than most do."

I rubbed my chin. "It still sounds like a lot of trouble to go through for what at the end of the day is still a rank three creature."

Kartara nodded. "I won't argue with you on that point. And you haven't even factored in the training the creatures must undergo before we return them to the void." She stepped closer. "But what value would you place on a scout who is able to move unseen through the void and see through the nether's mists as if it weren't there?"

I stilled, for a moment thinking it was me she was speaking about before realizing it was the collared stygians she referred to. "Your pets can do all that?"

Kartara stepped back. "They can. Our scryers can even see through their eyes. Sadly, though, we cannot pilot the creatures remotely."

I nodded slowly. "What about the void trees? Can they sense the hold you have over their minions?"

My question caused Kartara to scrutinize me anew. "You are remarkably well informed about the stygians. First your casual mention of netherstones, and now your talk about void trees. What do you know of the void?"

"Enough to believe them a menace that's been ignored for too long," I replied vaguely.

Oddly, my answer caused another smile to brighten the huntmistress' face, and she went on as if she hadn't just interrupted me. "We don't use the collars to dominate the stygians. There is no mind control involved, at all."

My eyes narrowed. "You don't? There isn't? How do you control them then?"

"Through months of rigorous conditioning that involves inflicting pain for disobedience and pleasure for good behavior."

"That works?" I asked, making no effort to mask my skepticism.

"Believe it or not, it does. And best of all, because we employ no mental trickery, the void trees cannot sense our hold over collared creatures."

I pursed my lips. Despite my doubts, I didn't fail to see the value in what the huntmistress was describing. "If your 'scouts' can do what you say, I agree, they would prove an invaluable resource in the nether."

The huntmistress' lips curved anew. "I'm glad you see it our way."

I took another long slow look around the room. "And is this what you wanted to show me?"

"This? This is just the beginning. There is far more to what we do, and more importantly, why we do it." Turning about, she strode toward the opposite end of the hall. "Follow me."

✻　✻　✻

Kartara led me through another set of winding passages, before coming to a stop in front of a steel-clad door.

The chamber beyond was crammed with long lines of tables overflowing with implements whose use I could not fathom. There were players aplenty in the room too, using the strange instruments.

The far wall of the room was stacked with cages. My eyes narrowed as I beheld the occupants—stygians. As I watched, two brotherhood members dragged one out and dumped it on an empty steel table.

Then they proceeded to cut into it.

My lips twisted in disgust. This is what the huntmistress wanted me to see? Her people butchering stygians? "Why are they doing that?" I demanded

Hearing the revulsion in my tone, Kartara followed my gaze. "Dissecting it, you mean?" she asked mildly.

"Call it what it is—butchery."

She shrugged. "Semantics."

"I'd still like to know what in hells you think they—"

"Have you ever wondered how the void creates its minions?"

My eyes narrowed anew. "Creates? You don't think the stygians are natural-born creatures?"

The huntmistress laughed. "There's nothing natural about the void nor its minions."

My lips turned down. "A poor choice of words on my part. Still, you must know what I mean. What has spurred your... theory."

"It's not just theory." She swung back to face me. "And we don't dissect the stygians on mere whim. There is a whole host of evidence to support the assertion of our top scholars that the stygians are created, not born."

"Such as?" I rasped.

"Such as the fact that despite us raiding thousands of nests over many decades, there has been no recorded sighting of a stygian young. Or the fact that the nether creatures bear an uncanny resemblance to ordinary beasts. Or the fact that at periodic, if rare, intervals 'new' stygians suddenly appear—and in such numbers, it beggars belief no one has encountered them before. And finally, if that were not enough, there are the chimeras to consider." The huntmistress repressed a shudder. "They, undoubtedly, are *not* natural creatures."

There was no arguing with that. Running my gaze over the far wall again, I rechecked the cages. But my initial assessment had been correct. There were no chimeras within.

Still, the very fact that the brotherhood made use of netherstone fragments in their collars meant they had run across the harbingers before.

I sighed. "So, how does dissecting lesser stygians help?"

"I'm not sure it does," Kartara admitted, "but it's an important step in learning more about our archenemies."

I studied the huntmistress carefully. I'd known the brotherhood and stygians were not on friendly terms, of course. Everything I'd seen in the castle had only reinforced that notion. But labeling the stygians archenemies? It suggested the stygians were more than a means-to-an-end for the brotherhood.

"That's a strong word," I said finally. "What makes you call them that?"

"Isn't it obvious?" Kartara countered. "The void has plagued the Kingdom for millennia, since even before the... well, let's just say forever and leave it at that. Over that time, the stygians have claimed millions of lives and hundreds of sectors, and yet the Powers don't seem to care."

I opened my mouth to voice a question, but Kartara rushed on before I could do so. "Do you know how many sectors are lost to the nether annually? Or how many ordinary people die from nether poisoning ?"

I shook my head. I didn't.

"The number of victims the nether claims every year runs into the thousands," Kartara said. "In a good year, we lose one sector. In a bad, as many as five." Her lips twisted. "And for all the Triumvirate's efficiency in closing down rifts in Nexus, that does nothing to help the rest of the Kingdom."

I could only nod wordlessly in response.

Kartara barely noticed as her words spewed out faster "Entire civilizations have been lost. Species eradicated. And what do we do when that happens? We move on, that's what. We seal this dungeon. Close off that sector. And move on to the next. As if there will be an endless supply of 'nexts.'" She shook her head sadly. "One day our inaction will catch up to us, and by then it will be too late."

"So... the brotherhood is on a crusade to save the world?" I asked quietly.

Kartara's eyes shone fiercely—and defiantly—as she leaned in closer. "Yes! From itself if needs be."

I didn't flinch from her gaze. "With all due respect, you cannot do it alone."

Laughing hollowly, Kartara backed away. "Oh, I know that. But what choice do we have? Everyone else—players, Powers, and factions alike— seem bent on ignoring the threat."

Now, seemed like the opportune moment to pledge my support for the brotherhood's cause, and I opened my mouth to do just that, but the huntmistress was already striding away—again.

"This way," she called over her shoulder.

Sighing, I hurried after her.

Chapter 559: An Education

The next room Kartara led me to was a library. Shelves lined every wall, each full of neatly stacked books.

Striding down the center of the chamber, the huntmistress spread her arms and turned around in a slow circle. "This is the work of centuries, and contains every last morsel of information the brotherhood has gathered on the void—every report, every sighting, every encounter described in exacting detail, and—" she smiled self-deprecatingly— "more than a few wild theories."

I whistled softly as I took in the wealth of knowledge in the room. "Is it safe?"

Kartara blinked. "Safe?"

I nodded. While the library was covered by the same dampening field filling the rest of the castle, there were no added defenses that I could detect. "Is it... uhm, wise to leave such priceless knowledge unguarded like this. Wouldn't it be better to store the books in a bank vault or—"

Kartara burst out into laughter. "Ah, Havick—that's what we're calling you, right?—don't you understand? No one but the brotherhood is interested in the information in this room. We don't hoard it. We've tried giving it away, many a time in fact, but the factions are simply not interested."

"Oh," I said, not knowing what else to say.

Kartara shook her head. "But it's not for the books that I've brought you here." Marching to an ornate table, she waved me over. "It's this."

Striding to her side, I glanced down at the table and the map prominently displayed on it. "What am I looking at?" I asked softly.

"The Nethersphere," Kartara replied, "or as much of it as we've managed to map."

My curiosity piqued, I inspected the map closely.

The parchment was peppered by small multicolored dots interconnected by thin lines. Leaning closer, I spotted a string of numbers beside each. The dots were sectors then.

But there were hundreds of dots.

I swallowed, imagining what that equated to in lives lost. "What do the colors mean?" I asked in a hushed tone.

"These circles—" Kartara's hand swept across the map, pointing out the green ones—"are sectors still free of the nether but in which a rift has appeared at one time or another."

I exhaled. At least a third of the dots were green. "Then there is still some hope of saving them," I murmured.

Kartara shook her head. "You would think so, but no. Few sectors have the resources of Nexus, and once the void finds them, it's only a matter of time before they fall."

"Surely, the Powers don't allow that," I objected.

"I told you the Powers don't care enough to intervene."

"Self-interest alone would—"

"Self-interest only goes so far. The void's incursions rarely touch the sectors held by the major Powers, and when they do, they are quickly squashed." The hunt mistress gestured at the map again. "But these green circles... none of them are a sector owned by one of the big factions. So why would the Game's elite bother helping?"

I wasn't ready to let the matter go. "What about ordinary players? I would think many of them would leap at the chance of earning the Adjudicator's favor. The Game rewards players for closing down rifts, after all."

Kartara snorted delicately. "You're right, players are all too keen to earn the Game's rewards. But rift-diving is dangerous enough—and venturing into a nether sector to kill a seed is as far as most are willing to go. How many, though, do you think are willing to tackle a stygian Power, or even an elite, in the selfsame sector—knowing full well there is no safe zone?"

She paused, waiting for my response. But I stayed quiet. The answer was self-evident.

"Not many, let me tell you," she went on. "And if you ask me, the risk of final death is likely the reason the Powers are themselves reluctant to enter the nether." Her lips twisted sardonically. "Why risk immortality, after all, for the sake of a few proles?"

I grimaced. The huntmistress words were deeply disturbing, yet for all that, I could not refute them. Not bothering to argue the point further, I moved the conversation on. "What about the other dots?"

"The yellow circles are sectors in which the mists have seeped in but are yet unclaimed by the nether. Red represents those taken over by a young void tree. Black is the domain of a mature void tree. And as for the gray circles... they are the ones that despite our best efforts remain opaque to us."

"Meaning?"

"We don't know what manner of nether menace occupies them."

I turned my attention back to the map. The gray and black dots were few and far between. "Then this is not a map of the Nethersphere but only of sectors threatened by it." I glanced at the huntmistress. "You misspoke earlier."

Her eyes glittered. "Did I?"

I nodded. "I have been to the nether as you must know." I placed a finger on a black circle. "Judging by the sector welcome messages, it is only the ones claimed by mature trees that are fully of the Nethersphere." My finger shifted to a red circle. "These can still be reclaimed."

For a drawn-out moment, Kartara said nothing, and though I did not turn her way again, I could feel the weight of her gaze upon my neck.

"So, it is to try and reclaim a sector held by a young void tree that you've requested our help?" she asked finally.

"Yes," I replied forthrightly, my gaze still on the map. Kesh should have already told her as much.

"Then it's a fool's errand you embark on."

I turned about to face her. "I disagree."

Unexpectedly, the huntmistress smiled. "How old are you... Havick?"

I blinked, thrown by the apparent non-sequitur. "Why do you ask?"

Kartara began walking away. "Oh, merely because it is only the young who are so foolishly optimistic."

I glared at her receding back. "That's not what—"

"The tour is not yet done," she said, cutting me off. "Keep up now."

My frustration mounting, I chased after the huntmistress.

✱　✱　✱

I barely paid the next set of passages we ventured through any heed. Instead, my thoughts turned inwards, I found myself questioning the wisdom of my current course.

Had it been a mistake to seek out the brotherhood?

While the huntmistress herself and everything she'd shown me was undoubtedly impressive, and a testament of the brotherhood's dedication to their cause, so far Kartara had expressed no interest in my mission or providing the help I'd requested from her people.

And I began to fear she had none.

Which begged the question: why had the huntmistress requested meeting me in the first place?

"We're here."

My musings coming to an abrupt end, I wrenched to a halt and looked around.

'Here' was an empty room of startling white with only a single decorative piece—a wall hanging in front of which the huntmistress had stopped.

"What's this?" I asked, as she clearly intended me to.

"The lifecycle of a void tree."

My interest sharpening, I gave the wall hanging my full attention.

It was a piece of intricately woven tapestry. At the top was a small black crystal—representing a stygian seed, I thought. Below the seed was a sapling, followed by six iterations of trees, each getting progressively bigger.

I swallowed. *Five? That must mean—*

Kartara's hand snapped out, and moving down the tapestry, she named each representation. "Seed. Sapling. Young. Mature. Old. Elder. Ancient. And finally, at the center of the web, the void fathers."

"Damnation," I whispered. "And they're all trees?"

The huntmistress hesitated fractionally. "We think so."

I threw her a sharp look. "You *think* so?"

"No brotherhood member has ever set eyes on anything greater than an old tree."

I frowned. "Then how do you know they exist?"

"From folklore and other bits of ancient histories we've managed to scavenge over the years."

I threw her an incredulous look. "You trust such information?"

Kartara folded her arms behind her back—to hide the sudden nervous tic of her fingers, I thought. It was the first sign of discomfort I'd yet seen from the huntmistress, and I didn't fail to mark it.

Or wonder as to its cause. But I had my suspicions about that.

"Not entirely," Kartara admitted, oblivious to my observations and thoughts. "However, despite our best efforts we've not been able to verify or disprove their claims."

"I see," I said, letting the matter lie. It was not a tangent I wanted to pursue right now. "What else can you tell me about the void trees?"

"They're sentient, uncannily smart, powerful psionics, but barely proficient mana casters."

I pondered her words. "What about the seeds?"

"Stygian seeds are psionics, too. But their mental abilities hardly need to be feared."

She was wrong about that, but sharing my own experience with the seeds in Draven's Reach would be too revealing. "What about sentience?"

"What about it?"

"Are the seeds... uhm, sentient?"

The huntmistress frowned. "In some sense they are living creatures, if that's what you mean, but if you're asking are they self-aware...?" Trailing off, she looked at me questioningly.

I nodded mutely.

Her frown deepened. "Some in the brotherhood seem to believe so, but there has been no conclusive proof one way or another." She shook her head. "Anyway, it's a moot point."

"Oh?"

"These days, it's brotherhood policy to kill any seed or sapling that comes into our possession. We've suffered too many unexplained accidents in the past for us to do otherwise."

"Ah, that's good."

My words earned me a strange look, but with a shrug, the huntmistress, dismissed the matter and moved on, "Void trees and nether sectors are inextricably linked. Wherever you find a sector lost to the nether, you will find a void tree."

"Because the trees are the ones creating the mists filling them?" I ventured.

Kartara nodded. "So, we believe. As far as the brotherhood has been able to ascertain, void trees have only two purposes: producing nether and creating rifts."

"Which in turn serves to expand the Nethersphere," I observed.

"Exactly. That's the void's ultimate goal: to consume everything in its path."

I pursed my lips. "So, why aren't you trying to stop it? That's your mission, isn't it?"

"Oh, we are. And it is. The brotherhood works tirelessly to close every rift we find—stopping the rot *before* it spreads." She shook her head. "But what we can't do, what we have never been able to do, is *reverse* the void's corruption."

I chewed over her words for a moment. "You're saying the brotherhood has never defeated a mature tree."

She laughed hollowly. "I'm saying more than that. Once the void's hold is so entrenched that the safe zone itself disappears, we consider it lost." She held my gaze. "No matter what the Adjudicator may say on the matter."

"But—"

Raising a hand, Kartara stopped me. "Havick," she said, almost wearily, "despite centuries of trying, no brotherhood force has ever managed to destroy a young tree. And if you let me finish, I will explain why."

Despite an almost compulsive urge to contradict the huntmistress, I sat back on my heels and schooled myself to patience. "Go on."

"Thank you." Kartara pointed to the chart in the wall hanging again. "By now, you likely know that the seeds can open rifts into a Kingdom sector. Such rifts start relatively small though and only grant passage to stygian creatures of tier four and below. However, as the seed grows, so too does the size of the rift, and by the time the seed sprouts into a sapling, its ley line is stable enough for the sapling itself to pass through."

I rubbed my chin, thoughtfully. The sapling I'd encountered in Draven's Reach had been rank twenty. "Following that logic, by that stage the rift must be... tier five?"

"Correct. So not only can the sapling pass through, so, too, can other stygian elites."

"I see. Go on."

"Once on the other side—in virgin territory, so to speak—the sapling begins producing nether mist in earnest. It still can't survive without the help of its parent though, so the rift remains open. But day by day, the mist around the sapling grows, as does the nest of stygians protecting it and the rift itself." Kartara's finger stabbed down on the representation of the sapling in the tapestry. "This is our last chance of stopping the void."

I was fairly certain I knew where she was going with this, nevertheless, I indulged her. "Why?"

"Because if we do not, if we allow the nether's touch to spread to every corner of the sector, the sapling grows into a young tree—and becomes a stygian Power. That, however, is not the worst of it. The rift itself stabilizes further, allowing *other* stygian Powers to enter."

"Like overlords and harbingers," I murmured.

Kartara's gaze grew piercing. "Quite. Under those conditions, it's only a matter of time before all remaining life in the sector is expunged and the safe zone itself destroyed." She paused. "You understand now what I'm getting at?"

"I do, but—" I inhaled deeply before going on—"technically, the young tree still cannot survive on its own. Correct? *That's* why the rift remains open. The tree still requires sustenance—however it's getting that—from its progenitor."

Kartara's lips thinned unhappily, but she didn't refute my words. "That is true as far as it goes. Only once a tree transforms into a mature one, does it become self-sustaining. At that point, the mist's concentration reaches critical mass, and the sector itself is pulled into the Nethersphere, negating the need for a rift anymore."

I nodded. "So, before that happens, we must kill the tree, close the rift, and reclaim the sector."

Kartara's teeth ground together in frustration. "You still don't seem to understand. What you describe is—"

"Impossible," I interjected. "Or so you believe. I get it." I paused. "But I believe otherwise."

The huntmistress sighed. "Then we have nothing more to discuss." Turning around, she began walking away.

CHAPTER 560: GETTING DOWN TO BUSINESS

"Wait!" I called.

The huntmistress kept walking.

"Goddammit, stop. At least do me the courtesy of hearing me out!"

Kartara drew to a halt but didn't turn around. "Why?"

"Because I have a plan—a workable one."

"Unlikely."

"I do," I insisted. "Really. Trust me."

The huntmistress finally swung round. "Why should I believe any lies you spew... *Havick*?" she asked with undisguised contempt.

I stared at her. This was not the first hint of mistrust I'd picked up from the huntmistress, but this was the first time she'd spoken my 'name' with such naked disgust. "You know I'm wearing a disguise."

"Yes," she said flatly. "I gave you ample opportunity during our little talk to reveal yourself. To come clean. But you chose not to. Leaving me with only one conclusion: you are up to no good, Havick."

It was the wrong conclusion, but I doubted anything I said would convince her otherwise just yet.

"How did you figure it out?" I asked quietly. "That I am not who I say I am?"

For a moment, the huntmistress didn't respond, and I thought she wasn't going to, then she shrugged, "We have a diviner watching the teleportation portal."

"A diviner... you mean a player who specializes in analyzing players?" I asked, recalling Wilsh, the blackguard captain who I had met so many months ago also alluding to one.

She nodded. "Fiona was unable to pierce your disguise. However, she *was* able to sense that you had one."

"And she told Texalo about it," I guessed. "By farspeaker link, presumably."

"Correct."

I had not sensed the mental communication between the diviner and the customs official, and as close as I had been to Texalo the entire time, that was disturbing in of itself. It was a timely reminder not to underestimate the brotherhood.

"So, you knew all along. Why bother meeting me in the first place, then?"

"I wanted to take your measure myself. Hardly anyone has succeeded in getting the better of Menaq and his mantises before."

I blinked, thrown by the unexpected reference. "Menaq and his ilk was a long time ago. Who told you about that? Kesh?"

Kartara shook her head. "No. But the connection was easy to make." The ghost of a smile touched her lips. "What are the odds, after all, that the emporium customer who bought a rare skillbook from us and the emporium customer requesting our aid in the nether are two different people?"

Hmm. When she put it like that...

Kartara watched the dawning realization on my face. "It is not often that Kesh takes it upon herself to deal directly with us. And the moment I received her recent missive, I knew. I knew the one we were dealing with this time to be the same one on whose behalf she approached us last time—the void mage with the nether absorption skill."

At the tail end of her words, an alert from the Game flashed for attention.

Your task: <u>Brotherhood Obligations</u> has been updated. You have kept your word to Kesh and the brotherhood, and have met with their huntmistress, albeit under the guise of someone else.

Objectives outstanding: Join the brotherhood on 3 expeditions into the nether.

I dismissed the message irritably. Now was not the time for it. "All that still doesn't explain why you won't hear me out," I pointed out to Kartara.

"I thought I made that clear already? You're a liar, *Havick.*"

I winced. The huntmistress appeared intent on wielding my assumed name like a stick with which to beat me. "Kesh vouched for me," I said stubbornly.

"She did," Kartara agreed, "And that's the only reason you'll walk out of here when we're done."

I ignored the implicit threat. "What can I do to redeem myself?"

"Reveal your true self," the huntmistress retorted instantly.

I shook my head. "I can't do that."

Kartara's eyes narrowed. "Why not?"

"There is more to fear in the world than stygians," I replied softly.

Surprise, suspicion, and a hint of calculation crossed the huntmistress' face. "You are being hunted."

I nodded mutely.

"By whom? Menaq?"

I chuckled, but it was a sound devoid of mirth. "Menaq is the least of my worries. Those that hunt me are not ones you want to tangle with—ever."

She stared at me searchingly. "And is that all you're willing to say on the subject?"

"Unfortunately, yes."

Kartara began turning away. "Then, like I said before, we're done here."

"Wait! What if I told you it was only one stygian Power your people would have to face?"

She threw me a sardonic look. "Only one? I thought it was—what was it again?—'four overlords and one young void tree?'"

Ignoring her tone, I pressed on. "And what if I told you it was a harbinger?"

That grabbed the huntmistress' attention, as I knew it would. Sadly, though, it was not enough to overcome her doubts. "I'd say you are a liar willing to spout whatever tale gets you your way," she stated flatly.

"I'm not asking you to believe me. I'll show you. In fact, I'll take you there right now."

She snorted. "Why would I go anywhere with you?"

"Because—" I held up the netherstone between my thumb and forefinger—"I'll do it with this."

The huntmistress shook her head. "I told you, I won't—"

She broke off, her jaw dropping open as she caught sight of the black stone.

I smiled. I had her. There was no doubt in my mind.

And about time too.

✳ ✳ ✳

That was not the end of the matter, of course.

In fact, it was only the beginning, and I got the distinct impression the real negotiations were yet to come.

Kartara had more questions—many more—all of which I pleaded off answering, repeating time and again that she was better off seeing the truth for herself.

Eventually, she agreed to withhold judgment.

She did not, however, accede to accompanying me on her own. Her advisors—the three I'd seen her sparring with—would be joining us as well.

"Are you sure about this?" Duskar, the orc voidknight asked the huntmistress for what felt like the tenth time.

"I am," she replied.

"But—" he began anew.

"It's a netherstone, Dusk," she interjected. "We *have* to see where it leads to." Her gaze found me. "No matter how objectionable we may find its owner's character."

I didn't let the insult faze me. I'd given the brotherhood more than enough cause to doubt me.

"We'll be the ones to hold the netherstone, though, won't we?" the elven nether witch asked.

This had been one of the sticking points during my earlier discussion with the huntmistress, but eventually I had conceded the point, realizing I wouldn't get her to trust me otherwise.

"Of course, Cait," Kartara replied. "You will be the one opening the portal." She glanced at me, and in response, I obligingly tossed the netherstone the elf's way.

Senzo and Duskar inhaled sharply, their eyes fixed on the black stone as it arced through the air.

I chuckled. "Relax, fellows. It's not as fragile as all that."

Cait caught it deftly, and the pair relaxed—but not before glaring at me, which only caused my grin to broaden.

"What will we face on the other side?" Kartara asked, ignoring the byplay.

I shrugged. "If things are as I left them, nothing but open desert and a whole lot of mist." I paused. "I should be the one to go through first, though. Just in case."

Duskar snorted derisively.

My amusement faded. "I mean it." I turned back to Kartara. "Will everyone be able to conceal themselves?"

"I'll handle that bit," Senzo replied.

I didn't bother asking how. "Very well." I paused. "Is someone going to lower the dampening field? If not, I suggest we depart from somewhere other than here. I need to cast my buffs before we enter the nether."

"Key him to the shield, Dusk," Kartara ordered, ignoring the mulish look on the orc's face.

Muttering resentfully, the voidknight complied, and a moment later a Game message dropped in my mind.

You have been granted temporary casting privileges while under the influence of the brotherhood spell: brotherly shield. Duration: 5 minutes.
You are no longer <u>ability-locked</u> and <u>scry-locked</u>.

"Thank you," I murmured. Drawing stamina, I wasted no time in cloaking myself.

You have cast vanish. You are <u>invisible</u>.

"I'm ready," I said from a spot of nothingness.

Senzo whistled softly. "Damn, is that... vanish?"

"Yes," I replied, enjoying the looks of amazement on their faces. "Now, open the portal and let's get this over with."

Cait looked at Kartara who nodded sharply. "Do it."

Closing her eyes, the elf summoned a doorway into being, and without hesitation, I slipped through.

Transfer through portal commencing...
...
...
Passage completed!
Leaving sector 45,104 of the Forever Kingdom.

✳ ✳ ✳

You have entered sector 30,199 of the Nethersphere.

I rolled out of the portal prepared for anything.

But just like I'd told Kartara, the area was devoid of mindglows. Rising into a half-crouch, I turned about and waited for the others.

Senzo was the first to come through.

You have passed a Perception check! You have detected a hidden entity. Senzo has failed to detect you!

The spymaster's head swiveled frantically from left to right, and back again, his eyes growing wilder by the second. He must have received an alert warning of danger, I realized.

"Relax," I whispered. "It's only me. There are no stygians nearby."

Senzo's gaze snapped to the spot where my voice was coming from. "You're sure?" he whispered back, but already I could see he was calming.

"I am. Where are the others?"

"They'll come through in a moment." Not explaining further, the spymaster closed his eyes and began muttering under his breath.

Sighing, I set myself to wait.

A few seconds later, a Game message unfurled in my mind.

Senzo has cast <u>covert lookout post</u>, concealing all allies within 10 yards beneath a tier 5 cloak.

You are <u>cloaked</u> (invisible to all entities outside the cloak). Duration: 5 minutes. Note, taking any hostile action will destroy the cloak.

"Impressive," I murmured, letting the weaves of vanish dissipate so that the others would see me.

Senzo grunted. "As is your own spell. Where'd you find it?"

I smiled. "Maybe I'll tell you one day—assuming all goes well, that is."

No disappointment marred the spymaster's face. No doubt, he'd been expecting such an answer. Glancing around, he took in the thick mists and the soft sand underfoot. "Where are the stygians?"

I pointed out a nearby dune—which I was not sure the man could see through given his lack of nethersight. "Beyond that hill."

"How—"

The spymaster broke off as the portal opened again and Duskar, Kartara, and Cait spilled out in quick succession.

"All clear," Senzo reported in a low-voiced whisper.

Nodding absently, Kartara turned about in a slow circle, bare blades in hand. "Cait?" she whispered.

"Working on it," the elf replied, before rushing through the weaves of another spell.

Cait has summoned a <u>witching eye</u>.

The witching eye is an ephemeral construct that grants its buffs to all allies within line of sight.

A moment later, a softly-glowing purple orb, that looked disturbingly like the eye it was named after, materialized above the elf's head.

Cait has activated a witching eye's clearsight buff.

You are now <u>clear sighted</u> (able to see through all non-solid obstacles) Duration: infinite. This buff will remain in effect as long as the source spell is being channeled.

My eyes widened. The elf's spell was another powerful casting and demonstrated how well-suited the brotherhood were at combating the void.

The huntmistress spun to face me. "Where?" she rasped.

Wordlessly, I pointed out the dune in question, and as one, the four brotherhood players raced soundlessly up its slope. I followed more slowly, watching my allies as much as I did the surroundings.

When I reached the top of the dune, no one turned around to acknowledge me. The four were too intent on the distant nether army to pay me much heed. Glancing in the rift's direction myself, I saw that nothing had changed since my last visit.

No, that wasn't quite true. There were fewer nagas this time around. Where had the others gone? Back to the other side of the rift?

Probably.

But it made little difference which sector the nagas settled in. They'd have to be dealt with either way. Shrugging, I made my way back down the slope. I'd seen enough. Let the four drink their fill of the nether army.

Once they were done, the negotiations could begin in earnest.

An hour later, my netherstone safely in my pocket, we reconvened in the brotherhood castle.

"So, you spoke truly," Kartara began without preamble.

The huntmistress, her three advisors, and I were sitting around the large ornate table in the library. The four congregated at the head of the table while I'd been relegated to the bottom end. The table had been designed to seat more than twenty and the space between us yawned wide—which was no accident, I thought.

"I did," I said simply.

She leaned forward. "But you failed to mention a few things."

"Oh?"

"Like the fact that the harbinger is accompanied by a few thousand lesser serpents," Cait replied.

"And seventy elites we know nothing about!" Duskar added with a growl.

I arched one eyebrow. So... the brotherhood had not come across the nagas previously either. That was interesting. The four had been close-mouthed during our time in the nether, communicating with each other primarily by farspeaker link, so these were my first insights into what they thought about the stygian army.

"I have information about the nagas," I said evenly.

Kartara's eyes narrowed. "You do?"

Retrieving a scale from my backpack, I slid it across the table.

"What's this?" Senzo asked, trapping the thing under his hand before it could skitter past.

"A naga scale," I replied laconically. "We've killed a few already."

Duskar looked torn between mocking my claim and demanding to know how. Letting the orc stew, I turned back to Kartara. But the huntmistress' head was already bent downward, examining the scale Senzo had handed to her.

"What is this stuff?" she murmured, more to herself than anyone else, I thought.

I responded, nevertheless. "I have it on good authority it's a void crystal composite."

Kartara inhaled sharply, Senzo's eyes widened, Cait's head whipped around to stare at the scale in the huntmistress' hand, and even Duskar looked stunned.

"I take it from your reactions that you all understand the significance of that?" I asked, breaking the sudden quiet.

Not deigning to answer, the huntmistress handed the scale to the nether witch who examined it minutely.

"He's right," she pronounced once she was done.

Leaning back in her chair, the huntmistress stared across the table at me. "You appear to have more resources at your disposal than you've led us to believe."

I tilted my head to the side. "How's that?"

"There are only a handful of people outside the brotherhood who could identify the scale's composition," she replied. "Who is your expert?"

"An ally," I replied vaguely. "One of many."

"And will your 'allies' be joining us on this expedition?" Duskar growled.

"Definitely," I said, hiding a smile. The question itself was a tacit admission that the brotherhood had been intrigued enough by what they'd learned to consider my offer.

Kartara threw the voidknight a warning look. "Our own participation is yet to be decided."

I shrugged. "That is why we are here, after all. Isn't it?"

Instead of answering directly, Kartara fielded my question with one of her own. "How did you find that sector?"

"Excuse me?"

She gestured toward the Nethersphere map still spread out across the center of the table. "The brotherhood has never heard of it before. We have no record of any rift forming between sector 30,199 and Nexus, or to any other sector for that matter."

"That comes as no surprise," I replied evenly. "I am the first player to set foot in sector 30,199."

Stark silence followed my response.

My gaze fixed on the huntmistress, I let it build. I could almost see the calculations running behind her eyes as she put things together.

"Where is the young void tree Kesh mentioned?" she asked finally.

"On the other side of the rift."

Kartara nodded. She had already worked out that much for herself, I realized. "And the four overlords?"

"Also on the other side."

Again, my response did not seem to surprise the huntmistress. "And what sector is that?"

I shook my head. "That you do not need to know."

Understandably, a chorus of protests followed in the wake of my words.

"Unacceptable!" Duskar declared, slamming a mailed fist down on the table.

"Ridiculous," Cait snapped.

"You cannot expect us to launch an assault with such crucial information lacking," Senzo said, shaking his head.

Only Kartara said nothing. Raising her hand, she silenced the others. "Then you mean for us to be decoys." It was not a question.

"Decoys?" Senzo wondered aloud. "Us?"

"What in blazes does that mean?" Duskar demanded, whipping around to pin his huntmistress with a hard stare.

"It means," Kartara explained, her eyes never leaving mine, "that 'Havick' and his allies intend on assaulting the void tree and the overlords on the other side of the rift while we stop the nagas and the harbinger from interfering." She tilted her head. "I've got that right, haven't I?"

I nodded expressionlessly. "You have."

Cait bowed her head. "Foolishness," she muttered under her breath.

Duskar was more unrestrained in his commentary. "Taking on a young void tree? And without the brotherhood's help? That's the most damnably stupid thing I've ever heard of!"

Once more the huntmistress reined in her subordinates. "What makes you think you and your allies can defeat a young void tree?" she asked when they subsided.

I sat back, deliberating how much to say. "I'm a psionic," I said eventually.

Senzo shook his head. "That won't help you against the tree nearly as much as you think. It's defenses are—"

"I know," I interjected. "But my own psi defenses are strong enough to resist the tree's mental assault. I will be able to approach it unimpeded."

Duskar grunted. "That may be. But you will still have to contend with the mists. The nether toxicity around the tree will be over—"

Kartara cut him off. "Havick has the nether absorption skill."

Cait raised her head. "He does?"

The huntmistress nodded.

Senzo put it together quicker than the others. "*He* is the one Kesh sold our skillbook to?"

Kartara nodded again.

"Well, damn," the spymaster said, sitting back.

The huntmistress turned back to me. "I grant you its plausible that you might get close enough to the tree to launch a physical attack, but you still haven't accounted for the overlord and the no doubt thousands of lesser stygians protecting the tree. How will you deal with them?"

I hesitated. I didn't know how the brotherhood would react to what I said next, but it was crucial I gained their input. "This is where I need your expertise."

"I knew it!" Duskar exclaimed.

Ignoring the orc, I went on. "There is a river."

A frown flickered across Kartara's face. "A river?"

"Yes. It borders the void tree on three sides. My people are fairly certain they can flood the valley the nest sits in." I paused, then added reluctantly, "The only thing we don't know for certain is what effect the water will have on the stygians."

The huntmistress' expression didn't change. "Tell him, Cait."

The elf turned my way. "You should know by now that the void's creatures, especially the lesser stygians, are not truly solid."

I nodded. The stygians' bodies were formed of a shadowy ichor that ordinary physical weapons passed through harmlessly. "Go on."

Cait shrugged. "It's simple really. Immerse a stygian in enough water and it will disrupt the internal bonds formed between the nether residue and plasma constituting the creature's body, reducing its cohesiveness."

I drummed my fingers on the table. "And what does that mean? Practically speaking."

Duskar laughed. "Practically speaking? It means water will weaken a stygian's attacks and defenses but will not otherwise hurt the creature."

I looked at Cait for confirmation.

She nodded. "That's another way of putting it."

I frowned. "I see."

"That is not all, though," the nether witch said.

I glanced at her questioningly.

"The water will not only disrupt the internal integrity of a stygian, it will remain in place, replacing many of the creature's internal nether bonds with water ones."

I threw her a blank stare.

Grimacing, the witch added, "In effect, a stygian drenched in water will be abnormally vulnerable to water-based attacks and spells."

I smiled. "Now, that is information I can use," I murmured.

"Then, you believe you and your allies are capable of destroying the nest on the other side of the rift?" Kartara asked, rejoining the conversation.

I nodded. "I do."

She pursed her lips, but didn't voice the skepticism I could see in her gaze.

"What else have you not told us?" she asked.

"The mature tree in sector 30,199 is a five-hour journey south of the rift." I paused. "It is guarded by three other harbingers and thousands of other chimeras."

"Chimeras?" Cait demanded. "What sort of chimeras?"

"Failed experiments," I told her. "Mismatched creatures that should prove no threat. I only mention them—" I glanced at Kartara—"because of our previous conversation."

The huntmistress nodded slowly. "You've found one, then."

"Found one?" I echoed.

"A stygian creche."

"I must see it," Cait breathed.

Kartara shook her head. "It is too far."

"But—"

"No," the huntmistress pronounced, ending the discussion. She turned back to me. "What else?"

"There is nothing left to tell," I said. "Now you know everything I do about the threat we're facing."

The huntmistress did not challenge my statement. "And what do you require from us—specifically?"

I shrugged. "All I need from the brotherhood is for you to stop the harbinger and nagas from entering the rift. How you go about that, we can discuss, but I will not dictate your strategy."

"For how long do you need us to hold the stygians at bay?" Senzo asked.

"Four hours—tops," I replied firmly.

Kartara nodded. "You don't want to risk the second nest involving itself." She pressed her palms together, thinking. "What are you offering in exchange?"

"What do you want?" I asked bluntly.

"The netherstone," was her immediate reply.

My denial was just as swift. "No."

Kartara opened her mouth, but I held up my hand forestalling her. "The netherstone is too valuable, I will not part with it. But there is a harbinger at the rift. Kill it, and an unmarked netherstone is yours for the taking."

"That presumes we will have time to harvest the black stone," Cait said.

I glanced at her. "Meaning?"

"Meaning, removing the stone intact is no small endeavor. It will take time, and more importantly, it must be done with exacting care—something nearly impossible to do during a raging battle or while fleeing a larger incoming force."

Senzo nodded. "It's why we ourselves have more netherstone fragments than we do actual stones. Invariably, we are forced to rush their harvesting."

I frowned. I'd not observed Ceruvax extract the black stone he'd given me, but I saw no reason for the nether witch and spymaster to lie. Besides, it would be easy enough to get Adriel to confirm the truth of their words.

"What about hiding the body?" I suggested.

Duskar's brows crinkled. "How would that help?"

I held up my netherstone. "Once things have quietened down, you can go back to sector 30,199 with this and retrieve the harbinger's corpse, then harvest it at your leisure."

"That requires you to survive the battle," he grumbled.

"No, it doesn't," I contradicted. "It only requires the brotherhood to survive." I held up the black stone again. "For the duration of the battle, this will be in your keeping. If I die, the stone remains in your possession and the point about the harbinger becomes moot. If I live, I get my stone back *after* you recover the harbinger."

Kartara cast me an appraising look. "You will trust the netherstone to our keeping?"

I grimaced, making no attempt to disguise my true feelings on the matter. "I have no choice but to. I will be on the other side of the rift for the duration of the battle."

She nodded. "What else are you offering us?"

My brows rose in surprise. "Isn't the harbinger's netherstone enough?"

She shook her head. "There is no guarantee we will manage to kill it. They are damnably hard to slay, and the risk is high it will flee before we manage the feat."

I pursed my lips. "Take the nagas, then. Their corpses are yours."

She eyed me. "All of them?"

"All," I confirmed, squelching the urge to negotiate further.

"That is generous of you," she murmured.

A wry smile touched my lips. "Not entirely. I will need something else from you in exchange."

Her brows drew down. "Like what?"

I ticked off points on my fingers. "Stygian weapons. Armor. And tier eight nether crystals or potions. Enough to equip a force of three thousand." I glanced at the nether witch. "Something to grant my people clearsight wouldn't go amiss either."

Duskar roared uproariously. "He's funny!"

"I'm not sure the corpses of seventy nagas will cover the cost of all that," Kartara said carefully.

I smiled. "I rather think it will. Especially once your people realize what they can do with the nagas' remains." I jerked my chin at the scale still resting on the far end of the table. "Keep that and show it to your crafters. I'm certain you'll be convinced thereafter."

Kartara inclined her head. "I'll think on it."

My lips turned down. The huntmistress was being more reticent than anticipated. "It'll be an investment too," I added.

She arched one eyebrow. "Oh?"

"If we succeed and close the rift, the brotherhood will have unfettered access to sector 30,199 for years to come. Imagine what you could do with that."

"That's a big if," she pointed out.

"I won't dispute that, but wasn't it you who was bemoaning the rest of the Kingdom's lack of interest in the stygian menace?" I spread my arms. "Well, here I am, trying to do what you said no player cared to—push back the void. And the best part? The risk to the brotherhood will be minimal. *You* will not be facing the void tree. *You* will not be taking on the overlords. My people will. And all I'm asking in return is that you arm us appropriately and stop the harbinger and the nagas from interfering."

I leaned forward. "Now, will you do it?"

The huntmistress' response was not the enthusiastic and immediate 'yes' I would have preferred. Instead, after scrutinizing me long enough to leave me doubting my impassioned plea, she glanced around the table, polling her advisors.

Cait nodded first.

Then Senzo.

Predictably, Duskar was the last to give his consent. "Hells, why not," the orc muttered finally.

Kartara turned back to me. "It seems like we have a deal."

CHAPTER 562: FORGIVEN

With a deal struck and the bare bones of a plan already in place, I had high hopes that matters would proceed swiftly thereafter.

Sadly, it was not to be.

Once the brotherhood officers and I got into the meat of things—the detailed logistics and planning—our progress slowed to a crawl. A whole host of decisions needed to be made: from how many fighters the brotherhood would commit to how we would get them into sector 30,199, and from how we would coordinate the twin assaults on either side of the rift to how the weapons deliveries would be handled.

And so on and so on…

The sheer number of decisions needed to be made was mind-numbing. Worse yet, the huntmistress insisted on multiple contingencies for every eventuality and that every decision be exhaustively examined before being finalized down to the very last detail.

This was not to say I disagreed with Kartara's approach.

It was the correct one, especially with so many lives at stake. Yet, that did not change the nature of the work. It was both drearily tiring and tedious.

But there were bright spots, too.

The brotherhood had a wealth of information—about the void trees, the overlords, and the tactics they'd employed against them in the past—all of which they shared unstintingly. I returned the favor, even though my own store of knowledge on the stygians was much smaller.

The hours flew by, lunch came and went, then evening arrived, and ever so slowly, our plans took shape. Finally, close to midnight, the last piece of the puzzle was set in place.

"That's it," I said, throwing down my pen. "That's the final contingency completed." I glanced around the table at the other drained faces. "Unless someone has something new to raise?"

Senzo groaned. "Hells, no."

Cait yawned. "I have nothing either."

A half-snort was Duskar's only answer.

I glanced at Kartara who shook her head. "No, I think we're done." She bestowed everyone around the table with a weary if heartfelt smile. "Well done, people. This is good work."

I rose to my feet. "I best be going then. See you again in four days."

"We'll be ready," Kartara promised.

✳ ✳ ✳

You have entered the safe zone of sector 12,560.

I stumbled into the Roost already half-asleep, but I retained enough presence of mind to exchange a civil greeting with the two forsworn on duty and ascertain that no emergency had befallen the forerunners while I was away.

Satisfied that the world could do without me for a few more hours, I climbed the stairs to my room, and sinking down onto my bed, I fell fast asleep.

✳ ✳ ✳

You have slept 6 hours.
Ghost's stygian claws have reached rank 15, her ash armor rank 16, her death magic rank 12, and her nether manipulation rank 10.
You and Ghost have reached level 262!

Despite the late night, I awoke early the next morning. Once more, Ghost had gained in level, improving most of her skills in the process.

She's training hard, I mused. Which was something I needed to do myself over the forthcoming days.

Rising to my feet, I slipped off the bed. I had accomplished more than I had any right to expect yesterday, but spending the entire day in a chair had left me stiff.

While I stretched, I reflected on the previous day's events. The brotherhood was not what I expected. They were less a mercenary guild of hunters and scavengers, clinging tightly to their monopoly over the stygian trade, and more an enthusiastic band of scholars and adventurers.

Idealists, I would have labeled them, if not for the abundance of cynicism and bitterness I'd sensed in the huntmistress.

Kartara herself was a leader worthy of respect. She was both passionate and astute, and I knew I had not won her over entirely. She had been reluctant to help throughout. And in the end, I suspected it was only because the brotherhood stood much to gain and little to lose that she had finally capitulated. What I asked of them was not much different from dozens of other expeditions they conducted. They would not be facing the void tree.

My people would.

Still, I could not fault the aid the brotherhood was rendering. They had been unstintingly generous when it came to the supplies we requested. And the forces they were committing... I foresaw no issues with them fulfilling their own role.

They will do well in the forerunners.

I smiled. But I was getting ahead of myself again. First, I would have to wait and see if the brotherhood lived up to expectations. If they did, then perhaps it would be time to attempt forging a longer lasting alliance.

Until then, I had a battle to prepare for.

Completing my stretches, I exited my room and descended to the floor below. It was time to return home again.

✳ ✳ ✳

A familiar grizzled figure greeted me upon my re-entry to the cave. Keros' poleaxe was already halfway to butting me in the chest before recognition sparked in his eyes.

"Oh, it's you again," he muttered uncharitably.

"Of course it is," I replied cheerfully, and somewhat loudly, as I clapped a hand down on the windknight's shoulder. "Who else would it be?"

Ignoring his consternation, I strode past, chuckling.

The cave was a hive of activity again. Everywhere I looked there were nagians hurrying back and forth. Their numbers had more than doubled since the last oath-taking ceremony I had performed. *Attending to them should be my first priority,* I thought.

"It should," a quiet voice replied.

I missed a step and nearly fell but caught myself in time. *"Ghost?"* I'd not sensed her, which meant she was shielding herself from me. *"Where are you?"*

"Here."

Turning to my left, I spotted a patch of languid darkness—Ghost. She was creeping through the darkness, her movements so slow and controlled that most would miss them. *"What are you doing?"*

"Stalking Stormdark."

My gaze drifted farther down the cave to the dire wolf in question. He was, to all appearances, sleeping.

"It's a game," Ghost added unnecessarily. *"Elise has been teaching me."*

I glanced around but failed to spot the werefox. *"Where is—"*

"Shh!"

I shushed. Resuming my nonchalant walk through the cave, I watched Ghost and her 'prey' from the corner of my eye. The pyre wolf was doing much better than I expected given her size and glowing red eyes which she had all but closed to avoid detection.

But even with her sight so impaired, Ghost did not fumble in the darkness. Every paw was delicately placed, and her movements were so sure and steady, she appeared to be gliding through the shadows. Four yards from Stormdark, Ghost drew back on her haunches.

She's got him, I thought.

But a split-second before Ghost could leap, the dire wolf spun to his feet, stiff and erect. *"I see you!"* he crowed.

Ghost's shoulders slumped.

"It was a brave effort," I told her sympathetically.

"I thought I had him," she groused.

I nodded. *"You nearly did."* Changing course, I made my way to Ghost's side. *"What's with the stalking?"*

The pyre wolf shrugged her massive shoulders. *"All dire wolves can stalk. It's something we all learn young."* She hung her head again. *"I never did."*

I swallowed. Because she had lost her body and been forced to exist as pure spirit. Dropping to my knees before her, I ran my hand through her coat. *"I wasn't just being polite before,"* I said, baring my thoughts so she could see the truth of my words. *"You really were doing remarkably well."*

Raising her head, Ghost stared at me with unblinking eyes. *"You think so?"*

I nodded.

That seemed to cheer her somewhat, but there was still a despondency to Ghost's thoughts, a sadness that sat heavy in her mind, and I feared I knew the cause.

Me.

"I'm sorry," I said, sitting down fully. *"I shouldn't have left you behind."*

"I understand why you did it, Prime. I can't do what you can. I would only have been a burden to you there."

Was that why she was training so hard?

"No, Ghost, that wasn't why I did it." I blew out a troubled breath. *"Leaving you behind was a misguided attempt to protect you."* I held her gaze. *"I shouldn't have done it. And I won't again. Promise."*

Ghost raised her head, painful hope in her eyes. *"Truly?"*

"Truly," I said firmly.

"Then I forgive you."

I squeezed my eyes shut, my own emotions in turmoil. I'd been thoughtless—no, worse than that, I'd been hurtful—and in the process, Ghost had suffered.

"It's alright, Prime," the pyre wolf said, resting her head in my lap. *"I understand now. I don't begrudge what you did."*

I sighed. *"Then you're a more generous spirit than I Ghost."*

"Of course, I am," she said smugly.

I smiled, gladdened by the renewed brightness of her thoughts.

"You better go," the pyre wolf said, getting up. *"The others are eager to hear your news."* Her gaze drifted to Stormdark. *"And it's my turn to play prey."*

✳   ✳   ✳

I resumed my journey through the cave, my heart lighter. I was glad I'd patched things up with Ghost. I'd taken her for granted, I knew. Something I resolved not to do again.

Reaching the campfire, I found it full.

All eyes turned my way as I arrived. They'd been waiting for me, I realized. Rising to her feet, Safyre approached me, the Cloak of the Reach in her hands. "Everything good with Ghost?" she asked quietly.

I nodded, taking the Cloak. "Yes, I begged for her forgiveness, and she was kind enough to give it."

Safyre smiled. "That's good news. Just don't grow too used to that attitude." She arched one eyebrow. "I may not be so kind."

"Duly noted," I murmured. My gaze darted back to the campfire. "What's going on?"

"Mariam and Deryn told me you were back. I knew you'd have news, and good or bad, I thought it best we discuss it and firm up our plans."

Mariam and Deryn were the two forsworn who'd been on duty at the Roost last night, I recalled. "Good thinking." I took in the faces arrayed around the fire. Only one was missing. "Where's Nyra?"

"Still in the Mind Trials."

I felt a flicker of concern. "How long has it been?"

"Almost a day, but Sulan is not worried—yet."

I glanced at the white wolf flopped down beside Aira and Duggar. Her eyes were closing sleepily.

"Oursk is keeping an eye on the Rings," Safyre said, noticing the direction of my gaze. "Sulan will take over again once we're done here."

Nodding, I strode forward. "Then we better hurry things along."

CHAPTER 563: WAR COUNCIL

DAY 5 OF MICHAEL'S DEADLINE

Seating myself between Safyre and Adriel, I scanned the faces around the campfire. Lucius and Elise were both present, as were all the Pack elders — Duggar, Snow, Sulan, Aira, and Leta. Terence, Teresa, and Sedgwick were also in attendance, as was Keros.

"The brotherhood has agreed to help," I said, getting straight to the point.

Sighs and gasps of relief echoed all around.

"What exactly does their help entail?" Duggar asked.

I waited a second before answering as Elise, acting as the wolves' translator, repeated the dire wolf alpha's question aloud for the benefit of everyone else.

"The brotherhood will assault the rift from the other side," I replied. "We will provide no support to them in that regard."

Adriel's brows rose. "Then you will give them the netherstone?"

"I will *lend* them the netherstone for the duration of the assault," I corrected.

"And you trust them to return it thereafter?" Lucius asked.

I nodded. "I do. But even if they don't, the loss of the netherstone will pale in comparison to what we'll gain by claiming this sector." Taking my time, I recounted my discussions with the huntmistress and her advisors.

"So, they have also agreed to supply us with weapons, armor, crystals, *and* clearsight potions?" Teresa asked more than half-disbelievingly.

I smiled. "Yes. Their willingness to do that had caught me by surprise too, I'll admit. But the good news is that, for the duration of the battle at least, we will be able to equip everyone with the necessary protections to fight in the nether." My gaze came to a rest on the wolves. "Assuming everyone still wishes to participate."

"We have not changed our minds," Sulan said complacently, her eyes still closed.

I glanced at the alphas for confirmation.

"The Packs will join the fight," Duggar agreed, a sentiment Snow echoed nonverbally.

"You struck a good deal with the brotherhood," Sedgwick mused, his head bobbing approvingly. "But I wonder... would you be able to extend the terms of your supply agreement? In the long run, it's sure to be profitable."

"Sedge," Safyre remonstrated, "this is not the time for that."

"Why not?" he asked, looking affronted. "Securing the faction's financial future is just as important as winning the battle."

Safyre leaned forward, her lips tightening.

I laid a restraining hand on her arm. "He's right. But a long-term agreement is impossible. We don't know where the nagas come from or how to find more."

"Oh," the dwarf said, deflating.

"Besides," Adriel added, "I'm not sure we'd want to trade away any further scales we acquire. There is much we can do with them on our own."

I turned the lich's way. "You disagree with the bargain I struck?"

She shook her head. "No, I think you did well to secure the supplies we required for the battle. But the scales are not something we want to give away—ever."

I nodded, accepting her advice. Adriel, better than anyone, knew the value of the scales.

"What is your plan, Wolf?" Keros demanded abruptly, bringing the discussion back on track. "You have one, don't you? It is all well and good that the brotherhood will secure the far end of the rift, but I still haven't heard how you intend on dealing with the enemy on *this* side."

"Our plan for the battle is exactly what we're here to discuss," I replied, unruffled.

"Nor is it Michael's responsibility alone, Ker," Safyre admonished. "You are no bystander." She swept her gaze across the campfire. "None of you are. The plan is one we must all contribute to and agree upon."

Chastened, the windknight subsided.

"Thank you, Saf." I turned to the twins. "What's the news from the Eastern Marches?"

"All's quiet on that front," Terence answered. "The Blades are still the sector's owner, but like you anticipated, they don't have full control of the region yet."

"Good. And the town?" I asked.

"It's still deserted," Teresa replied. "Terence and I have made camp in the portal tower."

I sighed. "Then there's no sign of our allies?"

She shook her head. "None."

Ceruvax and Farren were not late, not yet. Still... only three days remained before the battle. *It's going to be tight,* I thought.

Betraying no outward sign of concern, I turned to the nagians. "Before we get down to discussing strategy, can you summarize what you've learned about the nest, Lucius?"

The nagian inclined his head. "Gladly. Our people have spent the past two days examining the entire length and breadth of the river, and what we've discovered is..."

*　*　*

Our war council concluded before lunch.

Our planning was no less exhaustive than the brotherhood's, but all the forerunners were already familiar with the situation. And, in the end, this led to a speedier resolution.

"What will you do now?" Safyre asked as everyone began dispersing.

"Greet the new nagians for starters," I replied. Ghost had already truth-tested them, so thankfully their oath-taking ceremony would be quick.

"And then?" she probed.

Unexpectedly, of all the forerunners' leaders, I was the one with the least tasks remaining. Everything I could have done, I'd done already.

"I don't know... Probably go find something to kill."

Safyre wasn't fooled by my flippant response, though. "You're going to try leveling up before the battle," she guessed.

"Yes," I admitted. "It'll be the best use of my time, and until Ceruvax and the others arrive, there is not much left for me to do here." I smiled. "You and the others have things well in hand."

She nodded. "Just be safe."

"I will," I promised.

"And you will take Ghost with you this time."

It was not a question. I chuckled ruefully. "Definitely." I paused. "You'll let me know about Nyra?" While the probable fate of my apprentice troubled me, if I was being brutally honest, there was nothing further I could do to help her.

She either passed Atiras' tests or didn't.

"As soon as I hear," Safyre replied. "You plan on staying in the sector?"

"Yes, Ghost needs to train her nether manipulation, and my nether absorption can always do with improvement."

Sharp relief crossed Safyre's face. "Good," she breathed.

I looked at her curiously.

"I half-feared you'd enter Draven's Reach," she explained, seeing my questioning look.

"Ah," I said, nodding in understanding. "I won't deny I wasn't tempted."

I was convinced Ghost and I could traverse the elite dungeon fast enough to reach the final chamber and bring back the others in time to fight the final battle. But despite my confidence, I knew there was no accounting for chance or plain old bad luck. And the last thing the forerunners needed was for me to be trapped in the dungeon.

Just like the last time.

If it came to it, we could fight the final battle without Ceruvax, Farren, and the others—albeit with greater risk and less certainty of victory.

What the forerunners couldn't do was kill the void tree without me.

And that wasn't me being immodest. That was the cold hard truth. If Zekiel didn't return with the others in time, I couldn't risk myself to make it happen, not this time.

"So, you're going to the nest," Safyre concluded.

"I am," I confirmed. "But I won't enter the nest proper. I plan on staying in the foothills this time around." It was where Ghost had been training her skills for the past two days, and I saw no reason not to follow her lead.

"See that you do," Safyre cautioned. "I'll inform Lucius and the others you'll be heading their way." She pursed her lips, thinking. "It might be a good idea to take Elise with you."

My brows rose. "The were-druid? Why?"

"She and Ghost have grown close the last couple of days, and the pair have been working well together. I think you'll be pleasantly surprised by their tactics."

I nodded slowly. "I'll speak to her."

Stepping forward, Safyre squeezed my arm. "Good, and don't be too long, Wolf. I expect you back in time for dinner."

"Yes, ma'am," I murmured, returning the gesture.

✳   ✳   ✳

Before meeting the nagians, I invested my new attribute points and saw to Ghost's player progression—which in the end amounted to improving only one of her abilities.

Your Perception has increased to rank 117. Other modifiers: +4 from items. Available ability slots: 21.

You have upgraded Ghost's mist-thin ability to <u>greater mist-thin</u>. The third tier of this ability allows your familiar to reduce the toxicity of any free-floating nether in a 30 yard radius by 3 tiers. You and Ghost have 60 of 85 Magic ability slots remaining.

Upgrade complete. Class points remaining: 2.

Ghost's Class has advanced to rank 14.

Although the pyre wolf had other abilities available for advancement, her store of remaining Class points were low, and we agreed to save them for her most important ability—manifest. If our training went well, it would be ready for upgrade soon.

Thereafter, we met with the nagians.

It was a short meeting, quickly concluded. While Lucius' people were done investigating the river, they had a lot of preparations to finish before the battle and the mage hunter was in a hurry to get going.

Nonetheless, I did manage to come away with a trio of spells.

You have accepted 20 non-players into the Forerunners faction.
You have acquired the tier 5 spell, <u>disrupting ray</u> (stolen).
You have acquired the tier 4 spell, <u>fireball</u> (stolen).
You have acquired the tier 5 spell, <u>cold sphere</u> (stolen).

Finally ready, Ghost, Elise, and I teleported to the foothills.

✳   ✳   ✳

The nether toxicity at your current location is at tier 7.

Exiting Elise's portal, I stepped out into the familiar rocky terrain of the foothills.

"Where exactly are we?" I asked, glancing over my shoulder at the were-druid, who was already in fox form.

"About a mile due east of the nest," she replied. *"I didn't want to set our arrival point too close."*

"Good thinking," I murmured. *"Well, I best get ready."* Drawing psi, I began casting.

You have taken the form of a level 262 elder wolf, gaining primal resistance (+30% against all damage types) and health regeneration (2% per second). Your nether resistance has reached 100%. You are now immune to all hostile nether spells and effects.

You have cast engine of war, increasing your Strength, Constitution, and Dexterity by +20 ranks for 30 minutes.

You have trigger-cast quick mend.

You have cast imitate, assuming the visage of Ghost. Duration: 1 day.

Elise's face remained inscrutable throughout most of my casting, but she was unable to rein in her surprise at my last spell. *"You're going to fight looking like Ghost?"* she asked, looking back and forth between me and the much smaller pyre wolf. *"Why?"*

"To train my deception," I replied.

"Why choose Ghost's form, though?"

"For no particular reason." Other than that I didn't want the stygians suspecting I could disguise myself as one of them yet.

"Right," Elise muttered. She turned about to face the distant nest. *"How do you want to do this?"*

"You two are the ones with the experience here. I'll follow your lead."

Ghost did not hesitate. *"This way!"* she shouted, racing ahead.

Elise didn't let her get far. Dashing forward, she called, *"Come, Wolf. Watch and learn!"*

Sighing, I followed after.

CHAPTER 564: GROOVY VIBES

Elise and Ghost's training regime did not entail dashing wildly into and out of the nest as I half-feared it would. Instead, at the edge of the foothills, the pair drew to a halt.

"This is it," Elise said.

"This is what?" I asked, inspecting our surroundings. We were in a shallow dip surrounded by tall peaks on all sides. Tellingly, it stank of stygian.

"This is our killing ground," Elise said, voicing my suspicion before I could do so myself.

I glanced westward at the single mound of earth separating us from the nest. *"How do you lure them over?"*

"That's the easy part," Ghost said. *"When the stygians catch hold of the scent, they can't help themselves. Just watch!"* She turned to the werefox. *"Go ahead, Elise. Show him."*

The druid looked at me questioningly, and I bobbed my head, curious to see how Elise and Ghost had managed what I myself had failed to do.

Stretching out flat against the ground, the werefox closed her eyes and began casting.

Elise has cast fountain of life.
Elise has cast nurturing light.
Elise has cast rejuvenated earth.

Over the space of a few minutes, water began to bubble out of the ground, the barren soil grew fertile, and most amazingly of all, warm sunlight somehow managed to penetrate the thick mist to stream down on us.

"That's impressive," I murmured, lifting my muzzle to the sky and enjoying the play of the light on my face.

"The sunlight won't last long," Elise hastened to add. She was still casting, I realized. *"But it will last long enough."*

Long enough for what? I wondered, but didn't bother asking. I was sure I was about to find out.

Ghost has cast mist-thin, reducing the nether toxicity to tier 4 in a 30 yard radius.
Elise has cast arboreal guard.

Six pine trees burst out of the ground around Elise, and while they shrank away from the mist's touch, they drew strength from the warm sunlight, pooling water, and loamy soil, and second by second grew taller, filling the air with the crisp, invigorating aroma of pine.

"Get ready, Prime," Ghost said. *"It won't be long now."*

Turning away from the wholesome sight of the tree grove, I faced outward. *"The stygians can smell the pine?"* I guessed.

"Yes," Ghost replied, *"and they hate it."*

"It's not just the pines, though," Elise added, her voice dripping with weariness. *"The void seems to resent anything green and growing."* She paused, then conceded, *"Although, admittedly, they seem to hold an especial hatred for anything tree-like."*

"Good to know," I murmured and drew the shadows close.

You are hidden.

I didn't intend on staying concealed—that would only needlessly draw the spores—but using stealth for my opening attack couldn't hurt.

"What should I expect?" I asked, my gaze fixed on the crest ahead.

"Lesser stygians to begin with," Ghost replied, coiling back on her haunches. *"The nagas and flying serpents will only arrive towards the end."*

"I see," I remarked, doubly impressed. It seemed Elise and Ghost were the real reason some of the stygian elites had crossed back to this side of the rift. And if the two were killing nagas on their own... it accounted for my familiar's relatively quick leveling.

At a persistent tickle between the pads of my paws, I glanced down—then blinked. *"Is that... grass?"*

Elise chuckled. *"Yes, Lord Wolf, it is. These hills are not quite as dead as they appear. With only a little encouragement, they can be reseeded with life."*

"Now that is—" I broke off as a snaking shape crested the western hilltop. The lesser stygians had arrived.

A hydra followed in the wake of the first serpent. Then another and another, until eventually, the hilltop was swarming with stygians.

In silence, Ghost, Elise, and I watched them descend. All told, there were fifty-three stygians in the first wave. But despite the enemy's number, I didn't cast charm. While I was all but certain the stygian pack ahead was outside the void tree's protective aura—and thus mentally vulnerable—I didn't want to risk doing anything that would cause the Power to recall its minions.

And besides, it wasn't my telepathy that needed training.

As the stygians drew closer, the branches of the pine trees above rustled in warning. Ignoring the trees' ominous shaking, I kept my gaze fixed on my foes. Waiting.

Twenty yards.

Ten.

Five.

Now. Empowering my body, I rushed forward, unleashing the bevy of spells I held in readiness.

You have cast charge. You have knocked down 2 stygians (2 resisted).
You have cast stomp, staggering 3 stygians for 1 second (12 resisted).
You have activated fearsome aura. Range: 23 yards.
50 of 53 foes have failed a mental resistance check!
50 lesser stygians have been <u>petrified</u> (frozen in fear and unable to act).

I crashed headlong into the onrushing stygian wall, shattering it in one fell swoop and robbing it of all momentum.

You are no longer hidden.

Multiple hostile entities have failed to pierce your disguise.

I was only just getting started, though. Drawing yet more stamina, I flooded my limbs with energy.

You have cast wind daemon, multiplying your speed by 2x for 1 minute.

The world slowed—from my perspective, anyway. To Ghost, Elise, and the stygians, it no doubt seemed as if I was moving too fast to track.
Which indeed I was.
Leaping forward from a standing start, I pounced onto the closest of the three still-moving stygians—a serpent—and bit deeply into its neck.

You have killed a stygian serpent with a fatal blow.

Whirling around, I took a swipe at the hydra on my left.

You have cast stunning paw, stunning a stygian hydra for 5 seconds.

Then, I began killing in earnest.

✳   ✳   ✳

The skirmish was over almost before it began.
I did the bulk of the killing, affording Elise and Ghost barely any chances to contribute. *"Well,"* the werefox mused ruefully when the last stygian fell, *"that certainly went differently."*
"Sorry," I replied contritely. *"I'll hang back a bit next time."*
She laughed. *"Don't. This way, we'll kill more stygians."*
Ghost nodded. *"They won't stop coming, Prime—not until the trees are destroyed or dispelled."*
My gaze flickered to the tall pines looming over us. *"How long until that happens?"*
"One hour," Elise replied.
I turned back around. *"Well then, I guess that leaves us a lot more work to do."*

✳   ✳   ✳

The nagas didn't appear before the hour was up and the pine trees receded back into the earth. But that was alright. We killed plenty of lesser stygian packs in the intervening period.
Why the void tree allowed the creatures to be slayed in dribs and drabs like that was beyond me, but I knew the Power cared little about its minions—those it deemed expendable, anyway.
At the end of the first hour, Elise summoned another pine grove, using the identical combination of spells she had initially, and we resumed our slaughter.

She did the same again at the end of the second hour. Then, the third. After the fourth though, we were forced to call a temporary halt to the proceedings as a message arrived from the cave.

"Michael?"

"Saf, what is it?" I asked, recognizing her voice at once.

"Nyra's back."

"Thank Wolf," I murmured. *"How is she?"*

"Drained. Exhausted. She was mumbling incoherently when she emerged, but she subsided quickly thereafter. She's asleep now."

I nodded, recalling my own experience in the Trials. *"She'll sleep the rest of the day away,"* I predicted.

"Sulan thinks so, too. How are things going on your end?"

"Better than expected. I might just make supper, after all."

I sensed her smile across the link. *"See that you do. Later, Wolf."*

"Bye, Saf."

The rest of the afternoon passed slowly and uninterrupted as we resumed the cycle of killings. After each hour, the verdant growth of grass grew lusher and spread farther, because, while the trees' appearance was only temporary, the grass' was not.

And in the end, it was likely the hills' new carpet of greenery that drew the elites out.

"Nagas!" Elise shouted. *"On the hilltop!"*

The were-druid's warning was unnecessary, though. I'd already spotted the threat.

The nagas had not come alone. A pack of snakes winged aloft above them. *"You and Ghost deal with the flying serpents,"* I instructed. *"Leave the nagas to me."*

"You're sure?" Elise asked, uncertainty marring her voice for the first time.

You have cast wind daemon.

"He is," Ghost answered before I could. *"The Prime can handle those two."*

"Alright, Wolf, they're yours," Elise said as she peeled off to the left. *"Let's go get those snakes, Ghost."*

My eyes fixed on the nagas, I didn't bother answering. The pair had descended partway down the slope, but didn't seem keen on advancing further. Their shields were up, too, and they were already launching their first salvo of voidballs.

It was not me they targeted, though, but the pine grove. Padding forward, I launched my own offensive.

You have cast disrupting ray.
You have hit a level 244 stygian naga's shield for 5x more damage.
Two hostile entities have failed to pierce your disguise.

Hissing angrily, both nagas' gazes jerked in my direction. They had recognized the spell, if not my form, and I fancied I could see new hesitancy in their eyes.

Continuing my advance, I cast again.

You have hit a level 244 stygian naga's shield for 5x more damage.

My foe looked back over its shoulder—in the direction of the nest—and I knew it was contemplating retreat. Not about to countenance that, I leaped through the aether.

You have teleported behind a level 244 stygian naga.
You have cast overpowering blow and will deal 1.5x more damage on the next attack.

A nearly unseen blur, my paw rose and fell, shattering the remnants of my target's shield. Barely pausing for breath, I attacked again.

You have cast stunning paw, stunning a level 244 stygian naga for 5 seconds.

With a forlorn sigh, the naga collapsed in on itself and rolled bonelessly down the slope. Spinning away, I closed in on its companion, which was staring at me with something akin to shock.

This time, there was no mistaking the fear in my foe's gaze, and I knew with certainty, it was going to flee—or try to. Slipping into the shadows, I drew psi and cast.

You are hidden.
You have cast windborne.

Laying down the ramp of air in a spiral pattern around the naga, I rushed along the edges of its shield bubble—at six times my normal movement speed—and raked at the creature with one massive paw.

You have cast overpowering blow.
You have backstabbed a stygian naga for 7.5x more damage.
A level 240 naga's shield has blocked your attacks.
You are no longer hidden.
You have critically hit a level 240 stygian naga.
You have critically hit a level 240 stygian naga.
...
Your target's shield has been destroyed!

My spiraling assault was not even halfway complete when the naga's shield collapsed. Growling in satisfaction, I released the psi weave I held in abeyance.

You have activated fearsome aura, petrifying 2 stygian nagas.

Ah, ha. Perfect!
Leaping off the windslide, I took a moment to check on my companions. The duo had retreated to the pine grove, and from beneath the tree's sheltering embrace, were fending off the swooping serpents.

The trees were not passive participants either. They actively assisted the pair by grabbing onto and holding any flying snake that made the mistake of approaching too closely.

Ghost and Elise have things under control, I concluded.

That left me free to finish things off with the nagas properly. Drawing on long-dormant memories, I reawakened my blood.

You have cast enslave.

It was time to bind a stygian to our cause.
Or perhaps, two.

CHAPTER 565: WAITING

You have successfully dominated a level 240 stygian naga.
You have successfully dominated a level 244 stygian naga.
You and Ghost have reached level 263!

The blood-bindings went off without a hitch, but Ghost, Elise, and I weren't ready to call it a day yet—far from it. While my deception skill was progressing nicely, I still didn't have enough attribute points for what I intended.

So, we kept fighting.

And the stygians kept dying.

Wave after wave of lesser nether creatures assaulted the druid's grove, and time and again, we annihilated them. Sometimes the nagas joined in the attack. They always approached tentatively though, as if afraid to commit. Despite this, we managed at times to trap and kill a few. More, often, though, we had to be content with driving the elites back.

In this one regard, my presence served to hamper our training efforts. There was no helping it, though. The void tree had realized a powerful foe lurked in the foothills, and it was not about to needlessly risk its more valuable assets.

Still, the stygian Power continued to throw away the lesser stygians' lives as if they were of no account, and perhaps, they weren't. Regardless, though, a few hours before midnight, I reached the milestone I had been striving for all day.

Your deception has reached rank 25.

"Ah, I've done it."

Elise looked at me curiously but didn't ask for an explanation. *"You're ready to head back then?"*

I nodded. *"I think so."*

"How did we do today?" Ghost asked eagerly.

Turning my attention inward, I called up a summary of our efforts over the course of the day.

You and Ghost have reached level 264!
Your Perception has increased to rank 121. Other modifiers: +4 from items. Available ability slots: 25.
Your insight has reached rank 26.
Ghost's telepathy has reached rank 13 and her nether manipulation rank 11.
Your alchemy stone is full. Total stored ingredients: 500 / 500.
You have killed 7 stygian nagas.

"We didn't do too badly," I told her. My presence had slowed Ghost's own skill progression since I'd ended up doing the better part of the fighting. Still, the pyre wolf had managed to rank up two of her skills, and I, likewise.

My focus, though, was more on my overall player progression. I needed to advance at least three more levels before I had enough Perception slots to advance imitate to rank six.

But I wouldn't get there today. We were all simply too exhausted.

"Open the portal," I told Elise, *"and let's get out of here."*

✻ ✻ ✻

Getting out was a much more laborious process than I'd made out.

First, we had to find somewhere safe to leave the blood-bound nagas—I wasn't about to take them to the cave—and in the end, I decided the best place for the creatures was the Draven's Reach gate. It was at the other end of the sector, and about as far from the nest as you could get.

Next, we hauled the dead nagas to the selfsame spot—I didn't want to crowd the cave unnecessarily. It took seven portal trips, all told. Even with Ghost and I working in tandem while Elise kept watch, it was no easy task. But as back-breaking as the work was, it was simple, and eventually we returned home.

The cave was quiet when we arrived. Not even Keros was on guard when we stepped out of the gateway.

"So, he does sleep," I mused aloud.

"Who does?" Safyre asked, stepping out from behind a large crate in the area serving as our storeroom.

"Keros," I replied. "What are you doing up so late?"

"Working," she replied, stifling a yawn. "But I could ask the same for you."

I laughed. "A fair point." Turning around, I shooed Ghost and Elise away. "Go on, you two, go get some rest. I'm sure you're both exhausted."

"Will we be heading out again tomorrow?" Elise asked aloud. She was in nagian form once more.

I hesitated. "I don't know yet. I'll tell you in the morning."

Inclining her head in acknowledgment, the druid headed off, Ghost trotting amiably by her side.

"They make a good team," Safyre observed.

"They do," I agreed, turning around to face her. "How's Nyra?"

"Still sleeping."

I nodded, unsurprised. "Any other news?"

"The brotherhood's supplies have begun to come through, and they're as good as you promised."

"Excellent. You've received the full complement?"

"I wish," Safyre replied with a rueful shake of the head. "Since we're funneling everything through the Roost and trying to keep the brotherhood from tracing our ley lines, ferrying the supplies is going slowly. But we should have the last shipment in our stores by tomorrow."

I grimaced. "I suppose that will have to do. What about Ceruvax and Farren? Have you heard from the twins again?"

Safyre sighed. "I'm sorry, Michael, but there's been no news on that front."

"Damnation," I swore. If the Reachers weren't late before, they were now.

"What will you do?" Safyre asked.

I shrugged fatalistically. "What else can I do but wait? I'll give them another day."

"And if we still don't hear from them?"

"Then we'll have to assume they won't reach us in time," I said grimly, "and plan to proceed without them."

✳   ✳   ✳

Day 6 of Michael's Deadline

You have slept 8 hours.

Despite the exertions of the previous day, I rose early the next morning. The deadline for reclaiming sector 18,240 was drawing closer, and I was feeling the press of time keenly.

Striding through the cave, I made my way toward the mostly-empty campfire. Hardly anyone was awake yet.

"Prime...?" Ghost asked sleepily. *"Is that you?"*

"Yes. Wake Elise. We'll get going as soon as the two of you are ready."

A pregnant pause, but no argument followed. *"Alright, but you probably want to visit the Pack first."*

"Why?"

"Nyra's here."

I stopped mid-step. *"She's awake?"*

"Yes."

Swiveling about, I changed direction. *"Coming."*

✳   ✳   ✳

I found Nyra in the far-right side of the cave, being watched over by Sulan and Aira. My apprentice was sitting down cross-legged, her face buried in a bowl. Nodding in passing to the dire wolf elders, I sank down opposite her.

"Morning."

Nyra looked up. "Michael," she greeted, then resumed eating.

Consternation flickered across my face.

Aira's laugh echoed in my mind. *"She's hungry."*

"I see that," I replied. *"Is she okay?"*

"She is," Sulan pronounced.

"I can hear you, you know," Nyra said, still spooning food into her mouth.

"We know you can," Sulan said serenely.

My gaze fixed on my apprentice, I studied her intently. She was different today, more present, and more... dangerous. There was also a keenness to her that had been lacking before. She had changed, and I was sure the wolves sensed it too.

Reaching out with my will, I inspected her anew.

The target is Nyra, a level 108 virulent witch. She bears a false Mark of Lesser Shadow, a true Mark of Michael (hidden), and a true Mark of Wolf-brethren (hidden).

Nyra has awakened her blood and is an anointed scion bound to Wolf.

So. She had succeeded. "Congratulations," I said quietly.

The young woman looked up. "Thank you," she said with a tired smile. "It was more difficult than I imagined."

"But you succeeded," I pointed out.

She grinned lopsidedly. "I did, didn't I?"

I smiled, sharing her joy. "I'll want to hear the full tale, but later. For now, give me the highlights. What scion abilities did you choose?"

Holding up one hand, Nyra began ticking off points on her fingers. "Astral blade. Levitate. Hardened body. Mind shield."

I tilted my head to the side. "Why levitate? I thought for sure you'd pick shadow blink."

"I thought about it," she admitted, "but in the end, I decided I wanted to focus more on my ranged attacks."

I nodded. "Then levitate makes sense." Not only would the ability allow Nyra to strike her targets from afar, it would also help her maintain her distance from any melee-type foes that sought to close in on her. "What about your blood memory? What did you choose?"

"Revitalizing blood."

The blood spell was one I, myself, had been offered. Calling up the long-ago Game message describing it, I re-examined the ability.

Revitalizing blood: your blood can reinvigorate. This blood memory will grant you 4 abilities: recover health, recover psi, recover mana, and recover stamina. Each can be used once per day on yourself or another to fully restore any lost health, stamina, mana, or psi. Its activation time is instantaneous. This is a generic blood memory.

"It's a good choice," I said slowly, "especially since you didn't go with chi heal." I rubbed my chin. "But..."

"It's a defense-support ability, I know. But the battle is only a few days away. Revitalizing blood will let me assist you directly."

I frowned. "I appreciate the thought, Nyra. Still, you shouldn't be making decisions about your player progression for anyone's benefit but your own."

Nyra rolled her eyes. "I know that. You've said it enough times I'm hardly likely to forget it." She leaned forward. "But you've also said more times than I care to recount that it is our duty as Wolves to protect the Pack. And like it or not, *you* are Pack too, Michael."

Sulan laughed. *"She's got you there,"* the white wolf crowed.

I sighed. It was time to retreat. This was not an argument I was going to win, especially not with Sulan and Aira siding with her. "Sorry, Nyra. I meant no criticism. You've done the Pack proud. I'm sure your new abilities will serve the faction well."

"Thank you," she murmured.

I rose to my feet.

"Where are you going?" Nyra asked.

"To train," I said, walking away. "You should too, once you're feeling up to it. Time's running short."

✳ ✳ ✳

I had a few more chores to see done before the day's work could begin in earnest. To start with I located Sedgwick and shook him awake.

"Do you know what time it is?" the dwarf asked gruffly as he got up. "Never mind, just tell me what you want."

I tossed him the alchemy stone. "Extract the ingredients from this. Don't bother selling them now, you can do that later."

"Done," he grunted, handing me the stone back a moment later. "How much are you looking to get for them?"

"Nothing. Use the proceeds to buy more health potions." I paused. "At the same rate we agreed on previously, of course."

"Of course," he muttered. "Now is there something else you want? Or can I go back to sleep?"

"Yes, there is, actually." I slipped a piece of paper into his hand. "I need these too."

The dwarf frowned as he read my hastily scribbled note. "What do you want with all this?"

I smiled. "You'll find out soon enough. Now, don't mind me. Go back to sleep." Leaving Sedgwick to mutter discontentedly to himself, I hurried off to find Adriel.

✳ ✳ ✳

After informing the lich about the blood-bound nagas and the seven corpses waiting for her attention at the Reach portal, I met with Lucius and the nagians and took the newcomers' oaths.

You have accepted 15 non-players into the Forerunners faction.

Only then did Elise, Ghost, and I set off for the foothills.

Arriving at the site of yesterday's battles, we found all traces of our previous efforts vanished. The grass that had taken hold so nicely had been destroyed anew, and the corpses of the few stygians we'd not looted were nowhere to be seen.

"It's a good thing, we moved those nagas," Elise said, noticing the same.

"The void has no compunctions about devouring its own," I replied.

Elise nodded in agreement. *"So, same routine as yesterday?"*

"Yes." Drawing back the sleeve of my left arm, I activated the scoundrel's wristband. *"But today, we'll make an especial effort to make sure no naga escapes."*

✳   ✳   ✳

The rest of the day passed in a blur, with each cycle of killing following quickly on the heels of the previous, and I soon lost track of how many lesser stygians we killed.

It was as much as a thousand, maybe more.

My traps did their job well, too, and by midday, every remaining naga on this side of the rift was dead. Sadly, the void tree declined to bring more of the elites from the adjoining sector. That did not stop me and my companions from continuing our slaughter, though.

Safyre made sure I was regularly updated over the course of the day, too. I knew when Sedgwick's health potions arrived and when the last of the brotherhood's shipments landed in our stores.

I was also kept abreast of my apprentice's doings. Accompanied by a small pack of wolves, Nyra had chosen to re-enter the guardian tower. It was a wise decision. The young witch would have had a hard time keeping up with Elise, Ghost, and me in the nether-infested sector. The icy tundra, on the other hand, was a more suitable training ground for her.

Sadly, though, the one report I was most anxious to receive did not arrive. Hour after hour, I waited to hear word of the Reachers, but time and again, I was disappointed.

Something was preventing Ceruvax and Farren from answering my summons. That, or Zekiel had never reached them.

Had it been a mistake sending the psi knight alone?

In hindsight, it seemed so.

But it was too late to go back and do things differently. And one way or the other, I would have to live with the consequences of my decisions.

Thankfully, though, while my player level progressed torturously slow over the course of the day, by the time I finally crawled into bed for the night, it was with the certain knowledge that Ghost and I were as prepared as we could be for the forthcoming battle.

You have killed 11 stygian nagas.
Your alchemy stone is full.
You and Ghost have reached level 267!

Your Perception has increased to rank 127. Other modifiers: +4 from items. Available ability slots: 31.
Your shortswords has reached rank 23, your meditation and nether absorption rank 24, and your telekinesis rank 21.
Ghost's magma maw has reached rank 15, her stygian claws rank 16, her death magic rank 13, and her nether manipulation rank 12.
You have accepted 15 non-players into the Forerunners faction.

Chapter 566: The Mantle of Leadership

The next day began like any other.

But it was not just any other day. Today was the penultimate day before the battle for the sector—a battle that would determine the future of the forerunners.

The wait was over. And in more ways than one.

Reaching the campfire, I sank down beside Safyre. Everyone else was already there, and this time it really was everyone—all the nagians, all the forsworn, and both wolf Packs. The only ones missing were the ten still-unhomed possessed, Zekiel, Bacheus, Shael, Anriq, and of course, the Reachers. But despite the gathering's size, no one spoke, no one joked, and the greetings I received were somber and half-hearted.

They know as well as I that by day's end tomorrow, more than half of us are likely to be dead.

Because without Ceruvax, Farren, and the others, the chances of us minimizing our losses in the forthcoming battle were minimal. Despite this, I knew we had no choice but to forge onward.

Inhaling deeply, I began.

"We can no longer count on the Reachers coming to our aid," I said, getting straight to the point. "That leaves our forces short of Ceruvax, a player nearly a Power in his own right, Farren, a lich almost as strong as Adriel, five hundred wolfmen, and a fighting force of two thousand elite soldiers." I paused, letting my words sink. "And what do we have left to face the void with on this side of the rift?"

I swept the surrounding faces with my gaze, but despite the answer being obvious, no one ventured to respond.

"Me, Safyre, Adriel, Ghost, one hundred nagians, eleven forsworn, five other players, and three hundred and thirty wolves."

I grimaced. "Whichever way you look at it, the loss of the Reachers is a crippling one. Nonetheless, I still intend to take the fight to the void tomorrow. I will fight, not in blind hope, but because I believe we can still win—*even* without the others."

I paused. "We will have to curtail our ambitions, though. Without the Reachers, a straightforward victory will not be possible. Nor will vanquishing the void entirely be achievable. Instead, we will have to use subterfuge, feints, and a good old-fashioned bluff to accomplish our true goal—closing the rift."

I sighed heavily. "I fear the butcher's bill will be long, though. That is why I asked Safyre to call this meeting. I will fight, but you don't have to. Anyone who wishes to stand down may do so now."

I waited a beat, but no one moved.

"The fighting will be bloody," I warned. "And even with all our preparations, victory is by no means assured. I may die. So may you. We all may.

"And while I believe our cause worthy, that what we're trying to build here is worthy of sacrifice—be it your life or mine—you may not feel the same. If so, this is your opportunity to step back. I will not blame you if you do. No one will."

Once again, no one stirred.

I bowed my head, humbled by their faith. "Thank you," I murmured. "I will do my best to shepherd us all safely through tomorrow."

"For the forerunners!" Terence shouted.

"For the forerunners!" Teresa echoed.

Throwing back her head, Sulan howled, her voice echoing loudly across the cavern. Ghost joined in, and soon, all the wolves were howling.

A second later, so was everyone else.

Nagians, forsworn, it didn't matter, everyone began hollering and howling, filling the cave with a jubilant roar of sound.

It was almost as if we'd already won.

"LONG LIVE WOLF!"

"LONG LIVE THE FORERUNNERS!"

"FOR THE ANCIENTS!"

"FOR THE PRIMES!"

Sitting still and quiet under the noise, my lips curved up in a bittersweet smile. If nothing else, I had succeeded in raising the company's spirits.

But only time would tell what that would count for in lives lost.

✳ ✳ ✳

"Not the most rousing of speeches," was Sedgwick's comment when the gathering finally broke up, "but satisfactory nonetheless."

"I was not trying to rouse anyone," I said tightly. "I was *trying* to make sure everyone understood the reality of what we'd face tomorrow."

Keros chuckled. "A noble ambition, Wolf, but a word of advice. What soldiers need is hope—and not to be crushed by the weight of reality."

"He gave them both," Safyre interjected before I could respond, "and did rather well, I thought. Now, off with you two. Michael and I need to talk." Linking her arm through mine, she drew me away from the pair. "Ignore those two," she said, once we were out of earshot. "Life has made them cynical."

I chuckled. "Oh, but I will."

"It was a good speech," she said, eyeing me sideways.

"I wasn't trying—"

"—to give a speech, I know," Safyre finished for me. "Nonetheless, it was what everyone needed to hear." She paused. "They will fight better for it tomorrow."

I blew out a troubled breath. "I hope so." Glancing down, I inspected the bag containing my latest purchases from Sedgwick. We were going to lose people tomorrow, there was no helping that.

But the two days I'd spent training had not been in vain. Thanks to my recent level gains—and the items in the merchant's bag—I had one last opportunity to better our chances of victory tomorrow.

Safyre didn't fail to mark the direction of my gaze. "You're venturing out again, aren't you?"

I nodded mutely.

She sighed. "When do you leave?"

"Now. I've delayed my departure too long as it is." It was late morning already. The arduous training I had subjected myself to the previous two days had finally caught up to me, and I'd awoken later than usual. "I have to revisit the nest," I explained.

She nodded, already knowing what I had in mind. "You know we haven't spoken about what comes after."

"After?"

"That's right. Assuming we manage to close the rift—"

"We will," I interjected firmly.

"I'm not disputing that," she said gently. "But what will we do after? Without the Reachers, we don't have the numbers necessary to claim the sector."

"There are.... options."

She glanced at me. "Why don't I like the sound of that?"

"Because none of them are particularly *good* options." I grimaced. "Still, without the Bane Wolves and the others, we'll have no choice but to approach either the brotherhood, the bounty hunters, or the Blades for help."

Her brows rose. "The Blades, really? You'd approach them?"

"They would not be my first choice," I admitted. "That would be the brotherhood."

"I thought as much," Safyre said. "When will you speak to the huntmistress?"

"Only after the battle," I replied. *Assuming we win.*

She stared at me searchingly. "Is leaving it that late wise?"

"Speaking to Kartara before would be less wise, I'm afraid. She is already skeptical enough of the entire venture. I dare not give her further cause to back out."

My uncertainty about the Brotherhood's commitment was also the reason I'd not called off the assault entirely. If I asked Kartara to wait—be it for two days, five, a week—I wasn't sure she wouldn't simply call the whole thing off. And while I could still see a way to defeat the void tree without the Reachers, I couldn't see us doing it without the brotherhood stopping the harbinger and nagas from interfering.

So, we had to go ahead—albeit with a truncated plan that would see the rift closed, but not necessarily all the stygians banished from the sector.

"Kartara might not be pleased being lied to," Safyre pointed out, "even if your lie is only one of omission."

I sighed. "I know, but we are where we are. It's too late to change course now."

For a moment Safyre didn't say anything, but then rather than argue the point further as I was half-afraid she would, she moved the conversation on. "So, the nest. Then what?"

"Then I have to rendezvous with Shael and Anriq. It's past time I met up with them."

I would be setting out to meet the pair later than I'd originally planned, but that couldn't be helped. Revisiting the nest was equally important. Hopefully, the pair would not go on without me.

"You think they have reached the tundra's exit portal already?" Safyre asked.

"I hope so," I said fervently.

"And if they haven't?"

I didn't say anything. There was nothing to say, after all.

"What about the two nagas?" Safyre asked finally.

My lips turned down. "The hold I have over them will dissipate the moment I leave the sector, but if they're still in the region when I return, I'll enslave them anew."

Safyre nodded absently, but her thoughts were clearly elsewhere.

"Something else on your mind?" I prompted.

"Yes." A pause. "Take Nyra with you."

I frowned. "Nyra? To Nexus, you mean? Why would I—?" My eyes widened in realization. "No."

"Yes," Safyre retorted firmly. "Except for the twins, she is the only one you *can* take... and Adriel has already spoken to her."

My eyes narrowed. "When?" I asked sharply.

"This morning," Safyre replied calmly, ignoring my tone. "Nyra knows what must be done, and more importantly, she is willing to do what is necessary."

I shook my head. "I can't—"

"You can," Safyre interjected gently. "You know as well as I do that Nyra is the best candidate. Other than you, she is the only scion in our ranks, and for obvious reasons, it cannot be you."

"But—"

Safyre squeezed my arm. "You'll only be taking Nyra as a precautionary measure. If your original plan holds true, then all will be well."

And if it didn't all go well, I'd be faced with the choice of allowing Nyra to sacrifice herself. I closed my eyes. And as strong-willed as the young witch was, I knew she would take the decision out of my hands.

But given what was at stake, did I have the right to make the choice for her?

No. I didn't.

"Alright," I said heavily. "I'll take her with me."

✳   ✳   ✳

Before setting out for the day, I found a quiet spot to calm my turbulent thoughts. The conversation with Safyre was forcing me to face a blunt truth I'd been hoping to avoid: being a leader meant sacrifice.

And not necessarily my own.

Nyra was just the beginning. Tomorrow, I would face the same choice over and over again. Securing the sector would cost lives—lives *I* would have to spend.

Sending others out to die, putting them in a position where they would have to choose between their own lives and doing what was right for the faction, was not something I was ever going to be comfortable with, I knew, but it was something I would have to do, nonetheless.

"For the greater good," I muttered, the very words leaving a sour taste in my mouth. For the greater good, I would have to allow those I'd vowed to protect to sacrifice themselves.

Starting with Nyra—my apprentice, and a young woman who wouldn't even be in this position if I hadn't dragged her along.

"It's her choice," Ghost said quietly as she came up to join me.

"I know."

"We must all make sacrifices in the name of the Pack."

"I know that, too."

"Then you have made your peace with Nyra's decision?"

I sighed. *"I have."* And I had.

A pause. *"So, when do we leave for Nexus?"*

An apt question. Wrenching my thoughts away from my maudlin musings, I ran my hand through the pyre wolf's coat, giving her my full attention. *"Soon. But there are a few things we have to take care of first."*

"Like?"

"Like our player progression."

Ghost's ears flicked forward. *"You mean it's finally time to advance my manifest again?"*

"It hasn't been that long since we last upgraded it," I said, laughing at her impatience despite myself. *"But yes, it's time to upgrade your manifest—and my imitate ability, too."*

"Then what are you waiting for, Prime? Do it!"

Still smiling, I turned my attention inward and did as she bade.

You have upgraded Ghost's manifest ability to <u>superior manifest</u>. The fourth tier of this ability allows your familiar to leave her spirit vessel and take shape as a <u>master stygian pyre wolf</u>. When in this form, Ghost's <u>pyreborn</u> and <u>voidborn</u> traits will advance to tier 2.

The second tier of the pyreborn trait increases Ghost's fire magic resistance to +60% and the damage she deals with fire-based attacks to +60%. Additionally, the blast radius of <u>explosive entry</u> is increased to 10 yards.

The second tier of the voidborn trait increases Ghost's nether resistance to +60% and the damage she deals with necrotic attacks to +60%. Additionally, the mist column length of <u>necrotic wake</u> is increased to 20 yards.

Superior manifest also increases the distance from her spirit vessel that your familiar may materialize to 50 yards. It consumes psi or mana and can be upgraded. This is a Class ability and does not occupy any ability slots.

Upgrade complete. Class points remaining: 1.

Ghost's Class has advanced to rank 15.

Ghost's physical form has changed to that of a master stygian pyre wolf.

"Oh," was Ghost's only forlorn comment after trying out her new form.

I could well understand her reaction. This time around, Ghost's appearance had not changed. Nor had she gained any new traits or abilities. However, her existing traits and previous manifest variants *had* improved.

"It's not so bad as all that," I said sympathetically.

"I'm not so sure about that, Prime." Ghost muttered. *"I haven't changed at all!"*

"Oh? Well, there's the small matter of your nether and fire resistance."

"What about them?" she asked dejectedly.

"That percentage increase you earned in both? It's enough to push you over the top."

"Over the top of what?"

I smiled. "Over the top of one hundred percent. Congratulations, Ghost, you are now totally immune to nether and fire magic."

That caught her interest. *"Totally? As in…"*

"Completely. No nether or fire spell will ever hurt you again. Not even the mists can touch you now." Drawing up the relevant Game message, I read it aloud to her.

Ghost's nether and fire magic resistances have reached 100%. She is now immune to all hostile nether and fire effects.

The pyre wolf sprang to her feet in excitement. *"That's great!"*

I nodded. "It certainly is."

"I must go tell Elise!" Ghost whipped around, then hesitated, glancing back at me.

"Go," I said, correctly interpreting her look.

"I'll be fine here," I added, when she still didn't move.

"You sure?"

"I am. I'll finish up my player progression and join you in a bit. Now go!"

Ghost went.

I watched her for a moment longer, a smile still on my face. Somehow, the pyre wolf always seemed to know how to put me in a better frame of mind. I was fortunate to have her for a companion.

My smile faded. Ghost would also be one of those in danger tomorrow.

I knew I had no right to stop her—or anyone else under my care, for that matter—from placing themselves in harm's way, but what I *could* do was make myself strong enough to protect them when they did.

Lowering my head, I turned my attention to the waiting ability tomes.

It was time to see to my own player progression.

Reaching into my bag of holding, I hauled out my entire store of ability tomes. None of the Strength abilities I'd unlocked a few days ago had proved effective against the stygians so far, but I'd not expected otherwise. The three abilities were still only at tier one, after all.

Now, though, it was time to upgrade one of them.

But only one. Sadly, I didn't have enough ability slots for more than a single elite Strength ability.

Overpowering blow, charge, or stomp—which will it be?

Overpowering blow was nice. But it was only good for a single strike, whereas both charge and stomp were area-of-effect abilities. For charge to be effective, though, I would have to be constantly zipping around the battlefield, knocking down my foes.

And while there was nothing wrong with that when I was battling a large number of enemies, it was less useful when I was faced with a single powerful opponent... like a Power.

Stomp, on the other hand, would work equally well in either circumstance. It *also* had the potential to affect a larger number of foes—but only at the expense of the added mobility charge provided.

But then again, I didn't need more mobility.

Stomp it is, I decided, picking up the ability tomes for its tier two, three, and four variants. Opening the first book, I started reading.

You have upgraded your stomp ability to <u>improved stomp</u>. The tier 2 variant of stomp increases the ability's debuff duration to 2 seconds and its area-of-effect to a 5 yard radius.

You have upgraded your stomp ability to <u>superior stomp</u>. The tier 3 variant of stomp increases the ability's debuff duration to 3 seconds and its area-of-effect to a 7 yard radius.

You have upgraded your stomp ability to <u>greater stomp</u>. The tier 4 variant of stomp increases the ability's debuff duration to 4 seconds and its area-of-effect to a 10 yard radius.

Not bad, I thought. Returning the unused tomes to my bag of holding, I withdrew an upgrade gem. Now, for the final stomp upgrade.

Ability gem activated.

Creating ability tome...

...

Tome creation halted.

There are 2 elite variants for the stomp ability.

Variant 1: <u>ponderous step</u>. This variant causes the ground underfoot to quake with every step you take. Each tremor will stagger or knock down nearby entities.

Variant 2: <u>shockwave</u>. This variant creates a single devastating shockwave that injures and staggers all targets in a 50 yard radius.

Hmm, I mused, deliberating over the choices on offer. Ponderous step appeared to provide a continuous effect—but for how long seemed unclear—while shockwave was a supercharged variant of stomp.

On the other hand, ponderous step would *not* synergize with vanish. I could still use both abilities simultaneously, but every step I took would reveal my position—literally. I rubbed my chin. *That's a definite downside.*

Still, knowing where I am will be less helpful to my foes than they realize, I thought, recalling my battle with the Devil Riders from a few weeks ago. Even though the enemy had had a fix on my position, they'd been unable to hit me. And besides, if ponderous step became problematic, I could always disable the ability or not use it at all.

Ponderous step it is, I decided. The ability promised to disable my enemies for longer, and in the end, that outweighed any of its negatives.

Reaching out to the Game, I communicated my choice.

You have upgraded your stomp ability to <u>ponderous step</u>. This tier five ability grants you the <u>heavy</u> buff for 1 minute. While the buff is active, your footfalls will cause the ground in a 10 yard radius to shake, staggering or knocking down any target that fails a physical resistance check for 1 second.

Unlike its lower-tiered variants, ponderous step physically alters the terrain underfoot and will therefore affect magically shielded foes to the same degree it does unshielded ones. However, any target not in direct contact with the ground will be unaffected. Note, this ability can only be used when you are in wolf form.

You have 8 of 40 Strength ability slots remaining.

Perfect, I grinned. That ponderous step would disrupt even a shield-mage's concentration was not something I'd anticipated and only made the ability more valuable.

My Strength upgrades finished, I opened my bag again and drew out another two upgrade gems. It was time to advance the imitate ability. Closing my fist around the first crystal, I willed my intent to the Adjudicator.

Ability gem activated.
Creating ability tome...
You have acquired a tier 5 imitate ability tome.

Well, that was a waste of a good gem, I thought, my lips twisting unhappily at the lack of variants. Not wanting to dwell further on the matter, I opened the tome and began to read.

You have upgraded your lesser imitate ability to <u>master imitate</u>. The tier 5 variant of this ability enhances the spell's robustness allowing it to function in a safe zone and falsify all your analyze data.

You have 16 of 127 Perception ability slots remaining.

The Game description contained no surprises, and didn't tell me anything I didn't already know about the ability, and so, without further ado, I activated the next upgrade gem.

Ability gem activated.

Creating ability tome...

...

Tome creation halted.
There are 2 grandmaster variants for the imitate ability.

"That's more like it," I murmured, avidly reading the follow-up Game messages.

Variant 1: <u>doppelganger</u>. This variant allows you to take the form of any living entity of the same size and approximate mass as you. Your transformation is impenetrable to nearly all forms of detection. Additionally, your spirit signatures may be falsified.
Variant 2: <u>fake</u>. This variant allows you to take the form of any non-living entity of the same size and approximate mass as you. Your transformation is impenetrable to nearly all forms of detection. Additionally, your spirit signatures are completely removed during your change.

"Urgh!" I muttered, my excitement fading. The alternative the Game had offered up was less than appealing. There was nothing wrong with fake, it just wasn't the ability for me.

Fake sounded like the ideal ability for the patient infiltrator or thief, someone who could afford to spend hours mimicking a cupboard, or some similarly inoffensive piece of furniture, but it didn't serve my purposes at all.

It looks like it's going to be doppelganger, after all.

Ruing the loss of the two ability gems I hadn't needed to use, I willed my choice to the Game.

You have acquired a tier VI doppelganger ability tome.
You have upgraded your imitate ability to <u>doppelganger</u>.
Doppelgangers are amongst the most feared covert operatives in the Kingdom. Their disguises are not mere illusion nor are they only skin-deep. Cut a doppelganger and they will bleed the same blood as their subjects. Worse yet, a doppelganger is impossible to uncover by magical means and can only be detected by high-tiered Perception abilities.
The tier 6 variant of this ability allows you to transform your body to match any living subject of similar size and mass as you. Note, the doppelganger ability is not a shapeshift ability, and while your new form will exactly replicate your subject's, your attributes and skills will stay your own.
Additionally, while you are in doppelganger form, you can falsify all your spirit signatures or remove them altogether, thereby truly assuming the guise of a non-player or monster.
The transformation is permanent, and while stamina is required to effect the change, there is no accompanying spell duration, nor is any energy expended to maintain your new form. This ability can be upgraded.
You have 1 of 127 Perception ability slots remaining.

I rose to my feet, a smile on my face despite the two wasted upgrade gems. Doppelganger was everything I hoped it would be, and now, finally, I was truly ready to face the void tree in battle. Doing so, though, would have to wait until tomorrow.

Today, I had other tasks to complete.

And first up on the list was another visit to the nest.

✳   ✳   ✳

Only a little later, Elise, Ghost, and I were back in the foothills. Today's agenda, though, was nothing like that of the previous two days.

"Give me a few minutes to get ready," I told the others. Not waiting for their responses, I closed my eyes and cast.

You have taken the form of a level 267 elder wolf.

You have cast doppelganger, transforming your form into that of a level 150 stygian serpent, and concealing all your Marks. Duration: infinite.

"Wow," Elise said, edging away instinctively. *"Is that... him?"*

"It is," Ghost replied.

Opening my eyes, I surveyed my new form. My limbs were non-existent, and I... slithered. *Urgh,* I thought, suppressing my distaste the same way Elise likely just had.

As far as stygian serpents went, I was a bit on the large side—I'd not been able to reduce my wolf-size much—but hopefully, none of the stygians would have cause to inspect me closely. Worse yet, I reeked of the nether and my breath smelled equally foul. That, though, I expected was part and parcel of the disguise.

"It's uncanny," the werefox said, circling me slowly. *"You look and smell exactly like the real thing."* She lifted her gaze to mine. *"I bet you even taste the same."*

"Don't even think about it," I warned.

Elise laughed. *"You're no fun."*

Deciding not to indulge the were-druid further, I turned to my familiar. *"What about you, Ghost?"* I asked, rearing up tall as I'd seen the stygian serpents do. *"Can you sense anything amiss?"*

The pyre wolf shook her head slowly. *"No... if I didn't know better—"* she pawed delicately at my scaled torso—*"I'd think this was real."*

"In most senses it is," I murmured.

"Why did you change to a wolf first?" Elise asked curiously, her earlier humor vanished.

"I had no other choice. My human form is too small to mimic a creature as large as a serpent."

Nodding, she sat down on her haunches. *"Well, whenever you're ready, then."*

Leaning down, I reached down and picked up Sedgwick's bag.

You have acquired a bag containing 4 items.

The precious bag safely tucked inside my serpentine jaw, I drew the shadows close about me.

You are hidden.

"I'm ready. Let's begin."

✳   ✳   ✳

Elise has cast arboreal guard.

Five minutes later, another lesser stygian pack was cresting the rise to the west.

Multiple hostile entities have failed to detect you.

"Right on schedule," I murmured. Safely nestled in the shadows, I watched the nether creatures descend upon the unguarded grove.

"Do we really need to let them destroy the trees?" Elise asked from where she and Ghost were hiding. *"I hate to see the grove desecrated."*

"We do," I said firmly.

"But..."

Shutting out the rest of the druid's protest, I kept my attention focused on the serpent pack and their assault on the grove.

The pine trees did not go down easily.

They claimed the lives of more than one lesser stygian, but in the end, the enemy's numbers were simply too great, and the last tree expired. Then, of course, the stygian pack reversed course.

That was the moment I was waiting for.

Concealed on the selfsame slope the nether creatures were traversing anew, I let the shadows around me unravel and slid out from behind the boulder I'd been hiding behind.

"Moment of truth," Elise murmured.

Ignoring her, I kept my gaze fixed on the lead hydra in the pack. How would it react?

But the nether creature did not so much as throw me a passing glance as it stomped by on its way to the nest.

"Well, that was anticlimactic," Elise muttered.

"It was," I replied, allowing myself to breathe again. *"But remember, no talking once I leave the foothills. We can't risk the void tree realizing anything is amiss."* So saying, I slithered into the lesser stygian pack.

While the other serpents and hydras didn't exactly make way for me, none of the creatures protested my entry.

I was in.

Feeling Ghost's eyes on me and, through our bond, the worry coloring her emotions, I said, *"Don't worry, I'll be fine."*

"I know you think that," she began, *"but if you get in trouble—"*

"I won't," I assured her. *"But if I do, I will reactivate our link immediately. You have my word on that."*

"Alright," she conceded reluctantly. *"Good luck, then, Prime."*

"Thanks, Ghost." Turning my attention inward, I poured the entirety of my psi into the mental walls protecting my consciousness, cutting off every connection between my mind and the outside world.

Now, nothing could get in or out.

Your psi abilities are no longer available.

The precautions I was taking were extreme, and perhaps unnecessary, but no one, not even the brotherhood, understood the true extent of the void tree's psionic capabilities, and I didn't want to find out the hard way, I'd gambled wrong. Getting things right today was crucial if I wanted our plan tomorrow to succeed.

As mentally prepared as I could be, I crested the rise and entered the void tree's line of sight.

✷　✷　✷

Multiple hostile entities have failed to pierce your disguise.
Multiple hostile entities have failed to pierce your disguise.
...
...

The void tree did not react.

Nothing in the nest did, which was truly the best reaction I could have hoped for. Still, that did not make my journey through the nest any less nerve-racking.

The moment the lesser stygian pack crossed over the nest's outer perimeter, it split apart, the individual serpents and hydras heading in seemingly random directions. I kept my own path erratic. But there was nothing random about my course.

I had a destination in mind, and it was almost on the void tree's doorstep.

I slithered past untold clumps of hydras and serpents—some dozed, while others moved about as listlessly as I was pretending to do. None of them cast me a second glance. The overlords appeared just as uncaring. And the void tree...

Despite its oppressive and pervasive aura, the stygian Power was equally ignorant of my presence.

Well, that, or it was luring me closer.

But I rather doubted that. If the void tree's psi abilities were that far beyond my own, it would've had no trouble defeating me during our previous encounter.

The minutes ticked by.

And ever so carefully, I meandered my way to my targets: the overlords bracketing the void tree.

Both colossal creatures were still anchored firmly in the ground, puffing out a constant stream of thick nether. It didn't look like either stygian Power ever intended on moving again, which perhaps explained why so many lesser stygians had taken to crawling over the pair.

That made my task easier.

I would be just one more snake amongst many and of no import. Reaching the first overlord's side, I slithered on without pause—just like I saw so many other serpents doing.

The overlord didn't react.

There had to be a whole host of spores nearby too. But if there were, they were just as fooled by my form as every other stygian in the nest. Growing more confident, I increased my pace, snaking up the Power's near-vertical sides without pause.

This overlord was no different from the other two we had killed. Its hide was just as pockmarked and riddled with cracks. There were plenty of flying serpents about, too. For whatever reason, they preferred to perch on top of the Power. Passing a large clump of the creatures, I finally slowed.

My vertical ascent had come to an end. Now, the stygian Power curved beneath me like a gentle hill.

I had reached my destination.

Raising my triangular head, I scanned the surroundings. There were deep craters and spidery cracks aplenty in close proximity to me. Slithering to the side of a particularly deep one, I curled up tightly with my head in the center of my serpentine coils.

Then, pointing my mouth downward, I opened my jaws.

Sedgwick's bag slid out.

I'd deliberately left its drawstrings loose and it took only a few delicate nudges with my nose to fully open the bag.

Inside lay four items: two aetherstones, and two innocuous looking wooden balls.

But looks could be deceiving.

And while there was nothing special about the balls themselves, the same could not be said of what lay within their hollowed-out insides.

I'd spent a considerable amount of time seeding the two objects with trap crystals before setting out, and now they were each effectively... a bomb.

I'd learned from my previous failed attempt at cracking open the overlord's shell, and in hindsight, I realized I'd failed not because my traps hadn't been powerful enough, but because they hadn't been embedded deep enough.

A problem the wooden balls should see solved.

I picked up the first bomb gingerly with my jaws.

You have acquired a plain wooden ball inset with 30 dormant tier 4 traps, each formed of 5 trap elements: 2 x poison cloud enchantments, 1 x fire enchantment, 1 x remote control, and 1 x remote key. Dormant traps are harder to detect and will not trigger under any circumstances.

Lowering my head into the crack in the stygian's hide, I dropped the ball and listened intently.

The bomb fell for a long time before coming to a stop with a muted thud. I hissed in relief at the lack of a sharp crack. The wooden ball had survived the journey intact. *Perfect*, I thought, turning my attention back to the bag.

It was time to imprint one of the aetherstones.

I'd paid Sedgwick a pretty penny for the two gems, but I rather thought they were worth it. Like Safyre had told me long ago, under ordinary circumstances, a mage could open a portal to anywhere they'd been.

Or to anywhere they had the aether coordinates for.

And it was the coordinates of my present location I intended to capture. With such coordinates in hand, our mages could portal a strike force directly onto the overlord, allowing them to bypass the surrounding stygians and immediately assault the Power.

Of course they would just as immediately come under attack. If not by the void tree itself, then certainly by the thousands of other stygians nearby.

Still, the absence of the Reachers made it more imperative—not less—that we kill the overlords early. If my bombs worked as I hoped, the strike teams could do just that and vanish before the stygians overran them.

If, on the other hand, my bombs failed...

Well, then, at the very least, the strike teams would serve to keep the overlords distracted while Safyre, Adriel, the forsworn, the nagians, and I dealt with the void tree.

It would not be as easy as all that, of course, and no doubt there would be more than a few complications to handle, not least being the rest of the nest.

Still, I believed the plan was workable, even if it left us dangerously overextended. But, as I kept reminding myself, we didn't have to destroy the nest or even kill the overlords. It was only the void tree that was important.

Destroy it, and the rift would close.

Simple.

Or so I hoped. It was too bad I couldn't use my makeshift bombs against the void tree itself. But unfortunately, there was a limit on the number of trap crystals I could employ—a limit set by my scoundrel wristband—and I'd used all of them in making the two bombs. And besides, venturing close enough to the void tree to place a bomb near it was too risky.

Enough daydreaming. Picking up the bag again, I focused on one of the charged but unetched gems inside and willed my present location into it.

You have etched an aetherstone with the aether coordinates of an arbitrary location within sector 18,240. This location will henceforth be designated: Loc-A.

It was done, and none of the stygians had reacted.

I had done what I could. The rest would be up to the others. Uncurling, I slithered away to my next target: the second overlord.

I had one more aetherstone to etch and another bomb to place.

Chapter 568: At the Heart of Things Again

The second half of my mission in the nest went as flawlessly as the first, and it was only a little later that Nyra and I were heading to Nexus.

It was time to attend to the final piece of business still left undone.

You have cast doppelganger, transforming your form into that of Vulen, a level 187 elven phantom and concealing your Powerful Initiate Mark. Duration: infinite.

Ghost has unmanifested.

2 of 2 stygian nagas have been freed from enslavement. They are no longer dominated.

You have entered the safe zone of sector 12,560.

You have entered the safe zone of sector 1.

I stepped out of the portal at the Roost and into the bright and noisy environs of Nexus.

"By the ancients," Nyra muttered under her breath as she followed me through the gateway.

Glancing over my shoulder, I found my apprentice gawping at the teeming mass of players crowding the teleportation platform. "So many players..." she whispered.

"Be careful of what you say here," I warned. *"You never know who is listening."*

Nyra nodded jerkily. "Sorry." Her eyes darted to the right. "Who is that?"

Following her gaze, I spotted a triumvirate knight bearing down on us.

"That," I muttered, "is unwanted attention."

"No gawking!" the knight yelled, looking straight at me. "Clear the platform. Now!"

Pulling Nyra along, I did just that.

"Try not to lose sight of me," I cautioned as we slipped into the crowd. *"And don't be afraid to push your way through if needs be."*

Nyra didn't reply, but I felt her take hold of my cloak and not let go. Content to let her navigate that way, I cut south through the square, heading for the gate to the plague quarter.

No one threw me a second glance, nor Nyra for that matter. My disguise kept me safe and secret blood hid her Wolf Marks even more completely. So, it was no surprise when we reached the south gate without incident.

You have left a safe zone.

"Eew, what's that smell?" Nyra asked as we exited the triumvirate gatehouse.

"That's the plague quarter. You're in it now."

"You didn't tell me it would smell so bad," she accused.

"It doesn't, not to most people, anyway." I glanced at her sideways. *"It must be the Wolf in you coming to the fore."*

"Huh, really?" she asked, perking up. Turning her hands over in front of her, she inspected them minutely as if hoping to find them different.

"I don't think the smell is so bad," Ghost offered suddenly. *"The nether is much worse."*

I chuckled. *"That it is. Oh, and welcome back."* The pyre wolf had been silent since we'd entered Nexus—and not by choice. The Game had put her forcibly to sleep inside the Cloak, and she had only reawakened after we left the safe zone.

"Thank you, Prime," Ghost said, peering through my eyes. *"I don't suppose I can manifest here?"*

"You can't," I agreed. *"But don't worry, we'll reach the dungeon soon. And there, hopefully, there will be no one around to watch you—or us."*

✳   ✳   ✳

You have entered sector 105 of the Endless Dungeon. This sector is part of a closed region named the Guardian Tower. It consists of 5 unclaimable sectors and 6 one-way portals.

A maximum of 6 players may be in the Guardian Tower at any one time. The dungeon is repopulated daily.

Recommended player levels: 140 to 160.

Recommended party size: 4 to 6.

Current number of players in the dungeon: 4 (including your party).

Sector bosses remaining: 4 of 5.

Emerging in the entry chamber of the guardian tower, I stepped absently aside as Nyra stumbled in after me. My focus was nearly wholly consumed by the dungeon welcome message. On the one hand, what it had to say was comforting.

Four players in the dungeon... that had to mean Shael and Anriq were still alive. Didn't it?

But on the other hand, one of the dungeon bosses was dead already. Which one was it? And why only one? And would the dead boss ruin my schedule?

"Something wrong?" Nyra asked.

"I'm not sure," I replied as Ghost began streaming out of the Cloak. "I guess we'll find out soon enough."

Tiptoeing to the door of the chamber, Nyra peered out. "Interesting," she murmured, before glancing back at me. "How do you want to do this?"

"As quickly as possible." I frowned. "If I had to guess, I would say Shael, Anriq, and Bacheus have already exited the tundra and begun their ascent through the tower. If we manage it, I want to reach them before they get to Kolath."

Because, of course, there was only one reason we were here.

To awaken the guardian.

And replace him.

The only question outstanding was who would take Kolath's place. Bacheus or—almost of its own accord, my gaze drifted to my apprentice— Nyra.

"Michael?" she prompted.

I jerked free from my musings. I had been staring, I realized.

Nyra frowned. "Did you hear what I said?"

Ghost has taken the form of a level 267 stygian pyre wolf.

"Yes, I did," I replied shortly. "I'll take the lead. You and Ghost keep up if you can."

Not waiting for her response, I charged forward.

✳ ✳ ✳

I didn't halt my mad dash as I burst through the doorway and into a familiar underground basin, one filled with lava and populated with fire slugs, savants, and a pair of magma elementals. I barely slowed down in fact, and that was only to get a lock on my target.

And the moment I did, I released the psi I had been holding in readiness.

You have teleported into the shadow of a level 155 savant acolyte.

I rushed back into existence beside a black throne. The hooded figure ensconced in it jerked upright. But it was already too late for him.

Ebonheart was in motion.

You have killed a level 155 savant acolyte with a fatal blow.
The first sector boss has been slain! Sector bosses remaining: 3 of 5.

That quickly the 'battle' for the first level was over.

✳ ✳ ✳

The level wasn't cleared. Not yet.

While the sector boss was dead—and the magma elementals vanished— the fire slugs, and other savants remained. I paid them no heed, though. Rifling through the belongings of the corpse at my feet, I let Ghost and Nyra attend to the mopping up.

The duo were doing a fine job, too.

Diving headlong into the molten lake, the pyre wolf was killing the fire slugs and savants with abandon, while Nyra did the same from a platform of solidified air.

The dungeon denizens didn't stand a chance and soon the pair were standing beside me on the island of magma rock.

"Is that it?" Nyra asked, looking confused.

I nodded.

Her consternation grew. "The *entire* level?"

I chuckled. "If only you knew how long it took me to get through on my first try, you wouldn't be so surprised." I held up the amulet of fire I'd retrieved from the sector boss. "But I have what we need. Let's move on."

✻　✻　✻

You have entered sector 106 of the Endless Dungeon.

The second level's dungeon denizens fared no better than those from the previous one. However, given the labyrinthine nature of the ratmen's tunnels, it still took us hours to get through their domain.

But while our passage through the sector was long and tedious, it was not arduous. With me, Ghost, and Nyra working in tandem, we barely had cause to pause in our headlong rush. Using slaysight, charm, manifest, and a whole host of other abilities, the three of us bulldozed through every obstacle in our path—be it a trap, ratman, or savant—until we reached the final chamber and found a veritable army waiting for us.

But it was an army that was much too low-leveled to pose any serious threat.

"Cut your way through to the exit portal," I instructed Ghost and Nyra. "I'll deal with the sector boss."

"How are you going to—" Nyra began.

You have cast wind daemon, multiplying your speed by 2x for 1 minute.

Not waiting for her to finish, I blinked out.

You have teleported into the shadow of a level 161 savant disciple.
You have cast cold sphere.
19 of 20 targets have been <u>chilled</u>.

I smiled grimly. With my foes moving as slow as molasses, and me dashing about at twice my normal speed, killing the sector boss and his guards was going to be child's play.

Hefting my swords, I got to work.

✻　✻　✻

You have killed a savant disciple with a fatal blow!
The second sector boss has been slain! Sector bosses remaining: 2 of 5.
You have acquired an amulet of earth, the second piece of the guardian amulet of elements.
You have entered sector 107 of the Endless Dungeon.

It was only a few minutes later that our small party entered a familiar field of white.

"The tundra!" Nyra marveled. "I can't believe we're here already."

Nodding absently, I turned about in a slow circle, scanning the horizon in all directions.

Nothing.

Damnit. The trio should have been here by now. "Ghost?"

"I don't sense anything either," she replied. *"If they're still on the tundra, Shael and Anriq are too far away to detect."*

Let's hope not. Reaching into the farspeaker bracelet around my wrist, I called out, *"Shael? Anriq? Can either of you hear me?"*

Stark silence.

"They must have left the sector already," Nyra remarked.

"Maybe," I allowed. "That, or they are lost on the tundra and are in no fit state to respond." I sighed. "Either way, we have no choice but to continue on."

Waiting was not an option. Our schedule simply did not allow it.

"Which way do we go?" Nyra asked impassively. She had to know what it would mean if the trio were lost. Despite this, no fear or hesitancy colored her voice.

"This way," I replied with the same lack of inflection. Facing the direction I knew the portal to the fourth level to be, I marched grimly through the snow.

One way or the other, the forerunners were going to lose a valued member today.

✳   ✳   ✳

You have discovered the lair of the sector boss.
Deactivating its veil of concealment...

We reached the ice dome protecting the portal to the next level without mishap, and despite my hope of learning otherwise, we spotted no sign of Anriq or the others.

"How do we get through?" Nyra asked, tapping on the solid wall of ice in front of us. "Do we accept the Adjudicator's request to retract the barrier?"

I shook my head. "Not yet." I glanced at Ghost. "Materialize inside the dome using explosive manifest."

"Got it, Prime," she replied. *"And then?"*

"Wreak havoc," I instructed grimly. "We'll take down the barrier and join you as soon as the sector boss is dead."

✳   ✳   ✳

Ghost has killed a level 172 frozen savant adept. The third sector boss has been slain! Sector bosses remaining: 1 of 5.
You have acquired an amulet of ice.
Ghost has unmanifested.
You have entered sector 108 of the Endless Dungeon.

We emerged in the penultimate sector of the guardian tower on a cliff face.

But forewarned by my first run through the dungeon, we were prepared. Nyra had pre-cast levitate, and Ghost—who would have trouble navigating the narrow path along the cliff wall—had returned to her spirit vessel.

"We follow that," I said, gesturing to the slender ledge winding along the cliff face.

"For how long?" Nyra asked breathlessly, staring down into the yawning expanse of space at our feet.

"Until we find a wyvern."

Her head jerked upward to scan the wide blue sky. "There are wyverns here?"

"Yes, and savants riding them, too."

"Err... how do we fight airborne foes in this terrain?"

I smiled mirthlessly. "Easy. We get mounts of our own."

✳   ✳   ✳

You have successfully dominated a level 165 brown wyvern.
You have successfully dominated a level 162 brown wyvern.

Two hours later, Nyra and I were mounted on our own wyverns, both of whom were bound to me by ties of blood.

"You promise you will keep your word, Wolf?" the wyvern I rode asked for the second time. *"You will free us after you've killed the interlopers?"*

"Of course. I will not renege on the deal we struck."

The wyvern hissed disparagingly, but despite his disbelief, he knew he had no choice but to obey my commands.

We flew the rest of the way in silence, our destination the valley at the end of the canyon we raced down. Traversing the sector in this manner was much faster than the way I had originally crossed the level—by way of the ledges and bridges.

Still, I bemoaned the time lost.

Evening was fast approaching, and the day was nearly at end.

"There they are," the wyvern said.

Looking up, I spotted the sector boss, and the two savant aeromancers accompanying him.

"Then, let's go get them," I murmured.

✳   ✳   ✳

Nyra has killed a level 186 savant master!
The fourth sector boss has been slain! Sector bosses remaining: 0 of 5.
You have acquired an amulet of air.
You have entered sector 109 of the Endless Dungeon.
2 of 2 brown wyverns have been freed from enslavement.
Ghost has manifested.

Only a little later, with another sector boss dead behind us, Nyra, Ghost, and I crossed into the guardian tower's final level.

"We've made it in time," I said, exhaling in relief as I studied the sector's verdant plains and darkening skies. Evening was upon us, but one way or another, we would be done with the dungeon soon, leaving us ample time to return to sector 18,240 before the big battle.

Nyra, meanwhile, was studying the marble compound to the left. "Is that where he is?" she asked quietly.

I knew who she meant. Kolath—the Nexus guardian. "Yes, that's the final chamber. It's where we'll find—"

I broke off.

"What's wrong?" Nyra asked, her face filling with concern.

I licked my lips. "The chamber. It's open."

CHAPTER 569: A LONG OVERDUE RESTORATION

I stared at the white marble walls—and the gaping hole between them—my thoughts whirling. The compound's crystal door was open.

And it shouldn't be.

There was only one explanation: someone was waiting within. A sector boss was dead—and had been since before we arrived. Now, I knew which one it was.

The grandmaster savant—the level five boss.

"Is this a bad thing?" Nyra asked in a low voice.

I tore my gaze away from the final chamber. "What?"

"That the gates are open, I mean."

"No. No, it isn't. On the contrary, it's good news." It had to be Shael, Anriq, and Bacheus inside. But, on the off chance, it wasn't...

"We'll do this slow and quiet," I whispered. *"Here's what I want you to do..."*

✳   ✳   ✳

You have cast engine of war, wind daemon, vanish, and trigger-cast quick mend.

An invisible shadow, I followed in Nyra's wake.

The young witch was my stalking horse. She strode openly toward the final chamber, but with her buffs cast and defenses raised. And both Ghost and I were ready to jump to her aid at the first sign of trouble.

Reaching the missing crystal door, Nyra paused, her tension palpable.

Ten yards behind her, I stopped, too. I couldn't see what lay within the marble compound, and I ached to do so, but I dared not. If there was a trap, it was Nyra who would spring it.

"Nyra!" a familiar voice called from within.

My apprentice's shoulders relaxed, relief and recognition sweeping across her face. "Anriq! You made it." She dashed forward and out of sight.

"You know her?" a second voice asked in a hushed tone. I recognized it as well. It was Shael.

"It's Nyra, Michael's apprentice," Anriq replied.

"So, where is he?" a third asked—Bacheus.

It's them. It really is, I thought, finally letting myself relax. An analysis of their mindglows confirmed it. Using Shael's mind as a focus, I jumped through the shadows.

You have teleported 50 yards.

"Where's who?" I asked lightly, letting the shadows around me unravel. All three jumped.

"Michael!" Shael exclaimed. "You made it. We feared…"

I clapped his shoulder. "I know. I was afraid something had befallen you, too." Tilting my head to the side, I let my gaze flit between the trio. "Why didn't you wait for me?" *Like I asked.*

The three exchanged glances. "We reached the exit from the tundra early," Anriq replied eventually. "And we didn't think it wise to just hang around."

My brows rose. "Early? How early?"

"We got there yesterday," Bacheus said.

"Yesterday!" Nyra exclaimed, pursing her lips. "That means you crossed the tundra in… *four* days?" she asked, slightly disbelieving of her own calculations.

A smiling Anriq and Shael both nodded. "All thanks to Bacheus. You won't believe some of the spells he has."

The nagian couldn't blush, but I could tell the others' praise pleased him.

"Well done, you three," I said warmly. "Both for getting through the tundra so fast *and* for finishing the remaining levels."

"And how did you do that so fast?" Nyra demanded.

Anriq grinned. "I'll tell you later."

I rubbed my chin. "I assume you reached this level yesterday?" That would explain why the level three and four sector bosses had reappeared in the interim. The dungeon reset itself every day.

"We got here last night," Bacheus confirmed. "But we took the opportunity to sleep and recover before entering the final chamber and tackling its boss."

Shael shuddered. "And a good thing we did." He glanced over his shoulder at the compound's lone corpse. "That bastard was hard to kill."

"Since then, we've been waiting," Anriq said, concluding the trio's tale. "Just like you asked."

Nyra rolled her eyes. "You were told to wait on the tundra."

The werewolf ducked his head sheepishly.

"Never mind," I murmured. "It's done." Swiveling about, my gaze found the sculptured marble form of Kolath. "And we've reached him."

"Prime, can I manifest?" Ghost asked. She'd been following the conversation avidly but now was ready to explore the environs herself.

"Go ahead," I replied absently. Striding through the ankle-high grass, I approached the colossal statue while the pyre wolf streamed out of me.

The others followed silently on my heels.

Little about the guardian had changed in the intervening time. Perhaps, his statue body bore a few more hairline cracks, but other than that… there was nothing to indicate Kolath was a declining soul, a spirit who had spent overlong in this world, and whose mind was not quite all there anymore.

"How shall we do this?" Bacheus asked quietly.

I turned to face him. "Are you sure you still want to do this?"

"I am," he replied without hesitation.

I glanced at Nyra.

She raised her chin. "As am I."

Shael frowned and Anriq's eyes widened. "Wait, what?" the werewolf demanded. "Why would—"

"Nyra is only here as a precaution," I interjected, but it was to Bacheus, not Anriq, that I directed my response.

"A precaution?" Anriq repeated, not at all mollified.

"In case Kolath refuses my offer," Bacheus explained serenely.

The werewolf's gaze flitted to the nagian. "Why would he do that?"

Unexpectedly, Bacheus laughed. "Well, for one, the guardian is somewhat mad, so who knows what he might do?" His humor faded. "And for another, he might deem me unworthy. I'm not a scion anymore, after all."

"Oh," Anriq said, deflating.

Ghost has manifested.

"I will try to see that it does not come to that," I said firmly. My gaze returned to the looming statue. "But it's probably best if I awaken him. Kolath should still remember me."

Shael held out his arm. "You'll need this then." A guardian amulet rested in his hand.

"I have one of those, too," I murmured, removing the objects I'd collected from my backpack.

You have acquired all four pieces of the guardian amulet of the elements. Do you wish to combine the pieces?

I replied in the affirmative, prompting another response from the Game.

You have created the artifact: <u>guardian amulet of elements</u>.

I took the amulet from Shael's outstretched arm, nonetheless. The artifacts served as tithes that powered the guardians, and two offerings would eke more life into Kolath than one could—which would be a good thing.

Hopefully.

"You five better back up a bit," I said. "Kolath can be a little... touchy."

My companions retreated hastily, but it was only when they reached the far end of the compound that I stopped shooing them away. Satisfied that they were as safe as they could be, I turned back to the statue. The time had finally come to complete a task long overdue.

Kneeling, I brushed away the sand covering the statue's stone plinth base, exposing the carving beneath. It was exactly as I remembered. I inhaled deeply. *Here goes,* I thought. Touching the amulets to the carving, I willed my intent to the Adjudicator.

A Game message unfurled in my mind.

Analyzing offerings...

...

...

Analysis completed. The offerings have been deemed sufficient. Do you wish to tithe these two artifacts to the guardian?

I do.

Tithe accepted. Items lost.
Awakening guardian…

✳   ✳   ✳

Awakening guardian…
Awakening guardian…

The Game message replayed itself in my mind over and over, and still Kolath did not emerge. Finally, tiring of the wait, I sank down, cross-legged in the dirt.

Which, of course, was when the alerts changed.

The revival is complete. Guardian awoken.

I straightened. *Here we go.*

Bracing myself, I tightened the shields around my mind. My last encounter with Kolath was not one I was likely to forget. The guardian had nearly killed me with his mental assault then.

I couldn't afford to be incapacitated this time around. The stakes were too high.

Kolath's eyes snapped open.

"Welcome back," I greeted softly.

He did not respond. His expression inscrutable, the guardian's gaze flitted to my companions, then back to me again.

I held firm under his examination, and at the edges of my mind, I thought I detected a telltale tickle. I was being inspected—minutely—I imagined, but I couldn't be certain.

"Prime, is everything alright?" Ghost asked softly. *"I can feel—"*

"Shh!" I hissed. But it was too late.

His head snapping around, Kolath pinned the pyre wolf with a hard stare.

I wasn't sure what Kolath intended, but I couldn't risk that he would launch an attack next. I rose to my feet.

"NO!" I shouted, the word reverberating across the compound. "It is me you will deal with."

The guardian's head creaked slowly back in my direction. *"Then they are yours, Wolf?"*

I relaxed fractionally. *So, he does remember me.* "They are."

Kolath's lips twisted. *"Even the… stygian?"*

"Ghost is my familiar, and no stygian," I said firmly. *"Let him into your thoughts, Ghost,"* I added, knowing that Kolath was likely listening in. *"Let him see what you are."*

Mutely, the pyre wolf lowered her defenses.

A second passed.

"Ah, I see now." Kolath leaned forward, folding himself nearly in half to place his face inches from mine. *"It is good you do not seek to lie to me, Wolf child."*

I shrugged as nonchalantly as I could. "I have no cause to."

The guardian's eyes glittered. *"Then, will you not let me into your mind too?"* A gentle but firm prod against my shields. *"Your defenses have grown quite impressive."*

I ignored the request altogether. "I've completed the task you set me," I said, seeking to sidetrack the guardian.

Kolath frowned. *"What task?"*

"I've found out what has happened to your brethren." I paused. "I have even awoken one."

Kolath jerked upright so fast I barely saw him move. *"Who?"* he demanded, looming over me in unmistakable threat. *"Who did you awake?"*

"Draven," I replied succinctly.

The guardian's eyes flared. *"So, my brother lives. Thank the ancients."* His gaze jerked back to me. *"Tell me everything,"* he ordered.

Gathering my thoughts, I began my tale.

✳   ✳   ✳

"You've done well, Wolf," Kolath pronounced when I at last ran aground. He had listened to my tale in avid silence, not interrupting once, and for all my fears about the state of his mind, the guardian had shown no sign of the brittleness he had during our first encounter.

"Much better than I expected," he went on. He chuckled abruptly. His mood had lightened appreciably since hearing my tale. *"But then, Wolf was always being underestimated."*

I inclined my head. "I did my best to help."

"That you did." A pause. *"And now you are here again. Why?"*

I inhaled deeply. "To help you."

Kolath's brows crinkled. *"With the offerings, you mean? I appreciate the tithe but—"*

"No," I interjected softly. "I don't mean the tithes."

The guardian's frown deepened.

"It's time for you to go to your long sleep, Kolath," I said.

"Ridiculous," he scoffed. *"I don't need to—"*

"Draven thinks you do," I continued inexorably. "And so do I."

The guardian glared at me. *"I am perfectly capable—"*

Once more, I cut him off. "You are not. Like it or not, your faculties have deteriorated, Kolath. You have simply been too long out of stasis and at this task too long. It is time to hand the reins over to someone else."

"Tell me what it is you think I cannot do?" he roared.

"Where is the lost Prime?" I shot back without hesitation. I knew where she was. I had figured out the truth with Draven and Adriel, but I had not told Kolath yet.

The guardian's face grew perplexed. *"What?"* he asked less stridently.

"You heard me. Locate the lost Prime. She is hiding in one of the dungeons under your control. Draven believes the only reason you can't determine her location is because you are in decline." I paused. "Can you tell me otherwise?"

Silence.

"You can't, can you?"

Kolath hung his head. *"I can't,"* he whispered.

"I'm sorry, Guardian," I said sympathetically, "but neither of us can afford to shirk the truth: the time has come for you to give up this life."

Kolath's gaze rose to meet mine. *"Who will take my place?"*

I waved my companions over. Saying nothing, Kolath watched in silence as they gathered around me.

"Bacheus has volunteered."

The guardian's eyes shot to the nagian. *"The possessed?"*

Bacheus stepped forward. "Former possessed, Lord Guardian," he corrected, inclining his head. "If you will allow me the honor, I will serve in your place." He paused. "Perhaps, that way I can wipe away some of the stains besmirching my soul."

Kolath's gaze drifted back to me.

"He can be trusted," I said in response to his look.

The guardian's shoulders sagged. *"Very well. I will do as you ask."*

I bowed low from the hip. "Thank you, Guardian," I said sincerely.

Kolath sighed. *"No, Wolf, it is I who must give thanks. What you do today, what you may still do, could very well save the Kingdom and stop our relentless descent into the void."* Creaking into motion, he mimicked my bow. *"Hail Scion! Hail House Wolf! And may the ancients always favor your blade!"*

Straightening, the guardian grimaced as if in pain. *"Now, let us be done with this and see me to my rest."*

CHAPTER 570: A NEW DAWN

The process of replacing Kolath with Bacheus was not a short one, nor was it one Kolath was willing to let us observe. Banished to the exterior of the compound, and with nothing else to do, Shael, Anriq, Nyra, Ghost, and I sat down and exchanged tales of our respective journeys.

It passed the time, but slowly, and as the hours flew by, I grew more anxious. It was becoming more urgent that we returned to sector 18,240.

Eventually, though, a welcome Game message unfurled in my mind.

You have completed the task: <u>Restore the Nexus Guardian</u>. You have convinced the guardian Kolath to relinquish his hold on life and allow Bacheus to take his place. Nexus now has a new guardian.

Congratulations, Michael! You have completed a task crucial to the continued functioning of the Endless Dungeon and the survival of the Kingdom. By restoring the Nexus Guardian, you have shown yourself to be a <u>Protector of the Ancients</u>. This has become the second tenet of your burgeoning House.

Staying true to your House's tenets will deepen your Wolf Mark in the future. Straying from it will see your Mark weaken.

Another tenet, I mused, and an unexpected one at that.

It was the second tenet my 'new'—and yet unformed—House had earned. The first, Just Retribution, was more nebulous. Protector of the Ancients sounded straightforward enough, though, and it was easy to see how it would benefit me and the other scions in the short term.

Rescuing the guardians—and perhaps even assisting them with tithes—would deepen our bloodline Marks. More importantly, the tenet would give our disparate bloodlines a shared purpose, one with material benefits, and that would only help unify our House further.

Yet, I couldn't help but wonder how many other tenets the Adjudicator had in store for us, and if I would find them all as appealing.

No use worrying about any of that now, I thought, rising to my feet. The Adjudicator would act as he saw fit, and there was little I could do to sway him.

"It's done," I said, turning to the others.

Not questioning how I knew that to be the case, the others stood with me. Leading the way, I re-entered the compound.

I found the same marble statue gracing the inside. It was Kolath, yet not. The statue's features had changed, almost imperceptibly so, and at a guess, they now resembled Bacheus' true face—one I'd never seen. More startling, though, was the statue's new suppleness and vibrancy. It was reminiscent of the same energy I'd noticed in Draven.

The Nexus guardian had truly been reborn—and reinvigorated.

"Michael," Bacheus intoned. "Come closer."

That was another difference between Kolath and Bacheus. The former had only spoken to me through mindspeech.

I did as the guardian bade. "Everything went well?" I asked cautiously, not entirely sure what to expect of this 'new' Bacheus.

"It did," he replied vaguely.

I waited for him to go on, but he stayed silent.

"What's wrong with him?" Shael hissed as the seconds ticked by and Bacheus stayed locked motionless.

"How would I know?" Anriq muttered.

"I wasn't asking you," Shael retorted. "I was—"

"Shh! Both of you," Nyra snapped.

Nodding gratefully to her, I took a step forward. "Bacheus?" I prompted loudly.

The guardian shook his head. "What? Oh, sorry. There is a lot about this new form that I still have to process."

"Which is understandable," I said. "But the others and I need to get going again, and before that..."

"You need to know if I can do what we discussed," Bacheus finished for me. "One second," he said, bowing his head to think.

Patiently, I waited.

A minute later, the guardian shook his head. "I can't."

My shoulders sagged. It had been a long shot, and perhaps too much to wish for, but I'd been hoping—

"I can't make the guardian tower a private dungeon and bequeath it to you," Bacheus went on, oblivious of my thoughts, "but I can stop anyone who is not a forerunner from entering or leaving."

I straightened. "You can?" I asked breathlessly.

What Bacheus was proposing was nearly as good as what I'd asked for. We wouldn't own the dungeon, but we would be able to control access—if only through Bacheus.

And having a say in who could enter or leave the guardian tower was vital to our cause.

Because, notwithstanding the shield generator around sector 18,240, a hostile entity could still enter the sector through the tundra nether portal. Granted, the portal was hidden away on the icy plains and was almost impossible to find if you didn't know where to look.

But it was still a vulnerability.

One that we were now about to plug with the new Nexus guardian's help. It meant, too, that irrespective of how the battle went tomorrow, irrespective of whether the void claimed sector 18,240 or not, the Packs would still have a safe haven to go to—one safeguarded by a guardian, no less.

"I can," Bacheus confirmed, unaware of my musings. "Or I can permanently close the hidden portal, if that is what you prefer."

I shook my head. "I don't prefer." While the tundra portal was a vulnerability, it was *also* our backdoor into Nexus and a second haven. And the strategic value of both those things were not to be underestimated. "Tell me more about the first option."

Bacheus shrugged. "There is not much to it. I will key the guardian tower's entrance and exit portals to your faction tokens. That will stop any player not part of the forerunners from using them. I can also reconfigure the internal portals in the dungeon, making them two-way so your people can pass freely between levels. And finally, I can relocate the hidden portal to this sector—" he gestured at the verdant plains beyond the compound's walls—"and anywhere out there that you want."

"Wow," Anriq gasped.

I could forgive his astonishment; I was feeling no small measure of it myself.

"But doing all this will come at a price," Bacheus finished.

Ah, so there is *a catch.* "What price?"

"The forerunners must provide me with a steady stream of offerings. A tithe a month should be sufficient. That will keep me powered and awake."

That we could do. "Is that all?"

"No. You will also have to forfeit any rewards stemming from the completion of your recent task. In a very real sense, the privileges I offer will become your reward."

I grimaced.

"How can you even do any of that?" Shael demanded suddenly. "I thought dungeons were immutable. And doesn't the Game constrain your lot from interfering with players?"

"Dungeons are not immutable," Bacheus said. "You only have to look at the ones owned by the factions to realize that. As for my... constraints." His lips curved up in a dangerous smile. "I am less restricted in what I can do than you think. The new Powers' own violations have left me free to act if they—or their followers—dare enter any of my dungeons."

He paused. "But I take your meaning. When it comes to unaffiliated players, the Adjudicator will allow me to do what I've proposed only because it's in support of my primary mission—protecting the Endless Dungeon."

Shael's brows drew down. "I don't follow."

Bacheus sighed. "In the last few hundred years, do you know how many tithes the Nexus guardian received?"

Shael shook his head.

"Less than a handful," Bacheus replied. "It was this lack more than anything else that led to Kolath's decline. Without tithes, I, too, will fall asleep, and if I fall asleep, I cannot fulfil my duty."

Shael nodded slowly. "Which is why the Adjudicator is letting you strike a deal for tithes."

Bacheus smiled. "Precisely. But the deal is not yet struck." His gaze found mine again. "What say you, Wolf?"

For a long moment, I stayed silent, weighing up my decision. But honestly, there was not much to consider. What the new guardian offered was nearly priceless in its potential.

There were the ratmen mines in level two to consider, the wyverns in level four, and the green—and very fertile—plains of level five. Taken altogether, they would provide nearly all the resources the forerunners needed to flourish and grow.

And Bacheus had to know that.

Which, I suspect, was what had spurred his proposal. Despite his new status as a guardian, the former sorcerer was still married to the forerunner's cause.

"We have a deal," I said finally.

The guardian grinned. "Excellent."

✳ ✳ ✳

The status of the dungeon has changed.

The Guardian Tower has been reconfigured to consist of 5 unclaimable sectors, 2 one-way portals, 4 two-way portals, and 1 hidden portal that has been relocated to sector 109.

The dungeon status has furthermore been falsified to hide these changes and to report its current number of players as being 6 of 6. The actual status is only perceivable by a forerunner.

You have sealed a Pact with Guardian Bacheus. In exchange for exclusive access to the Guardian Tower, your faction will deliver 1 tithe per month to the guardian. Failure to deliver the agreed offerings will result in the removal of the forerunner's access to the dungeon during the month concerned. This Pact may be terminated by you at any time.

You have 7 / 20 active Pacts.

As an added precaution, I had Bacheus place the hidden portal ten miles from the level five exit. Doing so wasn't strictly necessary, but it made me feel better, anyway. This way, if the worst befell us, and an enemy somehow gained access to the dungeon, there was still a decent chance the entrance to sector 18, 240 would not be discovered.

Then, it was time to depart.

"Farewell, Bacheus," I said. The others had already set off for the 'new' hidden portal, and it was just the guardian and me left in the compound.

"Farewell, Wolf," he replied. "We shall see each other again, I'm sure."

"No doubt." I began to turn away, then paused. "You will contact Draven?"

"As soon as I've settled into this new skin," he promised.

I nodded, then hesitated, not wanting to overstep. "Any regrets?" I asked eventually.

I didn't have to explain what I meant. "None," Bacheus said firmly. "Although…"

"Yes?" I prompted.

"I wish I could be there for tomorrow's battle."

"Ah, well. But never fear, I'll do our best to see it won without you."

Bacheus grinned. "See that you do. I'd hate to think all this has been for nothing."

"Never that," I murmured. "And thank you again—for everything." Turning around, I strode away.

*   *   *

We completed the trip back home in remarkably good time, hopping first through the hidden portal, then through a second portal—this one of my own my making—and in short order, we were in the cave again.

Almost everyone else was there, bedding down for the night or already asleep. Despite this there was an anticipatory buzz in the air.

Tomorrow we would fight for the sector, and one way or the other, we would decide our fate.

Releasing the others and sending Ghost to truth test the last of the nagians—Adriel had finished rehoming them only an hour ago—I joined Safyre where she stood warming herself by the campfire.

"Adriel is asleep?" I asked.

"She's finally getting to enjoy some well-deserved rest," Safyre replied.

I nodded. Of all of us, the lich was the one who had worked the most tirelessly. And thanks to her efforts, we had one hundred powerful former-scions on our side. They would serve as the backbone of our company tomorrow. A company that was still a potent force, even without the Reachers reinforcing our numbers.

Still, I couldn't help but ask, "Any news from the Marches?"

Safyre shook her head sadly. "None. The twins' latest report was two hours ago. There's still no sign of the Reachers."

"Damn," I muttered. "You should recall them. The twins, I mean."

"I will. First thing tomorrow." She yawned. "But with everything else happening, I haven't had the time."

"Sorry," I said contritely. "You must be exhausted too."

She threw me a lopsided grin. "I am. But the good news is that everything is done. All the supplies have been delivered, and everyone has been drilled and knows what roles they'll play tomorrow." She tilted her head. "What about you? How did it go?"

"Extremely well," I said with a satisfied smile.

"Then we have a new guardian?"

I nodded.

Safyre's gaze drifted to Nyra who was in the midst of an animated conversation with Shael, Anriq, and two of the forsworn. "And I see Nyra's here. That must mean..."

"Bacheus is the new guardian," I finished for her, then launched into a condensed retelling of the day's events.

"Oh my," Safyre murmured when I finished. "You've outdone yourself this time, Michael."

I shrugged. "It was all Bacheus' doing. He came up with the idea, and however he did it, he managed to sell the whole thing to the Adjudicator."

Safyre shook her head in bemused wonder. "If you told me seven days ago that this is where we'd be, I would've laughed. Now look at us. The sector has been secured and ours for the taking."

"Only nearly," I pointed out cheekily. "There is still the small matter of one void tree and two overlords to deal with."

She laughed, her eyes sparkling with genuine humor. "Of course. How did I ever forget?"

Chuckling, I drew her in a hug. "Whatever happens tomorrow... it's been great."

She squeezed me back. "Only great?" she murmured.

"Well, er... what I meant was—"

Laughing, Safyre set a finger to my lips. "I know what you meant. Now stop talking, and let's enjoy what time we have remaining."

Chapter 571: Another Surprise

Day 8 of Michael's Deadline

I didn't think I would manage to get any sleep, but much to my amazement, I woke up feeling surprisingly rested and reinvigorated the next morning.

What time is it? I wondered, sitting up amongst the blankets forming my bed. *Did Saf let me oversleep?*

But before I could discover the answer to that, a distant shout drew my attention. A second followed it in its wake, then a third.

"Ghost, what in hells is that racket?" I muttered. I was not in the main cave myself and could not immediately tell what was going on.

She ignored the question. *"Sleep well?"* she asked, amusement tracing her voice.

"Excellently," I snapped. *"Now, what is going on? And what time is it?"*

"It's still early," she replied unrepentantly. *"Most of the company is still abed. And that noise is the sound of Keros' challenge. Teresa has arrived with someone in tow."*

"Someone? With Terence, you mean?"

"No, it's...."

"Ghost?" I prompted.

"It's Regus," she said, her mindvoice full of astonishment.

My mouth dropped open.

The Reachers had come.

Heedless of what further chaos my abrupt arrival might sow, I flung open my mindsight and shadow jumped directly to Teresa.

* * *

You have teleported 183 yards.

I stepped out of the aether and into a brewing fight, or at least I hoped it was only brewing.

Teresa was beside me, her face heated and her blades out. In front of me was the source of her ire: Regus and Keros. The ten-foot wolfman loomed over the windknight, the fingers of his clawed hands opening and closing as if he was only barely stopping himself from ripping out the smaller man's throat.

But despite the disparity in size, it was Regus who was at a disadvantage. Keros had his poleaxe pressed against the side of the wolfman's throat, and from the line of red dripping down the grizzled human's blade, he had already drawn blood.

Regus noticed me first.

"Michael!" he growled. "Thank the ancients you're here!"

Theresa spun to face me. "I was just about to call you," she bit off quickly. "There's news. The—"

She broke off as Regus snarled.

The big wolfman had tried to shift out from under the poleaxe, but Keros was having none of that, and now there was no mistaking the blood pouring down the weapon. Regus's eyes glowed ominously, murder in his gaze.

"Stop!" I barked.

The tableau froze.

I pointed a finger at Keros. "You. Back."

The windknight arched an eyebrow, his face smooth and unruffled as he glanced at me, and for a moment, I thought he would refuse the order.

But somewhat to my surprise, Keros complied, stepping back smoothly and retracting his blade. Dismissing the windknight from further consideration, I turned to Regus, who was tentatively feeling at the wound on his neck. It was already closing.

"Where are Ceruvax and Farren?" I demanded, getting straight to the point.

"Back in the Marches," the wolfman replied.

I exhaled in sharp relief. Then things had not gone as badly as I feared. "What kept you? We were expecting you days ago!"

Regus shrugged apologetically. "Your man—Zekiel?—had some trouble getting to us, and then there were a few unexpected delays getting the doors to the final chamber unsealed."

I sighed. I dearly wanted to know the specifics, but I realized, too, they were unimportant right now. "Why are Farren and Ceruvax still in the Marches?"

"Because they're waiting with the men." Regus jerked a thumb in Teresa's direction. "And because this one thought it would be a bad idea for all two thousand five hundred of us to suddenly appear in your base." His gaze sidled to the impassively observing windknight. "And now I understand why she felt that way."

I frowned. "All of them are just sitting around waiting in the Marches?"

"Not all," Teresa answered quickly. "I came as soon as I could. So far, only the Reachers' vanguard has emerged from the dungeon."

Regus nodded in confirmation. "But the others are hot on their heels."

That was not good. The longer our people sat around in the Marches, the greater were the chances someone would notice their sudden arrival from nowhere.

Worse yet, we were not prepared to receive them.

We'd altered our plans to accommodate our significantly smaller force— which was why the rest of the company was still abed. The battle was only scheduled to begin this afternoon, and with only five hundred odd wolves and humans to pre-position, I'd convinced Safyre it wouldn't make sense to start ferrying our people to the river before noon.

Now, though, we had a force six times larger to contend with.

And for all the undoubted benefits that brought, it was going to be a logistical nightmare getting them all geared up and in position in time, especially this late in the game. Not to mention the changes we would have to make anew to the plan.

I groaned. *Safyre is going to kill me.*

✳ ✳ ✳

The next two hours were chaotic.

But it was controlled chaos, and the stress—such as it was—was buoyed by the knowledge that the chances of us triumphing today had improved dramatically.

Every nagian and forsworn caster who could open a portal was pressed into action weaving gateways, and those who couldn't were either made to stand guard or cast concealment shields—because, of course, we had to do our best to hide what was happening in the Marches from its owners. The wolves were also set to work fetching weapons, armor, crystals, and potions from the stores that we had thought would go unused.

"So, this is your base," Farren observed. "It's... cozy."

Adriel laughed. "It's only temporary, brother."

I smiled. The siblings' reunion had been heartfelt and touching to watch. The two lichs, Ceruvax, Regus, Algar, and I were standing at the mouth of the west tunnels, watching the last of the Bane Wolves settle into place.

"But... did it really have to be another cave?" Regus lamented, with only the faintest hint of a whine to his voice.

Adriel arched one eyebrow. "Would you have preferred camping out in the nether above?"

Regus grunted. "Well, when you put it that way..."

Farren laughed.

"I prefer it here," Algar said softly, his voice going almost unnoticed beneath the laughter.

My gaze slid in the high captain's direction. He'd been unusually quiet since arriving. One thing that none of us had considered was the effect that leaving the Reach would have on the Bane Wolves.

The Marches' open skies had shocked most of them near-senseless.

It was the first time the former New Haveners had been out of the Reach, the first time they had found themselves in such an extravagant open stretch of space, and most were still recovering—or at least, I hoped they were. In hindsight, it was a good thing we had established our base in a cave.

"Will the men manage the battle?" I asked quietly.

"They will," Algar replied. "The mists are familiar." Almost unwillingly, his gaze stole upward to the solid stone roof. "As long as they cannot see the... sky, the men will be fine."

I nodded, accepting his judgment on the matter.

Ceruvax's gaze found me. It was not the first time I'd felt the weight of his stare. "We have not yet talked," the envoy said.

I knew he had questions—lots of questions. There had not been time to brief the Reachers fully yet, and what information we'd managed to impart was full of holes.

"I know, but further discussions will have to wait until after the battle. There will be plenty of time then," I assured him. "Right now, I have to leave."

Ceruvax's eyes narrowed. "Where are you going?"

"To meet our allies, the brotherhood." The force the huntmistress had agreed to commit to the battle—two thousand players—was smaller than our own but not by much. And it was nearly time to begin deploying them in sector 30,199.

Turning about, I surveyed the faces of the Reachers. There was a reason I'd summoned them here, and it was not simply to reminisce. "You will likely not see me again before the battle."

That got all their attention.

"Safyre and Adriel will share as many of the details as possible in the intervening time, including—" my gaze skipped to Algar—"the Bane Wolves' part and—" I picked out Regus—"what role the Reach Pack will play. But I want to make one thing clear: Safyre is in charge. I trust her completely. You will follow her orders to the letter. No exceptions."

I paused to let that sink in. "Understood?" I asked, my eyes resting on the two elites in particular.

Ceruvax inclined his head stiffly. "Understood."

Farren acquiesced more easily. "If Adriel has faith in this Safyre of yours, then of course, so will I."

"I will keep them in line, Michael," Adriel promised with a small smile.

I nodded. It was not that I distrusted any of the Reachers or thought them less capable than Safyre, but circumstances had conspired to leave them in the dark, whereas Safyre knew every intimate detail of the plan. Even Adriel was less caught up than she was.

And just like Algar had told me long ago, every army needed a leader. In battle, there should be no confusion about who was in charge.

And today that could not be me.

I expected to be in the thick of things for much of the forthcoming battle. Not only was the risk of me falling greater, but as preoccupied as I was going to be with my own fights, it was likely I would lose sight of the bigger picture.

That would be Safyre's responsibility.

She would be the one directing the flow of the battle. She would be the one making sure things did not go awry. And that was why I'd made certain to drive the point home with Ceruvax and Farren. I didn't need the pair trying to contradict her mid-battle.

"Good. Now that that's settled, there are just two more things to do." Stepping forward, I laid my hand on Ceruvax's arm.

Commander ability triggered.

Do you wish to pass on the <u>blood puppet</u> memory to your follower, Ceruvax?

"What's this?" the envoy asked.

I smiled. "A gift," I said, willing the Adjudicator to proceed.

Analyzing player...

...

...

Analysis complete.

Ceruvax is an awakened Wolf, and you may bequeath him with a less powerful variant of the blood memory. Do you wish to proceed?

Once more, I conveyed my answer to the Game and waited.

Ceruvax has been awarded the ability: <u>enslave (lesser)</u>. As a weaker variant of blood puppet, this blood memory will allow your follower to permanently enslave a single non-player subject whose level is equal to or lower than his own.

Ceruvax's mouth dropped open in astonishment. "A greater blood memory! This is from your awakening in the Combat Circle?"

"It is. Now, it's your turn."

He looked at me curiously. "My turn?"

I nodded. "I need your strongest spell." My gaze drifted to the lichs. "Yours, too, Farren, Adriel."

✻   ✻   ✻

You have acquired the spell, <u>oblivion</u> (stolen) from Farren. Oblivion (stolen) is a tier 6 death spell that destroys any living thing it encounters within a radius of 100 yards. Few can resist its touch, and for those that don't, death is instantaneous. Targets struck by the spell will <u>disintegrate</u>.

You have acquired the spell, <u>noxious vapors</u> (stolen) from Adriel. Noxious vapors (stolen) is a tier 6 channeled spell that decays the flesh of all living entities to feel its touch. The health of every target subjected to the spell will decay at a rate of 10% per second for 5 seconds.

Note, each subsequent touch from the vapors will increase the duration of the spell's debuff.

You have acquired the spell, <u>seeping shadows</u> (stolen) from Ceruvax. Seeping shadows (stolen) is a tier 6 buff lasting 1 minute. It modifies all your attacks, causing them to deal pure shadow damage. In addition, foes struck by a seeping shadow blow will suffer a +5% <u>shadow affliction</u> for 10 seconds. Successive seeping shadow blows will increase the affliction.

Note, as a target's shadow affliction increases, their innate shadow resistance and damage reduction will decrease, causing them to suffer more damage from successive shadow attacks.

It was unfortunate that I could not use void thief to steal blood memories yet, because of all the trio's spells, those were the most powerful. Still, the three spells I got from Ceruvax, Farren, and Adriel were tier six instances, and were powerful enough in their own right.

Oblivion had been particularly tricky to 'steal,' but with both Adriel and Ceruvax watching over me during the theft, I'd survived the experience *without* disintegrating.

"Thank you," I murmured. "I have a feeling these are going to come in handy soon."

The trio smiled.

I glanced at Adriel. "Final thing: the two nagas I enslaved. Do you know where they are?"

She nodded. "They haven't moved since being freed. They are still at the entrance to Draven's Reach."

"Nagas?" Farren asked, an inquisitive cast to his face. "Those sound interesting."

"I guess you could call them that," I murmured before addressing Adriel again. "Take Ceruvax to the creatures. He should be able to dominate one." I paused. "On second thought, take Farren, Regus, and Algar with you as well. It will be good for them to see some of what we'll be facing before the main battle."

The lich inclined her head. "I'll do that."

I clasped hands with each of the Reachers in turn. "I guess this is goodbye—for the time being, anyway."

Turning around, I hurried off to find Safyre.

There was time for one final goodbye before my rendezvous with the brotherhood.

CHAPTER 572: FIRST PRONG

You have cast doppelganger, transforming your form into that of Havick.

You have entered sector 45,104.

My entry into Sango went smoother the second time around. Texalo was waiting for me, and as soon as I appeared, he rushed me off to the brotherhood's castle.

"What's that smell?" Ghost asked, keenly observing everything from the safety of the Cloak.

"The sea," I replied as we drew to a halt outside the castle's entrance. *"The castle is built atop a cliff overlooking the ocean."* My gaze drifted back to the structure's steel-clad gates. They were sealed, I noted, but the brotherhood's spymaster was waiting outside. When had he slipped through?

"Right on time as promised," Senzo said, stepping forward to greet me as Texalo left.

I nodded absently as I searched for some sign of the promised brotherhood army, but the insides of the castle remained opaque to me.

"You sense anything, Ghost?"

"No."

A second ticked by, then another.

My gaze slid back to the spymaster. He still hadn't made any effort to open the gates. "We're not going in?"

"Nope, they're coming out." He cocked his head to the side. "In fact, I think that's them I hear."

I couldn't hear anything, which could only mean the brotherhood's shields were also preventing any noise from escaping the castle's walls. Schooling myself to patience, I waited.

A minute later, the gates were flung back, revealing a long line of brotherhood players armed and armored for war. At the fore, was Kartara riding a... stygian nightmare.

She wasn't the only one so mounted, though.

Five hundred other brotherhood knights followed in her wake, led by Duskar, their commander.

"Tamed stygians," Ghost marveled, studying the nightmares in fascination through my eyes.

I nodded imperceptibly, wondering what the pyre wolf would have made of the inside of the brotherhood's castle.

"So, what do you think?" the spymaster asked, drawing my attention.

I glanced at him. "When Kartara said you'd be bringing a cavalry company, I didn't realize this is what she meant."

"What? Did you think the brotherhood would go into battle riding ordinary horses?"

That's exactly what I had thought. I was spared from saying it out aloud though as Kartara dismounted beside me. The rest of the column trotted onward, into what I now clearly recognized as their mustering field.

"Havick," she greeted, handing the reins of her mount to an attendant.

"Huntmistress," I said, nodding in acknowledgment. "Are your preparations complete?"

With a small smile, she gestured at the passing players. "As you can see, they are. Five hundred cavalry. One thousand dedicated spellcasters. And five hundred infantry. As promised."

"Hey," Senzo protested, "don't forget the fifty scouts."

"And them," Kartara said, her gaze staying fixed on me. "What about things on your end?"

Despite the casual nature of the question, I did not miss the intent look in the huntmistress' eyes. Notwithstanding everything—the people she was committing and the weapons she had provided—her doubts had not been entirely assuaged.

"My people will begin moving into place shortly," I replied smoothly. "They will be ready when yours are."

I mentioned nothing of our recent hiccups, of course.

The huntmistress stared at me for a moment longer, then gave a clipped nod. "Good. Then there is no use in us standing around here any longer than necessary. If you will hand over the netherstone?"

Reaching into my pocket, I drew out the black stone. "Here, you—"

You have passed a mental resistance check! An unknown entity has failed to pierce your disguise.

My head whipped around to the gates. The cavalry column had finished passing through. Following in its wake was a much smaller group of fifty players, each clad in stygian leathers. *Senzo's scouts.*

At their fore was a blonde woman who was staring at me with something akin to frustration.

The target is Fiona, a level 201 human diviner.

Kartara tracked my gaze. "Ah, you've discovered Fiona, I see. You'll want to meet her, I'm sure."

"That's not necessary," I said quickly.

Paying my refusal no heed, the huntmistress beckoned the diviner. "This way, Fiona."

The blonde woman stomped over. My initial impression had been wrong, I realized. Fiona was not frustrated, she was seething.

Affecting a nonchalance I did not feel, I held myself still as Fiona bore down on me. I was not at all certain it was wise to let the diviner—a player whose Perception was likely on par, if not higher, than my own—get close, but what was I going to do?

Attack? Run?

Neither of those options were satisfactory ones, especially not with Kartara standing close by and watching me with hawkish intensity.

This is a test.

The entire encounter had been staged, I realized, almost clumsily so. But I didn't think the huntmistress cared if I deduced her intent.

I had two choices.

Flee, and likely lose the brotherhood's promised aid. Or grit my teeth, let myself be subjected to Fiona's probes, and hope she didn't discover a damned thing.

I went with option two.

"Ghost, whatever happens, do nothing. And say nothing. We're under observation." Not waiting for the pyre wolf's response, I shut down our familiar link and tightened the shields around my mind.

The diviner drew closer.

Matching stares with her, I folded my arms as she marched up and placed her face inches from mine.

Fiona has failed to analyze you.

"What are you?" she demanded.

"Don't you mean who?" I asked lightly.

The diviner sniffed.

Fiona has failed to analyze you.

My brows drew down. "What are you doing?"

Stepping closer, the diviner sniffed again, longer and deeper, and with her nose almost brushing against my Cloak.

Fiona has failed to analyze you.

She stuck her tongue out.

I recoiled.

"No," I said, glaring at the huntmistress. "Tasting is where I draw the line. She is *not* going to lick me."

Senzo chuckled.

Ignoring the spymaster's amusement, the huntmistress held up her hand, and with a grimace, Fiona backed away.

"Anything?" Kartara asked.

"He is human," the diviner replied grudgingly. "That much I can say for certain."

The huntmistress nodded. "What else?"

"Nothing."

"Nothing?" Kartara echoed, her voice strangely devoid of emotion. It was almost as if she'd anticipated the diviner's response. But that would mean...

She suspects something. But what?

"His spirit signatures *appear* genuine," Fiona continued, "his mind is impenetrable, and his magic seems non-existent." She paused. "Well, there is one other thing, but I'm not sure if it's relevant."

"Tell me."

"He stinks of the void."

"That's hardly surprising," Senzo said abruptly. "Considering where he's been, *what* he is, and where we're going."

I said nothing, but inwardly I wondered if Senzo was right, or if it was Ghost whose scent the diviner had caught.

Nodding slowly, the huntmistress turned my way.

"Satisfied?" I asked, scowling at her.

"For now," she replied evenly and stuck out her right arm, palm up.

Wordlessly, I dropped the black stone into her waiting hand. Drawing out something from her own pocket, Kartara held it out to me. "What's that?" I growled, my outrage still simmering.

"A farspeaker bracelet," she replied, ignoring my tone entirely. "It'll ease our communication in the Nethersphere."

For a moment, I considered refusing, but only for a moment. This was not the time or place for anger. And besides, I had little cause to be affronted. It was only my own deception that had spurred Kartara to act the way she had. Exhaling slowly, I took the proffered item.

You have equipped a farspeaker bracelet from the Brotherhood link set F05. Equipped items: 30 / 30.

Spinning around, Kartara marched off. "Let's go."

✳ ✳ ✳

You have entered sector 30,199 of the Nethersphere.

It took hours to ferry the brotherhood army to the sector. Most of that time was spent erecting concealment shields and other wards whose sole purpose was keeping the stygians from noticing the hostile force camping out on their doorstep.

Thankfully, the nether creatures on this side of the rift did not appear especially vigilant. Perhaps it was the lack of a void tree to goad them into action that accounted for their disinterest.

Whatever the case, the brotherhood force was able to move into place without detection. I hung around for the entire operation. Not because I wanted to, but because my presence was crucial for the coordination of our two-pronged assault from opposite sides of the rift.

It was only through me that both forces could coordinate their attacks, and even then, the coordination would be limited to ensuring both assaults kicked off simultaneously.

After that, the brotherhood would be on their own.

As would the forerunners.

"*Everyone report in,*" Kartara ordered from the dune top where she sat observing her people.

"*Cavalry mounted and ready to charge,*" Duskar replied. The nightmares and their riders were on the east flank. They had a singular task: hunting down and killing the harbinger.

"*Mages in position,*" Cait reported. "*Barrier dome spell prepped and waiting for release.*"

The nether witch was in charge of the brotherhood's spellcasters, their biggest cohort by far. The mages had two responsibilities. The first was to serve as the army's main damage dealers. They would be the ones killing the stygians en-masse. Their second task, and the more important one—from my perspective anyway—was to erect a shield barrier around the rift. As long as there were enough mages alive to keep the spell going, the dome would prevent the lesser stygians and the nagas from crossing the rift—in either direction.

The one downside was that Cait's spell was only tier five.

It would *not* stop the harbinger from getting through. Which was what made the cavalry's own part so important.

"Scouts deployed," Senzo reported.

The brotherhood spymaster had the smallest role of all the huntmistress' direct subordinates. He and the scouts were tasked with watching the army's flanks to make sure no unanticipated threats crept up on them. I'd been warned time and again that if that happened, the brotherhood would withdraw—irrespective of whether the agreed upon four hours had passed or not.

"Infantry also ready," Kartara said.

The huntmistress had taken direct command of the foot soldiers. Their only goal was protecting the spellcasters, which sounded simple enough, but was likely the most dangerous task of all since the nether creatures would almost certainly target the mages first.

"Everyone is in place," Kartara said, glancing down at where I waited in a shallow dip.

I rose to my feet. *"Then, I guess I better get going."* Turning to the brotherhood player waiting beside me, I whispered, "Go ahead, I'm ready."

Closing his eyes, the mage began intoning the words of a portal spell under his breath.

I looked back over my shoulder at Kartara. She was still watching me. *"Good luck, Huntmistress."*

"And to you too, Havick," she replied softly.

The portal opened before me, and I strode through without a second look back.

CHAPTER 573: SECOND PRONG

You have entered the safe zone of sector 45,104.
You have entered the safe zone of sector 12,560.
Your facial disguise spell has dissipated.
You have entered sector 18,240 of the Forever Kingdom.
The nether toxicity at your current location is at tier 8.

It took three separate portal transits to get back 'home.'

The first portal—created by the anonymous mage—deposited me in the safe zone of the brotherhood's home sector. The second involved an aetherstone jump to the Roost. The third was a portal I opened myself and took me straight to the riverside gully that was serving as the forerunner's mustering ground.

All in all, the trip took a little over a minute to complete.

"He's back!" Terence yelled across the forerunners' farspeaker link the moment I appeared.

I swiveled about to face him. The young arcane knight had obviously been tasked with keeping watch for my arrival. "Where are they?" I asked tersely.

"In the command post," he replied solemnly. "Waiting for you."

"And where's that?"

"Just head north along the gully. It's not far. You can't miss it."

"Thanks," I said, turning my steps in the direction he indicated. As I did, I prodded at my familiar, waking her from her slumber, *"We're here, Ghost. Start manifesting."*

"About time," the pyre wolf replied, shaking herself alert.

The gully was the same one I had designated as our forward base a week ago. It was about half a mile away from the river and distant enough from the nest that the void tree and the overlords were blissfully unaware of our presence.

But while the gully was the same one I'd used previously, it did not look the same. It had undergone a startling transformation in the interim. Not only had Lucius and his fellow nagians deepened the indentation in the earth, they had interconnected it with many of the adjacent ravines and gullies.

Now, the 'gully' was more in the nature of a trench—a *miles-long* C-shaped trench that bordered the river the same way the river did the nest.

And lining its length was the company.

All three thousand of them—bane wolves, wolfmen, dire wolves, arctic wolves, nagians, and forsworn—each and every one of whom turned to stare or salute as I strode past.

I nodded in acknowledgment of their greetings but didn't stop. Terence had said it wasn't a long walk to the command post. Still, I couldn't afford to dally overlong.

I didn't rush either, though, not wanting to give off the wrong impression and induce unnecessary panic. And besides, this was the perfect opportunity for me to get a sense of everyone's readiness. My head turning left and right, I scrutinized those I passed.

Nagians, wolves, people, one and all, they were armed to the teeth—in the wolves' case, literally so. Each wolf wore a specially designed muzzle fitted with stygian incisors. Some even wore studded harnesses—also formed from stygian material. Without the stygian gear, the wolves wouldn't be able to harm the nether creatures, of course, and great care had gone into their design.

All the wolves also had a thin leather strap fastened around their necks. Each held a single nether protection crystal, I knew. The wolves—and everyone else in the army, for that matter—had been allocated two crystals, but unlike the ones I'd used in the past, each of these lasted four hours. Everyone would have activated their first crystal before leaving the cave. And would do the same with the second prior to the battle commencing.

"How does it feel?" I asked Oursk as I spotted him among a small group of dire wolves to my right.

"Like a second mouth," he replied, knowing what I meant.

Shadetooth, beside him, grimaced, his mouth working uncomfortably. *"I don't like it."*

"You don't have to like it," the older wolf replied primly. *"You just have to use it to kill the enemy."*

Leaving sire and offspring to what sounded like a long-running argument, I marched on.

Ghost has taken the form of a level 267 stygian pyre wolf.

My familiar's sudden appearance attracted the attention of a pair of wolfmen on the left.

"There she is," one said, nudging the other.

"Told you she was big," the second replied.

While the pair inspected Ghost, I examined them in turn. The Reach Pack had brought all their possessions with them after leaving the dungeon, however their gear had been somewhat... lacking.

Now, though, the wolfmen bristled with stygian weaponry and armor that despite their lanky frames still managed to cover their furry torsos and limbs.

"Be careful," I warned, "she bites."

"I do not!" Ghost retorted indignantly, projecting her words directly into the wolfmen's minds and leaving them chuckling in our wake.

Next up was a squad of Bane Wolves. By contrast, their own mood was somber. But then again, the Bane Wolves were all professional soldiers, and this was the eve of a battle, and not just any battle but one against a stygian force the likes of which the former New Haveners had never seen.

They knew enough to be afraid.

The squad in question was a dwarven one, and currently striding down their ranks, conducting what appeared to be a spot-inspection, was Captain

Megtir, one of the warband's commanders. It was he who had first drawn my attention.

Catching sight of me, the dwarf snapped off a salute. "Hail, Milord."

"Megtir," I replied, slowing but not stopping.

Running my eyes along the squad, I inspected the dwarves' gleaming plate armor and polished weapons. Of all our forces, the Bane Wolves had required the least re-outfitting. "How are the men, Captain?"

"Ready and eager to wade into the enemy!" Megtir replied.

I doubted that but appreciated the sentiment, nonetheless.

"You remember our crazy run through the possessed prison complex, Megtir?" I asked, referring to the mass prison escape I'd orchestrated in New Haven after killing Castor.

The dwarf captain smiled. "It is not something I'm ever likely to forget, milord." His gaze drifted to the pyre wolf. "Ghost led us well."

I nodded. "She did. But this—" I pointed in the direction of the nest across the river—"what we do here today, will not be anything like that prison run, I promise. Today's fight has been carefully orchestrated and will be just as carefully executed. The deck has been stacked in our favor, Megtir. Heavily so."

The dwarf chuckled. "You never did fight fair, milord. I remember that much, and there's no reason to start now!" He glanced across the river. "Give them hell, Lord Wolf."

I bared my teeth. "I will." My gaze flickered to the silently watching squad. The dwarves were just as stone-faced as before, but I fancied the spark in their eyes burned brighter now, and that the lines drawn into their faces had faded a touch.

"Keep safe," I said in farewell before moving on.

"What was that about?" Ghost asked curiously.

"A timely reminder, I hope," I replied.

"Of what?"

"That this is not the first time we've faced such odds together and triumphed," I murmured.

Safyre, no doubt, had addressed the army before it had embarked from the cave, but the former New Haveners didn't know her, not like most everyone else did. Algar would've added his own encouragement too. Still, it was not Algar who had freed New Haven from centuries of possessed rule, nor was it Algar who had slain the archlich, or banished the stygians from the Reach. Like it or not, my words carried weight, and I could not be shy of using them.

A quicksilver shape, fast approaching, as it darted around the obstacles in its way, drew my attention.

"Elise!" Ghost called before I could.

The werefox rushed to a stop. *"Michael! Ghost! There you are."*

"Where are you off to in such a hurry?" I asked.

"The foothills," she replied. *"I've orders to scout it one final time."* Her gaze slid to Ghost, a question in her eyes.

"Ghost can go with you if she wants." I would have to release the pyre wolf to Elise's care soon, anyway. She would not be fighting alongside me during the battle.

"*Ghost?*" Elise asked, looking at my familiar.

"*Of course, I'll come,*" she replied.

Not delaying further, Elise raced off with Ghost hard on her heels. Together, the pair were twice as menacing, and more than one soldier started in surprise as they raced by.

Shaking my head at the pair's antics, I continued onward.

However, it was only a few seconds later, as I turned around a sharp corner in the gully, that I drew to a halt.

Before me, the trench-gully spilled out into a deep basin. At some point in the past, the basin must have brimmed with water. Now, though, the deep cavity was bone-dry.

But not empty.

The basin hummed with activity, leaving me in no doubt that I'd found the command post.

It did not take me long to spot Safyre either. She was at the center of it all, with Ceruvax, Farren, Regus, Algar, Keros, Lucius, Zekiel, Duggar, and Sedgwick alongside her. But it was not the ten forerunners that stole my attention. It was the twenty other inhabitants— large and unmissable— that did.

Nagas.

One enslaved naga I had expected. But where had the other nineteen come from? My gaze darting to and fro, I inspected the stygian elites closely.

And only then noticed an oddity.

Eighteen of the nagas were bruised, battered, and missing scales. Some were even lacking entire chunks of flesh. They were the selfsame nagas Elise, Ghost, and I had killed a few days ago, I realized.

And they're still dead. Or rather, it's undead they've become.

My gaze darted to Farren. He would have been the one to raise them. Unlike Adriel, whose death magic abilities were largely geared toward golem crafting, Farren's own specialization was undead summoning.

But speaking of Adriel, where was she?

One of the nagas stared right back at me, and something about it—the cant of its head, or perhaps, the look in its eyes—struck me as familiar.

Realization dawned.

The naga *was* Adriel.

The lich had made herself a new flesh golem.

∗　∗　∗

"This is a surprise," I said a moment later, after entering the command post.

"Do you mean the basin or the nagas?" Safyre asked, looking at me through eyes tinted a faint shade of purple.

The purple halo was a side-effect of the clearsight potion that she—and the other leaders of our somewhat-eclectic force—had already ingested. The rest of the army would follow suit once the battle commenced.

"Both." I looked up at the naga towering over me. "You did not tell me about this," I accused.

"It was a surprise," Adriel replied with what looked suspiciously like a naga-smirk.

I snorted. "It's a flesh golem, I take it?"

"Yes."

"When did you create it? I would have hardly thought you had the time to spare."

"I've been working on it since day one," she admitted. *"Ever since we killed the first overlord."*

I nodded, recalling the naga corpse she'd insisted we retrieve intact. "Well, I'm glad you did." Turning to Farren, I looked meaningfully at the eighteen nagas lined up behind him. "They're all yours?"

"Of course. Adriel doesn't have the skill for it," he said, throwing his sister a mischievous grin—which she ignored.

I didn't have to ask Ceruvax about the last naga. I could already tell it was his. I swung back to Safyre. "How do things stand?"

"We're ready," she replied simply.

"What about the brotherhood?" Ceruvax asked.

"In place and waiting for our signal."

I glanced at Lucius.

He stepped forward. "The water mages are ready to begin," he confirmed. "All they need is the order to go."

I inhaled deeply. Then this was it. All the long days, all the running back and forth, all the preparations, negotiations and worrying, they had culminated in this moment—with us ready to assault the rift from two sides.

It was now or never.

"Then the time has come to claim the sector," I pronounced.

Relieved smiles broke out amongst those gathered around me, even though they had to know we had long passed the point of no return.

Meeting Safyre's eyes, I nodded gravely.

It was all the signal she needed.

"Duggar, Algar, Regus, Zekiel, send word to your people," the aetherist ordered. "They are to ingest their clearsight potions and activate their second crystals." She glanced at Keros. "Ker, tell the others."

The four commanders hurried off to their respective commands, intent on doing her bidding. Keros—who didn't actually have a command— was the only one who stayed behind. Closing his eyes, he relayed Safyre's order to the other forsworn through the farspeaker network.

Of all our forces, it was only ten forsworn mages who were not gathered in the trench-gully—well, them, and Elise and her people who had ventured into the foothills.

The forsworn mages were still in the cave with the shield generator. The battle made powering the artifact even more important, not less. Still, there were several scenarios where the ten would be required to take a more active role in the battle—which was why Safyre had given the order she had.

"Ceruvax, Farren, Adriel, begin buffing Michael," Safyre went on. "Lucius..."

I stopped listening. Safyre had matters well in hand. And now it was time to finalize my own preparations. Turning my attention inward, I began shifting.

You have taken the form of a level 267 elder wolf, gaining primal resistance (+30% against all damage types) and health regeneration (2% per second). Your nether resistance has reached 100%. You are now immune to all hostile nether spells and effects.

Your current <u>nether regeneration</u> rate is: 20%.

You have cast engine of war, increasing your Strength, Constitution, and Dexterity by +20 ranks for 30 minutes.

You have trigger-cast quick mend.

You have cast doppelganger, transforming your form into that of a level 301 stygian harbinger, and concealing all your Marks.

I not only shapeshifted, I disguised my form thereafter, too.

It was not to mask my elder form from my allies that I used doppelganger. My shapeshifting ability was no secret amongst the forerunners.

No, the real reason I transformed myself into a harbinger—using a basilisk-dog chimera from the mature tree's nest as a subject—was to confuse the stygians. How long they would stay confused was anyone's guess, but initially at least, my form should give me the element of surprise.

Ideally, I would have preferred to assume a more anonymous guise—like that of a random hydra—and if I was fighting alone, I would have. But doing that in the midst of a raging battle risked my allies mistaking me for the enemy, or worse yet, hesitating to strike for fear of hitting me, and that I could not have.

Adriel has cast undead's champion (+100% damage inflicted) and warrior's boon on you (+20 to all physical attributes). Duration: 20 minutes.

Safyre has cast aether grace (+50% chance physical evasion) and aether protection on you (+50% reduced nether damage). Duration: 20 minutes.

Farren has cast lich's aid (+25% to the effectiveness of all your skills and abilities) and reaper's shield on you (+75% death magic resistance). Duration: 1 hour.

Ceruvax has cast healing wolf (doubling your health regeneration rate) and ancient's protection on you (+20% to all resistances). Duration: 20 minutes.

"All done," Ceruvax said, lowering his staff.

Nodding, Safyre glanced at Algar. He was the last of the four commanders to return. "I've received confirmation from my captains," the high captain reported. "The Bane Wolves stand ready."

"That's the final piece in place then." Safyre spread her arms to incorporate all four commanders in the gesture. "Go. Take charge of your people. It begins."

Saluting, Regus, Duggar, Zekiel, and Algar hurried off once more.

They would not return to the basin again, not until the battle was concluded. It was only the initial meetings that Safyre insisted be done face-to-face. During the battle itself, the four would communicate with Safyre through the forerunners' farspeaker network.

The four couldn't use the bracelets themselves, of course, for which reason, they each had a player assigned to them. Nyra was with the wolves, Anriq kept the wolfmen company, Terence was with the Bane Wolves, and Shael was accompanying the nagians under Zekiel's command.

That left only Teresa and Ghost to consider.

The blade priestess was already with the water mages, and would act as Lucius' second, while the pyre wolf was with Elise's small band, which had its own mission.

Safyre turned to Lucius. "Do it."

Bowing from the waist, the nagian elite wove mana and vanished. I knew where he was headed—to the water mages positioned *beneath* the river. Soon, the valley would be flooded.

And that meant it was time I, too, took my position.

Turning about, I began scaling the basin's eastern side. The slope was steep, but my paws found easy purchase and I flowed up the sides of the basin.

Ceruvax's gaze tracked me, his stare hard and appraising. *"You make a good wolf, boy,"* he whispered, his mindvoice tightly controlled and likely imperceptible to anyone else. *"So, why do you wish to give it up?"*

"I wish no such thing," I growled. The old envoy was almost certainly referring to my determination to forge the forerunners into a single House. Someone had obviously let something slip while I was away this morning.

"That's not what I heard," he said, confirming my suspicion.

"I will not renege on my oath to Wolf. Far from it. What I do will only make Wolf stronger."

"How?" he demanded harshly.

"This is not the time for this conversation. Like I told you, we'll talk—but after the battle."

"Tell me," he insisted.

I gnashed my teeth in frustration. But despite my annoyance I did not order Ceruvax to silence like I knew I could. It would not do to ill-treat him so.

"Fine," I snarled. *"If you want the truth, I think Wolf has walked its own path too long. We cannot do so anymore. To overcome the new Powers, we must unite under one roof. We must become one House."*

"So, you will bind Wolf to the other bloodlines?" he snarled. *"To Death? To Pestilence? Will you subject us to their rule too? Make servants of once proud wolves?"*

"No, old man," I snapped, my patience at an end. *"I will bind them to Wolf. Wolf will be subservient to no one!"*

Silence.

"Are you satisfied now?"

"I am," he replied, his voice serene and unruffled once more.

My eyes narrowed. *"Was all that a test?"*

"It was." He hesitated, then added softly, *"It is the bloodline I serve first and foremost."*

It was an apology of sorts—but only of sorts.

I bit off another growl. *"Do not forget, I do too."* Cresting the basin, I leaped onto the flat plain beyond. The river was half a mile to the east, and beyond that the nest awaited. *"Now can we leave off the tests, and just win the goddamn battle—please?"*

"As you wish, Wolf Lord."

✳   ✳   ✳

A few minutes later, Ceruvax, Adriel, Keros, and Farren—minus their new pets—followed me out of the command post. The battle was about to begin and the need for secrecy had passed. Safyre, though, did not leave the basin.

Of all the forerunner leaders, the aetherist—supported by Sedgwick, who was acting as her second—was the only one who would remain at the command post. It fell to her to monitor and direct the battle from afar using her scrying spells and the farspeaker network. It was arguably not the best use of Safyre's talents. Especially considering that she was the only other ascendant player in our ranks.

But someone had to serve as our reserve. And if the worst befell, someone had to survive to pick up the pieces. And given that Safyre *was* the only other Power in the forerunners, that person could only be her—something Safyre herself hadn't failed to recognize.

So, in the end—with more grace than I could've managed under the circumstances—Safyre had acceded to her role.

"Do you see anything yet?" she asked, only the faintest hint of strain peeking through her mindvoice.

I shook my head. *"Not yet,"* I replied, feeling the same tension she did.

Our entire battle plan hinged on Lucius and the water mages being able to accomplish what they promised, and while we had more than a few contingencies lined up, they all involved considerably higher causality rates.

Turning my head from left to right, I surveyed the nest anew. The stygians' numbers and deployment had changed little since my last visit. The void tree was in the center. Behind it was the black rift, and on either side of it were the two grounded overlords. There were no nagas—a welcome relief—nor had the void tree replenished the lesser stygians' numbers.

Courtesy of Ghost, Elise, and my own efforts, there were now a little under eight thousand lesser stygians in the valley, leaving our own forces outnumbered nearly three to one. But those were odds I'd take any day, especially considering that we had more than a few surprises in store for the void.

I scanned the valley anew, searching for the first such surprise. *C'mon, Lucius, where are—*

My eyes narrowed. Was that a wisp of steam I saw in the distance?

"I see something," Ceruvax reported on the farspeaker link.

"I do too," I added.

"Well, I don't," Keros muttered.

"That's because you lack wolf eyes," Sedgwick said primly. He, too, was on the communication network.

"Shut it, dwarf," the windknight growled, but the words lacked any real animosity. Keros' gaze was also fixed on the distant nest, and he was bouncing lightly on his feet.

He's looking forward to this, I thought.

"Michael?" Safyre asked, ignoring the pair's commentary.

"Something is definitely happening," I told her. I could pick out at least six different trails of steam rising from the valley now, and more were appearing every second. The stygians had begun to stir as well. They, too, realized something was amiss.

"But will it be quick enough?" Safyre asked worriedly.

"I think—"

I broke off as a geyser of water and superheated steam exploded out of the valley.

A second followed in its wake. Then a third. And a fourth.

"By damn," Keros whispered aloud. "I don't believe it, those creepy bastards actually did it."

My lips curled back in a doggy grin. Lucius and the water mages were certainly delivering on their promises.

The nagians had discovered a large network of tunnels and caves beneath the valley and had hit upon the idea of creating an underground lake—which they had done easily enough by siphoning water from the river itself. The next step had been sealing the lake and heating the water—this had been the most tedious and time-consuming part. The mages had been certain that once the underground lake had been heated sufficiently, its waters would explode upward at a prodigious rate, flooding the valley in no time.

The rest of us had been more skeptical.

Events were bearing out the water mages, though.

Over a dozen spouts had appeared all over the valley, each sending an incalculable amount of water gushing into the valley.

And more geysers were forming by the second.

I didn't have to report what was going on to Safyre, of course. She could see for herself what was happening. Many of the stygians were already ankle deep in water. And the nagians were not yet done.

"Lucius reports stage one complete," Teresa relayed tersely. *"Moving on to stage two."*

No one said anything. Instead, we watched with bated breath.

The ground rumbled.

And a second later, the previously quiescent river grew choppy. I knew what was happening, we all did. In the far distance, I spotted a mound of soil sink.

It was only the beginning.

As if that mound was the first domino, a ten yard stretch of ground to the south of it collapsed. Then the next bit did. And the next. And the next, until all along the river's horse-shoed shaped perimeter, the eastern bank... vanished.

Sending frothing water surging into the valley.

"Stage two complete," Teresa reported unnecessarily, and with more than a little glee in her voice. *"Valley successfully flooded."*

"Give Lucius our thanks," Safyre replied gravely. *"Sending brotherhood message now."*

On the tail end of Safyre's words, three roiling balls of lightning flew out of the command post, and arcing across the sky, sailed through the black rift.

It was the promised signal. Seeing it, the brotherhood would know to launch their own assault. It was my cue too. Drawing psi, I began my final preparations.

You have cast wind daemon.

"Begin stage three," Safyre instructed.

It was the command everyone had been eagerly awaiting and was the order to commence the assault-proper.

✳   ✳   ✳

Almost before Safyre finished speaking, portals started opening along the newborn lake's northern, western, and eastern shores as the nagians under Lucius and Zekiel's joint-command began ferrying our people to the water's edge. From there, the individual companies would unleash havoc on the lesser stygians.

But it was not to join in the main battle that Ceruvax, Adriel, Farren, Keros, and I had gathered on the basin's rim.

My gaze drifted to the two distant overlords. Neither had moved yet, but it was only a matter of time before they did.

"Opening portals now," Ceruvax and Keros reported in unison. The pair had the aetherstones I'd etched yesterday and would be leading the strike force against the overlords. Although it would have a very different composition from the one I'd envisioned yesterday.

Instead of a mixed force of nagians and forsworn, strike team one would consist of Ceruvax and Farren, and team two of Keros and Adriel. They alone would be taking the battle to the overlords.

Reaching into his pocket, Farren removed a pair of remote triggers—*my* triggers—and placed them under my clawed feet. I glanced from the triggers to the patiently waiting four.

"Go ahead," Adriel said quietly. *"We're ready."*

Inhaling deeply, I pressed down on both triggers.

You have activated 30 tier 4 traps.
You have activated 30 tier 4 traps.
60 tier 4 traps are no longer dormant.

"Bombs primed and ready," I reported.
"Do it," Safyre instructed.
"Yes, ma'am," I replied and pressed down on the triggers again.

A trap has been triggered!
A trap has been triggered!

Light flashed, and in the distance, the overlords shook. I wasn't done though. Pressing down gently again, I triggered the remaining traps one after the other, and in quick succession.

A trap has been triggered!
A trap has been triggered!
...

...

You have injured a level 325 stygian overlord!
You have injured a level 321 stygian overlord!

My mouth dropped open in a doggy laugh.
"It worked?" Ceruvax asked, correctly interpreting my expression.
"It did," I replied. *"By goddamn it actually did!"*
"Well, hells," Keros said, *"now, isn't that something."*
"Enough dawdling people," Safyre ordered. *"Go!"*
The four went.
The strike teams were numerically inferior to the originals, but they more than made up for that lack in raw power. Ceruvax, Farren, and Adriel's blood memories alone would carry the day, I expected.
Assuming, of course, that the third Power we faced didn't interfere.
Which was where I came in.
"I'm going in, too," I reported to Safyre.
"Stay alive, Wolf," she whispered.
"I'll do my best," I replied, and shadow jumped into the distance.

Chapter 575: A Battle Between Titans

You have teleported onto a level 340 young void tree.
The nether toxicity at your current location is tier 30, boosting your health, psi, stamina, and mana regeneration rates to 31% per minute.

I emerged from the aether atop my target—nestled amongst its very branches in fact—and in a cloud of nether that was the thickest I had yet experienced. With my clawed basilisk feet clinging to my slim perch of ash-white and my long snaking tail sweeping aside the nearby clumps of ebon-black thorns, I bent my canine head downward to glare at my foe.

For a split second, the tree did not react to my presence.

Which was not surprising, considering how much I resembled one of the grotesque harbingers. Then, too, I sensed its attention was wholly on what was going on in the valley—on the arrows and spells already raining down on the lesser stygians, on the water sloshing at its trunk, and on the four relatively small figures atop the two overlords.

I wove mana.

That drew an immediate reaction.

A young void tree has failed to pierce your disguise.

The branch beneath me quivered. The void tree suspected. While the stygian Power was not able to penetrate my guise, it nonetheless suspected I was no creature of the void. An attack was incoming, I was certain.

Still, I kept casting.

Attempted mental intrusion detected. A young void tree has failed to enthrall you!

Grimly, I kept weaving my spell.

If the void tree hadn't known what it was dealing with before, it did now. How would it choose to respond?

All the nearby branches rustled.

Realizing what form the assault was going to take, I tucked my head into my shoulders and wrapped my tail tightly around my body. But I didn't stop casting.

A moment later, a shower of ebony slivers homed in on my position. There was no dodging them. The range was too short. Besides, there was my spell to think about.

A stygian thorn has failed to injure you. The attack has been blocked by your impregnable mind, consuming 0.1% psi in the process.
A stygian thorn has failed to injure you.
You have evaded a stygian thorn.
You have evaded a stygian thorn.

...

...

Less than half the stygian thorns struck me. The rest—courtesy of Safyre's buff—simply passed through my wavering physical form. Still, the half of the black shower that *did* land was enough to wreak significant damage to my mental defenses.

...

...

Your psi is now at 64%.

I weathered the storm though and, more importantly, held onto my concentration. The last weave of my spell fell into place, and without hesitation, I manifested it.

You have cast oblivion.
Warning: your mana reserves are running low. Remaining mana: 25%.

The air around me flashed black, enclosing me in a small bubble of darkness so thick it was almost palpable. Mutely, I waited.
The darkness exploded outward, rolling over the stygian Power first—

A young void tree has passed a magical resistance check!

—and then, its unseen rings of escorts.

A level 4 stygian spore has died.
A level 6 stygian spore has died.
...
...

The darkness didn't stop there, though. It kept going, expanding into a sphere a hundred yards in radius that overran the two overlords and every creature in between.

Two stygian overlords have passed a magical resistance check.
Ceruvax, Faren, Adriel, and Keros have passed a magical resistance check.

But while the overlords and my allies—who had prepared earlier for the spell—did not disintegrate, many of the lesser stygians caught out by the spell did not fare so well.

A stygian serpent has died.
A stygian hydra has died.
...
...

The death notifications went on and on, but I stopped paying attention. I had accomplished what I'd set out to do, and even though it had cost me nearly all my mana, every spore within range—and perhaps even in the entire sector—was dead.
And no few lesser stygians, I thought with satisfaction, staring at the corpses below, many already half-covered by the heaving water.

My gaze flickered back to the void tree. I could tell from oppressive heaviness gathering around the shields enclosing my mind that I had its attention now.

Wholly and completely.

And while capturing the Power's regard had certainly been my intention all along, I couldn't help the ripple of unease that passed over me.

The damnable thing was angry.

Which meant things were about to get interesting—and not in a good way.

Drawing more mana, I readied myself.

✶　✶　✶

You have cast seeping shadows (modifying your attacks to deal shadow damage and increase your foe's shadow affliction by +5%). Duration: 1 minute.

I'd barely enacted my next spell—the one I'd stolen from Ceruvax—when the void tree struck anew.

A level 340 young void tree has cast <u>psychic scream</u>.

A wave of force, so powerful it left a shimmering haze in its wake, struck me. The attack bore all the hallmarks of a physical assault yet was not that. It wasn't magical either. No, what I felt was simply the void tree's seething fury, malice, and wrath, all mixed up in one and given impetus by the strength of its will.

You have partially resisted a psychic scream.
Psychic scream is a tier 7 psi ability that deals psi damage to all hostiles in close proximity to the caster.

My mental shields did nothing to stop the spell. The assault was not one against my mind, but my body. My void armor did nothing to combat it either.

Defenseless and naked against the vicious forces tearing at me, my bones shattered, my limbs crumpled, my eardrums exploded, and my eyes leaked blood.

A young void tree has injured you, inflicting psi damage. You are <u>bleeding</u>, <u>deafened</u>, <u>blinded</u>, and <u>crippled</u>.

If I had not resisted the spell somewhat, I was not sure I would have survived at all. As it was, stripped of all strength, my clawed feet lost their hold on my perch, and I plummeted downward.

But as devastating as the void tree's attack had been, it was hardly enough to defeat me—or even seriously injure me—and halfway through my fall, my defenses kicked in.

First quick mend triggered, restoring 50% of your health!

You are no longer <u>bleeding</u>, <u>deafened</u>, <u>blinded</u>, or <u>crippled</u>. Health remaining: 98%.

Mid-air, I twisted, and instead of crashing headlong into the choppy water below, I landed on my feet.

I couldn't say if my startling recovery surprised my foe, but I didn't wait to see how it would react. Drawing stamina, I sent energy coursing through my body.

You have cast ponderous step. You are now <u>heavy</u> (causing the ground to shake with each step) Duration: 1 minute.

I took a single step forward, my clawed foot plunging through the water to pound against the ground beneath.

Tremors rippled outward and waves danced anew. They extended all the way to my foe, causing its branches to shiver.

A young void tree has passed a physical resistance check. You have failed to stagger or knockdown your target.

I took another step, and the ground quaked anew.

You have staggered a young void tree, disrupting its concentration for 1 second.

Excellent. Surging forward daemon-fast through the knee-high water, and with my every step giving rise to new tremors, I launched myself at the void tree.

I covered the distance in less than a handful of seconds and without falling prey to any further spells. Whether that was due to ponderous step, I couldn't say for certain. But it didn't matter—I was within melee range of my foe again.

Lashing out with my right paw, I raked my claws down its ash-white trunk.

You have struck a young void tree with <u>stunning paw</u>. Your target has passed a physical resistance check. You have failed to stun a young void tree.

You have grazed your target (shadow damage partially resisted). Your target has failed a magical resistance check. You have afflicted your foe with shadow. Current affliction: 5%.

My left paw followed suit.

You have struck a young void tree with <u>stunning paw</u> (partially resisted), stunning it for 1 second.

You have grazed your target (shadow damage partially resisted), increasing its shadow affliction to 10%.

Next, my muzzle snapping forward, I bit into the tree's bark with razor sharp teeth that were brimming with as much shadow as my claws were.

You have attacked a young void tree with <u>lacerating bite</u> but have failed to deal bleeding damage.

You have struck your target a glancing blow (shadow damage partially resisted), increasing its shadow affliction to 15%.

My limbs replete with daemon-energy, I repeated the devastating combo twice more as I circled around the tree's base.
Step. Right paw. Left paw. Bite.
Step. Right paw. Left paw. Bite.
Most enemies would have been bleeding and dying by this point, but as it was, my attacks barely left a dent in the void tree's health.

A level 340 young void tree is 45% <u>shadow afflicted</u>. Its health is at 99%, its mana is at 0%, its stamina is at 100%, and its psi is at 50%.

I already knew why the Power's psi pool was so low. It was the psychic scream that was responsible. Casting the spell had been costly. But it was another facet of my foe's status that drew my attention—namely, its health. Only a meager one percent was missing.
It doesn't matter, I thought grimly. The damage I inflicted on the void tree would only increase the longer the skirmish dragged on. I only had to survive long enough to bring the fight to a conclusion.

An etheric lash has failed to injure you. 3% psi consumed.

I lifted my head. My foe was reverting to more familiar tactics, and already I spied, three more branches quivering.
Another black thorn shower was about to launch.
Forgoing further maw attacks in favor of keeping a wary eye on the branches in question, I kept up my relentless assault with my forelimbs.
Step. Right paw. Left paw.
Step. Right paw. Left paw.
…

…

The void tree's branches whipped back, then forward, firing off a long line of black thorns straight at me.
I didn't wait to meet them.
Digging my clawed feet into the stygian Power, I shot straight up its trunk and out of the way of the deadly barrage.

You have evaded a stygian thorn.
You have evaded a stygian thorn.
…

…

I felt like laughing as the black slivers vanished without a trace into the water below, but the battle had only just begun, and there was no telling what other surprises my foe had in store for me. Dropping back to the ground, I resumed my assault on its trunk.

* * *

Nearly a minute later, I was still dancing around the void tree while I struck at it with my paws. Thus far, I'd managed to avoid every volley of thorns it had sent my way—except for the first one, of course—and I could sense my foe's mounting frustration.

Evading the tree's etheric lashes was impossible, though, and I'd felt their bite repeatedly. But despite this, my psi reserves were growing—not depleting.

And, ludicrously, this was all thanks to the nether itself.

Your health is at 100%, your psi at 68%, your stamina is at 97%, and your mana is at 55%.

A nether regeneration rate of thirty-one percent per minute was nothing to sniff at and meant I gained one percent of my lost psi, stamina, mana, and health back every two seconds!

The mist was assisting the void tree as well, of course.

But either my attacks against the stygian Power were more effective than its own were against me, or its regeneration rates were not as good as mine, because over the course of the minute, the void tree's health continued to slip downward.

A level 340 young void tree is 100% <u>shadow afflicted</u> and its health is at 95%.

I had the void tree beat, and the stygian Power knew it, too.

Its eventual defeat was only a matter of time, now.

The next few minutes passed in a haze of concentration as I traded blows with the void tree. I struck at it with shadow, and every now and again, managed to land a physical disable—usually as a result of stunning paw or ponderous step.

It, in turn, threw a relentless barrage of psi spells at me, whether in the form of etheric lashes, stygian thorns, psychic screams, telekinetic blasts, or a whole host of other previously unseen abilities.

I weathered them all.

Not without help, though.

At the two-minute mark, a lance of concentrated purple lashed out from the void tree's trunk, and catching me off-guard, struck me dead center.

A level 340 young void tree has cast psi drain.
You have failed a mental resistance check. A young void tree has drained 60% of your mental energy. Psi remaining: 11%.

The attack, not unsurprisingly, left me shocked and reeling, but only momentarily. I was not entirely unprepared for such an eventuality. In fact, it was one we had planned for.

Sending my mind delving into the psi bracelet on my right wrist—a legendary artifact that I not previously had cause to use in battle—I released its enchantment.

You have activated the enchantment, _psi-feed_. Psi-feed is a tier 5 ability which allows you to refill your psi pool using either stamina or mana.
Stamina conversion activated.
Converting stamina into psi at a rate of 1% per second.

Much to my satisfaction—and my foe's displeasure—my psi was quickly restored to healthy levels once more.

Not long after that—in a fit of pique, perhaps—the stygian Power attempted to chain-cast psychic scream, but it managed only two successive castings.

Those two were devastating enough on their own, though.

A young void tree has cast psychic scream.
You have partially resisted a psychic scream. A psychic scream has injured you.
Second quick mend triggered, restoring 50% of your health. Health remaining: 95%.

A level 340 young void tree has cast psychic scream.
You have failed to resist a psychic scream. A psychic scream has critically injured you.
Warning! Your health is dangerously low at 15%.

A young void tree has 10% psi remaining.

I limped back from the tree, barely ambulatory. *"Code Yellow,"* I croaked into the farspeaker bracelet.

Wherever she was, my apprentice must have been keeping a close eye on me, because no sooner had I spoken the words than new life poured into me.

Nyra has cast revitalizing blood.
You have been healed of all injuries. Your health is at 100%.

"Thanks," I breathed, bouncing back into the fight. I didn't repeat my earlier tactics, though. The void tree had overextended itself, and in doing so, had erred.

And left me with a weakness to exploit.

Fashioning a spear of my will, I struck my foe at the very heart of its power: its mind.

You have cast slaysight (shatter).
Your mental assault has been blocked by a young void tree's mind shield, consuming 0.5% of its psi in the process. It has 9.5% psi remaining.

I almost howled in delight.

I'd guessed right. The stygian Power's mental defenses were just like my own. They, too, were powered by the creatures' internal reserve of psi—a reserve it had just flagrantly spent.

My eyes gleaming in predatory anticipation, I flung more psi at my foe.

You have failed to shatter a young void tree's mind shield. It has 9% psi remaining.

The void tree shuddered. It knew what I was doing, and it was afraid.
As well as it should be.
Drawing more psi, I struck it again and again and again...

A young void tree has 8.5% psi remaining.
A young void tree has 8% psi remaining.
...

...
A young void tree has 6.5% psi remaining.

My assault was unrelenting. I was so close. Once the Power's psi dropped to zero, its mind shield would fall, leaving it open to all sorts of mental manipulation. The void tree had to know this as well as I did, so...

Why was it not retaliating? *It must be conserving its energy for something,* I thought. *But what?*

A moment later, I had my answer.

A young void tree has cast <u>nether sacrifice</u>. Psi remaining 1.5%. Nether sacrifice is a tier 7 single-cast spell that destroys the minds of every stygian creature below tier 4 in a 200 yard radius, replenishing the caster's store of psi in the process.

Well damn, I muttered.
Hard on the heels of the first message, another Game alert arrived.

A young void tree has 100% psi remaining.

My foe's devastating spell crushed my hopes of a quick resolution, and with no other option, I padded forward through the water to pummel it anew with my shadow-touched paws. One way or the other I would see the thing destroyed.

No matter how long it took.

✳ ✳ ✳

My strange dance with the stygian Power resumed shortly thereafter. Once again it did its best to strike at me with psi while I gnawed and clawed at it with shadow. Notably, though, my foe avoided chain casting psychic scream again, and I, in turn, made sure to keep a wary eye out for its psi drain spell.

Throughout, I did my best to track the battle around me, although I only managed to do so in fits and starts.

As a result of my proximity to the void tree, the others had deliberately cut me out of the farspeaker network. They could still speak to me, and I to them, but we would only communicate in an emergency, and then only in code—like I had earlier with Nyra.

Nonetheless, from the few half-caught glimpses and bitten off cries I managed to pick up on, I got a sense of the battle.

Neither of the overlords on either side of me had gone airborne—which could only be a good thing. And all around me, arrows whistled, spells sizzled, and stygians moaned in pain or anger.

Few of the nether creatures sought to come to the tree's aid. Partly, I knew, this was because my allies were stopping them from doing so, but it also had to be partly the stygian Power's doing. Either the void tree didn't feel the lesser stygians' aid was warranted or felt the creatures had more important things to do—like killing my own people.

The rift did not open either.

Nothing came through, be it a lesser stygian, naga, or harbinger. And if that was any indication, it meant the brotherhood was doing its part.

The forerunners I heard more than saw. But that was to be expected. Other than for the strike teams, the rest of our forces had been ordered to stay out of the water—and not so coincidentally, out of the tree's psionic range. The Bane Wolves, supported by Lucius' group, were holding the northern and western flanks. The Packs—arctic, dire, and wolfmen—were guarding the southern front with Zekiel's people for support.

Ghost, Elise, and the rest of the nagian-weres were the company's roving support and, directed by Safyre, would go wherever the fighting raged hottest.

In general, the plan was for our people to hold the line at the water's edge, shooting down any flying serpents that overflew them and fending off any lesser serpents that managed to swim ashore.

And swimming was definitely required now.

The new-formed lake was as much as twelve feet deep in places, leaving even the hydras battling to keep their heads above water. Thankfully, whether by design or happenstance, the void tree had planted itself on a gentle mound, and at this stage, the water didn't reach my belly.

In particular, I strained my ears to listen for the cries of my people, and while I heard plenty of victorious howls and roars of triumph, what I heard much less of were anguished screams, tortured cries, pained whines, and lamenting howls.

We are winning, I thought. *And decisively.*

At least we were, until I heard one of the phrases I'd been dreading.

"Code Orange."

It was Safyre's voice, coming loud and clear through my farspeaker bracelet, and it could mean only one thing. The shield generator around the sector was going to fall in five minutes unless we did something.

The source of the attack was obvious too. It had to be the harbingers from the mature void tree's nest. They were on their way.

But as concerning as Safyre's message was, it did not drive me to despair. Code orange was not code red or code black. Those truly would have spelt disaster.

Safyre spoke again, her voice terse and strained. *"Code Green. Code Blue."*

Backing away from the tree for a moment, I assessed our options. Both of the new code words conveyed good news. Green meant the two overlords were dead, and blue that the threat posed by the lesser stygians was contained.

And that meant we had options—options only I was in a position to assess because they all hinged on my battle with the void tree.

The first option—flight—I discarded immediately.

The second—getting Safyre, Ceruvax, Farren, Adriel, and our other top mages to reinforce the shield generator—I dismissed almost as quickly. That would only buy us a finite amount of time, but as many surprises as the void tree had pulled out already, I had no idea how much more time I would need to kill it.

No, the best way forward was option three. *"Execute plan C,"* I replied.

A distinct pause, then, *"Executing."*

My gaze returned to the void tree. Plan C gave me and the others almost five minutes to prepare. And while they had tasks aplenty, my own boiled down to one: keeping the void tree occupied.

Which I intended to do in the best way possible.

Charging, I resumed my onslaught.

Chapter 577: Plan C

Over the course of the next few minutes, my world narrowed to one thing only: the void tree.

The chances were good that it had picked up on my farspeaker communications, but I doubted it knew what to make of them—other than that we had a plan—and I wasn't worried about how it would react.

The void tree also had to know the harbingers were on their way. Hells, it was likely the one to have summoned them. And that meant the stygian Power was probably keen to keep me preoccupied until its reinforcements arrived.

An urge I was more than happy to indulge.

Dance left, strike with my right paw, then with my left—that's how I restarted my skirmish with the stygian Power. I mixed it up, of course, often using shadow jump and windborne to relocate. I didn't want to fall victim to another black thorn shower. And if I became too predictable, I surely would.

A minute ticked by.

By the end of it, I had been barely hit. The same could not be said for the tree.

A level 340 young void tree is 100% <u>shadow afflicted</u> and its health is at 70%.

After what was now almost six whole minutes of continuous and heavy fighting, the void tree could no longer claim to be untouched. I'd stripped it of nearly a third of its health.

And it showed.

Fully a quarter of the stygian Power's branches were devoid of black thorns. Most of the missing thorns lay buried at the bottom of the lake, having sunk there after failing in their attempt to find me.

Another quarter of the tree's limbs were broken or had been gnawed off. To my surprise, I'd discovered that my ponderous steps could be an effective tool even when it was not on the ground that I trod. When I was buffed with heavy none but the stoutest of the Power's branches could sustain my weight, a fact which I had exploited by darting from branch to branch, shattering them in the process.

The tree did its best to shield itself, even going as far as to whip its limbs back and forth to keep me away. And the stygian thorns were always an effective deterrent.

Still, my tactics forced my foe to focus as much on its own defenses as it did on trying to kill me, which only served to spur on my own attacks.

Another minute passed.

A young void tree is 100% <u>shadow afflicted</u> and its health is at 64%.

While it pleased me to see how quickly I was whittling down the tree's health, I didn't let myself get too excited. I'd learned from the experience with the nether sacrifice spell.

And now, I more than half-expected the tree to restore itself when its health dropped too low. When and how it would go about healing itself I didn't know. Worst yet, I had no idea how to stop it from doing so.

Minute three came and went.

A young void tree is 100% <u>shadow afflicted</u> and its health is at 62%.

I finally slowed the tempo of my attacks. The complexion of the battle would be changing soon, and I had to be ready. Drawing on my energy reserves between attacks, I renewed my buffs.

You have cast engine of war, wind daemon, ponderous step, and trigger-cast quick mend.

Four minutes.

A young void tree is 100% <u>shadow afflicted</u> and its health is at 57%.

I backed away from the tree. It was nearly time. Any second now, an alert from—

An Aether Cloaking Device is no longer in place around this sector. Portals may now be opened at any location and the region's coordinates are no longer masked.

My heart dropped, and for a split second I felt fear strike. Then reason reasserted itself. *This is plan C,* I reminded myself. *This is what you asked Safyre to do.*

And the shield generator hadn't been destroyed, it had only been dropped—deliberately. While that introduced all sorts of risks in of itself, doing so had been necessary.

Another trio of Game messages flashed for attention.

I didn't need them, though.

The new shapes bracketing me on three sides spoke for themselves. The harbingers had arrived. And they had come hunting me.

✻ ✻ ✻

A level 301 stygian harbinger has entered the sector.
A level 303 stygian harbinger has entered the sector.
A level 341 stygian harbinger has entered the sector.
3 hostile entities have failed to pierce your disguise.

I didn't stick around.

Swiveling around, I darted quicksilver fast between the harbinger to my rear and the one on the left. They both snapped at me.

You have evaded 2 hostile attacks.

The two behemoths might be tier seven creatures, but they couldn't match me for raw speed, not buffed as I was, and I slipped easily beneath their searching jaws.

"Fleshling!" one roared.

"Deceiver!" the second cried.

"Face us coward!" the third yelled.

I paid them no heed, of course. My clawed feet sending water fountaining with every step, I fled as fast as I was able.

3 of 4 hostiles have passed a physical resistance check.
You have failed to stagger or knockdown 3 harbingers.

Sadly, the harbingers resisted my ponderous steps. That was of no immediate concern, though. I simply needed to get away. For now, my only task was escaping the lake.

Well, that and drawing out the three harbingers from beneath the tree's protective aura.

Let's hope they follow, I thought as I splashed deeper into the water. I didn't intend on swimming, though. Releasing the psi I held ready, I set down a windslide.

You have cast windborne.

Borne up by the ramp of air, I shot out of the lake to skim over its surface. Only then, did I risk a backward glance.

The harbingers were hard on my heels. But unlike the one I'd faced in Draven's Reach, the trio were not winged specimens, and much to their disgust, were forced to wade through the lake.

"I'll rend you from limb to limb for this," the largest shrieked.

Ignoring it, I turned my attention to the void tree. It had already fired off two volleys of black thorns, but as a result of the windslide, the Power had misjudged my speed and trajectory, making the twin barrages no threat.

My gaze drifted back to the harbingers.

The three were nearly identical to each other. Ordinarily, I would have thought nothing of the fact, but harbingers were chimeras and by nature, unique.

That must mean these three are... siblings? creche-mates?

Whatever the correct term, it likely meant the trio were used to working together. I grimaced. As if we needed things to get any harder. Setting aside my unhappiness, I studied the newcomers more closely.

Each had the torso of a lion, a manned, fanged, and horned face that was otherwise human looking, and the tail of a scorpion. Hmm... It was almost as if the void had been trying to fashion them into manticores but had somehow forgotten the wings.

Not that I was complaining.

Wingless foes were much easier to face.

All three harbingers were uniformly colored from the tip of their squashed noses to the business ends of their tails, and from the jagged points of their twin horns to their clawed paws.

The two smaller ones were males—going by their facial features, anyhow—and were gray and black, respectively. The largest one—a female that narrowly outstripped even the tree in raw power—was a striking cerulean blue.

Gray, Black, and Blue, I dubbed the three.

With their necks stretched and their chins raised, the trio were doing their damnedest to stop the water from soaking their faces—a futile task—even as their powerful limbs ploughed through the water. But the harbingers were not just doing that. Through the scruffy growth covering all three's faces, I spied their lips moving, almost imperceptibly so.

The harbingers were casting.

And they didn't want me to notice.

I didn't have much time, I feared. Swinging my head forward again, I scanned the horizon. The shoreline was still more than half a mile away.

I was fleeing eastwards, of course—towards the foothills. It was the only shoreline of the new-formed lake we had left unguarded.

And that wasn't by chance either.

On first glance, the crest of the foothills appeared empty. But I knew that was not likely to be the case. My sharp eyes roamed over the ridgeline, searching for a particularly distinctive rock formation.

There it is. Found it.

My gaze dropped minutely to the dark shadow at the base of the formation that was nearly indistinguishable from the rock it was pretending to be.

Ghost.

She was waiting for me. As planned. Crouching back on my haunches, I leaped.

I arced through the air while weaving psi. The spell took form quickly and was ready just as I reached the pinnacle of my leap. Without hesitation, I released it and—

You have cast shadow jump.

—came down, not in water, but on solid ground atop the ridgeline, next to my patiently waiting familiar.

"Welcome back, Prime," she whispered, not moving an inch.

"Thank you, Ghost," I murmured as I spun around to face the onrushing harbingers. They had not broken off their pursuit yet, but they still had a long distance to cover, over half a mile in fact. *Excellent.*

The trio could not fail to see me either. Silhouetted against the ridgeline, I was unmissable. *But just in case...*

Drawing in a deep breath, I raised my head and howled, one long, undulating cry that threatened never to let up.

AhhhooOOOOOoowhoooo... AhhhooOOOOOoowhoooo...

The sound went on and on, echoing across the lake and the hills. Gray, Black, and Blue did not fail to hear, and I sensed their thrashing through the water gain new impetus. No doubt the trio believed I was mocking them—and I was—or that I was celebrating my escape from their clutches—which I was not.

What the void tree made of my howl, I could not tell. Ever since the start of our fight, its ominous regard had not shifted once from me. Even now I felt its gaze. But it cast no spell, launched no attack.

Perhaps it realized such was futile, or perhaps it was content to let its hounds run me down. Whatever the case, killing the void tree would have to wait until after the harbingers were dealt with—assuming, we could in fact do that.

"What was that?" Safyre asked softly.

"A challenge," I replied just as quietly. *"A taunt."* I bared my canines. *"Or maybe just a little encouragement to make sure our quarry does not get distracted."*

She laughed.

"Don't get cocky," Ceruvax warned. *"This is no easy prey we hunt."*

"Never fear, old wolf, I will take no unnecessary risks," I replied easily. Staying where I was, I surveyed the battlefield. This was my first real opportunity to see what the others had wrought in my absence.

In the center of the lake sat the two overlords, still and unmoving. Dead, just like Safyre had reported. And already it seemed like the nether plumes around them were weakening.

Along the western, eastern, and northern shorelines the battle was still raging. I spotted Nyra to the south, surrounded by a pack of wolves, Shadetooth and Stormdark amongst them. Her arrows a blur, she was shooting down stygian after stygian from the sky.

A little further along was Anriq. The werewolf was fighting alongside a squad of wolfmen as they tackled a pack of hydras that had made it ashore.

Terence fought on the western flank. Dressed in Malikor's bright red legendary armor, he stood out like a sore thumb attracting stygians from far and wide. But he had Megtir's heavy dwarven fighters to protect him and looked in no danger of falling.

Shael was to the west too. With his head bent, his flute on his lips, and his fingers dancing along the instrument's length, the bard was lost in the music he was creating, the notes of which traveled far and wide across the battlefield, uplifting the company.

Teresa was standing tall in the lapping waters of the lake's northern shore, a giant spider—Lucius transformed—by her side. Her sword rising and falling, the blade priestess was butchering the stygians and doing her damnedest to tear them apart before they could drag themselves free of the water's clutches.

I turned my attention to the stygians next.

There were a lot of them in evidence—especially of the flying variety. Everywhere I looked I spotted serpents swooping down on the company.

But they didn't find my people unprepared.

The diving snakes were met by teeth, claws, arrows, and spells aplenty, and nowhere I looked did the line of defending forerunners appear ragged. And while I would not go so far as to say the skies were ours, the flying serpents' domain over them was being hotly contested.

The picture on the landbound front was entirely different.

There were lesser stygians aplenty in the lake, but the water had definitely stifled their mobility. And instead of the nagas and snakes descending on my people in an unstoppable wave, the lesser stygians only escaped the water's depths in small, isolated, ragged groups that were quickly put to the sword.

Despite this, none of the lesser stygians attempted to flee. We had deliberately left them a way out. The eastern foothills were free of threat. But none of the creatures fled this way. Instead, they threw themselves at my people on the southern, western, and northern flanks—futilely so.

Unless something changed drastically, the fate of the lesser stygians was sealed, and it was only a matter of time before the last of them perished. My gaze found the void tree again. But it didn't seem likely that anything would change. The stygian Power hardly seemed to care about the creatures. It was not even attempting to support its minions by spraying our forces with its stygian thorns.

Was that because it didn't care about the threat the company represented? Or because it was waiting for them to draw closer?

Which they would not.

Finding a way to assault the nest while not letting our people fall under the void tree's sway had been one of our biggest challenges during the battle planning.

In the end, we'd concluded there was simply no way to protect the three thousand odd forerunners from the void tree's beguiling influence. That had left only one option—keeping everyone outside of its mental reach.

Or rather everyone except me and the overlord strike teams.

The teams had been buffed with every type of psi protection we could think of. Unnecessarily, it turned out in the end. The void tree had paid them no heed.

And when it came to the void tree's mental reach, my own scouting had borne out repeatedly what that was: by and large, the range limit of the void tree's spells coincided with the nest's boundaries. Some of the Power's direct-damage spells—like stygian thorns and etheric lash—could be thrown farther, but we'd come up with more than a few contingencies to offset the expected damage.

What we'd not been able to compensate for was our forces becoming charmed or beguiled, and so we'd simply resolved to keep them out of the tree's reach.

Of course, such a strategy would not work when it came to the harbingers.

The harbingers were highly mobile themselves *and* of similar threat level as the void tree. And as consummate death magic users, they would be able to obliterate half or more of our entire force in one fell swoop—if they so wished, or if we afforded them the opportunity to do so.

A single oblivion spell was all it would take.

That was why Ghost and I were standing alone on the crest of the eastern foothills. And that was why only a small force was assembled behind us, each of whom was already buffed by Farren and Adriel to withstand the harbingers' death magic.

I was luring Gray, Black, and Blue into a trap.

But it was a trap in which only the forerunners' most elite combatants would participate.

And shortly—very shortly—I would find out if my small team was up to the task of taking down the three stygian Powers.

Chapter 578: I Alone Suffice

The three harbingers were less than halfway across the lake when I felt a change in the void tree's regard. I stiffened, immediately going to full alertness. Was another attacking forthcoming? Almost certainly.

"Ghost, ready yourself. We might need to—"

"YOU... CANNOT... WIN... WOLFLING."

For a moment, I was struck speechless. The mindvoice was the tree's. It—no, *he*, there had been a definite masculine undertone to the voice—was speaking to me, something I'd not been expecting at all.

No one—not the huntmistress, not Adriel, and not Ceruvax—had hinted that the trees were capable of speech.

"NOTHING... TO... SAY?"

Very carefully, I sat down on my haunches and took a moment to compose myself. The tree was speaking to me—why?

Was this some sort of trick? *Very possibly.*

Did I dare speak back to it? *No.*

I was not about to let a powerful psionic—and a hostile one at that—anywhere close to my thoughts. *"Ghost, stay alert, and don't take your eyes off those harbingers. The tree is speaking to me, but it's likely a trick, some sort of attempt to distract or deceive."*

"I'll watch them, Prime," she promised.

"SCARED... WOLFLING?"

"YOU... SHOULD... BE."

I wouldn't risk speaking mind-to-mind with the tree, but perhaps there was another way I could converse with it. "I am not afraid," I shouted, using ventro to project my voice as loudly and as far across the water as I could—I couldn't very well speak normally in my current form. "I have no reason to be. We're winning."

Around the corner of my eye, I saw the harbingers freeze, but only for a moment. A second later, they resumed their painstaking wade through the lake. But it was anyone's guess whether the void tree himself would be able to hear—or even understand—my words.

"HA... HA... HA... IT SPEAKS."

I said nothing, seeing no reason to respond to the insult.

A pause.

"YOU... ARE... NOT... WINNING."

"We are," I shouted back calmly. "Your nest is destroyed, and soon, every naga and serpent under your command will be too."

"HOW... LITTLE... YOU... UNDERSTAND.... WOLFLING. THEY... COUNT... FOR... NOTHING. I... ALONE... SUFFICE."

"You alone?" I mocked. "Is that why you summoned your dogs to hunt me down?

"MY... DOGS? I... COMMAND... NO— AH... YOU... MEAN... THE... FAVORED. BUT... YOU... ARE... MISTAKEN. THEY... ARE... NOT... MINE. I... DID... NOT... CALL... THEM."

My eyes narrowed. *The favored?* Was the void tree referring to the harbingers? *Almost certainly.* But what did the void tree mean when he said he did not call them? Was he lying? Why lie about something as trivial as that, though?

"MY... CREATIONS... ARE... SAFE."

"Your creations?" I asked, hiding my confusion. What was the void tree on about now? "What would those be?"

But either the void tree did not hear my question or chose to ignore it.

"YOU... WILL... NOT... GET... THEM. THEY... ARE... SAFE... BEHIND... THE... DOOR."

Door?

"HOW... DID... YOU... LOCK... IT?"

Creations? Door? Lock?

I was growing more puzzled by the second. What door was the void tree talking about, and how was it locked? As for, its creations, I had no—

My racing thoughts ground to a halt. *Unless...*

"By creations, do you mean the nagas?" I yelled. It was a guess—one inspired by intuition, but still only a guess.

No response.

"The giant snakes, I mean."

"THEY... ARE... BEAUTIFUL... ARE... THEY... NOT?"

So. The void tree *did* mean the nagas—and the implications of that were startling.

If the void tree was telling the truth, *if* his words could be believed, the 'door' had to be the rift, and the 'lock'... that had to be the brotherhood's barrier dome spell.

For some reason, the stygian Power seemed to believe the nagas, his 'creations'—*and what do I make of that?*—were safe on the other side of the rift, something that was patently not true.

And the only reason for the void tree to believe that...

Was if the brotherhood's spell was doing more than stopping the stygians from traversing the rift. It had to be *also* preventing them from communicating across it too. In which case, the stygian Power's claim about not summoning the harbingers also made sense. He would have had no way to do so.

So, why had the harbingers come?

The mature tree must've sent them.

It was the only thing that made sense. The mature tree would have surmised from the brotherhood's assault on the other side of the rift that the young tree was under attack, and fearing—rightly so—for its fellow, it had sent help.

But reading between the lines, it didn't appear as if the void tree in this sector cared for the harbingers.

"WOLFLING?"

In fact, it didn't seem like the young void tree cared for anything but himself and his 'creations.'

"DO... NOT... IGNORE... ME... WOLFLING!"

I opened my mouth to reply, then broke off as I saw Ghost shift. *"They're almost here,"* she whispered.

Following the direction of the pyre wolf's gaze, I saw she was right. The harbingers were only a few dozen yards from the shoreline.

"As enlightening as this conversation has been, I'm afraid, I'm going to have to cut this short," I told the tree. "It's time for me to deal with your Favored."

Not waiting for the Power's response, Ghost and I withdrew down the hill's eastern slope and out of his line of sight.

✳ ✳ ✳

Gray, Black, and Blue crossed the final stretch of the lake much quicker than I anticipated. Nevertheless, we were ready for them.

"Restore the shield," I instructed the moment Blue crested the western rise.

"Acknowledged," Keros grunted. The windknight was in the cave again with the other forsworn.

A second later, a Game alert flashed for attention.

An Aether Cloaking Device has been placed around this sector. Only designated entities may open portals in this sector and only at allowed locations.

Blue paused, as did the other two harbingers behind her, and almost in unison, the three raised their heads to stare skyward. I looked, too, but could spot nothing different. Still, it was obvious that even without a Game alert, the three harbingers had sensed the change in the sector.

"Get ready," I whispered to the others as I stared up at the three harbingers at the top of the hill.

This was a pivotal moment.

Gray, Black, and Blue had two choices. Retreat to the tree or advance onwards. For many reasons, I couldn't let them take the first option, and if they showed any hint of venturing down that path, I would have no choice but to spring our trap early.

"What's the matter?" I taunted, projecting my voice with ventro again. "Afraid?"

Blue's gaze swapped from the sky to me, but she didn't immediately respond or advance. "What are you?" she asked, her voice strangely contemplative.

I swished my basilisk tail and tilted my canine head. "Is that not obvious? I am a chimera like you."

"Liar!" Gray growled.

"You are not one of the Favored," Black spat. "The Chosen has told us the truth!"

"Favored? Is that what you think we are?" I asked, continuing my pretense. My voice hardened. "We are not that. We are aberrations."

"*You are not one of us,*" Blue countered. "You are a fleshling—a soon to be dead one."

"Then, why do you hesitate?" I challenged. "Come. Kill me."

Black's eyes drifted to the still and unmoving Ghost. "Do not think we do not see your pet."

"She is not hiding," I replied conversationally.

"Another perversion," Gray snarled, his eyes also on the pyre wolf.

Blue took a step forward, Black advanced left, and Gray right. *They're going to try and rush us from three sides,* I thought.

Ghost rose to her feet, hackles raised, but I didn't move. The harbingers hadn't committed yet, and until they did, I wouldn't either.

Blue raised her right forepaw and, leaving it hanging midair, pinned me with a steely gaze, almost as if she was trying to divine my intent.

"*These harbingers are far too cautious,*" I reported across the farspeaker link. "*They might not take the bait.*"

"*We're ready,*" Safyre replied. "*Whichever way things go.*"

The moment drew out, with Blue staring at me, and me staring back just as unflinchingly. "Come here and face us," the harbinger said at last.

"Why? Are you afraid to leave your precious Chosen's sight?" I mocked.

Black's eyes drifted past me to the hills at my back. "What is hiding back there?"

"Back where?" I retorted innocently.

It was the wrong response, and I could almost see the decision forming in Blue's gaze. *Damn, she's going to turn back.* "Ghost, get—"

Blue winced. A second later, Gray and Black did too.

For a moment, their reactions puzzled me, then I spied Gray's furtive glance over his shoulder.

Ah. They've received their marching orders. But what has the tree told them to—

I broke off as, in unison, the three harbingers charged.

CHAPTER 579: GRAY, BLACK, AND BLUE

I spun around, fleeing once more, with Ghost by my side. But this time, I didn't plan on going far. Drawing psi, I began renewing my buffs.

The three harbingers raced down the hill, moving faster over land than their passage through the water suggested they were capable of. Blue came straight on, while Black veered left and Gray cut to the right.

A classic flanking maneuver.

I slowed a touch, deliberately allowing the trio to catch up as we headed toward our ambush spot—which was the selfsame spot Elise, Ghost, and I had used during our training. I timed it just right too, and as we reached the center of the shallow dip, we found ourselves surrounded.

You have cast wind daemon.

Ghost and I skidded to a halt.

The three half-cats prowled closer.

"Why does it smell so funny here?" Gray muttered, lowering his head to sniff at the ground.

Blue ignored him. "This is the end of the line," she crooned.

"It is," I replied impassively, "but not the way you mean." Drawing stamina, I cast.

You have cast vanish. You are <u>invisible</u>. Duration: 5 minutes.
Ghost has unmanifested.
3 hostile entities have failed to detect you.

Ghost and I disappeared simultaneously, leaving the harbingers absent of any targets.

The creatures reacted quickly. Springing forward from a standing start, Blue landed on the spot Ghost had so recently occupied and found... nothing.

Copying her, Gray and Black charged my last known location. But they were a hair's breadth too slow. I'd already shifted position, leaving the duo with nothing but air to find.

Drawing psi, I retreated steadily.

"Find him!" Blue screeched.

I laughed, using ventro to cause my voice to emerge twenty yards away from my actual location. The trio spun around at the sound, giving me the precious few seconds I needed to complete my spell.

You have cast slaysight.
A level 341 stygian harbinger has resisted your spell.
A level 301 stygian harbinger has resisted your spell.
A level 303 stygian harbinger has partially resisted your spell.
You have paralyzed 1 of 3 targets for 30 seconds.

"Now," I instructed, speaking rapidly to the others across the farspeaker bracelet. *"Leave the black one, Saf. It's disabled."*

Blue and Gray, meanwhile, had realized something was amiss. Striding up to Black's side, Blue nudged him—hard.

The harbinger toppled over.

Blue spun around to face Gray. "Oblivion!" she ordered. "Now!"

Paying the harbingers no heed, I concentrated on my next casting. At the same time, the rest of the ambush team finally made their presence known.

Adriel has dispelled a tier 6 concealment field.

Adriel has cast <u>blood of the dead</u>. Blood of the dead is a lesser blood memory that resurrects the remains of any recent dead in the vicinity, up to a maximum of 100, transforming them into a ghostly army that fights on the caster's behalf.

Adriel has raised the ghosts of 25 nagas and 75 hydras to fight on her behalf.

Ceruvax has cast <u>rampaging pack</u>. Rampaging pack is a greater blood memory that buffs all allies around the caster in a 100 yard radius, adding fire damage to their attacks. Rampaging allies will deal 3x fire damage in addition to their normal attacks.

You are now <u>rampaging</u> (will deal 3x fire damage). Duration: 2 minutes.

Safyre has cast <u>tornado of light</u>. Tornado of light is a tier 5 Force ability that traps a single target in a vortex of light for 30 seconds, dealing sustained light damage to it.

A level 301 stygian harbinger has partially resisted a tornado of light and is <u>storm trapped</u>. Duration (reduced): 10 seconds.

"Focus your attacks on the gray and black ones!" I yelled as surging winds of pure Light descended from the skies and plucked Gray off the ground. "Get gray and black," I added for the benefit of Farren and Adriel who were not on the farspeaker network. "You have ten seconds."

My own spell completed, and I released it too.

You have activated fearsome aura. Range: 23 yards.

1 of 3 foes have failed a mental resistance check!

A level 303 stygian harbinger has been <u>petrified</u> (frozen in fear and unable to act).

My jaw snapped close in frustration as fearsome aura affected the same target as paralyze, leaving Blue unaffected.

But I had more cards to play. Darting forward, I leaped. "The blue one is mine," I snarled, weaving stamina as I rushed through the air. *"Ghost, take Black."*

"On it, Prime."

You have cast ponderous step. You are now <u>heavy</u> (causing the ground to shake with each step) Duration: 1 minute.

Ghost has cast explosive manifest.

Farren has cast <u>scythes of darkness</u>. Scythes of darkness is a lesser blood memory that manifests 2 dark blades into being for 1 minute.

As I arced through the air toward my target, I spotted the archlich's summoned blades appearing over Gray who was still trapped in Safyre's tornado. First one blade, then the other slashed down.

A dark scythe has critically injured a stygian harbinger.
A dark scythe has critically injured a stygian harbinger.

Adriel's ethereal army was moving too. Their limbs and jaws glimmering red—courtesy of Ceruvax's buff—they passed through Blue to converge on the paralyzed and petrified Black. Ghost was already there, attacking the helpless harbinger with tooth and claw and raking deep furrows in his sides. The female harbinger, meanwhile, was still casting, her lips moving rapidly.

But I soon put a stop to that.

Passing through the top of my arc, I rushed groundward. At the last second Blue looked up, sensing something amiss. But by then it was too late, and I landed directly atop the harbinger. The breath whooshed out of her lungs and her limbs splayed outward as she collapsed beneath my overbearing weight.

I didn't give her a chance to recover.

Bringing my clawed right foot down, I swatted Blue across the face. At the same time, I closed my jaws over the back of her neck.

A level 341 stygian harbinger has partially resisted your stunning paw and has been <u>stunned</u> for 2 seconds.
A stygian harbinger has failed to resist lacerating bite.
Your target is <u>bleeding</u>. Duration: 23 seconds.

I didn't release my hold on Blue's neck. Instead, I ground my teeth further into the wound I'd already inflicted, gnawing deeper. Nor did I let up with my paw attacks. My clawed forepaw rising and falling, I kept swatting at the downed harbinger.

Ceruvax has ordered a naga to attack a level 301 stygian harbinger.
Farren has ordered 18 undead nagas to attack a level 301 stygian harbinger.

I acknowledged the Game messages with barely a flicker of emotion. At this point, the introduction of Farren and Ceruvax's minions was overkill.

This battle could have only one outcome.

❋   ❋   ❋

The three harbingers put up surprisingly little fight.

It appeared I had misjudged my own strength and that of my allies. Even without Adriel and Farren using their strongest spells—as death casters themselves, the three stygian Powers were immune to the lichs' death magic—we still managed to keep the harbingers disabled for prolonged stretches of time.

Or perhaps it was simply surprise that carried the day.

Gray, Black, and Blue did not manage to get off a single spell, and it was possible the complexion of the battle would have changed completely if they had. But I doubted it. We were prepared for the harbingers' death magic.

In any case, the end proved anticlimactic, with alert after alert scrolling through my mind while my foe lay largely senseless beneath me. But eventually, the Game messages I was waiting for arrived.

You have killed a level 341 stygian harbinger.
You and Ghost have reached level 273!
Your dodging has reached rank 23, your two weapon fighting rank 21, and your thieving rank 18.
Ghost's death magic has reached rank 14 and her nether manipulation rank 13.

You've slain a tier 7 creature, deepening your Power Mark.
Congratulations, Michael! You have slain your 3rd tier 7 creature, thereby advancing another step down the paths of Power and acquiring the <u>Powerful Acolyte</u> Mark.
As a result of your new Power Mark, your <u>higher evolution</u> trait has advanced to <u>higher evolution II</u>. This trait allows you to evolve your ascendant Class to rank 2. But before you can do so, you must either deepen your Wolf Mark further or reach level 300. Note, once you acquire a legendary Class you will be prohibited from attacking players who themselves do not bear a Power Mark.

I stepped off the dead harbinger, my muzzle bloody and dripping gore. Looking up, I surveyed the battlefield.

The others were still fighting Gray and Black but appeared to have matters well in hand. Ghost had her jaws locked around Black's throat while the undead nagas and Adriel's ghosts beat at him. Farren, Ceruvax, and Safyre, meanwhile, were pounding Gray with spells.

"Michael?"

My head turned westward. The call had come from Anriq, speaking to me through the farspeaker bracelet. "What is it?"

"I'm not sure," he replied uncertainly. "But I think something is happening with the tree."

I inhaled sharply. "He has joined the battle?"

"He—? Never mind. But, no, that's not it. The ground around the Power is churning. And I think I see... roots."

"Roots?" I repeated blankly. "Why would—"

I broke off, realization dawning.

The tree was uprooting itself. I'd seen the sapling in Draven's Reach do the same thing. And the fact that the tree was digging himself up could mean only one thing.

He had decided to run.

I was sure of it. Despite the void tree's earlier evinced arrogance and all his talk of 'alone sufficing,' Blue's death must have shook him.

"They're definitely roots," Anriq added, unaware of my churning thoughts. "More have appeared, lots more."

"It's not just that," Nyra commented. *"The Power is rising too."*

"The trees can fly?" a baffled Terence asked. *"Why didn't it do that before?"*

"He's fleeing," I said numbly.

"Fleeing?" Teresa asked skeptically. *"Why would you think that? Maybe it's on its way to help the harbingers."*

"He's not," I said confidently.

Sector 18,240 was not Draven's Reach. It was a Kingdom sector and only reachable by the void through a rift—the very same rift that the young tree was anchoring.

Or *had* been anchoring.

Because there was a cost to a tree uprooting itself in a Kingdom sector. And that cost was the rift linking the sector to the Nethersphere. Without young void tree's roots to anchor it, the rift would not be able to sustain itself.

I lifted my gaze to the rift peaking above the top of the intervening foothills. It had shrunk—was shrinking *still*. The change was noticeable, leaving me in doubt that the rift was contracting. Its closure was inevitable.

And that meant we'd won.

No matter what happened from this point onward, the rift *would* close, the safe zone *would* reappear, and the mists *would* vanish.

Most importantly, though, it meant the sector was ours to claim.

But...

The rift was closing slower than any of us had anticipated.

And that meant the void tree had a way out—something that caught me equally off-guard. I couldn't see the stygian Power, but I knew that he wouldn't be uprooting himself if he didn't think he could traverse the rift before it was destroyed. The last thing he would want was to be stuck on this side of the rift with the foes that had hurt him so much. Which meant...

He's going to flee to sector 30,199.

Where even now the brotherhood was likely still embroiled in battle. The stygian Power would drop out of the rift and directly into their midst, leaving him close enough to strike at the brotherhood's army with his powerful mental abilities.

Enthralling some.

Killing others.

Doing to them the things we had been so careful not to let him do to our own forces. Even if the brotherhood managed to kill the void tree, they would lose hundreds in the process.

Turning my head to the left, my gaze found Safyre where she stood beside Ceruvax, Farren, and Adriel. I could see from her expression she already knew what I intended.

"I have to chase after him."

She sighed. *"I agree. We can't let the brotherhood pay for our failures."*

And it was *our* failure—I had no doubt about that.

We had all known there was a risk of the tree trying to flee at some point, but none of us had considered the possibility of him using the rift to sector 30,199 because the damnable ley line was supposed to close the moment the tree uprooted himself.

I'd promised Kartara that her people wouldn't have to face the void tree, a promise it looked like I would no longer be able to keep. Knowing the huntmistress, she and her people likely already had contingencies in place for such a scenario.

But no contingency was perfect.

And while many of the brotherhood might get away, many more would still die. Their deaths would be on my head. *"Unmanifest, Ghost. We have other prey to hunt,"* I said quietly before turning back to Safyre. *"You know what to do."*

She nodded. *"We will see the sector claimed."*

There were other things I wanted to say, but this was not the time for a protracted goodbye. Leaving things as they were, I dashed up the slope of the western hill, spinning psi as I went.

Ghost has unmanifested.

Cresting the rise, my eyes darted to my distant foe.

The void tree was fully airborne, and the base of his trunk was more than a hundred feet off the ground. A wormlike mass of fleshy white appendages hung below the Power—the roots Anriq had spied. But to me, they looked more like an overlord's tentacles, and as exposed as they were, the roots gave the tree a strangely naked appearance.

Is he more vulnerable this way? I wondered.

I would find out soon enough, I suspected. Of more concern right now was how fast my foe was moving. I had no idea how the void tree was propelling himself through the air, but he was almost at the rift.

I couldn't delay any longer. Releasing the weave I held ready, I blinked out of existence.

You have teleported into the shadow of a level 340 young void tree.

I emerged from the aether, nestled amongst the tree's branches once more, and not a second too early, either.

A heartbeat later, the tree made contact with the dark doorway and our transition into the void began.

You have entered a rift.

Warning: the rift you have entered is closing! The void tree that created the ley line between sector 30,199 and 18,240 is no longer anchoring the rift. Estimated time until the ley line is no longer traversable: 5 minutes.

...

...

Leaving sector 18,240 of the Forever Kingdom.

Transfer commencing...

✳ ✳ ✳

THE END.

Here ends Book 8 of the Grand Game.

Michael's adventures will continue in **Webs of Power**.
Coming 01 October 2025!

I hope you enjoyed the story! If you did, please leave a <u>review</u> and let other readers know what you think.
<u>Click here to leave a review</u>.

If you're enjoying the Grand Game, you might also want to check out my new series: **The Annals of the Runeguard**. It follows our protagonist, Dace Tolman, and is set in another universe altogether. Read on for an excerpt from the <u>Proving Grounds</u>.

Happy reading!
Tom Elliot.

MICHAEL AT THE END OF BOOK 8

Player Profile: Michael

Level: 273. Rank: 27. Current Health: 100%.
Species: Human. Lives Remaining: 4. Ghost's Lives Remaining: 4.
Active Pacts: 7 / 20.
True Marks: Powerful Acolyte.
True Marks (hidden): Worthy Adversary, Wolf Protector, Wolf Progenitor.
False Marks (fabricated): Lesser Shadow, Lesser Light, Lesser Dark.

Faction Data: Forerunners

Faction officers appointed: 2. Sectors claimed: 0 / 3 (+1 from Safyre).
Faction Leaders: Michael, Safyre. Faction Custodian: Adriel.
Players pledged: Nyra, Ceruvax, Terence, Teresa, Anriq, Shael, Keros, Sedgwick, +10 forsworn mages.
Non-players pledged: Adriel, Pack of the Reach (500), Bane Wolves warband (2,000), arctic wolves (200), dire wolves (130), nagians (100).

House Data

Governing bloodline: Wolf.
Core Tenet: Just Retribution.
Second Tenet: Protector of the Ancients.
Affinities: Renegades, outcasts, and criminals.
Followers: 2 / 200 (Nyra and Ceruvax).

Active Buffs

denotes boosts affected by items.
Damage reduction (DR) (reduces damage incurred only):
Life: 20%. Death: 25%. Air: 55%. Earth: 55%. Fire: 55%. Water: 55%.
Shadow: 40%. Light: 40%. Dark: 40%. Nether: 120%. Physical: 62%*.

Resistances (RES) (negates damage and/or rebuffs spell effects):
Life: 10%. Death: 12.5%. Air: 27.5%. Earth: 27.5%. Fire: 47.5%*. Water: 27.5%. Shadow: 20%. Light: 20%. Dark: 20%. Nether: 80%*. Physical: 0%.

Ghost (DR / RES): Fire: 85% / 102.5%. Nether: 85% / 102.5%. Physical: 91%* / 42.5%.

Stolen spells (3 / 3)

oblivion (tier 6), noxious vapors (tier 6), seeping shadows (tier 6): expires in 1.5 days.

Other Benefits derived from Items

Damage: +30% damage (ebonheart), +40% damage (faithful).
Abilities: perceive tier 6 spelled wards (sorcerer's coif), move soundlessly (wayfarer's boots), hands immune to hazardous substances (wayfarer's

gloves), spellhold: furious storm (mage's surprise), psi-feed (psi bracelet), penetrate tier 5 illusions (true-seer ring).
Traits: +20% aoe evasion (tiamaten vest).
Skills: +5 ranks in thieving (scoundrel's wristband).

Attributes

Available: 13 points.
Strength: 48 (40)*. **Constitution**: 56 (44)*. **Dexterity**: 166 (142)*.
Perception: 132 (127)*. **Mind**: 200 (188)*. **Magic**: 106 (85)*. **Faith**: 20.

Classes

Available (Michael): 1 point. 0 ascendant points.
Available (Ghost): 1 point.

Primary-Secondary-Tertiary tri-blend: voidstalker (fabricated). voidstealer XIV (hidden).
Ascendant Class: wolf lord (rank I, hidden), sire wolf (rank I, hidden).
Familiar: stygian pyre wolf XV (unique, hidden).

Traits

HFO: *denotes human-form-only benefits.*
WFO: *denotes wolf-form-only benefits.*

void heritage II (wolf, hidden): +4 Dexterity, +4 Strength, +8 Mind, +8 Perception, +12 Magic.
voidwalker II (wolf, hidden): improved senses in all conditions, nethersight, immunity to blindness.
arctic wolf II (wolf, hidden): +10 Constitution, +4 Mind, +6 Strength.
were's bite II (wolf, hidden, ascendant): 0 to 30% chance of granting another player the were-trait.
sire's strain (wolf, hidden, ascendant): boosts your other wolf traits by +1 tier.
elder form II (wolf, hidden, ascendant): +20 to all attributes, shapeshift.

house elite (bloodline, hidden): bound to House Wolf, detect dormant wolf bloodline strains.
secret blood (bloodline, hidden): conceals the wolf blood of yourself, your followers, and your familiar.
blood puppet (bloodline, hidden): grants you the enslave ability.

beast tongue: can speak to beastkin.
Marked: can see spirit signatures.
inscrutable mind: +8 Mind.
mental focus IV: increases effectiveness of Mind skills by 40%.
intrepid explorer: logs all locations in first-discovered sectors, and safe zone location in any visited sector.
spell illiterate: cannot cast mana-based spells.
potion resistance II: potency of potions reduced by 2 ranks.

spirit talker: can speak to spirits.
bold blood: +1 attribute per level.
higher evolution II: can evolve your Class to ascendant rank 2.
commander (ascendant): can share bloodline traits or blood memories with your followers.
champion (ascendant): increases the strength of blood memories.
spirit familiar: can bind a willing spirit as your familiar.
mage-host: +10 Mind, +10 Magic.
slip-through-shadows*: 20% chance to evade aoe damage.

spirit familiar (Ghost): mirrors player attributes and level, and shares ability slots with them.
psionic being (Ghost): retains telepathic skills and abilities from her former incarnation as a dire wolf.
free spirit (Ghost): can roam an unlimited distance from her host, but only within the same sector.
born again II (Ghost): grants your familiar 2 additional lives, will resurrect in spirit vessel.
pyreborn II (Ghost): +60% fire magic resistance and +60% fire damage.
voidborn II (Ghost): +60% nether resistance and +60% necrotic damage.
mirrored jewelry*: gains benefits of rank 7 rings, bracelets, and necklaces.

primal creature II (WFO, legendary): 18 feet long, +30% resistance, 3 attack types (physical, fire, poison).
regeneration II (WFO, legendary): health regeneration of +2% per second.

Skills

Available skill slots: 0.
light / hide armor (current: 180. Constitution, basic).

dodging (current: 232. Dexterity, basic).
sneaking (current: 249. Dexterity, basic).
shortswords / tooth and claw (current: 237. Dexterity & Strength (WFO), basic).
two weapon fighting (current: 213. Dexterity, advanced).
thieving (current: 180. Dexterity, basic).

chi (current: 208. Mind, advanced).
meditation (current: 240. Mind, basic).
telekinesis (current: 211. Mind, advanced).
telepathy (current: 237. Mind, advanced).

insight (current: 265. Perception, basic).
deception (current: 258. Perception, master).

channeling (current: 236. Magic, basic).
elemental absorption (current: 116. Magic, master).
null force (current: 82. Magic, master).

null life (current: 44. Magic, master).
null death (current: 53. Magic, master).
nether absorption (current: 244. Magic, master).

magma maw (Ghost) (current: 156. Magic, master).
stygian claws (Ghost) (current: 164. Strength, master).
ash armor (Ghost) (current: 171. Constitution, master).
telepathy (Ghost) (current: 137. Mind, advanced).
death magic (Ghost) (current: 141. Magic, advanced).
nether manipulation (Ghost) (current: 131. Magic, master).

Abilities

<u>Constitution ability slots used:</u> **15 / 44.**
greater load controller (HFO) (15 Constitution, master, light armor).

<u>Dexterity ability slots used:</u> **141 / 142.**
crippling blow (HFO) (Dexterity, basic, shortswords).
minor piercing strike (HFO) (5 Dexterity, advanced, shortswords).
deadly backstab (30 Dexterity, elite, sneaking).
superior trap disarm (HFO) (15 Dexterity, master, thieving).
superior lockpicking (HFO) (15 Dexterity, master, thieving).
greater set trap (HFO) (15 Dexterity, master, thieving).
wind daemon (30 Dexterity, elite, two weapon fighting).
vanish (30 Dexterity, elite, sneaking).

<u>Mind ability slots used:</u> **186 / 188.**
mass puppet (15 Mind, master, telepathy).
stunning slap (HFO) (Mind, basic, chi).
improved windborne (15 Mind, master, telekinesis).
lesser engine of war (30 Mind, elite, chi).
sentient shurikens (HFO) (30 Elite, master, telepathy).
shadow jump (30 Mind, elite, telekinesis).
greater quick mend (30 Mind, elite, chi).
impregnable mind (30 Mind, elite, meditation).
astral bite (Ghost) (5 Mind, advanced, telepathy).

<u>Perception ability slots used:</u> **126 / 127.**
powerful analyze (30 Perception, elite, insight).
greater trap detect (15 Perception, master, thieving).
conceal small weapon (HFO) (Perception, basic, deception).
mimic (HFO) (30 Perception, elite, deception).
superior ventro (5 Perception, advanced, deception).
doppelganger (45 Perception, grandmaster, deception).

<u>Magic ability slots used:</u> **20 / 85.**
superior draining bite (Ghost) (10 Magic, expert, death magic).
mist-thin (Ghost) (10 Magic, expert, nether manipulation).

<u>**Strength ability slots used:**</u> 32 / 40.
charge (WFO) (1 Strength, basic, tooth and claw).
overpowering blow (WFO) (1 Strength, basic, tooth and claw).
ponderous steps (WFO) (30 Strength, elite, tooth and claw).

<u>**Other abilities:**</u>
adept slaysight (hidden) (Class, elite, telepathy): paralyze, shatter, sleep, terrify, blind.
void thief extraordinaire (hidden) (Class, elite, any void skill and telepathy): 3x steal, siphon, negate, redirect on direct-damage, channeled, damage over time, aoe, wards).
manifest (Ghost) (Class, master): explosive entry II, necrotic wake II.
diresight (Ghost) (Class, advanced, telepathy).
direshield (Ghost) (Class, expert, telepathy).
enslave (hidden) (blood memory, greater): dominate 2 subjects per day.
shapeshift (hidden) (ascendant Class, legendary): twice per day, greater elder wolf.
lacerating bite (WFO) (ascendant Class, epic, tooth and claw).
stunning paw (WFO) (ascendant Class, legendary, tooth and claw).
fearsome aura (WFO) (ascendant Class, legendary, telepathy).

<u>**Known Key Points**</u>

Kingdom Sector 1 (Nexus) safe zone.
Kingdom Sector 12,560 (wolves' valley) nether portal and safe zone.
Kingdom Sector 18,240 nether portal 1 (guardian tower), and nether portal 2 (Draven's reach).
Kingdom Sector 75,172 nether portal 1 (Draven's Reach) and safe zone.
Kingdom Sector 65,231 (Korg Minor) safe zone and nether portals to Korg Deep.
Kingdom Sector 65,232 (Korg Major) safe zone and nether portals from Korg Deep.
Kingdom Sector 45,104 (Brotherhood sector) safe zone.

Dungeon Sector 101 (scorching dunes) exit portal and safe zone.
Dungeon Sectors 102, 103, and 104 (haunted catacombs) exit portals and safe zones.
Dungeon Sector 105, 106, 107, 108, and 109 (guardian tower) exit portals.
Dungeon Sector 14,913 (candidate's dungeon) exit portal and safe zone.
Dungeon Sector 73,102 (Draven's Reach) one-way entrance portal, safe zone, and exit portal.

Nether Sector 30,199 nether portal 1 (dead) and Rift-X.

<u>**Aetherstone Bracelet Stored Points**</u>

sector 24,401 safe zone.

<u>**Netherstone Stored Point**</u>

sector 30,199 (Rift-X: somewhere in dunes).

<u>Equipped</u> (30 / 30 Game items)
<u>Weapons</u> (2 equipped)
ebonheart (+30% damage) (soulbound).
faithful (+40% damage).

<u>Armor & Clothes</u> (12 equipped)
tiamaten scalemail vest (+32%, +4 Constitution, slip-through-shadows).
sorcerer's coif (perceive tier 6 wards).
ranger's kit (+24% damage reduction, 4 pieces).
bomber's belt (5 x acid bombs, 5 x smoke bombs, 5 x ice bombs, and 5 x fire bombs).
belt of the chameleon (8 x rank 4 nether protection crystals, 9 x rank 4 disease protection crystals, 6 scent concealment crystals, 5 x mental concealment crystals, 4 x rank 6 disease protection crystals, 2 x rank 5 poison protection crystals, 1 x rank 4 strength enhancement crystals, 0 x rank 4 dexterity enhancement crystals, and 2 x rank 4 magic enhancement crystals).
wayfarer's boots (legendary item, +8 Dexterity, move soundlessly).
wayfarer's gloves (legendary item, +8 Dexterity, hands immune to hazardous substances).
cloak of the Reach (legendary soulbound item, +10 Magic, +20% fire magic resistance, +20% nether magic resistance).
scoundrel's wristband (+5 ranks thieving, 0 / 300 trap-making crystals) (<u>triggers</u>: pressure plates, sound glasses, tripwires, motion pins, remote control, spell detector, psi detector. <u>elements</u>: lightning, poison clouds, fire, spring-coiled daggers, bear-trap clamps, small explosives, blots of darkness, ice, spiked-pit, hallucinogenic mist. <u>guides</u>: reflect, split, and funnel. <u>keys</u>: remote, timed.)

<u>Rings & Accessories</u> (13 equipped)
goliath's ring (+8 Strength).
acrobat's ring (+8 Dexterity).
sharpshooter's band (+4 Perception).
hale stone (+8 Constitution).
savant's ring (+4 Mind).
troll's talisman bracelet (+6% damage reduction).
mage's surprise (+10 Magic, spellhold: trigger-cast tier 5 spells).
psi bracelet (legendary item, +8 Mind, psi-feed).
simple potion bracelet (3 / 3 full heal potions).
aetherstone bracelet (1 / 5 stored locations, 2 stone charged).
jeweled pet (grants Ghost: mirrored jewelry trait).
true-seer ring (true-seeing: penetrate tier 5 illusions).
Forerunner bracelet (council set, 1 of 30).
Brotherhood bracelet (set F05, 1 of 10).

<u>Other</u> (2 equipped)
large bag of holding (200 slots).

seeking eye of sylvana (legendary item, +invisible, 4 hours use, track & scout).

<u>Ghost (1 equipped)</u>
Forerunner collar (council set, 2 of 30).

<u>**Backpack Contents (key items only)**</u>

<u>Money</u>: **223 golds, 5 silvers, and 3 coppers.**
1 x coil of rope.
cat claws.
20 x acid bombs, 20 x smoke bombs, 20 x ice bombs, and 20 x fire bombs.
small bag of hiding (tier 6 concealment ward).
a simple shovel.
stygian shortsword, +3.
stygian shortsword.
netherstone.
19 x greater portal scrolls.
packet of unrefined cynacilin powder.
farspeaker bracelet (Tyelin set, 1 of 15).
farspeaker bracelet (Safyre set, 1 of 4).

<u>Upgrade Items</u>
8 x upgrade gems.
piercing strike tier III, IV, & V.
ventro tier III & IV.
load controller V,
whirlwind V,
trap disarm V,
lockpicking tier V,
set trap V,
mass puppet V,
windborne V,
enhanced reflexes V,
trap detect V,
ventro V,
lesser imitate V,
charge II, III, IV & V,
overpowering blow II, III, IV & V,
stomp V.
2 x aetherstones (etched).

<u>Soulbound Items</u>
Tartan token.
Vivane token.
Kesh Emporium access card.
tavern bill of ownership.
BHG ID (junior member, 1 / 10 active jobs).
journeyman rogue's underworld token.

pioneer's compass (soulbound, attuned to safe zone).
unmarked chest key card (from Nicola).
Forerunner faction token (ID: 0001).

Miscellaneous Loot

None.

Alchemy Stone Contents

(500 / 500 ingredients stored).
310 x lumps of necrotic plasma, and 190 x vials of nether residue.

Bank Contents

Money: 655 gold, 0 silvers, and 0 coppers.
2 x full healing potions.
2 x full mana potions.

Tavern Money: 300 gold, 0 silvers, and 0 coppers.

Open Tasks

Heist in the Dark (steal chalice from the Power, Paya).
A Perverted Trial (stop the Triumvirate abuse of the Combat Trial).
Brokering Peace (establish peace in sector 12,560 within 4 months).
Brotherhood Obligations (join the brotherhood on three nether expeditions).
Revive the Guardians (awaken Draven's brethren).
Locate the Lost Prime (find the hidden Prime).
Resurrecting Death (make Adriel a scion again).
Found a new House (persuade two non-Wolf Powers to join your House).

Open Pacts

Deliver cynacilin. Status: pact obligations fulfilled. Blythe owes you a favor equivalent to the worth of sector 75,172.
Inner Council Pacts with Safyre, Anriq, Teresa, Terence, and Shael.
Guardian Tower Access Pact with Bacheus (deliver a tithe once a month for access).

Feats Accomplished (by book)

Solo your First Boss, Play the Game.
Novice Dungeoneer, Realize your Lineage.
Rift Defender, Pioneer of the Realms, Solo your First Dungeon.
(none).
Master Dungeoneer, The Bigger they Are, A Mighty Player.
Ascending to New Heights, Charging Headlong into Power, First of Many.
Apprentice Dungeoneer.
Solo a Power, Realm Explorer.

The profiles—heavily condensed—of the Forerunners are provided below. Only abilities, skills, and traits already revealed in the story have been listed.

Nyra

Level: 129. **Class:** virulent witch.
Mark: Mark of Michael, Wolf-friend, Shadow.
Traits: secret blood (lesser).
Skills: longbows, sneaking, focus, poisoning, light armor, daggers, herbalism, chi, meditation, telekinesis, telepathy, deception.
Blood memories: enslave (lesser), revitalizing blood.
Abilities: hobbling shot.
Equipment: Forerunner bracelet (council set, 3 of 30), Forerunner faction token (2 of 20).

Terence

Level: 127. **Class:** human arcane knight.
Marks: Minor Light, Lion.
Equipment: Forerunner bracelet (council set, 4 of 30), Forerunner faction token (3 of 20).

Teresa

Level: 129. **Class:** human priestess of the blade.
Marks: Minor Light, Lion.
Equipment: Forerunner bracelet (council set, 5 of 30), Forerunner faction token (4 of 20).

Anriq

Level: 146. **Class:** were-rampager (Darksworn Class).
Marks: Greater Dark, Lesser Shadow, Wolf pack-brother.
Equipment: Forerunner bracelet (council set, 6 of 30), Forerunner faction token (5 of 20).

Shael

Level: 148. **Class:** half-elf red minstrel.
Marks: Moderate Shadow.
Skills: Shadow magic, fire magic, life magic, channeling, music, deception, dodging, thieving, insight, focus.
Abilities: Guile, Shaten's Call to War.
Equipment: Forerunner bracelet (council set, 7 of 30), Forerunner faction token (6 of 20).

Ceruvax

Level: 299. **Class:** human were-mage.
Marks: Pack Alpha.
Trait: secret blood (lesser).
Blood memories: enslave (lesser), rampaging pack (greater).
Abilities: healing wolf, seeping shadows.

Equipment: Ritual Combat Circle (soulbound), Skull of Souls (soulbound), Forerunner bracelet (council set, 8 of 30), Forerunner faction token (7 of 20).

Safyre

Level: 225. **Class:** human aetherist (Lightsworn Class).
Ascendant Class: Bastion of Light. **Followers:** 11 / 100 (6 forsworn elites, 5 forsworn rank 4 players).
Marks: Supreme Light, Powerful Initiate.
Ascendant Abilities: call to arms, bastion of healing.
Force Abilities: Tornado of Light.
Abilities: aether grace, aether protection, warrior's boon, summon aethereal allies (drow phantom, feral specter, aether saint), greater portal, lesser portal, furious storm, purifying dome, supreme portal, devilish winds, aether bolt.
Equipment: Forerunner bracelet (council set, 9 of 30), Forerunner faction token (8 of 20).

Adriel (non-player)

Level: 262. **Class:** human lich.
Marks: none. Formerly of House Death.
Skills: possession, enchanting, golem-crafting.
Blood memories: Death's finger, Blood of the Dead.
Abilities: death's sheltering hand, noxious vapors, undead's champion, warrior's boon, veil of darkness, tier 6 containment field, repel-the-living, wraith winds, fly-trap (ward), reanimate.
Equipment: Forerunner faction tokens.

Lucius (non-player)

Level: 210. **Class:** nagian mage hunter.
Marks: none. Formerly of House Spider.
Skills: sneaking, dodging.
Abilities: fly-trap (ward), warding web, summon spiderling horde, darkness bolt, disrupting ray, concealing web (tier 4), polymorph (spider).

Zekiel (non-player)

Level: 206. **Class:** nagian psi knight.
Marks: none. Formerly of House Bear.
Skills: telekinesis, telepathy, chi, meditation, heavy armor, and broadswords.
Abilities: blink, levitating disc.

Elise (non-player)
Level: 170. **Class:** nagian were-druid.
Marks: none. Formerly of House Fox.
Abilities: shapeshift (were-fox).

Keros (forsworn)
Level: 210. **Class:** human windknight (Lightsworn Class).
Marks: Greater Light, Safyre.
Equipment: Forerunner bracelet (council set, 10 of 30), Forerunner faction token (9 of 20).

Farren (non-player)
Level: Tier 6. **Class:** human lich.
Skills: possession, undead summoning.
Blood memories: scythes of darkness (lesser).
Abilities: reaper's sanctuary, reaper's shield, purifying dome, darkness bolt, oblivion, lich's aid.

Sedgwick (civilian player)
Level: N/A. **Class:** dwarven merchant.
Marks: Lesser Light, Lesser Shadow.
Equipment: Forerunner bracelet (council set, 21 of 30), Forerunner faction token (20 of 20).

BOOKS BY TOM ELLIOT

BY TOM ELLIOT

The Grand Game (series page)
Book 1: The Grand Game: ebook | audiobook
Book 2: Way of the Wolf: ebook | audiobook
Book 3: World Nexus: ebook | audiobook
Book 4: House Wolf: ebook | audiobook
Book 5: Wolf in the Void: ebook | audiobook
Book 6: A Scion's Duty: ebook | audiobook
Book 7: Ancient Debts: ebook | audiobook
Book 8: The Lost Reclaimed: ebook | audiobook (coming soon)
Book 9: Webs of Power: ebook (coming soon)

The Grand Game Box Set (series page)
Book 1-3: Birth of a Player: ebook
Book 4-6: Rise of an Elite: ebook
Book 7-9: The Makings of Power: ebook (coming soon)

The Grand Game, Elana (series page)
Book 1: Empyrean's Rise: ebook
Book 2: Empyrean's Flight: ebook

Annals of the Runeguard (series page)
Book 1: Proving Grounds: ebook | audiobook
Book 2: Sector 52: ebook (coming soon)

BY ROHAN M. VIDER

The Dragon Mage Saga (series page)
Book 1: Overworld: ebook | audiobook
Book 2: Dungeons: ebook | audiobook
Book 3: Sponsors: ebook (coming soon)

The Gods' Game (series page)
Crota, the Gods' Game Volume I
The Labyrinth, the Gods' Game Volume II
Sovereign Rising, the Gods' Game Volume III
Sovereign, the Gods' Game, Volume IV
Sovereign's Choice, the Gods' Game Volume V

Tales from the Gods' Game
Dungeon Dive (Tales from the Gods' Game, Book 1)

AFTERWORD

Thank you for reading the Grand Game!

If you enjoyed the book, please consider leaving a review on amazon [click here]. I'm already at work on Michael's next adventure.

If you have any questions, comments, or want to support my writing, please feel free to contact me through my site, TomLitRPG.com or Discord.

Alternatively, if you wish to learn more about the world of the Forever Kingdom, understand the system of the Grand Game better, or are just looking for the latest news on the Grand Game, please visit my site at TomLitRPG.com or signup up here for my: Newsletter.

Regards,
Tom
Support my writing on **PATREON**
Amazon Author page | Goodreads | Facebook | Reddit | Discord |

DEFINITIONS

Accord: old agreement between new Powers ceding control of Nexus to the Triumvirate.

Adjudicator: controller and arbitrator of the Grand Game.

alchemy stone: a device used to store alchemical components.

ancient: old Power.

anointed scion: a scion who has bound himself to a bloodline.

ascendancy: process of being a Power.

ascendant: descriptor often applied to Game aspects involving higher evolution.

ascendant undead: term the Adjudicator used to describe Stayne, meaning unknown.

blended Class: a combined Class.

blood awakening: the process of recalling blood memories.

blood infusion: the absorption of the essences from former scions.

blood memories: gifts from your forebears containing the power of the ancients themselves.

bi-blend: a combination of two melded Classes.

bloodline: reference to the ancient from which the player is a descendant.

breaking: refers to the breaking of the world, the fracturing of the Forever Kingdom into sectors, aether, and nether.

Circle: aka Ritual Combat Circle.

civilian player: a player without a class or combat abilities. Civilians do not have a player level.

class-unique skill: a skill that is unique to a Class and can only be acquired through a Class stone.

closed sector: a landmass that does not physically border another, making the area inaccessible except by portal.

composite spell: a multi-stage spell made up of two or more individual spells.

controlled sector: a sector owned by a faction. Ownership of a sector gives the faction's players increased privileges in the region.

Class: a defined path or vocation that gives a player access to specific skills.

Class evolution: the advancement of a Class, generally to a better-ranked one, due to particular traits, skills, or Marks acquired by the player.

Dark: one of the three Forces.

Darksworn: a player pledged to the Dark who values the self over the collective.

deathwish: An ability that is triggered in the instant between a creature being dealt fatal damage and the spirit fleeing the body.

Elite: a tier five player, i.e. someone above level two hundred.

ebonblade: soulbound weapons found in the Twilight Dungeon.

envoy: a trusted representative of a Power authorized to speak on their behalf.

Endless Dungeon: A section of the Nethersphere where dungeon mechanics are active.

Everborns: term used to describe players.

evolution: the advancement of a player's core characteristics.

familiar bond: a permanent spirit binding between a spellcasting player and a creature, allowing them the transfer of Game-gifted knowledge from host to familiar.

follower: a player that has pledged themself in a binding vow to a Force or Power.

Force: Light, Dark, Shadow. The building blocks of the cosmos and energy in its rawest form.

Forcesworn: Collective term referring to Darksworn, Lightsworn, and Shadowsworn players.

Forever Kingdom: the world of the Nethersphere and Kingdom.

forsworn: a sworn who has betrayed their Power.

Game: refers to the Grand Game.

gatekeepers: holders of ancient lore, guardians of the ancients' trials.

half-form: the in-between state where the player is in a mix of his two forms (man-form and beast-form).

House: House of the Ancient.

House of the Ancient: a grouping of followers pledged to one Prime.

Kingdoms: the collective name given to sectors located in the aether.

lycan: werewolf.

ley line: magic threads connecting nether sectors.

Light: one of the three Forces.

Lightsworn: a player sworn to the Light that champions the cause of the many, even to his own detriment.

marshmen: mysterious dwellers in the saltmarsh district.

meld: the process of combining multiple Classes into one.

mindglow: the visible signature of a mind as seen with mindsight.

neutral sector: a sector unowned and unclaimed by any faction or Force.

Nethersphere: collective name given to the sectors in the nether.

Netherspawn: stygian creatures.

nethersight: ability that allows stygian to see through free-floating nether.

new Power: one of the Powers that usurped the ancients.

oath breaker: one who has broken a Pact.

Pact: a binding enacted between a Power and player, overseen by the Adjudicator.

Power: an evolved player.

power word: a blood memory ability.

Prime: head of ancient bloodline. An ancient.

Prime Conclave: a gathering of Primes referred to by Kolath.

Primehood: the act of becoming a Prime.

rift: unstable portal from the nether. Ley line created by stygian seed.

scav: short for scavenger. A player who loots kills not his own.

scion: one bearing the blood of an ancient.

scion abilities: the abilities Michael had earned during the Wolf trials: astral blade, chi heal, mind shield, shadow blink.

seeking spell: spell that distinguishes friend from foe.
Shadowsworn: a player pledged to Shadow.
stolen spell: a spell acquired from another and cast using their skills and attributes.
soulbound: an item that remains with the player after death.
sworn: as in sworn servant. A sworn is a follower of a Power who has sufficiently deepened their binding Mark to benefit from the binding.
the real: reference to the physical realm.
trap-making crystal: crystal in trapper's wristband. Can be manifested as different trap components.
tratin: underwater sentient species with gills and blue scales.
trials of the ancients: tests created by the Primes for their successors.
tri-blend: a combination of three melded Classes.
trigger-cast: a spell held in readiness and invoked under specific conditions.
unsworn: not a sworn servant, and not bound to a Power.
upgrade gem: a game item used to advance an ability a single tier.
voids: informal term used to reference players who possess a void Class.
void Classes: a rare subset of Classes that specialize in damage reduction.
void's chosen: term by which the stygians address the stygian seeds.
void fathers: void trees.
Watcher: a Game artifact typically used to uncover deception players.
windslide: ramp of air formed by windborne spell.
were-trait: a trait carried by all were-players, fueling their ability to shapeshift.
weres: short for werewolves and other were-players.
wolfmen: hybrid species, non-player werewolves.
wolf trials: ancient trials created by Wolf Prime.
wolfkind: used interchangeably with wolfkin.

Key Characters & Factions

Factions

Albion Bank: major non-aligned bank in the Forever Kingdom.
Awakened Dead: A Dark faction.
Axis of Evil: An alliance of Dark factions.
blackguards: Policing force in the Dark quarter.
dawn brigade: Policing force in the Light quarter.
Devil Riders: small Dark faction.
Forerunners: Michael's faction.
gray watch: Policing force in the Shadow quarter.
Mantises: A Dark faction of assassins.
Marauders: small Shadow faction.
Reaper Clan: small Dark faction.
Silent Blades: small Dark faction.
Shadow Coalition: A power bloc of Shadow, made up of like-minded Shadow Powers.
Tartan: the faction of Tartar, the god-emperor.
Tartan legion: the military forces of Tartar.
Triumvirate: A unique faction composed of Light, Dark, and Shadow that control Nexus.
Unity Council: the governing body of Light, made up of all Light-affiliated Powers.

Guardians

Bacheus: new Nexus Guardian, former possessed.
Draven: centaur construct in Draven's Reach.
Kolath: former Nexus Guardian.

Guilds and Non-Factions

Bane Wolves: mercenary band out of New Haven.
Bounty Hunters Guild (BHG): headquartered in the plague quarter, mercenaries.
Information Brokers: a gnomish organization in the plague quarter.
Pack of the Reach: wolfmen pack.
Kesh Emporium: merchant company owned by Kesh.
Stygian Brotherhood: headquartered in sector 45,104. Experts in all-things-nether.

House Wolf

Atiras: Dead Prime Wolf.

Keros: forsworn and human windknight.
Kesh: master merchant, owner of the emporium, human woman.
Lake: guard outside emporium, berserker, giant.
Malikor: Mammon's envoy.
Michael: protagonist.
Misha: Marauder tracker, aka the Hound.
Moonshadow: aeromancer, male elf.
Morin: Michael's companion from Erebus' dungeon, the painted woman.
Nicola: under-dweller and underworld merchant, civilian.
Nyra: virulent witch, Michael's apprentice.
Orlon: Triumvirate knight-captain in the plague quarter, human.
Pitor: rank 15 warrior, Kalin sworn, human, Marauder sub-boss.
Richter: constable in Triumvirate citadel, human civilian.
Safyre: human aetherist, formerly known as Cara.
Saya: apprentice alchemist, tavernkeeper in wolves' valley, gnome.
Sedgwick: dwarven merchant.
Senzo: brotherhood human spymaster, huntmistress' advisor.
Shael: red minstrel, half-elf.
Simone: sharpshooter, half-elf female.
Stayne: Erebus' henchman.
Stonebeard: Triumvirate captain, dwarf.
Talon: the captain, Tartar's envoy.
Tantor: Michael's companion from Erebus' dungeon, high elf male.
Teg: Michael's escort in citadel, human.
Terence: human fighter, arcane knight.
Teresa: human fighter, priestess of the blade.
Tevin: Marauder knight.
Toff: player outside haunted catacombs, ogre
Trion: Triumvirate holy knight, Herat sworn, human.
Trexton: herbalist in Triumvirate citadel, Simone's contact, dark elf.
Tyelin: Blythe's envoy.
Wengulax: mantis assassin, blade dancer, human.
Wilsh: Blackguard captain, human.
Yzark: Marauder boss.

POWERS

Arinna: Light Power.
Artem: Shadow Power. Goddess of nature.
Blythe: Dark Power, faction leader of the Silent Blades.
Erebus: Dark Power, leader of the Awakened Dead faction.
Herat: Light Power, member of the Triumvirate.
Ishita: Spider goddess, Dark Power, member of the Awakened Dead.
Loken: Shadow Power.
Kalin: Minor Shadow Power, faction leader of the Marauders.
Mai: Unknown Power and collector of artifacts.
Mammon: Dark Power, faction leader of the Devil Riders.
Menaq: Dark Power, leader of the Mantis faction.
Muriel: Light Power contesting Wolf Valley.

Mydas: Shadow Power, member of the Triumvirate.
Paya: Dark Power, junior member of the Awakened Dead ruling council.
Rampel: Dark Power, member of the Triumvirate.
Tartar: Dark Power, also known as the God-Emperor.
Viviane: Power owning the Albion Bank.

WOLFKIN

Aira: dire wolf dame.
Barak: dire wolf elder.
Cantur: half-mad wolf.
Duggar: dire wolf alpha.
Oursk: dire wolf sire.
Leta: dire wolf elder.
Monac: dire wolf elder and former alpha.
Moonstalker: Oursk's pup.
Shadetooth: Oursk's pup.
Snow: arctic wolf pack alpha.
Star: Snow's mate.
Stormdark: Oursk's pup.
Sulan: dire wolf healer.
Suva: dire wolf elder.

LOCATIONS

bounty hunters guild headquarters: in the plague quarter.
court of the dead: archlich's stronghold. Also court.
Dark quarter: eastern side of Nexus.
Eastern Marches: collection of open sectors that Draven's Reach exits onto.
global auction: auction in the safe zone.
guardian tower: public dungeon.
haunted catacombs: public dungeon.
highlands: arid northern grasslands and hills of the Eastern Marches.
information brokers office: in the plague quarter.
Kesh Emporium: merchant house in the safe zone.
Korg: collective name for the three sectors of Korg's Deep, Korg minor, Korg Major.
Light quarter: western side of Nexus.
lowlands: fertile southern lands of the Eastern Marches.
market square: square housing global auction.
New Haven: city in Draven's Reach.
plague quarter: southern side of Nexus.
saltmarsh district: area in the southeast of plague quarter.
scorching dune: public dungeon.
Shadow Keep: central castle in the Shadow quarter.
Shadow quarter: northern side of Nexus.
Sickening Ooze: dungeon in saltmarsh.
Sleepy Inn: Michael's tavern, aka Wyvern's Roost.
Southern Outpost: tavern in plague quarter.
Wanderer's Delight: hotel in the safe zone.

EXCERPT FROM THE PROVING GROUNDS

DAY ONE

My alarm beeped.

I didn't open my eyes. Whatever time it was, it was too early. Without looking, I reached out with my right hand to silence the damn thing.

My hand met cold stone.

What? I must still be dreaming. With a groan, I turned over onto my side.

That, too, felt wrong.

My bed was lumpy and unyielding, and felt nothing like my soft mattress should. Had I rolled onto the floor?

The alarm beeped once more.

I reached for the annoying clock again, but my hand only met more stone. "Bloody hell, where is that damnable thing?" I growled, my eyes snapping open.

I blinked. Then blinked again.

I'm not in my apartment. For a drawn-out moment, that was the only thought filling my head. Finally, the gears of my mind began turning again, and I processed what I was seeing.

I was lying on a straw pallet in a room bordered on all sides by unadorned stone. Turning on my back, I found more dull-gray stone staring down at me. Not only was I not in my apartment, I was somewhere I'd never been before—in a place you wouldn't normally catch me dead in either.

How did I get here? I wondered. Jerking upright, I gave my surroundings a second longer look.

The stone chamber was dimly lit. Nonetheless, I could make out a wooden door to my left and a table in front of me. Its contents, though, were hidden from sight. Stranger yet, a torch had been inset onto the wall to the right—an actual goddamn torch!

Where the hell is this?

The room looked for all the world like something extracted from a textbook on medieval history. Was this a prank? Someone's deranged idea of a joke?

BEEEEP! BEEP!

There was that annoying beeping again. Rising to my feet, I scanned the room anew. The sound wasn't coming from any clock I owned, that was for certain. Hells, there wasn't even an electrical socket in sight.

No electricity? How much weirder can this get?

I puttered around the room, perusing the contents of the table and tapping on the walls. No matter how hard I searched, though, I failed to find the source of the beeping.

Is it coming from outside? I wondered.

But despite the room's strangeness, I was loath to open the door and check what lay beyond. However I'd gotten into the room, it wasn't by accident. And whoever had brought me here was almost certainly waiting outside. I'd face them when the time came, but that time was not yet.

The beeping came again. Louder still.

Growing more perplexed, I kept searching. *I am not dreaming,* I thought, coming to the conclusion only reluctantly. Everything—the smell of the burning torch, the feel of the rough stone beneath my palms, and the crackle of the straw pallet—felt too real.

BEEP! BEEP!

I stilled. Bundling all my emotions together—my fear, my confusion, and my anxiety—I locked them away and focused on one thing only: the sound.

BEEP!

BEEP! BEEP!

BEEP! BEEP! BEEP!

My brows drew down. It almost felt like...

...the sound was coming from me. *I* was the source. As if spurred by the realization, words appeared in the air before me.

<u>Creche Notice 1050-01</u>

Welcome to the Proving Grounds, human Dace Tolman.

You and the rest of your species are now subjects of the Simian Galactic Empire. From this day on, your only goal is to serve the Emperor, glory to his name.

The Emperor's servant, the Suzerain, Al-Takor, has chosen to spare your species from annihilation and offer you and your fellows a chance at continued life.

To this end, you've been transferred to Sector 52 in Creche 1050 of the Proving Grounds, a hidden world configured for human testing and training. The first step in proving yourself worthy of the emperor's service is to: <u>Exit the Creche.</u> Any knowledge you earn while in the Proving Grounds will be carried over to the wider world.

My mouth worked soundlessly. *Alright, I've officially gone mad.*

Another window opened before my eyes. Like the first message, it floated in the air, superimposed on my sight.

Human Dace Tolman, please acknowledge receipt of Creche Notice 1050-01. Have you read the message in full?

I glared up at the roof, scowling at whoever or whatever was sending me the hallucinations. "Of course, I read the message," I growled. "How could—"

I broke off as both windows disappeared, and another took its place.

Thank you.

I sighed, not knowing whether to laugh or cry.

The last message disappeared after a second, and I sank to the ground. Bowing my head between my knees, I tried to figure out what was going on, and just as importantly, how I'd gotten here.

My memories seemed fuzzy, but I doggedly persisted until I wormed free the ones I was searching for.

I had been in my apartment—working as usual. At thirty years old, single, and living in the big city, my life was all about my job and slowly working toward the day when I didn't need one anymore.

That was the dream, anyway.

A client wanted the completion date of his project brought forward, and despite me knowing that meeting the new deadline was a near impossibility, I had agreed. The client was always right, after all.

More memories rushed back—quicker now.

That's right. I had been working on the project designs when something distracted me. What was it? Something on the news... Something so far-fetched, I nearly fell off my chair laughing...

I lifted my head off my knees, eyes widening. It had been a report on extraterrestrials. An alien fleet had supposedly appeared in Earth's skies. The reporter had been going on about black clouds of something—*nanites?*—dropping from the strange spaceships to blacken the air.

A startling thought hit me.

It had all seemed too preposterous to believe at the time. But now... I recalled the first message floating in the air before my eyes.

"The 'Simian Galactic Empire'," I muttered. Were those the aliens who had appeared over Earth? It sounded ludicrous. But what other explanation was there?

"By god!" I exclaimed. "Have I been abducted by aliens?"

No response was forthcoming.

✳   ✳   ✳

I don't know how long I sat on the floor, my thoughts circling in on themselves as I tried to make sense of my predicament. But eventually I came to the conclusion that it didn't matter.

No matter how or why I came to be where I was, I would have to find a way to make the most of my circumstances. If there was one thing I had learned in my life, it was that no matter how many times life knocked you down, you had to pick yourself up and keep going.

See to your survival first, Dace. Everything else, including understanding this crazy place, can come later.

Rising to my feet, I tried the door. It was locked. I didn't let that stop me. Bracing my shoulder, I rammed into it.

It didn't budge.

I backed up all the way to the far end of the chamber, and was just about to hurl myself at the door again, when another message arrived.

Human Dace Tolman, you cannot exit the starting chamber until you have been analyzed.

I frowned. *Analyzed?*

The System must assess your physical and metaphysical makeup to determine your Nodal Capability. This will limit the number of Essences that you may install.

My eyes narrowed. None of that made any sense, but it seemed that whatever entity was responsible for the floating messages was responding directly to my internal thoughts.

Was my mind laid bare before it?

I am not privy to all your thoughts, human Dace Tolman. Normally, I would only be able to sense those you direct to me or the System. However in this chamber, I have greater awareness of your mind. Such was deemed necessary by my Creators to guide new participants.

I puzzled over that for a minute. "Who are you?" I asked out aloud eventually.

I am personal administrator i-4-252-527. For the duration of your journey through the Proving Grounds, I have been assigned to your person, human Dace Tolman.

"Well, that's too long," I muttered. "How about I call you Ad-i or Adi?"

That will suffice, human Dace Tolman.

"And enough with this 'human Dace Tolman' nonsense. Call me, Dace."

As you wish, Dace.

"So, what are you, Adi?"

I am personal administrator—

I waved away the entity's response. "I got all that. I mean *what* are you? Who created you?"

Adi was silent for so long I thought it wouldn't respond. Eventually though, more words scrolled through my vision.

I am forbidden to speak of my Creators or of my exact nature. For your purposes, you may consider me a construct of the Proving Grounds.

I chewed over the administrator's words then hazarded a guess. "So, the Simians created you?"

No, the Simians are simply the Proving Grounds current owners. They did not construct it—or me.

I frowned. "But the Simians are the ones that put *me* here?"

Correct, Dace. The Simian Suzerain, Al-Takor, has registered you and the rest of humanity as participants in the Proving Grounds. Your entire species is now within its hidden world.

I sputtered. "That's impossible. How can an entire planet, more than eight billion people, be transplanted from Earth to this Proving Grounds? And what do you mean by 'hidden' anyway?"

The Proving Grounds' location is a secret that not even the administrators are privy to. You can rest assured, however, that the System is more than capable of accepting the quantity of participants introduced by Suzerain Al-Takor.

I let that pass. "And what are the Proving Grounds?"

I am forbidden from revealing more of the nature of the Proving Grounds than I already have.

I sighed. It didn't seem like I was going to get any quick answers. I set aside the mysteries surrounding this place.

"Alright Adi. You mentioned something about analyzing my abilities? What did you mean by that?"

On the table you will find a disc-shaped object. Place your hands upon it so that the System may determine your quantity of available Nodes.

I tried looking at the table to see the item Adi was referring to, but with all the text from the administrator's responses obscuring my vision, it was hard to make out what lay there. I brushed away the message windows irritably. "Is there no other way we can communicate, Adi?"

A pause. *"If you prefer, I can respond directly to queries through mindspeech. Like this?"*

I bit back a start at the strange—and distinctly feminine—voice in my mind. "Much better, Adi. Thank you." I hesitated. "Are you female, Adi?"

Another pause, much longer this time. *"I was. I am."*

I didn't question her somewhat strange response. Leaving well enough alone, I walked over to the table. Sure enough, a large flat disk was at its center. With a shrug, I placed my hands on the metal surface.

A thrill of energy rippled from the disk into my hands, prompting another spill of words across my vision.

I opened my mouth, but before I could get a word out, Adi spoke in my mind. *"Dace, the window before you is a System generated message. I can, of course, verbalize the information, but it is better that you view it directly."*

I closed my mouth with a snap. "Alright, Adi," I grumbled, then read the floating text.

<u>Player Profile: Dace Tolman</u>

Level: 1. Health: 10 / 10 HP.
Stamina: 10 / 10 SP.
Species: Human. Class: None.

<u>Nodal Capability</u>

Max Nodes: 17. Total Occupied: 3 / 17.
Available Essence Nodes: 13 / 17.
Class Reserved: 1 / 17.

Occupied Nodes

Strength, tier 1 Essence: 1.
Dexterity, tier 1 Essence: 1.
Constitution, tier 1 Essence: 1.

Skills

None.

I read the message twice. Then once more, just to be sure. A lot of the information didn't make sense, but enough did to shock me.

"Adi," I asked slowly, "is this a game?"

"No, it's the Proving Grounds."

"But—" I asked, waving helplessly at the window. The damn System had referred to me as a 'player' and while it had been over a decade since I'd touched a computer game, I knew RPG stats when I saw them.

I sighed. It didn't matter. Whatever the Proving Grounds was, I would figure out its inner workings. Then I would exploit it.

Like any good gamer would.

My gaming skills might be rusty and years out of date, but they weren't dead. I chuckled, good humor restored. "So, what now, Adi?"

"I am not permitted to advise you, Dace."

I shrugged. Seeing how much she was *not permitted* to tell me, I was tempted to ask Adi what use she was exactly, but I squashed the impulse. Why antagonize what was so far my only source of information in this world?

But from the System's response I could assume that this was a game, in some sense at least.

I'll treat it as such, anyway. And let's see if I can't beat the Simians in their own playground.

When I'm done with them, they'll rue the day they put me in here.

✳ ✳ ✳

To continue reading the <u>Proving Grounds</u> by Tom Elliot <u>click here</u>.

www.ingramcontent.com/pod-product-compliance
Lightning Source LLC
Chambersburg PA
CBHW051549100726
47898CB00001B/33